April, June and November

Novels

The Limits of Love
Lindmann
Two for the Road
Orchestra and Beginners
Richard's Things
California Time

Screenplays

Darling
Privilege
Far From the Madding Crowd

April,
June
and
November

Frederic Raphael

The Bobbs-Merrill Company, Inc.
Indianapolis - New York

Library of Congress Cataloging in Publication Data

Raphael, Frederic, 1931—
   April, June and November.

   I. Title.
PZ4.R217Ap   [PR6068.A6]   823'.9'14   76-11614
ISBN 0-672-52266-7

FOR BEETLE

Κύριε, ὄχι μ'αὐτούς
Lord, not with these people

GEORGE SEFERIS, 'Postscript'

What are the islands to me,
what is Greece,
what is Rhodes, Samos, Chios,
what is Paros facing west,
what is Crete?

HILDA DOOLITTLE, *Selected Poems*

APRIL

'I think she'll be absolutely right for Danny,' Virginia Playfair said. 'She's pretty, she's intelligent and she admires everything he's done.'

'Why can't you find me someone like that?' Adam Playfair said. 'I wish I knew why you always have to be so nice to Danny.'

'He needs somebody. No one ought to be thirty-six and not married.'

'Everyone ought to be thirty-six and not married. I can't imagine anything nicer. Except perhaps being twenty-six, and in the same condition.'

'He told me he wants to get married. It can't be very enjoyable, when you think about it, living by yourself, having affairs first with one girl and then with another —'

'The more I think about it, the more delicious it sounds,' Adam said, 'so you'd better shut up. Being forty is just about the most sickening experience I've ever almost had. Why we have to have a party to celebrate it, I cannot think. Celebrate, my God!'

'Don't moan,' Virginia said. 'It makes you sound menopausal.'

'It'll happen to you, so don't gloat.'

'God knows it will,' Virginia said, 'and it won't to you, so don't you gloat either. He's miserable as sin, Danny, half the time, you know he is, and when he isn't, he's deluding himself.'

'What makes you so confident?' Adam said. 'What makes you so sure you know what's best for everyone else?'

'It's a question of instinct.'

'Oh Christ.'

'And intelligence. God knows, husband dear, you spend a good deal of your time acting as though you knew exactly what was right for the world. I don't think it's fair to lay that one entirely at my door. You should hear yourself talking to your clients — and their publishers.'

'That's all bullshit, as you very well know. A literary agent who doesn't at least seem confident might as well shut up shop. And one who really was would chuck it in and do something useful.'

'Why would you want to stop doing something you're very happy doing and do better than anyone else? And as for useful—'

'At the age of forty,' Adam said, 'there are very few things one does better than anyone else. And the number diminishes daily. There's always some whizz-kid coming up on the rails. They had a winger last Sunday beat me for speed two times out of three. Believe me, at my age, one has to rely on positional sense or one's dead.'

'I'd still sooner go to bed with a man of forty than one of twenty.'

'Well, you'd better hurry up and make your reservations. I shall be forty-one in a year's time.'

'The other thing I was going to say was, as for being useful, where would your friends be without you?'

'With Curtis Brown, I suppose,' Adam said. 'Oh, I suppose I have my uses. I keep the wheels oiled. I supply the superlatives the critics fail to come through with.'

'You do a great deal more than that. I think you're very creative. *Very* creative. And so do a lot of people.'

'At least this party'll be on expenses,' Adam said. 'There is that to be said for it, even if it is for Danny's benefit.'

'You're not really jealous, are you?'

'One never knows, does one, until it comes to it?'

'Funny to have known someone for so long,' Virginia said. 'Do you realize he's the only one out of the whole lot of us who hasn't got married? Why do you think that is?'

'Perhaps he's smarter than we are,' Adam said, 'I don't know. I'm sure you do.'

'Probably the same thing that ultimately prevented him from getting a first. Ultimately he can't make up his mind. He lacks decision.'

'Is marriage a matter of decision?'

'I think Danny's very confused at times. I'm not saying he can't keep a lot of balls in the air, but he can't always decide which one he actually wants to catch.'

10

'I sometimes think,' Adam Playfair said, 'that you and I, dear wife, live in entirely different worlds.'

'Anyway,' Virginia said, 'everyone else is married and it's obviously time he was.'

'Oh damn Danny anyway.'

'And apart from anything else he wants children.'

'Why can't he have ours then?'

'That's vulgar and silly and anyway you know you dote on them. Candida's written another wonderful poem, by the way, did she show you?'

'I never thought my daughter would turn out to be Ezra Pound,' Adam said.

'Oh do you think it's Ezra Pound? I think it's far more Robert Graves, that shaggy use of the vernacular—I'm thinking of that line that ends "and an ultimate sixpenny bus".'

'You call that vernacular? You use a strange vernacular.'

'I do? Are you not aware how often you use the word ultimate?'

'Do I? I thought you did.'

'I get it from you.'

'Women always say that,' Adam said. 'Perhaps it was something to do with National Service. Why we all got married. One got used to the idea of conscription. Danny never went into the army, did he? He never got into the habit of doing his bit.'

'You do sound put upon,' Virginia said. 'No one's ever stopped you doing what you want. You all moan and groan—'

'Do we? Who do?'

'You and Paul and people. But the fact is, virtually all of you have ended up exactly what you wanted to be.'

'And what about all of you? Because presumably you're making a rather heavy distinction between the sexes.'

'Not really. I think the females all got more or less what they wanted as well.'

'Well then,' Adam said, 'that seems to be the particular curse of our generation. All our wishes have come true. What's the name of this girl you've found for Danny?'

'Perhaps we didn't have the right wishes,' Virginia said.

'Well, I'm sure you did. Accurate wishing's always been your forte.'

'I really sometimes wonder why I love you.'

'My body,' Adam said.

'Not entirely.'

'Thank God. Isometrics can't do the trick forever. Come on, give: who is she?'

'Rachel Davidson,' Virginia said. 'You've met her briefly.'

'Is that the dark girl who reads for Norbert Ash?'

'You're thinking of Ruth Leman,' Virginia said, 'although funnily enough this girl does read for Norbert occasionally and she is dark —'

'Then why the hell couldn't I have been thinking of her?'

'Because Ruth Leman's the one you were chatting up at Meredith's publication party. She reads more or less full time. Rachel's mainly been an actress —'

'Then Danny probably won't like her.'

'She went to Oxford. She just missed getting a first, but she's obviously bright. She read P.P.E. We met her that evening when Basil Brain did his tango.'

'Rachel *what* did you say?'

'Davidson. He thought a lot of her. They talked for a long time, so she must have some brains.'

'Or big tits,' Adam said.

'She has got a good figure actually, but that wasn't the point —'

'Your greatest mistake in life is to think that clever men like clever women.'

'Basil told me himself he thought she had a very lively personality.'

'I.e. big tits,' Adam said. 'The personality comes *en supplément*, like sauce Béarnaise used to at Raffi's.'

'What I'm trying to say is she isn't the ordinary kind of ambitious young actress that Danny bumps into directing his films and things. She's got brains *and* looks and that's rare. What's more she knows a bit about life.'

'By which I suppose you mean she's had an affair with Professor Brain.'

12

'Who told you that?'

'No one. You suggested it yourself; just now.'

'I never did any such thing. There's no evidence whatever that Basil's had an affair with her – or anyone else, if it comes to that.'

'There's Cynthia Chernov's twins. Two premises of a syllogism which provide a more than obvious conclusion.'

'That was before he married Gay. I think they're very happy.'

'I wonder what it is that makes a man marry a war-correspondent.'

'She's hardly simply a war-correspondent. She did write that book on the Roots of Realism.'

'And what was that all about?'

'You remember. It was a comparative study of Norris, Dreiser and Red Lewis. Of course you remember. About the alienation of the American populist writer from his material. Alfred liked it very much. It's really only since Vietnam that she's been scrambling round in helicopters. And you have to admit those pieces she wrote were something more than routine reportage –'

'About a hundred thousand words more, if memory serves –'

'I like Gay,' Virginia said, 'I think she manages to stay quite remarkably feminine.'

'So do I,' Adam said, 'considering the kind of man she is.'

'Cheap,' Virginia said, 'and unfair. The trouble with you is, you think women should always be soft and cuddly like Cathie.'

'Cathie is about as soft and cuddly as a hand grenade. Cathie! Jesus!'

'It's true, nevertheless. You still can't really accept that a woman can have a mind.'

'Like my authors,' Adam said, 'I can accept anything except criticism. Do you think I married you just for your nice short legs?'

'The reasons you married me may be complicated,' Virginia said, 'but they don't necessarily clash with what I just said. You are foul sometimes.'

'I expect you're quite right, as usual, but we won't talk about it. It might remove the magic.'

'People marry people for all sorts of funny reasons, but equally they often turn out to be very happy together. Which is what I'm saying about Basil and Gay.'

'The touching thing about you, Gin, is that you think everybody's blissfully happy until they fall apart in mid-air. And then, of course, you're the first one to grab the Black Box and tell us the exact cause of the disaster.'

'Perhaps I have to think people are happy, or at least that they can be. Perhaps I have to think that. Sometimes it's not easy for a woman to face the fact that ultimately she's entirely alone.'

'You'll always have your children to keep you warm.'

'I hope I shall,' Virginia said. 'Don't think that isn't part of the reason I wanted them. Why are you standing there like that?'

'There was something I wanted to do,' Adam said, 'but I can't remember what. Anyway, so the lot has fallen on Rachel. I hope she'll be agreeable.'

'I told you—'

'Oh yes, I know, but admiration isn't always a prelude to bliss. I must say though, I think it's very thoughtful of you to have found Danny a partner of the same faith. I hope he'll appreciate it.'

'You're not being very nice to me this evening. It's got nothing to do with *faith*. It never occurred to me. I never even thought about it—'

'Rachel when-from-the-Lord,' Adam Playfair said, 'and you never thought about it? You may not have thought about it, but it certainly occurred to you. I'm not saying you're wrong. God knows, Danny's made enough of a thing about being Jewish. I think you're entitled to take it into consideration. Only I'm not sure he'll ever actually go so far as to marry a Jewess.'

'I think they're fascinating. Jewesses.'

'Racist.'

'If you read Darlington,' Virginia Playfair said, 'you'll find there's a lot more in race than people like to think. I mean, they are different, we're *all* different, of course, that's what you eventually come to realize reading Darlington—'

'I did read the dust-jacket. You've heard the three biggest lies in the world, haven't you? "This car's only had one owner," "If you let me, I'll only put it in half way," and "I'm not ashamed of being Jewish."'

'Who told you that? I'm not sure I like it very much.'

'A second-hand car dealer told it to Jack Darwin. It's quite old actually.'

'When did Jack Darwin ever buy a second-hand car?'

'He didn't. He was doing some research for *Bangers*, you know Jack.'

'Naturally,' Virginia said, 'I might have guessed.'

'Only luckily you never do.'

'You wish you were in Danny's shoes, don't you? You don't have to tell me.'

'Having juicy dollies selected for me by the most intelligent woman in London? Who wouldn't?'

'Dollies! How I hate that expression!'

'Talking of which, where's that damned kraut cow? It's about time she was in, isn't it? Some English lesson she goes to. Roughly one hour and seven inches long, if you want my guess. It's a quarter to bloody eleven. Somebody's got her knickers in his pocket. Ultimately they're all whores, these girls.'

'Inge's a very nice girl, and by no means unintelligent. Her grandfather was an assistant professor at Heidelberg before he went into industry.'

'And what did you do in the war, grandpa — and so industriously too?'

'We'll leave Danny to ask her that, shall we?'

'Who else have you asked to this damned party?'

'You are ungracious when all I —'

'That's what we get married for, isn't it? So we don't have to be gracious any more.'

'I sometimes wonder where our generation got its ideas from. There's a piece for somebody. Paul perhaps.'

'We got them all from Paul, didn't we? Paul and *Lilliput* mostly, I'd say, speaking for the men.'

'People used to be polite to their wives.'

'Only when they didn't want to be bothered with them.'

15

'Do you really think that? I mean in Jane Austen —'

'If you trace the course of marriage through the English novel,' Adam said, 'you'll find out exactly why we're in the mess we are in. Deceptions that were once social and are now sentimental. It's the same with Christianity. You start off with an institution and you try to turn it into a machine which guarantees caring. It's transparently absurd. You still haven't told me, Mrs Playfair, who else you've asked apart from Danny and his fiancée whom he happens not to have met yet.'

'Must you go on?' Virginia said. 'Paul and Margaret.'

'Obviously.'

'Obviously. And Norbert and Babette. Dick Lucas and his wife. I can never remember her name —'

'Sandy.'

'That's right. And Basil and Gay.'

'Are you sure that's wise?'

'Wise?'

'In view of Rachel whatsit.'

'Oh I see what you mean. Well, I don't want her to feel that I'm throwing her at Danny. It'll be nice for her to see someone she knows.'

'And who else?'

'Am I deceiving myself or are you beginning to sound slightly more enthusiastic?'

'As long as there isn't going to be a cake.'

'Of course there's going to be a cake. How can you have a birthday party without a cake?'

'It only means everyone'll be as embarrassed as hell because they haven't brought a present.'

'Oh nonsense. Anyway, some of them probably will.'

'Meaning you've told them. You are —'

'Meaning a lot of them asked. People don't give parties that often any more. I suppose because of money. It's generally assumed there must be some special reason.'

'Well, go on. Who else?'

'The Doctors.'

16

'Not both of them? *Quelle richesse!*'

'And that rather impressive man from the French embassy is bringing someone. Jean-Claude Cénac.'

'Is he queer then?'

'Who?'

'This rather impressive man who's bringing Jean-Claude Cénac, whoever he may be.'

'Adam, honestly. Jean-Claude *is* the man, he is the man who's bringing someone, only I don't know who. He asked if he could. I presume it's a female. Oh, of course, you weren't there when I met him, I went with Paul, you were in Chicago. It was a reception for that rather overrated girl who'd won the *Prix Femina*. He rather impressed me. He used to be a violin prodigy and then his family pushed him into the Diplomatic. He still plays, but rarely.'

'Only while the Rome Treaty burns, I assume. Is he bringing his fiddle with him?'

'You might like him. He's very sharp. He was at the *Haute Polytechnique* and you know what that means — that immensely practical intelligence they all have. He's very pro-British, but in a critical way. I found him very sympathetic. Apart from having an excellent mind, he also has this artistic — musical side —'

'All right, all right,' Adam said, 'you don't have to feed him to me piece by piece, I'll nibble for myself when he gets here.'

'And there're quite a lot of other people as well, of course. Brian Stammers.'

'Has he got a wife?'

'There's not much evidence he's got anything in that respect,' Virginia said, 'but one's M.P. is one's M.P. After all, we did get him in.'

'Just. You'll have to find him somebody,' Adam said. 'Somebody who can type, I should think that'd be the main requirement.'

'All you care about's what's between a woman's legs,' Virginia Playfair said, 'but what's between her ears matters too. There are some marriages that're quite successful even though sex hardly comes into them.'

'Like Marks and Spencer,' Adam said. 'Where is that fucking girl?'

'She's very nice to Candida,' Virginia said. 'Which is what matters. If she goes back to Pforzheim after learning her English in this house, she's going to have learnt very little apart from fuck.'

'She knew it before she arrived if I'm any judge. She's damned late, blast her, nice or no.'

'We couldn't do without her, so —'

'We couldn't do without any of the things that drive us potty,' Adam said. 'I sometimes wonder why the hell not.'

'There she is.'

'And about time. Funny how often one talks about something and then it happens.'

'Probably you heard her coming along the street subconsciously.'

'Grammar,' Adam said.

'We always said we wouldn't have anybody, didn't we?'

'We always said just about every stupid thing there was to say. Strange really, when you think of all the brains involved.'

'I don't think we did at all,' Virginia said.

'Ah,' said Adam, 'that's because you said so many of them! Remember how marriage was going to be a free association? An agreement, not a contract?'

'In my opinion I've always been very undemanding.'

'Undemanding?'

'I think I have. I've always been afraid of being too talkative and boring you. I wanted more than anything else to be what you wanted me to be.'

'I suppose you have,' Adam said. 'I never thought of that before.'

'That's because I never said it before.'

'Thank you.'

'What I mean is —'

'Oh I know what you mean.'

'I'm going up to have a bath —'

'You'd better hurry before that Kraut whips all the hot water washing the marks of sin from her marbled limbs.'

'It's strange really, isn't it, to have someone else living in the house with you and sort of to agree not to see her except when we all want to? It reminds me of that story of Nabokov's, do you remember, where the wife and her lover live in the same house as the blind husband?'

'I thought you didn't like Nabokov?'

'I don't like the way he keeps winking at you all the time and asking you if you're managing to keep up with his allusions. It's all so gloating and deliberate, but he does have a certain cosmopolitan flash; it may be untrustworthy but it's undeniably brilliant. One can't deny him invention. Invention without heart, you might say.'

'I'll certainly try. I didn't actually know heart was a plus these days; is it?'

'What's writing without heart? *Littérature*.'

'True,' Adam said. 'Very true.'

'I certainly never denied him invention, because that he undoubtedly does have. À *outrance*.'

'You obviously can't wait for Jean-Claude whatsit to get here and start understanding what you mean.'

'Why do you say things like that? When you understand perfectly?'

'Years of professional caution I suppose. "You and I know what's meant, dear boy, but will *they*?" One way and another, dear wife, our whole existence is aimed at pleasing some idealized "they", ain't that the truth? And containing ourselves accordingly.'

'I think one can have standards,' Virginia said, 'without having to accuse oneself of kowtowing. Personally I think if any agent's got standards, you have.'

'Thanks,' Adam said, 'but unfortunately none of them have.'

'You certainly did as a publisher.'

'And look where that got us.'

'There are still plenty of things you wouldn't handle.'

'As for instance?'

'You know very well. Anything systematically dishonest. A pro-Powell piece, for instance. You wouldn't sell a pro-Powell piece if your life depended on it.'

'If my life depended on it, wife, I'd do anything.'

'That's exactly where you're wrong.'

'How can you possibly know what I'd do? If Meredith had

19

written it? And insisted I sold it or he'd quit? What gives you the right to know what I'd do? I don't know what you'd do.'

'I certainly wouldn't do anything I knew was intellectually dishonest.'

'Not even for Jason and Candida, wouldn't you?'

'No.'

'Or Tobe? How can you possibly be so sure? Might it not ultimately be intellectually dishonest not to do something to save them? Might that not be the ultimate vanity, the ultimate sell-out of the intellect you're so incredibly proud of?'

'You're wrong about that,' Virginia said. 'In many ways I'm ashamed of it. In many ways I wish I hadn't got a mind at all. That's one of the things life has taught me. I use it because it'd frankly be a betrayal not to, but—'

'The Frank in frankly not being hard to identify—'

'I think you'd be a lot happier if I had less brains and more—'

'I don't think so.'

'Oh yes you would. And because I'm the sort of wife I am, I wish it was true. Only unfortunately sometimes I think my brains are the only things I've got to hold on to.'

'Then you're an ass, aren't you?'

'Am I?'

'You'd better go and have your bath.'

'It's time we had a change,' Virginia said.

'You know you prefer it in bed when it comes to it.'

'I was rather hoping for both.'

'Christ, you've arranged for me to be publicly fortified on Wednesday and we've been married sixteen years, do you honestly expect me to make it twice in one evening? What do you think I am? It's either here or there.'

'What about me?' Virginia said. 'Don't you think I might have some influence on things?'

'Not enough,' Adam said, 'frankly.'

'We'll see about that, shall we? Later. Meanwhile, put these in your pocket, will you? I don't want Mrs Who finding them in the morning.'

'The funny thing is,' Adam said, 'you'd do this for the sake of the kids, wouldn't you, with almost anyone, and you'd actually be rather pleased with yourself, so why—'

'One's body doesn't matter,' Virginia said, 'in the same way as one's mind. What one does with one's body doesn't have any moral content. It's what one thinks that makes a thing moral or not.'

'You'll have to ask Basil Brain about that. I'm not sure he'd agree. Look, try putting your legs—'

'Morality's a question of judgment. What one writes, roughly speaking, *are* judgments. To give one's personal signature to falsehood is surely the final betrayal of what we generally think of as decent behaviour.'

'So what you said about what you did with the Chief of the Gestapo might be immoral, but the act itself—'

'Is a means to an end. If I save my children by making love to a Chief of the Gestapo, for the sake of example, that's my affair.'

'My dear Mrs Playfair,' Adam said, 'this is bloody awkward. It's these arms. And the cushion's too soft. We're sinking in too far. It's no good.'

'I like it,' Virginia said. 'It reminds me of when we used to do it in that Windsor chair in the kitchen at your grandmother's.'

'Look, I can't afford to risk doing my back again. We've got a match down at Ascot on Sunday. Paul's counting on me.'

'You don't understand women,' Virginia said, 'or you'd see that her body is the one thing she has absolute rights over, to do what she likes with. Silently. That's her pleasure. Without answering to anyone.'

'And where does that leave marriage, may I ask?'

'She also has the right to be faithful.'

'Which is the ultimate act of possessiveness.'

'I think this'd be better,' Virginia said, 'if we did it like this. How's that for you? It's nice for me.'

'Quite reasonable really. Rather good in the event. You are a clever girl. Ultimately.'

*

'If there's one thing I simply cannot abide, it's being first. I think we ought to walk round the block.'

'Oh listen, Basil, those kinds of things don't matter any more, do they? If we're first, we're first. We'll have a drink with Ginny and Adam—'

'You forget, I don't know them as well as you do.'

'She's a very intelligent woman. One of the most intelligent women in London.'

'I've heard about her references. No, I do hate being among the first.'

'At a party, my love, I think you should add that qualification. At a party.'

'I don't think of myself as a great leader,' Basil Brain said. 'Rather the opposite. I fancy myself, if I fancy myself at all—'

'You fancy yourself,' Gay Brain said.

'If I fancy myself at all, as a counter-puncher.'

'Paul says you specialize in the overlap.'

'Except that my legs aren't up to it any more.'

'He said you played very well on Sunday.'

'For an ageing Professor.'

'He didn't say that.'

'I don't flatter myself that I keep my place entirely on footballing merit. I hope they're going to feed us reasonably.'

'Virginia had a French training.'

'So presumably did the mother of a French family with whom I stayed in La Rochelle when I was an undergraduate. I believe Sartre must have stayed with the same people when he came to his rather swampy conclusions about the nature of reality. What time did it say on that invitation? Are you sure it said eight? I wonder if anyone's done a paper on Sartre and Plato. I bet it said eight-thirty.'

'It said eight. I don't make that kind of mistake. You should know me by now. I'm getting cold. Let's at least get out of the car. Is there a connection?'

'Put your flak jacket on. Plato's ideas are Sartrean decisions taken by God. I think we should wait till we see some other people going in. Certainly Sartre's ideas are less original than he thinks they are. You're sure it's tonight?'

'You can see. From the lights. They have an expectant air, surely, don't they? Oh come on, the heater's stopped working.'

'I do hate being first,' Basil Brain said. 'I like to hear a nice healthy continuo before I come in.'

'Soloists always do,' said his wife. 'They like to still the tumult with a few scathing cadenzas.'

'Funny, I've never been a musical man,' Basil said. 'I can understand the structure, but I've never actually managed to enjoy the sound.'

'The logical mind,' Gay said. 'There are one or two people. You can see.'

'Even logic has its music, to the true exponent. I never really cared for it myself. Venery and football are my only genuine passions.'

'Next to football, venery, if one were to give them an order.' She was his second wife. 'Are we locking the car?'

'Not particularly. Someone told me last week that Ivan Chernov has a Krooklok. Don't you think that's rather perfect?'

'I was thinking of leaving my umbrella. They always get pinched at parties.'

'I thought that was bottoms.'

'Only when you're about,' Gay said.

'I think I may honestly say, after but a moment's introspection, that I have never pinched anyone's bottom. Not, one might say, as an end in itself.'

'I was going to say you were a damned liar.'

'That's why I made the qualification. Bottoms are interesting only for what they lead to.'

'Balls.'

'In some instances, but not the ones that interest me.'

'Save it for the party,' Gay said. 'Save it for the party.'

'What I was trying to say was simply that I have never been a fetishist of that kind. Breasts, of course, are different.'

'Not according to Dr Morris.'

23

'I must say I think he was a trifle lucky to make his fortune for an observation of that degree of banality, but perhaps I'm jealous.'

'What he observed,' Gay said, 'was the appetite of the public.'

'You may be right. I hope our hostess does no less. Ah, thank God, some other people. Do you know them? If you don't, no one will.'

'I'm going to kick you in a minute. You know who that is as well as I do. It's that television man. Dick Lucas and presumably his wife. He chaired that chatterama programme you did once.'

'Oh my God,' Basil Brain said, 'if I'd known he was coming! I think we'd better address ourselves to the wrong number for a few seconds.'

'We can't. Smile and be sociable. He's not so bad, when he sticks to his last.'

'Unfortunately he always believes that his last should be first. If he starts asking me to define my terms, I shall beat him about the head with the nearest copy of the *Philosophical Investigations*. It's curious how one only has to be an academic for people to start teaching one one's business. He's a very tiresome man, Gay, truly he is. *Lucas a non lucendo*, I presume.'

'I think you probably intimidated him.'

'Intimidated him! He never stopped talking from the apple to the egg.'

'Enough,' Gay Brain said. 'Is the bell not working?'

'I don't know,' Dick Lucas said. 'We've tried a couple of times. It certainly doesn't seem to be ringing inside.'

'That is generally what we mean by not working.'

'Or perhaps they can't hear it. It might be working but they can't hear it.'

'That is a possibility.'

Gay Brain said, 'Excuse me asking, but that's not a parcel, is it? I mean —'

'Yes, it's Adam's birthday,' Sandy Lucas said. 'He's forty.'

'I might have known,' Gay said. 'I might have known. Damn. Well it's too late now. Nothing's going to be open at this hour.'

'There's always John Bell and Croyden,' Basil said.

'And Boots in Piccadilly,' Sandy said. 'Try knocking, Dick.'

'After all, it is your business, isn't it?' Gay said. 'Knocking.'

'I've given it up,' Dick Lucas said, 'since the last director I praised shot himself.'

'In self-defence no doubt.'

'He left no note,' Dick said. 'I haven't reviewed a film for the last—'

'I'm *so* sorry, I'm terribly sorry, the bell hasn't worked for ages, I do apologise.'

'How did you know we were here, Ginny, if the bell doesn't work?'

'We heard the feet and we waited and waited, finally I'd decided to come anyway—I must tell you a story about that—anyway, Basil, Gay, how lovely. Dick, and—oh you haven't gone and—I told you not to—'

'We on the other hand,' Gay said, 'haven't gone and you didn't tell us. I'll get Basil to write Adam a cheque. Or a book.'

'A *festschrift*,' Basil said. 'Why not? I'll start a collection right away.'

'Don't be silly, he'll be thrilled that you came. It's your company we want, not your presents.'

'We may as well take our blasted vase home again then, Sandwich, it's obviously not going to be appreciated.'

'Sandy!' Virginia said. 'I'm so glad you've managed to come this time.'

'I came last time,' Sandy said.

'We met once before,' Basil Brain said, 'at TV Centre. You were chief brain.'

'Chief *of* the brains, not quite the same thing. I may have been in charge of the class, but I never claimed to be a member of it.'

'Gay, come on upstairs, and Sandy.'

'What was this story?'

'It happened soon after we were married. We were living in a cottage down at Marlow. My grandmother lent it to us. We were poor as anything and we asked some people over to dinner from Oxford. This was when Joe had gone over there to teach and anyway we asked Joe and his then wife and this rather frightening character as I then thought of him—'

'I know who you're going to say, Gilbert.'

'Gilbert Masterman, you know how pompous he is, the most unsmiling man ever, and I was so nervous, because I was planning to apply for an assistant lectureship at the time, something Jason's arrival promptly put an end to, I need hardly say, I opened the door —it's in there, Sandy, if you want to powder your nose or anything —without waiting for him to ring the bell and there he was peeing in the bushes.'

'Gilbert? I don't believe it.'

'As I stand here.'

'Wait till I tell Basil. What happened?'

'Well, I didn't know what to do. Finally, I went back indoors and shut the door. A few seconds later he rang and I opened it again.'

'What did he say?'

'He said, "My dear Mrs Playfair, when I tinkle I tinkle and when I ring I ring."'

'Oh my God, it's too perfect. It's too perfect. You know what he said to Baz on one occasion? He said, "If there's another war, I have all my plans laid. I intend to be a wireless operator in Rangoon. I've kept up my morse, I think they'll have me." You know what Baz said? He said, "Gilbert, don't underestimate yourself, they'll jump at you." The sheer lack of imagination! It never occurred to him there might not even *be* a Rangoon in the next war. Let alone time to get him there. What do you give it? The next war? Eight minutes?'

'The extraordinary thing is, though, he's got such tremendous pull.'

'And absolutely no push,' Gay Brain said. 'It is strange.'

'How's Basil liking London after Cambridge?'

'He likes it. He's such a tremendous social climber.'

'I'd never have accused Basil of that.'

'Of course he is. The Sherpa of NW1. And he gets asked everywhere, the Palace—the Playfairs—'

'Oh God,' Meredith Lamb said from the hall, 'It's that terrible American woman. What's her name? Gay Slater. We were once on a train together to Manchester and I promised myself—pardon!— never again.'

'Meredith, you wait there, I'm going to come right down and take a bite out of you.'

'I'll go in the other room and take off my trousers.'

'No one would notice any difference,' Gay called, 'if you did. The funny thing is,' she said when Meredith had gone into the drawing-room and Francesca, his wife, had thrown one of her beautiful, comprehending smiles towards Virginia, 'he really and truly doesn't like me. And I'm not too crazy about him. His position and the Pentagon's don't really have two cents to choose between them.'

'All that belching and farting is really only a façade,' Virginia said, 'don't you think, really? Meredith's basically an old-fashioned romantic, one more sentimental *laudator temporis acti*.'

'He may be all of that,' Gay Brain said, 'and then some. But I don't see why that has to turn him into a supporter of Marshal Ky.'

'He's a frustrated Quixote,' Virginia said, 'turned grouch.'

'Listen, I've no doubt there are still a lot of saddled Rosinantes in the Pentagon waiting only for a short-sighted rider with a good windmill to tilt at. Unhappily in most cases the windmills turn out to be peasants' houses, with the peasants still inside. And the lances turn out to be napalm.'

'You don't need to convince me,' Virginia said. 'Adam and I both made our positions clear at least three years ago. In no uncertain terms.'

'Men like Meredith Lamb are only tolerated because somewhere along the line they represent our own fall-back position. They man the bastions of reaction while we sally forth on our supposedly liberal missions. When the going gets really rough they open the gates of the bourgeoisie's strategic hamlets and we all scuttle back inside.'

'I don't think that's true,' Virginia said. 'At least not for me. I think I can honestly say—'

27

'Oh yes it is. Meredith is our vulgar sub-conscious. That's why, really, if we were serious people, we'd do our best to throw him into outer darkness. Meredith, you know, is really quite a nasty noise.'

'You can't dismiss the novels. Paul thinks very highly of his fictional achievement.'

'I've started one or two. I've never managed to finish one.'

'They're getting shorter and shorter,' Virginia said.

'True, soon you won't be *able* to start one without finishing it. Someone said the other day they were literary instant coffee, made in a jiffy and impossible to tell from the real thing, except by the taste. It was me as a matter of fact.'

'I like them,' Virginia said. 'I don't necessarily go as far as Paul, but I do admire them. He's cut away so much. That's what Paul admires. He's like Henry Moore in his way.'

'As far as I'm concerned,' Gay said, 'he's all hole.'

'I think in general the detective story is quite scandalously treated,' Meredith Lamb was saying. 'Take yours for instance. The first thing I like about them is that they damned well teach you something. You know your stuff, my old son.'

'It's very nice of you to say so,' Jack Darwin said.

'I'm perfectly serious. I'd sooner have written that one you did about North Africa — Sands of something, was it?'

'*A Desert Fountain.*'

'Right. What's that come from? Goldsmith?'

'Byron.'

'Damn. Anyway, I'd sooner have written that than all of, well, who shall we say? Any of your fashionable worthies. I'm sick to death of pseudo-revolutionaries trailing their bloody faggots from one market place to the next, challenging every decent burgess to put a match to them. It's about time someone damned well did.'

'Poor old George Lansbury,' Jack Darwin said.

'He was a stupid old cunt,' Meredith Lamb said, 'and you know it. It's all sheer canting masochism. The booted and spurious, that's what I call them, all these prophets of doom. Whereas what you do

28

is take us out there and rub our noses in it, never mind theories and theses. You give us the genuine griff, which is—'

'I haven't heard anyone use that expression in years,' Jack Darwin said.

'Pardon! And then there's all this women's stuff we're supposed to take so seriously. You know, chapter one, please may I have my orgasm; chapter two, that was no good, but please can we try again; chapter three, the do it yourself abortion and welcome to it; chapter four—evening, Cathie and 'tis ravishing you're looking— chapter four, woe, woe, my man has gone away; chapter five, woe, woe (again), 'tis pregnant I am and by a married man to boot; chapter six, why did I ever leave (a) Central Africa, (b) the West Riding or more often than not (c) dear old Ireland; chapter seven, although no one could be expected to live more than twenty minutes with such a whining bitch as you must realize I am, it's all everyone else's fault but mine; chapter eight, a visit to the parents but they're still drenched in hypocrisy as the day I left; chapter nine, what is there left but me and my little son to battle against the sinful world. Whereas your stuff—'

'I hoped we'd be coming back to that.'

'Your stuff doesn't drag itself moaning from one bed to the next, it's full of action and information, which is what I want in a book. It tells you something, for God's sake. After all, what is a novel when it comes to it? It's narrative. Narrative's what keeps the pot boiling, and by Christ, that's what a pot ought to do. More writers have been torpedoed by art than were ever corrupted by the demon commerce. I like to learn something when I read a book. By Gad, sir, when I want art I'll put on some Mozart. Take something you mention in Desert thing—'

'Fountain.'

'Yes. Are you sure about Byron?'

'Adapted from, yes. "Stanzas to Augusta". I always check these things.'

'I suppose you would. You mention there how the sand was a greater hazard to the British army than Rommel was. I was in that war by Gad, sir, and I never knew that. Sand under the prepuce a greater menace to morale than the 88-millimetre recoilless self-propelled gun? I never knew that.'

'I don't think the comparative statistics were ever actually published.'

'I bet it's damned well true. I accepted it because by God I know what an itchy prepuce is, by George. Good evening.'

'This is Rachel Davidson. Jack Darwin and Meredith Lamb.'

'Good evening.'

'Good evening, my dear, I'm just singing the praises of this clever bastard who, under the deuced cunning pseudonym of Jack Darwin writes the best bloody thrillers, call them what you will, this side of the Atlantic.'

'I've never read them I'm afraid,' Rachel said.

'Then your education is incomplete. You'll learn more from one book by this mythopoeic master than in all the philosophical treatises ever composed.'

'If you're wondering why he's being so flattering, it's because he's drunk.'

'But not disorderly, never disorderly. I'm flattering because I know how bloody difficult it is to do, boyo. I know how difficult it is.'

'I read that chapter you did in that composite job Norbert published,' Jack Darwin said.

'The bald-headed Primo Donno? Is he here? Is he coming? Which chapter do you think I wrote? I bet you guessed wrong.'

'You wrote chapter eight,' Jack Darwin said.

'Thank God I didn't murder my first wife, you'd never have let me get away with it!'

'No, I certainly wouldn't. I liked her very much.'

'So did I, but she and Francesca just couldn't agree on who was going to sleep in the middle. Yes, it was a pity that. It was a pity. How the hell could you tell which was my chapter? I thought I'd been through it for dabs until you couldn't tell me from Stork.'

'Use of the word "urn".'

'Urn?'

'You referred to an urn on the garden wall, below where they found Von Platt.'

'So I did. Of course you realize if they'd not been anti-Semites, they could have recruited an Afrika Korps composed entirely of circumcised squaddies and probably have pushed on to Cairo by the spring of '42? One only thinks of the top Jews like Einstein—and those polysyllabic sods you used to meet at High Table—but the loss of the rank and file may well have cost them just as dear. I'm surprised Alan hasn't tumbled to that. Another one of those unacknowledged banalities he admires so much. An élite Panzer division of prepuceless Jewboys and the world might have been his.'

'You also referred, if you don't mind my pointing it out, to the Danish frogman—'

'I thought that was a nice touch though, didn't you, making him Danish? I mean of all nationalities. Danish, I mean, the last thing—'

'You said he was armed with a repeater.'

'And so he was, dammit. *Ego ipse ita feci*, as we used to say in the jakes of old Bombay.'

'Forgive me, but I wonder if you really know what a repeater is.'

'A repeater? Do I know what a repeater is?'

'I have a feeling you've confused it with an automatic.'

'A repeater is a type of gun—'

'Yes.'

'Which can fire one round after another.'

'Yes—and no.'

'It's clear enough, isn't it? It's normal English, a gun—'

'Which can fire one round after another, true, but—'

'But what?'

'You refer to the killing of the eight Trinidadians and you say that it must have been done by someone armed with a repeater. I think you meant by that a gun which fires continuously as long as the trigger is pressed.'

'Isn't that a repeater?'

'That's an automatic,' Jack Darwin said.

'*And* a repeater, surely.'

31

'Possibly. In the sense that an automatic is always a repeater, but a repeater is by no means always an automatic.'

'You're cheeseparing, sir, you're cheeseparing. Not to mention hairsplitting. Wouldn't you say so?'

'I'm afraid I don't know,' Rachel Davidson said.

'I'm a great one for yielding to authority,' Meredith Lamb said, 'but I still maintain that there's no necessary solecism involved.'

'Necessary possibly not. Strongly implied I'd say yes, quite frankly. The overwhelming suggestion is that the eight Trinidadians—'

'I thought that was a nice touch making them Trinidadians, don't you? I toyed with Guadeloupe, but I didn't know what the noun form was. Get that, girl, noun form, that's what keeps us in business.'

'Guadeloupe-holes,' Jack Darwin said, 'possibly.'

'That's the feminine surely,' Meredith said.

'A repeater,' Jack Darwin said, 'is any rifle which is capable of being fired again without new rounds being put in. Thus any magazine-loading gun is a repeater.'

'A repeater is any gun that repeats,' Meredith said. 'I quite agree.'

'Always depending on what you mean by repeating. The original repeater, as you will remember, was the Winchester. You will also recall the characteristic reloading action. Ke-joink, puch, ke-joink, puch, ke-joink, puch—'

'Ke-joink, puch, of course I do. Good heavens, I wrote a piece on Westerns only—'

'I know. The Winchester was the original repeater, but it was not an automatic. Very far from it. You only have to think of the ke-joink. If it had been an automatic, there would have been no need for the ke-joink.'

'Are you being bored to tears by these two?' Adam Playfair said. 'Come and meet someone else.'

'Pretty girl,' Meredith Lamb said, 'most fuckable on first inspection, but she doesn't seem to know much about the things that matter in life.'

32

'The Lee-Enfield .303, the standard British infantry rifle of the last war —'

'Don't tell me about the Lee-Enfield .303, my old son, I fired one of the damned things. Down, crawl, observe, sights, FIRE.'

'What's Meredith Lamb doing on the carpet?'

'I think he's kissing Jack Darwin's feet.'

'Darling, the Doctors are here. Do come.'

'I was just talking to Miss Davidson —'

'You know how shy Victoria is, you must come and talk her down or she'll spend all evening upstairs with the coats. You know Professor Brain, don't you, Rachel?'

'I don't know about know,' Rachel said. 'We —'

'Of course,' Basil said, 'I remember, even if you don't.'

'How do you think it's going?'

'Not bad, but isn't it time we ate?'

'Victor! Victoria! We were terrified you'd had a late call at the last moment.'

'Oh no,' Victoria said. 'No, not at all. I'm not on tonight.'

'I was doing a broadcast,' Victor said. 'They called me at six o'clock and asked me to do something on Horse Shows.'

'I never knew you knew anything about Horse Shows.'

'I don't,' Victor said, 'but they wanted a piece by someone who didn't know about Horse Shows, a sort of meta-Horse Show piece, so they got hold of me and that's why we're late. Who's here? Is Basil Brain here?'

'Yes, he is,' Virginia said. 'He's in there.'

'Because we met at a dinner party at Fred's the other night and he said he might be coming.'

'I don't know whether you're hungry,' Adam said, 'but there's food downstairs, isn't that right, Gin?'

'I've had it catered for the first time, because if you do your own food you never get a chance to talk to your guests. I've got two lovely little pouffes from round the corner. They're supposed to be terribly good and, of course, I chose all the main things and terrines and cheeses and sweets myself, and — well, do come and see —'

'We've eaten,' Victoria said.

33

'I have respect for him where he sticks to his own discipline,' Basil Brain was saying.

'But that book he did on American foreign policy—'

'I'm not unaware of the book in question, nor am I necessarily hostile to his analysis, where it involves reasoned argument and a broad spectrum of reading, not merely the quotation of what sustains his thesis, but what I am saying is that I can't accept that his undoubted merits in one field give any necessary support to his views in another. Because I'm a good gardener does not make my views on table tennis any more valuable.'

'I suppose that that's true,' Victor said, 'but—good evening—'

'This is Doctor Victor Rich.'

'I know,' Rachel said, 'I've seen you on the box.'

'Rachel Davidson.'

'Hullo. I think I know what you were talking about, because we were talking about it at Fred's, weren't we, the other night? Yes, what I was wondering was whether there wasn't an analogy of a sort between the "natural games player", so-called, you know the kind of person one used to meet at school who was good at all ball games, even those invented on the spur of the moment, and the intellectual who can, so to speak, take up any language game in the sense of any logical system or situation after only a few seconds to get the gist of the rules.'

'I did say "necessary" support and I'd like to claim some special status for that qualification—'

'Yes, of course, I did take that point, but we could go beyond it. And if one looks at the whole logic of the situation—if one tries to see the general form of the way bright people are bright, I do think there's a sense in which credentials in one field can be of weight in another and apparently unrelated one.'

'I'm arguing,' Basil Brain said, 'if I *am* arguing, against privilege. And surely that's unexceptionable. The man with the stripes or his heart on his sleeve doesn't—'

'Obviously we're not arguing,' Victor Rich said, 'that would be absurd and counter-productive. That's not the way I assume us to be going on at all. But don't you think there's a certain tendency

34

towards intellectual disciplinary Guilds, and don't you think that's something that ought to be resisted? I do think that we're in danger of losing the ideal of universal man and that surely isn't something either of us would want?'

'Hullo.'

'Hullo.'

'You must be Mrs Playfair. I'm Gil Timmis.'

'Oh. How do you do?'

'And this is Camille. Adam said to drop by if we were in the vicinity.'

'Oh absolutely. I'm so glad you managed to —'

'Gil!' Adam said. 'Come in. This is terrific.'

'This is Camille.'

'Hullo. Well, you sonofabitch, you made it. I told you about Gil. He's bought the new Oliver Samson.'

'Your husband screwed me right into the ground,' Gil Timmis said, 'and then some. I only just managed to extricate myself in time for the party.'

'We were just going to have something to eat,' Virginia said.

'We've eaten as a matter of fact. With Gideon Levy who sent his very best.'

'Oh God,' Virginia said.

'Don't worry. I was very discreet.'

'Don't worry,' Adam said, 'I don't believe you.'

'And I'll tell you who I had lunch with today, that was Bruno. You know, he's still got a hell of a head on his hunched little shoulders. I hear Danny Meyer may be coming.'

'I heard the same thing,' Adam said. 'But he hasn't shown yet.'

'How's the back today? Adam could hardly walk when we had lunch Monday.'

'Better.'

'Playing soccer at your age. You must be crazy.'

'It wasn't anything to do with soccer,' Adam said.

'Jean-Claude, vous êtes ici! Comme vous êtes gentil d'être venu.'

'Not at all, may I present Nancy Lane?'

'How do you do? How nice of you to come. Je parlais de vous

35

avec Paul Mallory qui était à la Sorbonne au même temps que vous pour deux années dans les dernières années Cinquante et qui, je crois, vous a rencontré à cette époque-là. Il se souvient de vous comme étudiant. Il était Professeur de la Littérature Anglaise, c'était après l'affaire Suez quand il a quitté le Foreign Office, dégoûté par les mensonges Édeniennes. I don't know if you want to leave your coat upstairs, but a lot of people seem to be slinging them in Adam's study now. The segregation of coats seems to be a dying cult, doesn't it? Oui, Paul est maintenant un des chef-rédacteurs d'un Publishing House très bien connu, très gauchisant évidemment, mais pas Communiste du tout. C'est Playfair, Marks. On se dégoûte de tous les manifestations d'une idéologie monolithique et sans souplesse. J'espère, à mon avis, qu'en dépit de toutes les tendances révolutionnaires, dont on se compte très sympathique en général, on n'arrivera jamais encore à une politique Européenne qui nie aux autres le droit de leurs opinions and qui insiste rigidement sur la seule autorité de ses propres dogmes.'

'I absolutely agree with you, Mrs Playfair. I hope you don't mind that I brought Mrs Lane with me —'

'Pas du tout. I said you should. Is she — ?'

'Divorced. We met at a musical evening and I thought she was very nice, so —'

'Elle me semble charmante, et elle est très jolie. Elle est Américaine, n'est-ce pas?'

'Originally, yes. You speak excellent French.'

'Oh, a little and very badly. It was never my subject.'

'You must define what you mean by privilege,' Dick Lucas said.

'With great respect, I don't really think that I feel that obligation.'

'If you're going to use a word, you must tell us what you mean by it.'

'On the contrary,' Victor Rich said.

'I wonder why it is,' Basil Brain said, 'that no one ever dances at things like this any more. When I was an undergraduate, people always used to dance.'

'It is funny,' Rachel said.

36

'If I define what I mean by something, that doesn't necessarily resolve the argument. It simply *is* an argument. The simplest way to discover what I mean by a term is to listen to the way in which I use it. By privilege, what we normally mean is surely —'

'If one's going to have an argument, one should define one's terms,' Dick Lucas said.

'But one isn't,' Victor Rich said. 'That's the thing. Arguments as such are merely counter-productive.'

'I really should like to dance, wouldn't you?'

'I'd sooner eat first,' Rachel Davidson said. 'I haven't eaten for three days.'

'Three *days*? You can't be serious.'

'I am actually.'

'A girl as pretty as you who hasn't eaten for three days, it's against nature. That something so pretty hasn't been —'

'Plucked?' Janey Darwin said.

'The first use of privilege, surely, is, in effect, a private law. A law acting to the advantage of a single person or group of persons. Of the kind, for example, which still operates in the U.S.A. for certain powerful interests and individuals. It puts them not so much beyond the law as safely within it.'

'The simplest thing is to take you downstairs and fill you up. Why haven't you eaten for three days?'

'No money,' Rachel Davidson said.

'Good heavens,' Basil Brain said, 'someone's slipped up somewhere.'

'What're you doing all by yourself, Janey?' Adam said.

'Nothing much,' Janey Darwin said. 'Contemplating suicide. Oh, don't tell me; I know, it's been done.'

'The M1 is a considerably better weapon in every respect.'

'Better than the old Lee-Enfield? Never, sir, never.'

'A tank compared to a scythed chariot.'

'I suppose you're going to tell me it's automatic.'

'It is automatic.'

'Which means that a man in a panic runs the risk of premature ejaculation and has nothing left to offer at the critical moment. It's a moral hazard, giving a decent British infantryman a weapon like that.'

'Surely you're not really so broke you can't eat?'

'I've been ill as well.'

'You don't look it.'

'All he has to do is fit a new magazine. Two seconds. Ke-klonk.'

'Thirty years ago my father stood on the beach at Folkestone armed with a pike and the British were never in finer fettle. Oh, sod it, I expect you're right, but it's a damned cumbrous weapon for presenting arms, that you have to grant me.'

'That I grant you. Willingly.'

'What's been wrong with you?'

'I don't know really. It could've been dysentery, I suppose. The water's not brilliant where I've been living.'

'Where on earth have you been living?'

'I've been living in a village outside Barcelona.'

'What on earth for? And why did you drink it?'

'I went with somebody. We were thirsty.'

'Oh, I see. Well, you'd better be careful what you eat. That looks like soup, that can't hurt you. Try some of that.'

'It's gazpacho,' Virginia said. 'Do.'

'Thank you, but I really couldn't.'

'You probably ought to go very easily, if it's the first time you've eaten. Have you only just come back from Barcelona then?'

'Oh no, I've been living in Chigwell for the last five weeks.'

'Chigwell.'

'Yes.'

'Why Chigwell?'

'I know someone there.'

'I suppose I might have guessed.'

'That man really has an absolutely pre-Wittgensteinian notion of fruitful argument. I've only just managed to get away from him. The idea that definition is the first stage in an argument! I've been trying to demonstrate to him that definition is, if you like, the sign that the argument is over, but he didn't understand.'

'It's his profession not to understand,' Basil Brain said. 'What

38

about a slice of cold meat? A profession which comes very naturally to him. Or the galantine? I would have thought the galantine very suitable, wouldn't you, Doctor Rich?'

'It depends what the trouble's been. I'm not really medical, you know.'

'This young lady has had dysentery. She contracted it in Barcelona and suffered the consequences in Chigwell.'

'Why Chigwell?'

'She knows someone there.'

'I assume that you were talking about credentials in relation to dissent from the policy being followed in South East Asia.'

'When? I should go easy on the salad, wouldn't you, Dr Rich?'

'Might be abrasive, yes. When I came in and you were talking. You used the analogy of the gardener.'

'Oh yes,' Basil said. 'Try that to start with, and I should go easy on alcohol, isn't that right?'

'You feel that it dilutes his credibility to take an overtly partisan line on Vietnam?'

'His credibility as what? Let's find you somewhere to sit down.'

'No, I'm all right, it's very nice of you, but I'm all right. This is luxury already; it's actually warm.'

'Where were you living in Chigwell exactly?'

'In a disused shop.'

'Good heavens. You are dedicated to self-destruction! Dysentery in a disused shop. Don't you have parents? I suppose you've quarrelled with them?'

'No, not really, but I just don't live with them. Are you in agreement with commitment then against U.S. foreign policy?'

'Well, I think you'd be in some difficulty to find anyone in this room who wasn't in some sense against it.'

'Difficulty in *this* room,' Basil Brain said. 'That seems to be going down all right. How about another slice of galantine?'

'No, I'm all right.'

'Meredith Lamb's upstairs,' Basil said, 'go and ask him what he thinks about the Pentagon. You'll find he's very far from subscribing to what you think of as the general view. The last I saw of him he was in the prone position defending his post when none but he had fled.'

'Meredith is an intellectual posing as a backwoodsman. He's fine as a circus turn, but one doesn't leap into the ring with him. One claps or laughs, but one doesn't leap into the ring with him.'

'Jean-Claude, je vous présente Paul Mallory. Oh et vous ne connaissez pas mon mari, Adam. Adam, Jean-Claude Cénac.'

'Hullo,' Paul Mallory said. 'They had that L.S.E. man on the wing and could he go! Like the clappers. He wasn't too skilful but Christ he could run and Basil just hasn't got the legs any more.'

'Basil sweeps intelligently.'

'He sweeps all right when the broom's shoved into his hands,' Paul said, 'but he can't recover once he's off balance. He can still shift in one direction fairly reasonably, but he's about as quick on the turn as a Mediterranean tide. I thought Daniel Meyer was coming.'

'So did I,' Adam said. 'What's happened to Danny?'

'Oh it's early yet. Lots of people aren't here yet.'

'Are you a soccer player at all?'

'No, I am sorry to say. I used to play rugby of course, before I went to live in Paris.'

'What we need,' Paul Mallory said, 'is a young inside-forward with a pair of balls on him, because I thought Mungo was pathetic on Sunday honestly, and at least one constructive player in the back four. Soccer's the game, once you get to know it.'

'I like to watch it, but I have never played.'

'How old are you?'

'Thirty-eight now.'

'Pity. What we really need is someone about twenty-seven who can run. I was thinking we could train you up, but—he's got the build for a striker.'

'Who would you like to meet?' Virginia asked. 'Do you know Brian Stammers? Nancy Lane, is that right? Do forgive me, but—'

'That's right,' Nancy said.

'Brian Stammers, who represents us at Westminster. He's our M.P.'

'I did understand,' Nancy said. 'Forgive me asking, but what party are you?'

'Guess,' Brian Stammers said.

'Unfortunately I don't follow British politics too closely.'

'How long have you been in England?'

'Eight years on and off. We used to divide our time between London and Paris.'

'Used to?'

'When I was still married to my husband.'

'And you still can't tell Stork from margarine? I'm a Socialist.'

'I suppose I should've guessed.'

'There aren't any obvious caste marks,' Brian Stammers said. 'I don't really see why you should.'

'I don't think a Conservative would be willing to let you guess what he was, that's why I should've guessed. Anyway, I don't think our hosts are likely to harbour a Conservative, are they?'

'You sound as though you don't count that in their favour.'

'Oh now,' Nancy said, 'don't start trying to tempt me into indiscretions. As a matter of fact I don't know them at all. I just came with somebody.'

'Lucky somebody. There's one over there, as a matter of fact. Stuart Melrose. A Tory.'

'Brian,' Adam said, 'what I wanted to ask you was who was it who was supposed to have said that the present Government would see no objection to selling arms to Nazi Germany provided the equipment was used for external aggression and not against members of the native population?'

'It could have been Tony and then again it could have been Humphrey. I hadn't actually heard it in that form though. It is rather good. Ask Stuart, he might know.'

'He's become so stuffy since he became a P.P.S., he probably wouldn't get the point. Brian, I had an idea I wanted to talk to you about, and that was I thought it might make an interesting series, to get a number of people, possibly like yourself, who used to be academic, and get them to do an "If only" piece on the supposition that we had not gone to war with Hitler and the Nazi régime had survived, without actually physically conquering the rest of Europe.'

'We might have been a lot better off,' Nancy Lane said.

'Well, that's exactly it.'

'Better off by what standards would you say?'

'Danny! You must've crept in like the tide. Have you seen Virginia?'

'I hear it's your birthday. Condolences and here.'

'I told Ginny not to tell anyone'

'To say it's nothing is an overstatement, so don't worry.'

'Nancy Lane — Daniel Meyer. Brian Stammers.'

'Are you Daniel Meyer the director?'

'I'm Daniel Meyer *a* director,' Daniel said. 'I was in Hollywood last year — visiting the tombs of the Moguls — you're American, aren't you? — thought so — and my producer, who is probably one of the most shameless people presently going broke, grabbed the confidential guest list, with all the remarks on it, from the desk clerk. Everyone was tabulated — star, famous producer, well-known producer, TV personality, and so on. Next to me was "an English director", lowest of the low. Like a hotel with a candlestick next to it in the *Guide Michelin*.'

'Are you working at the moment? I mean, is Parliament — ?'

'I'm working,' Brian Stammers said, 'but Parliament isn't.'

'The History of England,' Daniel said.

'What I felt about it,' Dick Lucas said, 'was that it was a gratuitous example of two people hugging each other in public — or possibly of just one person hugging himself. The director.'

'He's standing over there,' Gay Brain said, 'so be careful.'

'It wouldn't alter my opinion,' Dick Lucas said, 'if he was lying on his death-bed. Those who submit themselves to public judgment shouldn't expect the court to take their feelings into account. To resent one's critics is really a form of blackmail. Those who spend their time making love to their own image shouldn't hope for the kisses of the bystanders as well.'

'You look as if you've lost someone. Have you?'

'I was just looking for my wife.'

'Oh. Why?'

'Danny's here.'

'I haven't seen him.'

'That's why I'm telling you. He's upstairs.'

'I decided to cut the cake up,' Virginia said, 'so that no one would be tempted to sing. I think it's going all right, don't you?'

'All parties', Adam said, 'are goalless draws. The best one can hope for is no serious injuries. Yes, it's going fine.'

'You have to admit he was right about a lot of things,' Nancy Lane said.

'Are you saying that seriously?'

'Well a man who most people agree could have been either a Conservative or a Socialist Prime Minister can't be a complete idiot, can he?'

'I don't know what evidence you've got for that. In view of the collection we've had in the last twenty years.'

'Can you seriously think you can be the head of any country without having any sort of qualities at all? I just can't believe that. I'm sorry.'

'The man was a phoney. You only have to read his books. They're the real giveaway. Have you ever read anything he's written?'

'I've met him,' Nancy Lane said.

'And you were impressed.'

'I thought he talked a lot of sense. And of course he has the most terrific personal charm.'

'So did Goering.'

'Tom's slimmer,' Nancy Lane said, 'even now.'

'You knew him well.'

'He came to our house a couple of times and we met at friends.'

'I'm afraid I couldn't stay in the same room.'

'I think I could do that,' Brian Stammers said.

'The fascination with such people is like the fascination with executioners. To spend time trying to humanize them is an obscenity. It's really a form of sucking up, of trying to obtain special terms.'

'That's not the point at all.'

'It's my point,' Daniel said. 'Fraternizing with those people is simply –'

'Trying to understand the world.'

'No, it's trying to excuse one's laziness, one's failure to act. The man who tries to understand everything before he does anything is the modern Oblomov, forever burying his head under the intellectual bedclothes.'

'He's known all the famous people of his century. I have to admit I found him fascinating. And he doesn't deny he made mistakes. He isn't half as dictatorial as maybe you like to believe.'

'It's not honestly a question of what one likes to believe. I've read practically everything he's written—'

'Why?' Brian Stammers asked.

'I suppose because I wanted to make sure that there was nothing there.'

'Rather like Charlie Broad's Psychical Researches in which he devoted immense care to proving that there was no foundation for belief in the Supernatural.'

'Hullo, Victor, how are you?'

'I'm all right,' Victor Rich said.

'Well, God knows you're qualified to tell,' Daniel said.

'Danny!'

'Hullo, Gin, how are you?'

'What did you do to get in?'

'Pushed,' Daniel said. 'Isn't that what everyone does?'

'You were on the programme once,' Victor Rich said, 'when I was producing "Left and Right".'

'Oh yes, of course,' Brian Stammers said.

'It didn't really turn out the way I'd envisaged it unfortunately. I wanted it to be a sort of meta-political discussion, but it always got too acrimonious on a rather petty level. Also nobody watched.'

'I hear there's talk of you being made Controller of Programmes.'

'There's talk of me being made practically everything,' Victor Rich said, 'but I don't necessarily believe it. What is true is that we desperately need someone in the Company at the moment who isn't involved at a purely careerist level. Someone who can take a dispassionate—'

'Point of view.'

'Point of view. Someone who wants to be something more than simply Mr Television.'

'His modesty', Daniel said, 'will be his salvation.'

'At least he's intelligent.'

'At most, he's intelligent.'

'Basil Brain's downstairs—and so's the food. Poor Victoria Rich, she's been sucking the same empty glass for the last twenty minutes. He doesn't really treat her very nicely. He just leaves her standing. Danny, you go on down, you know the way.'

'The way down,' Daniel said, 'is never difficult to find. And it is far from the same as the way up.'

'Adam, poor Victoria's been standing there for the last twenty minutes. Can't you introduce her to somebody?'

'The best thing would be,' Adam said, 'if someone were to be taken ill. Preferably with something rather unusual. She's apparently quite a remarkable diagnostician.'

'Perhaps you could get her to come and eat. You notice Danny came alone?'

'But will he leave alone? That's the question.'

'Quite, but it obviously means that other girl really is over. How do you think he looks?'

'Fit enough to play on Sunday,' Adam said, 'according to Paul, which is what matters. I must say I think you've done very well for him. She's very pretty, this Rachel of yours.'

'You're thinking of Scipio Africanus,' Jack Darwin said.

'I tell you I'm thinking of Alexander the Great. Surely I must be allowed to know who I'm thinking of, by God, right or wrong.'

'The Liddell Hart monograph you're thinking of was about Scipio Africanus.'

'Well at least you'll grant me that the stirrup was first used effectively at the battle of Tours by the Franks.'

'It was published in 1927, if I remember rightly, and argued that Hannibal had learnt from Alexander and Scipio from Hannibal.'

'Which is far from saying that Scipio would have beaten Alexander.'

'Rachel Davidson.'

45

'How do you do?' Rachel said.

'You know, Virginia, I was just saying what a marvellous party this was, but what a pity there isn't any dancing.'

'Basil, do you really want to dance? Because —'

'With so many pretty girls about? Wouldn't you?'

'*Mutatis mutandis.*'

Rachel Davidson said: 'Are you doing anything special at the moment?'

'I've just been doing a telly film about the Elephant Man,' Daniel said. 'If that means anything to you?'

'Sounds like first cousin to Buffalo Bill. No, it doesn't really.'

'Which I'm editing at the moment. The Elephant Man was a Victorian freak. A poor deformed bastard that got toted around by a brutal showman and displayed like a, well, a freak.'

'Which he was.'

'Which he was. This surgeon — Sir Frederick Treves, his name was — took him in and cared for him, and it's the story of their relationship. The thing being that the surgeon, who genuinely cared for him, on the one hand, on the other had a sort of necrophilous interest in the proceedings because he wanted to have the body when the Elephant Man died, so he could dissect it.'

'Is this true, this story?'

'All my stories are true,' Daniel said. 'I found it in an old book. Anyway, that's what I've been doing.'

'I loved *Myself Among Others.*'

'It has its admirers. Among whom Dick Lucas over there is not included. I'd really like to crunch him as a matter of fact.'

'Do you crunch people?'

'Only semi-legally. On the football field. But I clench my fists a lot.'

'Oh you're one of those as well, are you? Do you play with Adam and people? For the whatever they're called —'

'The Canons. Yes, I do, even though I didn't get a first. Their original idea was only to field people who'd got firsts, didn't you know that?'

'How incredible!'

'Not so much incredible as impractical. They managed it for a time, but it was a case of too many heads and not enough legs, so they spread their net a bit. They take it very seriously, as a matter of fact.'

'And don't you?'

'Except when I'm jeering at them.'

'Very few English directors are as sympathetic to women as you were in that film.'

'Do you think one should be sympathetic?'

'It's not enough,' Rachel said, 'but it's a start.'

'Towards what?'

'Releasing women from the stereotype.'

'Don't you think we could all do with a bit of releasing? I mean, it's not only women who are forced to be something. We all are, aren't we?'

'Women suffer more. There's so much less they can do. Unless they're very talented.'

'Or very pretty.'

'I don't think that helps.'

'That's because you're pretty. It helps.'

'She was wonderful.'

'Yes, she was.'

'Is she nice to work with?'

'She can be marvellous,' Daniel said. 'No one's an angel all the time.'

'No, I imagine even you can be quite difficult.'

'I can be a shit,' Daniel said. 'I think I will crunch him; he looks fairly out of condition. Mind you, bald men can be deceptive. One assumes they're rather debilitated and it ain't necessarily so. The shorn Samson can still sometimes pack a punch.'

'I find it rather frightening. People wanting to hit people.'

'It's something about London,' Daniel said. 'People lose the faculty for action and then they get scared they'll never recover it. Hence the cult of the boot. And then there really are some critics that ought to be crunched. And probably want to be. The masochism of the impotent.'

'It was a big success, though, *Myself Among Others*, wasn't it? Surely you can afford to have one or two people not like it?'

'It's when they don't like *me* that it hurts,' Daniel said. 'And Lucas has a particular personal—'

'Most of my friends liked it very much, so—'

'I obviously ought to have most of your friends!' Daniel said. 'You can certainly have most of mine.'

'He likes her,' Virginia said.

'You're not an actress, are you?' Daniel said.

'Not really,' Rachel said. 'I have acted, but I don't like to think of myself as an actress.'

'How do you? Like to think of yourself?'

'I don't know. As someone with decisions still to make, I suppose. Difficult to say. Someone with a future, but not in the usual sense.'

'Well, you're right,' Daniel said. 'Don't be an actress. Be somebody.'

'That's the thing,' Rachel Davidson said. 'People start asking you what you've been in and not what you are or what you want. Having a career begins to be a substitute for being a person. The old Women's Emancipation people thought opening the professions to women would do the trick, but it's just another blind. Instead of turning them into cuddlies, it turned them into pseudo-men.'

'No one's ever going to do that to you,' Daniel said.

'You'd be surprised.'

'And disgusted,' Daniel said. 'But I must confess, I rather like cuddlies.'

'I'm going to rig up the gramophone and then people can dance if they want to.'

'I'm not dancing,' Gay Brain said, 'I'm too full of food.'

'Too full of shit,' Meredith Lamb said.

'*Meredith.*'

'What have you acted in actually?'

'I did a few things at Oxford,' Rachel said, 'and then I did some experimental work with a group.'

'And how was that?'

'It was interesting. They were trying to do something new.'

'Where was this?'

'We worked in Swiss Cottage for a while and then we spent a summer in Tunisia. In Hammamet.'

'Oh at the—'

'Yes. I enjoyed it, but then finally—'

'He wasn't quite the man you thought he was.'

'Partly, but not altogether. I think perhaps I'm just not ambitious.'

'That sounds too good to be true. An attractive girl—'

'Are attractive girls always ambitious in your world?'

'Oh I don't have a world,' Daniel Meyer said. 'I make do with everybody else's.'

'Only the thing is, we haven't really got many suitable records—'

'Excuse me, but—Daniel Meyer?'

'That's right.'

'Gil Timmis.'

'Oh, hullo. I had a message—'

'I've been trying to contact you for two days. This is Camille. Daniel Meyer.'

'Hullo. And this is—oh, she's—'

'I'm a great admirer of yours.'

'All admirers of mine are great,' Daniel said.

'*Myself Among Others* really knocked me out. I would really very much like for us to work together. Of course I know a lot of people must say that to you.'

'Never enough,' Daniel said. 'And the way things are—'

'We're working in a dying industry, Daniel. Everyone knows that. We're working in a dying industry. More empires are collapsing every day. We're like the Hapsburgs.'

'Worse,' Daniel said. 'The perHapsburgs.'

'I like that,' Gil Timmis said. 'I like that very much. In fact, I'll probably steal it. I really did want to talk to you because I have a proposition. Not much of a proposition, but a proposition. I hear you know Greece pretty well.'

'I go there,' Daniel said. 'Or I used to. I haven't been recently.'

'The thing being, we have some money there. Locked in. Money we have to use there, like it or not. Not too much, but then you won't need too much. Production is still relatively cheap out there. Until next week. What we need is a story. Something contemporary, because that seems to be what the kids want to see, something that says something to today's generation, but at the same time, of course, we can't make another Z, because—'

'They wouldn't let us get away with it.'

'And full frontal Marxism personally I can do without for a while. What I'd like to do, if you were interested, because I don't know how you're fixed this summer, is to finance you to go and take a look around and see what you can come up with. If there was a book you wanted us to buy for you, well, that would be another way we might get into this. I have a pretty flexible deal back on the Coast and this is something we could develop without too much interference—'

'All interference is too much interference,' Daniel said, 'but still. Do you know a writer called Robert Gavin?'

'I don't believe I do. What's he written?'

'Books.'

'No, I don't.'

'He lives on one of the islands.'

'That's something I plan to do one day,' Gil Timmis said. 'Go take a yacht and visit some of those islands. Someone asked me in New York only last week, but—No, I never heard of him.'

'There's a novel of his called *Rats*. It's about a couple who dream of a place away from it all and how they finally go and live on an island and how it's slowly—'

'I think I can guess,' Gil Timmis said. 'Frankly Rats were last year.'

'O.K.,' Daniel said, 'I'll think of something else.'

'Something the kids of today can relate to is the problem. And don't be afraid of sentiment,' Gil Timmis said, 'because—'

'I think I know what you're going to say. Love is no longer a dirty word.'

'Is right. Let's just leave it this way, if it's something you'd like to think about, get Queenie to call me and we'll try and work

50

something out to keep the thing alive until it becomes a reality. When do you finish editing?'

'When does anyone?' Daniel said. 'Soon. Soon. I hope.'

'Once one's *in* politics,' Brian Stammers said, 'everything looks completely different. Even Stuart Melrose.'

'Good evening, Brian, how are you?'

'Fair,' Brian Stammers said.

'An admirable condition,' Stuart Melrose said, 'but small recommendation for high office.'

'You should know. How's L.G.?'

'Gloomy, Brian, gloomy, but don't underestimate him.'

'I'll never do that, I promise you.'

'Somehow,' Daniel said, 'it makes one feel a little sick to see two supposedly sworn political enemies grinning at each other like old friends.'

'You don't really believe in art,' Francesca Lamb said.

'I don't see the connection.'

'Exactly. Sublimation isn't really something you approve of. You want wars to be to the knife, but the essence of civilization is that they're to the tongue and the eye as well. Do you really want to see blood that much?'

'I want to see truth,' Daniel said. 'Or at least fewer lies.'

'They go together,' Francesca said. 'Truth and blood. Personally I find the English way of politics totally acceptable. I admire all sides of the house.'

'I hate England,' Daniel said.

'Nonsense,' Francesca said.

'I do,' Daniel said.

'Where do you admire then?'

'That's not the point. Nowhere.'

'Having chosen to live somewhere, personally I make the best of it. I can't live with my bags packed all the time. I don't think any woman can.'

'Does that make you feel better or worse, to be in a nice big class?'

'Don't be sarcastic with me, please, because I don't really have to listen to that sort of thing.'

51

Daniel said, 'Sorry.'

'If you want to be rude, be rude to the politicians, as you despise them so much. There are other people I can talk to.'

'Look, I said I was sorry.'

'And if I want my intelligence insulted, I can always go to the cinema.'

'Stand by,' Stuart Melrose said, 'someone's going to insult us.'

'No, I'm not,' Daniel said.

'What've you said to her?'

'Nothing.'

'You were obviously misquoted,' Brian Stammers said.

'I was misunderstood,' Stuart said. 'What the man actually said to me was "Why haven't you kept your promises?" and I said, "In this country, thank God, we've never had political parties that kept their promises. Any government which did what it said it would in its election manifesto would be politically irresponsible and economically disastrous." So of course it came out that I said it was irresponsible to keep one's promises.'

'You can't win with these people,' Brian Stammers said. 'I never read them.'

'Nor do I. They don't want to understand, that's the thing.'

'Look, I'm truly frightfully sorry if I said something –'

'I wish you wouldn't apologize,' Francesca said. 'It only makes it worse.'

'Do you know that Paul once told Adam that he never realized that once you were married it was still possible to find yourself physically attracted to other women? This was when he was still in the Foreign Office.'

'Do tell me, is he faithful to Margaret?'

'Yes, I think he is probably, but he feels dreadfully guilty about it.'

'I suppose that's what all this football's about.'

'The funny thing is that at Cambridge they wouldn't've been seen dead kicking a football.'

'Listen, I think I'd better be going.'

'You can't! You've only just got here.'

'I've upset Francesca Lamb.'

'She likes to be upset. Someone once told her she had a tragic face.'

'No, I was very stupid. I'm just not very sociable tonight.'

'Come and meet somebody else.'

'No, truly.'

'Please, Danny, or I shall be upset too. Francesca's not the only one who can be tragic, you know.'

'Oh I know.'

'But the critic's office, after all, is to judge the dish that's put in front of him,' Dick Lucas said, 'not to show understanding over what went wrong in the kitchen.'

'God, I hate that man.'

'Is it really worth it?' Virginia said.

'Until I can find someone else,' Daniel said. 'I need the exercise.'

'I should have thought it was far more to the point to find someone to love.'

'Ah but everyone's taken that I love,' Daniel said.

'Liar.'

'Am I? Not altogether. Why do you give parties, Gin?'

'I don't know. I suppose because there's always the off-chance I might meet someone I liked.'

'What do you think of the underground?' Rachel said.

'It's a reasonably quick way to get home,' Dick Lucas said, 'if one hasn't got a car.'

'I meant the underground cinema.'

'I was afraid you did,' Dick Lucas said. 'I confess I haven't yet felt the vocation.'

'He's unbelievable.'

'Do you know Ivan Mills?'

'I've been invited to know him. So far I've resisted the temptation.'

'Because he's got this group of people —'

'I have seen some of their product.'

'I'm not saying it's good,' Rachel said, 'but the thing is they did at least do it without help from anybody else.'

'Precisely the attitude of the infant to his faeces,' Victor Rich said.

Basil Brain said: 'They've finally got the gramophone working. Come and dance.'

Rachel said: 'I'd like to. Excuse me.'

'You're Dick Lucas, aren't you? I'm Gil Timmis. I'd like to ask you something. Oh, this is Camille.'

'It's really rather funny,' Victor Rich said. 'Basil Brain's been following me around all evening. I think he wants to get in on this new format Sunday afternoon discussion programme I'm trying to push at the moment.'

'Oh, what's that?'

'Basically it's a sort of meta-religious programme – that's to say I'm trying to use a religious slot for a cryptically irreligious purpose. What I'm after is a series of confrontations but with a therapeutic rather than a polemic purpose. Not just shouting matches, something with a basically Wittgensteinian slant. To show the fly the way out of the –'

'Flybutton, I know,' Daniel said. 'That's quite a slant for Sunday afternoon viewing.'

'I think I can swing it, but it's going to take some doing.'

'Well, you can always go back to Research,' Daniel said, 'if you don't get what you want.'

'I'm often tempted,' Victor Rich said.

'And yet you never actually fall,' Daniel said. 'What a staunch character you are. The most self-effacing anchorite since Simeon Stylites. Just as long as you don't have Dick Lucas as anchorman.'

'I shan't let that happen,' Victor Rich said.

'I'm sure you won't,' Daniel said.

'Everything Daniel says sounds so threatening,' Adam said.

'It always has,' Paul Mallory said. 'As I remember. He's a master of the minatory consonant.'

'Look who's talking!' Bernard Morris said.

'Do you go on marches and things?' Basil Brain said.

'I have done,' Rachel said. 'I've even spoken at meetings.'

'You must be extremely brave.'

'Not really. Just mildly dotty, I suppose.'

'The funny thing about these academics being', Victor Rich said, 'that they aren't all that bright. They really are not all that bright.'

'Who is?' Daniel said. 'Christ, what the hell's going on?'

'Meredith, stop it. Stop it. *Meredith.*'

'I'll kill the bastard.'

'What the hell's going on up here?'

'One minute they were talking and suddenly —'

'Look, knock this off, will you? Break it up.'

'Adam —'

'Ow. Jesus. Ow. Ow.'

'Jack —'

'The sod was trying to gouge my eye out.'

'What is going on?'

'Jack Darwin's just bitten Meredith Lamb's ear off.'

'What a shame. With all that food going begging downstairs.'

'Ow. Fuck a duck, Jack, what the —?'

'You shouldn't have tried to gouge my eye out, you silly —'

'I was only showing you the drill, for God's sake, as learnt in defence of this realm. Christ Almighty, this is my only suit.'

'One would never previously have thought of Jack Darwin', Paul Mallory said, 'as someone who read Dostoevsky.'

'Victoria, I wonder if you'd mind having a look at Meredith Lamb's ear.'

'There's blood all over the bloody thing. You are an idiot.'

'You shouldn't try to gouge people's eyes out. I've only got two, you know.'

'What future is there for a one-eared novelist and fiction a dying art? One needs one's ears about one, you know.'

'Here's Victoria to have a look at you.'

'The bugger's really done me a mischief.'

'Let's have a look.'

'For Christ's sake at least switch that damned gramophone off.'

'If he's only got one ear, surely the gramophone's not going to —'

'If a man's mad and he bites another man, what happens?'

'Nothing,' Victoria Rich said. 'This is quite superficial.'

'I wish I'd been a doctor,' Adam said, 'and been able to tell Meredith that.'

'We shall all be in his next book now,' Gay Brain said, 'and in a lousy light. I bet he makes me an Australian. People always do for some reason.'

'Where's Victor?'

'Oh surely we don't need a second opinion already.'

'I just thought—'

'He's downstairs. Hogging mousse.'

'I'd better go and make sure he's all right,' Virginia said. 'Do you want boiling water or anything?'

'What's going on?'

'It's Meredith Lamb. He appears to be having a baby in the sitting-room.'

'We must phone the papers,' Gay Brain said. 'Isn't it always supposed to be news when man bites dog?'

'I heard that,' Meredith said.

'Be advised by me, Merry, be advised by me,' Bernard Morris said, 'don't ever say you heard *anything* until after we've agreed the damages. Please.'

'I don't know whether this is any good,' Adam said. 'It's all there was in the medicine cabinet.'

'You are a predatory sod,' Meredith Lamb said. 'I must say. I've got a feeling you've left a tooth in the bloody thing. It feels like a .303.'

'My God, Meredith, for one who takes such pride in being the sometime owner of a Lee-Enfield, you don't half make a fuss when you're hit.'

'Just patch me up, whatever your pretty name is, and I'll get back into the line.'

'Merry, Merry, how many times do I have to tell you? Collapse a little for the people.'

'I think we'd better go home,' Janey Darwin said, 'before there's further mayhem.'

'So that you can get it all down, you mean,' Robin Peto said, 'while it's still fresh in the mind. At least it'll give you a new subject for Janey's Day apart from vaginal deodorants.'

'A swift knee in your crutch,' Janey said. 'How are you, Robin? Don't keep going away.'

'I think the English politician he actually admired most was Nye Bevan, strangely enough.'

'I don't find that so strange,' Brian Stammers said. 'I would have expected it. Only he was Welsh of course.'

'That should be all right now.'

'What about tetanus? I'm a modest man and gladly give credit where it's due, but I don't want to go down as the first English novelist to be gnawed to death by one of the assets of Talent International.'

'The ear lobes bleed profusely, but the wound is very slight.'

'Listen, Meredith, I'm sorry if—'

'Forget it, boy, just wait for the clap of the letter-box. It'll be my solicitor. In person. *Cum writ in manu.*'

'Don't threaten, Merry, don't threaten,' Bernard Morris said. 'Just leave the details to me.'

'Seriously—'

'My seconds will call upon you. Whose is the choice of weapons in these cases? Is there a historian in the house? Where's that amiable Frog? He'll know. Because I shall insist on automatics at fifty paces.'

'You couldn't hit the Post Office Tower at fifty paces,' Jack Darwin said. 'Anyway it's my choice.'

'I don't want to hit the Post Office Tower. I want to hit you. What's the good of praising a man's books if he bites your head off? I might as well have given my honest opinion.'

'We were in the middle of a dance,' Basil Brain said.

'Maybe in that case it's just as well,' Gay Brain said. 'She's very pretty and it's very near your bed-time.'

'She's the only good-humoured partisan of Women's Liberation I've ever come across.'

'Enough. Go on. Get your coat.'

'I would have thought you might have a lot in common.'

'No one ten years younger than me is going to persuade me to throw my bra away. We've been through too much together.'

'I'd say twenty,' Meredith said. 'Years.'

'Do you want to get the other one pierced as well? Then you could go to your next party as a pirate.'

'If so, Gay my dear, you will be positively the last person with whom I'd choose to share my plank.'

'I hope the dysentery doesn't come back,' Basil said.

'I don't think it will.'

'We must finish that dance one day. Or one night.'

'Yes.'

'Well, goodbye.'

'Goodbye.'

'You can't go yet, please don't. Meredith, do you want to go upstairs and lie down or anything?'

'Who with?'

'Shut up. He's all right,' Francesca said. 'The best thing I can do is get him home while he's still in two pieces.'

'I don't feel as if I've talked to either of you!' Virginia said. 'Do at least have something before you go.'

'Yes, at least have a slice of champagne,' Adam said. 'As I'm now irrevocably and publicly forty. Christ, I think I'm going to cry.'

'Don't do that, the drinks are watered enough as it is.'

'Paul's drunk.'

'I've had two drinks,' Paul Mallory said.

'It happens suddenly with lapsed Presbyterians, everyone knows that.'

'I'm anything but drunk.'

'That aggrieved Scots whine is a dead giveaway.'

'Look, Adam, it may be your birthday, but I'll not be abused beyond reason and without cause.'

'Don't come into my house then, Paul, and start talking about watered drinks.'

'Oh for Christ's sake, can't you recognize a joke? For Christ's sake.'

'Especially when it's stamped authentic by the British Antique Dealers Association,' Bernard Morris said.

'Oh Christ, why does it always have to end in aggression? It's so depressing.'

'We're off,' Gay Brain said.

'Do you know,' Virginia said, 'when we were all at Cambridge we seriously considered forming a community on an island somewhere and living in perfect bliss for the rest of our lives? A communion of first-class minds.'

'Pantisocracies have often been mooted,' Basil Brain said, 'but they rarely mature. Had you a constitution?'

'Total freedom guided by intelligence. No money, of course.'

'Naturally not. Just a rich backer. I remember actually drafting a constitution for such a community when I was up.'

'Up is probably right,' Gay Brain said, 'because in the end what these communities are all about is getting people to go to bed with you for moral reasons. The Spanish anarchists actually proposed a law which would oblige a woman to consummate any desire she aroused in one of the opposite sex.'

'Where'd you get that? Thomas?'

'Brenan.'

'Good Lord.'

'Shows how hidebound they were,' Robin Peto said. 'Stipulating the opposite sex.'

'I think we all had in mind for Paul to be the philosopher king. He was always so sure of himself.'

'He still is,' Gay Brain said, 'but he's no longer sure of anything else.'

'Paul's got a wonderful mind,' Virginia said. 'We still talk about it from time to time. Going off somewhere, just a few of us. Not too few, but—'

'Not too many. What did Plato recommend? Two thousand and forty, wasn't it?'

'That would be too many,' Virginia said. 'Far too many.'

'You're really thinking of a sort of Gentile kibbutz.'

'I'll be off then,' Daniel said.

'We did go to a nudist colony once,' Virginia said. 'When I was very depressed.'

'What happened? I've always wondered.'

'I got even more depressed. Adam hated it. He wouldn't really take part at all.'

'And what else, after all, was there to take?' Gay Brain said.

'I was cold,' Adam said. 'You are a bitch.'

'Is it true,' Gay Brain said, 'that if you get an erection they ask you to leave?'

'Why are you asking Virginia?' Adam said, 'She's never had one. I don't *think*. No, they simply ask you to withdraw.'

'Very good.'

'I've never had anything,' Virginia said. 'If it comes to that.'

'Oh. Oh. Now. Secrets.'

'But seriously, aren't you supposed to be able to control yourself?'

'That's the theory. We must ask Victor Rich,' Virginia said. 'Victor—'

'We really must go,' Basil Brain said.

'Because he'll know the scientific facts.'

'Are there scientific facts as opposed to other facts?' Basil said.

'And are they inevitably wedded to "that clauses"? Wasn't that the burning question once upon a time?' Daniel said.

'I still believe that there's something right in the desire to form an ideal community,' Virginia said. 'London's ultimately so unsatisfactory. The thought of us all living together and teaching each other's children, holding things in common—I'd still do it if other people would.'

'It usually ends with a compromise,' Gay Brain said. 'Sharing country cottages for the summer and finding that there's only one loo and that's blocked and the swimming pool's full of dead mice. We once did it in Vermont and it was ghastly. With the David Sterns and Wallace—'

'I wasn't there,' Basil said.

'No, it was before you. Mary Hope Stubbs came out and broke her leg. I was still married to Rudolph. It must have been six years ago. Seven. My God. Virginia, thank you so much.'

'Yes, indeed,' Basil Brain said.

Rachel Davidson said: 'I think I ought to be going really too.'

'No,' Adam said, 'I forbid it.'

'So do I,' Virginia said. 'You must stay. Have you met Daniel Meyer yet?'

'Yes. We had a long talk. I really would like to go now, if you don't mind.'

'How're you going to get home?'

'It doesn't matter. I know someone round the corner.'

'Oh that's ridiculous. You know us.'

'I'll be perfectly all right.'

'She can sleep in Jason's room. Our son. He's away at school. Oh do. I wish people wouldn't go. Adam, you must persuade her.'

'Not if she wants to go,' Adam said, 'that's always where the trouble begins. If people want to go, they should go. I'm forty and I know.'

Rachel said: 'I have enjoyed it.'

'Mr Darwin?'

'Yes.'

'I'm Gil Timmis. I've waited a long time for this moment. This is Camille. I'm one of the most devoted members of your fan club.'

'You'd better be careful. He just bit the ear off the last one.'

'Who was *that*?'

'Don't you know? That's Robin Peto.'

'Do you know, I honestly mean I honestly couldn't tell whether it was a man or a girl. I still can't.'

'Nor can he,' Stuart Melrose said. 'They're having a recount.'

'Have you ever thought of writing an original screenplay specifically for the screen?'

'Not when I can write a book first and then sell the rights.'

'That's what I figured. On the other hand, there could be advantages. You know who I'd like to get you together with and that's Daniel Meyer? He was here just now.'

'He just left,' Janey Darwin said. 'I like your shirt.'

'Because you know his trouble. Do you? Thank you. I'm one of his greatest admirers, don't misunderstand me, but he has a hang-up about art. He doesn't want to have, quite frankly in my opinion, but he does. You and he could make a terrific team.'

'Unless, of course, we both wanted to play in the same position.'

'I don't believe there'd have to be any conflict.'

'People always say that going in,' Jack Darwin said.

'Hey, wait a minute, I know, you're a friend of Asa—'

'That's right,' Jack Darwin said.

'Do me the honour, please, of hearing my side of it for one second, because you know what I did to Asa? I had to come down between him and Hank—'

'I know. He told me.'

'And O.K. I chose Hank. Does that make me a monster? Does that turn me into Medusa?'

'It was Medusa,' Jack Darwin said, 'who turned people into things.'

'Someone's being sick in Inge's bathroom.'

'Christ, she can't be pregnant again. I don't believe it.'

'I think it's the Lucas woman—what's her name?'

'Sandy.'

'I think it's her. I shall have to go and clean the whole place. Perhaps he could go up and collect her in the meantime.'

'Let Inge clean it up.'

'Don't be funny. And leave?'

Paul Mallory said: 'Your goal can be between the two arm-chairs. Now there's a bit of space. Adam, come on, your back'll stand up to this. It's you and me against Bernard and Jack—'

'What about me?' Janey said.

'You be with us, Janey,' Paul said, 'and you can have Jean-Claude.'

'Where's our goal?' Janey said.

'The archway. Between the archway and the gramophone. Ready?'

'Balloons never last,' Adam said, 'but all right.'

'We shall slaughter them,' Bernard said.

'Our kick-off.'

'Whatever you do,' Adam said, 'remember no hands.'

'I'll try,' Jean-Claude said.

'Ready?'

'The curious thing about pantisocrats,' Basil Brain said, 'you find, is that they're very long on justice and liberty, but rather short on love. My God though, fresh air's a wonderful thing. I'm surprised there isn't a tax on it.'

'Love,' Gay Brain said. 'I suppose you're right about that. Of course, it's not exactly an easy thing to legislate for.'

'Indeed, and intellectuals, despite everything, I mean in spite of their yearning for freedom, are really very keen on rules, aren't they, and regulations? I didn't give you the car keys by any chance, did I?'

'I'm quite certain not. What I always feel about people like Virginia particularly is that they're waiting for something to be forced on them.'

'That's what I mean about laws.'

'She won't do what she wants unless she has to.'

'I haven't got the blasted things.'

'Try your pants pocket. They're willing to wait for disaster, but they won't actually go out and find it. Do you find her attractive?'

'Virginia Playfair?'

'She does you,' Gay said. 'I'm sorry for her.'

'Oh dear,' Basil said, 'bad as that? Look, I can't find the blasted things.'

'Then you'll have to send for the garage and have them prise it open. They're waiting for the bomb,' Gay said. 'The whole lot of them.'

'Well, I'm sure they can rely on you to drop it,' Basil said. 'Keys. Success!'

'I thought it was a disaster,' Virginia said. She caught sight of herself in the spotted gilt mirror above the mantelpiece and craned for a better view. She might have been someone she had not seen for some time. 'Well, perhaps disaster's rather an exaggeration, but these things never turn out the way one hoped.'

'What does?'

'I don't see that you've got much to complain about.' She was wearing a red woollen dress, too short for the fashion, white open-work tights and black patent shoes with square silver buckles. Her long throat was left bare by a schoolgirl collar. Her wrists, chalk white, stretched from under the lace cuffs without the cover of either jewellery or wristwatch. As she moved the telephone closer to her cheek, the stitches creaked under her arms. Her face could have been beautiful, but it seemed deliberately composed for melancholy. The brown hair with its streaks of gold was pulled back, loosely, into a bun which left the back of her neck naked. She was without make-up and her unforgiving blue eyes noticed every threatening symptom of a maturity she dreaded and expected.

'Anyway,' she said, 'you should see the debris.'

'Oh, I've no intention of seeing that, if I can help it. I'm very squeamish about debris. Virginia, the thing is—'

'Let me guess. You want her phone number.'

'You could put it that way.'

'No wonder Adam envies you.'

'Adam, does he?'

'Of course he does. Starting a new adventure whenever you want to.'

'I think that's pitching it a bit high. I hardly call phoning someone up an adventure.'

'Oh don't be so modest, Danny. You can start a whole new life whenever you want to.'

'Then why don't I? I've often asked myself.'

'Anyway, you liked her. I hoped you would. In fact, I'm surprised—'

'I don't know about liked exactly, I certainly thought she was very—what?—attractive, but I don't know that I liked her.'

'If I were—if I were meeting you for the first time,' Virginia said, 'I think you might frighten me, Daniel M. Do you know, after all this, I'm not sure that I've got a number for her, but you could always get her number from Norbert. She might even be in the office today. You know she reads for him?'

'Ginny, I'm not sure we're talking about the same girl. I'm talking about the American.'

Virginia sat down on the sofa and lost sight of herself. '*American?*
You don't mean Gay Brain?'
'The airborne cavalry? Hardly. I leave her to Uncle Baz. No, I
meant the one that —'
'Oh my goodness, that one —'
'That's right. The one that came with somebody.'
'With Jean-Claude. Mrs Lane —'
'That's it. I've been trying to think of her name all morning.
Mrs Lane.'
'Nancy Lane. I hardly spoke to her.'
'Me neither. Virginia —?'
'Yes, I'm still here. Did you get a chance to talk to Jean-Claude
at all? Because he's an extraordinarily interesting man. Naturally,
of course, I haven't got her number either, because she came with
Jean-Claude and —'
'Oh I see. I wasn't that sure which of them had come with the
other.'
'She might be in the book, of course, under Lane. Jean-Claude
got involved with Adam and Paul and some of the others in a
terrific football game after you left. With a balloon. Hence a
considerable part of the shambles in actual fact. Paul was rather
impressed by him until he got knocked into the fireplace by a
rather enthusiastic French tackle. Are you going on this Easter
tour?'
'Oh God. I said I would. Is it still on?'
'I think it's down to about two games and eighteen meals, but
Adam still talks as if it's on.'
'Are you going?'
'Me? I don't know if wives are going or not. I shall do whatever
Adam wants. You know what a meek wife I am.'
'Yes,' Daniel said. 'Why are you?'
'Because I was brought up that way, I suppose. Or because I want
to be.'
'Or because you don't want to be.'
'Well, the important thing is, I am.'
'Important to whom?'

'Don't, Danny, this morning. Try under Lane and meanwhile I'll see what I can do.'

'I'm at 437–2621.'

'I hate these all-figure things. And new pence. I'm trying to think what that is. It's not GROsvenor, is it?'

'GERrard,' Daniel said. 'Does it matter?'

'I like to try and visualize where people are, and what they're up to.'

'You must make yourself very unhappy.'

'What else can one do,' Virginia asked, 'when one can't get anyone else to do it?'

'I'm sure there's no shortage of candidates,' Daniel said.

'Danny, I did ask you,' Virginia said.

Daniel said: 'I'm sorry. Anyway, if you want to visualize, visualize a dusty, dirty, dark hole in Upper Poland Street hung with strips of celluloid and exuding a strong but unmistakable odour of disillusion and disorder.'

'Incidentally, another thing, I'm sorry about that terrible American producer and that girl he brought. Wasn't she incredible?'

'Nice body,' Daniel said.

'She never said a word all evening.'

'Gil Timmis isn't really as bad as he tries to sound. The thing you have to remember is how frightened they all are. Anyway, he's offered me a job, so he can't be all bad –'

'But things are going very well with you, aren't they? Everybody must be offering you jobs.'

'There are jobs and jobs. He happens to know of some money tied up in Greece –'

'Greece!' Virginia said. 'Paul won't go to Greece.'

'Paul won't go to Calais if it means he might miss a match. I think he's afraid the team might be strengthened by his absence. That's why he's made himself captain.'

'He won't go to Greece because of the régime,' Virginia said. 'He feels one shouldn't.'

'O.K.,' Daniel said, 'but that means no Germany, no Poland, no Czechoslovakia, no Hungary, no Russia, no Brazil, no Mexico,

66

no Argentina, no Portugal, not much France and definitely not certain parts of the Fascist-dominated Home Counties. Added to which some Arab countries aren't all that chummy. I admire Paul's morals, Gin, but they do seem to have condemned him to a lifetime of immobility. Except for his annual jaunts to the freedom-loving U.S. of A. No Spain of course either and certainly no Mozambique.'

'Paul's done a lot,' Virginia said.

'Not enough,' Daniel said, 'to judge from Margaret.'

'I'll try and find the number for you,' Virginia said. 'I was thinking of Playfair, Marks. It was flat on its back before he took over the list.'

'True,' Daniel said, 'true. And now, thanks to him, it's flat on its feet.'

Daniel said: 'Well, I certainly think that's much better, don't you?'

'That way round, I do,' Brian Ball said.

'Doctors are funny people.' They were drinking pale Nescafé out of Chelsea Supporters mugs in the windowless room behind Soho Square where Daniel cut his films. 'And we seem to be more and more obsessed with them. Presumably because they're the only dyke between us and death – and death seems a lot more final now that religion's on the skids.'

'I think putting Sir Fred's walk through the slums before him seeing the Elephant Man does a lot,' Brian said.

'It turns the Elephant Man into the personification of what he can't cope with, what gets away from him, the monstrous goitre of Victorian England. And this way we get the scene in the Treatment Room and the fight between the two ginnies after he first sees him. It must be right. What I'd like to try now is putting the Neurotic Lady in Harley Street directly after that, so we get the contrast –'

'Get the contrast, yes,' Brian said. 'I was thinking though, whether that wasn't a bit obvious in a way.'

'And unfair on the Neurotic Lady too. In the sense that she can't help being unhappy – I mean, this way we seem to be condemning her. I think that's a good point, Brian.'

'It just seems a bit obvious.'

'Yes, that's the danger of Trying To Say Something. What I want to get at is really two things. First, the Neurotic Lady is being deprived of something – a good healthy fuck, basically – at the same time roughly as Sir Fred is being deprived of the chance to do something for his fellow men.'

'I'm wondering whether we shouldn't try the Dying Patient earlier.'

'What's Sir Fred's conflict basically? He wants to rescue the Elephant Man and at the same time he wants to dissect him, right? He wants to help the dregs and at the same time to analyse them. He hates the society which creates the kind of scenes we get in the Treatment Room – which are absolutely true – and at the same time he wants like hell to be a successful surgeon. In the end, after all, he does become the King's surgeon and hits the jackpot. It's a classical story of the conflicts of an ambitious idealist in a society which frankly hasn't changed that much.'

'The other thing we could do is put the Neurotic Woman just before the Queen goes to visit the Elephant Man in the Hospital.'

'Thus suggesting –'

'I was only thinking we don't have much of Sir Fred's ordinary life and career towards the end. You get the idea he was concentrating entirely on the Elephant Man –'

'Whereas probably he wasn't too worried about him, once he'd got him safely into his soft little cage. Good point, Brian. I suppose that's pitching it a bit hard, but that was basically what he did. He did make him into a sort of comfortable captive and bided his time for the big carve-up. What do you think of Sir Fred yourself?'

'He does him very well, I think.'

'No, I meant the actual character. The surgeon.'

'Fairly reasonable sort of bloke,' Brian Ball said. 'He did what he could, didn't he?'

'In many ways he was a terrible snob and yet on the other hand he really did have a lot of compassion –'

'There was something I wanted to ask you. The tart who takes him for Jack the Ripper, did that really happen?'

68

'Not that I know of—but don't you think—?'

'In that case, wouldn't it come better *after* the Elephant Man moves into the hospital?'

'You don't think that's telegraphing it a bit?'

'It is, but otherwise it doesn't—'

'Let's try it, can we? I'd like to see it before I—'

'Sure, naturally.'

'Well—' Daniel put his mug on a tin shelf and pulled his stool up to the bench. 'Off we go then.'

'Phone,' Brian said.

'Fuck the thing. Still, you can get started, can't you? Shan't be long.'

'Sure.'

Daniel lunged for the phone in the outer office. 'Yes?'

'Hullo. Is that Daniel Meyer?'

'It is.'

'Oh hullo. This is Rachel. Rachel Davidson.'

'Oh yes, hullo. How are you?'

'They gave me your number, I hope it's all right. The answering service.'

'Don't flatter yourself, they give it to everybody.'

'Oh.'

'On my greedy instructions. What can I do for you?'

'The thing is, I was having lunch with a friend of mine—'

'Ah, eating's in again, is it?'

'And the thing is, he's directed a film.'

'I ought to warn you—'

'I know it's—'

'In common with others of my breed, I hate talent.'

'What breed is that?'

'Directors,' Daniel said. 'What other breeds are there?'

'Anyway, he'd terribly like you to see it and—'

'He asked you to phone me. What you may not realize, Rachel, is that he'd terribly like *anyone* to see it.'

'I just know he'd be very grateful.'

'He'd be very grateful—' Daniel dropped into a swivel chair

69

behind a dusty mahogany desk, 'if I told him he was a genius and that I had every intention of resigning in his favour.'

'He doesn't expect anything like that. He's perfectly willing to admit there may be things wrong with it, but it is at least something he's tried to do himself and I promised I'd at least call and ask you.'

'Yes, well – when does he want to show it to me?'

'Tonight, if you're free,' Rachel said.

'Tonight! He's not intending to waste any time, is he?'

'He can get the use of a projector tonight and the guy who owns it is coming back to this country tomorrow and then it won't be so easy. It's in a pad that he's borrowing at the moment.'

'Is that where you're phoning from?'

'Yes, actually.'

'I thought you were living in Chigwell.'

'I was, but it's not really very convenient.'

'Except for Chigwell.'

'Sorry?'

'I said except for Chigwell.'

'No, that's right. I know it's a terrible nerve and I honestly wouldn't have called except –'

'I know. What time does he want to do it?'

'Well, that's the thing partly, he's working till about nine.'

'A working director? I hate him already.'

'He's working as a shopfitter and they've got a bit of a blitz on. He's a carpenter.'

'Then why does he want to make films?'

'He's only being a carpenter until – well, that's what he wants to do, be a film-maker. He's not hung up about being successful or anything like that.'

'Do you want to eat first?'

'It'll make it so late.'

'I mean before nine. You and me.'

'Oh. There's no need.'

'You're not off it again? Food.'

'No, not at all, only –'

'Do you know the Venezia, in Great Chapel Street? Meet me there at half past seven.'

'O.K., only this pad's in Fulham.'

'I've got a car,' Daniel said.

'O.K. then. I hope you don't mind, me calling and everything.'

'I'll tell you after the movie,' Daniel said.

'Danny? It's Virginia —'

'Oh hullo, Gin, I'm sorry. I was half-way out the door, I —'

'If it's a bad moment —'

'No, it's O.K., I was just —'

'Only I've got that number for you. I only got Jean-Claude this afternoon and that's why —'

'Oh, how nice of you.'

'— I'm so late with it. If you've got a pencil, it's 352-2117. You needn't worry because she isn't — she hasn't got a relationship with Jean-Claude or anything, they're just —'

'I'm sure they are. I wasn't worrying about it actually.'

'Oh everyone's so sophisticated these days,' Virginia said. 'The things I worry about don't bother anyone any more except me.'

'I'm very grateful, Gin, thanks a lot.'

'I suppose you're going to the first night.'

'What first night?'

'Dick Lucas is going. He's standing in for Ronnie. It's the new Dream.'

'My God, how many new Dreams can there be? No, I'm not.'

'Well, let me know how it goes.'

'I said I wasn't going.'

'Mrs Lane,' Virginia said.

Daniel still lived in the same flat he had taken on his return from America. He had often left it, sometimes for months at a time, but he could not bring himself to part with it, even though it was dark and, now that they had installed meters outside, rather inconvenient. Chelsea no longer seemed so romantic as it had when he had first moved there, but where should he go? He had put himself on various house agents' lists, but his demands were so vague and his finances so uncertain that he never approached a specific purchase. The hall chest was littered with brown envelopes; those that were not bills, or desirable properties, contained further information from a whole range of suppliers whose advertisements had first excited and later surfeited Daniel's imagination. He was half-way through installing a complicated new hi-fi set (the room, with its wooden panelling and minstrel's gallery, was perfect for it) but he had never had time to spend the half hour with the expert, a boy called Geoff, who could have explained its correct use. However, it was all deductible. Outside was a yellow Lotus Two plus Two. It was heavily coated with dust and there were deep scratches on its offside.

She was wearing an old A.R.P. warden's coat with sergeant's stripes. Her hair had been chopped very short, so that the large, almost feverish brown eyes dominated her face. Her hands were raw and bony, long-wristed. 'Sorry,' she said.
   'I thought you weren't coming.'
   'Sorry,' she said. 'I got held up.'
   'With a gun?'
   'No, not really,' she said.
   'We'd better order.'
   'I'll have an omelette,' she said.
   'Well, have a look at the menu.'
   'I'd like a spinach omelette.'
   'I don't know that they even do a spinach omelette.'
   'Yes, a spinach omelette,' the waiter said.
   'O.K. then, we'll have two of those,' Daniel said. 'And a bottle of Valpolicella.'
   'Red or white?'
   'Red?'
   'Fine.'
   'Red. So, anyway—'
   'It's very nice of you,' she said.

72

'Not really.'

'Andy's going to be terribly grateful.'

'Look, forgive me,' he said, 'and no offence intended or taken, but why do you go to so much trouble to ask me to come and see your chum's movie and then roll up here three-quarters of an hour late?'

'I said I was sorry,' the girl said.

'I told you – I'm not complaining, I'd just honestly like to know.'

'I went with a friend to the vet,' she said. 'She had a pet that had to be put to sleep.'

'You really are the friend of the lame dogs, aren't you?'

'It was a cat,' Rachel said. 'She hasn't had much luck recently and this was the final straw.'

'Evidently.'

'So things aren't too good,' the girl said. 'At least not in my part of the forest.'

'He's not going to think we've forgotten or anything, is he, if we're a bit late?'

'Oh no, don't worry.'

'I've never had a spinach omelette before. It looks rather good.'

'It is,' the girl said. 'They do them very well here.'

'Oh, you've been here before?'

'You asked whether I knew it.'

'So I did. Do you want anything else after that?'

'Not specially,' she said.

'You're not afraid of getting fat?'

'I'm just not particularly hungry,' she said. 'I don't eat a lot as a rule.'

'Nor do I,' he said.

'But you are worried about getting fat?'

'*Faute de mieux*,' he said. 'How about a *zabaglione*?'

'Coffee,' she said. She took out a box of tobacco and a packet of cigarette papers.

'How did you come to know this character?' he asked.

'Andy? I met him with some friends.' She leant her elbows on the table and smiled at him and then wagged her shaggy cigarette at the waiter for a light.

'We'd better drink this and go,' he said.

She made no remark at the car. She seemed as secure as if they were married. He looked at her, without turning the key in the starter, and she smiled, white teeth, gipsy eyes, feverish flush on her powderless cheekbones, the end of the cigarette on show between her reddish fingers.

'How do you come to know Virginia?'

'I met her at Norbert Ash's. Why?'

'Interest. Why not? And Norbert? The Maxwell Perkins of Porn?'

'We met at a party. He's more than that.'

'Is he now? You'd better tell me where this place is. What is he then?'

'You go right on down,' she said, 'past World's End. He's a sort of Maecenas in a way.'

'Buying Virgil by the yard,' Daniel said, 'and paying for only five feet in every hexameter.'

The gritty smell of the river met them as they got out of the car. Rachel led the way up a play street and turned down an alley. Iron steps took them to a wooden gallery. Rachel knocked.

'There doesn't seem to be a light,' Daniel said. 'Nice place for a studio. Even nicer if one could get into it.'

'It's been converted,' she said, 'it's still a bit rough outside.'

'It's well after nine,' Daniel said. 'Haven't you got a key? I thought you were living here.'

'I was staying here,' she said, 'but there's only one key. I slammed the door when I went out, you know, and that was it. The owner's coming back in the morning and anyway, there only is one key and Andy's got that.'

'I see. I suppose you did tell him we were coming?'

'The other one got lost. I said I'd call you and see him tonight.'

'In other words, he doesn't even know we're definitely coming.'

'Not everyone's on the phone at work,' she said.

'Well,' Daniel said, 'if he isn't here by half past, I'm not stopping.'

'O.K.,' she said.

'Is there any guarantee he's coming back at all? I mean, if the owner's going to be here in the morning, surely it's possible —'

'No guarantee,' the girl said, 'no. Don't you ever smoke?'

'No,' he said, 'I'm preserving myself.'

She crossed her legs and leaned against the wooden gallery railing. 'I like it here,' she said, 'don't you?'

'It's all right until you get silicosis, I suppose.'

'It's nice,' she said. 'Silicosis!'

'Aren't you ever afraid?'

'Of what?'

'It seems bloody lonely. Aren't you ever afraid someone might — I don't know —'

'I don't live here,' she said.

'Where do your parents live?' he said.

She laughed at that. 'What's that got to do with it?'

'I'm just interested.'

'You're getting old,' she said. 'Where do yours?'

'They're separated,' he said. 'That's my little tragedy.'

'Mine aren't,' she said, 'that's my little comedy. I remember now. In *Split* —'

'I hated that title,' he said. 'I got talked into it. How did you come to see *Split* anyway? It didn't get shown much.'

'I liked it,' she said.

'And what about your friends, did they like it?'

'I don't know,' she said.

'He's not coming, this mate of yours. Have you actually seen his film?'

'Bits of it,' she said.

'You've got your nerve, honestly, haven't you? Dragging me up here and then having the chap not turn up. It doesn't occur to you, I suppose, I might have something better to do?'

'He's usually here,' she said.

'It's damned well half past,' he said, 'and I'm getting cold.'

'You can have my coat, if you like.'

'I'm not really cold. I'm just looking for a grievance. But

seriously, there's no sense in hanging round, because he's obviously not coming. Where are you going now?'

'I'll be O.K.,' she said.

'You can come back to my place and have some coffee if you like,' he said.

'O.K.,' she said.

Under the A.R.P. coat she was wearing a tobacco-coloured sari and heavy black sandals with block heels.

'I'll get some coffee,' he said. 'There should be some.'

She took a book from the shelf and crouched in the corner of the big leather sofa in front of the unlit gas fire. She might have been expecting a very long wait.

'Will you tell me something honestly?' he called from the little kitchen. It was up some steps from the corner of the room, like a control cabin.

'What?'

'This mate of yours, this Andy character, does he really exist?'

'Andy? Of course. What do you mean?'

He came down and looked at her. She was serious over the book. 'What're you looking at?'

She turned the book for him. It was a volume of photographs: *Self-Portraits*.

'Do you like them?'

'Yes,' she said.

'Why?'

'Because they're all questions,' she said. 'But accurate ones. Precise doubts. I like that.'

'You did go to Oxford,' he said, 'didn't you? Did you like it?'

'I liked it some of the time,' she said, 'but I never really felt I was there. I never really felt I'd got anything I'd gone for. Perhaps I was afraid of becoming too—well, academic, I suppose. But I never felt helped. More threatened if anything.'

'In what way threatened?'

'I was afraid they were going to take something away from me,' she said. 'I felt they were after me somehow.'

'Castration fears,' he said. 'You frighten me, do you know that?'

'Do I? How?'

'I feel as if you want something awful to happen to you.'

'Well, I don't,' she said. 'The coffee's boiling, shall I go?'

'It isn't actually boiling,' he said. 'The water is, but not the coffee. If it did, it would spoil the flavour. These machines are designed so that the coffee itself can't boil. If it does apparently the oils get dispersed or dissipated or whatever you call it. Some actor told me that. Actors are full of funny information.'

'Everyone is,' Rachel said, 'only actors let it out. They're not afraid to volunteer things.'

'People drink a lot more coffee than they really want, don't they?' he said. 'It's taking the place of cigarettes. The new oral vice. Do you want the fire?'

'If you like,' she said.

'Matches,' he said, 'blast.' He went back to the kitchen. As he was looking for the matches, the phone rang. The girl picked it up and read off the number.

'It's for you,' she said.

'Not surprising in the circumstances. Look, do this, will you? Hullo.'

'Daniel? Adam. Sorry if you were—'

'I wasn't,' Daniel said. 'What's up?'

'I'm trying to get Easter straightened out for once and for all. Are you still on or not? It boils down to the seventh, eighth, ninth and tenth and back here on the eleventh.'

'How many matches?' Daniel asked. The girl was on her haunches in front of the fire. She swivelled to look at him, her face warm with humour.

'Two, probably three. We can leave Bordeaux on the evening of the eleventh. But obviously if we get enough people not everyone'll have to play in every match. We might even make four.'

'Yes, well, that'll be O.K. unless—Who else is coming?'

'Most of the regulars, except Mike and Carlo. He can't because it's their busy time, you know.'

'Carlo's no loss,' Daniel said. 'I'll make a note of it.'

'Victor and Paul and Basil and Brian and I've asked that French character who came to the party –'

'Have you now?'

'Turns out he used to play wing three-quarter for Brive.'

'And what's Brive?'

'One of the top French sides and he might be useful since we're going to be more or less in that part –'

'We could put him in goal,' Daniel said, 'if Carlo's not coming. He couldn't do worse.'

'Well, we'll talk about that. I hope I didn't interrupt anything.'

'Tell me, is Ginny coming with you?'

'On the tour? She might. She might. She's pushing.'

'*Ci credo*. See you Sunday anyway.'

'Right. It's the Scrubs, right?'

'I'll be there,' Daniel said. He leaned forward and put his hands on the girl's waist, where the sharp bones strained the silk of her dress. She watched the clay of the fire as it deepened into thick orange.

'Why haven't you ever got married?'

'No one's ever asked me,' he said.

'Seriously.'

'I've never wanted to,' he said. 'It's partly childish. Because I like to get what I want without paying for it. And partly, I suppose, it's more complicated – though possibly even more childish – things. I'm afraid of giving hostages to fortune.'

'You mean children?'

'I want children as I want a lot of things, out of vanity and curiosity and because it seems a shame not to have them, and maybe because I want something defenceless enough to love, but I wasn't thinking about children. I was thinking about formal commitments. I've never really committed myself to anything.'

'Have you ever thought about going to Israel?' she said.

'By God, you're not a recruiting agent for the Negev, are you?'

78

'Have you?'

'Yes,' he said, 'but not with any confidence. I'm not that mad about Jews *en masse*. Have you been there?'

'I worked on a kibbutz during one of my long vacs.'

'And?'

'I liked it.'

'You really do like to expose yourself, don't you?'

'It wasn't dangerous,' she said. 'I've never felt so safe in my life, honestly. It was almost too safe.'

'We're very hard to please,' he said. 'Did you learn Hebrew?'

'They spoke English.'

'They speak English here,' Daniel said.

'Have you got any music?'

'In me or in the place? Over there. There's stacks of the stuff. Unfortunately the system's not right yet, but something comes out.'

She said: 'Do you like Monteverdi?'

'Yes, I do. God knows why. I really shouldn't, but I do rather. I bought a whole raft of it at one time. I find I do that. I go to a shop and I buy all my records for the year in one go, especially classical records. I get sort of crazily greedy and then I don't buy any more for ages. Are you like that?'

'No,' she said, 'not really. Nice place you've got.'

'It's best at night,' he said. 'It's bloody dark in the day, but it's fine at night. I'm not here that much. I've never been able to bring myself to part with it.'

She smiled at him as if he had made some generous declaration. Yet she seemed a long way away, on the far side of the room, where he had to turn to watch her as she fiddled with the gramophone. She had put on some Segovia.

'Do you live alone then?'

'At the moment, yes, I do.'

'From choice?'

'From chance. In the sense that most things in one's life are chance, starting with one's life itself.'

'Oh I see.' She was at the limits of the room, running her finger along the surfaces of things like a prospective buyer. He felt a sort

79

of distrust, a petulance he did not like in himself, at the detachment of this slim, strangely amputated girl. Was it just the short, chopped hair? She might just have come out of an institution.

Daniel was wearing a polo-necked yellow ski shirt; it looked casual but he could wear it anywhere. He liked clothes which qualified him for as many *milieux* as possible. It was not so much that he wanted many things as that he could resist few. His disgust, and it was real enough, with London and the world in which he had grown up, both inhibited him from positive appetite and made him undiscriminating in his greed. Victor Rich had once told him of a condition where the patient, suffering from acute dyspepsia, his stomach crying out for rest, feels the pangs of insatiable hunger.

'Are you staying the night?'

'I don't know,' she said. 'I hadn't thought about it.'

'Well, think about it.'

'I haven't got anywhere else to go,' she said.

She was under the gallery, in deep shadow. A steep staircase, with a carved yew balustrade, mounted to where Daniel slept. The girl was in that hooded darkness. The difficulty of framing her in his vision, the secrecy from his eye which she had contrived, made her remoteness seem an evasion, almost an assault. Her indifference was either agreeably casual, as he was inclined to think, or alarmingly calculated. He was torn between harsh generosity and defensive caution.

He turned on as many lights as he could reach. She seemed, like a bat, hardly to notice them. Her movements appeared to be guided by sounds; she hummed faintly and snapped her fingers softly in response to the music.

What did she find to interest her among the dusty files and heavy boxes? He could never throw away magazines and seldom Sunday newspapers. They stood in unstable stacks. She looked at them, these things published in their millions, as if they gave some intimate clue to his character, as if they were private letters or clandestine manuscripts. She looked at them and then back at him quizzically, as if, again, she were comparing his photographs with a model who had aged.

'Do you ever take photos, stills, I mean?'

'Occasionally. But never after thought,' he said. 'Just as I see things, so as to make a note of them. No artistic pauses. I know I'm not really any good at it.'

'That shows how pleased you are with what you actually do do.'

'I don't know,' he said.

'You know yourself very well, don't you?'

'I know the lines of my defences, I know their weaknesses. I don't claim to know the centre, if there is a centre. You may remember that was the point—or I thought it was—of *Myself Among Others*. The inability of the character to know himself except through the opinions and memories of others.'

'He was rather pathetic, I thought.'

'As if being pathetic were an uncommon or even faintly disreputable condition!'

'You're not pathetic.'

She had turned again and gone through into the largeness of the room. She might have been a detective searching for something, the uncriminal cause of a distant crime. He went up the ladder to the gallery. There was a zebra-skin rug on the floor between the marble-topped table and the big, low bed with its Mexican cover, orange and beige. Two large Edward Burra water-colours hung against the back wall. There was a door between them to the bathroom. She looked up at him and smiled.

He said: 'I'll sling you down some things if you want.'

She said: 'Can't I come up?'

'Sure,' he said.

When he came out of the bathroom with an armful of blankets, she was sitting on the bed, sandals dangling from outstretched feet, toes pointed. She cocked her head and he came and put the blankets beside her. He kissed her violently, as if she deserved it.

She said: 'Can you do the lights from up here or do you have to go down?'

'Some of them I can,' he said.

'What's the matter?' she said, when he had turned out most of the lights.

'You look so happy,' he said.

'Don't your women usually look happy?' she said.

'My women,' he said. 'I don't know. You're the only one I'm conscious of at the moment.'

'What is it about you?' she said. 'I wish I knew.'

'I've made some coffee,' she said. 'I hope that's O.K. I don't know what you have in the morning.'

'What time is it?'

'It's just past eight,' she said. 'Why? Are you going somewhere?'

'I'm going to cut Sir Frederick Treves,' he said. 'But not till about half ten.'

'I had a bath. I hope that's O.K.'

'The labourer is worthy of her hire,' he said.

'And I've made some toast, O.K.?'

'You're a very pretty girl,' he said, 'come here. I want to kiss you, come here. There, that wasn't so bad, was it?'

'Have you ever grown a beard?'

'I did once. I was twenty. But my beard grows inwards, I mean it curls inwards and gets tighter and tighter until eventually it pulls itself. Very uncomfortable.'

'Did it pull itself out?'

'No, I curtailed it. I cut it. I shaved. Do I smell toast? Or is that London Bridge burning down?'

'Oh God,' she said, 'sorry.'

'Bring the butter and the Oxford marmalade. Someone used the place and left the other kind but I don't like it.'

'I'll have it,' she said.

'Look, I'll come down.'

'No I'm coming.'

He said: 'What're you looking so pleased with yourself about?'

She said: 'Oh I like bringing people breakfast in bed.'

'Oh, you do, do you? It's quite a habit of yours, is it?'

'Well, you didn't think you were the first, did you?'

'No, by God,' he said, 'I didn't. You're quite something. I only wish I knew what.'

'Do you really?' she said.

'You don't think much of me somehow, do you?'

'I think you're great,' she said, 'smashing. Didn't I make that clear in the night?'

'I don't know that sex necessarily makes anything clear. I think that's one of our mistakes.'

'Oh have we started making mistakes already?'

'The mistakes of our time,' he said.

'Oh, those,' she said. She was sitting, knees together, on the edge of the bed, buttering toast on the flat of her hand. 'Shall I put the marmalade on for you?'

'You know, it's the first time I've seen you in daylight! It suits you. Tell me something, do you always — ?'

'Do I always?'

'No, the other,' he said.

'Oh yes, sorry. Do I always?'

'Where are your things?' he said.

'Things.'

'Clothes, things.'

'Some are at home, some are at the place I was staying. Why?'

'Tell me something honestly. How many other people are you involved with at the moment?'

'Am I involved with anyone else?'

'That's playing for time. In other words, who was I last night?'

'You!'

'Was I really? Who was I against then? I had the impression I'd come in in the middle of something.'

'That's horrible,' she said. 'I don't like that.'

'Nevertheless.'

'No, that's not nice.'

'Is it true though, that's what I want to know?'

'Please let go.'

'What're you going to do?'

'Go. To work.'

'Work?'

'It's Friday.'

'Oh you work on Fridays, do you?'

'I read for Norbert Ash. I thought you knew. Every Friday.'

'And what sort of things do you read?'

'Children's books mostly.'

'I see. I didn't know he did them.'

'Well, he does. And I think it's time I went.'

'Right,' he said. 'What time do you usually get in?'

'Tennish,' she said, 'but—'

'Then if you wait a bit I'll give you a lift.'

'I fancy a bit of a walk.'

'I'm sorry,' he said.

'About what?'

'You know. You're really great. I was a bit astonished. I'm sorry I tried to—make it something less than it was.'

'Forget it,' she said.

'One thing I shan't do.'

'In time,' she said.

'Come here. Please.'

'I really want to go now,' she said. 'Honestly.'

'Come here.'

'You have to win, don't you?'

'That's probably why I lose so often.'

'More than likely,' she said.

'You're very pretty and you're wonderful in bed. Really. Terrific.'

'I just happen to enjoy it,' she said.

'Come on,' he said, 'and I'll run you to Gordon Square. It won't take more than about ten minutes.'

'I've just got dressed.'

'Well, just get undressed. It didn't take you long last night.'

'I don't want to,' she said. 'So please don't—'

'And what am I going to do with this?'

'Save it,' she said. 'Put it in the fridge for later.'

'Rachel.'

*

'I think it's beginning to come now,' Daniel said.

'Definitely,' Brian Ball said.

'Apart from the very opening sequence. I'm still not too happy about that. I've just had another thought. Suppose we start with him — yes, this must be right — start with him in the carriage — it's obvious — riding through the East End and the trace breaks and he's forced to stop and sit in the thing, that bit, while the coachman repairs it and the slum children stare at him and call him names. Christ, it's so obvious —'

'And then the doctors talking in the hospital — the laughter —'

'Into the Treatment Room — the sense of revenge when he treats the burnt woman — revenge on the —'

'And from the treatment room back to the second Harley Street sequence, is that what you mean?'

'I'll have to think about that, because I think I'd sooner have him go over and look at the shop where the Elephant Man's going to be on show and the queue with the same faces in it that, you know, when the carriage broke down — and then go back to Harley Street. Otherwise it's a hell of a long time before we get to the main theme. I mean, *we* know where we're going, but does the audience?'

'They've got the title to go on.'

'Unless they think Sir Fred is the Elephant Man. They're not to know, are they? You know something strange and that is, the style of Sir Fred, prose style I mean, is amazingly like that of Somerset Maugham, the same rather sardonic banality if you know what I mean.'

'Where should he meet the tart then first?'

'Point. Well, it could be the same night. After he sees the queue for the Elephant Man, he walks on thinking how sickening it is and we cut and then we get the tart, then after the tart we get the first actual visit to the Elephant Man, then Harley Street — obviously — and then the empty shop and the police have moved the show on, right?'

'You're forgetting the scene where he gives his card —'

'When he visits the show, of course, sorry, I was sort of assuming.

85

Obviously that whole sequence goes in there and then we get the Neurotic Woman, right, and then the tart brought in all beaten up, back at the Treatment Room and his close-up then and we get the obvious inference that he feels responsible for her being beaten up because he wouldn't go with her or at least give her anything, and then we get the call from the police and the Elephant Man is back in England—then the station—the card the only thing he's got on him and the commitment to help him. End of act one. Great. Perfect that should be. Have we missed anything out? The thing I want to do above all is be fair to Sir Fred. I think we are being, though, don't you?'

'We've kept in all his close-ups,' Brian Ball said.

'I mean as a character, the historical personality, not the actor.'

'Oh I see,' Brian Ball said.

'Did you ever read any Maugham?' Daniel said. 'Because there really is a remarkable similarity.'

'I don't remember. I saw some of the tellies they did. They did them quite well. Terrific colour quality.'

'You don't really get the irony from the box, though. Both of them were medical men, with the same Edwardian attitudes, both were hot for success and yet felt angry at the hypocrisy of the rich. Interesting.'

'A friend of mine worked on that series. Gerald. You've met Gerald. Funny bloke with a long nose.'

'Listen, Bri, I'm going to leave you to try that, I'll be back in an hour or so, O.K.?'

'Right you are, sir.'

'Only I've got some calls and things to make.'

'It may take a bit longer, because that sequence with the break-down in, that isn't quite right yet and we've got to lose that bloody No Parking sign somehow.'

'I still don't know how that happened,' Daniel said.

'Life,' Brian Ball said.

Daniel went into the outer office. He sat at the mahogany desk and leaned back to stare at the swollen photographs of one-time British stars to be observed through the arch in the foyer, which led to the 'Spectrum' viewing theatre next door. He picked up the phone and asked the girl for a line.

'Hullo. Is that Mrs Lane?'

'No, this is the Nanny. I'm not sure if Mrs Lane is here at the moment. Who is that, please, speaking?'

'My name is Daniel Meyer.'

'If you wouldn't mind waiting one moment.'

Daniel tilted his chair and felt the sill of the frosted window behind him against the back of his head.

'Hullo.'

'Oh, hullo, this is Daniel Meyer.'

'Oh, hullo. How are you?'

'I'm very well, thanks. I hope you don't mind my phoning you like this, but—'

'Of course I don't mind. I'm delighted.'

'The thing being that I've been asked to a special screening of the new Bill Stern picture and I wondered—'

'*A Public Life*, have you? I'm longing to see it.'

'Well, if you did feel like coming.'

'I absolutely do,' Nancy Lane said.

'It's on the fifteenth of April.'

'The fifteenth. Just a minute because I have to look. The fifteenth would be just fine.'

'It's at seven o'clock at the Mayfair and then they're having a sort of buffet afterwards, but we can always—'

'That sounds fine, I'd like that very much.'

'Shall I pick you up?'

'If you'd like to come here for a drink,' Nancy said, 'about six, why don't you do that?'

'Where is that exactly?' Daniel smiled to himself and put his feet up on the desk and tilted the chair a little further under him.

'I live at nineteen Seymour Walk,' she said, 'if you know where that is.'

'I know. Off the Fulham Road.'

'Right, nearly opposite that hamburger place—'

'The Great American Disaster, I know. That's the fifteenth then.'

He reached to replace the phone, but the sudden movement rolled the tilted chair forwards on its back castors. It crashed down under him and there he was: his head on the ledge of the window, his feet on the desk, rigid as a girder. The desk supported him under the calves, the sill under the back of his head. He could not think how to move without falling. His face was thickening red.

'Brian,' he called, 'Brian,' in a conversational tone. Brian did not hear through the door. Daniel held for a moment and then plunged sideways on to the ground. The worst thing was his head on the radiator. He hated bumping his head. He sat there, looking up at Patricia Roc. No one came; as a child, he would lie immobile where he had fallen for several minutes, often it seemed an eternity, waiting for his mother. The sight of Miss Roc's face, belonging to the same era as his childhood, brought back to him the distant tenderness of his mother, at the times when he was with her, and her present remoteness. She had remarried and was living in California. Her husband owned supermarkets and piloted his own Cessna. Daniel rolled, with a reproachful glance at the glazed smiles on the wall, and sat up. He had come down on his hip. He scrambled up, resentful of the audience which had failed to appear and stood, massaging his sore side, in the dusty room. He picked up the phone again. The line was still open. He shook his head at the unknown operator's lazy generosity.

'Queenie? Danny. What's the word?'

'Well,' Queenie said, 'I've spoken to our lovely friend, Mr Timmis, do you see, and he's full of delightful enthusiasm—'

'But not of delightful money.'

'Well, it could be worse, because he does really seem to want to make a deal if you can come up with the right story—'

'He's beginning to sound more and more like a Chief Inspector offering the villain a lighter sentence—'

'No, it's not as bad as that really, do you see, because he is serious about sponsoring this lovely trip to Greece—'

'How nice! Or to put it another way, how much?'

'Well, as you know they none of them admit to having any money these days, but he is willing to put five hundred pounds where his mouth is and I don't think that's too bad really, do you?'

'With the expectation of what?'

'Nothing contractually, but what he wants is an outline of a story or a project that you would want to go ahead with and that falls within the sort of budget you and he talked about. On the other hand he does emphasize that he'd like it to be a big subject.'

'None of that art shit, I know. And what do you think we should do?'

'Well, if you feel like a trip, why not do it? It leaves you free, doesn't it? You can go when you like —'

'And it gives me an excuse —'

'For whatever you feel like doing, which is lovely, after all, isn't it?'

'And what's the news from the coast?'

'Well —'

'Say no more.'

'No, it's not as bad as that. In fact we had a telex in today asking when you were free.'

'And when am I? Aren't I?'

'When will you be finished editing the famous Sir Frederick and how's it all going?'

'Well, it's going rather famously, honestly, I think, much it matters —'

'Of course it matters, Danny —'

Daniel said: 'What was this telex about?'

'Just to query your availability. Doubtless we shall hear more.'

'And meanwhile we'd better grab Mr Timmis while we can.'

'Grab the lovely Mr Timmis,' Queenie said, 'that we shall certainly do. And meanwhile how are you and when are we going to see you?'

'I'll come in sometime,' Daniel said, 'perhaps the beginning of the week.'

'And I'll have the biscuit barrel on the desk this time.'

'Monday,' Daniel said. 'As far as temptation is concerned, Oscar and I are entirely at one.'

He returned to the cutting room and stood patiently behind

Brian Ball at the movieola. Again and again Sir Fred met his tart, crossed the road and spoke, walked past the Elephant Man's booth and retraced his footsteps. Random thoughts, like illicit sound piercing an insulated stage, began to disturb his single-mindedness. Over tea he had turned his mind, deliberately, to Nancy Lane, but it was Rachel who came unsummoned before him. The two women together made serious work impossible, or challenged its seriousness.

He slipped into the outer office (why this habit of stealth?), while making a long suggestion which grew louder and louder as he moved away. He stood over the phone, making provisional speeches. Then, as he reached out to pick up the receiver, the phone rang.

She said: 'Is that Daniel Meyer?'

He said: 'Speaking.' He was grinning at Miss Roc.

She said: 'It's me. Rachel.'

He said: 'Sorry?'

'Rachel. Rachel Davidson.'

'Hullo, how are you?'

'I hope I'm not disturbing you,' she said. 'Are you still working?'

'We never close,' he said. 'What can I do for you?'

She said: 'I don't know how you're going to feel about this –'

'You still want me to see your mate's film.'

She said: 'Oh, would you?'

'If I must. Must I?'

'No, of course not,' she said, 'but he would be grateful. And last night really wasn't his fault.'

'Whose was it?'

She said: 'It was a muddle really.'

'Ah, that's what it was.'

'It wasn't Andy's because he didn't even know for certain that we were coming –'

'I don't mind,' Daniel said. 'We needn't make a big thing of it. When does he want to show it to us? Tonight?'

'I don't know about tonight,' she said.

'Why? What're you doing tonight?'

90

She said: 'It's not what I'm doing. It's what he's doing.'

'Whether he's at it with his hammer and chisel, you mean.'

'I don't know whether he is or not,' the girl said.

'Well,' Daniel said, 'that doesn't have to affect whether we see each other or not, does it?'

'No,' Rachel said. 'I suppose not. If you feel like it.'

'What're your plans for the weekend?'

'I was going down to the country to see some friends.'

'Ah. Listen, I'll tell you what, when are you leaving the office?'

'In about twenty minutes.'

'I'll come and collect you.'

'No, it's O.K.,' she said. 'Thanks, but—'

'I'm not far. It's no problem.'

'No, really, because I've got some shopping to do.'

'Shopping? What're you shopping for?'

'It's honestly easier if we meet at Andy's. Hullo?'

'I'm here,' he said.

'It's honestly easier if we meet at Andy's.'

'Where is Andy's these days?'

'You know,' she said. 'Same place.'

'I thought the owner was coming back.'

'He didn't after all. He's staying on for a bit. So it's O.K. for the moment.'

'I see.'

'So I'll meet you there if that's O.K.'

'If I can find it. What sort of time?'

'About nine.'

'Never mind about,' Daniel said. 'I'll be there at nine and if he really wants me to see the thing he'd better be there. Hullo?'

'I heard you,' Rachel said.

'She's a funny girl.'

'Rachel?'

'Yes. Isn't she?'

'She's O.K.'

'I mean the way she's always late.'

'It doesn't matter. There's plenty of time.'

'But it's a funny thing *always* to be late.'

'I don't attach much importance to it as a matter of fact, personally.'

'I suppose I'm a bit compulsive. On the other hand, when you've got a unit waiting for you it does begin to matter a bit.'

'I suppose it does in a way.'

'It does.'

'What I mean is, it's only temporary, isn't it?'

'Time?'

'Depending on other people. Units and things like that. It's only a question of time and we'll be able to operate on our own. I mean, it's a bit like scribes, isn't it, before you could write a letter?'

'Excuse me asking, but what's your last name?'

The young man sat there biting his nails, one and then the next. 'Ford,' he said. 'Why?'

'It's just an old English habit, wanting to know people's names. Are you laced up?'

'Sorry?'

'The film; so we can start when she gets here.'

'Have you got another appointment?'

'Appointment? No,' Daniel said.

'We can start when we like,' Andy said.

The door from the gallery led into a luxurious loft. It was at once secretive and ostentatious; storage galleries had been converted, all along the far wall, into cubicles, each floored with thick, upholstered foam like an armchair for a giant. Curtains could turn them into bedrooms. In the centre was a round purple ottoman filled with polystyrene pebbles, an island of yielding comfort. Several mobiles, hung on wires from the long steel beam which crossed the room under the slanting skylights, clinked and swayed. A tree, large enough to shelter a picnic, grew out of the far corner. Andy slid aside two upholstered panels in the wall to reveal the screen. The projector was already in place on a draughtsman's table which had been racked down to take it.

'He's got some stuff, this chap,' Daniel said.

'Gordon? I suppose he has really,' Andy said.

'Gordon who?' Daniel said.

'A bloke called Gordon East.'

'God, I know him,' Daniel said. 'At least I think I do. He must've done himself some good.'

'You know William Stern, don't you?'

'I did,' Daniel said.

'Do you want something to drink?'

'What've you got?'

'Anything you like.' Andy leaned on a cupboard and it clicked open to mirror rows of bottles.

'How did you come across him? Gordon, I mean.'

'I worked with him for a bit.'

'I knew him in New York. It must be the same man. I expect he's bald by now. Worked at what?'

'Yeah, he is. I was his assistant, you know.'

'Where is this girl? Does she often do this to you?'

'Not often,' Andy said.

'It's science fiction, isn't it, this place?'

'It's O.K.,' Andy said.

'What's Gordon doing these days?'

'I don't know really. Did you work on *Proof Positive* then with him, Stern?'

'No,' Daniel said. 'You know him, do you?'

'Not really,' Andy said. 'I admire him quite a bit.'

'Then you obviously don't know him. It's raining. No, that's unfair. I worked with him on the one before,' Daniel said. '*Jerusalem, Jerusalem.*'

'Oh yeah.'

Daniel said: 'How did you meet Rachel then?'

'Rachel?'

'Rachel,' Daniel said. 'How did you meet her?'

'At Oxford,' Andy said.

'Were you at Oxford?'

'Yes. I was. For a year.'

'Oh I see. Why was that?'

'I didn't like it.'

'Ah. I hope she's all right.'

'All right?'

'Not had an accident or anything.'

'She said she might not come,' Andy said.

'What? She what?'

'When I spoke to her. She said she might not be along till after.'

'After what? She never said anything like that to me.'

'She said she might be busy and not come till after. She's O.K.'

'But I spoke to her this afternoon, this evening, just a few hours ago and she said she'd be here at nine. I told her not to be late and she said she wouldn't be.'

'Oh, did she?'

'Do you really want to show me this picture? Or did she make that up as well?'

'She doesn't make up much,' Andy said, 'that I know of.'

'How long ago did you meet her then?'

'Probably a couple of years.'

'She was in her last year, I suppose.'

'Suppose so, yes.'

'What were you reading?'

'That was it partly, I wasn't sure. I wanted to do Chinese, but then I decided I wasn't stopping anyway.'

'And since then?'

'It's been fine,' Andy said.

'Life.'

'Yes.'

'Let's see the film you've made,' Daniel said.

'It's not that special,' Andy said. He was lying on the purple circle in the middle of the studio, staring at the sound of the rain on the glass. He was thin, with pale skin and a narrow chest, long shanks and a colourless face surrounded with long fair curls. He wore a blue dye-stained shirt, patched jeans and sneakers the colour of dirty puddles. 'You probably won't like it.'

Daniel smiled. 'Then I'll tell you I don't.'

'Oh I'm not worried.'

Daniel walked to one of the alcoves and squatted down, smiling with anxious indulgence at the sprawled young man. Andy breathed regularly. Was he going to sleep? 'If you want me to see it, perhaps we'd better start,' Daniel said. 'Has it got sound?'

'Yes,' Andy said, 'lots.'

'What would you like me to say?'

'Nothing particularly.'

'Why did you want me to see it?'

'Rachel said you wanted to.'

'She told you I wanted to see it.'

'That's right.'

'But I never even knew it existed. How could I have wanted to see it if I didn't know it even existed?'

'That's what she told me.'

'Somebody's got something wrong.'

'What did you think of it?'

'It's really very hard for me to say.'

'Shocked you a bit, didn't it? I'm not worried. You can say anything you like.'

'I don't know about shocked. I just wonder why you made it.'

'That's the thing,' Andy said. 'That's what I mean.'

'I suppose it's mainly that I didn't have any idea what to expect. I somehow expected —'

'Something humble,' Andy said. His hair looked darker. He must have been sweating.

'It's not really that, no. It's just, I suppose, that that kind of film-making is completely beyond my experience, I suppose you could say.'

'I figured,' Andy said. 'Don't worry. Forget it.'

'You don't think much of the sort of films I've been connected with, I shouldn't imagine.'

'I wouldn't say that. They just don't interest me particularly.'

95

'You see film as an art, purely a form of personal expression. Quite honestly, I don't, not altogether.'

'I see it as something it's interesting to do.'

'I.e. not a profession. Not something to make money out of. That's not a side of it that interests you.'

'I haven't really thought about it.'

'Suppose I offered you a thousand quid for the film, outright. What would you say?'

'I'd say thanks a lot.'

'You'd accept.'

'Sure.'

'Then what's so wrong with doing it professionally?'

'I never said there was anything wrong.'

'And following from that, what's wrong with getting things in focus and having a coherent story and decent lighting?'

'I never said there was.'

'I'm just wondering myself.'

'Sorry?'

'Why you seem to put me in the wrong when, God dammit, I'm not in the wrong.'

'Sounds like your hang-up to me, that does.'

'What makes you think it's all so easy, this business?'

'I never said I thought it was easy.'

'There is a language apart from speech.'

'Oh ar.'

'Which you use very consciously, I'd say. This is a kind of attack, isn't it?'

'What is and by whom exactly?'

'This film of yours. You're lashing out at something. I mean, it only makes sense as a kind of protest, a kind of sneer really, doesn't it?'

'Makes sense? I never claimed it made sense.'

'That's what makes it a gesture, a kind of action.'

'If you like.'

'Like spitting.'

'If you like.'

'You make me feel bloody old-fashioned, and yet the people you people admire tend to be the commercial film-makers of the past, the really dead commercial Hollywood film-makers. Keaton, Keystone, Lang, Wilder, people like that. Ford.'

'I just like shooting,' Andy said.

'And they wouldn't have known what the hell to make of what you're doing.'

'I'm not bothered,' Andy said. 'Would Rembrandt have known what to make of Picasso? Or Pollock?'

'Oh Christ,' Daniel said.

'I don't think so,' Andy said, 'particularly.'

'I wonder where the idea came from,' Daniel said, 'that art was easy. Not that I necessarily believe all this about film being an art.'

'As you said.'

'As you noticed.'

'It comes from kids,' Andy said. 'Anyway, all those old pros, they made their pictures even faster than we do.'

'You and — ?'

'The underground,' Andy said.

'They came out of vaudeville,' Daniel said. 'They had their tradition already. They had their craft by heart. Anyway, what're we arguing for?'

'I thought you wanted to.'

'*I* wanted to.'

'I thought you did, yeah.' Andy released the spool from its clips and stood there with the leader hanging white.

'I don't want to argue.'

'No?'

'In spite of everything, I still think part of the fun of film is the public part, trying to reach a lot of people, trying to make something that's intelligible first time through. You can't look back in film, at least not in the cinema —'

'I was going to say —'

'Oh I know, I know. The cassette is upon us. In spite of everything I still think in many ways comedy is the heart of film. And the heart of comedy is timing, preparation, wit, intelligence, accuracy, a certain kind of accuracy above all.'

'I'm not too interested in laughs. I laughed at *Death In Venice*, though, I admit.'

'You laughed at *Death In Venice*.'

'Yeah, I laughed at that. I thought that was a lot of laughs.'

'You're kidding.'

'Am I?'

'Really? Honestly? You laughed.'

'Well, it was funny, wasn't it?'

'You didn't think it was art then?'

'That doesn't follow, does it? According to what you were saying. I thought it was funny. He looked like Mr Pastry, didn't he, the bloke? That was funny for a start.'

Daniel said: 'Where is this bloody girl?'

'It was sort of a one-joke picture, but I thought it came off O.K'.

'Are you hoping to do anything with it, this film of yours?'

'Do anything with it?'

'Have it shown.'

'Not really. I got the chance to do it, so I did it. As far as I'm concerned that's the finish really. There it is, if anyone wants it. Like people.'

'Can I ask you something else? Are you proud of it?'

'Why should I be?'

'Are you pleased with it?'

Andy sniffed and smiled and went, rather delicately, as if he were barefoot, across to a big suitcase with metal clasps and reinforcements and threw the spool into it. 'I've done it, haven't I?' he said. 'That's all there is to it.'

Daniel said: 'Why is it better to wave the camera around like a flag instead of holding it still and letting the audience see something?'

Andy said: 'Better? Who said it was better?' He answered reluctantly, sitting on the suitcase and working the locks. He looked first at one lock and then at the other; Daniel was reminded of a jazz musician, checking with his partners what they are going to do. 'I'm surprised you're so bothered,' Andy said.

'I'm interested,' Daniel said.

'I don't want to do commercial shit,' Andy said.

'Who does?'

'So I'm not worried,' Andy said. 'I do what I feel like doing. If I feel like waving the camera around I do it.'

'But how does one feel like that? I mean, what constitutes feeling like that?'

Andy got up and went to the door and opened it. The rain shone in the light. 'Thanks for coming,' he said. 'Sorry if you're sorry.'

Daniel said: 'Look, what's the idea?'

'Bad vibrations,' Andy said.

'Oh come on,' Daniel said, 'that was last year. What's the matter with you?'

'You wanted to see the film. I showed it to you. You're not happy, you may as well go. O.K.?'

'Very far from O.K.' Daniel said. He thrust himself against the door, but Andy did not resist. The door banged. Andy threw himself down on the purple patch again, legs apart, hands latched behind his head. 'She phoned here, didn't she? Now I want to know where she is. Where is she?' Daniel raised his voice. She might have been hiding in the studio. 'I want to know.'

'Maybe she went home,' Andy said. 'I don't know.'

'Doesn't it occur to you something may have happened to her? I'm worried about her.'

'Why?' Andy said. He was scratching his eye in a very thorough way.

'When she called, what did she say?'

'She said she didn't know if she could make it or not and to go ahead without her.'

Daniel said: 'Look, if you're hiding something —'

Andy spread his hands and surrendered with his legs in the air. 'What have I got to hide?'

Daniel said: 'Do you often do this kind of thing?'

'What kind of thing is this?'

'Try to make fools of people.'

'You don't usually have to try all that hard,' Andy said. 'I find.'

Daniel said: 'You take a lot of risks, don't you?'

'Risks? Not more than I can help.'

'Do you really want to work in films?'

Andy again seemed to count off some number of raindrops, then he said: 'I do already. Why, are you offering me a job?'

'Not if you're that easily satisfied.'

'I am,' Andy said.

'I'm going to tell you something because why the hell not,' Daniel said. 'I don't know whether you're a black belt or something, but I think you ought to know that you're a very provoking character. Very provoking indeed. And one day someone's going to be provoked.'

'I know,' Andy said. 'A lot of people have got problems.'

'Some day someone may actually do something. Not everyone is as inhibited as I am.'

Andy jumped up and Daniel, excited, was ready to defend himself. Andy grabbed his reinforced suitcase. Dressed exactly as he was, in cotton shirt and sneakers, he dived out into the rain and banged the door behind him. His footsteps drummed on the gallery boards and then he had slipped away into silence. Daniel had to act for a few seconds. He had to mime astonishment and surprise because he was left blank. He saw no sense in following the boy into the darkness and yet how could he stay in the studio? He walked round the room and examined the shelves of expensive paperbacks. How long was it before he heard footsteps? The fool was coming back. There was a double rap on the door. He went slowly across and opened it.

'What the hell's the big idea?'

'Oh hullo, you're still here,' the girl said.

'What the hell is going on?'

'I don't know,' she said. 'What is? I mean —'

'We were going to meet at nine o'clock,' he said. 'It's now — it's now twenty past eleven.'

'I told Andy to tell you.'

'Tell me what?'

'Because didn't he?'

'Tell me what?'

'I had to go and see my brother.'

'You had to go and see your brother? Where is your brother? And who, if it comes to that?'

'What's the matter? What's happened? Where's Andy? In the bog?'

'He may be in the Thames for all I know. Or care. What's happened to your brother? He suddenly barged off out of the room and that's the last I've seen of him. I hope. Well?'

'He got into a fight,' Rachel said. 'And they were afraid he was going to lose an eye.'

'What about?'

'Oh it wasn't anything to do with him,' Rachel said. 'He just got involved.'

'Well, where is he?'

'They've got him at Charing Cross at the moment.'

'And I take it he isn't going to lose an eye after all.'

'Apparently he was mistaken for somebody else and he was so amazed that he never bothered to tell the people he wasn't. It was absolutely horrible. How did you get on with Andy?'

'We had a communication problem,' Daniel said. 'I had the impression he was high. Could that be so?'

'Possible,' Rachel said. 'He's a strange boy.'

'And he made a very strange film.'

'Yes,' she said. 'What did you think?'

'I thought it was horrible. Absolutely horrible. You never told me you were in it.'

'I didn't see any point,' she said. 'I mean, what difference does it make?'

'To what?' Daniel said.

'That's right,' the girl said.

'That's right! What does that mean, that's right?'

'I don't know what you're angry about.'

'I'm not angry. I'm just trying to understand you.'

'It's the same thing,' she said. 'You're angry because I don't come out neatly, like an algebra problem in G.C.E.'

'I don't know anything about G.C.E.,' Daniel said.

She sat down on the purple patch and began to chew her nails.

'Let me ask you something,' he said.

'Anything you like.'

'I don't know where to begin.'

'Are you sure you want to?'

'Yes, because I'm interested.'

'In what?'

'In you. In people like you, you and Andy. Our youngers and betters.'

She seemed as interested in him. She turned her eyes on him. The eyelids seemed to leave her dark eyes unnaturally exposed. Daniel thought of the prisoners in Malraux tortured by the removal of their eyelids. She seemed not to be aware of the destructive light that fell on her. She was wearing a dye-stained shirt and ribbed black pants and a heavy pair of men's shoes, surely, with round laces. She had thrown off a rain-darkened sheepskin waistcoat.

'Did you want to do this film, this so-called film?'

'Did you tell Andy how much you disliked it?'

'I didn't pretend I was mad about it. On the other hand.'

'You did,' she said. 'Obviously. You are a sod.'

'Why am I supposed to be dishonest when everyone else is so honest these days? I tried to discuss it with him. I tried to make contact with him. I tried all that business.'

'If it had been another girl maybe you would have felt differently. If you hadn't known me, I mean.'

'What I'd like to know is why it seemed such a good idea to help him make it. Sticking roses up your arse!'

'It didn't hurt anybody,' she said. 'I didn't do anything that damaged anybody.'

'What about yourself? If I told you I thought you'd been conned, what would you say? If I said that you'd been persuaded to do something basically very nasty, very cheap, very obvious and very

102

bad in order to gratify somebody else's vanity, what would you say?'

'I'd say that's what women are supposed to do and like doing most days of their lives.'

'Being fucked in public? Balls.'

'I did what men do all the time,' she said.

'But you're not a man, for God's sake. Are you?'

'You must have seen things I didn't,' she said. 'I don't remember actually—'

'Give or take a few inches,' he said.

'Inches make a difference,' the girl said.

'What did you think when you were doing what you were doing?'

'Think? I didn't. Why should I have been thinking? Would you believe it if I said I was experimenting to see if I really wanted to be an actress?'

'Is that what acting is to you? Really? Is that what you think acting is? Did he give you notes afterwards?'

'Of course not. Why are you so angry?'

'I'm not, I'm just—'

'You're seething. I can see.'

He sat down beside her. The arms of her shirt were wet from the rain.

'He couldn't get anybody else,' she said. And then she laughed. He reached to gather a kiss. She looked at him with pity and huddled forward, enclosed in her own arms and felt for a cigarette in her waistcoat. He sighed and leaned back, but stiffly, affecting a sort of weariness with the very games he longed to play. 'I didn't enjoy it,' she said, 'not much anyway.'

'You're not going to make it your career then?' he said. 'Making blue movies. I wish you'd get this bloody shirt off.'

'It's not a blue movie.'

'Oh of course it is.'

'And what are the movies you make?'

'It's a funny thing,' he said, 'you're not the girl I met at the Playfairs at all are you?'

'No, I'm her sister,' she said.

He looked closely. Really she might have been. This girl's hair looked darker and longer and the open eyes were a different shape from those he had seen in Gibson Square. 'Who the hell are we?' he said. 'Don't worry, I know. We all know only too well.'

'I don't,' she said.

'You're one of those forms that're all blanks,' he said. 'You'll get filled in presently. Being blank isn't being free. Sooner or later you have to find answers to the same old questions.'

'Did Andy say he was coming back?' the girl said.

'He didn't even say he was going,' Daniel said.

'Only he can do funny things,' Rachel said.

Daniel said: 'You're against something, aren't you? You're at war with something. Everything you do is a kind of—gesture, isn't it? It doesn't really come positively from you. You are a *type* of person.'

'Why do you always have to prove things?'

'It's my education,' he said. 'You're right. I make shit. The movies I've worked on are all shit, you're quite right.'

'I never said they were. I like them. I told you I did.'

'Nevertheless,' he said. 'It's all a fraud. You work half honestly in a fraudulent industry and you believe you're doing something bold and true. It's almost worse than being a genuine fraud. Do you know I once saw a shop in New York City, it had a sign saying "Everything In This Window Guaranteed Fake". Somehow I found that rather touching.'

'Why don't you give it up?' she said.

'What else is there to do?' he said. 'It's all hatred, isn't it? The whole thing about this country is hatred. I'd like to find one really big, worthwhile subject and then—'

'Do you want a drink?'

'No. What's growing up, I used to wonder? It's staying up as late as you like, it's drinking and it's doing what you want. Fucking, naturally. What did you think growing up was?'

She shrugged. She had a tumbler of brandy.

'You're cold,' he said. 'Where're you going to stay tonight? Here? Do you—is Andy—?'

104

'He's a funny boy,' she said. 'I hope he's O.K.'

'He's O.K.,' Daniel said. 'He's probably found an audience by now.'

The girl sat in one of the cubicles, huddled over the glass like a gipsy.

'I'm sorry. I shouldn't have said that.'

'Yes, you should, if you wanted to.'

He went over and stood above her and finally lifted the glass from her hands and set it aside. He tipped her face up towards him.

'It's all right,' she said.

'What is?'

'The way you feel. I understand.'

'And how do I feel?'

'You want to hurt me,' she said. 'I suppose I must ask for it.'

'It happens that often, does it?'

'It happens,' she said.

'Old campaigner,' he said. 'Have you really got a brother?'

'Do you think I'm a liar?'

'O.K., you may have a brother, but was he really injured the way you said?'

'You do think I'm a liar,' she said.

'God, you make me feel ancient,' he said. 'You make me feel bloody ancient.'

'In what way?'

'Because you make me moralize. And feel a hypocrite at the same time, because every standard I judge you by is one I disapprove of, that's the real hell of it.'

The silence alarmed him. It was as oppressive to him as those periods when the phone never rang, when days and days passed without messages, without proposals and without ideas. He had then to accept that he was a man who could not endure his own company and was incapable of enjoying himself.

'The Quakers declare a concern,' he said, 'you've heard of that, haven't you, when they feel anxious about something? Well, I feel a concern about you. You frighten me honestly. Not personally; your situation.'

'Oh I'm O.K.,' she said.

'You don't believe me,' he said.

'Yes, I do. Up to a point.'

'Meaning?'

'The Quakers aren't necessarily all that great.'

'Oh, no one's necessarily great.'

'They were among the people most influential in destroying Robert Owen,' she said. 'Did you know that?'

'Robert Owen?'

'The Socialist, the Utopian industri—'

'Oh Robert Owen, were they? I didn't know that.'

'Yes, they were,' she said.

'Oh well,' Daniel said, 'the Jews killed Christ. You can't win 'em all. How far back are we going to go?'

'If we don't go back,' she said, 'how is anything going to be any more important than anything else, how are we going to judge things at all?'

'That's funny coming from you,' he said. 'He'd make a good subject, really, wouldn't he, Owen?'

'Who do you think I am?' she said.

He put out his hand and held her arm, just below the elbow. He bent and kissed it below where his hand was. He looked up at her and expected to find her older. The smooth, glistening face, the feverish eyes, the uneven eyebrows, the chopped hair, the face of a young girl, with all its prompt emotions, disturbed him; it offered such meagre defences against the world, for itself and for him. He longed for her to bring her lips down to his, but she did not. He had to stretch his neck to make contact with her. It pained him — he was positively sulky in the face of it — that she now showed none of the impersonal passion which had so staggered him the previous night. He sat down beside her and smiled into the room. 'What do you want to do?' he said. 'Do you want to wait here? Or do you want to come back with me? Do you think your mate's ever going to come back?'

'If he comes back, he'll be all right,' she said, 'and if he doesn't, there isn't much point.'

Now she wanted him to kiss her. He kissed her. Her mouth was soft and welcoming. She put her arms round him and he felt a vengeful gratitude. He was determined now to excite her, to give her every satisfaction except that of his own. He started to tremble and that passed for passion, with him and with her; it was, he recognized, a kind of imposture by his body, by the least personal part of himself, it was a sign of the body's hatred for the mind, a hatred of his thoughts, confused and childish and lamentable and sentimental, a revulsion of his body which his mind, cunningly double as ever, claimed to understand and to lead, so that he did not quite lose faith in himself, seeing that he was at least capable of hating himself. He made love to her then with a raging tenderness. He shook at the skill of his hands and his lips and his tongue, he trembled at the beauty of the girl whom he caressed into such credulity that she allowed herself not only to be invaded, for that was nothing now, but also to smile at him when it was finished and she was sleek with his kisses. This time, he thought, oh he thought, he had done it, he had done it, she was not only in his power, she not only wanted him, she was willing to allow that he was right and that she was wrong and that all the wise and true things she had said to him were refuted and pointless. Only then when she was satisfied did she realize, with a curious frown, that he had kept his cold bargain and taken no pleasure of her. Her hands, warm and pale now, reached for him and she moaned and said 'You ... ?' in a voice bleakly hopeful and inquiring. 'You,' she said, and blinked to see that he was actually still in his clothes, while she lay sprawled, in a damp mattress, her body flecked now with goosepimples. He stroked her chill back and shoulders and held her against him. Her eyes searched his face, as if, coming late into a crowd, she was looking upwards at a bank of strangers, stumbling towards the one she had expected to meet and who now failed to stand out and declare himself. She guessed some trick her innocence could not believe of him. She said, 'Please,' so politely that he could not refuse. He hated that politeness but he could not refuse it. It cut short that journey towards desperation and destruction on which he felt bound and he could love her for her kindness, for her humanity even at the same time as he despised and hated and dreamed of cheating her.

He said: 'Come back with me to my place.'

She said: 'You don't really want me to.'

He said: 'Jesus.'

'No,' she said, 'you don't.'

He said: 'Rachel—'

'Look, it's all right,' she said. 'You don't have to apologize or explain. I know.'

He said: 'Would you believe me if I told you that I wanted to love you?'

'Yes,' she said, 'of course.'

'Because I swear to God I do.'

'That's all right,' she said.

'What about you?' he said.

'What about me?'

'Have you ever loved anybody?'

'Oh yes,' she said.

'I suppose you love everybody,' he said.

'I'd like to,' she said, 'but there isn't time—'

'I don't know,' he said, 'the way you're going—'

'Why don't you go home?' she said.

'I wish I understood you,' he said. 'I wish I knew what you really wanted.'

'I really want a cigarette,' she said.

'Oh that's ridiculous, that's ridiculous. Rachel—' He ran to her and put his arms round her. He stopped her and held her. 'I wish I knew which the hell of us—'

'What?'

'Was trying to take advantage of the other.'

He truly expected her to smile. He expected her to play Beatrice now and smile at the invitation to toss aside their rapiers. She did not smile. She rolled her head as if she had a stiff neck. He was panicked for a moment. Miles of track seemed to slide into the abyss. His vision of the future was useless. He had to think of something new. He had to recover. And anger blinded him when he most wanted to see. He ran to anger. He was always ready for war. He understood it.

He said: 'Perhaps you'll explain to me why you wanted me to see his stupid, vulgar, unnecessary film? If you weren't after something, what was the idea?'

She was getting dressed.

He said: 'You've tried to put me down ever since we met — ever since we met again anyway. Now I want to know why.'

She stood with her leg slightly cocked and drew up her zip.

'I'm damned if I see why I shouldn't —'

She put her spread hands either side of her head and plumped her hair and then she went for the door. He grabbed her and threw her back into the room. She stood still. She looked down to her left and stood quite still.

He said: 'I'm asking you to help me. I need your help. I need you to say something. I need you to tell me something.'

She sighed and moved her fingers against her jeans.

'Did you simply want to humiliate me? Is that all you wanted? Was it all — did I do something once without even knowing it — I mean, what's the point of this?'

'Can't you believe in any motive except revenge?' she said.

'Rachel,' he said, 'I don't love you, it's quite true. I don't begin — no, that's not true, I do begin to love you, but then I begin to love all women I — have anything to do with. Let me try to be honest with you —'

'No,' she said.

'Why not?'

'Because you'll destroy yourself,' she said. 'And me, if you can.'

'Oh that's nonsense. That's nonsense. Don't flatter yourself, I'm not going to destroy myself. Maybe you're putting that on to me, does that occur to you, because that's what you want?'

'I don't want anything,' she said.

'That is wanting something,' he said. 'That's demanding something, you know that as well as I do.'

She walked over to collect her coat. He followed her and

grappled with her. He turned her to him. He had forgotten how to kiss; he butted and bruised his mouth against her lips and teeth. He couldn't remember how people kissed. He hurt himself against her. She broke from him. There was sweat on her forehead.

She said: 'I don't want to argue.'

'What are you trying to make me do?'

'I'm going,' she said. 'It's better.'

'Better than what?'

'It's all wrong,' she said. 'It's a mess. It's a messy canvas. There's no way we can put it right. It may be my fault, it may be yours, I don't know, but there's no harm done, not if we call it a day now, before it goes any further and we get any dirtier.'

'Rachel,' he said.

'What?'

'Come and live with me.'

'No,' she said.

'Please. Please.'

'Please don't ask me,' she said. 'Not now. At least—not so *quickly*.'

'Maybe I do want to destroy you, I don't know, but I want you, whatever I want. Please believe me.'

'It'll only mean this over and over again,' she said, 'until finally it hurts as much as you want it to.'

'Hurts who?'

'That's the question,' she said.

'What are you after?' he said.

'Oh,' she said, 'you have such faith in me.'

'In women,' he said.

'I had an idea,' she said, 'you're quite right, that you might be—what I wanted, what I was after. I really don't want to be an actress, but when I did, I thought perhaps you were the person who might make me—I don't know—important. That's what a woman wants maybe, to feel important, to feel she matters.'

'Couldn't we get out of here?' he said.

She said: 'Please don't worry about me. I mean it.'

'What is it? Have you proved whatever it was you wanted to

prove, is that what you're saying? Because I wouldn't be too sure.'

'You don't have to threaten me.' She said it good-naturedly. 'There's no need to threaten me.'

'What've I got to threaten you with?'

'Oh, the future,' she said.

'You don't want a future, do you? Not that I can offer you one, but isn't what you want a kind of eternal present?'

'Isn't that the ideal?' she said.

'Unfortunately,' Daniel said, 'there's an angel at the gate with a flaming sword.'

'What sort of thing ought we to be serious about?' Victor Rich said. 'I don't want you to worry about when we start or even whether we've started at all. That's something we can worry about when we've finished. What I mean is, I want this to be a serious programme, but I don't want it to be solemn. For the moment I'm going to make myself chairman, but that isn't by any means a permanent arrangement—'

'If it goes on like this,' Bernard Morris said, 'they'll have to send it out on splitscreen so he can be seen nodding encouragingly to himself.'

'What I do ask is that you don't overlap too much—it's a question of picking up the cues as it were spontaneously. It's not that difficult. Perhaps I could ask you this. Is there really such a thing as being serious at all? Or should there be?'

'If serious means anything,' Gay Brain said, 'evidently there are things that are serious. Certainly things we don't have any right to laugh about.'

'Such as?'

'World starvation, Vietnam, race—'

'Why don't we have the right to laugh at them?'

'Do I really have to spell it out?'

'What I'm after,' Victor Rich said, 'is what does and doesn't sanction us to laugh at things? Could it be that we can laugh at what we can cure and not at what we can't? In this sense, don't we look forward ideally to a time when we can laugh at everything? Won't that be the time when we have finally defeated the problem of the intractable? And isn't that the time when we shall be the true masters of our environment, when we shall really have inherited the earth?'

'You mean—'

'What I'm trying to get at here is that there are things we now laugh at which were once just as serious as the things we now feel we shouldn't laugh at. The best satire announced before it turned into showbiz that the time had come to face the comedy of certain things which were previously assumed important and that helped to rectify a number of errors of disproportion, didn't it?'

'In other words—'

'I'm only the chairman of this discussion in the most provisional way and I certainly don't intend to monopolize it, but what I want to put to you is that perhaps the whole idea of a serious discussion is a sort of unconscious, premature bow in the direction of metaphysics, religion, the whole idea of the right sort of life being a dying life, in the sense in which Jeremy Taylor looked at it. Isn't there, I mean to say, a sort of continuity, unacknowledged but undeniable, between religious ideas, which we would probably consciously reject around this table wouldn't we, and the ideas which support our notions of correct or sensible attitudes over matters of substance? We could talk about sex here—'

'I must say I was hoping,' Bernard Morris said.

Daniel said: 'I—'

'Let me just explain,' Victor Rich said. 'Isn't it, for instance, true that almost every idea we have concerning values derives from religious origins, that's to say from unproved, transcendental ideas, basically non-empirical and non-scientific? Now this is sometimes taken—I'm thinking of the arguments of Christian apologists, of various degrees of sophistication—isn't this generally taken as an argument for the preservation of religion, I mean as a warning against throwing out the baby with the bath water, but isn't that perhaps exactly what we ought to be doing? Ought we not consciously and deliberately to be dismantling the old value

112

structure, rather than waiting for it to dissolve as we've been taught to do—'

'Who taught you that, Victor?' Cathie Connolly said. 'Because it's nothing I've ever been taught to the best of my knowledge.'

'It's the basic Cambridge position,' Victor said.

'The missionary position,' Gay Brain said.

'I'm sorry Basil isn't here,' Victor said, 'because I think he'd bear me out, but you know what I mean, Daniel, don't you?'

'I believe I do,' Daniel said. 'Shall I be the first to mention Wittgenstein or shall I leave it to you? And how about Eysenck, shall I spit first or will you?'

'I don't necessarily spit at Eysenck. He rather lends force to my argument—'

'I wish I knew what it was,' Cathie Connolly said, 'and then I'd be the better able to disagree with it.'

'Are we really in any difficulty here?' Victor said. 'Seriously?'

'Frivolously,' Gay Brain said, 'we are a little.'

'What I want to ask you—Paul, you haven't said anything—'

'Don't worry, Victor, I will, I will.'

'What I want to ask you is whether, in spite of all the explosions of the enlightenment—explosions which turn out all too often to be mere fireworks, calculated more often than not to delight the courtiers they pretend to scarify and never seem to evict—in spite of all that, isn't the whole machinery of morals, whatever morals we're talking about, standing in the way of a new world rather than preparing the way for it?'

'I think he's stopped,' Bernard said.

'I wonder if you'd mind explaining how this relates to what you call the Cambridge position,' Daniel said.

'Yes. Basically, I think philosophy, the kind of philosophy which you and I believe or at least believed in, doesn't truly believe in itself. If it did, if it wasn't afraid of making itself obsolete, it would not just argue for the worthlessness of the whole metaphysical currency from which—and this is the basis of its hesitation—it still derives most of its revenues. Suppose that we really believe science to be the essential human activity—'

113

'God forbid,' Cathie Connolly said.

'Who?' Daniel said.

'Just let me try to try to finish and then—'

'How do you define science?' Jack Darwin said.

'I purposely avoided having Dick Lucas here in order to avoid being asked that particular question. I don't think I can define it, but I think the meaning will emerge—because what I mean by science—and I have worked as a scientist—is something to do with method not with field of activity.'

'Who sweeps a room as for thy laws,' Daniel said, 'makes that and the action scientific.'

'Good.'

'Thank you.'

'Look at it another way. What do we take to be the social consequences of a scientifically based society? What I want to suggest here is that the essential, the *essential* I want to emphasize that—'

'He wants to emphasize everything. I never knew such a man for speaking in italics.'

'—the essential feature of the moral consequences of a scientific society is to be found in the irrelevance for even the most life and death issues, for the most significant and vital research, I mean, of any sort of moral seriousness, earnestness if you like, off the job—'

'You get this—'

'Yes, Paul—'

'Ah, we have lift off!'

'You get this in Watson's book, don't you, *The Double Helix*? You get this already in the early 'fifties, with the combination of a book on the origins of life, because that's what it is roughly, with a diary of petty seduction or the hope of petty seduction. You get the godlike vision of Watson and Crick contrasting with the moral frivolity of a generation—our generation—which was enthralled with the pretty packages that the foreign girls provided but were damned if they knew how exactly to undo them. I think this comes across in Watson with quite remarkable, if shameful accuracy. I must say I thought the frivolity gave one a lot of confidence in

114

the scientific validity of their theory, which is rather interesting.'

'Nice of you to say so,' Bernard said. 'That'll reassure the Nobel Committee.'

'Frivolity of course,' Victor said, 'isn't the only alternative to seriousness. Frivolity, you could say—'

'If you got the chance,' Bernard said.

'Is only solemnity turned inside out. What we're after perhaps is a kind of divine lightheartedness. What do you think, Paul?'

'Could be,' Paul Mallory said. 'That could be.'

'What I want to put to you,' Victor Rich said, 'is that our models of the soul and of society (I do wish Basil was here, but Plato did, after all, show the connection between the two) are unduly, piously dependent on ideas of God and the nature of reality which have no necessary claim on our credulity. Plato, in spite of his strictures, was surely addicted, wasn't he, to artistic standards? His images of perfection were as rigid as statues. How are we for level, Kenny?'

'All right for level.'

'Good, so the the thing that I want to put to you is that perhaps the validity of the positivist position has been much too glibly and not always honourably denied. The solemnity of its ideological attitude has allowed reactionaries to discount its liberating aspect as if they, the reactionaries, rather than the positivists were the guardians of pluralistic liberalism. I want to suggest that when science abandons its claims to any jurisdiction over the traditional areas of philosophical ethics it is not showing modesty, but a proper and liberating arrogance. The reactionary, on the other hand, and here I refer to those who want to reinstate the significance of the traditional ways of doing philosophy, the traditional categories — these people have been quick to assume that science, or its negotiators, its plenipotentiaries, have conceded its incompetence rather than proclaimed its impatience, its conviction of the futility of developing those areas at all. What needs to be said clearly surely is that there is no evidence for the value of traditional disciplines at all.'

'How do we break out?' Daniel said.

'I'm sorry?'

'How do we break out?'

Victor Rich said: 'I do wish someone else would come in on this. I don't want to do all the talking. Paul?'

'Break out of what?' Paul Mallory said.

'Let's say the traditional categories. Who's going to lead the way?'

'Oh Daniel,' Cathie said, 'here was I assuming you were.'

'The best hope might seem to be, I say seem to be,' Paul said, 'the young.'

'Shouldn't we stand up?' Meredith Lamb said. 'When royalty are mentioned? If the young are our best hope, I shall repair to a cork-lined room and harvest my memories, such as they are.'

'I'm not making an entirely facetious point,' Paul said. 'The point being that if you want people to escape from indoctrination you might find your best hope in those who have not been long exposed to it —'

'Who is more thoroughly indoctrinated than the young?'

'Meredith, you must try —'

'I think what's being being said here is that those whose conceptual apparatus is not yet fully developed and hardened —'

'When I was eighteen,' Meredith Lamb said, 'my conceptual apparatus hardened at the slightest opportunity —'

'He's such a baby,' Gay Brain said, 'he really is.'

'What I think's being said here,' Victor Rich said, 'is that the masses have never had a great use for language and that the young in a sense feel a sympathy for the masses because they too are, literally, new to the game —'

'I'm not sure I was saying just that —'

'But I think this is the crucial point. After all, why do people start off radicals and end, so often, to the right?'

'Because they learn sense,' Meredith said.

'They learn a language, let's say,' Victor Rich said. 'To put it less emotively.'

'I'd like to put it more emotively,' Meredith Lamb said, 'personally.'

'The masses and the young have in common — couldn't we say? —

a willingness, a yearning even, to escape through new rituals, new passions, new religions, if you like, and they're able to do it much more quickly, with less heart-searching, than the articulate, than we can.'

'They have less packing to do,' Daniel said.

'That's probably it. They have less packing to do. The crisis in conceptual affairs always unsettles the middle class—including the intelligentsia, the language users *par excellence*—far more than it does the wealthy, who have more concrete values—or those to whom choices have never really been given, the poor and the young.'

'The young are swamped with choices,' Meredith Lamb said. 'They can go to hell by any one of a thousand packaged tours. It's not the lack of choices which cripples them but their inability to choose. Lack of values, God help us.'

'Isn't that just a little hasty? Haven't you railroaded us a little here?'

'Say it if you like, but be careful,' Daniel said, 'I can feel it coming.'

'Isn't the idea of choice as the crucial moral act more typical of the bourgeoisie—and I don't use that term in any necessarily opprobrious way—than of any other group? The institution of marriage alone, after all, is only a moral institution in the middle class, who, after all, invented love, isn't that true, Meredith, you'd agree there, wouldn't you?'

'Pardon. If I had to.'

'I think you do have to. The aristocracy and the old rich marry for dynastic reasons and the poor marry, if they marry at all, for the sake of the family—and they traditionally marry after pregnancy, which bears out my point. Only the middle class *choose* their mates because of feelings and imagine themselves betrayed if their feelings stray. The rich take mistresses, the poor yield to their impulses, but the bourgeoisie believe in the definitive nature of choice—'

'What exactly are we supposed to be discussing?' Jack Darwin said.

'Oh Jack, don't start playing Dick Lucas's part. We're just discussing. There isn't a subject, not as such. Do you really want there to be?'

'Why do we always have to spend our time attacking the middle class,' Meredith Lamb said, 'when we know very well that most of us and most of the people we know and most of the people we like come from it?'

'I'm absolutely not attacking it. The middle class is, I quite agree, the most adventurous intellectually and socially of all the classes, but surely precisely because of their great diversity of activities and involvements they are most vulnerable to any radical revaluation. They hold their assets in intellectual equities. A slump in values murders them. They have careers, not jobs; families, not dynasties; responsibilities, not power; culture, not traditions. They are the masters of small changes and the victims of great ones. The bourgeoisie may be opportunist—it must be opportunist—in the short run, but it inevitably must, mustn't it, become conservative, if only because efficient business—financial or intellectual—requires a reliable communications system, that's to say, language? Bernard, this is your field really. The middle class can accept new calls, new ramifications with some alacrity, but it is genuinely appalled to see the wires come down—shall we have some coffee?'

'Now you're talking,' Gay Brain said.

'You haven't said much,' Victor Rich said, while they were waiting for the boy to bring the coffee.

'I'm saving my ammunition,' Daniel said.

'Probably too many people,' Victor said.

'Possibly.'

'What I really want to get on to is the role of science in society.'

'We're a bit short of scientists,' Daniel said, 'except for you.'

'Management comes into this, too, doesn't it, Bernard? I want to talk about business later.'

'Then I'm sure you will,' Bernard said.

'I think I'm off,' Jack Darwin said.

'Please don't,' Victor said.

'Seriously,' Jack said, 'because this isn't my sort of thing, I know, and I'm only wasting your time.'

'I would regard it as a personal favour if you'd stay.'

'I'm off, truly,' Jack said.

'He wasn't really suitable for this kind of thing,' Victor said. 'What I also want to get on to is what is science's answer to ethics. Why did Wittgenstein want nothing to do with ethics? I think the answer is contained partly in the view that the scientific version of ethics is geriatrics.'

'Come again.'

'He will.'

'The extension of human life—we really may as well go straight on, if that's technically—good, we're on camera again, but there's no need to behave any differently—'

'Why does a discussion like this always have to be so general? Why does everything have to be generalizations?' Cathie Connolly said.

'If I could just make this point, what I want to say roughly is that the lengthening of human life, the extension of human vitality is the quintessential question of scientific ethics. It is, I mean to say, the solution of the problem of ageing which will enable mankind to discard most of its ethical preoccupations.'

'I have a feeling,' Bernard Morris said, 'that you're going to explain that in other words—'

'In other words, the institution of marriage, the idea of the privacy of sex, the notion of belonging in human relations, and the whole nexus of emotions and moral scruples connected with this area of life, all of these things derive their centrality in human life from the fact that they determine the shape of our lives during the twenty-five years, say, of our sexual, physical and mental peak. Now science has been used to support this view or that—some have tried to analogize human to animal behaviour, in order to separate out the essential features, and some have been quite successful—'

'Successful enough to have to go and live in Malta,' Bernard Morris said. 'If you can call that success.'

'And some have tried to spiritualize it, but what I'm saying is that science ought to be indifferent to these efforts and pursue its course in a quite undogmatic way. The problems of morals will simply be irrelevant and have no further hold on human interest, if we can extend life towards infinity. How can for instance infidelity matter to people who need not give up the best years of their lives to each other? How seriously will sexual morals be taken when people can take pleasure without fear of the pox or of procreation? The development of a simple retroactive contraceptive will make absolutely obsolete all the Catholic campaigners and the anxious consciences, much more effectively than arguments about when a foetus is really alive or what we ought to do about illegitimacy. When we no longer have to reckon with death all the time, when we cease to be born astride the grave, what grounds will remain for seriousness, for lamentation as a literary form, for privacy as a condition of pleasure? When men can stay vigorous for a hundred years and women beautiful for just as long, most of our present ethical preoccupations will be no more significant than whether thunder is on the right or the left.'

'That's very good news,' Meredith Lamb said. 'Now can we go for a jar?'

'The fear of frivolity is the fear of the future,' Victor Rich said, 'Because I personally believe that frivolity will be the key of man's future, and the sign that he has finally conquered his environment and ceased to be afraid of it. Seriousness is the attitude of man to the unknown and above all to the divine, which he fears to offend. I could say a lot more about this, because I think it's very important —'

'He could say a lot more about it,' Bernard said, 'because he thinks he's very important.'

'But I very much want to hear from all of you, what you think. Cathie, what — ?'

'I do wish you wouldn't generalize so much because to me the way you generalize is, if you don't mind my saying so, positively inhuman. It makes me feel so small, so defenceless —'

'She's going to turn into a flower,' Bernard said. 'I can see it coming. Woman Into Foxglove.'

*

Outside the building, they stood about awkwardly on the pavement. Having entered in daylight and come out to darkness, they frowned at the city.

'You may remember what Samuel Rogers said at Lady Caroline's,' Daniel said.

'And I may not,' Bernard Morris said.

'The first person who leaves the room leaves his reputation behind him. You're not going back to the country tonight, are you?'

'Absolutely.'

'How long does it take you, for God's sake?'

'Hour and a half, I enjoy it.'

'You don't want to come and have a drink?'

'No, I think I'll get back. Syl gets worried if I'm late. You know.'

'How is she? It's bloody ages.'

'I know. But you know what it's like, we're not often in town.'

'You are coming on this tour, aren't you?'

'I said I would. I'm not that keen on being away, but —'

'I'm thinking of driving down. Why don't we go together?'

'Just the two of us.'

'Yes.'

'It means a bit longer away, doesn't it?'

'Hardly. You could fly back, if you wanted to.'

'Look, can I think about it?'

'I'm going to drive anyway. You weren't thinking of bringing — ?'

'Syl? No, she's got the kids to look after, otherwise, you know —'

'How old's — the oldest one — David now?'

'Twelve. Nearly thirteen.'

'Jesus!'

'Jesus is older,' Bernard said. 'I'd quite like to come, it's just —'

'Then why don't you?'

'Can I get in touch with you, sorry butting in, can I get in touch with you when I've taken things a little further at the usual place?'

'I'm not thinking of moving,' Daniel said.

'In case of developments. How did you think it went?'

'You were in fluent form,' Daniel said.

'I was afraid I might have said too much,' Victor said.

'Not that I noticed, did you think so, Bernard?'

'Not a bit,' Bernard Morris said. 'I thought you were very self-effacing. For you.'

'The problem is to goad people into reacting.'

'Oh, I think they reacted.'

'What shall I do?' Daniel said. 'Shall I give you a call and see how you feel?'

'Yes, O.K. And I'll talk to Syl. I'd like to do it in a way, it's just a question of domestic arrangements. I'll see you anyway.'

'That woman runs him,' Paul Mallory said. 'She's got him exactly where she wants him.'

'Sylvia?'

'She's got him exactly where she wants him. Connolly said it years ago. In *Enemies of Promise*, there's nothing to ruin a man compared with the pram in the hall. You can see how he runs back to her. He's like a dog on a short lead.'

'He keeps it all together,' Daniel said, 'as the Americans say.'

'But at what expense?'

'How's Margaret?' Daniel said. 'She was looking very good at the Playfairs.'

'She's not too bad,' Paul said. 'She's O.K.'

Victor Rich was walking away towards the car-park with Cathie Connolly, his head bowed to listen to her, the occasional nod waggling the red tip of his cigarette. His driver got out of the Humber as he approached and opened the door, but Victor stood apart, arguing with Cathie, for as long as Daniel kept him in sight.

'Give her my love,' Daniel said. 'Margaret.'

'Yes, I'll do that.'

'Why wasn't Ginny in on this affair tonight? I expected her to be.'

'Probably being saved,' Paul said, 'for the real thing.'

The football pitch was under the walls of the prison. When Daniel drove up, Jack Darwin was sitting on the tail-gate of his petrol-injection Triumph 2500. He had used it for a sponsored drive to Tashkent; there was a big white target on the driver's door.

'Afternoon, Jack.'

'Morning,' Jack Darwin said. He stamped his boots on the tarmac and then bent to tighten the laces.

'What're they like, these people?'

'They're not a bad little side,' Jack said, 'We shall have to play it tight at the back.'

'Who are they exactly?'

'The Hoteliers? London hotels side. If they've got their strongest line-up they'll probably give us a run, especially if we've got the same front three as last week.'

'He hasn't given Victor another outing, has he, after last time?'

'You bet your arse,' Jack Darwin said. 'You know he can't leave Victor out.'

'And Carlo in goal again?'

'Carlo in goal,' Jack said.

'What're you working on at the moment?' Daniel said. 'Another book?'

'This Timmis character's asked me to do an original screenplay for him. What do you know about him?'

'He's asked me to go and scout a story in Greece. Perhaps we should team up on it.'

'Sounds to me as though he likes buying people,' Jack said. 'I rather fancied the bird he had with him though.'

'Camille? Nice body,' Daniel said. 'How's Janey?'

'Working away. She was very nice-looking. Her back division looked nice and solid and she had an excellent pair of front runners. But here comes our gallant skipper, what news?'

'News is,' Paul Mallory said, 'they play a flexible 4-2-4 and they've got a centre-forward who's played first-team stuff in the Isthmian league and you know what that means—'

'Ankle-tapping at an advanced level,' Daniel said.

'You two're going to have to work out some kind of a strategy.

123

Bernard and Basil'll have to take care of the wing men and you two prop up the centre.'

'You can chase back a bit yourself,' Daniel said, 'if you feel the call.'

'We're not exactly richly endowed up front.'

'At least Bernard's back,' Jack said.

'He's back,' Bernard Morris said, 'the man they can't gag. Good afternoon, sports fans, and welcome to another edition of Fuck Your Luck.'

The Hoteliers played in white. They were already practising moves by the time the Canons had changed and straggled on to the field.

'They do look a bit hot,' Daniel said. 'We're only eight, for God's sake.'

'Basil and Victor Rich are on the way,' Adam said.

'The definitive instance of eight and two makes eight,' Danie said. 'Who else is coming?'

'Harold Usborne said he was coming.'

'Harold Usborne?'

'He's pretty useful. Used to be a Ulysses first-team regular,' Bernard Morris said, lurching from side to side and then doubling on the spot.

'Don't waste all your fuel revving up,' Daniel said, 'will you? Which one's the centre-forward?'

'The black chap,' Paul Mallory said. 'Jamaican.'

'Well, at least we shall be able to pick him out.'

'Until it gets dark,' Jack Darwin said.

As they watched, the Jamaican breasted down a long ball and stroked it into the net, all in one movement. 'Fucking Pele we're up against,' Bernard Morris said. 'You won't catch me tipping *him* next time he brings me a club sandwich.'

'Here they are,' Adam said. Basil Brain's Alvis had arrived at the car-park. The referee was rubbing his hands together.

'Are you all here then?' the Hoteliers' captain said.

'Bog Irish,' Jack Darwin said. 'We're certainly seeing life in the raw here this afternoon.'

124

Robin Taylor, in his blue track suit, had completed three laps of the field and trotted back towards Daniel and Bernard Morris. 'This is the big one then,' he said, doing right hand to left toe and left hand to right toe.

'I hope you're fit, Rob.'

'Had two hours' squash yesterday, so I ought to be,' Robin said. 'And I was out for an hour on the heath this morning with the dog.'

'All right, all right. No intimidation.'

The referee blew his whistle.

'So much for the Ulysses first team,' Daniel said, as they lined up.

'We shall have to waste some time,' Robin said.

'What do you suggest? How about putting on a discussion programme?'

'Keep it tight at the back,' Paul said, before trotting up to kick off.

'Kicking off's his biggest contribution to the proceedings,' Bernard said, 'I'll give him tight at the back. Cunt.'

The first long ball for the Jamaican was that little bit too long. Daniel was quickly across and pushed the ball back to Carlo who threw himself on it and rolled it for Bernard Morris. Daniel smiled at the Jamaican, but there was no answering smile. The next cross was better flighted. Daniel went in at the same time as the Jamaican and was coming out with the ball when he was tripped. Basil Brain prodded clear. Daniel smiled again. His generosity met no response. 'One more like that,' he said to Bernard, 'and I shall apply to my friendly neighbourhood racist for a deportation order.'

'Thank Christ,' Bernard said. 'Here's Harold.' A man in fringed leather and a crash helmet had ridden up on a 500 c.c. Norton and hurtled on to the pitch. He leaped off, jettisoning gauntlets, jacket, leggings and the crash helmet behind the goal, around the horizontal Norton, and anticipated the referee's formal invitation to come on to the field by flattening the Irishman and clearing the ball into an adjacent game.

They held the Hoteliers for the first forty minutes and then the Irishman broke free in the centre and swung a long ball to their sprinting little winger. 'I wish I knew where they found them,' Bernard said. 'Every bloody team except us has got a winger who can shift.' The winger ran like one of the figures on the side of a Greek vase, flying arms and legs, down to the corner flag. Over came the centre and there was Carlo groping air. The Jamaican jumped with Daniel. The ball ran loose and the Irishman sidefooted it into the goal. 'From our own correspondent,' said Bernard, with a sour look at Carlo. They were about to kick off when Robin Taylor was seen to be lying on the ground.

'End of part one,' Daniel said. 'What the hell happened to him?'

'He must have been sitting in a draught,' Bernard said. 'He's lasted longer than usual all the same.'

Two minutes later, the Irishman came through again. Victor Rich should have tackled back, but he stumbled and fell and went down. 'Another dying gladiator,' Bernard said. 'An ever absent help in time of trouble.' The German assistant manager (Bernard Morris had so identified him) hit a short ball in full stride. The force of it all but carried the goalkeeper over the crossbar. He came down the right side of the line and threw the ball out towards Robin Taylor who had palmed himself to his feet and was making fiercely deprecating movements. The assistant manager was in with a waist-high boot, over came the short lob and the Jamaican laid it off for one of the Hoteliers' two dozen or so Italians and Spaniards. This time Carlo dived into an empty pool and the ball was under the back netting. 'Fuck,' Bernard said. 'Two-nothing.'

They got one back early in the second half. Dave Reece, the strongest and best of the Canons' forwards, made a long solo run, escorted by cries of 'Yes, yes,' from Paul Mallory, and finished with a swerving shot into the top right corner. Paul ran back with an air of modest elation. 'You'd think he'd won the fucking cup single-handed,' Bernard said. 'He never touched the bloody thing.'

'That's the way,' Paul said, 'we can win if we use our brains.'

The Hoteliers were unintimidated. The assistant manager came dancing past Victor Rich ('He doesn't seem to realize who Victor is,' Daniel said to Bernard, 'this kraut, does he?'), who again found good reasons to sit down, beat the limping Taylor, who was brave for all

126

to see, and was finally unloaded by Harold Usborne, who spat. Daniel said: 'Victor, for God's sake, funnel back, man, funnel back.'

Basil Brain said: 'I'm beginning to form quite a high opinion of this inside-left.'

The Jamaican had gone into a quiet phase. Suddenly he came to life again. He beat Daniel twice within a couple of strides and fed the ball into the path of the assistant manager who banged it against the bar. While Carlo was still scooping at its shadow, the Jamaican headed the ball across the face of the goal and Daniel sliced it over the top. The nippy little winger took the corner. Carlo collapsed on the ball and threw it out to Victor Rich who ran the whole length of the field without ever bringing it under control. 'The thing about Mr Television,' Bernard said, 'is that the ball dribbles him.' Having reached the by-line, with an acre of empty turf between him and the rest of the players, Victor paused and then sliced the ball into another game.

'Cunt,' Bernard said.

'A subtle summary,' Daniel said. 'Here comes the Hermann Goering division again.'

'Take the centre-forward,' Bernard said.

'And achtung to you, mate,' Jack Darwin said.

The Jamaican breasted the ball down, veered right and hit the shot just as Daniel came in. It took him full in the balls. He scrambled it away and went down. When he found the will to open his eyes, he saw the Jamaican grinning at the German. Bernard pumped Daniel back to life and he limped back into the game. He was just stamping out the last of the agony when one of the Spaniards flattened Paul and Victor, leaving them shouting at each other, and chipped a perfect ball for the S.S. man, who came haring forward, with his high-kneed run, blond hair flying, working for the left-hand flag. The Jamaican was off for the penalty spot, with Daniel after him. Basil Brain scuttled forward, sitting on air, both feet out, and the ball popped to the Irishman who smashed it first time across the centre. Carlo dived as the Jamaican came in. The black man went down and the ball rolled free. The Jamaican took his weight on one hand and tried to pivot the ball into the net. Daniel took the ball in one stride and the Jamaican's ankle with the next. 'Good clean fun,' he said, as the Irishman ran down to the flag for the corner.

'Dirty bastard,' the Jamaican said.

'You can't always be the only shit in a changing world,' Daniel said.

Over came the corner. Daniel and the Jamaican went up together. Daniel felt the other's ribs against his shoulder and punched upwards with the whole side of his body. The Jamaican went down on his face. Bernard gathered the ball and had it in the other penalty area before the referee had time for second thoughts.

'You'd better watch yourself,' the Irishman said.

'I always do when I get the chance,' Daniel said.

Meanwhile, Paul Mallory had won a corner by ducking cunningly under the ball. Adam took it, on the right. Daniel went up and headed it to the feet of Victor Rich who frowned and stumbled the ball into the net before falling flat on his back. Daniel offered him a hand. 'The danger's past,' he said, 'you've scored.'

'Two each,' Paul Mallory said, running back with the ball in his arms. 'Now!'

Straight from the kick-off, the Hoteliers' winger hurdled a succession of low obstacles and worked the ball to the by-line. The Jamaican and Daniel climbed for the cross. The Jamaican was on top when Daniel bundled him into the goalkeeper's arms. Bernard, with a cry of 'Victor', had passed it to Harold Usborne, but this time the referee had not moved. He was pointing to the penalty spot like a man who just discovered it. 'That's never a penalty,' Bernard said.

'I think it fair to say there is a case for this decision,' Basil Brain said. 'Strenuously though I shall deny it at the subsequent inquiry.'

The Irishman ran in and, as the Canons protested, hit the penalty against the post. It ran along the line and the Irishman darted in and put it into the net. 'Goal kick,' Bernard said.

'Goal kick,' Daniel said.

'I'll sort you out later,' the Irishman said.

128

'Dirty fouler,' said the assistant manager.

Robin Taylor was down again: cramp. 'For the fittest man on the field, he's not what you'd call long-lasting, is he?'

'Sorry, chaps,' said Taylor, 'but I shall have to go off.'

'When did he come on?' Bernard said. 'I can't have been looking. Cunt.'

Adam now ran up to take one of his long throws on the left. After elaborate flexing motions, he dropped the ball behind his back. Players from other games were already on their way to the showers. One of the warders on the corner tower of the prison had taken off his cap and was combing his hair. The sun was orange and lowering. Paul Mallory was saying 'Oh for Christ's sake,' and the ball had gone out for another throw, when the referee blew the whistle.

'Fucking horrible,' Bernard Morris said.

'We kept it tight at the back,' Jack Darwin said.

'Like a fucking rock,' Daniel said.

'Brighton Rock,' Bernard said, 'the same thickness all the way through.'

Daniel offered his hand to the Jamaican, but the black man was already walking away. Daniel heard the Irishman say: 'He played a filthy game. He should've been sent off in the first half. He should have been sent off before half-time.'

'Well, at least you scored,' Daniel said, 'and that's what strikers are for.'

'Question of the right place at the right time,' Victor Rich said.

'Dave's a terrific player,' Paul Mallory said, 'I'm the first to admit it, but I wish he'd give an occasional ball. He really has to learn to give a ball. It's an ungrateful task playing alongside him.'

'Without Dave,' Bernard said, 'we'd have been well and truly fucked.'

Victor Rich was already changed and ready to go when Daniel and the rest of the players reached the dressing-room. He was never seen under the shower.

'How do you think it went the other night?' he said.

'That's for you to say,' Daniel said, 'isn't it? It wasn't noticeably duller than one expects.'

'I thought we said one or two things that need saying and need saying rather badly.'

'In that case I don't suppose there's the smallest chance of our ever appearing on the air.'

'You're unnecessarily cynical, Daniel. I've noticed that with you. The bad doesn't necessarily drive out the good, not all the time, not if one puts one's weight behind it. How goes it with *The Elephant Man*?'

'We're worrying away. I've put the scissors in pretty hard and I think it's come down to the right length. Tell me, are you coming on this tour thing?'

'To Bordeaux? I doubt if I shall be able to. I shall probably be in New York. I've got a conference going on the ethics of communication—'

'The peaceful uses of television,' Daniel said. 'Sounds nice. In that case I might be able to show you Sir Fred when you get back, if you like.'

'Sir Fred?'

'My film. *The Elephant Man*.'

'Oh that, yes. Well give my girl a call. I thought it was basically a good programme myself. The other night.'

'Oh that, yes.'

'Coming back for some tea, Danny? Virginia asked me to ask you.'

The two teams changed in a single room with a wire mesh fence between them. Usually there was banter between the sides after such a game; this time there was none. Daniel showered and dried himself on his sweaty shirt. He had forgotten a towel. He dawdled, but the others were slow. Adam was shampooing his hair under the shower. Robin Taylor was unwinding a bandage with stoic apprehension from a thigh which emerged, at the end, quite unmarked. Bernard Morris, still in jockstrap and sweat-badged shirt, was giving an account of an incident at Stockholm airport during a recent International Management Conference; it involved eight people speaking five different languages, all of which he imitated with astonishing fluency.

Daniel walked through the building, where a dozen sides were changing and showering. Lights showed beyond the deserted fields. A groundsman was unhooking nets. The walls of the prison were black. As Daniel turned the corner of the brick pavilion into the car park, the Jamaican and the Irishman were standing together, unchanged, waiting, beside a Thames van. Daniel walked towards the Lotus. Were they going to attack him? He both doubted and expected it. In *Pay or Play* there was quite a famous joke, where the hero, running after a man who had stolen his passport, reached a fork in the path without knowing which direction to take. In the film, he went both ways, splitting into two of himself without a moment's hesitation. Now Daniel could imagine, with simultaneous plausibility, both a vicious attack and an anti-climax. The Jamaican was ambling after him, the Irishman behind. 'Wait a minute,' the Jamaican said.

'Sorry.'

'I said wait a minute.'

'Not now, sorry.'

'You want to see what you done?'

'It'll be better in the morning,' Daniel said.

'You wait a minute, sonny,' the Irishman said, 'if you're sensible. I'd advise you to.'

'Sorry,' Daniel said. He had his key out. But they were already at him. The door of the car was open but he had no time to get in.

'Filthy dirty Jew,' the Irishman said.

'Oh for Christ's sake.'

'Filthy dirty Jew.'

'Knock it off,' Daniel said. 'Don't be ridiculous.'

They had started to pull at him when there was an explosion of sound and the Norton charged straight at them across the car park, twin exhausts storming. Harold Usborne, gauntleted and booted, head down, crash helmet shining, managed to slow down with the sound of someone accelerating. The two men were already backing away when the Norton stopped, growling, and Usborne lined up beside Daniel.

'See you,' Daniel said, 'next Tuesday.'

'Am I the first again?'

'You know you're the fastest driver. Much too fast if you ask my opinion.'

'I think of myself as extremely cautious.'

'You're well known to be extremely reckless.'

'As long as you spell it with a "W". Hullo, Candida, how are you?'

'Still terribly shy. You know Daniel, Candy, don't you? Heavens! How was the game?'

'Scrappy. Written any more poems recently?'

'Well, Candy? She wrote one this morning, didn't you, Candida?'

'I didn't know you played the clarinet, Candida. Listen, I hope I really am expected. Adam said—'

'As long as Adam said. I'm just a meek wife,' Virginia said. 'I always expect whatever he says. She's really extraordinarily musical, so André tells us.'

'He said you particularly wanted me to come. I rather hoped it was true.'

'I want anyone who wants to come.'

'That's not very flattering, but never mind.'

'You don't need flattering. Take it upstairs now, Candida, will you, and play it there, if you must play it? And make sure Tobe's O.K.'

'You're anything but meek, Virginia, so—'

'You're wrong, you're quite wrong. Do you want tea or a drink?'

'Tea,' Daniel said, 'buckets of it. I ran my arse off this afternoon. And I did my ankle.'

'What was the score?'

'We scrambled a draw. Two each. We miss Sandy and Mick.'

'Mick never plays now, does he?'

'Well, they live so far out,' Daniel said. 'I mean *Shropshire*.'

'I wish we did.'

'Oh, do you?'

'You seem to imagine, Danny, that I don't mean things when I say them. On the contrary, I mean exactly what I say. I hate London. Where *is* Shropshire?'

'There doesn't have to be a contradiction between your sincerity and the fact that I don't believe you. Somewhere left of centre, isn't it? Near Mummerset.'

'You never believe women,' she said. 'You and Norman Mailer.'

'Poor Virginia! It's all lies about me and Norman. I really do feel sorry for you, though.'

'Why? You don't really have to feel too sorry for me, Danny.'

'Having to listen to all this chat about football.'

'How many people are coming back altogether, do you know?'

'Jack probably, because Janey does her piece on Sunday, doesn't she?'

'Yes, of course. I must say I think she's very lucky —'

'To have found someone who'll publish it?'

'That's nasty.'

'And you're never nasty, are you, Gin? So that can't be what you meant.'

'Lucky to have a chance to express herself.'

'If by self-expression you mean telling us all the endless and charmless details of her terrible marriage to that rather nice man, Maurice Stukely.'

'I think they're very interesting,' Virginia said, 'the things she writes.'

'If you like a diet of dirty laundry,' Daniel said. 'But then I suppose happiness isn't all that much of a subject.'

'I suppose not,' Virginia said. 'Assuming it exists.' She had one hand on the handle of the orange enamel kettle. 'Do you think it does?'

'It's not a thing, is it? It's what we used to call an epiphenomenon. Like steam. Try to capture it and it's gone. Stuff like that.'

'I hope you're going to make a great film one day, Danny.'

'Thank you. It would be nice.'

'Have you got any ideas?'

'Some. Not many. *Le grand sujet, c'est qu'il n'y a pas de grands sujets.*'

'I think you're one of the ones who might do something really good.'

'You're in a very benign mood this afternoon, Gin.'

'Because you're still – unsettled.'

'I thought you were trying to settle me. With a wife.'

'Who told you that?' Virginia said. 'I meant your mind.'

'That old thing,' Daniel said.

'It's still alive.'

'Thank you.'

'How did you manage finally with what's-her-name? You know, you called me up about.'

'Oh we're meeting after Easter, after this tour.'

'And meanwhile?'

'I rub along.'

'I bet you do,' Virginia said. 'You're going on the tour then, are you?'

'Well I said I would.'

'Then I'm sure you will. What's funny?'

'Nothing. Why? Are you coming?'

'Adam did say I should, only I don't think he really wants me. Do you think he does?'

'We could do with an attacking winger.'

'Or do you think he'd be much happier with an all boys together party? Janey's thinking of coming, but –'

'A funny piece about football widows coming up no doubt.'

'Paul!' Virginia said. 'If I'd known you were coming I'd've made some of my oatcakes! As it is, it's just the old walnut loaf. Candida made it from *The Pooh Cookbook*.'

'Tea's the thing,' Paul Mallory said. 'Christ, what a pisser, didn't you think so, Danny?'

'Who else is coming?'

'Jack'll be here in a minute.'

'And David?'

'No, Dave's not coming.'

'I wish he would,' Virginia said.

'He's coming on the tour, isn't he?'

'He said he might. I think he will.'

'One sees so little of him,' Virginia said, 'and I do think he's worthwhile. It takes a lot of guts to give up playing second leads at Stratford in order to become a hospital porter. Jack, I do hope Janey hasn't changed her mind?'

'She hasn't changed it. She just hasn't made it up yet.'

'What make-up is she using on her mind these days? It sounds like the basis for a new series.'

'Stop it, Danny. What about Margaret?'

'If we can fix with her mother to come and look after the boys,' Paul said.

'You see how lucky you are, Danny, not having children to worry about?'

'Ah yes, but think what a lonely old age I shall have!'

'You've still got time, haven't you?'

'A week or two,' Daniel said. 'How's everyone going to get down to Bordeaux? Are you taking cars?'

'I thought we could fly and hire a minibus down there. Much easier.'

'I think I may ship my car over and drive down. What're you smiling at, Gin?'

'Danny always walks by himself,' Virginia said.

'Have you heard anything of Meredith's ear, Jack? It's not true, is it, he's carrying it around with him in a bottle?'

'I think that's somewhat exaggerated. No, as a matter of fact I sent him some fruit—something he could get his teeth into—and he wrote me a jokey note, so it seems to be all forgotten until the next time.'

'Was Basil playing this afternoon?'

'If you can call it playing.'

'Oh I wish you'd brought him back.'

'Virginia always sounds as if she wants to mount people's heads in the hall,' Daniel said.

'Don't worry, that's exactly what she does want,' Adam said. 'Together with their balls if she can get them, of course.'

Virginia went out of the kitchen and up the new staircase (they had recently had the kitchen done, William Morris) and they heard a door slam upstairs.

Daniel said: 'Oh God, sorry, Ad.'

'It wasn't you,' Adam said. 'Leave her be.'

'Have we got enough people for this tour, Adam? That's what we've yet to be sure of. Carlo's not coming and—'

'We shall be O.K.'

'Look, Danny, don't worry about her—'

The sitting-room door was shut. Daniel hesitated and then turned the brass knob and went in. Virginia was sitting, in her glasses, reading Octavio Paz in the big armchair by the fireplace. Shaded light fell across the blue and purple Casa Pupo rug.

'Sorry, I was an idiot.'

'It wasn't you,' Virginia said. 'Not entirely.'

'Meaning it was me partly,' Daniel said. 'I'm not sure that isn't worse, having to share billing with person or persons unknown.'

'Oh you know them,' Virginia said.

Daniel said: 'What the Christ are you doing here?'

'Waiting for you.'

'How long have you been here?'

'Two and a half hours.'

'When I arrange to meet you, you don't come. When I don't, you do. You look frozen.'

'I am a bit.'

'You're bloody mad, you must be. Is something wrong?'

'Yes, it is rather actually.'

'Well, come in, sit down. I've got some brandy somewhere.'

'I don't want anything, thanks.'

'You look awful.'

'I'm O.K.,' she said, 'it's Andy.'

'What's the matter with him?'

'He's dead.'

'Dead?'

'He's dead.'

'When did this happen?'

'Today. I heard about it this afternoon.'

'Well, what happened?'

'He threw himself off a roof.'

'Threw himself—Do you know I remember a time when there wasn't a roof in London high enough to throw yourself off? They said you couldn't build high buildings in London because of the clay soil or something. Where was this? And why, for God's sake?'

'Teddington,' she said.

'God,' Daniel said, 'that's not even in London. What happened exactly?'

'He fell off this roof.'

'On purpose?'

'I suppose it must have been. No one knows.'

'I hope it wasn't anything I said,' Daniel said.

'He was probably high.'

'High enough, it seems.'

'A friend of his got hold of me—a mutual friend—'

'There's always one, isn't there? And now I suppose you blame yourself.'

'It just seems such a waste. Such a shame. He was twenty.'

'Look, have a brandy, for God's sake. You'll feel better.' He put his arms on her shoulders. 'You look wretched.' He bent and kissed her. 'Do you want something to eat?'

'I don't want anything,' she said.

'O.K.,' he said.

She was wearing her long sheepskin waistcoat and fawn corduroy trousers and a shiny black peaked cap.

'Where are you living now?'

'I'm staying at my brother's.'

'Is he all right now then?'

'He's not there,' she said.

'Look, take this off and I'll light the fire.'

'I'm all right.'

'I'm glad you've come,' he said, 'but why have you? Do you blame me in some way?'

'I don't blame you,' she said.

'You think I blame myself. I feel like Byron,' he said. 'He called Keats poor little Johnny-piss-a-bed because he went into a decline after what the critics said about him, and then he almost went mad himself when they weren't too keen about something he'd done. I just hope he didn't kill himself because I didn't say he was a genius.'

'Oh he wasn't worried about that,' she said.

'You saw him again then?'

'He was staying at my brother's until yesterday,' she said. 'It was all so garbled because she only had enough money for a minute. The girl who told me about it on the phone.'

'It's about time you came clean with me,' Daniel said. 'When did you actually hear about this?'

'I told you. This afternoon.'

'And what did you do then?'

'I sat down and thought about it. I tried to work out what it meant.'

'It doesn't mean anything. What it meant! What could it mean?'

'I mean, to kill yourself, it's a big step. It's a big decision.'

'I get you, and you thought a big step needed a big push. I'm afraid it's not necessarily so. A big decision because death is a big thing. Death isn't a big thing, Rachel, it's a nothing. Do you think there has to be a big unopened truth hidden somewhere? I doubt it. He was maybe high, he was certainly unbalanced, weird, just the kind of person to spit in his friends' eye with some stupid gesture —'

'He was my friend,' Rachel said.

'He wasn't mine,' Daniel said. 'What're you trying to use him against me for?'

'Against you? You're horrible,' she said. 'I'm not.'

'Maybe I am. I fear I may be, horrible. But why should you come round here and wait all this time to tell me about it? Wait for

138

two and a half hours, why? Because you thought I'd like to know? Or because you wanted to be the first to tell me the good news? Or was it because you wanted me to feel guilty because I didn't admire the way he photographed your arse? Have I been a traitor to the young, is that what you want me to feel?'

'I just wanted to come and see you.'

'You wanted to come and throw something at me.'

'You're horrible,' she said.

'Fine, I'm horrible. Let it be a lesson to you. You seem to think you can have it both ways, you can live this kind of crazy life of yours and still expect people to be kind and care about little you, why the hell should they?'

'I don't expect anything. I don't expect anything.'

'You're a goddamned bloody liar,' he said. 'You expect the lot. I didn't kill him. I'm sorry he's dead, like I'm sorry anyone's dead, because it puts us one space nearer the judgment seat and all that business—Jesus!—but why specifically should I give a damn about Andy what's-his-name deciding to make away with himself?'

'I don't expect you to,' she said.

'Where are you going?'

'I'm going.'

'It's after midnight.'

'I'm allowed out after midnight.'

'Oh don't be damned silly.'

'Why are you so angry? That's what I wish I knew.'

'I wish I knew,' he said.

'Because it's horrible.'

He said: 'It's pretty obvious really, isn't it?'

'Not to me.'

'O.K.,' he said, 'O.K.'

She sat staring into the fire, her shoulders narrowed, hands in her lap, legs tight together, knees against the edge of the sofa. 'I can't believe it,' she said.

'Nor can he, I don't suppose.'

She bowed her neck.

He said: 'By which I mean perhaps he didn't really think of it as anything final, perhaps he had that old fantasy about killing himself and then seeing how sorry everyone was. I often do – or did.'

'He wasn't like that.'

'What was he like?'

'He didn't care about what people thought. He always did what he wanted to do.'

'Then why be sorry for him?'

'Because it's such a horrible thing to want to do. And anyway I'm not sorry for him.'

'You're sorry for yourself.'

'Do you honestly not see how horrible the world is when someone like Andy goes and kills himself? How polluting it is?'

'Oh let's not drag pollution into this. He aborted the mission, that's all. He went into a lousy orbit and he aborted the mission. How about that for a tricky modern myth? Were you sleeping with him?'

'Not regularly,' she said.

'The last few days.'

'He was so difficult to talk to.'

'You went to bed with him to make conversation easier, I suppose.'

'Is that such a bad reason?'

He went and put an arm under her knees and one behind her and made to lift her off the sofa.

'Please don't.'

'Would you like a hot bath?' he said.

'No thanks.'

'Are you going to sit here all night?'

'Oh I don't know,' she said.

'That's the first time you've ever sounded annoyed. If you want to sit there, sit there. It's all right with me.'

'You don't have to stay up,' she said, 'if you don't want to.'

He said: 'Somehow –'

'What?'

'I expect you to realize –'

'Realize —?'

'How much I dislike feeling what I do, which is very little. I suppose it's because death never seems real when you aren't face to face with it. I was never in a war. I've never really seen it. Perhaps it's something I don't want to face. One tries to blame the dead for it.' He stayed near her, looking down at the knob of bone at the top of her spine. It shone like a boil. He touched it, gently, almost expecting her to flinch at the pain. He left his hand over the strong bar of her neck and stroked her behind the ear with his thumb. 'Killing oneself doesn't make much sense, not in England, not now, does it really? Camus said it was the crucial question, didn't he, suicide?'

'I suppose it's for whom the bell tolls and all that business. I don't know. It's like buying a paperback thinking it's a novel and it turns out to be short stories. I mean, that's all there'll ever be about him. It's horrible.'

He said: 'I'm going to make some coffee.' When he brought it, on a Florentine tray, she was still hunched by the fire. It had not warmed her. She lifted her head slowly, as he poured the coffee. She managed a weak smile and then drank, with her hands either side of the cup. 'Do you feel you did something to make him do it?'

'No, I honestly don't.'

'You didn't reject him or anything?'

'No.'

'You gave him what he wanted.'

'I liked him,' she said.

'Did he ask you to marry him?'

'Good heavens, no. Not a bit. I just hope—'

'What people do generally doesn't have as much to do with other people as other people think,' Daniel said. 'Christ, I played in a shitty game this afternoon and then I had to sit through another instalment of the unending story of Virginia Playfair, intellectual, mother and martyr.'

She seemed to laugh at that, but she was crying at last. Tears and laughter came together. She was smiling and laughing and the tears sprinkled down her cheeks.

He said: 'I keep expecting to see a rainbow.' He bent and sipped the tears. 'I credit you with too much, don't I?'

'Poor Andy,' she said.

'Hold on a minute,' he said, 'I want to show you something.'

'What?'

'I shan't be a second. It sounds funny but I've never shown this to anyone else before. I keep it in a box under the bed and I've never shown it to anyone.'

'It's nice.'

'Do you know what it is? It's not a test, it's all right. Only I find you tell people what things are and they're offended because they knew all the time or you wait for them to recognize things for themselves and they think you're testing them. It's Cycladic.'

'I thought it was,' she said.

'About two thousand B.C.'

'Where did you get it?'

'Oh in London, I'm afraid. I bought it just before devaluation. I thought it was a shrewd move.'

'And was it?'

'Not particularly. When the bill came it was in dollars, so it made no difference. Clever, these Chinese. Still, it's nice, isn't it?'

'Why haven't you got it out?'

'For people to see? Because it's my little secret.'

'Then why did you show it to me? Because we're two of a kind?'

'Because — I wanted to show you something I valued. Oh Christ, I don't know. A sign of favour.'

'I used to visit an uncle who had butterflies.'

'Who had butterflies when you visited him or — ?'

'Calm down! Who collected butterflies.'

'I know.'

'And he used to bring them out, the rare ones, and hold them for me to see. South American ones and things like that. I never used to know what to do.'

'You could have said "pretty".'

'Oh I did. And they were. But I never used to know how to look at him.'

142

'And now you don't know how to look at me? There isn't really anything to say about her, is there? Actually, very little's known about her. They say they're Goddesses, but of course that's begging the question because all figures had a kind of sacred quality, magic anyway, once they were made, so it doesn't get you anywhere. What I like about them—about her—is the anonymity. The self-sufficiency. The arms folded like that, they seem to be denying the need for anyone else at all. I suppose it is a Goddess. A female who doesn't want anything and doesn't demand anything and yet has lost nothing of her femininity. She doesn't even ask to be worshipped.'

'And that's your ideal, is it?'

'It's an ideal,' Daniel said.

'You like enigmatic women.'

'Not at all. An enigma is always asking to be solved. There's no such thing as a self-sufficient enigma. She's just something to be with, something to consider. The absolute opposite of the multi-breasted, squat Mother Goddesses you get in Asia Minor at the same period, roughly.'

'You favour flat chests.'

'I've been corrupted by modern life,' Daniel said. 'I'm not that pure, no. She's nice, though, isn't she?'

'She's very nice. She's lovely.'

'How little there has to be of a thing for it to be a presence! And yet if it were something in a book or a film we'd insist on knowing more. We'd want to operate on it. The thing about her is, there's nowhere to make an incision. There she is.'

'She's very nice,' Rachel said.

'You're beautiful,' Daniel said. 'Rachel, Rachel. What was that? *Rachel, Rachel*?'

'A movie,' the girl said.

'Joanne Woodward,' Daniel said.

'You'll never sell it, will you?'

'*Mon petit bagage?*' Daniel said. 'I hope not. No. You know what though? I sometimes have a tremendous desire to drop it.'

'To drop it?'

'They break very easily these things. They're very brittle. Perhaps it's just having something valuable, it's almost too much of a responsibility, a worry. Why not break it right away and be done with the tensions?'

'Well, I hope you don't. Perhaps you ought to give it away, if that's how you feel.'

'Here,' he said.

'I don't want it,' she said.

'Oh I know.'

'Or you wouldn't have offered it to me.'

'No. Because I would have known that you wanted it and then I would have suspected that you were angling for it—'

'And that would make me cleverer than you and you wouldn't like that.'

'I probably will break it one day.'

'You probably will,' Rachel said. 'But I don't think so.'

'The thing about art,' he said, 'is there's nothing you can do with it. Like people.'

'Oh you can do things with people,' Rachel said.

'You can damage them,' Daniel said, 'hurt them. Isn't that what we do? Try to make an impression.'

'I don't,' Rachel said.

'Then you're waiting for someone to do it to you,' Daniel said. 'You're tired. You ought to go to bed.'

'You're wrong,' she said.

'You're practically asleep now.'

'About me waiting to be hurt. I don't want to be hurt. I actually would quite like to be happy.'

'That's masochism personified,' Daniel said.

'Do you always have to be clever?'

'Never take your foot off one stepping-stone until the other is firmly on the next.'

'That way you'll never get across the river,' she said.

'Pulling crackers,' he said, 'and reading the mottos. It's an old-fashioned way of having a party, but it still works.'

'I don't like it, not really,' she said. 'It's hateful really.'

144

'Come on,' he said.

'Worship and knowledge,' she said.

'I'm going on this tour,' he said.

'Are you really?'

'Well, I said I would. What I don't really fancy is getting down there. I shall enjoy the games, but I'm not so keen on the social side. I'm thinking of driving down with Bernard Morris. You know who he is.'

'The writer.'

'Yes, I've known him for a long time. He wrote the story *Pay or Play* was based on, if you remember that.'

'Of course I remember.'

'I suppose I could cancel,' he said.

'Do you want to?'

'You can always stay here, if you like,' he said, 'while I'm away. Do.'

She said: 'No, I shall be all right.'

'When's the funeral?'

'I don't know,' she said. 'I shan't go.'

'Who's looking after it?'

'His family, I suppose.'

'Imagine how they feel. Oh don't tell me you blame them, do you?'

'I don't blame them. I think it's a good thing you're going on this tour. I don't think we should see each other again.'

'Why?'

'I'm frightened,' she said, 'of what it'll lead to.'

'Such as?'

'Oh,' she said.

'What's so frightening about me?'

'The part that never comes out.'

'There isn't any part that doesn't come out. You've seen all the parts that come out. They've come out as far as they can. There are no extra inches.'

'If you had your way, you'd be something completely different,' she said. 'I really feel that.'

'To that extent everything I do is a postponement, to that extent you're absolutely right.'

'I believe you could do something beautiful,' she said, 'if you'd let yourself.'

'Oh, oh, oh. Come on now.'

'Why the American?'

'Because that's where your last piece came from, about doing something beautiful.'

'I believe you could,' she said.

He said: 'You know what you should do? You should marry a nice young man, a nice reliable young man with idealistic tendencies, perhaps a teacher—you might even teach yourself—and you should have some children and you should make toys for them out of wood and cut paper. You should stop fucking the town and find yourself someone reliable and decent and just a little old-fashioned. It doesn't much matter who you screw. There are plenty of virile young men with ideals and not too much ambition. You could be happy, Rachel, and that makes you pretty rare.'

'And what about you?' she said.

'Oh me,' he said, 'I'm already pretty well fixed. My arrangements are made.'

'You're going on this tour for instance,' she said.

'And after that. I have one or two things maturing. I'm going to Greece in the summer. Have you ever been?'

'No,' she said, 'I told you I hadn't. I don't much want to at the moment.'

'The funny thing is,' he said, 'and I'm not saying this to keep you or anything like that, I can see this whole thing being quite different. I can see myself—' He stood in front of her and looked her up and down. 'I can see myself loving you very easily,' he said. 'Though I don't like to say so.'

'But you can't do things easily any more, can you?' she said.

'In comes the javelin,' he said. 'Boing!'

'I'd sooner be in your blue movies,' she said, 'than your life.'

'And another one,' he said. 'Thanks. And by the way, liar.'

'No, because it would be truer,' she said, 'and more interesting.'

146

'Truer than what and of what?'

'I'd know you better,' she said. 'And you'd be truer to yourself. You'd have fewer preconceptions.'

'I don't believe in the idea of basic truths, I don't believe in all that gutter stuff, the idea that life is more honest the lower you go. The lowest thing is the grave. Keep stripping and in the end there's a skeleton and what does that prove and what can it do? Why not come to Greece?'

'You don't want me to.'

'I'm asking you to. Don't be a baby.'

'It's not me personally you want; it's the proof that you're able to get me to do what you want.'

'We might as well be married,' he said, 'the way we're going on.'

'I won't give in,' she said. 'I don't care what you say or think. I won't give in. I've seen it happen and it's not going to happen to me.'

'You'd sooner die than be like your mother,' he said.

'You're a killer,' she said. 'And I'm not going to be the victim.'

'You're going to be somebody's,' he said. 'Why be such a snob about it?'

'You think I'm joking.'

'You think I am. But don't you see, Rachel, seriously, in other words please let me try and explain, don't you see that what you keep thinking is honesty is only a return to the brutal? You say that there's something brutal in me, and you're right. There's something completely unresolved in me, I admit it, and I think I'm afraid of resolving it because I have a feeling that when I do I shan't be young any more. I'll tell you very plainly, as one might someone one never expects to see again, a whore or a priest, or a stranger in a fogbound airport, the truth is I want to destroy the world because I hate it and when I meet people like you, young people, really young, who can still believe in openness and generosity I feel afraid for them, quite honestly, and I also feel fear and hatred of them, because they make me obsolete. They warn me how little time there is left and how unlike them I am. I'm a coward and a bully, Rachel. I don't say that for pity or because I want you to

147

deny it, I'm just telling you the truth. Now how do I work it out? In films we always say, work it out in action, but in England today, can one really do that? Without play-acting or rhetoric, without provocation or the sort of pointless stupidity that threw Andy whatsit off the roof in Teddington? I doubt it. I work it out each week, childishly, on the football field. I go in when I want to keep off, I force myself to run when I want to walk. Men are pathetic, I quite agree, but if Andy had actually upped and attacked me, he would probably never have killed himself. It was all that ridiculous adolescent idealism that made him so self-righteous he had to turn on himself. He made an idiot of himself, in the original Greek sense; a silly idiot. Suicide is the masturbator's murder. How about that?'

'I don't think Andy was a masturbator,' Rachel said.

'All men are,' Daniel said, 'that's what women can't accept. As far as men're concerned, everything's been rehearsed. Women're a lot better than we are. More natural anyway, as Michelangelo said. That's why we resent you so much. Antonioni. We deprive you of the chance of being what you hope and you deprive us of having what we remember. There's no real reconciliation possible. I truly believe that.'

Rachel said: 'So you're going on this tour.'

'So perhaps in the end the best we can hope is for each of us separately to get out of it whatever we can. Why not stay here? Use the place. Seriously. While I'm away. No one'll disturb you. You're welcome.'

'Sylvia, you look marvellous.'

'You sound surprised.'

'Don't start as soon as I get here. I'd forgotten how beautiful it was, this place. I really had. It's bigger than I remember. I lost my way through the village. It's such a long time.'

'You once said it wasn't. Beautiful.'

'I never said that. I've always envied you this place.'

'You did actually. There's some coffee if you want some. Don't mind Charlie, she may knock you down but she's quite friendly. Charlie, go on.'

'She probably smells some of my friends. Why do you call a bitch Charlie?'

'After that man in *Secret Life Of An American Wife*. He called all his women Charlie, do you remember? We saw it the night before she arrived.'

'Sensible plan really.'

'All women being the same?'

'Not you, Sylvia. You look better all the time. I really had forgotten what this place was like. You've done things to it, though. It must be five years. More.'

'Something like that. We've put in a few things and taken a few out.'

'You still haven't forgiven me, have you?'

'Bernard! Daniel's here. He's talking to Adam. He's always on the phone.'

'Comes of living down here, I suppose. He always was garrulous, Bernard.'

'He used to say you were the one who kept him talking.'

'When we were doing *Pay or Play*.'

'Yes. Charlie, go away now.'

'You haven't forgiven me, have you? For what I did. For changing it and everything.'

'It's a long time ago,' Sylvia Morris said. 'If Bernard's willing to forgive you, why shouldn't I?'

'Norbert Ash,' Bernard said, 'is really one of the biggest cunts. Hullo, Daniel, carriage at the door?'

'Carriage at the door,' Daniel said. 'What's he done?'

'I'll get my things together. Offers me no advance, no increase in the percentage, and tries to persuade me it's a gesture of true friendship. Jew.'

'They are together,' Sylvia said. 'I togethered them.'

'What would I do without you?'

'Go off and play football probably,' Sylvia said. 'Even more often than you do.'

'I'm sorry,' Daniel said. 'Perhaps I pushed him into it. He wasn't all that keen.'

'He was easily all that keen,' Sylvia Morris said, 'but he knew I wouldn't be.'

'I asked her to come with,' Bernard said, 'and she wouldn't.'

'Because I don't want to hang around some dingy hotel while you go off with the boys? I shall be happier here.'

'Anyone would be,' Daniel said. 'I don't remember this room at all. Are you sure, because Virginia's coming, and Janey?'

'Quite sure, thanks. It used to be a junk-room—it was the still-room before that—and we had it done out for the kids. You'd better go or you'll miss the plane.'

'How long will Southend take from here? Not much over an hour, surely?'

'Shouldn't do.'

'Well—' Bernard said. 'If we're going I suppose we'd better. Where's Dave?'

'He's gone next door to play soccer,' Sylvia said.

'They're all at it,' Daniel said.

'I did say goodbye,' Bernard said. 'I saw the others upstairs. They're in the Eagle's Nest.'

'Go on,' Sylvia said, 'or you'll miss the plane.'

Daniel said: 'Thanks for the coffee. I wish we didn't have to rush. Perhaps—'

'Come and see us,' Sylvia said. 'We're always here.'

'I haven't been asked,' Daniel said, 'recently.'

'That never stopped you in the past.'

'Christ, now I remember where the dialogue really comes from in this family.'

Daniel went outside and stood by the Lotus until Bernard came running out with his Adidas bag. 'She really looks marvellous.'

'Syl? She wears pretty well.'

'It's over five years. She still hasn't forgiven me. Have you?'

'It's in the past,' Bernard said, 'for fuck's sake.'

'So's everything we don't forgive people for. You haven't, have you?'

'I didn't take it as badly as you thought,' Bernard said, 'I just happen to have a gift for polemics. When there's a chance to cut loose, I tend to do it. Now I come to think about it, you didn't do anything most directors wouldn't do. You're a ruthless race.'

'Like you once said, directing isn't a vocation, it's a neurosis.'

'Did I say that? Have you got your passport?'

'Yes, have you? Tell me something. Did you circumcise your children?'

'Funny you should ask that. We did David and then when Mike came along we had him done too, in case David should think he was missing something. Ha ha ha. I'm not at all sure we should've. We went to a match, David and I the other week, I took him up to Stamford Bridge, and Syl sent him with a flask of soup. The bloke in front turned round and said, "I hope that's kosher." Dave gave him a big smile and then afterwards it turned out he hadn't the least idea what the bloke meant. I suppose you can always rationalize it and say it's cleaner or it gives the woman more pleasure or it lessens the likelihood of cancer, syphilis and sore throats.'

'You're not much of a Jewish writer,' Daniel said, 'any more.'

'I'm not much of a Jewish anything any more. Are you?'

'You've got a Jewish wife.'

'Fortunately,' Bernard said.

'Why fortunately?'

'Oh among other things because I don't have to worry about what she thinks. At least on that score. Makes it a dead issue.'

'The amount of time you and Sylvia've been together —'

'Oh come on. There's no safe period in marriage.'

'You're happy, though, aren't you? Are we going the right way? I always think of you as happy.'

'I always think of you as curious. You know how defensive married people are. We don't let out our secrets without a fight, and especially not to bachelors. People not in the club. Sexual goyim.'

'Bachelors!' Daniel said. 'Funny word.'

'Not as funny as husbands.'

'I always think of queers when I hear the word bachelor. It sounds like a cover-up.'

'Speak for yourself,' Bernard said. 'I heard Harold Usborne's coming. On the Norton.'

'Naturally. Give us a bit of solidarity in the mid-field department,' Daniel said. 'How long have you and Sylvia been together?'

'Since the beginning of time,' Bernard said. 'We've been married fifteen years. Crazy, isn't it? And what's your latest score?'

'I'm sorry I didn't have longer to talk to Sylvia,' Daniel said. 'What do you do about being Jewish? Seriously.'

'Do? I try not to walk with too much of a limp. What is there to do?'

'I was thinking of the children. You used to make quite a big thing of it. You used to address groups and things.'

'Oh God. I used to address groups to tell them why they shouldn't be in groups any more. I was trying to wind things up, but it takes a full A.G.M. to swing a thing like that. Annual General Millennium.'

'And weren't you in on that round-robin they got up when the June war was about to break out?'

'I didn't come out of that too well. Where were you then?'

'I was in Mexico,' Daniel said. 'I was going to do that epic about Cortés.'

'But it got too stout, I remember. They put my name on something I hadn't even seen and then they thought I was being shirty when I complained about it.'

'I could've told you they were—'

'I could've told you, my son, but I got carried away. Then, like everyone who gets carried away, I kicked and when I kicked they dropped me. *Curriculum vitae.*'

'I always thought the Israelis could take care of themselves without any signatures to help them,' Daniel said.

'And right you were, but at the time ... I don't teach my children anything. I just answer their questions, like when they ask, why is this night different from all other nights? I say, because tonight we're going to watch "Softly Softly". I'm an assimilationist, what else can I be. Aren't you?'

'I would be, except that I don't feel at home,' Daniel said.

'Where do you?'

'That's not the point. I don't feel at home because I don't associate myself, through pure chance perhaps, with half the things that the English simply have to accept, have to defend, have to put up with ...'

'I don't feel the strain of that at all. Like the man said, I like it here.'

'Do you really think it'll save you?'

'Why make waves?' Bernard Morris said. 'And save me from what? The next holocaust? There isn't going to be a next holocaust. And if there is, will keeping kosher save us? I think it's true, what they say about *shiksas*, you ought to get married. And then we can all ask you what you're going to tell *your* children.'

'You're sure we're going the right way?'

'I shouldn't know the way to Southend, the Monte Carlo of East Anglia? In a minute we go left if we live so long.'

'Of all the people to end up living in the country,' Daniel said, 'I never expected you to. Don't worry, I'm a safer driver than I look. You seemed the Londoner to end all Londoners.'

'It's true. I outHarrodsed Harrods. The fact is, we could buy sixteen times as much house down here for the same money. And besides, with children – Sylvia likes it a lot more than London.'

'But what about you?'

'She's happy, I'm happy,' Bernard said. 'There you are, left. Southend.'

'You didn't really want to do any more work on *Pay or Play*, did you, at the time? I mean, I know you were angry that I did some rewriting –'

'I was angry that you got someone else to do some rewriting and that it was done the way it was. But let's not rehash the rehash for God's sake. It's a long way to the Dordogne.'

'The funny thing is, I really wanted to say, that you can create a sort of morality of ruthlessness that doesn't just excuse what you do, it actually forces it on you. In many ways I'd sooner have gone on being friends with you both and let the film go hang, but I thought it would be chicken, I really did.'

'Listen, I believe you. But as it happened it formed the basis for a very nice little career and what's a couple of friends in a case like that?'

'Your gift for polemic again,' Daniel said. 'Don't think it doesn't still hurt. She never really wanted you to do films at all, though, did she?'

'Well, she's probably right. She thinks whoring in the press is whoring enough. Not that I don't like the money.'

'The money's the worst part,' Daniel said.

'Balls.'

'It's turned it into a shit's game,' Daniel said. 'Don't think I wouldn't like to give it up.'

'Don't worry, I don't. You've done some good things, son. You're internationally regarded —'

'Like hell —'

'You're internationally regarded, you've got a growing reputation, you're not liked, but you're well liked —'

'All right, all right.'

'It's on the left when we get to it,' Bernard said.

'So politically you're no longer involved,' Daniel said.

'I spit three times when I meet a Tory,' Bernard said, 'but quietly. Writing about the City, you'd run out of spit doing it too energetically. But after all, do we really want a new society? I've had twenty years trying to make myself at home in the present one. Do I want to take religious instruction at my age? When are things not so bad? Things are not so bad when there's time to think are things really so bad.'

'For an assimilationist you sing a lot of the old songs.'

'Because I'm an Englishman I have to lose my voice?'

'Two illusions,' Daniel said, 'that one is still a nice person underneath and that being Jewish is no longer important.'

'What's important about it? I can't even remember what we used to go on about. I think probably it was all part of being beastly to our parents. The kosher revolution. It went a lot further in the States than it ever did here. As for being a nice person, that's another kettle of *gefülte* fish altogether. What is a nice person?'

'Someone who'd be nice if only other people were.'

'On the contrary,' Bernard Morris said. 'That's a shit.'

'Sylvia resented me,' Daniel said, 'even before all that happened with *Pay or Play*.'

'She doesn't like anything that threatens to disrupt our life. Not even things she'd quite like for herself. Norbert Ash wanted her to read for him at one time—'

'He has a lot of faith in the literary opinions of women,' Daniel said. 'Or something.'

'*And* something,' Bernard said. 'He's heard they're cheaper. She wouldn't do it. I wanted her to, but she wouldn't. She thinks the children'll starve to death if they don't have her at every meal.'

'She must be well gnawed by now. You married a Jewish mother,' Daniel said.

'When you think of women like Virginia Playfair, I'd sooner have Syl. All that ambition. All that galloping presumption.'

'I don't think that's quite fair,' Daniel said. 'Gin looks after her children as well as the other things she does.'

'She reviews them, you mean? Sorry, am I treading on sacred ground?'

'Me and Gin? Not at all. She didn't like your last book, I remember now.'

'No, she didn't, I can forgive that, but if there's one kind of critic who really rubs me up the wrong way it's one who goes out of her way to be impartial.'

'I thought she was wrong,' Daniel said. 'I liked it.'

'I must've been out when you called,' Bernard said.

They saw the girl first not far from the Customs House at Le Touquet. She had not been on the plane. She gave no clear evidence of being English, but she wore the denim top and trousers, the ragged sheepskin waistcoat and the air of sour complacency which Daniel associated with English girls. She was sitting by the roadside on an ex-army knapsack. The Lotus was supposed to be a two plus two, but the shelf behind the main seats was small and, after a glance at Bernard, Daniel accelerated.

They spoke less, the two men, now they were in France. Bernard watched with extreme vigilance, as if everything were new to him, and Daniel, despite all his relaxed promises, had eyes only for the speedometer and the kilometre posts, computing again and again the relationship between miles and kilometres. Bernard recommended lunch at Foucarmont, where the proprietor shook hands with him and asked after the family. Daniel was jealous of Bernard's welcome. The meal came slowly, though it was good, and Daniel, in spite of his early intention of giving credit where it was due, became irritated at the long delays. The kilometres which he had killed seemed to revive and run ahead of them, where they waited to be conquered all over again.

Bernard described how they had first come to this particular restaurant and how David had run round and round, through the kitchen and the annexe, humming to himself and finally bumping into the girl who was carrying the cheese board, while Daniel tried to work out how far they could get that night and whether he should mention a stop at Chartres. It was strange; he could not tell whether he wanted to stop at the cathedral or not. Did he want to do Bernard out of seeing the glass or did he not want to see it himself and resent making a halt on Bernard's account?

Bernard talked of his family with a sort of mocking insistence. He spoke to the waitress with torrential fluency and obviously relished the opportunity to flirt; yet Daniel felt that he had brought his family with him and was piqued at the extra company.

'It's a funny thing about your pricks fix menu,' Bernard said, turning the cheese board for a wider angle, 'you always feel cheated if you don't eat your way through it. You spend your life waiting to be cheated, I suppose.'

'Or to cheat,' Daniel said.

'No, one doesn't wait to cheat in my experience. That happens suddenly and afterwards you think, Christ, that's done it. At least I do.'

'Do you often cheat?'

'You're talking about sex now, aren't you? No, I don't actually. It's too complicating. As G.B.S. pointed out, one fuck's much like another when it comes to it.'

'Ah yes, maybe, but what about the way you come to it?'

'I've been married a long time,' Bernard Morris said. 'I'm institutionalized. You don't get Camembert like this in England, Daniel my son, I don't know why you don't, but you don't.'

'You believe in being faithful,' Daniel said. 'Do you still?'

'Prod prod.'

'I'm not prodding,' Daniel said.

'You're prodding, you're fact-finding. I recognize the signs. Don't forget, I'm in the business myself.'

'I'm interested,' Daniel said. 'Have you finished?'

'You don't want coffee?'

'Not unless you do.'

'We sound like an old married couple,' Bernard said, 'already so soon. I don't mind going, if you want to go.'

'Nice place,' Daniel said, 'but it has taken a bit of time.'

The girl was waiting at a complicated intersection, in the middle of open country. She was sitting on her knapsack eating her fingers.

'What do you think? Shall we?'

'What?'

'Give her a lift. Did you notice her before?'

'Yes, at Le Touquet. Up to you.'

'She looks quite fuckable,' Daniel said. 'Do you think she's English?'

'I was wondering,' Bernard said.

'Probably shouldn't,' Daniel said, 'but still.'

She was bending over, buckling things back into her knapsack.

'Are you going to Paris?' she said.

'No, we're not,' Daniel said, 'we're going on down. You

should've got onto the autoroute, you'd have been there by now.'

'Can't you get to Paris this way?'

'It's a long way round, but you can. We'll put you down where we turn off.'

'All right then,' she said, holding out the rucksack. Daniel squeezed it in behind him and the girl climbed into the remaining space. Her face was streaked with dirt; she had freckles and dark-rimmed eyes and she sniffed. 'I got a lift this way, see, first thing, and he said I could get on to Paris this way.'

'What are you going to do in Paris?'

'I've got a friend.'

She sat sideways, head ducked, with no eyes for the two men. She might have been looking out for her stop.

Bernard Morris said: 'Do you do a lot of this?'

'Hitching? A bit. It's quite a good way to save money.'

'Aren't you scared at all?'

'Scared?'

'Hitching on your own. It can be dangerous, can't it?'

'I'm not worried,' she said. 'I don't do it at night.'

'I'm told there are some people who like doing it in the day,' Bernard said.

'I'm not worried,' she said. She turned her head now and Daniel could see her face in the mirror. She sniffed and wiped her sleeve across her face.

'What does your friend do in Paris?'

'Works there,' the girl said.

'Are you going on holiday?'

'I'm going to have a bit of a look round, you know.'

'Is she expecting you, this friend?'

'I said I might come. She said I could.'

'How did you come to be in Le Touquet?'

'You have to come to somewhere,' the girl said. 'And I got this special rate. I work for a travel agent, see, or I did.'

'I see. But you weren't on the plane.'

'I came over yesterday,' she said. 'I was on what they call stand-by. I stayed last night.'

158

'You've got a friend in Le Touquet as well?'

'Yes,' she said. 'Where are you going then?'

'We're going down to the Dordogne. We're going to play football.'

'Oh,' she said, 'you're footballers. Who do you play for then?'

'A team.'

'Not Birmingham,' she said, 'do you?'

'Tottenham,' Bernard Morris said.

'Is that right?'

'What're you looking for?' Daniel said. 'I'll tell you when we get to where you get out. We're not there yet.'

'I was looking out for a boy,' she said.

'What do you need a boy for? You've got us,' Bernard said.

'A boy I know,' she said. 'Tottenham Hotspur?'

'No,' Bernard said. 'Tottenham Nothing. Just a bunch of people who play soccer together.'

'He set off this morning before I did and I said I might see him.'

Daniel said: 'I could drink some coffee. How about you?'

Bernard said: 'I wouldn't mind. Fancy some coffee?'

The girl said: 'I don't mind.'

'That's what I like,' Bernard said, 'enthusiasm.'

'Funny,' the girl said. 'As a matter of fact, I wouldn't mind going to the toilet, if they've got one.'

Bernard and Daniel sat at the chipped table in front of the café. 'Toilet, aren't they funny? What do you think of her?' Daniel said.

'She's not exactly what you'd call in mint condition. I'd say her underseal was a little dented, wouldn't you?'

'What do you think the chances are we could get her to stick with us?'

'If you fancy your chances for a quick ram, I'll catch the train. I don't mind. I'll go into Paris, if you like.'

'Don't be silly,' Daniel said, 'what would I do with her on my own?'

'Read the instructions and don't exceed the stated dose. What would you do with her? If I'm cramping your style, Danny my boy, come out with it. You said yourself she was fuckable. She's fuckable. Hullo, feeling better?'

'It wasn't very nice,' the girl said.

'Tell me something quite seriously,' Daniel said. 'Don't people sometimes assume a girl on her own is fair game?'

'Some do,' she said.

'And what do you do if they do?'

'Depends.'

'On what?'

'What they're like, of course.'

'You're not afraid of being raped or even murdered? That doesn't bother you.'

'Life's too short, isn't it?'

'It can be shorter some ways than others, though, can't it?'

'I'm not worried,' she said. 'Have you got a light?'

'Neither of us smoke,' Daniel said. 'You don't, do you, Bern?'

'I've got my methods,' she said. 'It's nice coffee.'

'I'm glad you like it.'

'First drink I've had today,' she said.

'They're all the same,' Daniel said, 'these young girls. They don't know how to take care of themselves.'

'You're married, aren't you?' she said.

'Who?'

'Both of you.'

'One of us is and one of us isn't,' Bernard said. 'For this week's star prize all you have to do is guess which.'

She sucked a coffee-drenched sugar and then blew her nose on a dirty handkerchief. 'I should be in Paris tonight, shouldn't I, with luck?'

'What's she like, this girl friend of yours, if it is a girl friend really? Do you really want to see her that badly?'

Bernard said: 'Presumably.'

Daniel said: 'Because we're driving right down and you could come the whole way with us and no extra charge.'

'Don't you like the idea?' Bernard said.

160

'It's you, isn't it,' she said, 'who's married?'

'No,' Daniel said, 'it's me.'

'I thought it might be.'

'I've been married a long time. Fifteen years nearly, so you can imagine—'

Bernard said: 'Shut up, Daniel, stop it. I'm the married one actually.'

'I reckon you both are,' she said.

Daniel said: 'It doesn't make any difference to you, does it?'

'What do you mean?'

'Whether people are married? You don't bother about things like that, do you, people of your age?'

'Course we do,' she said. 'How much further is it? What're you stopping for?'

'A quick slash, as you ask,' Daniel said. 'Any objections?'

'You could have gone back there.'

'I forgot.'

'Don't worry,' Bernard said. 'Nothing funny's going to happen.'

'He could've stopped back there.'

'I prefer pissing in a hedge,' Daniel said. 'It's cleaner.'

'Don't worry,' Bernard said, 'it's only an act.'

'That's right. We're a couple of out-of-work actors.'

'I thought you were footballers.'

'Footballers,' Bernard said, 'actors, you name it, we'll give it a whirl, give it a go, eh Danny?'

'Shan't be a minute.'

The girl said: 'He is the married one, isn't he?'

'No, as a matter of fact. I am. Does it make any difference?'

'What *to*?' she said.

'How you feel about us.'

'I don't feel anything,' she said.

'On we go,' Daniel said. 'Where are we going to stop the night? Chartres, what do you think?'

'We could eat in Chartres. There's quite a good place we often go to.'

'Come and eat with us,' Daniel said. 'You'd easily get a lift back to Paris. You don't mind if she has dinner with us, do you?'

'No thanks,' the girl said.

'That's not very adventurous of you,' Daniel said.

'Do you know who we are you're turning down?'

'No.'

'He's a very famous film director,' Bernard said.

'Let's not exaggerate. Famous will do.'

'He really is.'

'Have I ever seen any of the films you've done?'

'Unfortunately I don't have that sort of intimate knowledge. You might have. *Myself Among Others*.'

'Sorry?'

'Was one of them. *Myself Among Others. Pay or Play. Split.*'

'I might have seen that one, I don't know.'

'About a couple breaking up and how it affects their child.'

'There're a lot like that, aren't there?' the girl said.

'Well, I've done my best for you,' Bernard said.

'And he's a writer.'

'Oh. Are you really a film director?'

'He just told you. Yes, I am.'

'That must be very interesting. What do you write about?'

'People,' Bernard said. 'What do I write about?'

'There he is,' she said. 'The boy I was telling you about. Would you put me down here, please?'

'We're by no means there yet,' Daniel said. 'And it's nothing like as easy for two people to get a lift as one.'

'Come on,' she said.

'You can't fight charm,' Daniel said. 'Only we can't take another one in here, you know, if that's what you're thinking.'

'No, I didn't expect it,' she said. She was fighting past Bernard, who had to get out before she could. 'Thanks for the lift.' She stumbled back along the lumpy verge towards the young man.

'Bang goes the gangbang,' Bernard said.

'Have you ever been involved in one?' Daniel said. 'There's a guy on the coast arranges orgies. He's one of those second generation producers, you know, and that's basically what he does. He invited

162

me to one when I was over, I was sort of tempted, but in the end I chickened out.'

'How far were you willing to go with this girl just now?'

'I was more interested to see how far she was willing to go,' Daniel said.

'Not very, my son, as far as I could judge.'

'You have to keep chipping away,' Daniel said. 'You have to persist. Above all, you have to be willing to make a fool of yourself.'

'You reckon you would have made it if I hadn't been here, do you?'

'You could imagine killing a girl like that,' Daniel said.

'You could imagine anything,' Bernard said.

'But quite plausibly. You could imagine a situation like this, a couple of friends picking up a girl, one of them engaged or involved, one of them married, let's say —'

'Are you engaged? I didn't know.'

'Let's just assume for the sake of the story — after all, this is a business trip — I told the Chancellor we were going to look for a story with a continental background — say these two men're on the way to play football or meet a bunch of people — they can't turn up with the girl, certainly not with that girl —'

'My friend the snob,' Bernard Morris said.

'Let's be honest, for God's sake, we couldn't take her to have dinner with Margaret and Virginia and Janey, they'd never let us hear the last of it. That girl, come on. So assume these two friends pick up this girl and she's a little more forthcoming than this particular Judy was, let's assume they have some hold on her, she wants to be an actress or she's always wanted to know a writer —'

'I'd sooner she just fancied me,' Bernard said. 'To keep it within the bounds of probability.'

'O.K., now what happens? The truth is, isn't it, maybe neither of them on his own would have too much to do with her, or if he did he'd find some way of getting rid of her, but then suppose that they egg each other on, that each of them is a lot more — well, outrageous, than he might be if he were giving her a lift on his own. It becomes something between them, although neither of them

163

realizes it, and she thinks she's on to a good thing, nice car, good meal, maybe a good fuck, it's all experience, she's only a kid, but in order to get her, in order to impress her, they tell her more about themselves than they really want to, they start off just a couple of studs, they have this fantasy of omnipotence that comes from being no one in particular, just the men in black, but in spite of what they intend, they have to boast about who they are, they have to display themselves personally, and so, although it doesn't seem to matter when they're getting her, they've put themselves somehow in her power once things have gone too far. That's just one strand in the story, another is obviously the competition between the two of them; in the first place to be the one that makes it with her first and then not to seem to chicken out when the chips are really down. And then there's another thing that comes out, entirely without premeditation, which is that they really want this girl and that they're willing to do anything to get her to do what they want, basically because they like to win. They're bad losers. She doesn't mean a thing to them, they seduce her, that's one side of it, with blarney and charm and display, but they also overpower her. They tell themselves to begin with that she could perfectly well reject them and check out, if she wanted to, because all men ultimately think — maybe know — that women can get out of a situation if they want to, how'm I doing?'

'I like it, Danny, I like it.'

'But then when she shows signs of second thoughts, they discover that they've got her where they want her. They can make her do anything they want. She's not the little fighting cat they made her out to be to make the fight seem a fair one, she's a frightened little mouse. O.K., so now they change their plans. They've been talking of a dinner and some kind of three-in-a-bed thing, a sort of little secret the two men can share when they meet again, but there's also this repressed sadism thing going on and this dare situation that makes each of them wonder in turn how far he can push the other one. Take me, I never went in the army or anything. I was deferred and then I went to the States and when I got back, luckily the whole thing had been stopped, but of course — you know this very well, Bern—there's that bit in me which feels guilty and wonders whether I didn't maybe run away from something. Killing is a kind of test of manhood, whether we like it or not. You remember the bit in Malraux—'

'I don't accept all that rant,' Bernard said,

'It's not a question of accepting. Fear of death is fear of killing. We're afraid of the dark because we've never been in it.'

'I was in Cyprus,' Bernard Morris said.

'I didn't know that.'

'Not for long and I didn't see much, but I saw enough.'

'Did you kill anyone?'

'I shot at people. I don't think I ever hit anyone. Luck, not judgment.'

'You tried.'

'Nobody shoots to miss.'

'Well, there you are. I never knew you were in Cyprus. Have you ever been back?'

'No.'

'I'm going to Greece in the summer. I never knew you'd been.'

'What do they do, do they kill the girl?'

'First of all, they offer to take her to a slap-up hotel, routine Edwardian seducer stuff, and then they get greedy, I'm making this up as we go along—'

'What else?'

'And you're not forbidden to help, by the way. They decide to have her without paying for the privilege, which is what it comes to, and if she were willing, if she'd laugh and enjoy herself probably they'd treat her quite decently, because they're not monsters or anything.'

'A couple of nice fellers like you and me, I should say not—'

'This is a story, Bernard, for God's sake, don't keep turning the spotlight on yourself. Let's forget ourselves. What happens is, they fancy her before dinner not after, it's mentioned quite casually, like do you fancy a drink, only she doesn't, she wants to go a bit slower, maybe from her side she's enjoying seeing what she can get before she agrees to enter the Common Market, she's trying to improve her deal, so then there's a sort of jokey element, except that they sense—and we know, as the treatments say—that she thinks they're a bit old, a bit passé and it's this sort of contempt they sense coming from her which brings out the beast. So the driver whips the car off the road and into the proverbial wood. Again, if she will nicely, they might even be too embarrassed to go through with it, think of his wife, think of his fiancée. In a pleasant atmosphere some things won't play—'

'Who is this girl you're thinking of marrying?'

'Here's another thought—I'm not thinking of marrying anyone, forget all that—suppose the other one, the me character, if you want to put it that way—suppose he's having an affair with the wife of someone they both know, someone like Gin, for the sake of example, one of the typical tortured Canonbury affairs, all classical quotations and anguished talk about the morality of freedom—'

'I'm just a country bumpkin,' Bernard said, 'not too many shocks please. I've got the hay to get in when I get back—'

'Hay, in April?'

'Purist. At least I have to get my fork tuned.'

'This could be quite interesting though, don't you think?'

'The trouble with these things is, either they're too general—and become a sort of allegory or something, which God forbid—or they're too specific and you spend the whole film casually giving people information, which is a bore.'

'You just do it,' Daniel said.

'And what does it tell you?'

'It tells you about sexual competition, guilt, jealousy—'

'And there but for the grace of God, go we—'

'Exactly. Suppose they do rape her, or the next best thing—but always somehow with the assumption that she understands, that she's playing along with them—because if she thinks of them as passés they think of her, in spite of everything, as sort of tolerant, sort of maternal almost, in the way that men do expect women to be, age notwithstanding—'

'You ought to have a tape recorder going on this—'

166

'With your famous facility for dialogue, Bern, I'm relying on you to reproduce the whole conversation verbatim—'

'Don't use that filthy language with me, Daniel, please. Verbatim already. Well, let me tell you something, if I do it will be in a work of fiction and I shall swear on a shteck bible I made the whole thing up myself while suffering from a high fever.'

'No, suppose they realize after they've got her in the woods, suppose they realize that already it's gone beyond the point where they can pull out—'

'Please, no frankness—'

'Short cut it then, can't you see how they could have all the reasons in the world to destroy her? She isn't real to them, they aren't even real to themselves, because they've been living out a kind of fantasy and neither of them could face the humiliation of this girl, this girl above all, pursuing them out of their joint dream—which would basically be what it was—and making a mess of their lives. And at the same time, at the same time, the sadistic thing would be working too and they'd rationalize their destructive urge—'

'These long words, Mr Meyer, they frighten one—University boy, are you?'

'This is really a very relevant story I'm trying to work out here—they'd only use force slowly, to get her to strip, or do this or do that—and only when she wouldn't would they get nasty and set about hurting her, always within the context of a dream, a situation where torture was part of pleasure. They'd make her their whore and then tell themselves that whatever they were willing to pay for they were entitled to have. And only when she resisted, when she fought them in a non-sexy way, by running or shouting or being just plain uncooperative would they go beyond play and become really nasty—this is really one hell of a good idea, Bernard, seriously, isn't it?'

'And meaningful to boot. So why not boot it?'

'For God's sake, it's about all the things that interest us! It's about the limits and limitations of all our lives. The married man, the supposedly free man, the civilized and the uncivilized—it's about why people do and don't do things. Nothing any of them do is ever implausible, but each thing leads to something else, which would be, if it weren't for the first thing—'

'Except that we didn't in fact do a damned thing. Except say "Hullo, what's your name" and that's basically all we wanted to do—'

'Can you honestly tell me that you wouldn't have screwed that girl if she's been a bit more willing?'

'You never know where she's been, a girl like that. I'm not going home and giving anyone an unbirthday present.'

'Syph you mean.'

'I can't just drop out of circulation for a few months of quiet reflexion. I've got family commitments, as they say.'

'So you would've ducked out?'

'Almost certainly.'

'But surely you can imagine not doing so.'

'Imagining and doing are very different things, my son. Suppose they killed her, what would happen then?'

'Aha, you're interested in the story.'

'I'm interested in what you say,' Bernard Morris said.

'In the land of subtle distinctions, Morris is king. What would happen then? In the end they'd just go on with their lives.'

'What about the body?'

'It'd never be found. We could establish that the girl had left home, she was on the bum, anyone who knew about her would assume she'd gone somewhere else. People must disappear like that all the time. Two intelligent men could surely find somewhere to dump a body where it wouldn't be found. They could take her miles away from the scene of the crime. God knows there must still be uninhabited tracts of France where you could get rid of a body.'

'And carry on exactly as before, would they?'

'What they'd done would always have been a part of their potential character. It wouldn't be as if anything really new had happened, that would be the whole point really.'

'That's a cop out,' Bernard said, 'Danny boy, that's a cop out. You're going along with all that Blakean crap about better stone a baby to death than nurse unacted desires. We all nurse unacted desires and a good thing too. It's the best thing to do with them. That's what civilization's all about and whatever we say we wouldn't be without it.'

'Chartres,' Daniel said. 'Do you want to stop?'

'For the night? No.'

'For food or anything.'

'The Cathedral you mean? Do you?'

'Don't mind. I really don't mind. Up to you.'

'Five minutes wouldn't kill us,' Bernard Morris said.

They climbed the steps to the cathedral at different speeds, Bernard craning to inspect the sculptures which hooped the side door, Daniel watching him, almost mockingly, with a sort of professional, measuring directness. An American was taking photographs. Daniel walked into the cathedral. The soft walls of light behind the high altar attracted him more than the flash of the rose windows. He walked on towards them, dreaming now of losing his companion and then sickened by his wish to find Bernard false in his response. The organist was practising. The sighing pipes offered a reproach to the whispering tourists.

Daniel was glad to be dwarfed by anonymous masters. Yes, he told himself, he was willing to be humble, he was willing to confess himself a child, he was willing to concede the mastery of others, especially when they were dead and nameless. How much did he know about glass, how much about colour, how much about buildings? Could one appreciate anything one did not know? As he walked round the empurpled cloister, Daniel was surrounded with the ghosts of his friends, all of them inhibiting and, finally, crushing his pleasure in it. He had never had a religion, he had emerged from no shadows into the clear light of reason. He did not belong to this Europe he was ready to venerate but unable to love. His birth into cynicism had been too easy. His mother no longer reminded him of the pain which had borne him into the world or of the hope others had of him.

'Had enough?' he said.

'If you have.'

'After a while, there's nothing more you can do, is there?'

'They certainly knew how to make pictures in those days,' Bernard said.

He looked bigger, more angular than Daniel wanted to remember. They might have been apart for several years. He looked older.

'What if they brought the girl in here,' Daniel said, 'first.'

'Would it help?'

'Help what?'

'To get her knickers off.'

'It would show something. The irrelevance of beauty perhaps. What do you think? How would she react?'

'She'd yawn,' Bernard said. 'She'd look around and then eventually she'd yawn. And they'd smile, even though both of them had been stifling yawns for the last ten minutes.'

'Aha, do I get the impression the hook is sinking in?'

'Unless she's a Catholic and they yawn before she does. Or maybe she yawns but they feel she's got the real message and they haven't.'

'Do you really give a shit about the stained glass, honestly?'

'I don't like it all,' Bernard said. 'I like the West window and the North one best. I'm not so keen about the East. Too gaudy. Being impure, I like things to be pure. I prefer Bourges, actually. The funny thing is, I don't really feel as if we've been there. It's like trying to learn a poem, they take the text away and you can't remember a line.'

'The thing about these places being,' Daniel said, 'you think there's going to be so much to see and you go in and there it all is, plonk. It's all there, but it's also all at once.'

'Your story's really the story of the two men, isn't it? I mean, they aren't necessarily queer or anything, but there's something unsaid between them and it ends in the death of the woman, that's the real story, isn't it? Couldn't it, for example, be that the one who isn't married is actually having an affair with the first one's wife, but is really a genuine friend of the other one? He tries to confess how he feels about the wife by sharing the girl, but it

170

doesn't work and when they go on each of them is more hopelessly committed to deception then he was before?'

'I wish you'd write it,' Daniel said. 'Talk to Syl about it, see how she feels about it. I'm willing to give the whole credit to you, if you'll do it, you can have the copyright, everything, so long as I have the first option on it.'

'Talk to Adam about that side,' Bernard said. 'He's the negotiator.'

Daniel said: 'Syl thinks I don't like her, doesn't she?'

'This bloke's going it a bit,' Bernard said, 'behind us.'

'Bloody motorcyclists,' Daniel said, 'they're all meshuggah.'

'Please,' Bernard said, 'nothing parochial. He is though, isn't he?'

'Oh no, you don't,' Daniel said. 'Did you see what he was trying to do? This thing can shift a bit too.'

'Remember I'm a family man, with very little insurance.'

'It's all right, if anything happens it'll be his fault.'

'That's what I'm afraid of. Could we just stop him and check that he's fully paid up and comprehensive with it?'

'He's English.'

'Then kill him,' Bernard said. 'He's got a Green Card in which case we're covered. Kill him by all means.'

'I thought you were in favour of assimilation.'

'O.K., have it your way. Assimilate him.'

'Not unless you want to die you don't,' Daniel said. 'Fucker's trying to come on the inside.'

'There's fire coming out of his nostrils,' Bernard said. 'Are you sure we ought to keep goading him like this? Did you ever see Cocteau's *Orphée*?'

'I loved it, God help me.'

'Victor Hugo, *hélas*,' Bernard said.

'Never saw it,' Daniel said. 'I don't like that noise.'

'It's only my knees. I'll put my head between them in a minute, that should give them something to do.'

'There's surprisingly little on the road.'

'Maybe the function was advertised.'

'If he goes now, he's bonkers.'

'He's more than bonkers, he's pancakes. It's not Shrove Tuesday, is it? The Christian Calendar, I have to admit it, is not one of my fortes. Nor one of my Joe Lyons either. Thank you. Look, Danny, for Christ's sake. All theology to one side.'

'We've got the legs of him.'

'We'll have his backside in here as well in a minute. I'll tell you what, concede. Concede, Danny, give him a graceful wave and tap your hard old head in honest amazement and give up, willya?'

'Are you really scared?'

'Who needs to be raspberry jam? Why do we always have to risk our lives for something useless? Would you go like this if it was going to help someone? Shit you would.'

'Oh shut up.'

'Suddenly it's the Battle of Britain. It's the First of the Few. Or in our case the Last of the Many. I'm supposed to cheer you on, I'm supposed to admire your virility, I'm supposed to make my will? In this weather? I'm supposed to witness your skill and maybe write you a testimonial. You're relying on surviving even though you're a cunt, and that's risky. That's vanity, Daniel.'

'Dial-a-sermon, that's you, Bern.'

'Trouble *sur commande*, and that's you, Herr Direktor. Listen, enjoy yourself. I can't see our story ending like this. What kind of a twist is it to end up an accident black spot? Round a tree, is that my destiny, my Newfoundland? To have come so far and end up a statistic? My children should remember me as a nasty mess on the road?'

'Blast it, he's got us. Son of a —'

'Danny, for —'

'We're still here.'

'What would you do if he went over the side?'

'Scramble down and collect him.'

'In twelve baskets, no doubt, not to mention the small fishes. You would too.'

'He knows what he's doing on the road and so do I.'

'Of that I have no doubt. It just happens to leave one question unanswered. What the hell am I doing?'

'Gathering material, Bern, gathering material.'

'Material for a cardiac seizure.'

'All right, you bastard,' Daniel said.

'Go a bit faster,' Bernard said.

'I can't you twit. If I could—Damn, he's got us. After all that.'

'Awaw,' Bernard said. 'And he's pulling up. Now comes the hand-to-hand stuff.'

'I'll take care of him,' Daniel said. 'Lock your window.'

'I'll help you throw the body to the *piranhas*. I've been around.'

'Big bloke,' Daniel said.

'The Phantom of the Autobahns is no five footer.'

'Afternoon,' Daniel said.

'What the fuck do you think you're on?'

'Christ Almighty,' Bernard said. 'It's Harold. Didn't recognize you with your armour on.'

'You really are a bloody maniac.'

'You should have run up your colours,' Daniel said.

'Next time I'll run up your bloody arse. Weaving around like that.'

'A pleasure postponed,' Bernard said. 'Just imagine if the three of us had gone over the side. It wouldn't have left them with much of a defence against the forces of Burgundy.'

'Bordeaux,' Daniel said.

'At a time like this he discusses vintages.'

'Anyway, how are you, Harold?'

'Pretty fair.'

'Where are you stopping the night?'

'I shall probably go on and get there. Otherwise I shall kip by the road. I've got my roll.'

'Bloody iron man, you are.'

'No cash,' Harold Usborne said.

'Only we're going to have dinner later.'

'I've got some sandwiches. Anyway—'

'We'll see you down there then.'

'There's one thing,' Harold Usborne said, 'I shan't be running into another lunatic like you.'

'Don't rely on it,' Bernard said. 'His father was a traveller.'

'Those things of yours can certainly move anyway,' Daniel said.

'You can't beat 'em when they're properly tuned,' Harold said.

'I bet he could play the Well-Tampered Caviare on those exhaust pipes,' Bernard said. 'Look at the damned things.'

'She does think I don't like her, doesn't she? Sylvia. It's not true.'

'I don't honestly know. Maybe she just thinks she doesn't like you.'

'In that case, I'm sorry,' Daniel said. 'Surely you either like somebody or you don't.'

'The thing about you, Daniel, is you absolutely make it impossible to be tactful.'

'Tactful. Since when were you tactful? And what did you mean about my father?'

'To give you the whole inside, now-it-can-be-told story: nothing. Absolutely nothing. I never even knew you had a father. Why, do you want to take offence?'

'No,' Daniel said. 'He's a strange fellow, Usborne, isn't he? What do you know about him? Apart from his having been in the Ulysses first team.'

'Nothing much. He's a bit of a loner, he's not what you'd call gregarious—and he doesn't like crowds either. That's three things.'

'Oh Christ, give it a rest,' Daniel said.

'He's a homosexual geologist and he's number seven on the best dressed breast list, now what do you want, blood?'

'Is he really? Homosexual?'

'You name it, he'll fuck it,' Bernard said. 'I haven't the least idea. A geologist he is, a tit he may be. He's a damned good player, that's for certain.'

'You defend yourself even against me,' Daniel said. 'Why?'

'I've got nothing to hide,' Bernard said.

'I suppose that's it,' Daniel said.

*

It was dark when they reached Orleans. The lights of the lorries glared on the windscreen and showed where impacted insects had raised their last lumps. They had chosen a hotel by the Loire, at the top of a rise where they had to turn across the traffic. There were iron gates behind a broad, earthen verge. As they reached the place, a motorcycle was lying in the road. A man was full length on the verge, a coat over him and a red and white crash helmet beside him. A lorry flashed its lights for them to cross. They slipped through a steaming gap. From far off they could hear the trumpeting of the ambulance. Attentive shadows surrounded the damaged man. Daniel drove down an avenue of cool trees and pulled up in front of the hotel.

'Shall we go back?'

'It wasn't Harold. I don't think there's much we can do,' Daniel said. 'The ambulance was coming.'

'There's always a reason for doing nothing,' Bernard said.

'I'm happy to walk back,' Daniel said. 'If you think there's any point.'

'You're probably right,' Bernard said.

'What do you want to do about rooms?' Daniel said.

'Do about rooms? See if they've got any.'

'You don't want to share, I mean, do you?'

'No, I don't. I once shared a room in a *pensione* in Naples with an asthmatic American and I have always said to myself from that moment, I'm going to get rich enough not to have to share a room ever again.'

'O.K., point taken.'

'Unless you want to.'

'After such a seductive speech?'

'You said yourself we were on business. Let the Chancellor pay, Danny, let the Chancellor pay. Call your accountant.'

'Let's not make a meal of it.'

'Talking of which, lunch is a long time ago. I could eat a horse. And don't worry, you probably will, thank you and good evening, fight fans.'

'You're willing to have dinner together, are you?'

'Oh come on, Meyer, what's the matter with you?'

'Me? Nothing.'

'You don't need to save thirty bob that badly, do you?'

'Of course not. I'm sorry, Bern. I feel exactly the same way you do about it. I don't like sharing except with a woman.'

'Well, there we are, thank God we're normal. It is Carruthers, isn't it?'

'I don't really think that,' Daniel said. 'To be honest.'

'The ambulance is there now,' Bernard said, 'so you can turn off your conscience. Why don't you? Think that? This seems O.K., doesn't it?'

'It's just one more inhibition, isn't it? Don't get me wrong, I don't fancy men, I never have, but it seems rather a pity sometimes, like not liking curry. I mean, it's not hard to imagine what it would be like to fancy them, is it? And so there's one more country you'll never visit.'

'I take an old-fashioned view, Danny my old mate, I take an old-fashioned view, over Lord's Cricket Ground and into Mrs Blumgarten's bedroom window. Be tolerant if you like, but don't have nothingk to do with fairies because they're not nice, that's what I say. They're a different world, they're a whole different thing, and from where I stand, sit.'

'Haven't you ever been on a beach and seen someone very sexy lying with her back to you and fancied her and then gone up and she's a he?'

'That's optical illusions. Anyone can make a mistake, take Hitler for example, but that's not fancying boys. Your trouble, Danny, is an overactive, too easily aroused imagination. You can imagine everything, but can you imagine living a single life? Have you ever imagined that?'

'In other words, I should get married.'

'I can't lay my hand on my heart and endorse an extreme measure of that kind, Daniel, that I can't do, but the way you're behaving this trip, you're a desperate man and you don't much care what you do, you're on a destructive line of argument, Daniel, and tell me the truth, how often have your bowels moved in the last coupla weeks?'

'Oh come clean, Bernard, talk like yourself for a change. Come out from behind it all for once.'

'Well look who's talking,' Bernard Morris said. 'Chameleon Schlemieleon.'

They were given adjacent rooms at the top of the hotel. When Daniel went downstairs, silently easing his weight on the rope handrail, Bernard was on the telephone to England. Daniel made his automatic professional inventory of the hotel lobby while he waited. He wondered whether to call his own number and discover whether Rachel had accepted his invitation.

'All right?' he asked, when Morris came out of the cabin.

'Sorry, did you want to call someone?'

'No, not at all.'

'I'm ready to go home now,' Bernard said. 'I don't know about you. We seem to have been away weeks. It's all right in the park, but it seems a bit pretentious really, doesn't it, a tour? The standard of game we play.'

'She gives you a conscience.'

'I've always had it,' Bernard said. 'Don't worry, if you didn't have it as a child, you're not likely to catch it now. Food time, right?'

'Unless you want a drink.'

'I never do. I've never enjoyed drink. I get hangovers, or I used to. At Cambridge we used to get drunk on Madeira, can you imagine? In college. The smart set. Turps is better for the liver. Do you want one?'

'I don't drink,' Daniel said.

'What are your vices, Daniel? Egotism, vanity, greed and ambition to one side, I mean.'

'Docility,' Daniel said. 'And undue respect for others. Shitface.'

For Daniel's taste, there was too much laughter on the tour, though some of it was his own. Once the party had gathered, there were nearly always several of them together. The absurdity of the expedition did not escape them, but 'the coach party spirit', as

Jack Darwin called it, was an accepted ingredient. The loss of privacy led to a relentless jocularity at which each could sigh separately but none could avoid when they were together. The small hotel where they made their base was in a quiet village. Jack Darwin had found the place during one of his gastronomic tours. He and Janey (who was then married to a barrister) had stayed there on their first clandestine week together. Daniel guessed that Jack had hoped to do a good turn to the proprietor and gently revive his memories. Darwin was a large muscular man who liked to climb mountains and make money and had discovered 'action fiction' as the likeliest means to both. He was not one who impressed by his subtlety, but the tourists' loud invasion of his memories, though he himself had engineered it, caused him such palpable distress that Daniel was quite touched. He had never much liked either him or Janey, but now he found himself as aware of their secret dismay as if the machinery of their emotions had been made in Switzerland and encased in glass. Paul Mallory's border ballads and the heavy midnight tramp of the forward line up the stairs were hardly more agreeable to the patient Madame Dusol than Harold Usborne's attempt to ride the Norton into the front hall or Bernard's loudly accurate impersonation of the chef. No sooner had they arrived at the hotel than Bernard seemed to become another person. Though their journey had hardly recreated a friendship which was warmer in memory than it ever had been in fact, Daniel had imagined that there would be a sentimental deposit of some kind. It occurred to him that it would not have hurt Bernard to buy him a meal on the way down or once to have put his hand in his pocket for petrol. At the same time he reproached himself for such pettiness and wondered whether he could persuade Bernard to make the return journey with him. He had earlier dreaded that the other might make the same suggestion. Daniel tried to lose himself in the communal activities of the tour, but even the games lacked the hoped for light-heartedness. The first was a goalless draw on a bald, hard ground against a team of officer cadets whose trainer, Bernard observed, had not fed them for a fortnight. The second, against Bordeaux University, was a farce; half of the opposition failed to

178

arrive because they had gone home for Easter and the tourists were obliged to divide against themselves. Most of them appeared to enjoy it, but Daniel played a hard, unsmiling game.

'It all seems to be a great success,' Virginia said, coming upon Daniel reading *Le Monde* on a bench in the little square where the long-distance lorries parked. 'Are you enjoying yourself?'

'Quite,' Daniel said.

'Most people seem to be,' Virginia said.

'Amongst whom, I gather, Mrs Playfair is numbered.'

'I adore France,' Virginia said. 'Anything interesting in *Le Monde*?'

'There's always something interesting in *Le Monde*,' Daniel said. 'That's the advantage of its being written in French.'

'I could so easily live here.'

'Of course, you've always had the *maladie française*, haven't you?'

'Couldn't you?'

'If no one else was here,' Daniel said.

'Yes, well, of course, the company – but I can never get Adam to come away when we're on our own. I thought you might have brought your girl.'

'I haven't got one,' Daniel said. 'They're all for export. Delivery's very slow on the new ones.'

'Is it not working out? I thought it was.'

'What do you want to know? Or alternatively what do you know that you want me to know?'

'Nothing.'

'You're looking much too glittery for me to believe that.'

'Am I?'

'There's a light in your eye. Or is it a beam?'

'It could be all kinds of things. Not necessarily to do with you.'

'As a matter of fact, Gin, I'm in the middle of a spiritual crisis.'

'Aren't we all?'

'All? You're not going to tell me that Harold Usborne is about to be received into the Church.'

'Harold Usborne! How did you and Bernard get on coming down?'

'Have you been talking to him?'

'No.'

'Has he been talking to you? That comes a lot cheaper, on the whole, doesn't it? He gushes God knows how many tonneaux per annum.'

'He's secretive through being garrulous, you're secretive through keeping quiet. You're both rather unknown quantities in the end. However I gather it was as competitive as one might expect. You're much too alike.'

'Thanks. Where's Adam this morning?'

'They've gone on a trip to Rocamadour. Him and Harold on the Norton.'

'I hope he's wearing a crash helmet.'

'Oh he'll be all right. Harold's ridden in T.T.s and things.'

'Yes, but has Adam? I'm surprised you didn't go.'

'Three on a motorbike? As a matter of fact, I'm waiting for Jean-Claude. He's coming over to take me to lunch.'

'That accounts for it. It is a beam. As a matter of fact, I'm very sorry. I'd rather like to take you to lunch myself.'

'There's always another day,' Virginia said.

'Oh, are you filling your book? You really are looking very attractive today.'

'There's no need to sound quite so surprised.'

'I always think of you as someone who'd wither if she was transplanted, but here you are blossoming.'

'I've never really been at home in London,' Virginia said. 'I think I'm really a continental. I was never so happy as the year we spent in Paris.'

'I never knew you spent a whole year.'

'Well, there you are, you went away, you thought everyone else stayed put, but they didn't. Adam was preparing a thesis on Vichy educational policy and I worked at Unesco until he decided not to go on with it.'

'And Paul was at the Sorbonne, of course.'

'Yes, we had a marvellous time. One was so alive. I've always regretted it. And Dave was over for a time, writing pornography.

180

We used to laugh and laugh. He wrote quite a lot. It was rather good.'

'It excited you, did it?'

'I don't think women are often stimulated by porn,' Virginia said, 'though I wouldn't deny it can have an effect. Of course it isn't usually angled for women.'

'The pornography that's angled for women is called literature,' Daniel said.

'That's very cynical,' Virginia said, 'that's very cynical, and I'm not even sure that it's true. Do you really think literature caters to female fantasy? I don't think most women would agree. Most intelligent women, anyway, think that literature's quite shamefully slanted the other way.'

'What do you think the basic female fantasy is?' Daniel said.

'You tell me.'

'The basic female fantasy is a fantasy of attention,' Daniel said. 'Someone paying very elaborate attention. That's why women like Henry James. You can't be more elaborate or more attentive than he is and no one is better at postponing climax for yet another orgy of meticulousness.'

'You may be quite right about that,' Virginia said, 'but why so bitter? That's the thing that puzzles me about you, Danny, you're so sour. I think I'd better wander back, because it's nearly noon and you know the French, they do like to satisfy their appetites promptly.'

'Get you! I hope Adam's going to be back in time for the match this afternoon.'

'He's going straight to the ground. He said.'

'Is Jean-Claude playing? Or is he going to be too busy satisfying his appetites? He did very well yesterday in that depressing bloody travesty of a game.'

'I don't know whether he's playing or not, I must ask him. But he's only satisfying one appetite as far as I'm concerned.'

'If he is supposed to be playing and he's late,' Daniel said, 'I shall know which door to knock on, all the same. I'll walk back with you.'

'What I like about him,' Virginia said, 'seriously, is that he's so —'

'Cultivated? Mature? Informative?'

'Partly.'

'He's got a lot of old blood, of course, hasn't he, cooling in his veins?'

'His grandfather knew Marcel. It isn't only that. He's rather like you, now I come to think of it. He's so secretive.'

'Be careful,' Daniel said, 'so was Bluebeard.'

'That sort of man is never violent,' Virginia said.

'Bernard and I killed a girl on the way down here, did he tell you?'

'Killed a girl? How? What do you mean? You're joking. In an accident? You didn't.'

'No, we strangled her, I think. I think we strangled her eventually. She knew too much.'

'You are joking.'

'How can you tell? We picked her up and — you know — and then we had to get rid of her. English girl.'

'Daniel, stop it.'

'Do you want to have a drink while you wait? Or would you sooner be alone when he comes?'

'Daniel, don't be childish, please. Was there really a girl?'

'We did pick up a girl, yes. With an accent like she had blotting paper in her sinuses.'

'But you didn't kill her.'

'Only with kindness. We dreamed up a movie and killed her that way. With retakes.'

'Men together really are horrible.'

'I'm afraid that's very true. Women are *toujours les civilisatrices*.'

'Oh the female sex can be quite base too, you know, quite serpentine. Don't feel too safe, Danny, will you, too cherished?'

'You have taken on a new lease of life,' Daniel said. 'I don't feel safe at all. I feel thoroughly exposed. My mental zip's quite undone.'

'That's because you haven't made up your mind about things, I suspect.'

'And how accurate your suspicions are! Though not necessarily

182

in the areas you think. It's mainly because I don't know what I'm going to do next, I think, professionally, in the way of a film.'

'Haven't you got anything in mind? I thought you had lots of things.'

'Oh I've got things in mind, but as Bernard points out, that's not actually the same as having them. *Au contraire*, as *Le Monde* would say. I may be doing a film in Rome, there's one possible in the States and then there's this Greek expedition, about which I've already talked more than enough.'

'You expect a lot from it.'

'I'm hoping if I mention it to enough people it'll become respectable. I've also got in mind a strange little film, very short, which I want to make, but I need a London house —'

'Have ours,' Virginia said. 'I should love to have a film made in my house.'

'No, you wouldn't, and anyway what I need is a Victorian terrace house, rather crummy, in Norwood or somewhere. Somewhere dusty. And Norwood, though I don't know it, sounds about as dusty as anything can conveniently be. So you can see, I'm arranging to fill my order book. And I've still got music to do on *The Elephant Man*.'

'Do you enjoy doing the music?'

'As much as anyone who's tone deaf can. It's rather strange, sitting in judgment on a musician when one literally can't read a note or even hum the national anthem without a frown.'

'Why aren't any of us musical? I've often wondered that.'

'If you played anything, Gin, it'd be the flute.'

'I used to like that game. We don't play intellectual games any more, we always used to. You know, what would he be if he was a fruit and all that and you have to guess who he is.'

'That was when we were competing. Now we're being competed against. We're the holders! And wise examiners never go in for exams.'

'How effortless you make it all seem, the things you say, Danny, how do you manage it?'

'I should like to say hard work, but it isn't that, assuming you're not being snide. I speak English like a foreign language. I always imagine that there's another language that would really suit me better, that would be closer to my natural tongue. I speak English like a spy, Gin, truthfully, always conscious that I'm deceiving people, or trying to.'

'Why do you think that is? I'm not being snide, as you put it, by the way, because it's not my style, as you ought to know. When I want to say something, I say it.'

'Which is why you're not an artist.'

'You do like to wound people, don't you?'

'I didn't know you wanted to be one.'

'That's an evasion, Danny. You meant to hurt—a little.'

'You invite it a little, Gin, surely you know that.'

'Appetite and invitation aren't the same thing. I have very little appetite for pain, as a matter of fact. Pain isn't really what I'm after at all.'

'Here he comes,' Daniel said. 'I'll leave you to it.'

'Have you ever really talked to him? Stay and have a drink with us, I think you'd like him.'

'No, I'm going for a walk down to the river,' Daniel said.

'If I was really having an assignation with him I'd hardly arrange to meet him here in front of the hotel where everyone can see. Give me a little credit.'

'I give you all the credit, Gin. You'd be quite gratified to know how much credit I give you.'

'That sounds very loaded. Bonjour, Jean-Claude, quel beau temps! C'est bien agréable, n'est-ce pas, pour notre petite promenade?'

'Morning, Jean-Claude,' Daniel said.

'Good morning, Daniel, good morning, Virginia.'

'I was just on my way,' Daniel said. 'Are you turning out this afternoon, Jean-Claude?'

'If selected,' Jean-Claude said.

'You will be,' Daniel said. 'Robin Taylor's pulled his other muscle, haven't you heard? While doing his relaxation exercises! See you later.'

'Dîtes-moi quelque chose, Jean-Claude, je crois qu'il y avait partout dans la France, à l'époque, les petits trains du type que Marcel a rendu si renommé. Connaissez-vous s'il y en avait un dans cette région, parce que je crois que j'ai vu hier une petite gare que pouvait être d'un service de petit train, type Balbec, c'est possible ou non?'

Jean-Claude arrived in time for the match, which was against a South-Western Press Eleven. The Canons expected a collection of rounded journalists, but most of the opposition were in their twenties and had come from the presses, not from their typewriters. They were not as hard as the officer cadets but they were more boisterous and less aware of the reputation of their opponents. The daring of distinguished intellectuals in venturing on the field at all did not impress them. They played neat pattern stuff, after their own fashion, and never noticed the honour being done them. Jean-Claude and Daniel saw a lot of action. Daniel made things easy for the Frenchman, rolled the ball to his hand as neatly as possible, while Jean-Claude, with the adaptability of the natural games player, soon demonstrated all the deceptive simplicities of a good goalkeeper. Nothing suggested anything but honest team-work unless it was the faint glint of mockery with which each so loyally served the other.

They came off the field together, after winning three-two (Harold Usborne, Dave Reece two), with large grins on their faces. Daniel felt, while they were playing, that the tour was, after all, enjoyable. As soon as he was dressed again, he decided to leave at once. He invented a professional excuse for his departure (he was down to play in the last game, at Bordeaux, the following after-noon), and apologized to Bernard Morris for not taking him back. 'Not a bit. Personally I'm flying home,' Bernard said, 'it may be slower, but it's safer.' Towards six o'clock, Daniel drove across the river and headed north. Virginia was walking through the village on the far side of the valley and waved to Daniel as he stormed up the hill. He faltered and then stopped.

'Where are you off to?'

'Home,' Daniel said. 'I've got to.'

'Home? I thought—'

'I've got to,' Daniel said.

'This minute?'

'If I hadn't seen you,' Daniel said, 'I'd have been in Calais by now.'

'What a funny time to go! Where will you stop the night?'

'I shan't. I shall drive all night, when the roads are empty, and I shall be across the Channel first thing in the morning.'

'Have you had a row or something?'

'No, I haven't had a row. It wasn't a bad game. You didn't do Jean-Claude any harm satisfying his appetites. He kept his eye on the ball.'

'You are silly,' Virginia said. 'Can't a woman have a friendship with an intelligent man without being accused—?'

'No one's accusing you,' Daniel said. 'Give us a kiss, Gin.'

'What're you talking about?'

'Oh for God's sake. A kiss, what am I talking about? I said give us a kiss.'

'I'm perfectly willing to kiss you,' she said, 'but I want to know what for.'

'That means you're not,' Daniel said.

'You haven't taken a bet with someone, have you?'

'A bet? Are you crazy? Who would I have taken a bet with?'

'Yourself,' she said.

He opened the car door and scrambled round to where she was standing on the narrow pavement. From inside the car, she had seemed altogether different; the shape of her face, the colour of her hair, the style of her body. 'Forget it,' he said. 'I like the sandals.'

'They are nice, aren't they?'

'I'll see you back in London,' he said. He held out his hand. They shook hands. Her mouth wavered, as if she were conscious of his embarrassment. He waved and ran, on tiptoe, round the car again. A trailer truck, entering the village, showed convenient impatience. He slammed the door and, buckling his seat belt, accelerated up the narrow street. Virginia did not watch him go. She was looking at the headlines on a rack of newspapers outside a *Papeterie*. 'Why on earth should I want to kiss that?' he said, cocking an eyebrow at himself in the mirror. He had known Virginia for years, ever since they had both had poems in an undergraduate magazine at Cambridge. He had found himself several times on the verge of passionate declarations to her. All of them had been formulated in a period of gloomy desire during which he did not actually see her or when she was involved with someone else. First there had been Paul Mallory and then there was a Professor of Anthropology whose wife was in an institution and then, triumphantly, there was Adam, whose Cambridge career promised a life glittering with prizes. Adam had started his own publishing house soon after their return to London. There had been a bright beginning, an anxious middle and a calamitous end. Friends remembered the beginning; Adam, as an agent, was able to rely on a publishing reputation which was more remarkable in retrospect than it had ever been at the time. The original Playfair, Marks, had indeed published a few books which people remembered, but the truth was that those who had subsequently bought the firm (and imported Norbert Ash to run it) had made the imprint sufficiently famous for Adam to draw a continuing dividend, at least in admiration, from an enterprise whose greatest success had occurred since his departure. Virginia compounded the confusion by reading French fiction for the new Playfair, Marks, so that the illusion of continuity had some slender substance. Paul Mallory was the editorial director, though the backing came, as so often, from television. The thing about Virginia, the attraction of Virginia, was that she gave one ideas. The more one thought about her, the more of a judgment it seemed on one's taste that one had not possessed her. She did not invite love (strangely, one found oneself pitying her) nor did she inspire devotion (she was too astringent) but she did, through her very qualities of demanding intelligence, provoke the aggression which, in a childish form, Daniel acknowledged he had just displayed. Her ceaseless interest in classifying one's intellect made her into the sexual object her first-class mind was so determined that no woman should be.

Her eagerness to associate herself only with those whose brains were equal to her own had always seemed part of an intellectual snobbery where academic achievement took the place of high birth, but now Daniel saw it quite differently. It was her contempt for men which made her choose only those with the best qualifications; it was doubt concerning her own physical charm which set such elaborate standards for those who were to share her bed and made her a prize, not a person. She had seduced them like boys, all of them, and they had vainly accepted that sex was secondary to intelligence, when all the time it was not them she was judging but herself she was protecting. She had guessed that the men of her generation could be sexually intrigued by and would never fail to compete for any prize provided it was wittily enough veiled.

Daniel stopped at a Routiers' café for dinner. He was given slabs of heavy, elastic sausage, a plate of tepid pork with white beans, salad, a choice of dry cheeses and a large, watery coffee. It was not much cheaper than the little hotel in the Dordogne, but its roughness gratified him. He was resolved to sever his connection with all of those with whom he had tried so long to ingratiate himself.

When he came out to the car again, it was hedged with parked trucks. A few young men and girls, in shiny plastic jackets, were standing by the verge, between the tall lamps, looking for lifts. One of the girls detached herself from the others and came smiling towards him. 'Paris?' Daniel shook his head, got into the Lotus and drove back on to the road. He was cured, he felt, of a crippling disease, he had shaken off the shadow of some unknown assailant, without ever knowing exactly what had threatened him. As he threaded the car more quickly through the traffic on the main road, he imagined a story in which a man, through the usual inadvertence heroes display in films, has acquired a suitcase and becomes the target of relentless agents. At first he is terrified and seeks to assure them of his innocence, but he cannot convince them. They are implacable. He is involved with a suspiciously tawny but luscious girl of exhilarating and shameless ruthlessness and the two of them are chased through all kinds of frightening locations including, perhaps, the organ loft of Chartres cathedral. (A false note from the

188

practising organist shows in which pipe the contraband is stuffed.) The man has always been inclined to paranoia. Now his fantasies are fleshed out by real danger. He survives, despite silent shots, poisoned pâté, hurtling automobiles in narrow alleys, sinister hotel elevators, misleading roadsigns, corpses in the car boot and a full panoply of bully boys; he is just beginning to relish his heroic centrality to the plot when the chief of his pursuers realizes that it is true that our hero knows nothing and is simply an innocent nonentity. He is, accordingly, dismissed from the plot without apology, tribute or reward. His pursuers abandon him, unharmed and unwanted. The tawny girl leaves but the faintest fragrance on the air to show where she has been. He is returned to ordinary life. It has been a near thing. At first he is hugely relieved but then, cheated of his nightmare, he is haunted by the desire for it. He tries to read into the simplest events the most sinister explanations. He seeks, vainly, for access to a new intrigue. The heroin which he has never touched (or even known he was carrying, perhaps) has turned him on. The absence of fear has become more obsessive than fear itself.

He breakfasted at the Connaught. No one knew he was in London. He had caught the first ferry in the morning. Mayfair was deserted; there was a meter free opposite the side door of the hotel. He had driven most of the night, except for an uneasy nap between three-thirty and five. He had come through the customs as tense as a man carrying contraband, but the truth was he had not exceeded the proper allowances by one drop. He had the illusion now, sitting alone in an angle of velvet, that he was engaged on some cryptic mission, that his paper, cocked against the marmalade pot, gave notice of singular purpose and distinguished him from the newly powdered Americans and well-shaved businessmen at the other tables. He excused himself from his porridge (with brown sugar) and went into the lobby.

There was no answer at the flat. It was never likely that Rachel would be there. Yet he could visualize her so clearly that he seemed to see her running down from the little kitchen and sitting on the

Chesterfield before she answered the phone. He could hear the little-girl note in her voice. She was wearing his silk dressing-gown. He waited and waited while the phone purled. Finally the phone was picked up. The girl gave the number. Daniel said: 'Rachel?' 'There's no one here at the moment,' the girl said. 'Oh,' Daniel said, 'that must be the answering service, is it?' 'Yes, it is.' 'This is Mr Meyer's number though I'm ringing?' 'Yes, that's right. Is there a message I can give Mr Meyer?' 'Yes, there is actually,' Daniel said, 'you can tell him, if you would, that Mr Meyer phoned. That's M,e,y,e,r.' 'Mr Meyer.' 'That's right,' Daniel said, 'no message.' 'Have you finished?' said the Hotel Operator. 'Yes,' Daniel said, 'finished. Definitely.'

He imagined a man who returns to London before he is expected or known to have arrived in the country. As long as he doesn't speak or make contact with anyone, he is able to see through walls and to have knowledge of all the secrets of the city. Nothing is hidden. How long before the pressure of his loneliness becomes unendurable and he is forced to betray himself? Daniel was like a solitary invader who had broken through the defences of his enemies and occupied their city. He wandered through the morning streets with an air of insolent secrecy. His movements were as dramatic as if a specially composed score accompanied him. He walked along Oxford Street waiting for some desire to breach his contentment. As he came level with Selfridges, he saw a young man with a khaki satchel over his shoulder come out of a half-finished shop. He crossed the pavement scanning the buses and swung himself aboard a number 2. It was Andy. Daniel blinked. The music stopped. He looked at the passers-by, none of whom were conscious of the drama. He blinked again. Surely someone had noticed? It was Andy and Andy was dead. He was wearing the same jeans, the same dye-stained shirt. His hair was lighter, from the dust no doubt. But it was Andy. Daniel ran along the street, which was now void of traffic, so that the bus was able to move quickly away. The pause, the silly pause which he had always tried to avoid in his films, between vision and reaction, had been too long. He ran along the street with all the strength and violence of failure. The bus had turned and was away down Park Lane. He chased it and, panting, saw it at the distant stop, but it was already going, though he waved and shouted. A bystander said: 'They never wait. They've only got to see you want them and they're gone.' He looked for a taxi. His car was back in Mount Street, at a meter. He was going to exceed his time. He ran, chest aching, towards the car. Could he have caught the bus? And was it Andy? And if it was, who was deceiving whom and why?

The warden was looking at the Lotus.

Daniel said: 'Here I am, it's O.K.'

'It's ten minutes already you're over,' the girl said.

'The most amazing thing just happened. Look, as you haven't even started.'

'I've got my job to do,' she said.

'I just saw a dead man,' Daniel said. 'Surely once someone's in his car.'

'Accidents happen all the time,' the girl said. 'People get killed.'

'Alive; he was alive. I saw a man I was told was dead and there he was getting on a bus.'

'Then he probably wasn't ever dead at all. You'd better go now, if.'

'I'm on my way. I promise I won't boast about it.'

'It doesn't make any difference to me,' she said. 'Are you sure it was him? Probably wasn't him at all.'

'How can you ever be sure it's anybody?'

'There's always fingerprints,' the girl said.

'You're right,' Daniel said. 'I should have taken his fingerprints.'

'Well,' he said, 'at last.'

'At last,' she said. 'I suppose it is really.'

'I wondered if you'd even remembered. That's why I called. I wondered if you'd still be here.'

'Oh I don't go anywhere,' she said. 'I have two children in school. A mother doesn't have too much time to go any place during school term.'

'No, I suppose not. Except that presumably you have someone you can leave them with. Like now, for instance. Where are they now?'

'They're in their room, with Rhoda, the nanny.'

'I remember. I spoke to her. They're very quiet.'

'I can have them make a noise,' she said. 'If that'd make you feel better. She's reading them a story.'

'I like the way you've done the house,' he said. 'Where do you sleep?'

'I sleep upstairs. Want to see?'

'Later,' he said. 'This room's very nice. And much bigger than it looks from outside. Did you have someone do it for you?'

'I have a little experience doing houses,' she said. 'I took a course in New York City and I worked with a decorator before I married Charles.'

'You know, you're not like I remembered.'

'Are you going to have a drink? Do we have time? Sure we do.'

'Do you have any wine?'

'Wine. Not up here.'

'I'll go,' he said, 'if you'll tell me where it is.'

'No, I think I'll go,' she said.

The drawing-room was on the first floor. The stairs went through it; it was a comfortable platform set between the ground and the roof. Two chesterfields, upholstered in royal blue silk covered with a fillet of crochet work, faced each other over a low, mosaic table. On the table were several French paperweights. A roll-top desk in the alcove beside the stairs was a still-life of bills, invitations and letters. On the wall above the mantelpiece was a painting of a huge green garden. A woman was crouching, naked, on the lawn, her cheek against the brilliant grass, her face averted. Between the double windows which looked on to the quiet street the wall was mirror from floor to ceiling. An iron sculpture, about a foot high, stood on the table. There were stiff, fresh tulips and narcissi in a blue Berber vase. The room was lit with a perspective of lamps. Whorls of light encircled and overlapped each other like lilies on the surface of an ornamental pond. The room was not large (Daniel paced from one end to the other in a few strides) but it was so artfully put together and so certain of its style that it gave an impression not only of wealth but of generosity. There was nothing provisional. Not a single wire showed, not a single scratch on the paintwork, not a single misplaced thread. It was the kind of set which might once have earned a round of applause at a first night (it even had a chandelier) but which would not distract attention from the actors when, after a polite hesitation, they actually stepped forward and began to speak.

'I hope this is all right,' she said. 'Because I don't really know about wines.'

'I'm sure you do,' he said. 'What a nice room this is!'

'It's some Beaujolais we had downstairs.'

'Do your children ever come in here?'

'Yes, of course,' she said.

'And what are they by the way?'

'Boys. Francis and Boris.'

'I like Boris,' he said. 'What's this?'

'It comes from Nigeria,' she said. 'From the Yoruba. I believe it has some religious significance, I think it's a prayer staff, but I don't know exactly. I once told someone that if you could get that iron ring off, everything you touched turned to gold. He nearly broke the thing.'

'I believe it,' Daniel said. 'I remembered your hair as much lighter.'

'Want to break the date?'

'On the contrary. I prefer it the way it is.'

'Then my afternoon wasn't wasted,' she said.

'It's naturally that colour,' he said.

'Naturally,' she said. 'What time do you think we ought to leave? What time does it start?'

Daniel said: 'Oh there's plenty of time. We don't have to be there till eight. And I know somewhere we can park.'

'Oh, that's fine,' she said. 'I had an idea it was earlier.'

'These things never start till eight,' he said.

'What do you hear about it, the movie?'

'I hear it's the most sensational thing Billy has ever done. It's harsh, it's uncompromising and it's going to gross twenty million domestic.'

'I'm looking forward to it,' she said, 'very much.'

'So'm I,' Daniel said, 'I like going to the movies. How old are they, the boys?'

'Eight and ten,' she said.

'In that order?'

'Boris is eight and Francis is ten.'

'You married very young.'

'I was nineteen,' she said, 'when I married Charles.'

'He's not in ships, is he?'

'No, he's not. That's Arthur. His cousin. Charles is in money.'

'I see.'

'He was a banker.'

'I thought you divorced him.'

'I did,' she said.

'I mean he's still alive.'

'I guess he's still as alive as he ever was.'

'Was he older than you?'

'He was. Still is. He'd been married before.'

'I see.'

'But then so'd I, I guess.'

'Before him? I didn't know that.'

'I got married my first year in college. I was crazy. It didn't last more than a couple of months, but I guess it counts. I was seventeen.'

'Why? Were you —?'

'I was just plain romantic. He was a flyer. Very handsome. It was one of those crazy midsummer things. He proposed to me when I was actually at the controls. It all seemed like it had to work. The big blue sky romance.'

'My goodness me, you've really had a life!'

'Think so?'

'So then along came the banker.'

'I figured like I'd made a fool of myself, which I had. He wasn't just a banker, Charles, he was a very attractive man, or seemed like one: nice age — mid-thirties ... '

'Absolutely,' Daniel said, 'nicest age there is. What went wrong?'

'Oh it's a long story,' she said, 'and I'm not telling it. We have a movie to go to, don't we?'

'He was American then, your husband. How do you come to be in England?'

'A lot of American banks operate in Europe. We were in Paris first and then we came over here.'

'Is he still here?'

'Why?' she said. 'Want to meet him?'

'I just wondered. I can always use a tame banker.'

'He lives in South Street. He isn't that tame.'

'That was when you met your famous politician friend then, when you were living in Paris, was it?'

'I hoped we weren't going to talk about that,' she said. 'And anyway, shouldn't we really be going?'

He put down the iron sculpture. 'That thing really doesn't come off, does it?' he said.

'It was never meant to,' she said. 'That's just my story.'

'Christ,' he said. 'Jesus Christ. Shit.'

'I had a feeling,' she said.

'Shit,' he said. 'What a fool! What an idiot! How long's it been running?'

'Over half an hour now,' the doorman said. 'And please —'

'What an idiot! There is such a thing as having too much notice. What shall we do, shall we go in all the same?'

'Nearly three quarters,' the doorman said. 'And I don't know —'

'I hate being rude by mistake,' Daniel said. 'And walking in now, it'd seem so calculated, like all miscalculations.'

'I did say,' she said.

'You did too. What a fool! And you look so beautiful. I mean —'

'Oh that doesn't matter,' she said.

'What do you want to do? I'll do anything you want to do.'

'Wait a minute, that's a big offer.'

'I mean it. Absolutely. Anything. Truly. What a fool! What a beginning! What shall we do? Shall we get married?'

'Careful,' she said.

'Why should flyers have all the fun?' he said.

'You don't know what you land yourself in, talking like that.'

'As long as it isn't— Listen, if I promise to get Billy to show you the picture within the next week, what do you say we go and have dinner?'

'And I thought you were going to be reliable,' she said.

'I am,' he said, 'from now on in. Promise. Where do you want to go?'

'Anywhere,' she said.

'I should've checked the goddamned invitation. I was so certain. Starting at seven, I never heard of such a thing. We could come back and go to the buffet,' he said, 'if you want.'

'That doesn't sound too tactful either,' she said.

'I'm glad you said that. Do you like Chinese?'

'I'd say come back to the house, but that seems kind of ridiculous. Yes, I love it. Chinese.'

'After all, how would we explain ourselves to oh, Rhoda, was it?'

'Rhoda, that's right. Oh she's been with me a long time now.'

'She sees 'em come she sees 'em go, is that it?'

'She takes what comes.'

'All the same, I have my pride,' Daniel said. 'Or will you tell her about what's happened whether we go back or not?'

'It's none of her business,' Nancy said. 'Of course not.'

'And how old is she, this Rhoda?'

'I guess her late twenties. Why?'

'I'm interested. I like to discover the shape of the ground. If you like Chinese, I know a good place in Poplar you might like. I'll have to call, but—'

'The Good Friends,' she said.

'Now I suppose I have to say no, somewhere else, and take you to a dump. Yes, I was thinking of the Good Friends actually, but if you know it —'

'I don't necessarily not like the things I know.'

When they were in the car, Daniel said: 'Have you never been an actress?'

'No,' she said, 'should I?'

'It seems a shame so few people get to see you.'

'I do move around the town from time to time,' she said. 'I'm not entirely sedentary. Occasionally I even visit people.'

'What happened with your marriage?' he said. 'I mean —'

'You mean you want to know the gaudy details.'

'Are they gaudy?'

'Nobody's talked to you about it.'

'Nobody knows I know you. That's —'

'What?'

'One of the things I like about you. You don't come out of my usual —'

'Trout stream?'

'You're no trout, Mrs Lane.'

'I'm sure you do know people I know. Because I've heard people talk about you.'

'More people know Tom Fool than Tom Fool knows,' Daniel said.

'I met Willie Maugham once,' Nancy said, 'when we were in the South of France. We were asked to the house.'

'And was he rude to you?'

'No. He used to say that. About Tom Fool.'

'He was always supposed to be rude to people. And yet they went on toadying to him and sponging on him. That part of it never seemed to worry them. How did you come to go there?'

'We were neighbours one summer. We took a place on the Cap. He was very sweet. He had a test he used to give people, you know, he had a picture he was very proud of and he used to take people into the room where it was and ask them to identify the artist. He did it with me. He took me in and showed it to me and the thing was, I did know who the artist was. It was —'

'It was Toulouse-Lautrec, wasn't it?' Daniel said.

'That's right, it was. I was a lot younger then—'

'I don't believe you could be a lot younger,' Daniel said.

'Anyway, I was standing there in front of this picture—thank you—and I knew who it was by, but at the same time I could see how pleased he was that usually no one could give it the right attribution—'

'Yes, that must have been a nice feeling.'

'Tremendous feeling of power I had. And then I remembered a story of his—I was thinking to myself what an impression it would make if I hesitated and then gave him the right answer, as if I really had deduced it, you know?—but then I remembered that story of his, Mr Knowall, I don't know if you recall it.'

'"Mr Kelada",' Daniel said. 'They made a movie of it. Nigel Patrick.'

'I don't remember, but you recall it hinged on a diamond—'

'A pearl—'

'You're right, a pearl expert who had to look a fool in front of everyone in order to keep a girl's secret—'

'Because the pearls were real and they'd been given to her by her lover and if he didn't say they were fake, then her husband'd know she was unfaithful.'

'Which of course would be terrible, that's right. And so I swallowed my pride and I said I didn't know.'

'Very white of you!'

'Only afterwards I did say that I should have guessed from the drawing of the head, which was actually the giveaway. It was a sprinter, two sprinters at the start, I don't know if you know that, this particular picture.'

'Thanks for telling me,' he said. 'Now I can bring it casually into my memoirs.'

'The head was really very Toulouse-Lautrec. I studied art appreciation when I was training as an interior decorator—'

'Was that how you met Charles?'

'That was how. I went with my friend Alexander Rapaport to his office. I did the measuring up and stuff like that—'

'And you obviously measured up extremely well.'

'I guess so,' she said.

'Did you fall in love with him?'

'I fell in something,' she said. 'I guess I thought I did. He was a pretty dazzling character.'

'I'd like to drive on right through the night,' Daniel said, 'but here we are already.'

'I think I'll have a cigarette before we go in,' she said. 'If that's all right. Anyway, so far as Mr Maugham knew, Sir Kenneth Clark was the only man who ever identified the artist correctly.'

'You did the right thing,' Daniel said. '*Noblesse oblige.*'

'I don't know about *noblesse*,' she said, 'but *oblige* certainly. He was very nice actually, the old party, not a bit snappety, as I'd been warned. I admired him. Do you admire him?'

'Sort of. He's Lord Clark now, isn't he? Has Charles married again?'

'You know, I don't really know. No, I'm sure he hasn't. He could have. In spite of everything.'

'In spite of what?'

'Oh let's just say in spite of—well, not liking to live with some-one, you could say. A woman, anyway. He likes to build barriers round himself.'

'And what about you?'

'Oh, I guess I was one of the barriers,' she said. 'How about eating?'

When they were sitting in the restaurant, Daniel said: 'What do you mean, you were one of the barriers?'

She smiled at him across the table, a smile at once flattering and unnerving. It promised candour, but it refused something else. It admitted Daniel's right to ask the question, but it avoided an answer. It was both very cool and very wanton. Above all, it seemed very special. When she repeated it, almost inadvertently, for the waiter, a moment later, he was shot with jealousy. The she turned the smile, unextinguished, once more on him. He was reassured. It was as if, seeing him coming, she had switched on a lamp in a darkened room and then turned to welcome him. She lifted her arms and joined her slim, white hands, with their mother-of-pearl nails, and leaned her chin on the backs of them. She was wearing a white shirt and flared silk Cossack pants over rust coloured boots. Her face was quite pale, the lips the same colour, almost, as the boots. Her cheekbones were shaded; her eyes, with their thickened lashes, had the same cool nakedness as her face. They were pale green, the shade of stones under water. Her beauty, she managed to suggest, by the steadiness of her stare and the patient humour of her mouth, was not to be held against her.

He said: 'It's over two weeks since I first saw you. You'd be surprised if you knew how much I've thought about you.'

'Would I?'

'Oh, perhaps you wouldn't. Perhaps you'd only be surprised if you knew *what* I've thought about you.'

'Something good, I hope.'

'Not altogether,' he said.

'I know. I remember. You were very angry with me at that party. Have you been storing up your anger then all this time? Is that what you've been doing?'

'I wasn't angry exactly. And it certainly isn't all.'

'What were you? Hurt?'

'Hurt, no. I'm not hurt by the things women say, at least not about general topics, not about politics. The truth is, I expect women to behave well. I expect them to be bright enough not to be stupid. About big things. I don't expect them to know a lot —'

'My goodness!' she said. 'I'm terrified.'

'I'm glad we missed the movie,' he said. 'What I mean is, there's something so vulgar about admiring cruel and dishonest ideas, I always hope there's a whole slice of humanity — the female slice — that's instinctively repelled by them. And I feel disgusted when I'm disappointed. And more than disgusted. I always think that the woman is really pretending, is trying to please by agreeing with what she secretly despises. And that seems even more despicable than anything else, but at the same time a lot less — what? — incorrigible.'

'My,' she said, 'what a lot you expect of us! What you expect most of all, I would guess, is that we should all love you.'

'You could lead a completely different life from the one you do, though, couldn't you? The London social bit, you could do without that, I mean. And the money.'

'I like the money,' she said. 'Don't get too starry-eyed.'

'I'm not starry-eyed,' he said.

'You know something? I don't altogether trust you, Mr Meyer.'

'Flatterer,' he said.

She wore no jewellery on her shirt, but there were gold bracelets on her wrists and matching hoops in her ears. She lifted her chin as she ate; he had the malicious impression that she was already doing exercises to prevent the aging of which she showed no sign.

He said: 'What do you do with your day?'

She said: 'I'm a woman of leisure. I don't do a thing. I just pamper myself. Is that what you want me to say?'

'I was interested,' he said. 'I don't want you to say anything except what's true.'

'I count my money—or some of it—in the morning and I go to the Beauty Parlour in the afternoon and I play with my children between half past five and bedtime, which is half past six, and then I go out to dinner or the theatre, usually a first night, of course, and then I come home and I drink a large Scotch and I go to bed.'

'Alone?'

She said: 'A divorced woman has to be very discriminating. Usually alone. Sometimes with a couple of friends.'

'And is that satisfactory?'

'What?'

'Living the way you describe.'

'I don't know,' she said. 'I've never tried it.'

'Haven't you? I get the feeling it's quite close to what you actually do.'

'I'm a partner in two businesses,' she said. 'I'm quite a busy woman.'

'What businesses are those?'

'I thought you might have known. I'm involved with Douggie Negus and I also have a share in White Associates.'

'You're back to your old tricks,' he said. 'You really are an indoor girl.'

'I play tennis,' she said.

'And you ski, of course.'

'Of course,' she said. 'Indoors.'

'I'm glad we can laugh,' he said. 'We were getting very staccato.'

'And what are you working on right now?' she said.

'You,' he said.

'Seriously.'

'I have an awful feeling that, yes, probably.'

'No, I mean it. What?'

'I told you, didn't I? I'm just finishing this film on *The Elephant Man*. Just a little film for the box; I got the money out of Victor Rich to do it. It's quite nice.'

'Victor Rich,' she said. 'He's brilliant, isn't he?'

'Yes, I suppose so,' Daniel said.

'He's really the only person around,' she said, 'in that particular field, who has any kind of appreciation of quality.'

'He hasn't seen it yet. No one has.'

'I'd like to,' she said. 'But what other plans do you have? Do you have something big coming up? You should do something really big.'

'I certainly hope so,' he said. 'Only I need a banker. What do you want now? Do you want ice cream or something? Or Ly-chee?'

'Just coffee,' she said.

'Why does that always sound so positive. Just coffee! It somehow suggests a wealth of experience. Just coffee.'

'Do you have brothers or sisters?' she said.

'Do I have brothers or sisters. Yes, as a matter of fact, I do. I have a brother.'

'What does he do?'

'Well, I'll tell you, he doesn't do anything very much. He's in hospital as a matter of fact.'

'Oh, what's wrong with him? Is it something serious?'

'Yes, it is really. He's in a mental hospital as a matter of fact. It's O.K., it's O.K., don't bother about being sorry. He's been there a long time.'

'That's awful,' she said.

'He's Mycroft to my Sherlock,' Daniel said.

'I'm sorry?'

'Holmes. Mycroft was Sherlock's brother. He was a lot brighter than Sherlock but he'd never get off his ass — or in his case leave his club — and so Sherlock solved all but the most difficult cases and then he went to Mycroft, who'd give him the clue without even leaving his armchair.'

'What's his name,' Nancy said, 'your brother? Is he younger or older?'

'James,' Daniel said. 'Not that he answers to it. He calls himself Jacob. He's two years older than I am.'

'And what's — you know — wrong with him?'

'He suffers from delusions,' Daniel said.

'Such as what?'

'It's one rather long and complicated delusion basically,' Daniel said. 'He believes that Hitler won the war and he's still in power. He believes he's in a concentration camp and it's only a matter of time before he's — you know — put in the gas chamber.'

'How ghastly! When did it start?'

'It's not only ghastly,' Daniel said. 'It's also — what? — extremely well argued. He has an extraordinary memory. He's read everything there is to read about the Nazis and he hasn't forgotten anything. He can't. And he really knows. He's had correspondence with scholars and people. He knows exactly what happened in all those places. He knows the names of the staff, everything. He's really an authority. People write to him.'

'That's tragic, but surely in that case —'

'What?'

'He must know that the camps were finally —'

'No, you —'

'He surely realizes some of the time —'

'I don't know. Perhaps he does. I don't see him that often. I don't see him as often as I should. He's been like this for a long time and with the best will in the world—'

'Where is he?'

'He thinks he's in Auschwitz and that it's—well the last time I saw him it was the winter of 1943. Time goes very slowly for him. In fact it hardly goes at all. In fact, sometimes I think it actually goes backwards. You see—oh, well, let's—'

'No, it's fascinating, it's—'

'It doesn't have much in common with interior decoration,' Daniel said. 'I don't usually tell people about it.'

'When did it first start?'

'He was going to go up to Cambridge. He was a scholar, Modern Languages.'

'Brilliant, I suppose.'

'Not as brilliant as Victor Rich, of course, just ordinary unique. He was a scholar anyway, and during the summer before he was due to go, he had this breakdown. It happened to coincide with my parents' parting, but I think it had been coming for some time. But then again, maybe so had their parting. Anyway. It seemed like it might be just a temporary thing. It started with a very funny essay he wrote which purported to be a minute from the Foreign Office explaining why H.M.G. could not interfere with Germany's internal affairs. It was like a revue sketch. Only unfortunately it didn't end there and finally he's had to be kept in this place. I don't see him as often as I should.'

'Isn't there anything they can do?'

'Oh, they have a whole menu of things they can do; the thing is to stop them doing them. Leucotomies, lobotomies, stuff like that. They have all kinds of things they can do, but I don't think we have any right to—to take away his ideas. Who's to say they're wrong? O.K., they're wrong. He's a critic, really, that's the thing. Trying to silence him is like running away from criticism. Which, incidentally, I would very much like to do. He's even learned Hebrew in there. Sometimes he's a Rabbi. He discusses the Talmud with someone who goes up from Willesden, or used to, every week, a genuine scholar. Who really finds it worthwhile talking with him.

Who's to say that he should be declared a fake because he identifies with a man who was gassed nearly thirty years ago? And yet on the other hand —'

'What?'

'He's a nut,' Daniel said.

'Where is he actually? In this country?'

'Yes,' Daniel said, 'he's near Ipswich. Want to go and see him?'

'What do they think about him? Do they think it might clear up?'

'You make it sound like roseola,' Daniel said. 'No, of course, it won't clear up.'

'These things sometimes do,' Nancy said, 'don't they?'

'These things. Do they?'

'You hear of cases. Anyway, you've certainly explained a few things.'

'Such as?'

'Why you were so angry when I said what I did about Tom —'

'As if there'd be no reason to be angry ordinarily, you mean?'

'I only said he was a fascinating man,' Nancy said, 'and he is. He knows everybody. He happens to be one of the most interesting people I've ever met. I wasn't saying I agreed with him. But then I think it's a little facile to equate him with everything that happened you don't like.'

'I don't equate him,' Daniel said.

'Now I've loused up the evening,' she said. 'Or anyway the evening's loused up. And I was really enjoying it.'

'Aren't you now?' he said.

'No, I'm definitely not.' She lowered her hands to the cloth and left them lying there while she looked, for the first time, around the room. Had her nose been bobbed? In profile it had an almost absurd shortness. Her teeth, so white and dazzling in full face, now seemed to push forward against her upper lip. He was conscious of her skull. The low light shone through her hair and its angle seemed to shave her head. She might have been bald. He saw her mortality. He saw through the accident of her beauty. She was transformed, for a moment, from a goddess to a victim. He smiled to himself and pressed his thumb into the crumbs of noodle which surrounded the

205

soya sauce bottle and then rubbed them away on the floor. He looked at the still bracelets which had chimed so prettily as she ate. 'We should have been in time for the movie,' he said.

'You're wrong,' she said. 'This is more worthwhile. Not so nice but more worthwhile.'

'I don't think so. You dressed to be seen.'

'I didn't do it to sit in the dark,' she said.

'You're beautiful,' he said. 'It's no good.'

She half skipped across the pavement to the car and tapped her feet while he opened the doors. They were both breathless as they settled in their seats, slammed the doors and turned, panting and amused to look at each other. He smiled without parting his lips and she lifted her chin towards him and he was kissing her lips. The strong barrier of her teeth seemed suddenly removed; his tongue passed, sweetly swollen, into the warmth of her mouth and was lost in softness. He touched only the sides of her arms, with the palms of his hands, aware now of the silken sheerness of the simple shirt. Her knees were sharp in the short front of the car and the folds of her Cossack pants fell to the floor. She held her hands up, as if the nails were drying, and sipped the careful tenderness of his kiss.

'Home?'

'Up to you,' she said.

He said: 'Do you like tunnels?'

'Tunnels?'

He drove through the Blackwall and then back again through the Rotherhithe.

'And now what?' she said.

He stopped the car and kissed her again and again it was the same, the same softness, the same fragrance, but now, as he withdrew, her teeth were there to pinch him as he parted from her.

He said: 'God, this is awful.'

'Is it? What is?'

'I love you,' he said, gulping down the word, almost coughing, and started the car. And then, when they were moving, and she was looking at him with a kind of wary conceit, he smiled,

206

mockingly, at her, as if between them they had deceived someone whose naiveté deserved it.

'Where are we going?' she said.

'So this is you.'

'This is me. I don't want you to think you've been misled.'

'In what respect?'

'The style in which I live. The sort of person I am. I'm sure someone with your eye will be able to read this room better than—'

'Better than I can read you? What shall I do? Take an inventory?'

'It is what it is,' he said. 'It can't smile at you or flatter you.'

'Were you flattering me?'

'When?'

'Before. When you said you loved me.'

'Did I say that? Anyway, what's flattering about it?'

'I'm mad about you,' she said. 'I was at the party.'

'Then we ought to be very happy,' he said.

'Ought to be doesn't sound quite as promising as it should somehow.'

'I've always been suspicious of beauty,' he said.

'Why?'

'Because it seems to promise something the person who possesses it usually can't deliver.'

'Which is?'

He shrugged. 'I can't say, and anyway, I still do expect it. Let's say quality. Quality.'

'I want you,' she said. 'Daniel Meyer.'

'You've got me,' he said.

She was sitting on the broad chesterfield in front of the fire. She spread herself diagonally across it and leaned her head on the back and looked round. Daniel turned on lights.

'It's a nice place you've got,' she said.

'It's yours,' he said. 'It's all yours.'

*

'Well,' he said. 'You're awake.'
  'I haven't been asleep,' she said.
  'I didn't want to disturb you. You looked so marvellous.'
  'I was just thinking.'
  'The first time's never—what you think it's going to be.'
  'None of them are, if you ask me.'
  'I mean to say, I'm sorry—'
  'It wasn't your fault.'
  'It wasn't too special.'
  'I enjoyed it,' she said. 'It was just what I wanted.'
  'It's a start,' he said. 'And it gives us something to look forward
to. I must have been nervous. It was my fault.'
  'What was?'
  'Well, you didn't, did you?'
  'I often don't,' she said.
  'We shall have to change all that,' he said.
  'I promise you it doesn't matter. What is it?'
  'I want you,' he said.
  'So soon?'
  'Completely I mean. I guess I shouldn't say it—'
  'It doesn't hurt, that I promise you.'
  'You're not cold, are you?'
  'No, it's nice in here, just right. I have to go home.'
  'Not yet. Stay just like that. Let me look at you a little longer.'
  'If these walls could talk.'
  'What do you think they'd say?'
  'Here he goes again.'
  'Oh no. Not again. This isn't something that's happened before.
I promise you.'
  'The phone's ringing.'
  'Let it.'
  'Aren't you going to answer it?'
  'Five rings and someone'll answer it for me. See?'
  'As soon as I leave you'll be ringing to ask them who it was.'
  'In the morning.'
  'It might be California.'

'That's Carolina—in the morning. If it's California they'll try again.'

'One day you're going to be very very famous.'

'Don't start the accusations so early in the day. I love you, Nancy. Truly, I feel as if everything that's happened between the party and now is just a sort of—parenthesis. A sort of prologue. Pre-titles, if you like. It's all been about you really.'

'Has it? That sounds very nice, only what has?'

'My life until this minute.'

'And what's it going to be about now in that case?'

'Us,' he said. 'What else? You and me.'

'I'm willing,' she said.

'Do you know what I saw this morning? I saw someone I thought was dead walking in the street. Running, even.'

'In that case,' she said, 'maybe there's hope for us all. Who was it?'

'No one of any consequence,' Daniel said. 'A bloke.'

'Oh that's all right,' Nancy said. 'I was afraid it might have been a girl.'

JUNE

'Iskios,' the sailor was shouting, 'Iskios.'

'Next stop the original Greek Island,' Nancy said.

'It's not so original any more,' Daniel said. 'Too many people have done it.'

'It's beautiful. You forget: I never saw one before.'

'I keep thinking you must have. A woman in your position.'

'I don't have a position. What position do I have?'

'I'm thinking of the past.'

'That old thing.'

'Married to a banker, living the big international life.'

'Will you quit that?' She smiled at him. 'I'm not married to anyone. Anyway there are bankers and bankers.'

'He did himself pretty well, didn't he? Among other people.'

'You don't turn into any less of a bastard, do you?'

'You're not defending him, are you?'

'Defending him? No, I'm attacking you.'

'That's what I like,' Daniel said. 'I like them to come to me.'

'They will, they will. Keep it up and they will.' She stood staring into what remained of the night, deliberately motionless, the wind pushing back a cuff of hair from her forehead, like some third, impatient hand. Her own hands, long white fingers slightly crooked, rested on the moist rail. Suddenly she gave him her beautiful smile. He went and kissed her, a long kiss broken by the blast of the ship's hooter above their heads.

'Jesus!'

The steamer altered course, on a wrangling of bells from the bridge, and aimed for the island. Blades of light twitched from the lighthouse on the promontory. An absence of stars defined the headland.

'I'll go down and get the bags,' Daniel said. 'You stay and watch the show. There's still plenty of time, but then that's the best time to go.'

'Want me to come?'

'No, I told you.' He walked along the deck towards the entrance to the first class. He stopped, by a stack of spray-darkened deck-chairs, and watched her. Pride and a sort of angry fear worked in him, pride that she was his, fear that she was planning to make him hers. Her immobility, the clear shape of her face, in which even the shadows seemed something solid and reliable, the remoteness which so perfectly set off her humour and her beauty, gave him that feeling of good fortune, of triumph over others, without which no one could ever be quite enough.

He was about to step through the doorway into the first class when three or four bent figures came running, whinnying, on to the deck. Holding their middles, as if they were clutching stolen property or had been struck in the stomach, they ran along the deck, behind Nancy, and up to the tall gate at the end. Finding it locked, they began to climb the squared bars and hauled each other over the top under the slatted curve of a lifeboat. Daniel blinked, with a sort of deliberate astonishment, and actually had a foot on the raised storm-step of the first class when he was faced by a large, bearded man kicking and shouting as he tried to clear himself of the two white-jacketed stewards who had him by the arms.

'Will you let the fuck go of me? How can I get out if you won't goddam well let go of me?'

'What the hell's the trouble?'

'Trouble? I'll say there's trouble. So help me, I'm going to throw these two motherfuckers right in the ocean if they don't let go, do you hear me?'

'Enough,' Daniel said. '*Asta, asta ...*' He could always seem the master of a language, except to a master.

The two stewards may have understood, but they were not persuaded. They went on pumping the arms of the bearded young man.

'What's it all about, for God's sake?'

'It's about the fucking class system on this fucking stupid boat.'

The young man grunted and heaved but he had no lack of breath for speech. 'It's about the fucking overcrowding, that's what it's about, and the lousy insanitary conditions. This ship ought to be condemned, it ought to be forbidden to sail. It's goddam well not safe.'

'They third class, they try to trip in first class,' the senior steward said.

'I'm not trying the case,' Daniel said. 'I just—listen, we're virtually there now, it's hardly worth—'

'They're packed like fucking animals. It's goddam well inhuman. It's barbaric.'

'Well, trust the Greeks,' Daniel said. 'After all, they invented barbarism.'

'Why don't you go and fuck yourself?'

'I was just on my way,' Daniel said, 'but you're hindering my career—'

'ASS-HOLE!' With sudden energy, the bearded man threw off one of the stewards, who crashed back against a framed map of the Cyclades. Then frowning like someone trying to shake off a piece of Sellotape, he began to swing the other, a dignified man with grey hair, against the bulkhead.

'You're going to hurt that man—'

'Hurt him? I'm going to kill him—'

'And then you'll really be in trouble. Why don't you—?'

'What else can you expect in a fucking Fascist country? This is a fucking Fascist dictatorship, so what else can you expect?'

'Look,' Daniel said, 'if you don't pay the right fare, you could be in Utopia and someone would throw you out. You could be in Cuba.'

'Don't tell me who's in trouble. You're in trouble. Ask not for whom the bell tolls, my friend, because it tolls for thee.'

'Look, don't be a cunt,' Daniel said.

'What did you say? What did you say?'

'Did anyone make you come here? Who asked you to come here?'

'I wanted to come here. I felt like coming here and I goddam well came here and that's it. These people are in temporary possession, in strictly temporary possession and that is all. I mean, that is all.'

'That man is a steward,' Daniel said. 'And there have been stewards on this line ever since Pericles. What's more, his head is not designed for hammering rivets. Look, will you stop? I really think —'

'What makes you think I give a fuck what you really think?' The steward at last came unstuck from the end of the bearded man's arm and went flying across the lit interior before braking himself on the stair-head. 'I don't give a fuck what you think.'

Daniel smiled with a nervousness he detested. The bearded man was very big. For a second he towered over Daniel and then, abruptly, he fell at his feet. In his place was a short, powerful and even more furious man holding a wrench wrapped in an oily rag. His engineer's epaulets were twisted off his shoulders by the thickness of his upper arms and the swell of his chest. He wore green overalls, curled and cracked two-tone shoes and an officer's cap, off-white at the circumference, black at the domed centre. Daniel stepped past him as the two stewards returned and grabbed the arms of the fallen man. They bumped him, moaning horribly, against the storm-step like men driving a wheelbarrow against a kerb.

People were beginning to come upstairs with their luggage. Some yawned; other mustered an unnatural vivacity. It was a quarter to five in the morning. Daniel went down to the airless cabin and sat on the lower bunk. The stubble grated on the flat of his hand. Nancy's two white leather suitcases with their snug, flat locks stood under the porthole like a pair of well-groomed brothers waiting for the taxi to take them to a party. Daniel's scuffed, shapeless brown holdall (bought at Montgomery Ward, in Chicago, on a recce for an abandoned film) was still unzipped; idle pyjamas hung out. Daniel picked it up by the handles and jolted the contents until the pyjamas disappeared. His teeth were grey; he was about to uncap his creased toothpaste when he saw that the bristles of his toothbrush were crawling with beige insects.

The plastic shelf was loose. In the cavity where it joined the wall, dozens of the pale creatures were falling over each other. Daniel looked reproachfully at the two white cases, in one of which Nancy's doubtless immaculate toothbrush had already been stored, and held his own brush under the bronchial hot tap. The insects fell, wriggling, into the basin. He dropped the brush into the vomit-box by the bunk, squeezed some toothpaste on to his finger and rubbed it over his teeth and gums. When he combed his hair, it seemed as brittle as uncooked spaghetti.

He took all three cases through the narrow door at the same time, his own bag wedged under his armpit. More and more passengers were banging out of their cabins. The corridor reeked of urine and cheap powder. Despite the calm sea, a mountainous woman was contriving, with anguished effort, to be sick into a cardboard box. The stairs undulated with luggage. A German, festooned with cameras, was coming down against the tide. 'There's always one,' Daniel said to a man beside him. The German pressed on, smiled at the sideswipe Daniel managed to give him with one of Nancy's cases, and disappeared below. The German's cases were also of white leather and had snug, flat locks.

'Christ,' Daniel said, 'it's daylight.'

'It's daylight and it's beautiful and I've never been so happy in my life.'

The sea was the colour of pewter. Light from the east was cancelling the stars. Even the lighthouse had lost its sharpness. The island spread slowly round the ship. Shelves of grey and brown rock had tilted and slipped into the water which boiled and slopped at the impact. The door of the wireless room was open. The sound of morse suggested some secret commentary on the ship's simple manoeuvre.

'Imagine,' Daniel said, 'it could be giving the orders for our immediate arrest and we'd never know.'

'Imagine it isn't,' Nancy said, 'because it isn't.'

'Nothing could ever happen to you, could it? How do you manage to be so sure of yourself?'

'I keep my nose clean,' she said. She crossed her long legs in their off-white raw silk trousers and shook her head free of her green, peasant-style chiffon scarf. The new light settled around her golden head like a halo. 'O.K., buster?'

'Jesus, you're beautiful. It's not enough to make love to you, you need to be carefully peeled and eaten segment by segment. You need to be nibbled to death.'

The steamer eased off and churned the harbour to green cream.

'Look at that church,' Nancy said. 'Will you look at that church?'

'Will you *listen* to that church? If you could, you'd probably hear them praying we don't come ashore. The clergy reckon that the tourist revolution is going to undermine the morals of Christian Hellas. Which, of course, constitutes a serious infringement of their monopoly.'

'I heard about that,' Nancy said. 'Did you ever hear of anything so ridiculous?'

'To tell you the truth, I have a sneaking sympathy for it.'

'Hell,' she said, 'for once I thought we were on the same side of the barricade.'

'No, it really is a form of sublimated imperialism, when you come to think about it, tourism, isn't it? You get the same contempt for the locals, the same sense of grievance when anything goes wrong, the same unwillingness to learn the customs of the people or their language and the same conviction that the natives ought to love us and at the same time keep their places. It's all the same old European game, only with money instead of guns.'

'That's quite some difference you just slipped in there. Holding someone up with money and holding them up with a gun aren't exactly the same thing. Anyway, they need our money. They'd be lost without it.'

'In which case, you can hardly be surprised that they hate us.'

'They don't hate us at all,' Nancy said. 'I don't believe they hate us one little bit. Are you sure we're going to go off from this deck? It seems a long way down to the dock. You thought I was hateful the first time you met me.'

'That was just one of your many attractions. What good is bait without a hook? *Fevgome apo 'tho?*'

'*Kato*,' said the green-overalled officer. He was leaning against the rail, apparently satisfied that his engines had finished another journey.

'Shit. I might have guessed. They're going off from down below.'

'Oh that's all right,' Nancy said.

'You're not carrying the crown jewels,' Daniel said, 'or whatever you've got in here.'

The crowd, getting wind of Daniel's discovery, now began to jostle back through the first-class doorway. The officer showed no sign of supporting Daniel's claim to lead the way.

'The next person who pushes me is going to get done,' Daniel said. 'Provided he's small and unarmed.'

'In view of the fact that we're due to be met, why get trampled to death? Will you recognize him, do you think, your friend Mr Gavin?'

'He's a writer,' Daniel said. 'And writers are never friends. I never even met him, for Christ's sake. All I have are a few fragments of his uncollected correspondence for which, in due course, the University of Boston will no doubt appeal to my generosity. I shall recognize him if he looks like the back of his book jackets. Otherwise not.'

'He'll probably recognize you,' Nancy said.

'In view of his appetite for *belle donne*, you're a good deal more likely to catch his eye. Shit, that damned Kraut's made it first off the boat. Someone's actually *helping* him. A *policeman*.'

'I'll goddam get off this fucking boat wherever I want to get off it. What do you mean permission? I don't need anybody's permission.'

'My God,' Daniel said, 'another old friend. He's made a quick recovery.'

'Who's that?'

'That character. The bearded guy. Surely you saw what happened?'

'And no fucking Fascist pig is going to tell me any different.'

'No hotel, no get off.'

217

'Didn't you see what happened?'

'No.'

'I don't have a ticket to go any further. I have to get off. You can put me in gaol, but I am not going any further.'

'When he knocked down those stewards?'

'I must have been thinking about you.'

'I am not going back on that stinking, insanitary tub. You can do anything you like—'

'David, don't you think maybe it would be better—?'

'Muriel, will you do something for me? Will you shut the fuck up?'

'Maybe we should make our way off before we're killed in the rush coming back on board.'

'You listen to me, Mr Pig. I have a ticket here and I intend to stay here. I have some people I'm planning to meet here, *comprende*? And I intend to meet them, whether you like it or whether you don't. Not on the boat, not in Timbuctoo but right here, like I fixed. I have a letter here which I picked up in American Express in Athens—'

'No hotel, no stay.'

'I'll carry one of those,' Nancy said. 'Happily. The light one.'

'No, you go ahead like John the Baptist. We may need you to smile at the man or maybe they won't let us ashore either.'

'Muriel, what the fuck are you crying about? Will someone please get the stupid bitch out of here?'

'David, why won't you realize—?'

'Muriel, I've realized, I've realized. Suddenly I have absolutely and completely realized. Like for good this time.'

'They are just simply not going to let us land without a hotel.'

'I feel as if you're my hotel, Muriel. You're ugly, you're expensive and you give lousy service. For one small, dark, smelly piece of accommodation your price is entirely too high.'

'It is their country.'

'Their country? Crap it's their country. Since when did any country belong to a collection of jerky janitors in uniform with guns instead of balls? Their country? Shit, it's their country.

218

Countries belong to the people, for Christ's sake, not to some set of jerky janitors.'

'David, it just isn't going to work. You know it isn't going to work.'

'Do you want me to slap you? Is that what you want me to do, slap you?'

'We may as well try and get by, because—'

'Because I will. I will, very happily, if that's what you want. I'll slap you right into the water.'

'Look, excuse us—'

'Where are you staying, please, on Iskios?'

'We have a friend meeting us. Mr Robert Gavin.'

'You have a hotel reservation?'

'No, I said, our friend Mr Gavin is meeting us. We're going to stay with him. Mr Gavin, the English writer. He's lived here for some time, I believe, and—'

'You must have a hotel reservation, I am sorry, or you cannot land on Iskios.'

'You're a bunch of fucking cowards, the whole crummy collection of you. A bunch of fucking cowards.'

'David, I wish I knew what you were trying to prove—'

'I don't have to try and prove a goddam thing, least of all to you. As far as I'm concerned, it's proved right now. You and I are through, but through. Now split, willya, vamoose, git.'

'We are going to be guests of Mr Gavin in his house.'

'If I just knew what I'd done to make you so hateful—'

'Muriel, for once in your overweight life, crying is not going to help. Mommy is not going to come. Mommy is in Peoria. One of these days you're going to have to grow up and so why not make it today? Make today like your big day.'

'I daresay he's actually waiting for us if you'd just let us—we've had a long journey. No one told us—'

'You've been just as hateful as you know how to be ever since we left Amsterdam. You were fine in Amsterdam. You were even fine in Wiesbaden. I didn't want to come to Greece. You were the one who wanted to come to Greece.'

'Uncouple, Muriel. Uncouple. Beat it. Go open your stubby little legs to some other lucky fellow. Sometimes even something for nothing can seem like a bad deal. I am therefore exercising my right to check out before noon, without obligation. Go be somebody else's room service.'

'You bastard, you bastard.'

'Oh now, who's this? Who's this? Heinrich Himmler? Is this Heinrich Himmler?'

'Perhaps we'll get some sense out of this chap,' Daniel said.

'I love you and you have to go and humiliate me in front of everyone. Why? What've I done?'

'I don't know you. I don't know who you are. And please, I don't want to get involved, I really don't.'

'I've never been able to talk to a woman like that. It's really quite a knack.'

'You aren't even a *natural* bastard,' Nancy said.

'Surely you mean, you aren't even a natural *bastard*?'

'My lover the Director!'

'I am sorry. Mr Gavin is not here. No one has seen him.'

'Here we are back among the Sophists,' Daniel said. 'I really can't believe that. If no one has seen him, someone soon will. He invited us to come. He does live on Iskios, doesn't he? He's lived here for years.'

'You think you're so damned fantastic in the sack, well I want you to know you're not all that fantastic. You're by no means all that fantastic.'

'Muriel, that fat little ass has already seen more action than it ever had any right to expect. Why not quit while you're ahead?'

'The obvious thing is to send a message to his house. Maybe he didn't get my telegram, but I can't do anything if you won't even let me on to the dock.'

'You must have a hotel reservation. It's the rule.'

'And we're the exceptions, surely you can see that?'

'O.K., I'll go back on the boat. I'll go back on the boat. I won't contaminate your shitty little bourgeois paradise. Only the

day will come. The day will come, and when it does, my friend –'
The bearded man managed to make going aboard seem a struggle,
even though his escort was going in the same direction he was.
'Ask not for whom the bell tolls.'
The steamer blew a blast on its hooter. 'Or for whom the hooter
hoots.' The Master was looking down, his cap at a Beatty tilt,
at the confusion on the quayside. Two bullocks were being hustled
aboard, their tails wrenched to one side by their drovers. Daniel,
mindful that fifth-century Athens was said to have remained
democratic because of the preponderance of sailors in its population,
threw the Captain a conniving glance. Was he not Cimon's
heir? The Master shouted abuse, his two fists rigid in front of him as
if shaking invisible irons. Nancy sat on a fluted bollard and looked
at herself in the little mirror she took from her white P.V.C.
shoulder bag.
'I have an invitation actually on me,' Daniel said, in a public
tone, 'from Mr Gavin. You can read it.' The soft-spoken official
in the rimless glasses took the letter; Daniel derived a silly pleasure
from his pretence to read it. 'My – my – my fiancée and I would
hardly have come all this way if we weren't expected. What
exactly do you expect us to do?'
'No one may land without a reservation. That is the ruling of the
Tourist Board.'
'In that case, I should like to talk to the Head of the Board.'
'The Head of the Board is in Athens.'
'In that case the Head here.'
'You are speaking to him.'
'Your name please.'
'And I have given my ruling.'
'This is too fucking stupid for words. We've been travelling for
two days.'
'Fuck you and fuck your island and fuck your government and
fuck your literature and fuck your landscape and fuck your Parthenon
and fuck your goddamned Greek light and your *ligo nero* and all the
goddam crap that goes with it.' The bearded man was leaning
over from the top deck of the steamer.

'If you'd just allow me to make a few inquiries,' Daniel said. 'Or maybe you could make them yourself.'

'And Long Live the Revolution. Muriel, for the last time, I told you to go away. I told you to beat it. Now beat it. *Exo*, for God's sake. *Exo*. Uncouple, can't you?'

'If it'll help to clear things up, I'm perfectly willing, although it's absolutely ridiculous, to take a room somewhere in the village while we clear this up. Or I'll leave a deposit, if that'll help, in cash. Only we're very tired. My fiancée—'

'There's a man here,' Nancy said, 'who says he can help us.' She had been talking over the guard-rails to some nodding Greeks whose grasp of English seemed to improve when Nancy was the speaker. 'He says his name is Dmitri.'

'Dmitri Bracheotis. Mr Gavin live on the other side of the island, beyond the *chora*, on Kalamaki Beach. I take you there. I work for Mr Gavin many times.'

'*Oreo*,' Daniel said. 'Fine, if you could just persuade them to let us through.' A few words from their new friend, a short thickset man with a rolling limp, persuaded the Athenian to widen the gap in the steel hurdles. Nancy strolled through the crowd with the air of someone who knew exactly where she was going. Daniel made to take the cases. Dmitri had already lifted them and looked round for more.

Nancy found an empty table at a crowded café. Though it was not yet six o'clock, the arrival of the steamer had brought the harbour to life. Those who had embarked left no noticeable gap. The bullocks had now been run aboard; the ship's cables were being freed from the marble thumbs which braced them to the quay.

'Coffee? Orange? Lemon? What you like?' Bracheotis' face was composed for pain; his leg was thickened with arthritis. He leaned his knotty stick against a kiosk selling chocolate and postcards and old newspapers. The smile he turned on them drove wedges of flesh in unaccustomed directions.

'What I'd really like,' Daniel said, 'is to get on over to Mr Gavin's. What about you, Nance?'

'Coffee would be wonderful.'

Dmitri grinned at Daniel's frown and limped into the café, clattering his stick for attention. 'Congratulations,' Daniel said.

'For – ?'

'Getting us through customs. If it weren't for you, we might still be in bond. Not that I'm a hundred per cent sold on our new friend.'

'A hundred per cent is an awful lot,' Nancy said. 'I have friends I'm not even ten per cent sold on. What matters is, will he get us to where we want to go?'

'I'm where I want to be right now.'

'The nights can be very cold,' Nancy said, 'sitting at café tables.' She leaned forward in charming challenge. 'And I don't like that.'

The steamer had fallen away from the quay and stood ready to charge the unseen gap beyond the white domes and tiered belfry of the church. It gave two blasts on its hooter and then seemed to slide directly, without a sound, into the grey rocks.

'End of reel one,' Daniel said.

'I may go out of my mind,' Daniel said.

'You won't.'

'Do you realize it's now half past eight? Nearly twenty-five to nine. We've been sitting here for over two *hours*. Where the hell has he gone now?'

'He'll be back.'

'Do you have to be so patient? I don't think Dmitri whatever-his-name-is even knows Gavin.'

'Have another yoghurt,' Nancy said. 'They're the best ever. He knows him.'

'If his place is on a beach, maybe we could take a boat round. There doesn't seem to be any shortage.'

'Remember Ulysses,' Nancy said. 'Boat trips can take longer than you think in these waters.'

'Ah but Penelope's with me this time. Well, Circe anyway. One of those characters. I always call him Odysseus.'

'*Ta zoa erchonte amesos*,' Dmitri said.

'I told you he'd be back.'

'What the hell do we need donkeys for?'

'For the *kiria*,' Dmitri said.

'Donkeys are fun!' Nancy stood up and smoothed her white trousers. Daniel hurried into the café to pay for the drinks and the yoghurt. The wrinkled widow smiled and pointed at Dmitri: he had paid already. Dmitri grinned and limped away across the square with the luggage. 'Don't worry,' Daniel said, 'we'll pay in the long run.'

'I'm not going to worry about a thing.'

The donkeys were tethered under a rust-scabbed tin sign bidding visitors WELKOM TO ISKIOS. The attractions of the island were THE TUMB OF HOMER—THE BIG SANDY BEACH KALAMAKI— THE BIG SANDY BEACH TRIS PETRES—THE MONASTERY OF MELISSA—AND THE MOUNTAIN WALKS. Tourists Informations were available in the house of the Mayor.

The penis of Nancy's donkey reached almost to the ground, but after a few whacks from Dmitri it retracted. Daniel's donkey was a mule. Dmitri signalled him on to a low wall in order to board, but the animal recoiled each time he tried to mount. Dmitri denounced it ostentatiously and whacked it into line. When Daniel at last scrambled up, the mule began to rotate, rolling its eyes and snapping at his legs. Dmitri banged it, left and right, and it steadied, whisking its tail. Meanwhile Nancy was installed on her small, grey donkey. She sat with her feet up on the front of the saddle, her behind against the wooden block at the back, hands in her lap. Despite its phallic display, her donkey blinked with gelded docility. Daniel had sat himself side-saddle, in the Greek fashion; Dmitri motioned that he should sit astride. Daniel pretended not to understand and then simply shook his head, but Dmitri kept twisting his hand in mid-air until he was forced to obey.

'Are you actually going to ride like that?' Daniel said.

'Sure. Why not?'

'Our friend obviously has more faith in your sense of balance than he has in mine.'

'You have further to fall,' Nancy said.

'And higher to climb. These saddles are more like luggage racks. I'm damned if I see why we need three animals. Never mind, *coraggio*, we shall soon be inspecting the tumb of Homer. How many English villages do you think could put up a notice in Greek?'

Dmitri was lashing the suitcases to a second, twitching donkey. He seemed able to leave a case temporarily floating in mid-air while he fetched a loop of rope under it. He muttered continually, a suspicious sergeant-major, vigilant for mutiny. Finally he thumped each of the animals, although they had already started along the dusty road, scrambled on to the extreme rump of the baggage donkey and set about rolling a cigarette.

'You remember those two little Cycladic figures in the National Museum, the ones in the narrow case at the end of the long gallery? They came from here.'

'I know,' Nancy said.

'I'm sure there must be others. There must be people digging all the time.'

'Be terrific to get one really from here. Or find one ourselves.'

'Not a chance. On the other hand, I found you, didn't I?'

'I have legs,' Nancy said. 'From where I sit, *I* found *you*.'

'Don't think I haven't noticed. The legs, I mean. We must ask around. It's not like robbing a church or anything. There's more stuff than anyone will ever have time to dig up. And more forgeries too, I must say.'

'*Sas aresoone ta palea pragmata?*' Dmitri licked his cigarette and fished for his lighter. 'You like old things?'

'He understands bloody good English, this bloke. Obviously I like them, otherwise we wouldn't be in Greece.'

Dmitri made no answer. He lit his cigarette from a gas lighter and drummed his heels on the donkey's pretty hips. The road to the village wound round to make a thick ziggurat of the hill above them. They soon branched off, however, by a gleaming war memorial of imported grey stone, and took a narrower track between stone walls. As the slope steepened, it was broken by broad white-edged steps; Dmitri slipped off the little donkey and limped after them, cadging a mild lift from its tail.

The island flattened out below them. The sea was the colour of damsons. In the distance, the ghosts of other islands lifted into view and then spread back into the sea. The village came more steeply at them; its deep-socketed windows stared down like black, unseeing eyes. The hill seemed to twist and totter as the animals veered from side to side, making the gradient more shallow, but more dizzy, with their cunning. Daniel's mule stopped before a tall step and then lurched suddenly at it. Though they were climbing, it felt as though he were going over a series of precipices. At each, the village leaned and swayed.

A man with a handlebar moustache, wearing a panama hat festooned with peanuts, a gondolier's shirt and striped bathing trunks, came bustling down the path towards them on a pair of muscular bow-legs. He was swinging his arms and humming to himself. When he saw Dmitri he raised his hand and grinned. '*Yasoo, Dmitri. Kala?*' He was followed by a bespectacled pink woman, taller than himself, in a pink dress and a pink hat. He smiled at Daniel and Nancy, as though the mere sight of them with Dmitri was already an introduction. He managed somehow to have a whispered conversation with Dmitri without ever shortening his pace.

'That's where we ought to go.' Daniel pointed to the island alongside Iskios. It seemed no more than a good swim away. Grey, unmarked sides rose to where a few houses highlighted the summit. 'I don't suppose they've ever seen a white man.'

'Agoria,' Dmitri said.

'Men only,' Daniel said. '*Agori* means male.'

'Maybe we should go,' Nancy said.

They skirted an elaborate, empty playground, full of bright equipment coated with the fawn dust of the hillside. Dmitri whacked the mule; the white buildings fell forward once more. At last they came level with a white and gold church at the entrance of the village. It reminded Daniel of one of those models which suppliants hold out in their cupped hands in pictures commemorating the dedication of churches. It destroyed all conventional sense of scale, appearing at once palatial and diminutive, even when they passed under its towers. The stiff path to its door was as impassable as the sharp triangle that stands for distance in some naive perspective.

They entered a funnel of white walls. Although they continued to climb, Daniel had a sense of falling. The main street was wide enough for a trail of donkeys balanced with paniers of sand to pass them on its way down, but the sides seemed to close tighter and tighter. As the village thickened above them, in tiers of heat and shade, they could have been plunging into the heart of the hillside. Nancy rode comfortably, her chin on her knees, with plenty of time to look right and left along the alleys on either side. Whitewashed steps, eroded by the footsteps and the constant brushing of their owners, cheesed into the sides of swelling walls and led the eye up to geranium-decked terraces or brilliant green gates and doorways. Nancy held her sandals in her hand. Her body nodded in agreement with her mount. When they reached the square, shining like a brilliantly lit room at the end of the shaded corridor along which they had come, Daniel jumped down to massage the dents out of his legs. Nancy stayed on until Dmitri took her hand. He made them sit at the dingiest of the cafés. Black bent-cane chairs and lame tables fronted a grey room void of all furniture except an old wooden ice box and a baize-covered table, recessed for cards, where old men in Turkish caps and baggy pants were at play. At the next café, a few paces away, the Priest, in a faded blue cassock and high-crowned black hat, stood talking to a Corporal of Police and another man, in a black suit and a stiff collar, whose thick briefcase leaned against a leg of his chair. The Priest had a bold, reddish beard and a chapped, vinous complexion. He prodded the flagstones with a long staff, reinforcing his point with the annihilation of ants. He found time to offer Nancy an impersonal, but flattering benediction. She returned him one of her dazzling, generous smiles. Daniel twisted in his seat and frowned at the old man who had shuffled out to take their order.

'Now what?' he said to Dmitri.

'Sit down, relax, have a drink. I will go and find the man who works for Mr Gavin.'

'I thought you worked for Mr Gavin.'

'The man who oversees his property. Please, sit down.'

'We don't really want to sit down. We want to get out to Kalamaki as soon as we can.'

'Sit.'

Dmitri tethered the animals to the railings in front of a small, barrel-vaulted church built on a platform just below the level of the square. Eucalyptus trees forked from the narrow surround of rammed earth and put up a spiky, inconclusive shade. From his doorway, under a blue and white striped pole, the barber watched them, razor in hand.

Nancy walked across the square. She looked at no one; everyone looked at her. She stood herself in front of a wire cage of postcards which creaked as she turned it. Two young men in very short shorts and leather pork-pie hats came racing out of the darkness of the street behind her and found themselves in sudden need of postcards. Nancy strolled back across the square, sharing with Daniel a joke he had not heard, and sat side-saddle on the chair next to him.

'I must write to the children. Trouble being I never know what to say. I wish I had your fluency.'

'Fluency!'

'You tell marvellous stories, you know very well you do. I wish you'd write to them. They'd much sooner hear from you.'

'Unfortunately they're not my children. Tell them from me Poseidon was in a good mood.'

'I'll never forget the story you told them in the car that first weekend we went down to see those friends of yours.'

'Bernard and Sylvia. That was a pretty good disaster.'

'Only because she was sick.'

'She was only sick because it was a disaster.'

'You should have known better.'

'Than what?'

'Than take another woman down there. You might have known

she'd put something out. As it couldn't be me, it had to be her back. She hated you having someone.'

'Sylvia? I don't believe a word of it. She's always had her knife in me.'

'Maybe that's because you never had yours in her.'

'You mustn't say things like that! That's a male fantasy, sex as assault. You don't go along with that, do you? Cathie Connolly would have you struck off the female register, *instanter*.'

'Has she really been the mistress of a Cabinet Minister?'

'Cathie? Who told you that? Like for instance what Cabinet Minister? Or the *enemy* of what Cabinet Minister?'

'Do you like her things?'

'I've never been privileged.'

'Her *books*.'

'Are no privilege at all.'

'I don't know so much. She has some insight.'

'You mean she looks at herself a lot. She's like Mary Magdalen trying to play the virgin.'

'What makes you so cynical?'

'A cue for the story of my life, which I shall resist. Which I have resolved to resist. Only Field-Marshal Montgomery sells his serial rights twice over. Listen, I wanted to ask you something.'

'Well?'

'Will you marry me?'

She put in the kisses at the bottom of her postcard. 'Why do you ask? Are you beginning to have doubts?'

'You never actually signed anything.'

She took his hand and turned it palm upwards on the table in front of her and marked it with a large biro cross. 'O.K.?'

'Nancy.'

'I think of us as married already,' she said.

'I know,' Daniel said, 'that's the thing. We're not. You know, this sonofabitch is going to keep us sitting here all day. I'll bet you anything you like it's no distance whatever to where Gavin lives. There must be a thousand people around here who know the way to Kalamaki. What do you say we step it out?'

229

'What about the bags?'

'Two more coffees,' Daniel said.

'Excuse me, you have to forgive me, I know I'm interrupting, but I just had to ask you something. Did you get those pants here?'

'No, as a matter of fact, I didn't,' Nancy said. 'They come from Firenze.'

'Oh wow because someone just told me there's a man here makes the best pants in Europe and when I saw yours—'

'I always thought he was on Mykonos,' Daniel said.

'That's another one, they have one here too now apparently. They say he's fabulous. Well, thanks and sorry if I ...'

'Can she really believe it matters who makes her pants? It's the people who made her legs she ought to be looking for. With a hatchet. Aren't women pathetic?'

Dmitri was standing with another man at the top of the shadowed street. A Sergeant of Police, judging his beads, had stopped to talk to the barber. The Priest was climbing the steps to his house, tolling his slow weight, step by step, up the handrail. Further down the hill, at the corner from which Daniel had first seen the square, a single slim man, in faintly tinted glasses, was watching the scene from under the marble balcony of an old Venetian merchant's house. He wore a well-cut suit and held a grey newspaper in a slim, almost fleshless hand: *Le Monde*. His lips, though quite pale and narrow, had a very precise definition. They twitched like those of a man who, having thought of a witty remark, hesitated to waste it on the present company.

'What would you say, secret policeman?'

'Who? Oh. Do you think so? Cycladic figure!'

'Right. The mouth.'

'Do they have mouths?'

'And newspapers. Of course. The remoteness, that's the real thing. Probably the postman, but I don't really think so. He's somebody all right.'

'You are Mr and Mrs Meyer? I am Mr Gavin's overseer. My name is Stelio Varis. I am so sorry there has been this difficulty.

I will take you right away to the house. On the way I can explain to you—'

'Oh that's all right,' Daniel said. He was fumbling with the roll of notes in the pocket of his blue linen jacket. Would fifty drachmae be enough for Dmitri, or would it have to be a hundred? Stelio Varis wore khaki shorts and shirt and a cotton cap with elastic at the back and a long stiff peak, like a racing cyclist. He had a clipped, untypical moustache. He might have passed for a minor Colonial Administrator.

Daniel offered Dmitri fifty drachmae. The Greek raised his eyes in ritual refusal. Daniel offered the money again. One hand and the eyes went up once more. '*Poso thelete?* How much do you want?'

'Nothing.'

'Nothing is too much.'

'Nothing.'

Daniel sighed and doubled his offer, Dmitri doubled his refusal: both hands came up. Stelio Varis switched his leg with a eucalyptus twig and smiled, as if this were a conversation in a language he did not pretend to speak. Daniel put away his money and they started for Kalamaki. They had not seen the last of Dmitri: the baggage donkey followed Daniel and Dmitri followed the donkey. A butcher, quite young and handsome, with two gold teeth, smiled at Nancy from his doorway as if they were old friends. She smiled back at him; Daniel frowned into the fly-dark shop.

As they reached the end of the long alley which twisted through the village, they were forced to stop. Daniel was on tiptoe, trying to see the reason for the hold-up, when he felt a hand on his back, firm and confident. Could it be Gavin? It was the Priest, still in his patched cassock, but now carrying a long shepherd's crook. For a moment, Daniel imagined that he had come with a message, but he simply wanted to get past. The villagers seemed a whole size smaller than the Priest, like minor figures in an icon. He was able to adjust his expression and the hang of his cassock before falling in, with perfect timing, behind the coffin which now appeared from the left and was carried, above the heads of the bearers, away towards a clanging bell in the distance. The lid was open, a wizened body inside. It seemed to Daniel that the usual laws of optics had been waived. The corpse was at once borne away and presented to him in extreme close up, tilted as if a head waiter were displaying a dish before its dissection. It was an old woman. Her hair fell over her forehead and her shroud was twisted. The crowd was drawn after her and soon drained away. Stelio Varis went into a cavernous shop and came out with a basket, covered with muslin.

They went on towards the slaughterhouse. Empty hooks hung over scrubbed shadows of blood. Opposite it, broad steps went up to a saddle of ground on which stood several windmills. On two of them, the sails were set and turning slowly. Others were bald of thatch; their spokes lacked canvas. Dmitri was leaning on the rump of Nancy's donkey with both hands, forcing him past the sparking blue doorway of the local Hephaestus with his oxy-acetylene burner. When Nancy reached the steps, she slipped off her donkey and went springing up towards the windmills. Daniel, decisively on foot, was already past and her empty donkey blocked him from following her. Up ahead, he could see the pitted wall of the cemetery. From behind it came the keening of mourners and the thin tinkle of incense-bearers, overlaid by the mindless grating of crickets. Nancy reappeared as they rounded the corner, coming out of one of the derelict windmills. Chickens had gathered at her feet. Even they earned her smile. She waved and came nimbly down through the rocks and rubbish. 'What's this, is this the cemetery?'

He looked up at the black crosses. 'Well, I hope it's not the hospital.'

They rejoined the dusty main road which had taken a more circuitous route around the hillside. Below the junction, there was a nightclub, the Poseidon, secluded in split bamboo. A picture of the earth-shaker, his beard full of crabs and lobsters, was painted on the white gatepost. The road went past a church no bigger than a four-poster bed, with a white portico, and then a shuttered house next to a chaff-silted threshing floor, and soon they were over the ridge and looking down into Kalamaki. The beach was a shallow crescent, half a mile long. A rocky cape closed the far end. Behind the sand, stone walls defined a geography of fields, their wild flowers stiffened by the summer heat, grass fading to fawn, vines huddled like green victims by their black stakes. A pebbled river bed spread into a dense pubis of low bush. The fields grew steeper and broke up into terraces which yielded to bald hillside, brown at the base, grey and silver and shining towards the peak, where beehives stood on narrow ledges. White houses, vines trellised before them, stood about the valley in puddles of shade. The sun was burning the blue sky to transparency.

Stelio branched off to the right down a deep incline. They followed a contour about a hundred feet above the sea. Dark bruises showed the path of the rocks beneath the bay. Beyond the far headland, the pale profiles of more islands teased the eye. They came to a gate propped shut with large, flat stones, which Stelio pushed aside with his boot.

'This must be it,' Daniel said.

A barbed wire fence ran on down to the cliff's edge. The ground was rough. Daniel stopped to shake pebbles out of his desert boot. Dmitri limped past. The caravan climbed the slope ahead of Daniel and vanished. He was alone. He retied his shoes and ambled down towards the cliff. He could see into a private cove of sea adjacent to the bay. A shifting white iridescence, just beneath the surface of the loose water, made him squint for a clearer view. He stood there, listening to the silence, wondering whether he was happy, and then turned and chased the others.

As he climbed the long slope, a winged horse rose out of the blue and breasted the sky. It was as white as the house below it. Its long throat and hooked head stretched for something above and beyond Daniel. It stood by a green gate on a coffin-shaped base at the corner of the walls surrounding the house. Many steps led up and down, through arches and under terraces, up to roofs and down to cellar doors. Confused by the cross-hatching of stairways up and down, Daniel could hardly distinguish where the actual buildings were. Paved platforms overlooked the sea. More statues were on

233

show beyond the house which, as Daniel watched, slowly revealed itself, like a photographic plate developing a new dimension of detail.

The padlock on the green gate was not rusted, but it showed no sign of having been opened recently. Was there another way in? Daniel vaulted the gate into a paved courtyard; flagstones went between low beds of succulent greenery. A stairway without a balustrade took him up to a barrel-vaulted hall. On the terrace outside, whitewashed benches flanked a tiled table; glossy magazines, a pair of Japanese binoculars, fumed Venetian glasses and a jug of half-finished orange juice formed a casual still-life. Daniel raised the clawed knocker and let it drop. The door was not latched; the clap of the knocker budged it.

Narrow windows allowed slices of brilliance into the tiled room. Marble figures were mounted on low pedestals. The air was cool and faintly perfumed. The change of light and his own state of mind made Daniel see the place in a series of cuts: the crouching woman, the headless man, the black roof-tree, the emperor's head, the locked door, the sphinx, the black and white tiles, the Aphrodite.

'Yes?'

The accent was American, but Daniel was so certain that it was Robert Gavin (perhaps, like Auden, he had acquired a transatlantic accent) that his ear and his eye tried to force the sensations they received into his likeness. The speaker was short, close-cropped, and dressed in a T-shirt stretched across the stomach, tartan Bermuda shorts and basket-ball sneakers. With him, in Daniel's perplexed perceptions, wrestled the image of the Robert Gavin he had expected, a tall, grey-haired, elegant Englishman. The two figures fought for a moment in the gash of light from the open door before the stranger detached himself and stood alone.

'How do you do? I'm Daniel Meyer.'

'I'm glad to know you.'

'Forgive me, but is Mr Gavin at home?'

'I really don't know. That's something I really can't tell you. It might be an idea to try his house.'

'Oh Jesus,' Daniel said.

'Listen, forget it. You're not the first person to walk in here like this. Maybe I should put up a sign, "Not Bob Gavin's", think I should? Daniel Meyer. Would that make you the film director?'

'I direct films.'

'I'll say you do. *Split*? Everybody's story.'

'That's not what the Box Office said.'

'Would you believe me if I said I saw it four times?'

'I'd try. I promise you I'd try.'

'Four times. One of the great movies; I'm serious. How about some coffee or some juice now you're here?' He was not much over five feet six inches tall, but his arms and legs seemed curved; Daniel felt that he would be a big man, if he would only straighten. The hand he now held out was small, and there were several rings on it, but his grip was a challenge.

'I'd love to,' Daniel said, 'but we've only just arrived and I think my – my girl will be wanting to know where I am – we kind of lost contact –'

'I understand. Why don't you both come by, later in the day? Say five, five thirty. Bob's place isn't more than ten minutes away. Come on over then. I'm Larry Pleasure.'

'You have some pretty nice things here.'

'I always did like to live with beautiful things.'

'You didn't find these here?'

'Most of them come from Asia Minor. I ship more things in than I buy here. The Greek Government can be very sticky over antiquities. I always try to do everything the right way, on the up and up, always did. *Tacktikah*.'

'Any Cycladic figures ever come your way?'

'I'm mainly a Hellenistic man. Cycladic is a rough market. They're appreciating very fast, but you have to know what you're doing. Personally, anyway, I'm not greedy. I play the orthodox market. I buy to keep. You're a Cycladic man, are you? Because I do have a couple.'

'I have this sort of dream,' Daniel said, 'of finding one sticking out of the sand.'

235

'Well, be careful how you pull it out. It could just blow your head off.'

'In that case I shan't bother. No, I just wondered whether there was any local stuff knocking about.'

'Want me to ask around?'

'If you could. Discreetly.'

'That's the only way I know. I'm not about to upset anybody. Meantime, don't for heaven's sake buy anything without talking to me. Some of the shopkeepers have gotten very clever in the last couple of seasons, ever since the cruises started putting in here. Trust no one, my friend, and you won't have anyone to curse, old Greek proverb. How long are you staying?'

'That depends. Maybe a couple of weeks, maybe less, maybe more. Do you know a character called Bracheotis, is that his name?'

'I know Dmitri,' Larry Pleasure said. 'I know Dmitri. Has he gotten on to you already?'

'Without him we'd still be sitting on Ellis Island. They wouldn't have let us land, if he hadn't—'

'He's a cunning old so and so, Dmitri. He's O.K. if you know how to handle him.'

'Only I don't,' Daniel said.

'Well, don't let him treat you like you were one of his donkeys. Don't let him lead you by the nose. You're going to stay with Bob? Do you know him well?'

'We've corresponded, that's all. Is it far from here?'

'Ten minutes. Less. I'll show you the way. You can cut through my place now you're here. You'll like him. A scholar and a gentleman. He lives right down on the point. I'm high on the hog up here, that's what Bob says. Oh he's an original, Bob. A real original. And does he love this island! The real old-style Britisher. I like him.' Pleasure was leading the way down the steps and along an arcaded walkway into another courtyard. Water surged fatly from a low marble fountain set in the middle of a wide, circular table. Rolls of split bamboo, lashed to the skeleton of a trellis, promised shade. They went through an arch into another walkway.

'Hi. How are you this morning?'

236

Below them, a couple carrying orange and blue towels were going down long steps towards the sea. They turned and mouthed a reply, but no sound came. The man was grey-haired but slim, with skin the colour of oiled steel. He had a spear-gun under his arm, flippers and goggles over his wrist. The girl was blonde and young and seemed shy. She turned away quickly.

'You really built yourself a Pleasure Dome here,' Daniel said. 'Did you design it yourself?'

'I gave the architect a whole raft of ideas and left it to him to come up with what I wanted.'

'You were the producer,' Daniel said.

'I was the producer.'

'Did you ever have anything to do with movies?'

'Nearly, but never quite. In other words, to my sincere regret, no.'

'It's never too late.'

'It's always too late, Meyer. You know that.' He looked at Daniel with wan, appealing eyes. Then his expression hardened, before breaking into a smile. He had even, pearly teeth set in a neat red jewel box of a mouth. He touched Daniel, in a sort of proprietary apology, and went on through a Moorish arch before turning so abruptly down a stairway cut in the side of the rock that Daniel was left on the edge of a precipice. Below him was a sort of inverted acropolis; Larry Pleasure's citadel was below the skyline.

Daniel said: 'My God, did you blast this out, or what?'

'Mostly My God,' Larry Pleasure said. 'My guess is this was a by-product of the great earthquake that put an end to the Minoan empire. The same one that finished Thera, because Thera was a pretty important island at one time, you know.'

'I saw the reports,' Daniel said. 'Mikros Knossos, you've got here, I must say. It's fantastic.'

'I wanted to buy that place one time. Knossos. I want to buy it. Or at least lease it. Have you ever been to India?'

'It was in Crete last time I heard.'

'Have you ever heard of the Lake Palace Hotel in Udaipur? Because that's what Knossos could have been. I could have made

237

that place into one of the seven wonders of the world, if they'd let me. Well, that's all in the past, like everything else.'

'It's getting hot. Don't you boil down here?'

Larry Pleasure held open the perspex door of the nearest building. They went through a cooled marble hall into a sitting-room furnished with low settles. Under the windows, wedges of white-washed cement were covered with foam rubber and coloured cushions. A lustrous crimson Rothko hung over the fireplace above a pair of wickerwork lobster pots filled with flotsam. The next room was furnished at floor level with Moorish divans and low brass tables on gate-legged stands. Plaster tablets of Arabic writing were bracketed to the walls. A pair of cedar-wood doors gave on to the hub of the building, a patio paved in alternate squares of pink and black marble and hung with flowers in white Tunisian cages and shrubs in fibreglass tubs; two fig trees grew out of breaches in the marble. In the centre was a small, deep swimming-pool. Double doors stood in the centre of each wall.

'Well, here we are in Los Angeles,' Daniel said.

'Oh no, this isn't L.A.,' Larry Pleasure said. 'Give me some credit.'

'I can't see you needing it,' Daniel said. 'It's the most fantastic short cut I ever took in my whole life.'

'Tell your girl to bring her swimsuit tonight, if she feels like a plunge. And if she likes to wear a swimsuit.'

'It certainly looks very inviting.' Daniel started through the next set of doors.

'It is,' Larry Pleasure said, 'and you're invited.'

The end of the passage gleamed like a silver furnace.

'Do you like sports?' Larry Pleasure opened a cedar-wood door. He pressed a switch and blackness bloomed into a squash court, the walls bruised by lozenge-shaped impact marks. 'There was a flaw in the rock, so —'

'I imagine you're pretty good,' Daniel said.

'I always liked games. I always liked to keep in shape.' Larry walked on towards the mouth of the silver furnace: a sash of light had been reflected on the perspex end of the corridor from the rock wall outside. When Daniel stepped into the open, heat struck like a brand. 'All you do now is, you go up the steps, on past Cerberus and Bob's place is the other side of the hill, through the olives; it's hard to miss.'

'Well, thanks a lot.'

'Pleasure. See you tonight. And I hope you find him.'

'Oh I will,' Daniel said.

There was a niche half-way up the steps; water burbled in a marble mortar. Daniel looked down and saw Larry still in the doorway, his forehead corrugated, eyebrows drawn together, and forced himself past the tempting water. At last a sea breeze cuffed his shoulders and he could breathe what seemed, by contrast, cool free air.

Up beyond the sunken palace, sections of paved ground alternated with tufts of burnt and straggly grass; then came the skull of a grey building, rods rusting in concrete, unglassed windows facing the sea. From the edge of the terrace, it was like looking into a well. The water was a black disc. On it floated a 72-foot Bermuda motor cruiser, an arrowhead of blond wood and winking chromium. The muscular grey-haired man was crouching over a hatch in the stern. A narrow gangplank with a single orange rope rail made a flat ladder to the shore. Next to the cruiser was a Chriscraft, a scoop of blue fibreglass, its engine cocked out of the water.

Rounding the unfinished building, Daniel saw the blonde girl's head and shoulders slip away along the clifftop. He stopped, looked and saw another white sculpture, unmistakably Cerberus, three heads with lolling white tongues. Passing a pit half-filled with tin cans, he climbed the hill beyond the gate and soon saw the roof of another house set in an olive grove further down the point.

As Daniel approached, he heard laughter: Nancy and a man. He smiled at the sound and stepped, without hurrying, over the octopus roots of the olive trees. Lizards darted. The house stood on two terraces overlooking Agoria, the island they had seen from the road. Every rock and bush on it was as unnervingly clear as the petals of crust on a loaf painted by Dali. On the far horizon, the double humps of another, distant island reminded Daniel of a couple of coats thrown down for goals. A steamer heading back for Iskios was cutting a long groove which healed slowly behind it.

The shoulders of Robert Gavin's house were turned away from Daniel. He could see the left half of Dmitri's body, leaning against the corner of the house by the stamping donkeys, casual and insolent. Daniel rounded Dmitri, frowning, but ready to smile if Gavin was on the terrace. An open door led into a big room with a double bed under wide, shuttered windows. The terrace was pierced by two other green doors, both closed. Whitened steps led down round an olive tree into a second terrace which was simply a room missing two walls between a pair of rooms whose doors faced each other across a tiled floor. A cement table, inset with shells and blue tiles, looked out over olive, fig and cactus. A sagging leather chair had been pushed aside.

'Isn't it divine? It's divine.' Nancy appeared in the door of the bedroom.

'You lost me,' Daniel said.

'Have you ever seen anything so perfect? Come and meet Flora.'

Nancy held out her hands and pulled him inside. Flora, presumably Gavin's woman, was working in the corner.

'Any sign of our host?'

The hoot of the steamer, startlingly close, swamped Nancy's answer. Stelio smiled, tested the hinge of a shutter and slipped from the room. 'He's not here. He's gone to Athens.'

'He hasn't gone to meet us, for Christ's sake, has he?' Daniel frowned, imagining the echo of the laughter he had heard. 'What's he gone to Athens for?'

'It's a kind of a mystery,' Nancy said. 'No one seems to know.'

'Isn't there a note or anything? He isn't the sort of man who'd go without leaving a note. We know he was expecting us.'

'They just say we should make ourselves at home and when he comes back, they're sure he'll put us in the picture.'

'Terrific.'

240

'Isn't this a lovely guest room? We have our own bathroom, everything. And the view. Have you seen the view? Oh Daniel!' She threw herself on the bed, hands behind her head, and smiled up at him. 'Flora comes down every day from the village, but otherwise we can be absolutely alone. In many ways, though I'm sorry to say it, I'm quite glad he isn't here. Maybe it's tact. Some people are naturally tactful.'

'What do we do about food?'

'She'll cook midday for us and night-times we can have just a salad or something like that or we can go out. We can do whatever we like. You're disappointed.'

'Put out,' Daniel said. 'It's stupid. I'll get over it. When I go from A to B, I always expect to find B waiting for me. You're quite right. It's beautiful.'

'We even have a mosquito net.' Nancy pointed with her eyes at the white cloud tethered above the bed. 'Paradise ought to be a little old-fashioned.'

She made friendly room for him on the bed. He went to the door. The two men were talking at the far end of the terrace.

'I had a strange experience on the way here. I wandered into the wrong dream.'

'I guessed something had happened. Where did you go?'

Daniel opened the shutters beyond the bed. 'There's this character has this, well, it's kind of a palace really. What you saw wasn't the half of it. He was very nice, very welcoming, considering I just blundered in. By the name of Larry Pleasure.'

'Larry Pleasure.'

'I think he said Pleasure. It sounds vaguely like someone one ought to know, like Ghirlandaio.'

'Oh I know Ghirlandaio,' Nancy said.

'And Larry Pleasure, do you know him? Who was Larry Pleasure?'

'I thought he was dead,' Nancy said. 'I thought he committed suicide or got murdered. I thought he was murdered out on the Coast, years ago. In a parking lot somewhere. It was about a girl, wasn't it?'

'Were you there at the same time?'

'What, when he was murdered?'

'When he was in the news, when he was well-known.'

'Otherwise I don't suppose I would have heard of him.'

'No, I don't suppose you would.'

'Daniel! Wasn't he supposed to have taken a lot of people for a lot of money?'

'You're telling me, remember?'

'I'm straining to remember anything at all. I don't really want to think about Larry Pleasure or the Coast. Frankly I had other ideas.'

'Now? Before lunch?'

'Won't it improve your appetite?'

'It is my appetite,' Daniel said. 'Remember?'

'I love my lover,' Nancy said. 'I really do.'

'Can we lock the door? Joinery isn't their strong suit.' He had been trying to fold the shutters. 'I don't want to shock anybody.'

She arched her back and slid out of her white trousers. Daniel turned the key in the lock. Her desire created his. When she was naked she rolled on to her elbow; it made more of her breasts. Her arms were cool, but the warmth of her thighs, as she wrapped them about him, confirmed her desire. When she twisted her body to draw him up on to her, he resisted. He hated to be dominated, even by submission. He kissed the little maternal badge of rucked skin below her navel and was kindled by the flattered tremble she gave at his touching what, somehow, he thought of as a mark against her. She pulled at his shoulders and brought him to her.

'That was all a bit of a surprise.'

'Nice one?'

'Very. I should now like to sleep for several hours.'

'We can,' she said. 'If you want to. We can do whatever we like.'

'Why does that always sound so intimidating?'

'Because pleasure isn't really your thing.'

'Must be because I'm so busy giving it to others. Are you going to shower or what?'

'I think I'd sooner go swimming. Eventually. When you're ready.' She gave him a slow smile without parting her lips and

242

stood with her hands folded under her breasts. He bent down and kissed her tuft of amber fur. 'Or are you always ready?'

'*Toujours prêt*? Hardly. Only don't you gloat. I know all about the famous female capacity for unlimited orgasms. What's the most you've ever had?'

'I don't count,' she said. 'But then I'm not a famous female.'

'Not orgasms, you mean.'

'Daniel, I forbid you to be cruel.'

'Why? Don't you want me to enjoy myself?'

She lay in a saucer of sand, one knee crooked, her hands by her sides, blue plastic pods over her eyelids. She was wearing a black one-piece swimsuit, cut deep at the back. Daniel sat, cross-legged a little distance from her, frowning at an open book. Sand fattened the pages.

Steps in the rock, and flat stones at critical stages, made half a spiral staircase in the face of the cliff. A jagged edge of shadow receded slowly across the beach to leave them stranded in the heat. Nancy lay so flat in her dish of sand that it was as though she had left a two-dimensional image of herself to keep her place and gone elsewhere. Daniel was reading a political novel about Greece; it increased his sense of shallowness and evasion. Nancy lifted her head an inch from the sand in search of the sun-oil and allowed it to fall back again, before drawing a careful line along the bridge of her nose.

Daniel went to the edge of the water.

'How is it?'

'Perfect. For polar bears.'

She tucked her hair under a yellow rubber bathing cap. Her face was made very naked by it, her eyes bulging and empty as she hid the last of her hair. She tugged down her swimsuit and ran up to him. 'I've been thinking.'

'I wondered what you were doing under your visor.'

'We should maybe go and find this trouser man later on. What do you think?'

'If you want to, why not?'

He threw himself on to the sea as if it were an enemy. Nancy strode into the water, leading first with one shoulder, then with the other, plunged and reappeared ahead of Daniel. He swam strongly on past her, but she was the natural swimmer. They swung to the left, in an unofficial race, and rounded the point. Larry Pleasure's place seemed to drift out to meet them. The sea was firm and springy. A breeze drove them across the bay, so that they seemed to have raced Pleasure's domain to a standstill. Daniel eased off. Nancy swam on and then came back towards him in a slow circle, resuming her stroke as easily as a victorious sculler.

'Oh,' she said, 'I love it! I really love it!'

'Maybe we should make love out here. Maybe this is your element.'

'My element is wherever you are,' she said. 'Or didn't I give you that impression just now?'

He grinned and struck out for the shore. She dawdled and then came after him. He could hear her clean, regular strokes. When his head came up, he glimpsed the bob of her yellow cap and the tireless pedalling of her white feet. He punched and punched at the greening water. She was gaining. He worked to the left, forced himself from her. Finally, exhausted, panting so that it sounded like a strange, high-pitched laugh, he dropped his feet and felt the soft ground beneath him. He had won. He stumbled up the shore and there she was behind him, tearing the yellow cap from her head. She gasped and fell towards him and he had just enough strength to appear strong. He took her in his arms and she put up her cold lips and smiled so lovingly, with such conviction, that his heart was turned to stone.

She broke away with a gasp of laughter and ran, high-kneed, up the beach and threw herself down. Almost instantly she sat up. Twenty yards away, a man was standing in his underpants, up to his thighs in the sea. A small dog was swimming towards him, neck craned. As it reached him, he caught it, held it for a second, and then stretched back his arm and threw it as far as he could into the waves. It struggled back towards him. Head working, it reached him again. Again he held it a second and threw it as far as he could into the deep water.

'What's he doing to that puppy?'

'He's drowning it,' Daniel said.

'You have to stop him. Daniel, you have to.'

'Do you want it?' Daniel said.

'Daniel, you have to save that puppy.'

He lunged forward through the low water towards the man. The dog was coming back again towards the shore, slowly. The man waited, like a fielder.

Daniel said: 'Why are you doing that?' The man, whose underpants sagged with the water they had absorbed, caught the dog once more in his fist. 'Can I buy the dog?' The dog flew through the air. 'Oriste ...'

The man frowned. He had a thick, broken nose and bulging, cracked lips. His hair was fairer than that of most Greeks, his eyes pale grey. 'Tha sas ton thoso. You can have it if you want it,' he said. 'An yirise. If it comes back.' The two men stood side by side, waiting. Daniel waded in and caught the puppy round the chest. 'How much do you want?'

The puppy snapped at him. Its teeth were small and pointed, like a fish's. The peasant scampered out of the sea, squeezing the water from the bottom of his pants. 'I don't want anything,' he said. 'It's not my dog. I was doing it for a friend.'

'If he bites me again,' Daniel said, 'I'll bloody throw him in.'

'He's just frightened,' Nancy said. 'He's darling.'

'Well, you've got yourself a puppy. I hope you'll be very happy together.'

'We can take him up to the house,' Nancy said.

'Or make a gift of him to Larry Pleasure.'

'I wouldn't make a gift of anything to Larry Pleasure.'

'I can now see us having to get a baby-sitter.'

'God forbid. I don't ever want to have to go through that again. I'm just beginning to see daylight over that particular problem.'

'I think your children are very nice,' he said.

245

'Other people's children are always nice.'

'It's not just the children. I also love pregnant women.'

'Do you really? Is that really true or is it something you've heard?'

'Skip it,' Daniel said. 'Have a puppy. What do you say we go have a drink? No, I want children. You forget, I have to have someone to leave my money to.'

'What money?'

'All the money I'm going to make when the movies come out of their coma. All my world-famous money when one day I actually make a success.'

'The day you're rich,' Nancy said, 'we'll have a child to celebrate.'

The beach looked a comfortable walk, but they laboured through tiny pebbles up to their ankles. For a few yards she held his hand, but then they parted and fought the yielding shore separately, Nancy with the puppy in her right hand, out for balance. A train of donkeys went by, drivers side-saddle, two skinny mongrels running behind. Below the *taverna*, a group of men were forking rubbish on to low, blown flames. Brackish smoke swirled. The rubbish was clots of oily flotsam. When the lumps were too big, the men, their faces varnished with sweat, covered them with sand. The puppy grew fluffy as it dried in Nancy's hand.

'They must really love the place.'

The Corporal of Police was standing at the mouth of the rocky track which mounted, between stone walls, towards the village invisible behind the thick hill. Sentinel chapels punctuated the long zigzag up to where Stelio had branched off towards the point. Cicadas made a glare of sound. Sunbathers littered the sands like victims of some hot accident. The sea was glassy smooth under the shelter of the cliff. Nancy and Daniel clambered up the rocks to the blue-shaded terrace of the *taverna*. The owner was putting a plate of peppered cucumbers, tomato and *feta* cheese in front of the man with the handlebar moustache. The bespectacled woman in the pink dress was prodding a plate of meatballs. Her dress was un-buttoned, revealing a yellow bikini.

'My God, doesn't it all look good?'

246

'It is good,' said the man with the moustache. 'On Iskios, everything is good. Even Paniotis is good.'

The *taverna* owner, glowering at the plates he was carrying to another table, gave a wan smile, eyes still on the plates.

'May I introduce Miss Long?' The pink woman nodded. 'And I am Vassili Vassiliotis.'

'Daniel Meyer, and this is Nancy Lane, my—'

Daniel was waiting by an empty table, but Nancy had drawn a chair over to join Vassili and Miss Long. He went inside to order the drinks.

'Vassili's a painter,' Nancy said, when he came out again. 'He's shown in Paris and New York and Minneapolis, but never in England. That's something we have to change. I can't imagine gallery people not being interested in paintings of a place like this, can you? I can't imagine Ira not being interested for instance. Or Nazar; I'm sure Nazar would be.'

'We haven't seen the work yet,' Daniel said.

'Mr Vassiliotis has shown in New York,' Nancy said.

'I once met a painter who made a big thing of having shown in New York and it turned out he'd shown in his father's furniture store in Queen's. Now of course I'm not—' Vassili Vassiliotis was not offended. He was leaning down over the parapet, talking to Dmitri Bracheotis, who was slumped on the grey donkey.

'He says your lunch is ready.'

'How the hell did he know we were here?'

'I'd love to see some of your work,' Nancy said. 'Do you have anything here?'

'A few sketches. I come here to enjoy myself. In the winter I paint like a bastard. In the summer ... ' He took Miss Long's thigh in his hand and shook it. She was reading a thick, handwritten letter. She looked up briefly, as if she were on a bus and might have reached her destination. The light caught her glasses; her pupils were like nail-heads. She finished the letter, folded it and put it in the straw shoulder-bag on the floor beside her.

'Are you here on holiday?' Daniel said.

'I am. And I'm also looking round, doing some field work.'

'You're an archaeologist?'

She gave a fluting laugh. 'Only in a metaphorical sense. I do dig, but for characters and situations, not for antiquities. Not that that side of things doesn't interest me in an amateur way. I write.'

'Professionally?'

'I hope so.'

'What sort of thing? Under your own name?'

'Of course. Davina Long. I write stories and novels. Thrillers sometimes, of a kind. I write in whatever form seems most appropriate.'

'After Greece perhaps you'll write an epic poem,' Daniel said.

'I've been to Greece several times before,' Davina Long said. 'I haven't yet branched into epic. However, there are other verse forms apart from the epic. Remember Sappho for instance.'

'You do reviews,' Nancy said. 'In a woman's paper. I've seen it at the hairdresser's. I've seen it at Leonard's.'

'I do do a stint in *Madame* from time to time.'

'We've come to Iskios to meet a writer, as a matter of fact: Robert Gavin.'

Davina Long thought. 'I've never heard of him,' she said.

'I'm surprised. He's written some very fine novels. I'd have thought you might have reviewed some.'

'I draw my net in confined waters. Our readership requires pampering. I usually write about historical or domestic subjects.'

'You're both staying with Mr Gavin?' Vassili said.

'Yes, of course. If he ever turns up. You haven't heard where he's gone, I suppose?'

'I am afraid not.'

'Or whether there's been some kind of trouble? Because he's — well, he's disappeared. They say he's gone to Athens.'

Vassili grinned and spread his hands before clasping Davina's thigh once more. 'He'll come back. They all come back to Iskios!'

Paniotis ran out of the kitchen, leaped down the rocks to the beach, ploughed into the water and scrambled into a dinghy moored in the flat water. He pulled up the four-pronged anchor and began to row himself with one oar, like a gondolier, towards a *caique* which now appeared from round the point.

'Here come the tourists,' Daniel said. 'Time to check out.'

'I like tourists,' Davina Long said. 'I like to observe them.'

'*Gnothi seafton,*' Daniel said. 'Know thyself!'

'I am familiar with the expression,' she said, 'but which one of us, in the last analysis, does know himself?'

'The last analysis,' Daniel said, 'is like the last trump. With any luck, we shall none of us be here long enough to hear it.'

'You really hated her, didn't you? Why? Because she's clever?'

'Because she's awful. I like clever women. What do you mean, because she's clever? Because she's pretentious.'

'And happy,' Nancy said.

'Maybe she's a great writer,' Daniel said. 'I don't know.'

'She writes quite well.'

'You never said you'd read anything.'

'I read one of hers. *The Queen of Aquitaine.*'

'God help us. Dumas *mère.* I'll bet he's a lousy painter too. He's much too cheerful to be any good. Are they sleeping together?'

'Well of course they are! He enjoys life. I like people who enjoy life. He's one of those people who likes to make women happy.'

'And never mind what woman.'

'Daniel Meyer,' she said, 'look who's talking!'

'You didn't exactly come off the rank, Mrs Lane. Christ, this bloody path doesn't get any less steep, does it? Do you really think I don't mind what woman I have? Would I have chosen you if that was the case?'

There was no one new at the house. Flora served lunch under the arcade; she agreed to give the puppy some scraps. She had cut twigs of bougainvillea and laid them with the cutlery. She gave them *dolmathes,* fists of spiced meat wrapped in leaves from the vines below them, and *pastitsio,* a flat round metal dish of baked macaroni. The macaroni was tepid; she had carried it from the baker's oven in the village. Afterwards came strawberries, cheese and coffee. '*Poli oreo fayito*,' Daniel said. 'Great meal.'

Flora smiled her sad smile. Everything that was said seemed, with her, to fulfil some hard prophecy.

'Wow, I'm really flaked,' Daniel said. 'I'm trying to remember when it stops getting hotter. Round four or half past, it should do.'

'That'd be the time to go up to the village. To see about those pants.'

'*Posa lepta ya na pas sto chorio?*'

'*Me la pothia? Misi ora. Saranta lepta.*' Flora took the last dishes into the kitchen.

'It's almost an hour's walk. Makes it a bit tight. And aren't tight pants out?'

'Tight for what? I'm not with you.'

'If we're going to see Larry Pleasure.'

'Is that really the kind of person you want to know?'

'I have this in common with Davina Long, I like to observe. A man like that I don't meet every day. How old do you think she was?'

'Not too old. Not too young.'

'Old as that you think? It's just that the guy asked us and I did accept.'

'You think he'll be doing the bun dance from *The Gold Rush* if we don't show? He's a pretty tough egg, Larry.'

Daniel said: 'You know those people on the beach, cleaning up. They'd been press-ganged. They'd been brought down from the village. Didn't you see your friend the butcher?'

'Friend?'

'The butcher who smiled at you in the village.'

'Oh the handsome one! Was he there? No, I didn't.'

'That's because he wasn't smiling.'

'You should take sugar in your coffee, maybe you'd be less acid. I'm going to sleep, are you coming? I thought you were tired.'

'Maybe in a minute. You go ahead.'

There were initials, D.H., set in the table on the lower terrace.

David Herbert? It was just the sort of place Lawrence might have romanced about the peasant. Or did the Greek, with his sly traditions, not fit the fantasy of the dark unconscious? Flora's watchfulness made Daniel feel like the officer of an occupying force. He was stiff with the effort to be casual as he opened the door of Gavin's sitting-room and went into the cool.

The room was fitted with wooden shelves and cupboards on the long wall opposite the shuttered windows on to the cliffs. Cane armchairs and a cane sofa were grouped about a square, lacquered table, possibly Chinese. A pair of paintings, green and leafy and very English, hung above the sofa. Daniel was reminded of the Constable country, though not of Constable. Could Sylvia Morris really have been jealous of Nancy?

The furniture had orange cushions; an orange fleece rug covered the floor. A brass oil-lamp with a milky china reservoir and hood hung from the central beam. Other antique lamps adorned the walls, each under a tapering shadow of soot. A glass-fronted case in the corner, its glazed doors shuttered with reflections, proved to contain only a few disappointing fragments of pottery and some tiny bronzes. A gramophone, wired to two large dry-cell batteries, was in the open cupboard under the bookshelves. The shelves were only a quarter full; the books were paperback thrillers in yellow jackets. There was no quality writing; no reference books; no classical texts. What a formidable memory Gavin must have! Or did he keep his proper library in the bedroom? His own work was full of an obsessive amateur scholarship, at once enthusiastic and dandyish, which, at its best, provided witty solutions to old enigmas and at its worst ran to footnotes longer than the text. (It was Gavin who had pointed out that Lawrence Durrell, in one of the volumes of his quartet, had given a Moslem funeral to a Coptic Christian: 'An imaginative touch.') Did he keep all his knowledge in his head? There was not a single copy of his own books, neither of those intricate travel journals in which hardly a step was taken but it excited a reference to Pausanias, to Ali Pasha or to the Venetian empire, nor of the novels with their embroidery of anthropological anecdote and allusive wisdom. Did Gavin so dread his dark heroines with their haunting reserves of sensuality that he would not give them house room? Where the hell was he?

Daniel jumped up from his chair and went back to the antiquities. Miniatures lay in a heap at the back of the case: several goats, some joined in the push-me, pull-you position, a chariot and two horses, a mirror (green and opaque, but unmistakable), a wolf, a small knife (perhaps a toy) with a deer's-head handle, and a tiny rabbit. The collection was probably Persian, of the seventh or eighth century. It might be petty, but why was it so carelessly jumbled together? The baize on the shelves had once been flattened by other, more substantial exhibits, some with bases of three or four inches square. There was a good foot between the shelves, generous for the pieces actually on show. A dagger of light shifted in the glass. Flora was in the doorway. She had removed her apron and put a scarf over her head. She carried the *pastitsio* dish wrapped in a cloth.

'There's no need to come back tonight, if you don't want to,' Daniel said. He put the bronze rabbit back in the case. 'Flora, you do know, don't you, that we expected to find Mr Gavin here? Have you any idea when he's likely to be back?'

She pressed her lips together and lifted her chin in the rite of ignorance.

Daniel said: 'When did you last see him?'

'Yesterday,' she said.

Daniel was startled; the house felt so deserted. 'Did he often go suddenly to Athens?'

'*Otan ithele o kirios,*' Flora said. 'When he wanted to.'

Daniel said: 'I'm a friend of Mr Gavin's, Flora. If there's some kind of difficulty I'd like to help him. When do you think he might be back?'

She said: '*Avrio, methavrio.* Tomorrow, the day after.' It was the polite way of saying she had no idea. '*Alla an theli tipota o kirios ...* But if the gentleman wants anything ...'

Daniel was struck by the ambiguous use of '*o kirios*'. It might refer to the person to whom one was speaking, or to the person he was speaking about, or to a third person altogether. '*Otan ithele o*

kirios' might have meant when *he* (not necessarily Gavin) wanted.
'Did they take much luggage with them?'
Although she shrugged, as if she failed to understand, Daniel
looked at the empty cabinet. 'And where is the—the—lady of the
house?' One could not imagine Gavin without a woman. 'And his
books? What happened to his books?' Flora huddled herself together
and, with a look of passionate scorn, ran up the steps, past the olive
tree, and out under the arcade.

Soon after four o'clock, Nancy appeared. Daniel was reading
Seferis in the canvas-backed chair on the lower terrace.
'Did you sleep?'
'Like the dead. Why didn't you?'
'That bloody dog's been yapping most of the time. Anyway,
I've been looking round. It's all very strange.'
'Why, what did you find? He's sweet. He's nice.'
'Nothing. That's what's strange. You look great.'
She was wearing a plain black dress of an unusual, lustrous
material which broke the sunshine into whorls of muted prismatic
colour. There was a buttoned pocket over either breast. She had
brushed her hair back and caught it in a fat, low bun. 'I'm all set,
if you are.'
'We're not going to Larry's then?'
'I thought I was the one who overdid the social side.'
'Aren't you going to wear any shoes?'
'Quit being so square, Professor.' She caught his hand and pulled
him up the steps. They had reached the little chapel, where the path
joined the road, when two helicopters began to chop the silence.
They came in low, rattling the sky, never silhouetted against blue
until they were all but overhead. They crabbed round the village
and veered off again down Kalamaki. They spun away and returned,
up out of the sea, from the direction of Agoria. After a half circle
over the windmills, the leader bolted down wind. The second plane
loitered along the far shore and then followed, skating on the icy
blue rink of the sky. As Daniel and Nancy approached the village,

253

people were still looking. 'It was him,' Daniel heard someone say. 'In the first one.'

'No,' said another. 'It was him in the second. The one that looked again. *Ton aresoone ta nisia.* He loves the islands. I saw him with my own eyes.'

One of the governing junta, as they were forbidden to be described, had been on a journey of inspection. Messages of welcome were strung on houses round the perimeter of the village. The Venetian mansion which housed the Post Office, the Municipal Offices and the Doctor's surgery, stood by itself at the side of the earth road round the village. Dmitri Bracheotis was sitting on the marble steps, chin on the top of his stick. He squeezed a smile. 'He must be psychic. Either that or just plain ubiquitous.' A paved path, shaded by cypresses, went across from the Post Office to Agia Eirene, the church with the gilded domes. Below the avenue was a dusty square where a floral message celebrated the ΕΠΑΝΑΣΤΑΣΙΣ, the famous uprising: ΖΗΤΟ Η 21 ΑΠΡΙΛΙΟΥ 1967. The letters were laid on a row of stretchers to ensure regular calligraphy.

'*Ton ithate?*' Dmitri said. 'You saw him?'

'I suppose so. Whoever he was.'

'The General.' Dmitri looked squarely at Daniel. Two policemen, tunics badged with sweat, carried a stretcher of flowers patiently towards the building. 'For next time!' A group of men in shorts had raised a pair of goal-posts from the ground where they had been laid so as not to impede the helicopter, and were slotting them into concrete shoes. Dmitri tittered as the flowers were carried past. 'He was going to land,' he said, 'and all he did was —' His hand zoomed past. 'He was going to stay for four hours. They've been sweating all day.'

'I've forgotten the kids' postcards,' Nancy said. 'Would you believe it?'

'Buy some stamps and write some more.'

'Oh I can't. Damn. I can't.'

'*Pios ine aftos?*' Daniel said. 'Who's this?'

The man in the pale-tinted glasses and the narrow suit was walking up the road from the harbour, the folded newspaper under his arm. His lips trembled on the verge of an unspoken witticism. A Sergeant of Police followed respectfully.

'*Enas politikos*,' Dmitri said. 'A political character.'

'In other words a secret policeman,' Daniel said. 'He must be disappointed they didn't land, after making everyone prepare a welcome like that. Is he from here?' Daniel watched with unintimidated scorn as the man turned along the cypress avenue towards the village.

'He comes from Athens,' Dmitri said. '*Ine enas politikos.*'

'Oh Daniel, ask him about the nightclub, ask him if it's any good.'

'I don't suppose he does a lot of dancing. You mean he was sent here from Athens? Oh my Christ, he's not a political *prisoner*?'

'*Etsi*. Right.'

'Shit! And I thought—How many of them are there, for God's sake? Are they really going to play football in this heat?'

Dmitri shrugged. 'Two, three. A few.' The other exiles were of no interest to him; perhaps they belonged to the wrong party. The lonely man, whose shadow had stopped to make sure that the decorations were being shifted with proper care, had now reached a bulbous church which squatted, like a blanched cactus, below the gilded towers of Agia Eirene.

Daniel said: 'Christ, and I gave him a hell of a look. He must've thought—'

'I'm sure he didn't,' Nancy said. 'I'm sure he didn't think a thing.'

The game was Greeks against tourists. Daniel stopped to retie his desert boot long enough to see it begin. The Greeks played clever, ostentatious stuff, while the foreigners, giants against their opponents, were soon red with the cost of unintelligent defence. An American, in combat boots and wide-belted jeans, fell over again and again, buying the dummy, until his knees were raw, but he never stopped laughing and charging and falling again. The Greeks scored regularly. The visitors were like Demosthenes' barbarian boxer; they rushed to the place where the ball was last played, by which time it was somewhere else.

'Wish you were playing?'

'That full-back's going to go off bang in a minute. Poor bastard's the only man with any idea. Catch me. They must be mad. Bloody concrete they're playing on! Come on, we'd better go and get you measured.'

Zeno, the trouser man, was in the street leading up to the main square. Once it had contained ordinary village houses; Zeno's fame had turned it into a bazaar. Nancy was soon in conversation with the more elegant proprietors. She won their confidence instantly. While she declined to buy anything in particular, something in her style suggested that she just might make an offer for the entire stock. Daniel loitered in the street. Eventually, Nancy came out of one of the boutiques, Artemis Arts, and beckoned him inside. 'Daniel, this is Constantine Mersenas. He has some really beautiful things.'

'You sound like you've already awarded him the Royal Warrant.'

'I am very pleased to meet you, sir,' Mersenas said. His voice was soft, his English fluent. He had a narrow, alert head, brown hair and amused blue eyes. He was a big man from waist to shoulders, but short legs reduced him to below Daniel's height. 'May I get you some coffee or a cold drink? *Niko, grigora, pethi moo.*' He sent a small boy on his way. '*Kathiste.* Please sit down.'

'Look at these materials. Look at that brocade. Isn't that exquisite?'

While they were examining Mersenas' fabrics, an American couple came in and had a conversation in dollars over a case of icons and Turko-Hellenic curios. 'I'd like to know how much one of those is, the one with the two figures on it?' the woman said.

'That is not for sale, Madam,' Constantine said.

'I'd like to know the prices of some other things you have in there.'

'They are none of them for sale.'

'Then why do you have them here?'

'Because I like them, Madam, and this is my shop.'

'Well maybe you could tell me the price of that white and gold number you have in the window. Is that for sale?'

'That is five thousand drachmae, Madam.'

'I just saw it down the street for three thousand.'

'That's right, we did too. Three thousand. Down the street.'

'Then I advise you to go back at once and buy it.'

'Well, will you take four?'

'The prices are all marked, Madam.'

'You're not very polite. It seems like a lot of money, that's all. I like the dress, but it does seem like a lot of money. Could you take off maybe five hundred?'

Constantine said: 'If you would like to come into the store-room, I will show you another weave in the same process.'

Nancy followed him into the back of the shop. Daniel waited on a *taverna* chair behind the counter. The boy whom Constantine had sent out for drinks came back with coffees on a round brass tray suspended from a round handle on three brass rods. He put one cup in front of Daniel and took the others through to the store-room.

'Young man, would you please take the dress out of the window for me?'

Daniel looked up. He was alone with the American woman.

'Do you have somewhere I can try it on?'

Daniel indicated the curtained recess by the store-room door.

'If it fits I'm going to have it. I don't care.' She came out calling, 'Harry? Harry! Have you seen my husband any place?'

'I believe he went up the street, Madam. Shall I go and see?'

'Oh, here he is. Harry, what do you think?'

Harry came in with the short, stabbing steps of a man lighting a cigar, eyes on the flame. 'Helen of Troy.' He looked up through a flash of flame. 'If that doesn't beat Helen of Troy!'

'Think so? Couldn't you really do it for a little less?'

'I'm sorry, Madam, I have no discretion.'

'I haven't seen another dress I liked a quarter as well. At least you'll take a traveller's cheque? What's the rate? What rate?'

'Thirty drachmae to the dollar.'

'They're giving thirty-two up the street.'

'In that case, Madam, I advise you to go up the street.'

Nancy watched, open-mouthed, from the door of the store-room. The American was signing one cheque after another. Daniel folded the dress and made a flattish parcel from the roll of Artemis Arts paper behind the counter.

'I really have to compliment you on your English. Your English is really extraordinary. Where did you learn it?'

'In England, Madam.'

'Well, I have to compliment you. You have scarcely a trace of an accent. Harry, we've got to go or we'll miss that boat. I can just see that Captain sailing without us. Well, goodbye now and F. Harry Stowe polly.'

'*Parakalo*,' Daniel said.

'Why, you—Daniel Meyer, you—you—' Nancy threw her arms round his neck and bumped her forehead on his chest. 'You lowdown—you really are!' Daniel held the money out to Constantine. 'You missed your vocation! Constantine says will we come by for a drink later? He's got some things he wants to show me. You know he was going to open a place in London. Wouldn't that have been something? Only the revolution, you know, came along and bang. His wife designs all the fabrics and the clothes. She has to look after the Athens shop, she sometimes manages to come out weekends. Imagine these fabrics in London. Imagine people like Catherine and Janey and Erica. Imagine Erica. Constantine was saying could I model some of the things for him? Maybe we could interest some English or American magazine. Maybe *Harper's*, maybe *Vogue*.'

Zeno had removed the floor of the room above his shop and substituted a narrow gallery. A twist of spiral staircase took the customer up to where bolts of cloth were slotted in cubbyholes. Zeno announced his price as a sort of joke: one fitting now, one tomorrow, thirty dollars. It was cheaper than Daniel feared but more than he had hoped. Zeno's charm was not Greek, but French. He went each winter to Paris. He was short, but so slim and so well-balanced that he seemed quite the tallest of short men. His wife stood behind a high, narrow desk, *à la Française*. Zeno was not drawn by Nancy's knowing questions. He tucked the end of his tape up between her legs; his wife noted the figures.

'I only want to have a dozen pairs,' Nancy said, 'from what I hear.'

'Certainly, Madame, no problem. A dozen pairs for Madame.'

'I can't really. How can I? I don't have the space.'

'When we have done the first pair, if Madame is satisfied, Madame can write and order as many pairs as she wants. Provided Madame's measurements don't change —'

'They won't,' Nancy said.

'I want to ask you something. Have you ever asked anyone to marry you before?'

'Not asked. Offered.'

'I can imagine.'

'In the days before the pill. An old story.'

'But still playing in the sticks from what I hear. Even the pill isn't all that infallible.'

'Unlike His Holiness. For some people these still are the days before the pill. I wonder if they're still playing football. We're not in the same world as these people. They're just scenery, frankly, aren't they?'

'They'll change,' Nancy said. 'Daniel, look at that moulding up there under the cornice and then think of some of Constantine's designs. Can't you see a relationship? What happened, did she get an abortion?'

'One way or another, the thing fell through,' Daniel said. 'I'd sooner not talk about it.'

'Because it hurts, or because it's none of my business?'

'It hurts because I met her again and her mouth smelt like a pigsty. A few months ago I heard she was dead.'

'Oh that's horrible. Dead! That's horrible.'

'Surrounded by cats. Listen, it's her tragedy, not mine. You don't have to be sympathetic. It's nice of you, but you don't have to.'

'I was thinking about her,' Nancy said. 'They *are* still playing.'

'Not really. That's the victors proving they weren't extended. How did it go?'

The red-faced full-back was limping towards them along the path under the cypresses. 'Murder.'

'What was the score?'

'Twelve-one. And the one was a penalty. I awarded it myself.'

'And banged it in?'

'As you ask. God, talk about unfit. If we'd had some defence we could have taken them apart. They always crack if you go at them. Bloody Yanks though, they've got no discipline. Courage but no discipline.'

'Courage without discipline is mere rashness.'

'Ah, a Platonist! If you're ever looking for a game, they play every Monday and Thursday. Five o'clock until the first fatality. It's time we got some people together and took these bloody Greeks apart. Monday, if you feel like it.'

'He recognized a fellow-addict,' Nancy said. 'They obviously need you.'

'Fellow-addict! He fancied a long look at you, that was all. He couldn't take his eyes off you.'

'They were so small I didn't notice,' Nancy said.

The political exile was walking down past the Post Office towards them. As he drew level with it, a group of six or seven girls, in jeans or Bermuda shorts, came laughing down the steps, tearing at airmail envelopes and clutching on to each other in their amusement. They engulfed the solitary man, with his folded newspaper; his head was dubbed with laughter. Daniel frowned; Nancy smiled. One of the girls was saying, 'But two pairs at the same time. I never saw anything like that in my whole life! I never in all my life saw anyone with two pairs at the same time.'

'Do you suppose she's talking about tits?' Daniel said. '*Kalispera.*'

'*Kalispera.*'

'Thus are blows for liberty struck.'

'Who was that?'

'The man Dmitri was talking about. The political prisoner. Perhaps you were in the Post Office. He's been sent here from Athens, exiled. He has to stay here indefinitely.'

'Think we could get in on the same deal? What do you think he did?'

'At a guess, probably failed to throw himself at the feet of the

Great King with a cry of *Ellas Ellenon Christianon* and other ethnic slogans.'

'He what? I guess politics just don't mean anything to me.'

'I wonder if he ever thinks of escaping.'

'Where would he escape to?'

'To Archimedes' platform. Only then there would be the problem of where to get the right-sized lever. The big lever suppliers are the Russians and the Americans and neither of them are likely to be too helpful.'

'Suddenly you're talking a language I absolutely fail to understand.'

'I'd like to see these bastards chucked out,' Daniel said. The road was empty. 'I'd like to spit in their stupid eyes. I'd like to see somebody do something about them. I'd particularly like to see *me* do something about them.'

'Well, you can. You above all people. Jesus, you're a film director.'

'Don't call me Jesus like that; I don't want it to get around. I get crucified enough as it is. So I'm a film director. So are a hundred other guys cruising around with their flags up and their hands out. Tell me, Nancy, can you name me one book, film, play or mixed media cock-up that ever actually made anybody do anything? Except, of course, to imitate it if it was successful? You can take the greatest book in the world—let's say *Anna Karenina*—did it ever dissuade anyone from committing adultery or lead them to take up the simple life? Because that was the idea behind it. *Au contraire.* Levin's a bore and Anna is the proof positive that even the loveliest married fruit can still be picked. So she ended under a goods train. So you can't win 'em all. Did *Citizen Kane* improve the morals of newspaper proprietors, did *On The Waterfront* put an end to graft? Did *Guernica* stop air raids? People queued all round the block to see *Z*, so now look around, can you see the tide of world indignation sweeping away a régime based on force and fear? I wish it was true, I wish I was a revolutionary at twenty-four frames per second, but I'm not and no one is. Either you do something or you've done nothing. People remember the pram, baby, but who can tell you what the hell they were doing on the Odessa steps in the first place?'

'I never saw *Z*,' Nancy said. 'Was it really as good as everyone says?'

Rock music burst out like fireworks behind them. The night-club was testing its power.

Nancy said: 'They've got a boutique as well!'

Daniel said: 'Pretty soon the Golders Green Crematorium's going to have a boutique.'

'You know you really ought to direct a comedy.'

'Hullo, would you like to come in and look around?' The young man was wearing glazed mustard velvet pants and a floral silk shirt, open to the navel. He was barefoot. A gold fist hung on a chain over his curly chest. His hair was short and he had the sly, wide-eyed look of an archaic ephebe. The few articles in the boutique were either locked in the window or pinned to the hessian walls. 'Overdisplayed and understocked,' Nancy said. In the patio, two girls were setting out chairs and tables by the basket-work bar. Nancy rattled a chain-mail vest and smiled to herself. Daniel looked at the bottoms of some olivewood chessmen. 'One time in Morocco I bargained with a guy for hours and finally bought some coasters from him he said he'd taken five days to make. When I got home I found they'd been made in India. Bloody Jews.'

One of the girls had a splinter in her heel. She sat and looked at it while the other one ran past the bar to fetch something. Both girls were slim and dark.

'May I see?'

The girl offered Nancy her heel.

'Oh, nasty! Has your friend gone to get a needle?'

'Either that or a gag and a kitchen knife,' Daniel said.

Nancy took the needle from the panting girl. The young man was busy banging the double doors of the ice box behind the bar. Nancy caught the thick flesh of the girl's heel on the needle and jabbed it open. The patient sighed and squirmed and then cried 'Aiee' as Nancy changed her grip and dug deeper with alternate prods and flicks. The wound reddened. 'Aiee.'

'It's coming,' Nancy said. She held the slim ankle and worked the needle.

'*Je vous prie, je vous prie.*'

'*Vous êtes du Liban?*' Daniel asked the spare girl.

'*Non, Monsieur, nous sommes d'origine Alexandrienne. Mais à ce moment nous habitons Athènes.*'

'*C'est votre soeur?*'

'*Ma cousine.*'

'How much longer, Doctor, do you think before the baby's born?'

'She's got half a tree in here. If I could only —'

The girl was rolling her head and grinding her teeth; her hands comforted her forehead and rubbed at her neat ears. The lobes were pierced with fine gold sleepers.

'There we are. Done. Look at that.'

'A prick with no balls,' Daniel said, 'A common Mediterranean hazard.'

'*Merci, Madame, merci.*' The patient leaned her head against Nancy's shoulder. Somewhere a donkey brayed until its breath expired in a choking sigh. '*Merci.*'

Daniel said: 'Pretty girls. Pretty boy too, if it comes to that. And I should think it does, wouldn't you? Maybe it'll be Androcles and the Lion all over again one day when we're thrown to the Arabs. Correction — when I am. You were very cool and calm, I must say, going on through all those Aiees. Did it really hurt her that much?'

'She wanted everyone to know how brave she was being.'

The donkey was on a ledge of turf above the road. It looked out at Daniel through two white patches like a prisoner staring through the peepholes in some terrible, exemplary dungeon. Daniel thought of the last sequence in *Jew Süss*. As they went by, a boy ran out of a dun-coloured stone hut; it seemed that he ran directly out of the underworld. He went straight for the donkey and began to belabour it, yelling in a harsh, theatrical voice, eyes now on the donkey, now on the couple watching from the road. The boy was ragged and dark; his head was shaved. He hit the

263

donkey again and again, raging at it with his harsh, bragging cry.

'Iskios contributed three ships to the Athenian fleet,' Constantine Mersenas said. 'It never became a mere tribute-payer like so many of the bigger, lazier islands.'

'An appropriate place for a rebel to be exiled,' Daniel said.

Nancy said: 'Someone told us—'

'It's perfectly true, George Akrotiri among others.'

'I don't know him,' Daniel said.

'He's a writer, a journalist, as well as a deputy at one time. He was a supporter of the old Papandreou.'

'Hardly a Red.'

'Reddish,' Mersenas said. The colloquialism sounded quite scientific in Mersenas' precise English.

'He's not imprisoned, is he?' Nancy said.

'He has lodgings. He lives in a pension.' He pronounced the word in the English way.

'Tell me about this one,' Nancy said. 'Isn't that beautiful, Daniel? Is that Macedonian too?'

'That is another double icon from Macedonia, yes.'

'Are you religious yourself?' Daniel said.

'Religious, no.'

'You have a reverence for beautiful things,' Nancy said.

'Of course.'

They stood for a minute in front of the icons.

'What would happen if he left the island? Akrotiri.'

'He would be brought back. Perhaps put in prison. I cannot say. Their minds work in strange ways.'

'And if he went abroad?'

'What could they do?'

'They could rage,' Daniel said.

'That they would probably do. You are not a friend of theirs?'

Daniel said: 'Is anyone?'

'Unfortunately.'

264

Daniel said: 'Are people forbidden to talk to Akrotiri and the others?'

'No. Not strictly. No doubt it's noted when they do. If they do it often.'

'Can he go into people's houses?'

'He can do anything he's not prevented from doing. If they wish to show their power they forbid something; then they forget to forbid it and people do it again. In the summer, they have many things to think about. Even now there are only seven, I think, policemen on Iskios. They cannot do everything.'

'Luckily.'

'In the old days for instance, when I first came here – my mother's family was from Iskios – no one ever locked anything. You could leave your wallet on the bitch –'

'On the beach –'

'Yes, and when you went back, either you found it still there or someone was on his way to return it. Now is different. Last year a tourist was robbed. This year one was attacked. Greed has arrived. This year is better so far because they have restricted who comes.'

'Is that partly because of the exiles?'

'I don't think so. Perhaps.'

'Did it come as a surprise to you, the – the Junta?'

'Yes, a surprise. Well –' Constantine looked at his watch.

Nancy said: 'Daniel, we have to go. I wish your wife was here. I'd so like to meet her.'

'Yes, well, perhaps she will come. I hope so.' Constantine left them and went to the corner of the room. He returned with a small icon, no bigger than a playing-card. 'I would like very much for you to have this,' he said. He held it out to Daniel.

Daniel said: 'We couldn't possibly –'

'Please.'

'It's beautiful,' Nancy said. 'Who is it?'

'I think Saint Luke.' Constantine wetted his forefinger and rubbed the grey-bearded face to life.

Daniel said: 'You know, I really don't want to take it.'

Constantine said: 'Greece needs friends. I give it to you as a friend of Greece.'

'Constantine …' Daniel bit his lip. 'No, it's not right.'

'Please. I want you to have it.'

Daniel said: 'Nancy mentioned something about taking some pictures, modelling some of your clothes. I don't know if you really want to go ahead, but if you do, maybe we could do some tomorrow. In the afternoon.'

'Oh yes, that would be all right.'

'Tomorrow then. And thank you. Thank you very much.' Nancy took the icon from Daniel. 'It's really exquisite.'

The square was filled with a rustling crowd. The sky had paled. The shadows were mauve and grey. Gas lamps hissed in the *tavernas*. Nancy and Daniel sat where a gap-toothed Socrates went back and forth with six or seven plates at a time. A boy of no more than eleven, perhaps his son, in a white coat, napkin over his arm, comb, pencil and bottle opener in his top pocket, carried bunches of sweating bottles and tin panniers of thick bread. Groups of young men and girls drifted between the tables, saying goodbye, whispering or shaking hands, as if commiserating over some communal bereavement.

'Constantine's very interested in film,' Nancy said. 'He was talking about it earlier. He thinks it's *the* medium of our time.'

'I think fashion's the medium of our time. Film's the medium of last time. People want to be their own shows now. You only have to look. I don't know why they wouldn't let the bearded guy land. There doesn't seem to be any shortage of freaks.'

'You'd hate it if I'd said that. You know what would make a sensational nightclub and that's one of the windmills. Can you imagine what a nightclub would be like in one of those windmills?'

'Round, hot and stuffy. Like so many people I could name. You want to go back to the Poseidon on our way home?'

'I'd kind of like to see it in action, if you would.'

He took her hand. 'Happiness scares me,' he said. 'It's like something so precious you're bound to drop it. You know the way parents say to their children, "Don't drop it". As if that will somehow prevent them, or at least switch the blame.'

'"I told you not to drop it."'

'Right. Don't let's drop it, Nancy.'

'I hope you are having a good time. You were an excellent surgeon just before, with my sister.'

'Once you have children,' Nancy said.

'Oh, you have children?'

'*She* has children,' Daniel said, 'in England. I have hopes. Is this your place?'

'I designed it, but it's not mine. It belongs to a rich man in Athens. I am here only till September.'

'What happens in September? Are you a student or what?'

'September I go back to the army. I am an Egyptian officer. Last month I was on the Suez Canal, killing Israeli soldiers.'

'I didn't know any Israeli soldiers were killed last month.'

'They are keeping the figures quiet to avoid causing panic.'

'Panic in Egypt or panic in Israel? Nice long leaves they give you in your army. They must be very confident.'

'Extremely confident. We are preparing a new secret offensive which will finish the whole Zionist adventure for once and for all.'

'That's very alarming news. Can I get Tel-Aviv from here?'

'You think I am joking; I am not joking. The Egyptian army is now something it has never been before.'

'You mean it's the Russian army?'

'Please, you are talking to an Egyptian officer. I have seen service on the Suez Canal.'

'Your sister was saying she lived in Athens. How come you're still in Egypt? Look, sit down and have a drink.'

'Never when I am on duty, thank you. An Egyptian officer is always on duty. Next month I shall be back in the firing line. Meanwhile I remain alert. Vigilant. Ready.'

'Egypt's somewhere I've always wanted to go to,' Nancy said.

'You will be received with open arms.'

'And open tombs. Tell me something, seriously, because I should love to go to Egypt too, why with all the problems and all the treasures you have do you go on worrying about Israel? You're never really going to beat the Israelis.'

'Within twenty years international Zionism will be completely eradicated. Look at what is happening to the dollar. We defeated England, soon we shall defeat America. Since 1956, what is England? A frightened child knocking at the door of Europe. England is finished. Finished. Soon it will be America.'

'Give me a company of jocks and your heels wouldn't touch, Coco, you insolent trouble-making whore-raiser. The Egyptian army, so called, won't stop running before Cape Town.' The full-back had flattened and darkened his hair with brilliantine. He had on an old cricket blazer — I Zingari, was it? — and creaseless, yellowing flannels. 'Christ, he's not telling you how he held the line when all but he had fled, is he? Coco, I'm going to have to have you committed to the galleys for gross elephantiasis of the imagination. Get me a large Gordon's and lemon and look sharp about it. I'm Piers Cobbett. He's quite an amiable little bumboy, Coco, but not to be taken seriously. If you think he's impressive as a wog officer, you should get him to tell you how he killed the French Resident in Oran under his mosquito net with a dagger. It's one of the best free translations of Malraux I've ever heard. Without attribution, of course, but that's the tradition of the market place. Thank you, Coco. *Je te vois plus tard, n'est-ce pas?* What are you, on your hols?'

'*Mezzo, mezzo.*'

'Daniel's a film director. Daniel Meyer.'

'And a nice one to be.' Piers said. 'And who are you? One of his stars?'

'My only star, Nancy Lane.'

'I'm not a star at all. I don't even act.'

'Is Coco really an Egyptian officer?'

'I think you are, you know,' Piers said. 'A star. Coco? The last time Coco saw Egyptian soil was when he was five years old. When Nasser, the late, the unlamented, kicked out the Copts, or at least nicked most of their valuables, the wisest of them saw the amber light and decamped to Athens and points west. Coco's been at the Sorbonne the last couple of years studying French and I'm rather afraid he's learnt some. *Par conséquence*, he's become a revolutionary *à outrance*, except of course in the country where he happens to live and it might lead to a swift kick where it hurts. I refer, of course, to Daddy's hip pocket. Once bitten, no thank you very much. Daddy, I hear, has fallen tidily on his feet and is doing very handsomely in the building biz. He built this. You direct films. You must know Billy Stern.'

'Very well.'

'No call for intimate revelations. He asked me to do something for him once. Something about Heliogabalus.'

'Don't flatter yourself, he asks all the boys. I thought I knew your name, of course: you lecture at East Anglia. Aren't you an ancient historian? The late Roman Empire.'

'I do shove the odd, squealing undergraduate, or student as I am obliged to call them, into that sadly despoiled quarry. There's still enough debris about for a bent-backed gleaner to make a living.'

'I read you on the Milvian Bridge,' Daniel said.

'As Belloc might have said, I don't care where you happened to be standing, just so long as you read me.'

'Belloc isn't one of my favourite men.'

'He was basically a sort of Ur-Deutsch pretending to be a Frenchman who knew what was best for England, but he had a nice line in Jewish humour.'

'Not a line I care to travel on. I really enjoyed the Milvian Bridge though. You made Constantine's conversion to Christianity seem about as spiritual as the devaluation of the pound. Didn't someone say that you were the first man since Julian the Apostate to say that the Olympians ought to be given another chance?'

'So you're the man who still reads the *T.L.S.*! It requires some knowledge of the background to know why Simon said that. You recognized Simon, of course? All those fourth-form jokes. It's all in the tradition of Housman on revenge. I reviewed his last book, which was quite bright but a trifle blousy, if you know what I mean, in the *J.R.S.* this was, so naturally it was Buggin's turn.'

'What happened to the Heliogabalus idea? It sounds rather hot.'

'Someone backed out, clutching the ducats to his chest. I was in it strictly for the mun, so I backed out too, unhappily in the opposite direction. It was going to be one of those tripartite films.'

'I know,' Daniel said, 'two parts tripe to one part art.'

'Yah! Is that an old one? What did you think of the *Fellini Satyricon*?'

'I've got one for that too,' Daniel said. 'One part satire and two parts con. I don't suppose Bill Arrowsmith approved.'

'It was a very extraordinary piece of montage, I thought,' Piers said, 'from the technical point of view. Nice little ingle, I liked him, didn't you? You must've been a Classic.'

'For a brief season. I never really knew what I was doing. I was clever enough to be a scholar, but not scholarly enough. Sad.'

'I wouldn't say so. You must make a lot more bunce where you are than you ever could've in the academic racket.'

'There's more to life than money.'

'Well, you seem to have that too. I wouldn't have any regrets. When I think of my colleagues' wives and other attachments.'

Nancy said: 'Do you have a place here or what?'

'Christ no, not me, ducky. I never have places. I'm strictly a boarding-house man. Advantages of bachelordom. I just thought it was time I had a sniff at a new island. I prefer Amorgos personally in the Cyclades. Elsewhere, Ithaca used to have a lot to be said for it until someone went and said it in one of the glossies.'

'You know Robert Gavin's got a place here, I suppose?'

'Bob Gavin, does he really? One more of those gentleman Hellenists who never got over being a wartime Klepht. I last met him years ago at a classical shindig in Yannina. My clearest memory of a very alcoholic occasion's of a plan to sew Basil Brain in a sack and drop him in the lake. Unfortunately came to nothing.'

'À la Ali Pasha! What had Basil done apart from committing adultery, which surely can't be charge enough these days?'

'With Cynthia Chernov, wasn't it? He'd read us an extremely long lecture on Philosophy and Mathematics, starting with the Republic and the Theaetetus and leaving no equation unequated between them and Wittgenstein. All stand. Tedium unconfined.'

'I like Basil,' Nancy said.

'We couldn't find a sack big enough for his head.'

'Talking of Republics, how do you regard the present set-up? The *hunta*, I mean?'

'Look, aren't you going to drink? Cross between Cromwell's Major-Generals and the Peisistratids.'

'I always think of the Peisistratids as a form of haemorrhoids. You know, he's got a nasty attack of the Peisistratids, but he'll be up and about in a week or so. Why the Peisistratids?'

'Obvious really. Someone had to come in and clean up the stables and it couldn't be anyone from inside the system, because that was the origin of all the *merde* in the first place. At least if you get invaded by your own army, as opposed to the Reds, you get a benign dictatorship and not just the knout.'

'Benign, you think?'

'An internal takeover at least has this to be said for it, it may be silly, it may sometimes be vicious, but in the long run it can only prove itself by bettering the condition of the country. At least it isn't serving Moscow.'

'It's serving Washington instead.'

'And a good job too. Where's Bob's place? I'd like to see him.'

'So would we. We're staying in it and he hasn't shown up yet. What've they actually done then, these people? Apart from put people in prison?'

'Look, personally I rather liked the old noisy, *louche* Athens with all the marches and the high-speed gas. Compare Batista's Havana.'

'Oh come on.'

'The old politicos were always talking about hydroelectric schemes and God knows what, pie in the sky, sometimes they even voted for them like well-trained seals, but nothing ever bloody got done. The present lot may be high-handed and slightly risible, Puritans generally are, but the dams are being built. And when they've been wheeled away in due course, the dams'll still be there. It's only fair to mention that they have already greatly improved the trout fishing in the Pindus. The hoi polloi no longer have free access and the stocks have improved dramatically.'

'Thus silencing all criticism,' Daniel said.

'Ah poo. Vichy was a pretty squalid episode, but the French've got more solid advantages, in terms of reforms and institutions, out of it than ever England got out of Our Finest Hour. Personally I'd sooner take the glory, but if you want to count the social pluses, it's no contest at all. *Les temps passent, les choses durent. Triste*, but true. The thing about dictatorships being they can never solve the problems of succession. Luckily for the rest of us, or we should still have the Roundheads. They get corrupt, they ossify, finally they die; and when they go their whole rhetoric goes with them, leaving, if you're lucky, a few essential reforms irreversibly grafted on to the commonweal.'

'Hitler being justified by the autobahns, presumably.'

'The Lord save us from analogizers. These people here, so my sources tell me, have probably been no nicer than a big company involved in a shake-out and not noticeably nastier. The people who've been spun off have probably grazed their knees and, if they hung on too tight, they've probably had their knuckles rapped too, granted. But Papadop is no Hitler, look you, and it's sheer sentimental masochism to think he is. All the trendy lefties go around trying to make Pattacake and Papadop into the thirty tyrants so that they can pretend to play Socrates, *sans* hemlock, of course. Your chum Gavin wrote a book called *Rats*, didn't he, all about the old earth-Gods still living in their dark little holes?'

'Christ, I never read it in that sense.'

'Oh surely,' Piers said. 'Look, I've promised to go and play some poker. Let me know if Bob shows up. And I expect you Monday on the football pitch. Five pip emma, and fail not our feast, unless you want to be permanently heckled by hags.'

'I'll try,' Daniel said. Nancy's foot was soliciting his under the table. 'Time we were going too.'

'He's rather fun,' Daniel said. 'Mad, but fun in a way. Didn't you think?'

'Ouch,' Nancy said, 'ouch, ouch, ouch. I thought he was a bore. Jesus, I've hurt myself.'

'What's happened? What've you done?'

'I've stubbed my toe.'

'We never bought espadrilles, fools that we were. Let's have a look. You haven't broken it, have you? Look, come and sit down and —'

She hobbled to Larry Pleasure's wall. Light showed in the deep recesses of the windows, but none spilled. The landscape had the chalky pallor of a dead bulb. Daniel took Nancy's foot to his face. The nail of the big toe had been torn back. He put his lips to the bubble of blood. Nancy tilted her head back and braced herself on stiff arms. Daniel could taste the salt of the blood and the flavour of dust. He kissed her ankle and her instep. She uncrossed her legs; Daniel sensed a softening of her whole body. Trembling, he kissed his way up her leg. She lay back on the wall, soft thighs lapping. Her breath sighed in the darkness. Anger and subtlety timed his movements. She sprawled inert, fingers dangling from the hard ridge of the wall.

'Come on.' He pulled her up and kissed her with salty lips. 'Let's get you home. I'll carry you if you like.'

When they arrived, the house was dark. Daniel put Nancy down on the bed and lit a lamp. She rolled her head on the pillow like an invalid.

'There's no bloody water,' Daniel said. 'How does this thing work, do you know?'

'It doesn't matter,' Nancy said. 'I can do without.'

'I suppose she's gone and switched something off. The pump or something.'

'Well, she'll be here in the morning.'

'I'll tell you what,' Daniel said, 'there's nothing like salt water for cuts. Why don't we go down and have a swim? It's terrific at night. I'm going. Hot work carrying women. Talk about sweat: it's not often you get the chance to see me in liquid form.'

'Darling, you go if you want to. I couldn't.'

Was it as a demonstration that he went or out of desire? How could one ever know the answer to such a question? He stood naked. His body was dry now and cut the darkness like a wire, humming with the cold. He cried out and swam towards a pleasure that seemed to loom ahead like an island. He was at home in the silent silkiness of the water. He looked up and faltered. An instant before, he had been at one with the sea, then he seemed to trip, to be swallowed, drawn down by a muscular throat, frictionless and prehensile. A slow group of stars, unmatched and unsymmetrical, glowed in the sky. They detached themselves from the heavens and came closing in upon him. Dull gold, dull red, dull silver, they drifted in, silent and fateful, until they hovered ahead of him. His mind raced; his imagination, usually so prompt with possibilities, abdicated. The sky stood full of accusing lights. The land, as he twisted in the water, was tilted away from him; he was on a crest of the earth, face to face with the inexplicable. And then, as quickly as a fresh angle in a film dispelling a mystery, all was explained. The low triangle of a yacht's hull swung between him and the sky. The converging stars were nothing more than riding lights. When the boat first appeared, she had been against the background of Agoria, black against black, the old trick of the illusionist. Now she was in the clear between the two islands; the lights, previously independent of all order or support, took their places at the ends of spars and the tops of masts. The throttling water disgorged Daniel, his panic subsided, and he headed back with a smile towards the shore, slipping through the night like a fat needle. He stumbled up the beach and watched the yacht's lights stub themselves, one by one, against the headland as she passed behind it into Kalamaki Bay. He threw himself down in a furious spasm on the wet beach and rolled and punched at the yielding sand, slapped arms and feet in the indifferent shallows until his body was coated with stinging damp. He stood, ashamed, huddled in his strange wrapping, his passion unassuaged, and tried a variety of cries on the empty night, like an actor rehearsing a death.

'Bloody fool,' he said. 'You stupid, fucking fool. You stupid fucking idiot. You stupid fucking cunt.'

He rinsed himself in the sloppy waves, grabbed his clothes and ran, scalded with the cold, up the steep steps to the house.

Nancy was asleep. It was too late to dry himself. The towel could not absorb the chill. He had to hug himself warm. Too charged for sleep, he walked along the terrace. A lozenge of light glinted on the tiled table outside the sitting-room. Daniel went down to find a bottle of Vodka, an envelope under it. He took them both into the sitting-room and lit a lamp.

Sorry you couldn't make it this evening. I thought if you couldn't come to drinks, maybe you wouldn't mind if drinks came to you. Enjoy Iskios, L.P.

P.S. How about tomorrow—same time? Wish you would. What news of R.G.?

Daniel filled a dusty glass with vodka, drank it and then set himself to search the room. The cupboards next to the gramophone yielded a stack of old *Country Life* magazines, a clip of bills, some of them in Spanish, two decks of playing-cards, shuffled into one, a travelling chess set and some empty tobacco tins. Right at the back, at the bottom of a box was an off-print of an article in a Classical journal; an acknowledgment to Robert Gavin had been under-lined. An illegible note in the margin, generous with exclamation marks, bore the author's initials. Daniel sat cross-legged on the floor and read the article. It concerned the method of taxation for mercantile imports at Athens in the five years before the first Megarian decrees. Traces of old discipline required him to translate the Greek quotations before he could continue his search. One cupboard was locked. He jabbed at it with the paper clip from the bills. A deep moan sounded from somewhere outside. A donkey or a cow? He was about to resume his prodding, when he saw a key

275

sticking out of another cupboard door. The same one fitted them all. As soon as it turned in the lock, a slithering wave of old photographs (why were all photographs old?) burst out like vomit, coughing and splashing over his hands and wrists and falling in glossy puddles on the floor. The moaning resumed from below the house, a groaning bellow. Daniel went outside and frowned from the terrace. The darkness was now silvered with wedges of moonlight; cactuses were profiled like flat, upturned feet. Far away, there was music, but between it and Daniel lay a ditch of loneliness, in which lay some moaning creature whose pain accused and annoyed.

The photographs had no obvious order. Some were polaroid, some 35-millimetre; all but a few were in colour. Daniel began to sort them into groups. The majority, he began to realize, had not been taken in Greece, though the climate was hot, even tropical. One of the men who appeared frequently was very dark, though not Negro. Several sequences took place on a restaurant terrace overlooking a wide, but dwindling river. Another set was of a party on horseback. The landscape was a vast plain. Then came a batch including a parade; there were Spanish names on the shops and offices in the square. It was South America, probably Argentina. Here was a collection taken at the seaside. A handsome woman, typically Robert Gavin, with a dark, demanding sensuality was seen alone in the garden of a villa. Sometimes she was asleep, sometimes she sat, a magazine or newspaper beside her, in a deck-chair, often languid and heavy-lidded, with jacaranda and poinsettia thick behind her. A number of the photographs could almost have been enlarged sections of others, as if the photographer had crept closer and closer. Was he serving some surreptitious obsession? Had it been done in secret or was there laughter behind it? Had they enjoyed the game or was it all done solemnly, hotly, with no sound but the sizzling of insects? The silence was blinding. How could one ever put the pictures in the right order? Thousands of permutations contended.

The black-and-white photographs were all taken in Greece: Athens, Delphi, Epidaurus, Mycenae, Olympia. Someone had taken a full record of the obvious. Daniel had done the same thing himself in his time. No one had posed for these pictures, but Gavin himself, in a wide straw hat and yellowish tropical suit, was occasionally to be seen, though never centrally. Daniel pored over these Greek pictures as if over some difficult footnote. In one of them, Gavin was looking back, under the brim of his hat, with a twisted, conciliatory smile, at once patronizing and submissive, on his ill-focused face. He had been caught at the same time as he was catching someone else, the watcher watched.

Daniel attempted to edit the photographs into some sort of story. He imagined that Gavin had gone with the dark woman to the seaside (perhaps it was Punta del Este, about which he had written) and that he was deeply in love with her. They seemed seldom to leave the villa, but that could have meant only that he rarely took his camera. There was one batch of photographs of her naked against coarse green grass. Gavin seemed to prefer to take her as she moved, so that her nakedness was humanized by the shifting of weight, by an expression of mild effort on her face. Once she was half-way to the ground, her heavy breasts hanging separate, her narrow knees almost pointed below her thighs. Now came a day of smiles. What she gained in humanity she lost in dignity. Though alone, she might have been at a party; her smile appeared by request. The woman looked younger, but she also looked more vapid. There were a dozen pictures of her fighting to get out of a flowered dress in order to sun herself. The actual incident could not have taken long and Daniel could guess that both of them had been laughing, but the separate images of it had a sort of prolonged and silent poignancy. The dress became a shirt of Nessus from whose burning folds she fought ever more feverishly to be free. It was a positive relief to see her lying, at last, beside her crumpled adversary. The dark man and a fair, slim girl, whose braids made Daniel think of her as La Tedesca, now came into the story. La Tedesca was often in fawn riding-breeches and carried a leather riding-crop. At first (if one chose this order of events), the dark man had his arm round her. Then came a couple of dozen snaps of the girl alone, on horseback. Some were out of focus, shot from another horse perhaps. They had a haunting weirdness, as if reality

277

could never be clear. On another occasion, she was wearing a black dress, low necked, and high heels. It might have been taken before a ball; her hair was elaborately piled and studded with emerald pins. Then she was walking through Buenos Aires. Here she was walking down the Calle Florida, almost swallowed in the crowd. Her face grew more suntanned; the darker she became, the less German she looked, the more Spanish and the more remote. Daniel could imagine that her voice thickened, became more harsh and more husky.

One day they all went sailing. The camera must sometimes have been wielded by the dark man, for Gavin himself appeared in wide, shapeless blue trousers, a toggled waterproof top and an old panama hat, turned down all round. He was usually doing something rather crucial, with an air of unemphatic competence. The dark man, in his turn, wore the embarrassed look of someone accustomed to shine who finds himself out of his element. Suddenly he was back on land and in the uniform of a Major, taking part in a show-jumping competition. Then he was playing polo. There were several shots of him holding a silver cup. The dark woman (Daniel had decided, provisionally, to call her Rosa) was among those applauding. She wore a red floral dress and a white hat filled to the brim with cherries. Her social smile was as operatic as the angle of her raised hands.

Daniel arranged the sorted pictures in a rough continuity, with generous space between them. He searched more and more greedily for the punctuating incidents which might make sense of them all. He stared at the bare sections of floor until they seemed to stir under his eyes. The silence caused him to mumble and mutter. His own mad commentary was supplemented by the moaning from outside. From time to time, he could see, as clearly as if her picture was among those in front of him, the sleeping figure of Nancy, calm and contented, her back to the space he might have been filling.

Back at Punta del Este, a ship had been wrecked and was breaking in two. Daniel found a whole bundle devoted to the wreck. The photographer had taken them at regular intervals, morning,

278

afternoon and night, as the ship disintegrated. The sequence continued for over three months. At first the boat looked capable of salvage. Groups of men and tugs attended it. The tugs worked and failed. Some men remained; some were replaced. Then there were no men at all. The ship bent and creased and cracked and split and fell open. The sea worked inside. The rigging tautened and then snapped. Rust ran like mucus from the boat's split jaws; weed bearded her anchors. And every morning, every afternoon and every night, whatever his other concerns, Robert Gavin went and photographed it; spring and summer came and still he persisted. Where did these pictures come in the continuity? Should they be intercut with another set showing Rosa and the dark man, El Caballero, playing *baby-foot* against two beach boys? The boys were naked but for their blue slips and the fine gold chains about their throats and their peaked Coca-Cola caps. Rosa, in one shot, had thrown back her head and was laughing, hands up. One hand rested, pleading and dependent, against El Caballero's shoulder. They had just lost the game; El Caballero was not amused.

Daniel intercut the sequence of the ship with the others. Imagine, for instance, that Gavin's obsession with the woman began with their arrival at the villa and that soon afterwards the ship was wrecked. Whose collapse was being symbolized? Daniel stared and stared at the picture taken after the *baby-foot* defeat. Rosa's intimate yet almost casual gesture seemed full of significance. At first Daniel took it as an omen of Gavin's coming loss of the woman, but somehow that reading failed to convince. Suppose, he thought suddenly, that Rosa was El Caballero's wife? What possibilities of subtle pain and sophistication! Then was La Tedesca the Caballero's mistress? Or was she his second wife and Rosa his first? Or was Rosa Gavin's wife and El Caballero her lover? Where was La Tedesca when Rosa and the dark man partnered each other at *baby-foot*? Daniel sat cross-legged over the puzzle, a composer with his favourite instrument.

Was Gavin the victim or the master of ceremonies? The whole reading depended on that decision. La Tedesca could have been beside him as he snapped the other couple; if so, had she been bored or did she share a secret mockery with him? The boat trip, where did that come? It might have preceded the whole Punta del Este sequence. The sea looked so blue and so unthreatening that it was hard to match it with the angry waves that battered the beached steamer. The silly pictures of Rosa at the polo could serve equally well as evidence of Gavin's disenchantment or prove the moment when he realized that Rosa could be detached from her self-satisfied husband. Daniel looked again at the garden. If he intercut the solitary woman with the chronometric progress of the steamer's ruin, Rosa could be seen as the victim of an icy sadistic game. Her flesh, previously so pointlessly itself, took on a new vulnerability. Her demanding sensuality was being slowly poisoned by the secret malice of her lover, just as the ship was by rust. He loved her, but he could not satisfy his love without souring and conspiring against it. He wished to find her faithless and vapid. He observed his own disillusion with a meticulous delight he could never find in true pleasure. What use is happiness to an artist? But then did he take up with La Tedesca, or was that a fantasy of Daniel's, as perhaps it had been of Gavin's? There were no shots, of course, of the two of them alone. Who could have taken them? The Greek pictures, all of them less clear and less well shot than the average postcard, seemed at first of no importance, but then by whom and for whom had they been taken? They came, presumably, at the end of the story; they might not be the climax, but they were certainly some sort of coda. In them, Gavin looked older, but he had a certain detachment, a sort of ravaged serenity.

As an appendix he assumed of no consequence, Daniel had laid aside some street scenes in Buenos Aires and Mar del Plata. (The name of the resort was included in a shot of a bank). They could have been taken at the beginning of a reel, before the camera reached the official first print. On second viewing, Daniel noticed that some included La Tedesca, others the two beach boys, apparently inadvertently; if one looked at them first, there would be no clue as to who was being featured. In one, El Caballero, on the other side of an avenue, was reaching in his pocket to pay for a newspaper;

his head was cocked as if at that moment he had been hit by an assassin's bullet. And that was the lot.

The moans were a demand. Some beast in agony was wandering in the darkness. Daniel bundled the photographs into the cupboard, keeping them in rough order, and re-locked the door. Then he went out on to the terrace. A dark figure was shambling between the upturned soles of the cactus. He made some incomprehensible noise and came into the light. The cropped hair and large ears reminded Daniel of the man who had been throwing the puppy into the sea, but the face was so lumpy, the jaw so grotesquely prognathous that, for the first time since leaving England, Daniel was reminded of the Elephant Man. The man held his face with both hands. His eyes were yellow with pain. Was he drunk?

'*Ti pathate?*' Daniel said. 'What's wrong?'

'*Ponothodos*,' the man said. It was indeed the man who had thrown the puppy into the sea. His face was so distorted by toothache that only his hair and ears were recognizable. He did not have a toothache; he was a toothache. Even his feet were hobbled by pain. Daniel went for aspirin. Nancy still slept, her shoulders, in a white nightdress, above the sheet. When Daniel returned to the terrace, the man was slumped against the table, his head sunk into the centre of his body for comfort and protection, like an octopus. Daniel was conscious of surveying him with something of the moral superiority which Sir Frederick Treves might have shown to the East End drabs who came to the Treatment Room of the London Hospital. The helplessness Daniel felt in the face of such suffering made him manufacture a metaphysic to rationalize it: the man's cruelty had brought proper punishment. Daniel made a stern business of dissolving the Codis. He was judge and physician in one.

The patient improved quickly and pulled out a roll of black banknotes. Daniel waved them away; he expected virtue, not payment. The man shrugged and climbed over the terrace wall and went down into the darkness. '*Tora ipno*,' Daniel said. 'Now sleep.'

Daniel woke to an empty bed. Nancy was on the terrace, wearing

281

pre-faded denims and a red tartan shirt. Her pen was flying across a green writing-pad. 'Hullo darling, you're awake!' She threw down the pen and ran and threw her arms round Daniel. 'I'm so sorry. I've been waiting to apologize about last night. The last thing I remember is you going down to swim. Were you terribly angry when you found I was asleep?'

'Furious. Flora not here?'

'She hasn't showed yet. I don't mind. It means I can prepare you breakfast myself. At least there's some Nescafé or tea and some of that toast in a packet—'

'*Paximathi.*'

'There's some of that and there could be some eggs, I don't know. I thought when we'd eaten we could go on an expedition, right up to the end of the beach, I thought, and maybe into the hinterland. Maybe we could visit Homer's Tumb.'

'Who were you writing to?'

'Virginia.'

'Playfair?'

'Is right. I promised I would. Adam won't come to Greece, you know, on political grounds and she's always dreamed of it. It seems a shame. Anyway, I was sending her a few first impressions. You know the water's still off.'

'Shit.'

'You can say that again, because of course we can't use the loo either. There's enough in the kettle for coffee, but that's about it.'

'Flora'll have to get someone to come from the village, if she can't do it herself.'

'If she comes.'

'She'll come. Greek time isn't like English time. She'll come. After all, we need provisions as well. Incidentally, I have some news for you. A big yacht came in last night.'

'I know,' Nancy said, 'I saw it.'

'You saw it?'

'You were still asleep, so I walked up to the point. She's anchored right in the middle of the bay. She's fabulous.'

'You mean you went up by Larry Pleasure's place?'

'I guess. It's not exactly going to be your dream breakfast, but at least it's made with love.'

'I'll bet Larry's got a loo like the throne room at Buckingham Palace.'

'Complete with low-pedestal Brenda's and Brian's? I'll bet he has too. You know something actually, the guest toilets at the Palace aren't really all that marvellous.'

'Palace? Oh, really? Thanks for the tip, I'll remember to take a leak before I go next time. When were you at the Palace? With Charles, I assume.'

'We had to go a couple of times.'

'I wish you'd brought your coronet, I've always fancied going to bed with a crowned head.'

'I'm sure you'd make her very happy. Snideyboots. I don't have any coronet and you know it. Diaphragm yes, coronet, no.'

'And what did the Queen have to say?'

'Not too much. We were at opposite ends of the table. Aren't you a bastard?'

'You know something? I'm damned jealous of that letter. I never knew you were on writing terms with Virginia.'

'You can read it if you like, only it'll probably turn your head. If it has any further to turn.'

'I don't think I've been too much to write home about so far.'

'Fish, fish.'

'I mean it.'

'You're a great lover and you know it.'

'How do I know? I've never seen the competition.'

'Believe me.'

'You'd recommend me, would you?'

'Oh Daniel.'

'Because I really want you—'

'What?'

'To be as happy as you can be.'

'But I am,' she said. 'I am. Aren't you?'

'Yes,' he said. 'I am. If you are.'

The yacht was called the *Leto*. She was moored in the calmer section of the bay, under the lee of the promontory. Daniel and Nancy had more coffee and fresh bread and honey in the *taverna*. Davina Long was serious over a spiral notebook. She looked across at them a couple of times, like a copyist in a gallery. 'Just doing my morning stint.' She wore an orange towelling coat, unbuttoned over a black swimsuit. Now and again she threw her head in the air and waited for a phrase.

Three women went down into the speedboat bobbing below the *Leto*. They wore similar, flowered one-piece bathing costumes and their heads were capped by peach-coloured silk scarves. A young man, his skin almost as dark as his sunglasses, dipped the outboard motor into the water and pulled the cord. The cold engine misfired. The boat accelerated unreliably. The first woman to water-ski could hardly draw herself erect. Nancy came slowly up the steps, her eyes on the boat; the note of its engine grew more thrustful. The woman who had seemed so ponderous now flew along behind it, straight as a thorn ripping the blue and purple bay. Soon she was holding the bar with one hand, riding her skis back and forth as if she were stitching the wounded water. The boat lost way. The woman sagged and melted into the water. One of the others dived in and swam back to her. The boat gained speed again and the two of them were drawn out of the water, side by side. They laced back and forth, plaiting the sea. 'Pretty good.'

'Nice, unostentatious little pursuit,' Daniel said. 'Short of being ferried in on the backs of a couple of whales you couldn't really draw much more attention to yourself, could you?'

'Oh I love water-skiing. You know who they are, don't you?'

'I have a feeling you do.'

'I was just talking to Vassili. It's Princess Astrid. She's been on Crete with the Schleswigs and the Stavro Stavropoulos crowd.'

'Power to the People,' Daniel said. 'A real princess. Well, a real fake princess anyway.'

'Daniel Meyer, one of these days! You can't help feeling sorry for her.'

'Wanna bet?'

'Seeing your husband's plane actually blow up right in front of your eyes? And then the way they treated her, his brothers, the way they persecuted her, treated her like some kind of a public enemy –'

'No fun being a gold-digger when the mine falls in,' Daniel said.

'She loved that man. She really loved him. Vassiliotis was saying the same thing just now. You just have no sentiment at all. Daniel, it was horrible; you have to admit it was horrible. Imagine having what she had and then, in a split second, nothing.'

'Except a million pounds and an invitation to Frank Sinatra's farewell concert. That's real bad times.'

She bent down and kissed Daniel on the mouth and shoulder. 'You think money's everything. What kind of compensation is a million pounds when you love somebody?'

There was a conference in the water. The two skiers were holding on to the side of the boat, the driver sat sideways, knees under his chin, feet toying with the dead steering-wheel. The third woman was behind him, her hands arranging her hair.

'Which of the three is our tragic heroine? Oh, and how was the loo?'

'Sordid, but what can you do? She has to be the one in the back, doesn't she?'

'Oh yeah, now I can see. She's the one with the number of her Swiss bank account tattooed on her wrist.'

Nancy took Daniel's hand and sank her teeth into the thick of his thumb. 'You're just jealous.'

'It's true,' Daniel said. 'I'll never have tits like hers. They really look like three instances of the same thing, don't they? Like in those old movies with Monroe and Bacall and whoever the third one was. Three Cohens in a fountain. Grable, was it?'

'She has to be the one who hasn't skied yet.'

'Right. They put the other two in to warm the bath for the royal ass.'

'She was so beautiful in the wedding pictures.'

The third woman also skied with only one hand; she also made spirographs on the grape-dark sea; but she ended by turning acrobatically round and round, one hand and then the other, riding now backwards now forwards, first on one leg and then on the other, jigging like a skater. She never looked at the shore.

'I don't feel she's enjoying it exactly, do you?'

'Do you think she enjoys anything any more? Imagine having a thing like that happen to you and having to go on living. In front of the whole world.'

'I can't help feeling it must be a lot easier to go on living in front of the whole world.'

'Well, I think it needs a lot of courage.'

'When all she really wants to do is throw herself face down on her bunk and cry and cry! I mean to say, she was entitled to five cents on every barrel that little old sheikdom exported and now—'

Nancy slapped his face. She smiled, her nostrils flared, lips compressed, and the slap carried little strength, but tears were ready in her eyes. Daniel caught Davina Long's eye and had to lean forward and make it a game. He sat looking at Nancy's glittering face, searching for humour. He put his mouth to hers and felt it quicken. Her lips were soft and welcoming. He turned his face, frowning, to kiss her more deeply. As she closed her eyes, a tear rolled down. He squashed it like an insect and left its blur on her cheek.

Nancy said: 'I know what you're thinking.'

'Do you?'

'What she really needs is you.' They sat together, Nancy's face sketching and cancelling a dozen expressions. 'Come on, we're going for that walk.'

Daniel said: 'You'll have to give me a minute. I can't get up as suddenly as you; I might break something.'

As they walked along the beach, the wind crowded around them. Daniel armed himself against it with a stick of driftwood. Nancy spun away on a scarf of wind and sailed down a long sandy slope towards a pad of brackish water where a spring had dried. Daniel fought after her—the wind that carried her seemed to resist him—and fell, laughing, down the softness. Nancy cuffed sand from her ears and hair.

'This always happens when I leave the camel in the garage.'

286

'I hate it,' Nancy said. 'I just hate it.'

'It seems much worse up this end, but all we have to do is get off the beach. It'll be fine back there. I love you.'

'Please, don't.'

'No one can see us. And I don't really care if they do. Why should the Princess get all the notice?'

'Daniel. I feel horrible.'

'Well, I'll tell you something, you're not. Doesn't the pulsing sand attract you? Think of Lawrence and the Arab boys.'

'All I can think of is my hair.'

They stepped over a rough wall into a field covered with brittle grass. There was a stone cottage at the back of the field: a dry door between unpainted windows. It had a dusty well to one side and a paved patio enclosed by a low wall. A grape vine was scaling rusty wires over the doorway. Nancy sat on the wall and brushed sand from hair and ears.

'I feel horrible.'

'You don't look it. Think there's a bed in there?'

'Who needs a bed?'

'You didn't fancy the sand.'

'Oh I see. You're still thinking about last night.'

'I'm thinking about right now. What do you mean last night?'

'When I fell asleep.'

'I wasn't thinking about that at all. You have some very strange ideas about the things I think about.'

'Well maybe that's because you don't tell me. What do you think about?'

'About you? Well—I think I'd like to give you a lot more pleasure than I do.'

'You give me a lot of pleasure.'

'I'd still like to give you a lot more. You know what I mean. I still don't really—'

'How many times do I have to tell you?'

'It doesn't matter how many times you tell me; I know.'

She said: 'You're really thinking about yourself. It's really you who isn't happy.'

'Yes, I am,' he said. 'But I know there could be a lot more for you.'

'I told you you were perfect, what more is there to be than perfect?'

'You can tell me anything in the world,' Daniel said. 'Anything.'

She sat there for a long time, the sand falling on to her legs. 'You should really have somebody else,' she said.

'You won't shock me,' he said.

'I know that.'

'So is there anything? Is there anything you want me to do? You can say, you can show me—anything you want—'

'Suppose I want you to guess,' Nancy said.

He said: 'Hold it. Hold it. Don't move. Just don't move.'

Daniel walked along the wall and took a large quartz stone from the corner. The snake was curled like a flattened ziggurat, grey on grey against the glittering stones. Daniel put his feet far apart on the wall and crouched down for aim before jabbing the stone downward. It covered the snake completely. Daniel sat on his heels, expecting cunning.

'What's going on out here? Is everything O.K.?'

'Jesus Christ,' Daniel said.

'I'm sorry, did I startle you?'

'No, I always have heart attacks like this.'

'So you found the snake.'

'Yes, I did. Don't tell me it was a friend of yours?'

'No, I saw it there and I figured it wasn't harming anyone, I'd leave it. People on Iskios rarely have heart attacks. That's a statistical fact. No cars, no vehicles, they're always going up and down, always exercising. There's a very low incidence of heart disease. Remember that poem of Lawrence's about the snake at the water hole? I figured it had as much right to be here as I did.'

'You were alone,' Daniel said.

'True. Hullo. I'm Larry Pleasure.'

'Hullo. We owe you an apology—not coming last night.'

'Yes. And thanks, for the bottle. We seem to owe you a lot.'

'You don't owe me a thing. Are you aware of the quite substantial

288

relationship between health and architecture? That was quite some wind suddenly.'

'We got involved up in the village.'

'Listen, there was no firm commitment. I just admire the hell out of this man's movies. And now I have to admire his taste in women as well. You know, we've met before.'

'It'll have to have been a long time ago.'

'Lew Leftwich, Malibu Beach 1958. Am I right?'

'Heavens, I can't remember that far back. I don't even want to remember that far back.'

'September 1958. They had a barbecue. They'd just moved into the house, Lew and Joan he was with then. They had a new barbecue pit. I can even tell you who you were with. You were with Tom York. And were you gorgeous! You weren't as beautiful as you are now, but were you gorgeous? What were you, for God's sake, seventeen? I bet you weren't more than seventeen. And were you stuck on that guy! You couldn't get an oyster pick between them. Well, am I right?'

'Could be.'

'And am. I'll tell you something and that is, I'm not letting any goddam real estate hustler turn *this* place into Malibu. Have you been there in the last three, four years? No one's going to do to this place what they did to Malibu. I'll tell you something, why don't you come back to my place and have some lunch? I have some langosta Stelio caught for me and we can drink a bottle of chilled Samian white wine and a salad. Please. I love to be with people who love each other. I'll tell you something, I won't have people on my place who can't be good to each other. People who snap and snipe? I show them the gate.'

'We have lunch waiting for us at home,' Nancy said. 'She's expecting us.'

'I'll tell you what we can do, that's we can send someone across, one of my people can go across and tell her to take it home with her. Is that Flora Loti he still has out there? Bob still not shown up?'

'No sign of him.'

'You know he tried to have me run off the island?'

'I thought you were friends.'

'He tried to have me run off the island one time. He told them I was running guns, did you ever hear of such a thing? Believe me, guns are the last things I want to have anything to do with, but that's what he told them. I had all kinds of trouble convincing them. All kinds of expense as well.'

'Was this the present people?'

'This was three years ago.'

'I thought they were supposed to be so incorruptible. I thought that was their one genuine claim to fame?'

'I had a whole lot of trouble. I don't let it get to me, I don't believe in grudges. I know how Bob felt, a newcomer moving in, making changes. That's what I want to avoid myself. That's why I keep buying up these properties. I bought this whole section last month, right back as far as the church you can see with the palm tree in front of it and over as far as the *stremma*, behind the wall there, the little stream. It's dried up right now, but it'll be back in business come October, November time. What I aim to do is beat the developers. The developer is a man I distrust and he's a man I despise. You know what I want to do? I want to turn this into an island of love; I'd like people to come here and fill this place with love. I figure eventually to put up maybe a dozen really cohesive, really sympathetic houses, and then rent or maybe sell them to people I can trust. I'm not looking to make a profit necessarily. Eventually of course property is bound to appreciate, but that's not my purpose. Love isn't something that just happens; it can also be created. And it can rub off. Love makes love. It isn't just a condition, it's a process.'

'Martin Luther Pleasure,' Daniel said.

'O.K., I accept that. You know the hardest thing in the world to sell people? A bargain. If I built some kind of a plush beach club here and put up some swanky chalets I could clean up, I'd be sold out in a week, sight unseen. But I don't want that at all. I want to attract people who'll love the place and love each other and I have a terrible feeling that I'm not going to find them.'

'Oh I think you will,' Daniel said.

'I can't imagine anyone not jumping at a place like this. I would.'

'Consider yourself invited. The first in the line. You know something? If you tell people you don't want to make a profit, all they do is ask you what the hell you do want to make. They get frightened.'

The *taverna* at the end of the beach, where Larry had moored the Chriscraft, was as dull as Paniotis' was lively. The owner sat at a table opposite a wizened old man in Turkish trousers and a cloth cap. An old woman was peeling green potatoes. The interior was bare except for several crates of empty bottles and a double portrait of the King and Queen measly with damp. The two men's heads were sunk between their elbows. '*Yasoo Kosta*,' Larry said as he went down the steps to the jetty. No one replied.

'These Chriscraft are only the most useful pieces of equipment anyone ever invented. I wouldn't know how to live here without one.'

'That cruiser of yours looks pretty useful too,' Daniel said. 'He seems a pretty miserable character.'

'Kosta? He has his problems. First drink, then Eleftheria, his daughter, he has his problems. I have to know I can move,' Larry said, 'that's the only way I can make myself stay still. 1958, wow! That was another planet, wasn't it? Malibu in those days. Talking about cruisers, remember the *Betty Smith*? Did you ever go out on the *Betty Smith*? Lew's yacht. Jesus, the things that went on on that boat. I was in a fight at that period, a proxy battle, trying to get control of one of the big studios, so I spent quite some time on the *Betty Smith*. You were on her a couple of times, weren't you, Nancy Jane?'

'I haven't thought about those days for such a long time. And I'm not Nancy Jane.'

'Pity we didn't get control,' Larry said. 'You could have made some pictures for us. I'm sorry.'

'I'm available.'

'You know what beat us? The banks. The banks had no imagination. They only wanted to go so far. They were willing to fill the tank, but it scared shit out of them when we told them where we wanted to go.'

'You must've been pretty young in 1958?'

'America's a wonderful country, right, Nancy J.? I say that in spite of everything they did to me personally. As soon as you have legs, you can run. Out there on the Coast, in spite of everything, those were some of the happiest days in my life. Aren't I right?' He put his arm round Nancy. The boat bumped arcs of spray over their heads. 'You and Tom York, you couldn't get an oyster pick between you.' The sea banged the fibreglass hull like an angry neighbour. Nancy took Daniel's hand between her thighs. 'There's nothing to worry about,' Larry said. 'I'll get you there.'

As they approached the *Leto*, the mirror image of the Chriscraft charged out towards them. The two boats converged at right angles. The *Leto*'s contained only the dark young man. He and Larry raised arms to each other. The dark man cut his motor and his boat slewed in under the *Leto*'s stern. The Chriscraft went on at full speed, bumping and leaping. Daniel was winking at the spray when suddenly the boat lurched and the motor whined out of the water. Larry had fallen overboard. The cliffs seesawed. Nancy cried out, hand over her mouth. Daniel caught the wheel as the boat lost way and subsided. He scrambled over Nancy and touched the accelerator. The wheel jerked as he tried to control it. Nancy twisted to look for Larry. The sea was empty. 'What are we going to do?'

'What the hell was he doing? All we can do is — *Larry*! Larry?'

The boat stuttered forward. 'Bloody fool.'

'Hi! O.K.?' Larry was shouting from behind the stern of the *Leto*'s speedboat. 'I just wanted to say hullo to Niko. He's an old friend of mine.'

'Are you planning to swim home then, or what?'

'Think you can manage the boat?'

'You might have thought of that before.'

'I had you down for seaworthy.'

'Unwisely. You'd better come and drive. I might miss the garage. Or overshoot it.'

'O.K.' Larry swam back to the boat and hauled himself aboard. 'It's really very simple.' Nancy pushed against Daniel as they started up, but he gave her no room. He pressed her against Larry's wetness. She gave him a bemused, unoffended look and spread herself between the two men, jeans and shirt darkening as if from exertion. 'You know she won't let a man on the boat except for the crew?'

'Lucky crew,' Daniel said.

'Oh listen, they had to check their valuables before they sailed. Anyone steps out of line and he's over the side. Since that day at the airport she hasn't looked at another man. She worshipped that guy. I knew Astrid before she married him. Insecure? Beautiful, but lost. Absolutely lost. He turned her right round. I used to see her in nightclubs. You know who the other two are?'

'Who?'

'It's quite a story. One of them used to be one of the stars of the Athenian ballet. She gave the whole thing up to be with Astrid, take care of her, look after her.' The Chriscraft slid alongside the jetty and Larry hurdled ashore, in a running crouch, the nylon mooring rope in his hand.

'And who's the other one?'

'I was about to say. The other one only happens to be married to George Ralli and she won't go home either.'

'Sympathy's a beautiful thing,' Daniel said.

'She refuses to go back to Evia, where they have this fantastic estate, you've heard about their estate, she'd sooner be with Astrid. They've been together, the three of them, for the last four, five months, all around the Mediterranean, never left the boat.'

'I thought they were on Crete,' Nancy said.

'They never slept one single solitary night on shore. That's what Niko told me. Never a single night. Not even for royalty. They really live for her.' Larry unlocked an orange gate in the side of the cliff. 'Without them, she'd have taken the shortest way to the bottom of the bay. Don't think she hasn't tried.'

'What've you got in here? The Guns of Navarone?'

'Just a simple, old-fashioned Waygood-Otis. I believe in having all the modern aids I can get, so long as I can keep them out of sight. What you can hide, you can have; isn't that the world today? You know the most tragic thing of all, of course?'

'What's that?' Nancy said.

'She desperately wanted a child; but desperately. You know how much importance a man like that attaches to a child. To a son, particularly. She wanted more than anything in the world to give him a son. Well, the first thing she was going to tell him when he came off the plane —'

'I can't bear it. It's not true. I can't bear it.'

'The first thing she was going to tell him when he came off the plane was that finally she was pregnant. You can guess what seeing a thing like that happen did to her. She lost her husband and their child all on the same day.'

'And you don't think that was tragic?' Nancy said.

'I haven't said a word.'

'Daniel doesn't find that tragic.'

'It's certainly very unfortunate.'

'Kings and Queens aren't allowed to have tragedies any more.'

'Well, they've had a pretty good innings, don't you think? And then what use is a son without a father? At least she's all set to go with the next one unencumbered.'

'There won't be a next one. I don't believe there'll ever be another man in her life.'

'What about that as a subject for a movie now, Daniel? A woman who has everything and loses it all. Think of the amount of public interest there is in a woman like that. She can't go anywhere without being mobbed.'

'Well,' Nancy said, 'this is really something. This is beautiful. The view!'

'I told you,' Daniel said.

'*Mi casa es su casa*,' Larry said. 'Be at home always, please, I mean that. I'll go get them to send someone over to Bob's place and let Flora Loti know you're not coming. Please—drinks are on the way.'

'I told you it was pretty impressive, didn't I?'

294

'She had everything in the world to live for and now she's waiting to die,' Nancy said.

'Nancy, Nancy, Nancy,' Daniel said. 'Do you remember him from your Malibu days?'

'Listen, I hardly remember my Malibu days. He was one of dozens.'

'Dozens of what?'

'People who were in and out. You really ought to try and meet her.'

'She's not interested in men. In and out of what?'

'In and out of everywhere. Daniel, do you have to be silly about it? You're just the sort of person who could help her.'

'I could help the whole world,' Daniel said, 'if I could get it to stand still long enough.'

'You're a movie director, why does it have to stand still? We really ought to try and get you to meet her.'

'I make it a rule not to try and meet people who don't want to meet people. I'm serious. I have no great wish to force myself on people.'

'Which means that you wait until people force themselves on you. You didn't tell him to get Flora to do something about the water.'

'Nuts. What were you doing out there though? In California? Was Tom York your flyer? Maybe I should run over.'

'She'll probably have discovered it for herself. She'll realize. What was I doing in California? I was living there. A lot of people do.'

A slim girl in a black dress and white apron wheeled out drinks on a rubber-tyred barrow; there was Campari and *ouzo* and Chivas Regal scotch and Polish vodka, ice in a blue glass bucket, twists of lemon.

'She'd look at you,' Nancy said. 'Astrid.'

'I have strange tastes,' Daniel said. 'I prefer you. He certainly remembers you all right.'

'He makes it his business to remember people. He sort of has the evil eye. He can swallow you with his eyes.'

'That sounds very voluptuous somehow. A woman who had that trick would never be short of friends.'

'If you were going with her, you'd have a film all set up in no time, no trouble at all.'

'It's pouring with rain on the French Riviera,' Larry said. 'I just had the report through. They have flooding in Cannes up to two and three feet in some places and they have a force eight gale. Yorgo's over at your place explaining the situation, so we're all set. You haven't helped yourselves to drinks! Now that's stupid. What can I give you? Personally I'm going to make a vodka Martini. Just like the old days, Nancy. Maybe you weren't even seventeen.'

'Never mind what I was,' Nancy said. 'You know our problem? We have no water. Over at the house. We can't even use the toilet. There hasn't been a drop of water since yesterday noon. There should be, because there's a big tank and everything, but it just isn't coming through.'

'Well, this is ridiculous. Why don't you just move in here? I only have a couple of people staying, delightful people, Buck Lehman and his girl, and I'd be really glad if you would. I think you saw them this morning. There isn't another soul here except for Yorgo and Stelio and Despina and her mother. I have plenty of room—and plenty of water.'

'It'll sort out,' Daniel said.

'At least feel free to come and have a bath when you want to— or a crap. Nancy, you don't want to get too much salt on your skin, it'll dry you out, with this wind blowing. Or go use my house on the beach. I can have that house put in shape for you in next to no time. It's kind of primitive, but you'd be absolutely on your own. It's an earth closet down there, but I'm told they've discovered it's just as hygienic.'

'I'm still hoping Robert Gavin will show up,' Daniel said. 'I'm sure we can get the water fixed. It just needs someone—'

'Tell me something, how much do you think people would be willing to pay for a place on the beach here? Everything taken care of, I'm talking about, on a condominium basis, with no worries about general upkeep, so you could just arrive and move straight in. What would be the sort of figure say somebody in the movies would be prepared to pay for a place on a Greek island?'

'I thought you wanted people you could love. It's not easy to love people in the movie business.'

'I have to try to work to a price,' Larry said. 'Shall we eat? It looks like it's ready. Are you ready for us, Despina? There's no sense in building something and then finding no one can afford it, even if it's a paradise. It has to be a practical proposition. Would fifty thousand dollars be too much? That would include a land-scaped plot about a third of an acre, a modern house, with three bedrooms or more if anyone wanted more, and rights to a whole range of communal facilities at a nominal figure. Would fifty thousand be too high? Would that turn people off?'

'Not if they had it.'

'Someone like Billy Stern, someone like that.'

'He could take a dozen, if that's the kind of person you're talking about. I'm sure there are lots of people, but then they'll expect maid service, they'll expect a kind of Piccola Marina. They're not going to form this loving colony you were talking about.'

'I love this island,' Larry said. 'I want to see it turn into something that isn't horrible.'

'You could always try keeping it exactly as it is.'

'You think that's possible today? Listen, have some more. Have another claw. Nancy, go ahead. Stelio catches me three or four of these a day. Please. The pressures are fantastic on a place like this. A crowd of hotel people came in from Athens a couple of weeks ago, cheque books open. Who can resist pressure like that? Unless we act fast, we're going to have a little Miami here. Hotels. I've even heard talk of a casino.'

'Why here?' Daniel said. 'Why Iskios in particular? Why not Agoria, for instance?'

'No one ever goes there,' Larry said. 'Hitler lives there.'

'I'm sorry?'

'Aydolf Hitler lives there.'

'Oh? Says who?'

'You think I'm kidding? I saw him. I was over there on the boat, oh maybe six months ago and I saw him. He runs a shop in the village. He's still got his moustache, it's a little grey now, but I have absolutely no doubt it's him. He lives very simply. He doesn't bother anybody. I guess he's reconciled.'

'Look, what is this?'

'I was a little surprised myself. I hope you like strawberries. They come from Naxos. He keeps himself pretty much to himself, of course. And he's not too well; he has this sciatica in the left shoulder. Too much paper-hanging as a young man.'

'What did you actually see?'

'Hitler. I was walking down the main street, this guy looked out of a shop, I recognized him instantly. He looked at me and I was all set to shake hands when he went back inside and shut the door. He'd changed, of course. At this point he has to be a very old man. Agoria really makes sense for him as a hideyhole when you think about it. I mean, South America was basically out, wasn't it? Inconvenient and too many people with the same idea. Also he wouldn't want to sit around with a lot of old associates, all of them blaming him for what had happened. Someone would be sure to put the finger on him just for something to do. No, it had to be somewhere no one would ever think of. Logically, Agoria.'

'Wouldn't it be funny if it was really true?'

'Killing,' Daniel said.

'What would you do? If it was him?'

'Kill him,' Daniel said, 'slowly.'

'He's considerably over eighty years old. He couldn't take a lot of killing. And then, of course, you have the problem of torturing someone who's in pain already. Sciatica's no gas. I guess you'd be safe to rib him a little.'

'I don't think you'd ever do it,' Nancy said. 'Kill him at this stage.'

'Maybe we should just leave him on Agoria. In the end, who's it hurting? All right, so he made a mistake.'

Daniel said: 'Real people died. Real people like you and me. Well, like me anyway.'

298

'The only people who died are the people who died,' Nancy said. 'Everyone else survived. Here we all are to prove it.'

'Some of us,' Daniel said.

'Let's say it wasn't him. Let's say it wasn't Hitler at all. Hell, you're supposed to be on holiday. Drink your coffee and then I want to show you the library. The light wasn't too good; maybe it was Bormann. Seriously, I have some beautiful books. One thing I always promised I'd have for my children, beautiful books and beautiful pictures.'

'Oh you have children?'

'I have to tell you I have two of the most beautiful children in the world. They're in school in Switzerland. Dotty is seventeen — Jesus, Nancy, she's the same age as when — and Bobby, he's fourteen. I did everything too young; married, divorced, had kids. It's like I was already an old man.'

'You and Hitler,' Daniel said.

'I have some pictures I have to show you I took. That was taken in poor light, but would you ever know? They're in school at Schloss Ingelstadt which is probably one of the two or three best schools in the world. If it wasn't, do you think I'd let them out of my sight? Isn't she beautiful?'

'She certainly is. You're a lucky man.'

'You know how often I get to see them, my own children? I get to see them maybe two months in the year. Otherwise they're either in school or they're with their mother who has to be one of the prime leeches of all time, bless her heart.'

'They do come out here, do they?'

'They were here all last summer. They only had the best time they ever had in their whole lives. They loved this place. They went with the Greek kids, they rode donkeys, they went out in the boat, they did whatever they had a fancy to do. She said I corrupted them, can you imagine? She said I corrupted my own kids. How can you corrupt something when you love it? Bobby wants to be a moviemaker, he wants to be like you. He's already made a movie this year. He's made a documentary about ski-ing; he's made a documentary about ski-ing I'd really love for you to see as a matter of fact. I gave him a Beaulieu sixteen-millimetre for Christmas and my God has he made a documentary. And I'm supposed to have corrupted him. If you've finished your coffee—'

Daniel said: 'Larry, tell me something. What do you know about the people they're keeping here on Iskios, the political prisoners? George Akrotiri—'

'All I know is, the only thing that ought to get involved in dog fights is dogs. Listen, I keep right out of politics. I was only bitten once, but was I bitten.' He pulled his shirt out of his shorts and showed them his back. The white skin was puckered into a healed pit. The scar pointed upwards under his ribs. Suddenly, he swung round and pulled the shirt up under his chin. There was another scar, longer and more ragged, under his right nipple. 'That's what you get for involving yourself in politics. At least that's what I got.'

'What were you running for?'

'When I got this? My life, my friend, my life.'

The library was a cool, shadowy room; light fell, sieved through thick roundels of glass, from deep recesses in the ceiling. Chart tables stood in each quadrant of the room. Glassed shelves lined the walls.

'I meant what office,' Daniel said.

'I never ran for office. That's not what I mean by politics. That's just the top dressing. I'm talking about the nitty-gritty. I'm not talking about Mayors and dog-catchers. Very simply what I was doing was I was trying to buck the Unions. I thought they were wrong and I tried to fight them. I was young, maybe I was foolish, but I was an idealist and I tried to fight them.'

'What unions were you fighting and why? These are nice.'

'They're Coptic.'

'I know.'

'Open the drawers, there's some more. Only it's really the books I want you to look at. Did you ever read Rilke? Rainer Maria Rilke, did you ever read any? I think you should. They were organized and I wasn't. I should have known I could never break them. The man who did this to me, you know what he is today? Today he's the head of the Governor's special commission on crime.'

300

'I don't believe it.'

'Nancy Jane, your lover never lived in California. It went in there and it came out here and the man who did it is head of the Governor's special commission on crime. A salaried employee of the State of California and a charge on the taxpayer. I was nineteen weeks in the hospital, eleven of them with a tube in my side. I was catheterized for over five weeks. I still have one lung half-collapsed.'

'And you play squash?'

'I play squash, I go sport-fishing, I do everything a man can do. What do I have to lose? I'm on the far side of time. There isn't anything they can do to me any more. I never had a prayer. Who fights the Unions and wins? You'd be surprised the people who chickened out on me when they heard who I was fighting. I was young, I was stubborn, I thought I could be different. You know something? No one is different. I had a dream though, I had a dream. I wanted to create towns, whole cities, why be modest? I wanted to improve the quality of life of ordinary people, only like right away—'

'At a stroke.'

'Right. I wanted to give them the future right away, that was my slogan. And a damned good one. I had some bright people working for me. I had all kinds of people working for me and some of them were damned bright. The best. Did you ever read Freud on names?'

'A long time ago.'

'Only he had this theory about the significance of names for people and Pleasure is a hell of a name when you think about it.'

'He was thinking of you when he invented the Pleasure Principle, I assume?'

'Probably. I have to check that out. My ancestors were Huguenots. They fled persecution, probably, just like your people did. What are you, Ashkenazi?'

'God knows. I suppose so. I never think about it.'

'Think about it,' Larry Pleasure said. 'It matters. It matters who you are, where you came from. Don't ignore it. Those things weigh with a man. My ancestors came from Aquitaine, if you know where Aquitaine is, in south-western France. Maybe they had some British in them too. Their name was Pré-Sieur, if you can believe it, because I had a guy check this whole thing out for me at one time. You know what Pré-Sieur means? It means Lord of the Meadow. Somehow it got changed to Pleasure when they were driven out after Saint Valentine's Night—excuse me, Saint Bartholomew's Night—Pré-Sieur turned into Pleasure. Isn't that amazing, because I've always had a thing about land? What I wanted to do basically was give the land back to the people. And that's how I landed up fighting the Unions.'

'You have some beautiful pieces here,' Nancy said.

'I wanted to give the land to the people and I wanted to give pleasure to the people too, I guess, and that's how I came to have a hole drilled right through the middle of here by a sonofabitch who's now the Governor's special assistant. You believe me, don't you, Nancy? If I call you Nancy?'

'I never saw one like that outside the National Museum in Athens,' Daniel said.

'And you'll not see another. You know how much money I've been offered for that flute player? For that one piece? Thirty-five thousand dollars.'

'Don't you ever worry about someone coming and—?'

'What would he do with it? What could he do with it? He'd eventually have to come back here and sell it back to me. No one else would touch it. A piece like that, it's too unique to have a price.'

'He might keep it for himself,' Daniel said. 'You never told me you had anything Cycladic—'

'You know something, a man who could take that and keep it to himself, this sounds silly, it sounds phoney, but I mean it, a man who only wanted it for himself, he'd be welcome to it. I'd try and stop him, but if he succeeded and he could keep it quiet, he'd be welcome to it.'

'What you can hide, you can have.'

'Right. You know how I think about these things? I think of

302

them as on loan. I don't believe in ownership. Beauty can't be possessed. It simply cannot be possessed. When I was building Pleasure City, I told people, investors, I told them, no one's going to own this place, that's not a concept that interests me, and I won't have any part of it. They're going to live in it; it's going to be theirs, but own it they shall not. I worked like a bastard trying to sell that concept to the Unions. I told them right out they were standing between the people and what was already theirs, but would they listen? They thought I was dangerous; the banks thought I was unreliable; between them — well, when you lose the Unions and the banks on the same day, you've got to have problems. I asked them to let me address the membership — that's all poetry over there — but would they? One hour with the membership, that was all I asked; I never saw grown men so scared. Of course now I know what I should have done. I should've let them take their cut, the bosses, and accepted it as the price of a dream, but at the time I couldn't bring myself to it. I was unrealistic. I wanted the pleasure without the pain and that's not to be found, not in this world.'

'These weaves are unbelievable. Do you know Constantine Mersenas? Daniel, wouldn't Constantine love these weaves?'

'He has that shop in the village, right? I know him.'

'He gave us a beautiful icon.'

'The Copts are really fascinating people. One of the oldest Christian cultures in the world. Mysterious, isolated, insular, yet, until recently, immensely rich and immensely powerful. I hope you want to be rich, Meyer.'

'I'll take fame,' Daniel said. 'And influence, which is much the same thing.'

'You know what money does? It leaves you with only yourself to blame.'

'But it also leaves you with only yourself.'

'Who in shit else did you ever have? Love? Love is the confession, no, the enjoyment of the other person's existence as a separate entity, that's my version. Never possession. How can you possess other people? It's an impossibility. You can't possess them. What else was *Split* about? Fear of money is fear of criticism, fear of opportunity, fear of life. I truly believe that. That's where I crime Europeans, except maybe the ones who live round the Mediterranean. They're so goddamned frightened of being wrong. They'd sooner do nothing than be wrong. You should have your own finance, your own studio, your own unit and then you could make movies without relying on anyone's say-so but your own. You'd have no one to blame but yourself. You'd be free.'

'I doubt it. All that would happen would be that you'd worry about not losing money. You'd become a businessman. I'd sooner stay a pirate and ply the seas for a rich trader, scarce though they may presently be. My God, you've got a copy of *Themis*. This is only Jane Harrison's first and rarest book. She was a famous Cambridge classical scholar at the beginning of the century. One of the first women to break into the monastery and shake up the microcosmographs a bit. I've never seen a copy before.'

Larry said: 'Nancy, you haven't seen the pool. Oh I have all kinds of stuff I keep meaning to get around to reading. Daniel saw it yesterday. It's yours whenever you want to use it. Now, if you want to.'

Daniel opened the fly-leaf of the book: R.M.G.; Gavin's initials.

'*Hullo, it's me. I don't suppose you ever expected to hear from me again. I certainly never expected to write to you, but suddenly I feel what the hell. I'm sitting by the Dead Sea, having got away from the kibbutz where I've been working for the last little while. Earlier, I was in a hospital for women with mental problems. It was rather nasty, really. We were working as orderlies and you can imagine which end of the stick we got to hold. It got me down. I began to think I'd sooner be a patient than a helper.*

It was only three weeks ago I left, but already it seems ancient history … Like you and me. If you and I ever had a history, which I begin to doubt. I still think about you, if you can believe it, without much thinking about us. I mean, I see you on your own and think about you on your own.

Does that sound like bullshit? I suppose so, but I honestly think I wish you well until I think of having anything to do with you. Sour grapes? I'm actually interested in you, principally I think as a film director. I'd like to go to a movie this evening when it gets cool, a nice outdoor movie, and find it was one of yours and it was one where you'd done what you can really do. No, I don't imagine myself in it, not at all. I'm still sorry about you getting involved with Andy's thing. Sorry you were so bugged anyway.

Especially when I thought he was dead! That was really when I liked you least. You were so annoyed it wasn't you who was dead! The Israelis aren't like that at all. They don't want to be dead and they don't respect the dead. They take them as a lesson, that's all, of what can happen if you don't watch out. Like they say the only good advice a parent can give you is, Don't do what I did. The Israelis seem different this time. They're always spoiling for a fight. They seem absolutely determined not to be charming. It's struck me particularly this time.

So what? I suppose I've grown up a bit since the last time I was here and I can see them more clearly. But in a way, and a sad way, I'm glad to be able to find something wrong with them, glad and sad at the same time, as with parents. Why am I talking to you like this? Why shouldn't I? It seems wrong that just because we've been together I should be forbidden to talk to you.

I ought to say clearly: I don't want you back. (As I say, if I ever had you.) But that sounds like an old ploy, doesn't it? The old female game of turning away from what she really desires. Well, will you believe me if I say I really wouldn't want to go with you again?'

'No,' Daniel said.

'Pardon me?'

'I was just—'

'Oh, excuse me. I thought you were talking to me.'

'At least try to believe this isn't meant to do anything, just to be something. Because I do care for you. I don't think you ever cared for me, even in

bed, maybe particularly there. I think having someone on your own embarrasses you; you want to change everything, the whole world, everyone, but not particular people. You want women to encourage the warrior. Only when is the warrior actually going to do some fighting? What worries me about you is the way you wait. You wait and wait. When are you going to make something happen for yourself? I can't get you out of my mind, not because I want you, I'm O.K. in that department, but because you're a victim. I feel like I've left you to walk into a trap. I don't know but you seem to be waiting for an excuse not to do anything. You can put all this down to bitchiness, of course, the woman spurned. Actually I didn't feel too spurned; I enjoyed you and I left you, or you left me, no one has to be marked down for a loser. I think about you because it's easier to think about you than about me, easier to work someone else out than work yourself out. You're my victim if you want to look at it that way.

I thought I might stay in Israel when I first got here, but I shan't. I remember the first time I came I seemed to be something wonderfully small and unimportant. I picked fruit in the heat and I seemed to melt away to nothing, I was so inconspicuous. I worked so hard I never saw beyond the sweat on the end of my nose. I felt very unthreatened, absolutely at home, beyond the possibility of being singled out. I felt more vulgar, do you know what I mean? I wasn't special. Men didn't fancy me just because I was dark and foreign-looking; there are too many like me here — dark and at home-looking! I felt insignificant and much much freer. That was before '67. I was impressed too, by the people, their determination, their manliness, their togetherness, the whole bit. They seemed without doubts. England is all doubts, isn't it? Doubt and hostility and resentment; all the symptoms of age. Israel was young; you didn't have to reassure it, it went right on without you. Now? Now, I don't know; they seem to be looking for their enemy, looking for the danger that will make normality heroic again. They have a grudge against the world because the world won't give them the spoils that a victor ought to have. I'm thinking particularly of David Levin, who's an American and also now a lieutenant in the army. I've known him since he was nineteen and he'd been here a couple of years. When he first came here he was strong for coming to terms with the Arabs, he even talked about marrying an

306

Arab girl. He had love to spare. Now he's impatient. He's married and they have a child and it isn't working all that well and he just wants everything to stop. He wants the Arabs to admit they're licked and to go away forever. He wants them out of the way because they're so unreasonable. His wife too, whom I like, also a Rachel.

Well? How are you? Are you frowning as usual? Or smiling because I'm a fool? I'm not a fool. I would really love to see you make a great movie, something that gave you away and forced you to give yourself away. You're so conservative really. I can see it now, knowing you and knowing your films. You're so tight-assed, as David always says. Did you get tired of me because I enjoyed you so much? I sometimes think that was the reason. I think you were a bit scandalized, a bit frightened. Can you honestly say you weren't? I think you want to force women to enjoy you and it worries you when the force isn't needed. True? Not even a little bit true?

I shall probably stay here until the autumn. I have a lot of thinking to do. How are things in the film world? Any better? They're making quite a few things out here, or planning to. They say Billy Stern may be doing something here in the spring. Why not you? I met the head of the Cultural Department at the Ministry of Tourism. Sweet man; he'd heard of you. Naturally.

Well, I'm going to go now. Maybe one day we'll meet and have a drink and talk about old battles! One day, when we're old and grey ...

I'm reading Rilke. Have you ever read him? You should. Be healthy and strong, as the Israelis say.

Love, (Why not?)

RACHEL D.

'I posted the cards,' Daniel said. 'What's going on?'

'No one here,' Nancy said. 'I've been waiting.'

'All this time?'

'I went down to Constantine's and then I came back and there still isn't anyone.'

'I see your pants are here.'

'You think those are mine?'

'It's your material, and we said we were coming this afternoon. Obviously they're yours. Why don't you put them on and save time? If you still want to do the photographs for Constantine.'

'I guess I may as well. Only, Daniel, he doesn't want to shoot the pictures this afternoon. He has things he has to do. He says could we make it tomorrow?'

'And here have I been dangling my camera all around town like your average package tourist.'

'You can still take my picture,' Nancy said. 'How do they look, the pants?'

'Oh, the pants! A bit tight at the back, unlike the Canons' usual defence.'

'Sorry?'

'They look a bit tight across the back. Don't sit down is my advice. At least not before you've spoken to your solicitor. You really have to come to the Post Office sometime and see the postman. He wears two pairs of glasses at the same time. I've never seen that before. Do-it-yourself bi-focals. One pair sort of protrudes above the other, like a small boy's underpants coming over the top of his trousers. They look terrific. How do they feel?'

'Your Highness I am so sorry. Oh. Excuse me. Where did you get those trousers, please?'

'From the chair,' Nancy said. 'They were on the chair.'

'Please, take them off at once. Please. Those are the Princess's trousers. Please. I must ask you not to try anything on until I am here. Please.'

Daniel said: 'We said three-thirty. We've been here nearly half an hour.'

'I have your trousers ready for you in a few minutes. A few minutes and I am ready for you.'

'Surely we were here before the Princess?'

'You must forgive me, but they sail first thing in the morning, I promised Her Highness that I would have her trousers ready for her this evening. She has ordered several pairs and it means that my work staff are — I'm sure you understand —'

'In other words, my—ours—the ones we ordered haven't been started yet.'

'They've been cut, they're working on them now. The girl is working on them now.'

Nancy said: 'Please, don't worry about it. Daniel, it isn't important. *Nous avons tout notre temps.*'

'*Madame est trop gentille.*'

'*Pas du tout. Je comprends bien votre problème. Je me cède devant la Princesse avec grand plaisir.*'

'Virginia Playfair couldn't have put it better.'

'If they're sailing in the morning.' Nancy eased the trousers down her legs and sat on the low chair to draw them over her feet. 'It doesn't hurt us.'

'You're getting yourself in a tangle for some reason,' Daniel said. 'Let me help. You're like the postman, only with four legs instead of four eyes.'

'Your trousers will be ready in one hour,' Zeno said. 'In one hour, I promise you.'

'When is the Princess coming for her fitting? Is she having a fitting?'

'This evening. We are making her six pairs. She will be here at six o'clock.'

'We might see her,' Nancy said. 'I'm sure she's going to be very pleased with them. Aren't they beautiful?'

'Madame's will be just as beautiful, that I can promise. *Je les ai coupé moi-même.*'

'That's what we're paying for.' Daniel said. 'Well, what do you want to do for an hour?'

'Anything.'

'The post's really amazingly quick,' Daniel said, 'from England.'

'Oh did you get something?'

'My girl forwarded a few things, the day after we left; but still — four days isn't bad. I thought there might have been something from Gavin, but there wasn't. I still think he might have done your trousers before Astrid's; first come, first served, dammit. Old six-eyes asked me to take a telegram in to Larry on the way back. I didn't realize we were going to be so long. I hope it can wait.'

'You'd think they'd send it straight down.'

'Via your friendly neighbourhood Western Union man, I suppose? Old six-eyes doesn't have the staff. Oh Jesus, look who's here.'

'*Cherete! Ti kanome?*'

'I suppose we could ask him about the water.'

'She may've done somefink abaht it already like,' Daniel said. 'If we tell 'im, 'e'll be dahn vair messin' abaht, 'anging arahnd, pushin' 'is nose in, woan' 'e?'

Dmitri grinned; he might have understood Daniel's cockney perfectly.

'What news of Mr Gavin?'

'*Avrio, methavrio, etho,*' Dmitri said. 'Tomorrow, the day after, he'll be here.'

'I've heard that one before.'

'*Methavrio to proi,*' Dmitri said. 'The morning of the day after tomorrow.'

'That sounds like a final offer,' Daniel said. 'What else is new?'

'What are you doing now, *me tin kiria*, for the next hour?'

'How does he manage it?' Daniel said. 'He always catches us when we're between shows.'

'*Elate sto spiti mou.*'

'He wants us to go to his house.'

'*Na kathiste, na parete ena kafethaki ...*'

'We're going up to the top,' Nancy said, 'up to the church.'

'*Eki isichia ...*'

'*Pame epano, echome ena philo poo mas perimeni,*' Daniel said. 'I told him we're going up to meet a friend.'

Nancy smiled, with an affectation of regret, and somehow she managed to do Dmitri a favour by leaving him so reluctantly. Though she dragged Daniel round the corner, it was as if he were dragging her.

'Do you really want to go up to the church?'

310

'I love side streets,' she said. 'Highways and byways. I love doing what other people don't.'

The thickness of the snowy walls gave them a virginal, undisturbed air. The edges of the paving-stones were whitened too. Only the occasional pile of donkey dung punctured the untrodden illusion. They went under wooden lintels, concave with old buildings; flags of fresh washing blew like the banners of an unseen garrison. The shuttered houses and sightless windows were full of an amusing menace, so that the two of them smiled together, toiling against the slopes and steps, conscious of dim noises, animals and children, cribbed behind the walls. Once a donkey cried out, its passion expiring on a sigh, as if inside the cloistered darkness it had found some desperate satisfaction. The cement was moulded, one wall softening into another, one house into another, by years of white-wash. It was as though the weight of the sun had rounded the top coats into a sparkling drift of masonry. The path might have been shovelled out of this massed whiteness and the walls heaped up on either side. They reached the square at the top, where a palm tree hung down like the spokes of a broken green umbrella.

'We could do with Larry's pool right here.'

'We could too.'

'Except you still haven't got your things.'

'That wouldn't worry me.'

'It worried you before.'

'It was too soon after lunch.'

'What a good girl you are!' Daniel said.

Nancy said: 'You feel like you could go striding from one island to the next. One big step after another and you'd be all the way to Crete.'

'Like Poseidon on the way to the wars.' He had his arm round her, measuring her waist, and she leaned her head against him. 'What was he like in California?'

'He was a hustler. One of thousands. Satisfied?'

'No. What about Pleasure City? Did it ever really get off the ground?'

'Pleasure City was a sort of Levittown for moneyed morons. He sold a lot of plots, I believe, but no one ever saw the houses, or their money back.'

'He *was* railroaded though, was he?'

'Not before he'd gotten a lot of money from a lot of people. He was riding for a fall, because only a fall could get him out of trouble. He had reached the point where he had to deliver and there was nothing in the delivery truck.'

'So he staged an accident.'

'And said the other guy had ruined the merchandise. It's not a new story.'

'You mean he never intended it to work? He was just a swindler? He doesn't strike me like that. He may be a phoney, but surely he was a genuine phoney? He really did have a dream.'

'Sure he had a dream. All hustlers have a dream. He wanted to make a million *and* be hailed as the saviour of the people, both. Who doesn't? Alternatively, he was willing to take half a million and forget the people. When things are good, the hustler wants the sun to shine on everyone. When the clouds start building up, he takes the sunny patch for himself and nuts to the rest of you.'

'Sharp stuff, sharp stuff! Your memory's staged a remarkable comeback too.'

'Isn't everything supposed to be there if you try hard enough? For me, it's as though it was all written right there on him anyway in letters that big.'

'From where I stand it looks like more than half a million. Couldn't there just be another nought on there? Look again.'

'Probably so. No respectable bank turns nasty on you for less than five million.'

'The horse's mouth is remarkably beautiful, but it remains the horse's mouth. You know something? You have very nice writing. I was reading your postcards. Never trust a director with a postcard. I found myself wishing you were writing to me. You've never written me a letter.'

'Nor have you me.'

'People seem so much more real in letters than they do in the flesh.'

'Who are you thinking of?'

'I suppose McLuhan would say it's just a hangover from the age of print. After all, the first novels were written in letter form, weren't they? You always believe a letter. Love letters, after all, are somehow more – what? – enduring, certainly, but also more serious, than the love they celebrate. Your writing's very confident, as if you never had to hesitate.'

'You saw me writing them,' she said. 'You saw how much I hesitated. Perhaps that was why people were so often disappointed in wartime. They exchanged all those wonderful, generous, passionate letters and they came home and found old whosit.'

'Or old whosit and friend. Letters are always about the past or about the future and never about the limited, cramped old present, maybe that's the thing. Everything's terrific except what's actually happening. Life's like an hourglass and we always have to live where it's narrowest.'

'What should I do – pack my Basildon Bond and creep stealthily away to the next island and begin a passionate correspondence?'

'Basildon Bond,' Daniel said. 'He's the Civil Service brother of James Bond, isn't he? Basildon is the respectable, faintly pin-striped one with the hair *en brosse* who always reaches the last sixteen in the Captain's Prize at the golf club and has the wife with the ankles and the weight problem who pours half glasses of sherry, as if it was some kind of dangerously inflammatory liquor.'

'Living for the knighthood that might just come before he retires and might just not.'

'That's right,' Daniel said, 'If he gets his K, he'll die contented. How do you know about the secret dreams of a Civil Servant? Homework of a hostess, I suppose. You're a clever woman.'

'Knowledgeable,' Nancy said, 'not clever.' She turned her back on Agoria and put her elbows on the parapet behind her, and confronted the square. The flagstones shimmered in the sun. The triple barrels of the church closed off the side to their right. Above them, a narrowing ladder of houses scaled the hillside. To the left, the square sharpened to a dark path which sloped down, like a stream gathering weight, towards a reservoir of shadow under the lee of a large mansion. 'There's that man.'

'Man?'

'You saw yesterday. At the football.'

'Piers?'

'No. That Greek man.'

George Akrotiri came forward from the cupboard of shadow in which he was standing. He crossed the square, under the rattling palm, and, though within a few yards of them, contrived to bring his solitude with him. He carried a folded newspaper under his arm and wore on his lips the same smile of subtle reticence.

Daniel said: '*Kirie* Akrotiri, *cherete*.'

Akrotiri nodded slowly and then removed his tinted glasses, as if disguise were no longer necessary. He glanced around the square (Daniel was reminded of the last reel of *Viva Zapata*; would armed men people the skyline?) and then, replacing his glasses, went on into the church.

'We really ought to have a look inside,' Daniel said. 'While we're here.'

The church was lined with the soft smell of incense. A triangle of sunshine fell awkwardly across the foyer, emaciated by the dropping sun. Candles burned below the iconostasis; thin smoke tested the unblinking eyes of the saints.

'Mr Meyer.' Akrotiri was behind the screen where the villagers hung votive offerings. 'I'm sorry; I startled you.'

'Not at all. Only how do you know my name?'

'A friend told me you were here. He pointed you out to me.'

'Did you follow us up here?'

'No, of course not. I was thinking of you and then I saw you and the lady standing in the square.'

'And I just told someone that I was going to meet someone, when I actually wasn't, though I too was thinking of you.'

'Ah. Mr Meyer, as you may know, I am temporarily what shall I say?—inconvenienced.'

'I understand very well,' Daniel said.

'My freedom is somewhat limited.'

314

'But not for long, I hope.'

'I hope not. Mr Meyer, I want to ask you a favour.'

'Anything,' Daniel said. 'I hope you know how I feel.'

'Thank you. Mr Meyer, my wife and my two boys are now in London.'

'In London!'

'Yes. Naturally it is not easy for me to communicate with them. My letters are censored. Sometimes they are stopped. This is a fact.'

'You speak fantastic English,' Daniel said. 'Where did you learn it, here?'

'In London. I was for three years the correspondent of *To Vrathi* in London.'

'I'm sorry,' Daniel said. 'Do go on.'

'Yes. I am wondering whether you would do a service for me and when you go back to England take some letters for them from me.'

'It would be a privilege,' Daniel said. 'Is there anything else I can do? Anything?'

'Yes,' Akrotiri said. 'As you know, quite apart from my particular difficulties, which I believe will be temporary –'

'We all believe that,' Daniel said.

'Yes, apart from that, for all Greeks it is very difficult just now, for those who have a family abroad to get money to them. The restrictions are very severe. I am wondering therefore, Mr Meyer, if you could possibly give some money to my wife.'

'How much?' Daniel said.

'About five hundred pounds.'

'Five hundred.'

'If you could. I am asking a lot.'

'Not a bit. On the other hand, you are asking five hundred pounds.'

'Yes.'

'Tell me something, if you don't mind –'

'Of course.'

'What decided you to ask me? What made you think I'd be – willing – or able?'

'I know something of your reputation. I read the reviews of your last film in *Le Monde*. Also in *Sight And Sound*.'

'My God,' Daniel said. 'They slaughtered it.'

'On the contrary. On the contrary. It was very perceptive.'

'We must have read different numbers.'

'Daniel, I'm going outside.'

'I'll be right out. Is there any reason why we're having this conversation in church? Are you being shadowed or anything? Because—'

'I simply prefer to have private conversations in private. No, no one is following me, not today. But the villagers can be very curious. I was a film critic, you see. I have actually reviewed your films a few times.'

'Perhaps I should see what you said,' Daniel said, 'before I make up my mind. No, listen, of course I'll make sure your wife gets some money. If I can make it five hundred, of course I will. But I'll certainly make sure she gets something. Does she have somewhere to live, because—?'

'Oh yes, she is living in Moscow Road, Bayswater, of course. She is quite happy. As far as the money is concerned—'

'Please don't worry. She'll get whatever she needs.'

'And I, of course, will let you have whatever you can give her here in Greek money.'

'Oh I see,' Daniel said, 'in that case—'

'Yes?'

'Well, I could probably manage the five hundred. I mean, from friends and people. People who feel the same way I do. How long have you been apart?'

'Nearly three years.'

Daniel said: 'Did you want her to go? Did you want them not to stay in Greece? Under the present people.'

'I was hoping to follow, but then I was arrested.'

'How are things here?'

'Dull.'

'Do you have enough to read?'

'To read, yes; to do, not.'

'Have you ever thought of getting away?'

'Yes, of course.'

'Would it be that difficult?'

Akrotiri said: 'It would take some arrangement.'

'Would you want to go back to the mainland or to get away—abroad, I mean?'

'I have nothing I can do on the mainland at the present time. The *maquis* is not effective. But then this is rather academic. Unless you have a helicopter in your luggage?'

'Surely there are boats?'

'The harbour is patrolled; my house is watched. Not only by the police.'

'Informers?'

'Busybodies, shall we say?'

'But it could be done.'

'Of course.'

'The thing would be to get you to England presumably.'

'That would be very nice,' Akrotiri said.

'How long would it take you to be ready, if the chance came?'

'Shall we go now?'

'Why were you actually arrested? What was the charge?'

'That I belonged to an illegal organization. An illegal organization being, of course, any organization that was formerly legal. The organization to which I belonged was and is a political party equivalent roughly to the right wing of your Labour Party. There were, of course, those much more to the right than I who were also arrested. No one is safe; although it is true that no one is necessarily unsafe. It is a matter of caprice.'

'Caprice. I like that. But, of course, it isn't funny to live under.'

'It is as a matter of fact quite funny, but not very pleasant.'

'How do the people here regard you?'

'Oh. They vary, naturally. It is so easy to damage them. And the tourists have brought them something they don't want to endanger. They have waited a long time for it. I don't blame them. After all, we politicians never worried our heads greatly about them, certainly we never emptied our pockets for them. To come from a village is bad enough in Athenian society, but to come from an *island* village ... We have our expiation to do.'

'And when you've done it?'

'We shall hope to improve our record.'

Daniel said: 'I envy you.'

'I beg your pardon?'

'*Sas zilevo*. I envy you.'

The door creaked. Daniel expected Nancy. The corporal of police was outlined in light, clinking his amber beads. Akrotiri touched Daniel on the arm and walked towards the door. Daniel followed, somehow defying Akrotiri more than the corporal.

'*Yasoo, Michali*,' Akrotiri said. 'Mr Meyer, this is Michalis Lefteris. It is time, yes?'

'It is time,' said the corporal, shaking hands with Daniel.

'Every afternoon I give Michalis an English lesson. He is in the Tourist Police. Promotion depends on learning a language. *Pame*. Perhaps I shall see you again. Perhaps one afternoon you will come and give us a little conversation? The real thing. Meanwhile I must remember envy, of course.'

'*Efcharistos*,' Daniel said. 'With pleasure.'

'I've got this telegram to deliver,' Daniel said. 'I told you.'

'Surely you could find a boy to take it down? Constantine's boy would take it down for you.'

'They look terrific anyway, don't they? The pants. They really do. Look, if you want to stay up in the village, why don't you? I'll wander down to Larry's and deliver the telegram and see you back at the house.'

'If that's what you want to do.'

Daniel said: 'We've already waited around for an hour.'

'I saw her once in Paris,' Nancy said, 'with him. I'd like to see her again just once, close to.'

He put his arms round her. 'I'll see you back at the house.'

He walked heavily, dizzily, as if he had had an afternoon of drinks. He was hardly conscious of walking at all. Though he

318

seemed soon to be at Larry's gate, the hours had lost their firm proportions. The sun seemed higher now than when he had come out of the church with George Akrotiri. He vaulted the gate and walked softly down the steps towards the house. He found a side door and was in a passage leading, he thought, towards the library. How many of Robert Gavin's books had found their way on to Larry Pleasure's shelves? Recognizing the door, he went in. As he crossed the threshold he heard a distant clamour. For a moment, he was pleased; everyone was occupied elsewhere. Then he heard running feet. He turned, embarrassed at being empty-handed but too far from a shelf to grab a modest book, and the door burst open.

'I—'

The man who faced him showed no sign of having run. It was the grey-haired man, wearing only a pair of flowered shorts. His flat stomach hardly moved.

Daniel said: 'I'm Daniel Meyer. I'm a friend of Larry's. I was just hoping to find a book. Is he here?'

The grey-haired man moved his head, several times.

'I've got a telegram for him.'

The grey-haired man held out his hand.

Daniel said: 'You must be Buck Lehman. Larry mentioned you were staying, at lunch. I'm Daniel Meyer.'

The man nodded, his hand still extended.

'It's addressed to Larry,' Daniel said. 'I think I'd sooner give it to him personally, if you don't mind. You're staying here, I gather? Fantastic place, isn't it? Look, I'd really sooner give it to him personally. He is here, isn't he?'

'I'll take it.'

Daniel said: 'I was hoping to see him actually anyway.'

'He went out.'

'Oh? I've just come from the village. I didn't see him.'

'He didn't go to the village.'

'In that case, I'll come back later. I'll come back and see him later.'

'I'll take the telegram,' Buck Lehman said.

319

'I wonder if I left something on the terrace,' Daniel said. 'I think I may have dropped something. We were here for lunch. Larry and my—my fiancée are old friends.'

'If you'll just give it to me.'

'Look, I'm sorry if I gave you a start the way I came in here. Only Larry did say to come by when I wanted a book. Did I set off some sort of alarm system or something?'

'That's O.K.'

'You'll make sure he gets it.'

'Sure.'

'I'm sorry he's not here. I was hoping for a dip in the pool.'

'Shit,' Daniel said, when he had climbed the gate and was back in the open. 'Shit, shit, shit.'

He walked along the tilted hull of the island. He considered going back to the house. He was able to imagine himself there, so clearly that when he found himself stumbling down the polished rocks towards the *taverna* it was as though he had split in two. He could see himself in the deserted house, he experienced the slow minutes until Nancy returned, and at the same time he was looking down at the bodies on the beach below him and the salted blue of the sailcloth Paniotis spread over his terrace.

The hotel was silent. Daniel went round to the lavatories. When he came out, he stood staring over the geraniums at the mounds of clean sand below the *taverna*. A narrow terrace ran along outside the rooms on the first floor and formed a ledge above his head. He had a vision of a film set in South America. An American, the liberal President of a College who has been forced to a bitterly outspoken resignation by a reactionary State Governor, is appointed to some consolatory mission in a Republic where urban guerrillas are more and more active. During his troubled reign as President he has been loyally sustained by the woman, now his wife, with whom he was having a necessarily clandestine affair. Although she assures him that his new appointment, as Chief Environment Consultant to the Good Neighbour Project, is both a genuine promotion and a recognition by Washington of the injustice he has suffered, he is obsessed by a sense of weakness. Perhaps there was no way in which he could successfully have resisted the Governor, who had all the levers in his hand, but he fears that he has failed through cowardice. He narrows this down to a belief that he was wrong to resign; he should have waited to be kicked out. It would, of course, have made manifest the weakness which his defiant withdrawal has obscured, but it would also have made unmistakably clear the ruthlessness of the Governor. As it was, he received an embarrassingly fulsome farewell and a mildly eulogistic release from the Governor's press office, the standard reward of the defeated liberal who has made peace with his conscience without rocking the boat. He feels himself too elaborately praised; less written up than written off. The Republic to which he is now sent, on an increased salary and with an impressive diplomatic title, is in the grip of raging inflation. Ordinary political activity has broken down. With his semi-ambassadorial status, he seems to have been appointed the conscience of a society which he is powerless to influence. If President Verdugo were more autocratic he might qualify for greater aid from Washington, but his charmless democracy earns only the lukewarm endorsement of which the mission the ex-President heads is the typical symbol. He is trying to initiate a programme of systematic contraception, which meets the opposition of the Catholic Church, whose more enlightened leaders are otherwise at one with him in the desire to bring the country back to political stability. The ex-President and the moderates are divided from each other by a metaphysical barrier which both acknowledge to be temporary. The crisis, however, is less polite. The *guerrilleros* become daily more outrageous. The ex-President's programme is hampered by the collapse of Verdugo's authority. He can control neither the students nor the workers. The ex-President realizes that goodwill cannot succeed without the direct economic intervention of the United States government; possibly secret police help is needed too. He writes to a friend in Washington, explaining the seriousness of the situation. Soon afterwards, the first American official is abducted. The

321

abduction is ill-planned. The victim, a C.I.A. adviser to the local police, is able to escape. He gives an interview in which he dwells on the youth and ineptitude of his captors. Then a Brazilian diplomat is kidnapped. The guerrillas give notice that they will release him when fifteen of their comrades are released from prison. Verdugo is determined to show himself strong. The guerrillas will never dare to carry out their threats. The deadline is reached; the diplomat is found murdered. Verdugo announces that he will now take ruthless measures. But what can he do that he has not done already? The ex-President's programme is even more severely threatened by the new tension and by those in Congress who would now suspend all aid to the republic. The ex-President attempts to explain the contradictions in the American attitude to a visiting deputation from Washington. He is sharply snubbed. They are looking to him, they say, to prove that the local people deserve the generosity they are being shown. He is once more in the dilemma which faced him in the College. He begins to take brave risks. He goes among the shanty-town dwellers at the edge of the city and tries to persuade them of the humanitarian merits of his mission. He is warned by Verdugo that the local police can no longer guarantee his safety. When he is bundled into a car as he walks past the Fountain of the Martyrs, he suffers an extraordinary sense of release. The dark basement in which he is now held is like a new world. He feels exceptionally alive. His captors are young and unsmiling. One of them is a girl. His efforts to be unpolitically friendly are coldly rejected. At first he tells his gaolers how hopeless it is to hold him and how ill-judged, but he is aware that he is strengthening their resolve by his mild protests. The more stringent the measures for his detention the more helplessly happy he becomes. He is moved from one flat to another. Only when he has crossed the city bundled in the back of an open motocyclette, with a bicycle over him and his mouth stuffed with rag, does he realize that he has missed several easy chances to draw attention to himself. The death which he sees coming towards him is frighteningly attractive. Or does he think that he can join those who have captured him? He delights in goading them, in forcing them to defend

322

their ideas. He becomes, whether they like it or not, a sort of Socrates. He nags them to a logical defence of their position. He argues the policies of America with a greater zeal than he could ever show among Americans. He wants to make plain to them what it is they are rejecting when they turn aside from the liberalism which has failed him. Meanwhile, they have given an ultimatum to the government over the fifteen prisoners. Pressure is put on Verdugo by Washington. Verdugo resists; he is afraid of seeming weak and he hopes now to extract more aid from the U.S. government. To cave in without gaining either money or prestige is more than his reputation for *machismo* could endure. The ex-President, unaware of the exact date set for his execution, proceeds with the slow education of his captors. Do they really have a viable social programme? Are their ideas for a new university really feasible? Is their very seriousness a sort of mask to enable them to hide from themselves the frivolous and impractical nature of their plans? Reluctantly they come to realize the strength of his intellect. He is careful not to propose any solutions to their problems. His position would be ruined if they thought that he was attempting to intrude his own ideas or subvert theirs. He is valuable only because he can be no part of their revolution. His happiness comes from a sense of involved impotence. He opposes, with belittling derision, the melodramatically violent ideas of the young woman. She takes petty revenge by bringing him bad food and by denying him cigarettes. He grows leaner. He gives up smoking. He refuses to appeal or to toady. And she responds by falling in love with him; or rather, in hatred. For ideologically she will not yield; her love for him humiliates her. His exhilaration is amazing to him. He is thin, weak, garrulous, but he is proud to be alive. Resignation restores his vitality. One day he makes them laugh; their good humour frightens and disturbs him. The deadline draws nearer. The young people now dread that their demands will not be met. He thinks that they dread killing him (he is aware of their dilemma) but they insist that their fears are less about killing him, which has been openly discussed as a sort of charmless necessity, than for their comrades. He offers to go and negotiate with the President. Either he will succeed in obtaining the release of the San Fernando fifteen or he will return. He doesn't really want to die. He only wants, he realizes, to be free of the life he previously led. Because of that desire, because of his indifference to his old life, he has become strong. He no longer wants the capable woman who so loyally supported him in his battle with the Governor. The guerrillas want to save their friends and, no doubt, they have little stomach for murder. They agree to put it to Verdugo that the ex-President be allowed to come and plead personally for the release of the San Fernando fifteen. They trust him to return, should he fail. Finally an agreement is reached and the ex-President, imagining himself a kind of sacred herald, is delivered to the Palace. He is promptly snatched from public view and transported to America. The San Fernando fifteen are taken to a new prison and fresh hostages are arrested as a result of the 'interrogation' of the party who drove the ex-President to the rendezvous and met a road block on the way back. They include the girl. The ex-President tries vainly to escape from the U.S.A. and return to the Republic. He refuses to go back to his wife. Liberty weighs on him like a life sentence. The title of the film is *The Prisoner Of Freedom*.

The sounds of the afternoon, the calls of children and swimmers across the water, the chafing of insects in the field beyond the stone wall, the complaints of a drover barracking a reluctant donkey, a man hammering in the *taverna*, the pumping of a *caique* engine, induced a sort of trance in which reckless ideas and the dream of success worked together in Daniel's mind. Now he was planning a savage but hated masterpiece, now he was being acclaimed for a timely blockbuster, made on a shoestring and grossing in Billy Stern proportions. And among the sounds, like some phrase entering a concerto, he heard a sort of mewing, at once denying and encouraging, a plaintive moan which faltered and then became as regular as the *caique*. He waited, knowing what it was and yet suspended in amusement and alarm. It reminded him of the girl when Nancy attacked the splinter, the rhythmic 'Aiee', stereotyped and passionate. Memory brought the dark girl to life, the beads of sweat on her charmingly downy lip, the movement of her hands against her ears. He could imagine the ears, soft and moist. The woman cried out, 'Lover, oh *lover*!' and Daniel stood rigid below the terrace. In the silence which followed, he trembled. He put his head down on his arms and the pissy smell of geraniums filled his nostrils. He yawned his dismay and smiled to cover it, to excuse it to himself. He heard a little laugh, like a glass bell, and a hyphen of sound, a low, flat murmur and then the laugh was repeated. A door opened on the terrace. He stood back under the lip of grained concrete. Could he see arms, the shadow of folded arms on the parapet above? He heard the whisper of slippered feet. He kept in the lee of the terrace and dodged round the corner and up, under the blue sailcloth.

'Did you see her?'
'Did I see—?'
'Anyone. The Princess, I meant. Who else?'
'No, I didn't. I didn't. Nuts, she never came, did she?'
'Flora, no. We needn't have worried. Or rather perhaps we should have worried. There still isn't any water. Did she not have a fitting after all?'
'She was never going to have one apparently, at least not at the shop. Zeno took the pants out to the yacht.'
'Ah. But then why were they on the chair?'
'Vanity? I don't know. They had to be somewhere, I guess. What have you been doing?'
'Thinking. Watching the sun go down.'
'Did you swim?'
'I didn't swim and I didn't fly. Actually I thought up a film.'
'Just like that?'
'It's the only way,' Daniel said. 'Either it comes or it doesn't. Like so many things, isn't that right?'
'You've had a bad experience,' Nancy said.
'No, I haven't. Maybe somebody else has had a good one, that always depresses me.'

'You sound like I ought to know what you're talking about, only I don't. I was hoping I could wash my hair.'

'There's a bucket Flora used, I was going to say uses, but probably that's optimistic. Do you think we offended her in some way? Should we have given her money or something? I could try and get into the cistern through the trapdoor in the roof. All we have to do is find the key for the padlock. It wouldn't be plumbing, but it'd be water.'

'We ought to be able to find what makes it go, two intelligent people.'

'The pump's down below the terrace, I found that, but it's locked. I'll bet Flora takes the keys with her. That's probably what Dmitri was grinning about. I should have gone and found her when we were up in the village. God, everything on this island seems a long way from everything else.'

'I really would like to wash it.'

'We could always go down to Larry's.'

'Before we go down to Larry's, I'd like to wash it.'

'Ah. In that case, I'll try and open the padlock. After all, I've already cracked one crib in this house. Why not another?'

'What was the film about?'

'Impotence really, I suppose,' Daniel said.

'That doesn't sound much like you.'

'We'll have to go somewhere else if we want to eat. Damn the bloody woman, why the hell couldn't she come? Why the hell couldn't she either come or say something? We can always eat at the *taverna*, I suppose.'

'That's actually what we said we were going to,' Nancy said. 'In the evenings.'

'Beauty is all very well,' Daniel said, 'but I still like things that turn on when I want them to.'

'Have you decided what you're going to do about your friend?'

'Have I decided what I'm going to do about my friend. What friend? I have so many.'

'You met in the church. Are you going to give her some money, his wife?'

'I don't know about give. He didn't say give. I would give her some, if necessary, but that's not the deal he asked for. If he wants me to, I will, obviously. The question is how much. Christ, would you believe it, the key's under the lock thing. Running water as soon as I get the bucket in, never despair. You don't think I should help him.'

'It isn't anything to do with me,' Nancy said.

'Can you take it if I lower it over the side? Let it right down or it'll spill, let it down on to the ledge. Then if you empty it in the basin, I'll get another one. You're still allowed to have an opinion.'

'Sure you should help him, if you want to.'

'What would you think if I wanted to help him get away?'

'Does he want to be helped to get away?'

'I think so. But what would you think?'

'What're you going to do? Buy him an outboard motor and a reliable map and point him in the right direction? Or lend him your passport and ink in the eyeglasses?'

'You think I should leave him where he is.'

'I never said that.'

'The dialogue implied it.'

'Of course,' Nancy said, 'if you did get him away, he could take care of his own wife.'

'If we got him far enough, I suppose he could. Stand by for bucket number two. How many are you going to need? Obviously it's something that would take a bit of arranging. I can't think passports are that important. I wasn't exactly thinking of him going Olympic Airways. There are always boats. He says the harbour's watched, but Paniotis has got a boat, Larry's got a couple of boats. The Princess has got a boat. You must admit that would be a nice touch. Maybe we could dress him as a woman and smuggle him aboard; that way, they'd have a fourth for bridge.'

'It's funny,' Nancy said. 'You're so keen to do good, but you don't think anyone else is any good at all.'

'That's not funny, old man, that's what it's all about.'

'You really want to hurt people. I noticed that the first time I saw you. The way you talked to that girl.'

'Well, there we are,' Daniel said. 'While you're doing that, I'll go and see if I can jemmy the pump house. I don't frankly give much for my chances. What girl?'

'Oh some girl at Virginia's party that night.'

'What did I say to her?'

'I don't remember what you said. I only remember the way you looked.'

'I can't see any key down here. It's either brute force or Open Sesame. Open Sesame! It's brute force. She may've left the engine key inside. If it's locked. Shit, this is a bastard. Can't be done. It's still rather a shock that there are some things that really can't. I wonder what the nearest free territory is from here.'

'Sorry, I had my head under.'

'The nearest free territory from here. Israel? Probably Israel. Or Turkey. Turkey. I don't suppose they're too keen to help the Greeks.'

'My ears are full of soap.'

'If we heisted Akrotiri.'

'You're not serious.'

'That's what I'm afraid of. That's why I'm beginning to think I am.'

'Is that really a good reason? Boy, that feels better.'

'Want me to come and rub? I'm not going to do any good down here. Come on, let me. I shall have to go up and find Flora, find out what's happened because this is ridiculous. Maybe she's sick.'

'What about that man who brought us here? He seemed responsible. Maybe he's the man to get hold of.'

'Nancy, maybe we should leave. Maybe we should go somewhere else. Either somewhere really simple, like Agoria, or maybe we should just go to Mykonos and find a good hotel. It's up to you. Or Crete we could go to.'

'And what about Mr Gavin?'

'I don't want to waste our time waiting for Gavin. He may never show. I'd like to see him, but I'm not about to spoil our holiday waiting for him.'

'I like it here,' Nancy said. 'I'm happy.'

'Are you really?'

'You sound like you want me not to be.'

They skirted Larry Pleasure's house and went down to the cliffs. The sun was sinking behind the *Leto*, reddening the sea and turning the yacht into a black vessel of flame. The motorboat had been hoisted inboard; a dinghy floated under the stern. The spars were bare.

'What do those flags say, Daniel, do you know?'

'Let me see now. Ah yes, if I remember my Admiralty codes correctly they say — it's coming back now — "Three hundred pounds a week". That's it. That's what they say. Exclusive.'

'One day —' She grabbed his arm and they began to wrestle, grinning, out there on the edge of the rocks, with the sea clapping faintly below them. She played and then, surprised perhaps at how strongly she had him, how effectively she could turn and twist his arm, she threw herself against him, as if he were a stiff door, and drove him to the ground. He yielded, remembering Alexander at the Issus, not to mention Hannibal, and let her spend her first charge. He enjoyed her awkward aggression, enjoyed making her think that she was winning. She scampered after him, when he dodged, hands out, and slithered down the mild precipices along the cliff top. On a level plate of barnacled rock, he turned against her. Her breath came rawly in his face, peppermint-flavoured; her teeth flashed, grinning with effort. He caught her wrists and forced her to the right, away from the sea, down on to the coarse floor. She went on one knee and then back with a bump. He straddled her and sat on her biceps, like a schoolboy. 'Daniel,' she said, 'these are my best pants.'

'You'll have a new pair tomorrow,' he said. 'And the day after.'

'There's also my hair. Please let go of me.'

'Rape is no easy science, is it?' he said.

'That's why men learned to tell lies,' she said. 'Now I've lost an earring. Daniel, I've lost one of my earrings. Please look.'

'Pax? That's what small boys used to say when they'd had enough. Latin Peace. *Pax, pacis*. Remember *The Go-Between*? What was really missing in that, now I come to think about it, was the pleasure the two lovers must've got in corrupting the boy, the subtler pleasure they must have got in enmeshing him in their affair. The film made out that they only wanted each other and only used their power over the boy to keep in touch with each other. But surely it went deeper—look, you are funny, don't look where I'm looking, look somewhere else—surely the affair grew deeper and more exciting because they were actually consuming the boy, enslaving him. It changed from love to something else. The Master never seemed to realize that. The boy became their meat. They ate him up. What movies one can always make out of other people's work! The man seduced the boy and the girl seduced the boy. He cheated him of the truth about sex and she cheated him of true affection. He wasn't the catalyst; catalysts don't change. He was their battlefield. And ze shape of ze battlefield alters ze nature of ze contest fought over it. Clausewitz. It's a funny thing, but it's true: relationships begin between two people but they end up with three.'

'And who's the third person in ours, if you please? We're not going to find it.'

'Wait a minute. Hold it. Stand still. It was snagged in your sweater all the time, half-way down your back.'

'Do you think?'

'Maybe they haven't turned up yet. Your lover. Our son. Who knows?' He watched as she re-attached the earring, face tilted, her ear listening to her two cupped hands.

'You'll have to get them to give us more time.' The voice was at the cliff-top beside them. Daniel shied at the sharp kick of sound. Nancy released her earring and looked round. Where did the voices come from? 'You know how it is in a place like this. It has its advantages and it has its disadvantages. They have to appreciate that.'

'You're two whole months behind schedule.'

'I'm doing what I can. You're doing what you can. What more can we do?'

'Behind what you promised. They're understandably concerned.'

'Buck, will you please try and understand? Will you make that much of an effort for me?'

The two men were in a small boat in the cove below where Daniel and Nancy were standing.

'You know what this water reminds me of? Flat Coca-Cola. A whole damned ocean of flat Coca-Cola. Buck, will you see it from my angle? Will you just try and do that for a moment?'

'I don't have to tell you what's in people's minds.'

'Buck, have I ever failed to keep my word to you personally? Have I? Answer me please.'

'You've had their money.'

'Part of their money. I've had part of their money. And I have also delivered part of the merchandise. Can anyone say I haven't?'

'Larry, it's two months now.'

'Buck, I'm asking you as a friend, I'm asking you as an associate, I'm asking you as someone who knows the way I work.'

Nancy said: 'The puppy. Daniel, the puppy. Have you seen, him?'

'What in hell are they doing down there? Surely they're not fishing? No, I haven't, now you mention it. Not all day. He's probably gone home. You see a lot of them running around. Have they got lobster pots down there or what?'

'These operations aren't that simple.'

'Maybe they're in the seaweed business. Supplying seaweed to Mr Chow's. That could be big trade. We couldn't have taken him home with us, anyway, the puppy. So it's just as well if he's decided to make his own way in the world. We'll probably see him around. Better carry a pocketful of biscuits in case. Come on, let's go eat. What the hell do you think they're doing?'

Nancy said: 'Oh, Larry's always got something on the stove.'

'I got the impression that Larry's on the stove and Mr Lehman's turning on the heat.'

'Maybe Larry needs someone like that to keep him going. He needs to feel menaced. He can't function without adrenalin.'

'He likes to run risks, is that it?'

'I guess he doesn't feel alive unless he's in danger. Something like that.'

'In that case, maybe he's the man to wheel Akrotiri to freedom. He's got the cruiser.'

'I don't really think that'd be dangerous enough to interest him.'

'Small-time stuff, huh? You're probably right. Only what exactly is so big deal about fishing up stones? That's what it looked like to me, they were fishing up stones.'

'We'll have to ask him,' Nancy said.

'You wouldn't?' He pulled her back to him and kissed her and turned the kiss into a longer question. When she leaned away from him, he raised his brows. 'You couldn't. If that Lehman character's on holiday, I certainly wouldn't like to see him when he's working.'

'What would you do if you were on your own?' Nancy said. 'Would you go down to Larry's now? Would you move in?'

'I'd be tempted,' Daniel said. 'But probably I'd do nothing. That, of course, is what being tempted usually comes to. And you?'

'I'd run,' Nancy said.

'Run? Would you? In which direction?'

She smiled. 'Ça, c'est mon petit bagage.'

'If you'll forgive me, I don't think Skinner is saying the same thing as Eysenck at all; not at all. I think the Skinnerian thesis is a completely different thesis. I give you there's a relationship, but it's very far from being a one-to-one or even a parallel relationship. Skinner believes that all mental phenomena can be reduced or translated into behavioural phenomena — into behaviour — '

'We used to call him Watson in my day,' Daniel said. 'Would it cause a conditioned hostility response if I were to take this chair?'

'Please go right ahead.'

'Thanks. Does anybody ever read Watson any more?'

'I don't think I ever heard of him. Did you ever hear of Watson?'

'How about Hitler? Did you ever hear of Hitler? A. Dolf Hitler? He was an Austrian philosopher. He lives right over there. Retired now, but still influential.'

332

'Is that right? Eysenck seems to me to be more of an élitist than Skinner does. Almost a moralist. Skinner isn't really either of those two things.'

'There's something very reassuring about hearing young men arguing,' Daniel said. 'They act like there was no greater enemy in the world than a false idea. They still believe that no one can willingly err and that you'd no more turn away from truth than you would from beauty. And you know something? I still half believe it myself. I wish someone would come out and take a bloody order.'

'*Parakalo*—' Nancy said.

'*Amesos*. Right away.'

'Partly, I think, that's what gets me into so much trouble with women.'

'Oh?'

'I can't help thinking that if they're beautiful they must also be good.'

'That sounds very unwise.'

'As I've discovered. Hullo, *kalispera*.'

'*Kalisperasas*.'

'Hullo, how full it is tonight! Vassili, how full it is!'

'I'll get some chairs from inside.'

'Have you had a good day?' Daniel said.

'I've had a quite superb day,' Davina Long said. 'I've worked, I've swum, I've done everything. And you?'

'We haven't worked, we haven't swum, and we've done nothing. Why haven't we swum?'

'There wasn't time,' Nancy said.

'That's right; there wasn't time.'

Vassili came out with a brace of chairs and handed one to Davina, who took it with outstretched arms and swung it over Daniel's and Nancy's heads. Vassili handed her the second chair, which she put down hardly a foot from where he was standing. He sat down, as triumphant as an acrobat.

Daniel said: 'We walked up to the other end of the beach this morning. It's much better up there in many ways.'

333

'Better? Is it? How? How better?'

'Fewer people. And much the same sand. There's even possibly a better view. You can see all the people up here who aren't down there.'

'That sounds very complicated,' Davina said.

'You tidy up the syntax,' Daniel said. 'Is the *taverna* up there as bad as everyone says?'

'*Etsi ketsi.* He fills up in July and August. Kosta—Kosta is a bit of a character. In the war, he used to take people from Athens to Turkey in his *caique*. Refugees, Jews, from Piraeus to the Turkish coast. He made several trips. He is a great navigator, or was. Now—' Vassili made a cup of his hand and tilted the thumb, like a spout, towards his mouth, once, twice, three times. 'He never goes to sea. He has a *taverna*, but he spends no money, the food is so-so. Mainly—' The tipped hand and the jutting thumb repeated their story. 'He was a great navigator and quite a brave man, but now ... no good.'

'He's also a monarchist, isn't he?' Daniel said.

'A monarchist? Oh, you mean the portraits. It was once a law to have these portraits. Kosta can't be bothered to take them down. He's out of date with the laws like he is with everything else. Kosta is not a monarchist.'

Daniel said: 'How does the régime affect you personally?'

'On the moon,' Vassili said, 'six kilos have the same weight as one here. Yet here we don't think six kilos very heavy. If they got lighter perhaps it would be nice, but as it is ... '

'And then, of course, one's not obliged to try and lift them at all. I suppose he's very bitter?'

'Possibly,' Vassili said, 'possibly.'

'You're not sympathetic?'

'You're looking quite striking tonight,' Nancy said. 'I love those dresses.'

'Sympathetic? No. I admire Kosta—for what he did—'

'Oh, do you like it?' Davina said. 'It's only Liberty's.'

'I know,' Nancy said.

'One does a thing and then it's done. Then one must do

something else, isn't that right? One can't sympathize with someone for his achievements, surely! That would be too much.' Vassili burst into an explosion of laughter. His assumption of good humour brought smiles from those who had heard nothing of the conversation. Food was passed between him and the table, as he leaned back, until he seemed to have made an operetta of the whole scene. His liveliness acted like the crash of an overture. Paniotis, plates all up his arm, managed a smile of effort, like a non-singer embarrassed into joining in a well-known chorus. 'And the wine, Paniotis, *to crasaki*? *To echis*?'

'*Amesos.*'

As the darkness came down around them, the terrace became a silver tent in the blue desert of the night. The *retsina* came in its frosted, salmon-pink can, followed by another can, and then another. Vassili presided like the Bacchus in a painted revel. The pace of the voices rose as if everyone on the terrace belonged to a single party. Though people still sat in their ordinary places, two by two, four by four, back to back, their separate humours struck a common rhythm, a common crescendo of expectation which was met at last when Paniotis turned up the gramophone and the pluck of a mandolin, the bray of a bagpipe, promised the dance. The diners, almost all of them, breathed out together, 'Aaaah,' and turned their chairs to see who would begin. The old man whom Daniel had seen at Kosta's lurched out of the kitchen in his ragged trousers and elbowless jersey. His face was shrivelled like an old glove, his eyes were those of a lizard. His ribbed hands, like paddles, fended away the air and his body, wooden shoulders, locked waist, teased the onlookers like a knowing girl. The diners smiled and sighed once more. The stiff old knuckles rippled; the fingers tested the nap of the night. The old feet sketched a figure and came back over it and moved towards a table. The hissing gaslight flashed dramatically in the narrowed old eyes. The gramophone needle rasped harshly but its dusty caw seemed only to add a proper, rustic note to the hoarse clarinets and the dawdling bouzouki. Chairs moved, the attentive apology of those whose feet pretended to remember what their heads denied. The smiles grew flatter, toothless, for fear of being called out too soon. The old man taunted them with his shuffling confidence. He danced; it was a parody that was the genuine thing, just as the music, grating through the cheap gramophone, was the echo of something lost, and in the loss regained. Oh, this old man mocked them all right. His slithering steps and tottering pauses reminded Daniel how gladly he would be rid of them. No wonder he was the friend of Kosta, gloomy Kosta, whose terrace, far down the beach, showed a light no brighter than a single candle. Daniel at any rate could imagine the distant gloomy room full of whispering men and women. He could intercut with these crass tourists the file of Jews going down to the *caique* in the deep night. He could imagine the gasp and stumble of the children in the darkness. He could hate the tourists along with the leering old man whose arms went up now and seemed to take the weight from his comic feet until he scarcely touched the floor, this scarecrow in his faded clothes and his ill-fitting, unironed skin. He could hate them, but he recognized himself, oh yes, as always among them. The old man haunted their table like a stripper, turned and teased them with the woolly holes in his back, advanced on Nancy and retreated, looked away and then back at Davina, who took Vassili's hand, who nodded and retrieved it. He stalked round the terrace and found none to match him. Then up out of the darkness, straight from his mule, came a young man, curly-haired, ruddy as a Poussin hero, hefting two crates of beer. He laughed at the old man, as if at a rendezvous well kept and let the boxes down, crash in the corner, and came forward flexing his back. The old man stamped his rubber-tyred foot and sat them all up with a bang and pulled his handkerchief from his pocket, crumpled but white, and stretched it, like a magician, to prove his powers, and stamped again and the young man took the end, smiling with the company, smiling for the last time as one of them before he took the challenge. The record stopped. The two men stood, heads down. Paniotis skipped to restart the machine; the same tune hesitated and caught once more. The old man waited and then shuffled, to begin. They circled; paused and circled again. Did they know each other? Had they danced before? Were they friends? Were they enemies? Their glances answered none of these questions, but they knew them to be in the air. They juggled with them, turned their backs and slid past each other, came together, hung apart, snapped their fingers, bent the back, threaded the white handkerchief like silk in a wound, under and over. Paniotis, tongue wetting a new cigarette, stood watching. He brought more wine and watched again. He frowned and then he began to shuffle, the cigarette behind his ear. A ripple of laughter went through the tourists. Paniotis twitched and one foot trembled in the dance. His shoulders rose. His face lightened. And three men were dancing on the concrete floor, under the hissing lamp. Inside, someone restarted the record before it had ended. Suddenly chairs were flung aside, tables pushed back, and the tourists jostled, like cattle for water, in the full light of the music. They strung themselves into a circle, a sagging circle, panting, and all began to sample the rhythm, all began to sidle, all were lifted, one against another, and began to dance. The circle breathed, now backing against the forgotten chairs, now meeting in an unspoken secret, faces close and rapt. The bodies buckled and rose; the leaders were lost in the movement they created; everyone was together. Daniel saw Davina's face, he saw Nancy's face, he saw Vassili and the two young philosophers, and he seemed released from all of them, content with all of them, needing nothing, taking everything, all of them swimming freely in the music.

'The ship,' someone said. 'Look at the ship.'

'They're having a party,' Daniel said.

'Look at the ship.' The dance lost way. The music stopped. 'What's happening?'

Nancy said: 'Daniel —'

'Jesus Christ,' Daniel said. He ran through the crowd, which was entangled like a rope twisted on itself, and down the steps to the water.

'Daniel, be careful —'

The *Leto* was burning. Chains of sparks and coughs of flame wracked the darkness. Daniel raced into the water, throwing aside his shirt and stumbling out of his jeans. He was ahead of the others, who came as spectators to the edge of the beach, most of them,

337

excitedly appalled. Paniotis and Vassili were working Paniotis' boat down from the top of the beach, on its wooden rollers. The two philosophers asked if they could do something. Daniel swam out. Two other men were running along the cliff with a torch, looking for a closer place to dive in. Daniel called out 'Hey, hey.' Could they be asleep out there? The *Leto* was further than he thought. Impatience weakened him. He thrust the water behind him and promised himself that the burning yacht would be a refuge. The fire seemed to be only in the stern and even now, when he saw its rawness, the huddled intensity of the flames, he cautioned himself that perhaps it was all intentional, some extra, luminous amenity, and that he must beware of sophisticated derision. He heard the double spash of something dropped from the deck and, almost at the same time, he saw and grabbed at a dinghy, floating empty towards him. He caught the rope and tried to pull it after him. There were two figures on the deck of the *Leto*, forward, leaning into the darkness. Someone started to scream, too late to shock, an embarrassing sound in the confusion of calls and cries from the shore and the cliffs.

'Jump. Get everybody to jump. *Jump.*'

He felt for oars in the dinghy and pulled himself aboard. The noise of the fire, reminding him of the hissing gas of the lamp in the *taverna*, seemed almost that of a tap left running. Surely a single hand could turn it off. The screaming stopped. Figures were moving like ghosts on the deck. Then the screams began again, but an angry voice answered, and they stopped. Daniel shipped his oars under the lee of the yacht and reached for a purchase. The gangway was down; a face peered at Daniel. 'Nikos?' It was one of the women hoarse in the gloom.

'No, it's not Nikos. It's someone else. What the hell's going on? You'd better get down into the boat.'

The fire was at the stern. Amidships it was still an irrelevance.

'What's happened? Where's the crew?'

A woman in a wrapper, her face smeared with grease, was hauling a box out of the companionway.

'Ashore. They went to the harbour. Nikos and the engineer.'

'Where are the extinguishers? The fire extinguishers, where are they?'

The pumping of Paniotis' engine punched out a loud line from the shore. The flare of lamps and the shouts of those lining the beach made a battle of what was happening on the yacht.

'Look, get down into the boat. Who's in charge here? How many people are on board?'

Another woman, in a flowered wrapper, appeared in the light. Flames broke out of the stern hatchway and blew towards them. Daniel took the first woman and pushed her down the steps towards the dinghy. He took the other in his arms (how soft, how small she was!) and bundled her after her friend.

'Is there anyone else? Where's the Princess?'

The *caique* with Vassili and Paniotis bumped the side; unintelligible Greek grated in the shadow. Daniel went to the companionway and admired the polished wood, lacquered to richness, and the brass fittings. There was no smoke, no heat, no danger. He flung open the doors and called out. 'Abandon ship.' It seemed absurd and melodramatic, until there was a bang and a flag of flame swamped the passage with smoke. A woman was tearing open the drawers of a built-in dresser in the cabin at the end of the passage.

'Your Highness,' Daniel said, 'beat it. Out. *Amesos.*'

'Please—' the woman said. 'Please.'

'Look, fuck off out of it, your Highness, will you? Now. Get going. *Grigora*, sweetie.' Daniel urged her out and pushed her down the corridor towards Vassili, whose face frowned from the entrance to the companionway.

'Get the royal ass into the boat, Vassili, will you?'

Vassili said: '*Kirie Meyer, grigora. Ela, grigora.*'

The second explosion was followed by a clash of metal and the roar of new flames. Daniel pulled open the dresser and filled the case the woman had been forced to leave. He took handfuls of jewellery, pots of make-up, brushes, combs, handkerchiefs, the valuable with the worthless, and came out into the smoke.

'Shit, I've left it a bit,' he said. 'I really have.'

'*Kirie Meyer—*'

The passage was no longer than five or six yards. One strong run through the smoke must be enough. He held the suitcase in front of him for a shield, ducked his face against his shoulder, and threw himself into the black. There was nothing, nothing to breathe, nothing to break, he was through on one long held breath until he barked himself against a solid door, it seemed, which swayed and held out against him. He gasped, a kind of angry prayer, and shrugged to be past. It was a door of flesh. It was a man, fighting to keep him back in the choking corridor.

'The case,' the man said. 'Give me the case.'

'Don't be an ass.'

Daniel drove his knee between the man's legs and pinned him against the side of the corridor. Flames jabbed the sky behind the doorway, but there was a chink of air now, enough to strengthen him against the man whose face, almost politely, he peered to see. 'What the hell's the idea?' The man butted forward and Daniel, with incredulous pleasure, diverted the head under his arm and against a brass fitting. To his astonishment, a light came on; the light in the corridor came on and he was fighting with a dark, grey-haired man, dressed in white trousers and a striped T-shirt.

'Give me that case, you faggot.' The light sizzled and went out.

Daniel said: 'Get out of my way, you stupid prick. Have the bloody case.' He threw it into a hole in the night and heard it bang, rattle and splash.

'Faggot.'

Daniel kicked the man's shins and landed a punch in the hard stomach. Hot ash blew over them. The man lashed out, left and right. The right glanced off Daniel's cheek and carried the man behind it. A second later he plunged into the water after the case. Daniel coughed and winced at his cheek and realized, with painful humour, how odd he must have looked, wrestling in his sodden underpants with the neat Mr Lehman.

There were more boats around the *Leto*. Vassili, his feet half into a pair of furry slippers, was directing a fire extinguisher at the galley door. Resin bubbled between the narrow planks of the stern.

'Nice smells from the kitchen,' Daniel said. 'Where'd you get that?'

'*Kato.*' The extinguisher withered as Vassili answered. It had made little impression.

'Come on,' Daniel said. '*Pame.* We're never going to stop it now. Is everyone over the side? That's all that matters. She's going to go. Nothing's going to stop it now.' The crackle of candied wood and the heat beating back at them through the galley door proved it was senseless to stay any longer. Daniel pushed Vassili towards the ladder. 'I'll make sure there's no one else.'

Paniotis was holding the *caique* to the side. He helped Vassili and Daniel aboard and then pushed the yacht away. '*Tipota na kanome,*' he said. 'Nothing to be done.'

'*Tipota,*' Daniel said. 'Another blow for Lloyd's.'

Nancy said: 'You must've been crazy. Did you hear me shouting? You must've been crazy, I thought you were never going to leave. Did you hear me shouting at you? I was shouting and shouting.'

'No,' said Astrid, 'I am sorry to say I did not.'

'It was my fiancé who swam out first.'

'Oh, I must thank him.'

'Princess, we're staying up on the point. Why don't you come up there and get away from everyone?'

'Where's Buck? Has anyone seen Buck? Hi, Nancy J., O.K.? Princess, are you all right? Have you see Buck?'

'Have you managed to save anything?'

'Very little, I'm afraid.'

'I have things I can lend you,' Nancy said. 'I have things up at the house that'll fit you. It's really a beautiful house. It belongs to a writer. Larry, if you see Daniel —'

'Tita? Where is Tita?'

'You can all come up there,' Nancy said.

'Eleni, have you seen Tita?'

'At least there's one relief,' Nancy said, 'there isn't any press.'

'Where's Buck?'

'I don't give a fuck where Buck is,' Daniel said. 'I hope he's drowned himself.'

'What's the matter with you? What're you talking about? I'm talking about Buck Lehman.'

'Me too. Reminds me, did you get a telegram this afternoon?'

'Yes, of course. What in hell are you washing your jeans for?'

'Look, don't be a cunt,' Daniel said. 'I threw them into the water when I swam out.'

'You went out there?'

'Of course I went out there.'

'Vassili, have you got Buck there in the boat?'

'Look, he can swim, can't he?' Daniel said. 'Why get your knickers in a twist?'

'Daniel, I don't recognize you. I simply don't recognize you.'

'Your friend and I—' Daniel said. 'Maybe I've done you a good turn, who knows?'

'Larry, I think I'll go back up to the house,' the blonde girl said. 'Maybe Buck swam back to the rocks. I think I'll go back up.'

'It really is the night when everyone comes out of the woodwork, isn't it?' Daniel said.

'Sweetie, everyone's coming up to stay at our place, the Princess and the girls,' Larry said, 'so if you do go back, tell Despina she should open the other bedrooms, get it all together, will you do that, sweetie?'

'I'm surprised you didn't get the cruiser out,' Daniel said. 'And the private fire brigade. Crassus would've.'

'Crassus? Daniel, I think you're drunk.'

'What's your name?' Daniel said. 'I've seen the body, but this is the first time I've come in contact with the mind.'

'This is Nuala. She's a very nice girl. You be nice to her. This is a famous director in a lousy mood.'

Nancy said: 'I've had them make some tea. There's plenty of sugar in it. I think you should drink it.'

'I'm really perfectly all right. I am not even wet.'

'It's still a shock,' Nancy said, 'losing all your things.'

From somewhere down the bay they could hear yells of laughter, a deliberate show of derision, rolling out like the cry of some Homeric God over a battle. The voices on the beach, always self-conscious, faded before the coarse confidence of the sound and then rallied unconvincingly, to drown it. 'Kosta,' Daniel said. 'I'll bet you.'

'You were very bold,' Davina Long said.

'Bold?' Daniel said. 'Dotty more like. I'd have thought you'd have your notebook out at a time like this. Where is it?'

'Full,' Davina Long said. 'How long will she burn for, Vassili, do you think?'

'A couple of hours,' Vassili said, 'perhaps more. They've sent round to the harbour, but by the time they get here with a pump it'll be too late.'

'Write-off time,' Daniel said.

Vassili dusted his hands one against the other in agreement. Flames now covered the *Leto*, like sagging saffron sails. The glow carried to the faces of the onlookers and gave them an excited and shifty gleam.

Daniel said: 'Have you found your suitcase?'

'This is my fiancé.'

'Because there's a bloke out there somewhere with your suitcase.'

'I'm sorry? With my suitcase?'

'With all your stuff in it.'

'I had no suitcase,' Astrid said.

'I was the one with the suitcase. Are you the man who threw me off the yacht?' Eleni Frangakis put her hand on Daniel's shoulder and laughed. 'He came into my cabin and evicted me, just like that. Very forceful, he was. Out. Didn't you?'

'You're a very confusing trio,' Daniel said. 'You ought to wear numbers.'

'He was so kind and chivalrous,' Eleni said. 'He threw me out like a burglar.'

'Well, someone's got that case,' Daniel said. 'Talking of burglars.'

'Oh, they will bring it,' Eleni said, 'they will bring it. I was only collecting a few things.'

'You're either very cool, very rich or very insured.'

343

'Daniel, I want them all to come up to the house.'

'By all means. How many beds have we got? The fewer the better.'

'Daniel!'

'Princess, the boy's here with the torches. Buck has your suitcase—'

'Buck has the suetcase,' Eleni said. 'There!' She held on to Daniel's arm. 'The mystery of the suetcase is solved. Buck has it. Who is Buck?'

'I like you,' Daniel said. 'Buck is a strong-arm man. He goes with the little blonde girl. The butterball.'

'Oh yes, she is so pretty. *Pame sto spiti, Astrith?*'

'I thought they were coming to ours,' Nancy said.

'Nancy Jane,' Larry Pleasure said, 'don't you start being greedy now. Everyone's coming to me. It's fixed.'

The Princess was sitting at the table where Daniel and the others had had dinner. She had a hairy grey blanket stretched across her knees; half a glass of lemon tea steamed in front of her. She was in her late thirties. Her blue eyes were as large as the photographs promised and her head had all the erect alertness of someone who, when she was not watching others, always watched herself. She seemed, despite her present situation, as aloof as she had in the days when she was seen only in royal company. Daniel was eager to strip her of her pretensions, but he could not deny her the suspicious, delectable isolation of a chosen person. The heavy brows and lips, apparently so sensual, had something of the scarred rigidity of an old boxer's. The truth was, she was a Danish beauty who had had a little success in Hollywood; a little success in the sense of much disappointment. She had not even been the first choice of the Prince. According to those magazines which no one ever read but of which everyone knew the contents, he had been rejected by a more famous lady and his choice of Astrid was said to have been as brisk as a final rush through a duty-free shop. Her wedding had been avoided by genuine royalty and her right to her present title was doubtful.

The procession went with torches up the rocks towards Larry

Pleasure's house. Blades of light switched the darkness. Nancy held the blanket up to the Princess's shoulders. It trailed behind her like a robe.

'I'm sorry I was a bit rough in the yacht,' Daniel said. 'Only there really wasn't too much time.'

'You were very masterful,' Eleni said. 'I'm sorry that I was not who you thought I was.'

'Oh that wouldn't have made any difference.'

'No?' She caught his hand as she stumbled nimbly over a ridge of rock.

Daniel said: 'I thought we were going to our place, but it seems not.'

'Oh you have a place? That's nice.'

'You used to be a dancer, I gather?'

'Yes,' she said, 'so you see—I'm used to being thrown around, though I must say your language was unusual.'

'You weren't offended, I hope?'

'Offended? Offended! No, I was not offended.'

'I once had an affair with a ballerina,' Daniel said. 'Though not from the Royal Ballet, of course.'

'Daniel?'

'Who did you expect?'

'Darling, hullo.'

'Hullo. What time is it?'

'Were you asleep? I am sorry.'

'What the hell time is it?'

'You must have slipped away without telling anyone. I never saw you go, nor did anyone else.'

'They forgot to play my exit music. Heads are going to roll in the morning. The ones that haven't split already. That was turning into quite a party. Just the kind of coronation I can do without. What the hell are you doing?'

'Packing a case.'

'It's three in the bloody morning. What the hell's the idea?'

345

'I'm taking it over to Astrid. She hasn't got a thing to wear.'

'Maybe you shouldn't try to change that. The last time she was in the same condition, *ut dicunt*, she won herself a kingdom. Well an oildom.'

'Daniel, I'm really tired of that line of talk.'

'Well, what the fuck are you packing a bloody case for? Put the bloody thing down and come to bed.'

'I must say I've had nicer invitations. I don't know what went wrong with you this evening. Everyone was admiring you and saying how brave you'd been and all you could do was skulk in a corner and finally disappear altogether.'

'I wasn't brave. I was angry. Which is quite another thing. Plato again. My actions were not the result of good intentions. By no means.'

'Buck was saying how brave you'd been and how quick.'

'Fuck Buck. There was something decidedly fishy about the whole affair, if you ask me.'

'I think maybe you should go back to sleep. I'll see you in the morning.'

'For Christ's sake take your goddam clothes off and come to bed. Or are they waiting for you back there?'

'I promised she'd have something to wear when she woke up in the morning. She's got literally nothing. You made a terrific impression on Astrid.'

'I shall probably wake up and find I'm famous, if I ever manage to get back to sleep. Nancy, if you take that case out of here I'm going to turn very nasty, I'm warning you now. Are they still awake over there? What's been going on all this time?'

'We had some food. Really appetising, I must say, which Despina prepared. And then we had some music. That little blonde girl sang. Really rather nicely. Nuala.'

'She had to do something nicely.'

'Daniel, it'll take me five minutes to get it over there. Please.'

'Then five minutes in the morning will be time enough.'

'Please be careful what you're doing.'

'Why, are these pants destined for the royal arse? Come to bed, will you? I've been waiting for four hours. Nancy, I'll take it over in the morning. This really seems to be my night for wrestling with suitcases. Suetcases. What's the symbolism in that, do you think?'

'Daniel, I warn you —'

'Of what? Of what do you warn me, mistress mine? *Digame.*'

'I promised.'

'Tell me, what's Madame going to do now — you'd better let go — wait around at Larry's until Harrods send her a new yacht? Let go, Nancy, let go. I've already been hit by a gorilla once tonight. Don't think I can't cope with a goose. Jesus Christ, you bloody cow. Are you all right?'

'Now, Daniel,' she said, 'now. Now.'

'Okay, all right. On the way up.'

'Now, darling, please.'

'All right, all right.'

'You bastard.'

'Damn right.'

'You stinker.'

'Stinker!'

'Aren't you?'

'I'm everything you want me to be, my darling. *Toujours à la disposition de Madame.*'

'Is that right? Is that nice?'

'You tell me. You tell me. You do the talking.'

'I don't — want to — much — really —'

'That's good, that's good, that's good. That's good. Is that good?'

'Stinker. Christ, you stinker.'

'Okay then, okay then.'

'God, I love you,' she said. 'I *love* you. You.'

'Thanks,' he said. 'A bit late, but thanks.'

'What a funny place to end up,' she said.

'Well,' he said, 'that's show business. We had to find some use for the bathroom. You can't build a set and then not use it. It wouldn't surprise me — Christ almighty, you're not back with that suitcase routine? Why can't you leave the bloody thing where it is? And tell me the story of Nancy Jane instead. I'm dying to hear it.'

'Story!' Nancy said. 'What story? There is no story. You always want the past. Some people used to call me Nancy Jane, that's the sum total of the story. Like it?'

'I'll take the suitcase. Give me the suitcase, Nancy. I'll take it.'

'No.'

'What a long word you can make of no when you want to!'

'None of it belongs to you,' Nancy said. 'What's it to you?' She went with such a quiet sense of purpose that she could have been a young girl again. She touched the side of her cheek with the flat of her hand and gave him a smile different from her usual, a smile that was shy and even pleading, but with a sort of glee in it, the smile of a child leaving a parent for a party. 'See you later.'

'Murder,' Daniel said.

He could not stay in bed. He took Jane Harrison's book and Rachel Davidson's letter into the bathroom and lit the lamp. He sat on the useless lavatory and read the letter once again.

'One is humiliated,' he said to himself in the mirror, 'when no action one can take, no available choice can prove one genuinely strong.'

When he woke, the light was false to his eyes. He blinked to make sunshine of the grey. His watch said eight-fifteen. A thick roll of sound drummed the air. He went to the window and looked out. The sky was the colour of a landed fish. Between the clouds were pallid scales of faded brilliance. A glum sea, like sour soup, fermenting and brackish, churned against the rocks. Its noisy froth was freckled with black fragments. A warm wind turned the olive leaves silver. Daniel went across the room and out of the door. Perhaps the weather would be better on the other side. There was no sign of Nancy. Had she slept beside him? His dreams were so real, reality so doubtful, that he could not be sure. The bed suggested that she had been there, but he had woken to find himself on her side of it. He might have taken his own impression for hers. A cup with the stain of some Nescafé in it was on the table in the kitchen.

A man was standing on the terrace, a cup to his lips, by the leather chair, one hand flat on the tiled table, his back to Daniel. He wore creased flannels and a blue windcheater. His grey hair blew in separate strands, fine and almost invisible against the unhealthy sky.

'Mr Gavin?'

The man turned and smiled and spread his hands.

'I'm Daniel Meyer.'

'Mr Meyer, you must be a very angry man.'

'Not at all.'

'You must be. I've treated you abominably. I trust you had my message?'

'I knew, of course, you must have left one, but —'

'Oh, but this is dreadful. That you should have the house? Make yourself at home?'

'Oh, I'm sorry, yes, of course. As you can see, we have. My — my fiancée is over at Larry's.'

'Oh yes?'

'We had a bit of a drama here last night.'

'So they were telling me at the harbour. I hear you distinguished yourself.'

'I did nothing. I swam out. I had a boat back. I did nothing at all. Believe me, if I had, I'd be the first to admit it. You've been in Athens?'

'I went to Athens. I hoped to be back in time to greet you and then unfortunately — in the first place, I had to see my doctor —'

'I had a feeling.'

'Nothing. Nothing. I seem to be all right now, but he insisted I go into a nursing home, they had to take tests, I was forbidden any contact with the outside.'

'What was it all about?'

'A long story. An old trouble.'

'I don't know what's happened to Flora incidentally,' Daniel said. 'She was here the first day, she was terrific and then she seemed to disappear. I hope she isn't ill too.'

'She came to Athens,' Gavin said. 'She heard somehow I was in hospital, she put herself on the boat and came. She's an exceptionally devoted woman.'

'Oh I see. Has she come back with you?'

'She'll come back to Iskios in a day or two.'

'Only we've had no water.'

'That's easily remedied. And now the weather's gone back on us. You haven't had much of a welcome.'

'It's been very interesting,' Daniel said. 'You know what film directors are like. They like to taste a lot of different flavours. *Hors d'oeuvres* is our national dish.'

'It's a race, is it, being a director?'

'A foot race or a chosen race, do you mean? It's actually a bit of both. I'm very glad you've come back, I must say. Are you really all right now? Health-wise, I mean?'

'No,' Gavin said. 'But I feel very well.'

'Selfishly, I'm looking forward tremendously to talking to you. I've had an idea, actually, while I've been here that I'd like to talk to you about, for a film. Set in South America. I don't know whether you'd be interested.'

'We shall have to see.'

'I'd like that very much. Look, have you got any luggage or anything I could fetch for you? If you haven't been well—'

'I've brought only a rucksack,' Gavin said. 'I'm not staying very long.'

'Oh I see. Well, I hope we shall have time to talk a bit anyway. In any case, of course, I couldn't go on staying in your house indefinitely.'

'Do you like it, the house?'

'Very much. Very much indeed. It quite puts Larry's place to shame. I gather you're not too keen on his presence.'

'Oh—' Gavin waved a hand and went for a cigarette from his hip pocket which was squared with a box of matches. 'Men like that ... ' He turned and looked up at the house. 'Yes, it's a decent enough place. Of course, I've done a certain amount to it. Men like that have their uses, Mr Meyer.'

'He's got quite an extraordinary collection of stuff over there, one way and another.'

'He has an excellent cheque book,' Robert Gavin said. 'So you want to make a film of *Rats*.'

'Well, it's not quite as simple as that.'

'Oh?'

'As I tried to explain in my last letter, I don't think *Rats* itself is going to be a starter—'

'Did I receive this letter?'

'Well, that of course I can't say. I know I sent it. I had some post myself this week from England, so it seems to be coming through all right.'

'I thought your purpose was to make a film of *Rats* and you wanted to solicit my help over the necessary—what?—adjustments required for its translation to the screen. I'm sorry.'

Daniel said: 'I think you know how much I admire your books. I don't know if you've seen any of the films I've done.'

'I don't think I have. You direct them under your own name?'

'Well, yes.'

'I don't believe I ever have.'

'You might have seen one called *Split*, which was about—'

'I don't think so. I'm rarely at the cinema. I generally prefer reading.'

'Yes, of course.' Daniel glanced at the door of the sitting-room. 'I gather you read a lot of detective stories? Quite a lot of people—'

'Oh rarely, rarely. My favourite is Pausanias. I'm very self-indulgent, you know, in my tastes. I read and reread old Pausanias. I sometimes feel we're contemporaries.'

Daniel said: 'Have you ever thought of writing a film?'

'The cinema used to interest me,' Gavin said. 'I was once approached by a distinguished director, or is it producer?'

'Producers are never distinguished,' Daniel said.

'Director, who wanted me to work with him on a film about the Crusades—'

'Blind Dandolo on the walls,' Daniel said, 'terrific stuff.'

'But he found himself financially straitened and the whole thing was allowed to lapse. The cinema interested me mainly because of its rhythms—'

'Ah.'

'It seemed to me, and I may be wrong, a sort of verse form. Is that a cliché in your business? A matter of stress and line. Is that a common view?'

'No, but it's an interesting one. Hence the significance perhaps that music's always had in it.'

'I know very little about music. You're thinking of acquiring somewhere here, I'm told?'

'I'm sorry?'

'You're thinking of acquiring a property. It's certainly likely to prove an excellent investment.'

'Who told you that, for heaven's sake? Larry's trying to interest us in a cottage he's got down on the beach—and some sort of wild programme for a development, but I'm certainly not—'

'Because of course you couldn't possibly find anything better than this. This is probably the best site in the whole island.'

'Absolutely. You're not threatened, you're completely safe, they can do what they like on the bay. With your beach, you've got no worries at all.'

'I've no doubt he's asking a great deal of money.'

'So far he's only asked how much I think he can ask.'

'He'll get it, of course. What about some of my other books? What about *A Greek Light*?'

'I liked it very much. That's the one about the war, isn't it? But I can't see anyone letting us make it.'

'Make it in the Mani,' Gavin said.

'I'm thinking of the money,' Daniel said. 'And I do think there'd be political problems. I don't think anyone would give us the money.'

'This place must be worth over ten thousand pounds, I should think, wouldn't you? Together with the land. There's quite a deal of land.'

'I should think easily. I really wondered if you had any un-published stories, or any ideas even. What I really want, I think, is a

352

love story of some kind, but with a modern setting. Well, a love story that says something, shall we say? You have some of the sexiest heroines I know. But I'm open to absolutely anything. Love in the widest sense.'

'Tell me Mr — Mr Meyer, tell me, how soon would it be possible for you to get some money for me? If, for instance, you were to decide to do *A Greek Light*? I mean, it could always be modified. It could always be adapted. Do you have money with you? Have they given you some sort of *carte blanche*?'

'All their *cartes* are very *grises* these days,' Daniel said. '*La carte blanche, c'est le dodo*. No, what I was hoping—'

'I must sound quite intolerable. You must forgive me. I'll be frank with you, if I may.'

'I'd be pleased if you would.'

'You may, you may not, be pleased. The fact of that matter is, I'm a very poor businessman. I discover, for instance, that I've been very badly bilked by a paperback firm in whose spokesman I put undue trust. The consequence is, I'll be quite blunt, I'm somewhat strapped for cash.'

'There is, as someone said to me in London recently, a great and universal shortage of coin. We're all in much the same boat.'

'I fear we may be at some cross purposes here. I had a wrong expectation of you and you of me. Perhaps you're the one who has been the more grossly disappointed. I hope you'll forgive me. The truth is, Mr Meyer, you are welcome, at almost any figure you mention, to make of any book of mine that strikes you as suitable any film you want. You mentioned in your letter that you would be as loyal to my ideas as you could, or vision, did you say? I am embarrassed to say that, in the particular circumstances in which I find myself, I don't give a rap whether you're loyal or not.'

'I understand,' Daniel said.

'I doubt it,' Gavin said. 'Have you ever been in love, Mr Meyer?'

'I rather thought that might have something to do with it.'

'You're probably too ambitious, probably too successful. I'm talking about a love that is absolutely demanding, a love you'd do

353

anything to — to keep, to which, in order to keep it alive, you are willing to make absolutely any concession.'

'I don't think I ever have,' Daniel said.

'You're thinking of getting married,' Gavin said. 'I was married twice, no, three times, myself.'

'You've had a lot of experience of love.'

'I thought I had. I thought I had until this spring. This spring has been a very remarkable one for me. Not that that need be any concern of yours. I wouldn't care to wish it upon you, but I have had a very extraordinary time, these last months. I sold my library, you know, all my books. Everything.'

'The antiquities too,' Daniel said, 'I know. All except the little bronzes. I hope Larry gave you a good price.'

'I've even found Pausanias a rather garrulous and confused old person in the last little while. Oh he paid me a reasonable fraction of what I asked, your friend. You know that sort of person. They must bargain, they must also seem generous. They're caught between avarice and the demands of *la bella figura*. I rather like them for it; it gives their faces a marvellous greedy innocence.'

'Is she Greek?' Daniel said. 'The lady?'

'The lady? Ah well, yes, that's rather the thing, really —'

Daniel said: 'I'm afraid —'

'It actually happens not to be a lady.'

'Oh listen, it's nothing to do with me —'

'And that's why I want to get back to Athens as soon as I can. Unfortunately the weather's turned. This'll probably last a couple of days. I've got rather a delicate stomach at the moment. Anyway the boats'll probably hole out until the worst of it's over. It's something that's come as rather a surprise, but there it is. At my age one must — one must learn to accept things as they come — and be glad when they do.'

'You're not really in any mood to sit and talk about films at all.'

'To tell you the truth, I'm not. You see, one never knows how long one has and one doesn't want to waste a moment.'

'I can understand that. Only, of course —'

'I've wasted yours. I can see that.'

'Coming to Iskios can never be described as a waste of time exactly.'

'You must know a lot of Americans. Surely you must know someone who'd like to buy this house?'

'Surely—well, surely you'll come back here—I can't believe—'

'I should really like to find someone to take it on.'

'I'm sorry to say I don't have anyone in my pocket.'

'You're in films. You're interested in Greece. You want to make films here.'

'I don't have the right kind of money.'

'Oh surely. I don't insist on all of it right away.'

'I'm sorry,' Daniel said. 'If you hoped that I was coming here with a fat cheque book, either on my own or anyone else's account—'

'My dear chap! Of course not. Of course not. I've expressed myself with remarkable ineptitude.'

'No, that's all right. You haven't got a Cycladic figure you want to get rid of, though, have you?'

'A Cycladic figure.'

'Because that's something I could be interested in buying. If it was reasonable.'

'We should have to make sure that it was, wouldn't we? We should have to make sure that it was.'

'We shall have to leave,' Daniel said. 'The house.'

'My dear chap, why? Stay on by all means. It's the least I can do. Just because I'm not here—'

'It all seems to have been a bit abortive, I must say. We can't stay if you're not here.'

Gavin said: 'I must make it up to you. You simply must let me make it up to you. Do you know, it's very strange really, I'm getting on now, I don't like to admit it, but I am, and I've suddenly discovered the most extraordinary happiness. I should be feeling tremendously generous, tremendously open, that's how I've always imagined it was when one was in love. But I really think that up until now it's not been love at all, even when I've written

355

about it, it's been the joy of possession and that's something else again entirely. My loves until this spring have been entirely sterile, entirely public, entirely ostentatious. I've only written about them when they were over, when I had felt the pain or the triumph. Often both. And yet I've always assumed they were potentially good, genuine. They weren't. This boy, you'll forgive me for talking frankly, meaning, of course, that I don't give a damn if you forgive me or not, this boy—' Gavin sat on the parapet of the terrace, the wind grabbing smoke from the cigarette at which he pulled with an almost adolescent haste, and stared down at the cactuses and the figs below him. 'This boy, this young American, Bob, it's as if it's something I've always waited for. He chose me, that's the remarkable thing, he chose me. We met at a dealer's, he'd just come back from Constantinople. You know what he said about Santa Sophia? He said it was crepuscular. I recognized the quotation and I must say I laughed. He was talking to Margoulis, who doesn't need to be told what Santa Sophia is, and I had to laugh. We went and had a coffee together and I was telling him about Mystra and the last of the Palaeologues — what a story for a film that would be — and a woman came along, a Greek woman with those superb eyes and the rather disappointingly short legs, but a splendid woman, a woman you could have chosen—I could have chosen — for a heroine, and I made some chaste but appreciative observation, and more politely than anything else, so far as I was aware, this young man—his name happens to be Bob—did I say?—which is rather odd—he agreed she was beautiful and then he said "You don't like women really, do you?" I was astonished. I was absolutely amazed. I said I'd been married three times and that wasn't exactly the end of my experience and he nodded, rather brusquely to tell you the truth, and he said "doesn't that kinda prove it?" It amuses me the way they say "kinda". "Doesn't that kinda prove it?" he said. "You're not happy with them." "Well," I said, "I'm bound to say I don't know about that, but then what's happiness?" "You know what it is," he said. I was absolutely amazed. He didn't say anything else, just that. "You know what it is." This was April. We've been together ever since.'

'Does he love you?'

'Do you know I don't give a damn? I tell you, I don't give a damn about anything that describes what we are. Not a damn. We're together. As long as I can be with him, I'm beyond caring, certainly about words. I know his faults. I mean, I'm not in the least likely to be upset by being told what they are. I don't care a hang. The only thing I'm remotely interested in is being with him. Everything else is a bore, honestly. He wants to go down to Mystra and into Mani and we need some ready cash, it's as simple as that. I want to hire a car and raise some scratch.'

'Has he got any money?'

'He went to Turkey hoping to buy some cocaine, but he doesn't know half enough and it's a difficult market to break into. No, he's got no money. Just about enough to get back to California.'

'Does he want to get back to California?'

'Eventually,' Robert Gavin said.

'He hasn't come with you,' Daniel said. 'To Iskios.'

'I thought it better,' Gavin said. 'He was here before, but—'

'Flora? I get you,' Daniel said. 'Well, I find myself—'

'I shall never write another book,' Gavin said. 'I shall probably never write anything else at all. To tell you the truth, at this moment I find the whole thing—not so much false as absurd. There are better writers, read them. There's great art, let's rely on it. There is not much of life, why not live it?'

'And Greece, this absurd Greece?'

'Greece? Is it so absurd? I can't even discuss it, you know. I really don't care.'

'And this is what being in love means for you, is it?'

'Oh my dear fellow. My dear fellow.' He lit another cigarette and held it to the wind. 'I'm living in the middle of an explosion, Meyer, that's the amazing thing. I'm living in the centre of an explosion.' The wind clapped him on the back and ruffled his hair. 'It's the most marvellous thing I can imagine. Time, space, they don't mean a thing.'

'So Bradley promised.'

'Not a thing. I'm absolutely beyond caring about a thing.

However, as I say, I could do with some money. That I really could do with. Earthquake weather, that's what this is. Shall I tell you something, Meyer? It's only the shameful which is really worth a damn. It's only the utterly unspeakable that's worth risking a penny piece for. It's only the unprintable that's worth writing about, because it's impossible. I've wasted my time, I knew it when I was doing it, but I told myself I was wrong. I was right. I've suffered, not for love, not for what I'd lost or hoped to gain, but because I was wasting my time. Everything that's communicable, everything that can be said is public, do you follow me? It's show, it's repetition. You're absolutely right to make films, because films are all about money, am I not right? Make the money and use it to blow yourself to pieces, use it for what can never be repeated or captured in any form whatsoever. This young man, this Bob, do you know why I'm so happy with him? Because I don't give a damn who he is or what he is, only *that* he is.'

'In which case, of course,' Daniel said, 'there is nothing more to be said.'

She was leaning over the parapet of Larry's terrace in the raw silk trousers. Her legs were crossed, and the top half of her body was out of sight as she watched whatever was happening below. Daniel went softly over and put his arms round her and caressed her. He could have sworn that there was a long moment before she reacted. She straightened and turned, blue eyes blank, neither pleased nor outraged.

'God Almighty,' Daniel said. 'Sorry about that. Seen Nancy anywhere?'

'Oh it's you.'

'Yes, I'm sorry about that. I thought I recognized the view. Where is she, do you know?'

'Perhaps she is inside. They were all having breakfast.'

'What's happening? Anything interesting?'

The shell of the *Leto* had been towed close to the shore. The hull had retained its rigidity; the burnt-out blackness had an oily sheen. Whorls of smoke had worked over and over, lapping fantastic trails, on what was left of the superstructure and the melted Chriscraft. Paniotis was standing in his *caique*, phlegmatic as an undertaker, directing the operation. The greasy sea was lumpy with wreckage.

'Horrible sight,' Daniel said. 'Better if she'd folded up and disappeared completely. I hate corpses.'

'Yes, it is. Horrible.'

'You haven't had much luck, I must say. You really haven't.'

'Luck? No.' She walked along the terrace, keeping pace with the slow haul of the yacht.

Daniel said: 'What will you do? After the weather changes. Larry could probably ferry you somewhere. I'm sure he'd take you anywhere you wanted to go.'

'He has already offered,' Astrid said.

'You didn't own the boat yourself, did you, the *Leto*? It was chartered, wasn't it? I mean, it's still nasty, but at least it wasn't something —'

'I have lost many things,' Astrid said. 'Personal things.'

'I saw you in an old film on the television a few weeks before we left England. *Water Wings*.'

'Oh you didn't! I hoped perhaps they had burned it.'

'You had a pageboy and you were wearing Bermuda shorts. You looked very good.'

'Oh please. Where we were this troupe of girls on a cruise? Aquabats. I hoped they had destroyed all the copies.'

'You and —'

'Esther and Barbara Dean and who was the man? No, don't tell me. It was Jean-Pierre. Of course Jean-Pierre and Jack Craven.'

'As the millionaire. I wondered whether you'd remember.'

'But of course. The highlight of my screen career. Of course I remember. I even sang a song —'

'I'm sorry to say I didn't stay for the song.'

'I was extremely sultry. I frowned so hard I gave myself a headache. I had to have manipulation. And then, after all, I was dubbed. But the frown at least was still mine!'

'You must've had offers to go back into movies.'
'Never to do anything worthwhile.'
'What's worthwhile?' Daniel said.
'Oh for instance, if someone like—'
'Billy Stern?'
'Yes, someone really good.'
'Kurosawa,' Daniel said.
'You think?' Astrid slitted her eyes and they both laughed.
'No, you see, there is always the idea and then the fact. The
idea is sometimes enchanting and the fact is—well—a disappoint-
ment. A person like yourself, you see for instance, would never
want me.'
'Oh my dear,' Daniel said.
'Because you would know that really I am not an actress. I
could never play a part. Certainly not now. I am—what's the
expression?—they used to say it about contract artists—'
'Locked in?'
'I'm locked in. That's right.'
'Do you really think so? What about the Italians? Almost any
of the top Italians could use you marvellously. They don't seem to
have the same inhibitions—or is it the same illusions?'
'They don't think in terms of parts,' Astrid said. 'They give
parties. It's the Italian tradition. Some are happy and some are
unhappy, but they are all parties.'
'That's very good,' Daniel said, 'I like that. Where did you get
that from?'
'You're not very flattering, Mr Meyer.'
'Yes, I am,' Daniel said. 'If you knew.'
'Darling! I thought I heard your voice. How are you? Are you
all right? Have you had any breakfast? Princess, can I bring you
some more coffee? You must be frozen out here. Good morning,
darling, I hope I'm forgiven.'
'Why, have you done something?'
'It's so tragic,' Nancy said, 'the wreck. I can't bear to look at
it. I hate to see things like that. Did you sleep? I thought the best
thing was to leave you to sleep.'

360

'Ah, that's why you left me. I slept very well indeed. Did Gavin arrive before you left?'

'No. Princess, I thought you'd like to know, Nikos has spoken to Athens. They're going to send a replacement, as good as they can manage, as soon as the weather is reasonable.'

'I should think they will hang Nikos from the yardarm,' Astrid said. 'It was all because of him that it happened. He and that fool of a cook leaving the gas.'

'Because he's actually arrived.'

'He hasn't? Gavin? This is the man we were supposed to be staying with.'

'On the overnight boat. He's going again though, as soon as the weather clears. It's not exactly going to be the cosy creative week I had in mind.'

'This is a writer Daniel was planning to work with. Princess, I'm going up to the village later this morning, can I tempt you to join me? Zeno's promised to have the pants ready. Alternatively I could always go and collect them. How do you feel? Darling, you could come with us.'

Daniel said: 'I have to find somewhere to sleep. We can't stay on at Gavin's.'

'Has there been some kind of a ruction? Because Larry'll always find us somewhere.'

'We could always sleep in the squash court, I suppose. You don't happen to play squash, do you?'

'No, I don't,' Astrid said.

'We'll talk about it later,' Nancy said. 'Darling, you really ought to have some breakfast. I wish you would, I feel so guilty about you. Go and eat—and shave—and then later we can go up to the village, Princess, if you—'

'I don't really want to stay here,' Daniel said. 'I think I'll go and ask Vassili if Paniotis can find us somewhere.'

'But darling—with a toilet. If not a bathroom, I must at least have a toilet.'

Breakfast was in the patio: a big copper pan of scrambled eggs and drying bacon, toast, rolls, marmalade and jam, a bowl of strawberries glistening with sugar. The blonde girl was in the pool, floating with her eyes closed, her fingers moving up and down as if she were drying her nails. Daniel took a cup of coffee and sat on the floor, in the corner, under a white tub of greenery.

'Mr Meyer, I have to apologize to you.'

Daniel said: 'Oh hullo. Do you know, I was just wondering why my cheek ached. What the hell were you playing at?'

'You know what I did? I thought you were that stupid sonofaso-andso who started the whole thing.'

'Nikos.'

'I thought that was who you were.'

'Oh, is that right?' Daniel said.

'And then when I sort of realized my mistake, we were already too far in to explain –'

'You hit me, if memory serves, after you saw who I was. After the light went on.'

'It was sort of too late. We were too deep in. You caught me with a good one too, you know.' Lehman pointed to a trio of purple bruises under his ribs. 'You're a pretty dangerous man.'

'I wish you meant it. I think you were playing with me.'

'Not at all.'

'Then why weren't you, if you knew who I was? Skip it, skip it. What you're saying is, you didn't mean all those nasty things you said, right?'

'What did I say? Did I say something?'

'You said I was a faggot,' Daniel said. 'And you weren't too friendly yesterday in the library either. Also with the lights on. Though not as unfriendly as that. Always assuming faggot is unfriendly in your language. It's not an easy word to say charmingly.'

'Mr Pleasure particularly likes me to take care of the place when he's out. I guess I was over-anxious and failed to cool off fast enough. What can I say? I'm sorry.'

'You've said it,' Daniel said. 'Have some coffee. Is she doing something important in there? She seems to be concentrating very hard.'

'She's working on her stomach,' Buck Lehman said.

'Oh well, it makes a change, I suppose. Tell me something –'

'Gladly.'

'Easy now. Don't come out of character too fast, you'll lose credibility. I wanted to ask you something. Oh yes, how long does it take from here to the Turkish coast?'

'To the Turkish coast?'

'To the coast of Turkey or, as we English say, the Turkish coast. Larry gets quite a lot of his stuff from Turkey, doesn't he?'

'What're you talking about?'

'Forget it.'

'What exactly are you trying to say?'

'I'm really asking you how long it takes to go, for instance, in the cruiser from here to the coast of Turkey. Is that such a tricky question? You know, I have a feeling that even now our friendship is not destined to prosper.'

'You want to go to Turkey?'

'I know people who might, that's all. Please don't worry about it. It's only a little plot I'm trying to work out in my mind. Larry told me he got a lot of his antiquities from Turkey.'

'It takes around eight hours, but it could take less, of course, in the right circumstances. Possibly as little as six.'

'Where are you from?' Daniel said. 'Are you from California too?'

'I come from the state of Washington,' Buck Lehman said.

'How difficult is it to handle, Larry's boat?'

'Pretty easy,' Buck said, 'if you know where you're going.'

'With a good navigator,' Daniel said, 'there'd be no real problem?'

'I don't imagine,' Buck Lehman said.

'Darling, we're ready, if you are. Hullo, Mr Lehman. Darling, if you've finished, Astrid's just getting ready and we're going to wander up. I thought we could take her to Constantine's. It'd be so nice if we could, well, bring her out a little bit, and he's such an interesting man.'

'What do the other two think of this excursion? Have they given her an exeat?'

'They're just so happy to have her go. They'd like nothing better than have her enjoy life again.'

'Well,' Daniel said, 'if we can't make her happy, who can?'

'The thing she really dreads, she was telling me, is publicity. She hates being portrayed as a kind of gloomy recluse, the Queen Victoria at Osborne image, but equally she dreads coming out of purdah because of the idea of all those photographers.'

'*Qui a fait vivre la Princesse Astrid*? I can imagine *France-Dimanche* already.'

'I've suggested something, I don't know if it can possibly work, and that is, she should come to stay with us in England. Incognito. She terribly wants to visit London and buy clothes and look around, go to galleries, the theatre. I thought maybe we could have her come over some way no one ever travels, like maybe from the Hook of Holland. She's still a Danish national, which means if she gets a new passport she won't even need to have her title on it. She could stay with us, no one would ever know, she could give the press the slip entirely.'

'Would you really want her to stay? Wouldn't she really be much happier at Auntie Clara's? Claridges.'

'She jumped at the idea of somewhere simple and uncomplicated.'

'You make Seymour Walk sound like a kibbutz.'

'Where she could just see people she wanted to see. Daniel, you have to admit, she's been through a lot. This on top of everything. She's lost almost every stitch she owns. And it would be kind of fun, to smuggle her in. Imagine going to shows and the big shops and everything. This is somebody who's suffered. Somebody we can really help.'

'Fine, terrific. Nancy, I don't want to stay at Larry's. We'll go to Paniotis and if he can't help us, then we'll go up the other end, to Kosta's. The place where Larry tied up the Chriscraft.'

'Oh but that's miles away! At least don't go now. **Darling**, please. Later, if you have to.'

'From what? Miles away from what?'

'That beach is like walking in quicksand. And it's endless.'

'I'm sure it's excellent exercise for the ankles. An anti-varicose must.'

'Larry would be very insulted if we went right up there. I think he'd really feel very insulted. I don't think I could do that. To rescue somebody who really needs to be rescued, Daniel, can you think of anything more worthwhile than that?'

Daniel sat in the square drinking coffee while the two women went through Constantine's stock. He had written cards to Queenie and the Morrises and Virginia and was tapping his teeth with his biro when Robert Gavin dropped quietly into the chair next to him. 'May I?'

'Of course.'

'I'm afraid I've quite messed things up for you. But I must tell you I think I've had an extraordinary bit of luck. I'm not sure, but I may have.'

'I can't wait,' Daniel said.

'On your behalf you understand. It's about this, this Cycladic figure you said you were interested in acquiring. I feel I owe you something, after all. It so happens I was talking to one of the people I know here and this chap's got something he swears is the real thing—I'm not vouching for it myself, because I haven't seen it yet—but he swears it's genuine and he wanted to know was I interested. I thought of you at once.'

'When can I see it?' Daniel said.

'You really will have to promise to be quite extraordinarily discreet,' Gavin said. 'It's not his, you see, he's handling it for a friend. He's got it at his house. He's in his shop till about noon, but he could show it to us then.'

'Will you know if it's genuine when you see it?'

'I shall have a better idea than I do now.'

'I know a bit about fakes,' Daniel said. 'They tend to have a reddish—'

'Well, then, you can best judge for yourself. It really is the most unusual coincidence, because these things don't turn up that often. However, as I say, this came absolutely out of the blue. Of course it's unlikely to be a prime specimen. It's not that absolutely clear white marble you sometimes get—'

'You'll be better able to say when you've seen it, I expect,' Daniel said.

'Incidentally, I was going to say, I do hope you'll stay in my house for just as long as you want to. I hope to leave tomorrow night, if the weather changes, but I'd hate you to feel—'

'We shall move out tomorrow,' Daniel said. 'Thanks all the same.'

'Oh why? Why? I shall probably advertise it in *The Times* shortly, I'm told that's the best place. However, if you know of anyone who'd like first bite, do let them know.'

'And where will you live when you've sold it?'

'I shan't,' Robert Gavin said.

'You'll just keep on the move?'

'If possible.'

George Akrotiri came out of the house with the marble terrace and stood on the step with his newspaper. He looked up the road at Daniel and inclined his head so faintly that he might have been assenting to some subtle but murderous proposition. Daniel actually felt himself blush. Akrotiri turned and went down towards Agia Eirene. Gavin had looked the other way, with what Daniel took to be conventional tact but when he looked up again, it seemed more like boredom. He was not offering Daniel an alibi, he simply wished that he himself were elsewhere.

'Perhaps you'd sooner meet here later,' Daniel said. 'I've got one or two things I'd like to do.'

'By all means. Twelve noon, if that suits.'

At the Post Office, Daniel leaned on the counter to write his last card: *'Today's a strange day, cloudy, "earthquake weather" according to a supposedly knowledgeable English writer. Otherwise it's been the expected, merely fabulous Greece. Colonels thin on the ground but thick in the air, helicopterized but so far gunless. I have yet to catch my crucial subject, but I'm living in hopes.*

You'll see it one day. Comme toujours.' He had left a little space at the bottom, in which he wrote, in almost illegible script, '*Thanks for your letter. It's too late to change and too early to regret. I'm happy; I'm happy you are. D.*' The words became smaller and smaller, like the tail of Alice's mouse. Daniel slipped the cards almost secretively into the upright tin box at the top of the marble steps and had to find Dmitri standing at the bottom, his straw hat secured under his chin by an elastic, the usual mocking laugh cooking in his throat.

'*Ti kanome?*'

'*Kala, kala,*' Daniel said. '*Pao sto chorio.*'

'Kirios Gavin is back.'

'Right,' Daniel said.

'Tomorrow he's going again.'

'You know it all,' Daniel said.

'He has his friend in Athens. *To mavro.* The black one. He's come back for money.'

'Who's *mavro*? What's black?'

'His friend! Has he sold you anything?'

'Not yet,' Daniel said. 'Is he really? *Black?*'

'*Mavros ine. San afto.* Like this.' He snapped the elastic under his chin.

'*Pao sto chorio,*' Daniel said.

'*Prosechete, prosechete,*' Dmitri said. 'Watch out.'

'*Yati*? What for?'

'*Prosechete,*' Dmitri said.

The bell-shaped shopkeeper had been on the boat with Daniel and Nancy. He wore the same dark suit and carried a black plastic briefcase. His face was pasty white and closely shaved. When he shook hands, he looked away, as if to be able later to deny that he had ever seen Daniel. Yet he made a procession of their passage through the village, mopping his face with his handkerchief and bowing to people who came by and talking on at them when they had passed. His house was large and shuttered, its shadowy rooms stiffly furnished with set pieces of furniture; a three-piece suite, under plastic; a dining-room suite of eight lacquered chairs; plastic flowers in vases everywhere. He whispered to his wife in a side room and came back, sweating apologies, to turn on light brackets all round the shuttered sitting-room until it glared like an electric shrine. When he had proved that every light in the room was working, he opened his briefcase and brought out a crinkled brown paper parcel. 'Christ,' Daniel said, 'it's like the fishmonger opening the whole damned shop and then pulling a mackerel out of his hip pocket.'

'They haven't had electricity for very long,' Gavin said.

The shopkeeper undid the string, which he rolled into a careful ball, and opened the paper. He lifted aside the cotton wool like a doctor over an interesting wound. '*Oriste*,' said the shopkeeper, inviting Daniel's diagnosis.

The figure was so unlike what he had expected that all his prepared knowledge seemed futile. The marble was greyish yellow and the figure had square shoulders and a bullet head. The face was squarish too, with an abrupt Cycladic nose. The legs were cylindrical and ended at the ankle. The declivity between the legs was a crude furrow. The arms were straight to the sides and delineated by similar furrows. Daniel said: 'I've never seen one like this in my life.'

'*Oriste?*'

Gavin said: 'It's certainly unusual.'

'Is this Cycladic?'

'*Kiklathiko, kiklathiko*,' said the shopkeeper.

'*Apo poo ine afto? Apo tin Iskio?*'

'*Iskio, Iskio*.'

'What date is this, would you say?'

'He says it's about 3,000 B.C.'

'Do you believe him?' Daniel said.

'Perhaps a little later,' Gavin said. 'I'd like to have a closer look.'

'*Oriste*.' The shopkeeper handed the figure to Gavin.

'I used to make quite a point of these at one time. Of course it's not the classical Cycladic. He'd be asking a lot more than he is, if it were.'

'What is he asking?' Daniel said. 'I didn't hear him ask anything.'

'He wants ten thousand drachs for it,' Gavin said, examining the figure with suspicious care.

'He'd take less?'

'What I'm thinking is, it just could be a very early cult figure. In which case it could be worth a good deal more. It's got no obvious sex which is rather intriguing.'

'Surely one would expect some female markings?'

'Not nec-ess-air-ily,' Gavin said, 'not nec-ess-air-ily. Of course if it had feet we should be able to tell a lot more. On the other hand, if it did have feet, as he was saying, it'd be worth a great deal more. The price seems to me about right, frankly. For a genuine piece. Less, I'd be dubious; more, I'd say too much for an intelligent buyer; sucker stuff. Ten thousand drachs sounds about the right mark. Very hard to say. What do you make of it?'

'At least the earth in the cracks looks authentic,' Daniel said. 'Second or third millennium crud without a doubt. It's not exactly a thing of beauty, is it? Hardly your spiritualized marble. Isn't that what you said about one of these ladies?'

'Did I? Possibly. Of course, I may have been speaking ironically. You know, the more closely one looks, the more unusual it seems. One has to bear in mind these people probably find it easier to get hold of the real thing than they do a fake. Added to which, why should anyone fake something so crude and untypical? I've seen some quite remarkable fakes in Athens and elsewhere. Why should anyone try to pass off something as rough and ready as this? I'm bound to say, I've got a feeling it's probably right, you know.'

'*Oriste?*'

'*Ena lepto.*'

Daniel said: 'I'd like to show it to somebody.'

The shopkeeper clicked his nail against a gold tooth.

'He's afraid of the wrong people hearing about it.'

'In that case I think perhaps I'll let it go. After all, it's not that cheap.'

'Absolutely up to you. I'm bound to say, though, I don't think it's expensive. If it is right, *if*, then it's probably going to be worth almost a thousand pounds in the open market.'

369

'It's very tempting, but I think I'll let it go. I think I'll definitely let it go.'

'Absolutely up to you. One has to trust one's own judgment in these cases.'

'And you think I haven't?'

'My dear chap, I didn't mean that at all. Not at all. *Then ton theli o kirios.*' Gavin indicated that it was no use continuing.

'*Opos theli o kirios.*' The shopkeeper closed the cotton wool and took the ball of string from his hip pocket. Daniel craned for one last look. Had he done the wrong thing? Until he refused the piece, he was sure that he was being duped, but once it was put away, he was convinced it was authentic. He walked back to the square with Gavin. Although the other had, in a way, made a fool of him and should, by rights, be making amends, Daniel was nagged by a sense of owing Gavin something. He wished now that the man would go or that he could go himself. Despite Gavin's disappointingly mercenary style, Daniel feared he had proved insufficiently interesting to engage the older man's attention.

The two women were drinking coffee in Constantine Mersenas' shop. Daniel saw them through the window. Nancy's hand was out, her fingertips just touching the brocade round the neck of the ornate tunic Astrid was wearing. Constantine was sitting at his desk, his head at an angle, writing in a notebook. When he saw Daniel, he closed the book. The two men smiled.

'He has many beautiful things,' Astrid said.

'Astrid looks magnificent in them,' Nancy said. 'Better than anyone else could possibly look.'

Constantine said: 'She exaggerates.' His soft smile excused him from any criticism of Astrid; he had merely complimented, and yet criticized, Nancy. Daniel recognized the tone and again the two men smiled together.

'You ought to get the Princess to model them for you in the magazines,' Nancy said, 'if she would.'

'Oh no,' Astrid said.

'Of course not. Only I obviously couldn't possibly now.'

'We couldn't today anyway,' Daniel said, 'not in this light.

On the other hand, I don't know. It might be rather nice for once to have a Greek island without the famous Greek light. No sharp shadows, no squints.'

'We'll come back tomorrow then, Constantine. You're sure the girl will have done the alterations? And meanwhile we'll take these.'

'Quite sure. With pleasure.'

'You go on,' Daniel said. 'I'll bring the parcels. I want to ask Constantine something. You go on, I'll catch you up by the Poseidon.'

Nancy took the Princess's arm.

Daniel said: 'I've just been offered a Cycladic figure.'

'Ah.'

'A somewhat rustic specimen. I wondered if you knew this man Tselementes, is that his name? The fat shopkeeper. Because he's the chap who's offered it to me. Is he straight, do you think?'

'I don't know that he is not,' Constantine said. 'He is a little man—how do you say?—a middle man. He buys, he sells. It would not be fair to call him dishonest, nor yet to call him honest. He buys, he sells.'

'I get you,' Daniel said. 'Would you know if a Cycladic piece was genuine or not?'

'I might.'

'I thought I knew a bit, but when it comes to putting one's money where one's mouth is, I'm not so sure. Actually I've said I wouldn't have it. I've turned it down, but now that nothing depends on it, I'm beginning to wonder if I was right.'

Constantine said: 'There are so many beautiful things which are authentic, why buy what seems doubtful?'

'Oh I shan't,' Daniel said. 'I shan't. But there's always the hope that one might have been clever and found a bargain. Not only a bargain, but something really valuable one's discovered for oneself.'

'I cannot advise you. If I saw the piece, perhaps I would know. But then, of course, if you are interested in bargains, there will always be another piece, won't there?'

371

'I should either become a connoisseur or shut up, you mean? No, you're absolutely right. Absolutely right. You said you knew Robert Gavin, I think?'

'A little. He came in once with his friend.'

'*O mavros*. What was he like? An American?'

'Yes. To tell you the truth I didn't like him.'

'The black man? Didn't you? He thought it was right, Gavin, the figure.'

'He's an intelligent man,' Constantine said. 'It probably is.'

Daniel said: 'Constantine — damn, I really ought to go — I'd like to talk to you again sometime. I wanted to talk to you about something else.'

'Please.'

'I'll try and come by on my own.'

'I shall be here,' Constantine said. 'Until September the fifteenth.'

The clouds remained heavy. Daniel ran down the street and along the avenue under the cypresses, past the football ground where two shaven-headed boys were kicking a soggy white ball, and up the dirt road towards the Poseidon. Beads of sweat condensed and rolled down his chest. The two women were standing at the gate of the nightclub talking to the Egyptian officer.

Nancy said: 'Daniel, the parcel.'

'Shit. Piss. Fuck. To name but a few. Bugger.'

Astrid said: 'Please, we'll send someone — '

'I saw it right there on the counter as I left the shop. Shit. I'll go back.'

'He is an absent-minded professor,' Coco said.

'*Ni l'un ni l'autre*,' Daniel said. 'Unfortunately.'

'My sister can go,' Coco said. 'I'll send my sister.'

'I'm going,' Daniel said. He was no further than the football ground when he saw Constantine's boy carrying the parcel towards him. He found two drachmae for the boy and hurried back to interrupt the women's conversation with the Egyptian.

The surf was rolling, almost cylindrical, along the bay. The sand was steepened by its continuous motion; the pebbles tumbled like flails and ate the softness. There was a smell of death. By the water's edge, stiff, glazed fish lay drowned in the air. Where the river bed had already scored the surface, the foam spread and congealed, as if the whole sea had curdled. Lunch had been laid on the terrace. Larry told the company that there had been a tidal wave in the mouth of the Po and there was a full disaster alert in Venice. It did little to dispel their listlessness. The dishes succeeded one another with a reproachful clatter. Nancy was the brightest of the guests; she described to Larry the clothes which Astrid had bought and how much they did for her—and she for them.

Daniel said: 'What news of the rescue expedition?'

'They have problems. Everything's pretty booked up.'

'What's going to happen? Is everyone going to sit here and do nothing until the Pope draws it to the attention of the world's conscience?'

'Oh Daniel, stop it, darling.'

Despina was offering second helpings of the veal stew when Dmitri Bracheotis burst on to the terrace. 'Kirie Meyer, tilegraphima.' Dmitri limped round the table and unbuttoned his shirt to extract the telegram from next to his heart.

'Oh shit; Gil. He's phoning me from London at two o'clock. My producer.'

'It's five of now,' Larry said. 'You'd better get your skates on.'

'Amesos,' Dmitri said. 'Pame.'

'I somehow don't think the contents were too much of a secret.'

'Grigora.'

Dmitri had his donkey and the big mule tethered by the green gate. Daniel shook his head, but Dmitri pointed to his watch and chopped the air with the side of his hand. 'Pame.' Daniel jumped on to the mule, Dmitri encouraged it with the end of his stick and they went galloping across the hard ground. Dmitri drummed his heels and jabbed the donkey with the sharp piece of bone on a string behind his saddle. Daniel tried to keep the mule to the path,

373

but Dmitri prodded its neck and turned it towards the cliffs which barred the direct line to the village. Daniel was jerked up and down on the wooden saddle. Every time the mule faltered, Dmitri leaned over and whacked it, left and right, and it scuttled forward, hooves glancing on the polished stones. The cliff was surely too steep for direct assault. Daniel prepared all sorts of speeches about the unimportance of telephone calls, but Dmitri lashed out with his stick. The mule snorted and snatched at the slope, grabbed a hold, took two more solid whacks, left and right, and rose like Bucephalus, pawing and pawing, back legs braced, and sprang straight up. Dmitri was right behind it, ready with another solid blow when the mule teetered on the edge of the roadway. The gallop to the Post Office jolted Daniel raw. Dmitri, grinning, leaped down, grabbed the mule's bridle and, with a cry of '*Grigora, grigora,*' hustled Daniel into the Post Office like a prisoner late for his execution.

There was an hour's difference between London and Greece. Two o'clock in London was three o'clock on Iskios. Daniel waited. Dmitri waited beside him. Daniel told him that there was no need to stay. He stayed.

'You saw it,' Dmitri said.

'Saw what?'

'At Tselementes'.'

'Yes, I saw it.'

'It's very old. Very old. *Para poli paleo.*'

'Do you think so? I'm not so sure.'

'*Po po po.* Very old. Very good. Very beautiful.'

'How do you know?'

'*Kalo ine.* It's O.K.'

'I didn't buy it,' Daniel said.

'You didn't buy it? *Oreo ine. Paleo.*'

'I didn't want it.'

'*Ti na kanome?*'

They waited.

'You don't think it's fake then?'

'Fake?' Dmitri rolled his eyes. 'Fake?'

'Well, that's your opinion.'

'Fake? It comes from *tris petres*.'

'Well, I'm not buying it.'

'*Then ine pseftiko*.'

'All the same,' Daniel said.

'*Kirie* Meyer. *Lonthino*.'

'Danny? Gil. I hope you don't mind me calling you like this.'

'Delighted,' Daniel said. 'How are you?'

'Very good. I just came back from California.'

'You're back from the dead then.'

'Back from the dead and I have something I wanted to talk to you about. I hope I'm not screwing up your holiday doing this. The weather's lousy here. It's like November. Where are you, you lucky bastard, on the beach?'

'No, actually I'm in some kind of a miniature steam room. Colour me molten. So what's new?'

'I don't know how you're making out out there, whether you're making any progress—'

'Some, some.'

'Because just in the last forty-eight hours something's come up I think could interest you. I don't want you to feel pressured—'

'I like to feel pressured.'

'We have someone gargling on the line here. I said I don't want you to feel pressured, but I talked to Queenie and she said to go ahead and call. The thing is, I don't know how you feel about directing a caper—'

'I never really have,' Daniel said. 'It rather appeals to me.'

'Because I have a script the company want to go with. It's set in South America. Could be Brazil, could be Guatemala, could be Chile or Peru. It could be Argentina. I guess even Mexico. I'll tell you the reason, briefly, I thought of you. It has a potential political angle to it, in the widest sense. It's a caper, but it's in *Wages of Fear* country; it could have and I believe it should have up-to-the-minute significance. You know where else we could do it, and that's Paraguay. What we have are these six guys, two of them aren't too important, piranha fodder, and they're out to find this Nazi war criminal who's hidden himself and his whole operation somewhere out in the forest with enough gold to bail out the entire motion picture industry. And, believe me, that's money. Anyway these guys set out to get the gold maybe for some idealistic purpose—one of them maybe is a guy who's lost his whole family in the gas chambers, another one's maybe some kind of romantic revolutionary—and they think they're the only people in the race, but then they realize they're being trailed, they're not alone and that what they are is the rabbit that's been put in to get the ferret out of his hole—'

'An interesting concept,' Daniel said.

'Isn't it though? Listen, Daniel, I can't tell you the whole story, but the thing is these are not the usual Wild Bunch, the two main characters are scared shitless, one of them keeps tough for the other and the other keeps going because he thinks the first one can make a man of him. It's a case of who's kidding who. It's called *Dog Eat Dog*. Jack Darwin wrote it. You know Jack? The plot ends up with a whole slew of double doubles. I don't know how that grabs you as a title, *Dog Eat Dog*?'

'Pretty good,' Daniel said. 'Not bad.'

'What I want to do is get you in the same room with Jack. It's an original and I'd sort of like to let him see it through, I think you two could maybe spark ideas off each other. On the other hand if you have somebody you want to bring in to give some of the dialogue a little more snap, fine. Overall, I think it's got one helluva good premiss, I really do, and some excellent characters. We want to go in February. Oh listen, I never mentioned the girl. There's a girl.'

'That's a twist,' Daniel said. 'Tell me about her.'

'The daughter of the top Nazi. She's young. She's the daughter of this Nazi chief who's been in the jungle twenty-five years, his daughter by some native woman he's been shacked up with. So you get the question of inherited evil, all that stuff. She's learned English from fan magazines, which I really think is a nice touch. She's never talked to anyone English or American, but she's

376

heard the radio and she's read every magazine you've ever heard of. Turns out she believes in all the ideas we've lost faith in. It's kind of a nice idea. And not so impossible. Listen, I'm digressing, because the basic story is a straight caper, but with modern overtones. Like Che Guevara meets *The Treasure of the Sierra Madre*. Isn't that an interesting premiss? I'll tell you who I thought for the girl.'

'Tell me.'

'Camille.'

'Camille.'

'She's just done a picture in Spain, I saw some of the cut material last night, she's going to be a sensation. She never looks less than beautiful, she acts, she's fresh, she's unspoiled, she's sexy, I don't think we have to look any further. Daniel, listen, I hate to do this to you, but if you're interested, how soon can you be back in London? Have your friends shown yet?'

'How the hell did you know about that?' Daniel said. 'He finally turned up this morning.'

'Jesus, this is a god-awful line.'

'Have someone shot,' Daniel said. 'Or shall I?'

'I hate to pressure you, but if I said like be back the end of next week, would that make me the heavy?'

'Listen, Gil, it sounds very attractive.'

'And Danny, I ought to tell you, we're going to pay you for this one.'

'Even more attractive. As a matter of fact, I had an idea for a picture in South America myself.'

'Sounds fascinating. I'd like to hear about it. Maybe we could do the two of them back to back. Tell me, how do you feel about Jack?'

'Very much in favour. Listen, Gil—'

'I can't wait for you to talk to him about it. Daniel, forgive me interrupting your pleasure like this, but I'm really delighted and the sooner you and Jack—'

'Me too, me too.'

'Because after all our talks, here's something right in our laps—

I always hoped this would happen. You'll be back here Thursday evening? Can I rely on that?'

'I have to get back to Athens first. What's today for Christ's sake?'

'Today is Saturday, I believe.'

'I'll call you Thursday evening,' Daniel said. 'Just don't tell me that you've got Billy after all. Get your people to get me two seats out Thursday, will you? B.E.A.'

'Will do. Listen, I wouldn't have Billy Stern on this; it needs somebody ballsy. It needs you.'

'And you'll talk to Queenie, will you?'

'I have a call into her as soon as I put the phone down. I'm excited; I hope you are.'

Dmitri said: '*En daxi*? O.K.?'

'*En daxi*.' Daniel took a hundred drachmae from his pocket and pressed it into Dmitri's hand. The donkey-man took it, but never lost his old mocking smile. Daniel ran out of the Post Office and down the dirt road. Dmitri did not take a single step to follow him. He stood at the top of the marble steps, tucking the drachmae into his purse.

Daniel walked round the village. The sun at last began to burn through the top of the clouds. The sea in the harbour was barely wrinkled now. Puddles of blue showed between the islands. In the distance, a steamer caught a glint of sunshine. It grew hot. Daniel walked slowly. He was bruised. He lifted his head and smiled; he lowered it and frowned. The clouds split and shadows sprang from ambush.

'Well, I bought it,' Daniel said.

'*Vevea*,' Constantine said.

'I began to have doubts, so I thought what the hell. What do you think? Don't tell me it's a standard piece of tourist fodder or I may do myself an injury.'

'Let's see.'

378

'The guy particularly asked me –'

'*Then pirazi*. Don't worry.' Constantine opened the brown paper behind the ledge of his desk. He smiled and then smiled at Daniel. 'Most interesting.'

'Well? Am I an idiot? The fact is, I had a bit of good news and I thought what the hell. What do you think?'

'*Apo 'tho ine?*'

'So they say. It's like nothing I've ever seen. On the other hand, at least there aren't any tool marks on it.'

'Of course, forgery is a very old art here in Greece. It's nice. It's pleasant. He has a face like your Dmitri.'

'His head's as hard. Dmitri says it's right. Or he did when I said I wasn't buying it.'

'Possibly he is correct,' Constantine said. 'He often is.'

'Constantine –'

'*Oriste?*'

'I'm probably going to have to go back to London next week. We probably have to leave on the Wednesday boat.'

'I'm sorry.'

'I'm going to try and get George Akrotiri out before I go. If necessary, obviously, I'll go with him. What I have in mind is to get Larry Pleasure to lend us his cruiser. I reckon we could get Akrotiri to the Turkish coast and be back here by daybreak. What I need is a Captain. This is something I really want to do. Something I really feel I've got to do.'

'Why Akrotiri?' Constantine Mersenas said.

'I seem to have got involved with him. He's the only one I know. I've talked to him. And he's got the sort of personality that'd go down well with the press. He's been a London correspondent. I think he'd make a good impression. I like him.'

'I see.'

'Look, I don't expect you, obviously, to do anything unless you want to.'

'*Then boro*,' Constantine said. 'I can't. I make no excuses. I can't, I won't. The price is too high and the reward too small. *Then boro*.'

'Fair enough.'

'Furthermore, I am strictly an amateur sailor. Daniel, tell me, why do you want to do this?'

'Isn't it obvious? Because I'm tired of doing nothing. We live in a society that always finds a way to do nothing. Either because we know too much or because we know too little. We never know the right amount to make us actually act. Greece is a simple instance, forgive me, but it is. We know who the enemy is, we know what can be done. We know what they're doing, we know who supports them and we know who is against them. It's a straightforward case where something can be done. Instead of which, we find endless ways of getting in our own way.'

'You're an impatient man,' Constantine said. 'You're a very impatient man.'

'Yes, I am. But also in normal circumstances a very docile one. Impatience doesn't entail action; unfortunately. Christ, I'm talking as if doing — doing what I was talking about —'

'Excuse me one moment. Can I help you, madam?'

'That icon — that one in the case with the two figures on it — how much is it?'

'It is not for sale, madam.'

'I'm sorry?'

'It is not for sale, madam.'

'Oh. Not for sale. Honey, it's not for sale.'

'What I was thinking of doing isn't anything very earth-shaking, that I grant right away.'

'I like you very much,' Constantine said. 'But I must say —'

'Ah, as long as there's a but.'

'You will never solve your own problems by trying to solve ours.'

'I'm not so sure. Byron —'

'Byron, as you know, achieved immortal fame for himself, but his services to Greece were not very great. Because he was famous, his death was a symbol, but it was his fame he gave to us, nothing more.'

'You suggest I go away and become a little more famous? Akrotiri, apart from that, did ask me to help him.'

380

'I like George, I like to see him, I like to talk to him. He's amusing, he's lively, he's intelligent.'

'But —?'

Mersenas smiled at the small objects on the top of his desk. 'He is rather Ovidian,' he said. 'Ovidian? Is that a word?'

'Like Ovid. The poet.'

'Who was exiled from Rome for being indiscreet, I think.'

'No one quite knows. Possibly for writing a scandalous poem implicating the Emperor's family. No one quite knows. Is that what Akrotiri did?'

'Please, Daniel, believe me, I am your friend, I want all the things you want.'

'Are you? Do you? And if you are and if you do, pleased, delighted as I am, why are you and why do you?'

'As you know, one does not explain these things. That is how I feel. George is a very indiscreet man. He talks. And he is very easily flattered. He is an actor. Like many political journalists, he thinks of politics as being all a matter of secret agreements, secret talks, secret alliances. He loves inside stories; he loves to get them and he loves to be known to have got them. His only reason for telling you that he knows a secret is that he enjoys seeing how you will go about extracting it from him and what titbit — titbit?'

'Titbit, yes.'

'Titbit he will acquire in exchange. He is not a man for whom to risk your life.'

'I wasn't thinking of an investment on that scale,' Daniel said. 'I was thinking more in terms of lifting my little finger. A small but definite gesture.'

'It's not always possible to limit one's investment in that way.' Constantine moved the chairs behind the counter and bent to look out of the window.

'Or honourable, I grant you,' Daniel said. 'But it's all I had in mind. You think I'm a fool.'

'I understand your feelings. I share your impatience.'

'Forgive me, but what are you actually doing? Is it really

impossible to do anything? If it is, how did they manage to do something?'

'I am waiting,' Constantine said. 'How does one prevent people from breaking the rules? They won the game by breaking the rules. They were in a perfect position. Now, shall we give up the rules, in which case there can never be another game, or shall we wait until they find that the game cannot be played without rules? People imagine that a game will become easier when one is not hampered by the rules, but in fact, I think, it becomes more difficult, it may even become impossible.'

'You know what this argument reminds me of—it reminds me of many things—but for some reason it reminds me most of the Colonialist argument at the time of Suez. The British and French honestly imagined that the Egyptians would never be able to run the Canal, that they would be physically and mentally incapable of piloting the ships through it and that in consequence they would be obliged to hand it back. Only a white man could ferry a ship through a canal.'

'And how many ships now pass through the Canal, please?'

'That's my whole point. Actually, the Egyptians piloted ships perfectly well for several years—but even if the Canal is now closed to traffic, the old pilots have not been recalled. The thing's silted up, it's closed for all sorts of reasons, but no one's gone back to playing the game by the rules. It's not a game, Constantine, and there aren't any rules.'

'I disagree with you. I disagree with you. We shall not, of course, go back to where the game stopped when the rules were broken, but there is a game, in the sense of—'

'I understand the sense,' Daniel said. 'I spent two years doing nothing else at Cambridge. You're invoking the idea of some kind of sensible equilibrium to which the ship of state must eventually revert. But ships sometimes sink, or burn, or simply become obsolete. Sometimes their captains become landbound and turn into shopkeepers and there's no one to take the helm when it's needed.'

Constantine said: 'You speak well.'

382

'I'm sorry.'

'But I still believe you know little of the realities.'

'Sometimes one is left with no one to hurt but one's friends,' Daniel said.

'I am not hurt.'

'Then it's only because I missed my mark. The intention was there.'

'You are a very frustrated man, Daniel.'

'Yes, I wish I understood it.'

'A very frustrated man. What is it that is frustrated in you?'

'People who know the answer to that are theoretically released from their frustration. I don't know. Perhaps it's just that there are too many people who believe they're Jesus Christ and I'm a bit thrown to find I'm not alone in the illusion. Frankly, Constantine, I don't know.'

'You're torn between gifts and blows,' Constantine said. 'You don't know which to offer people.'

'Or myself,' Daniel said.

'Oh, of course. Oneself is only one of the people one treats well or badly.'

'You're a philosopher, Constantine. No, I mean it. You're a genuine Greek philosopher. Well—you're probably right. You're probably right about everything. In which case, of course, don't expect me to forgive you!'

'I hope very much that you will. Nor do I think necessarily that I am.'

'Not nec-ess-air-ily,' Daniel said. 'I do forgive you. I was only joking. I want us very much to be friends. It's only with strangers that one really can be friends. What I wonder, Constantine, is why people never do what they want to do? Why, when we are alive for so short a time, do people so rarely do what they want?'

'But what do they want? You said yourself—'

'In the end, it seems always to come back to sex.'

'And is there something there that you want and cannot find, cannot do?'

'Even if there were, would it solve anything? The big bang,

does that really solve everything? Does it really solve anything? Does it even exist? Somehow, I don't know whether I'm right, I always associate it with death. I suspect there's no real ecstasy unless it's a final ecstasy. Anyone who plays around with the idea of the big bang is really playing with the idea of death, don't you think he is? He doesn't trust life. He's afraid of the quotidian. And that's the way life is measured. Why are you smiling? You think I'm talking about myself.'

'There are those who play the big game for little reasons, and those who play the little game as if it were big. The dabblers and the melodramists. You should decide what you are.'

'A dabbler or a melodramist? Not much of a menu, Constantine. Melodramist or melodramatist, do you think?'

'You are a clever man, *un homme très vif*, you're accustomed to being everything at the same time. You take office in every government everywhere, you have better ideas than everyone. Often you do. You can make all the women happy—'

'Ah, I wish!'

'You want to spread yourself everywhere. You are here three days—you are ready for a decisive stroke.'

'You're saying I'm a playboy. I wish I was. I'm not even that.'

'You believe only in what you are not.'

'Oh, for Christ's sake, what does one *do*? You're right, you're right. You're right enough, but what does one *do*?'

'Something excellent,' Constantine said.

'They'll piss on it,' Daniel said.

'Something excellent shows that excellence is possible. I believe that excellence is the enemy of everything that is wrong. And in this way, always worth while. Always. I believe that if you were to make a truly excellent film, it would do more for Greece than starring—is that what you say?—George Akrotiri in a melodrama.'

'I've had this conversation so many times—the idea that committed cinema—'

'I'm not talking about commitment—'

'Christ, you speak fantastic English—'

'I'm talking about excellence, even if it seems quite unconnected

384

with politics. Excellence rebukes them better than argument, better than force. Excellence remains intact; it is not a missile, it is an alternative world altogether.'

'The World of Ideas. Plato lives! What the hell are you doing running a shop?'

'I have a wife and a family,' Constantine said. 'And I like it. So.'

'You're not happy,' Daniel said. 'Any more than I am. Why do we do it?'

'I am very happy,' Constantine said. 'I am not satisfied, but yes, I am happy. I am not impatient as you are. I like my shop. I like the things I sell. I like my friends. I love my family. I am happy.'

'You're happy! With Greece like it is? You're really happy?'

'Really, really! At the centre I am happy. I am not happy with Greece, but yes, I am happy *in* it.'

'And that's why you won't help me get Akrotiri out?'

'Can you pretend that it is important?'

'Between us. I don't know.'

'It is an act of fantasy, Daniel, an act of frivolity. I understand what makes you think it worth while. But to me, I must tell you, it is the act of a frustrated man. A shot at the Gods. Nothing more.'

'You know you're a man,' Daniel said. 'You can turn me down and be certain you're not a coward. You decide not to do something; that's it. Me, I can't pass a crossroads without trying to go in all directions. Why?'

'Your centre is art, but you won't acknowledge it.'

'It's not an art, Constantine, film. If I don't get Akrotiri out how am I going to feel when I get home? You see? It'll only take so long to do the job, so why not do it? Better do it, and then not feel bad about not having done it. One puts things off in order to avoid being accused of putting things off. I shall have to go through with it now. I wish I'd never thought of the idea, but now ... Story of my life.'

'You're going to marry your girl?' Constantine said.

'Oh, darling, you're just in time. Come and tell me what to bid.'

The four women were sitting on the terrace, under the split bamboo shade, playing bridge.

'You'll have to tell me the story so far,' Daniel said.

'It's gone a club from the Princess, a spade, and then I said three clubs—'

'Quite right.'

'Four spades from Eleni, pass, pass and now it's me again.'

'If you think I'm going to take the responsibility now, you're absolutely mistaken. You get to the crisis and then you turn to me. Decide for yourself. That's the fun of the thing.'

'Pass,' Nancy said.

'With an overtrick,' Daniel said.

'You should have told me what to do. That's rubber. Sorry, partner dear. Why didn't you?'

'It's not playing the game,' Daniel said. 'When you let an outsider make the crucial decision. Listen, Nancy, I spoke to Gil and I've got to be back in England Thursday of next week.'

'In which case there's no sense in going all the way down the beach to find a room. Larry says we'd be crazy anyway. He insists there's no problem at all. He's delighted. What should I have done, now it's all over?'

'Bid five clubs and the Princess would have doubled five spades.'

'They made five spades.'

'Not if you lead a diamond and the Princess holds off the first one. You come in with the ace of trumps and she gives you a ruff. Gil's got a picture he wants me to direct. Big one.'

'Darling!'

'Set in South America.'

'Just like you've always wanted! That's wonderful. Come and see the room, it's so pretty.'

'And the water runs like wine, I've no doubt.'

'You have to admit!'

'Nice room,' Daniel said. 'I admit. What are we on? Modified American Plan.'

'We've got—what?—five days, couldn't we just try and relax and enjoy ourselves?'

'Should we limit ourselves when there are so many other people to enjoy as well?'

'I love you,' Nancy said. 'Whatever you may think. What's the movie about?'

'Absolutely everything according to the spiel. It's a caper basically.'

'That's exactly what I always thought you ought to do. Exactly. It'll give you a chance to break out.'

'You make it sound like impetigo. The water works. The chain pulls. It's paradise. Actually, it could be fun. But first I have to read the script. Still, today a movie is a movie is a movie. You takes what's going because it's a long wait between trains. I was afraid you might be sore. At the prospect of leaving.'

'Who wants to be here if you're not? And they're all going on Monday. They hope to have a boat here for them Monday morning.'

'We could hitch a ride.'

'If you want to.'

'Gil wants to go in February. Which means a Christmas recce in the jungle. How does that grab you? Honeymoon in the jungle if you like.'

'How long do you think the picture'll take?'

'Sixteen weeks at least. These action things always do. Probably more like twenty. Billy took twenty-eight to shoot *A Public Life* and it had just three sets. Mind you, he has tenure. And deserves it, and deserves it. He can shoot and reshoot and they still sign the cheques.'

'I guess it must be a big budget. I hope they're going to pay you.'

'Gil promises. This time I get full adult fare. What're you thinking? We've had the honeymoon already?'

'Of course I'm not. Not at all.'

'Make love to me,' Daniel said. 'And then we'll go swimming. Come on.'

'What if I don't feel like it?'

'Feel like it,' Daniel said. 'I feel like it. Make love to me. Be nice to me. Be nice to me and I'll be nice to you, isn't that what they say?'

'Have you completely—?'

'Come on, Nancy Jane. Come on, Nancy J.'

'Daniel, I truly—'

'Every time I mention getting married, I encounter the same kind of—'

'That's unfair and you know it.'

'So what is the problem? What is the big barrier? Is it the budget?'

'I'm not going to continue this conversation when you're in this mood.'

'Isn't it about time you came out with it?'

'Damn you, Daniel Meyer, I won't have you make yourself out to be some kind of—of investigator, some kind of detective entitled to the truth, whatever the truth is.'

'The truth is, Nancy Jane, that you don't want to marry me because you're afraid of losing Charles' money.'

'Daniel, I'm just—'

'Now be very careful what you do, because Astrid thinks we're a darling couple. Don't fracture any of her painfully recovered illusions or you may find her burning at both ends come nightfall.'

'Who have you seen? Who have you been talking to? If it wasn't so unfair and so cruel and so vulgar—'

'It probably wouldn't be so near the truth.'

'Shall I tell you what you're afraid of? You're afraid I *will* lose my money if I marry you—'

'Do me a favour—'

'You've been digging ever since we met. Was the house mine? Was there a trust for the children? Oh it's always been as though it was something I ought to be ashamed of, it was always asked as if only delinquents owned houses or had trust funds, but haven't you been interested? Boy, have you! You talk about money all the time. You're obsessed with it. You play with it like kids play with dirt. You can't stop. For God's sake put some clothes on.'

'Let's interpret that for the populace, shall we?'

'I've had enough of your stinking sarcasm. I don't have to take it and I won't take it. I will not be made to feel ashamed.'

Daniel said: 'You'd sooner be independent. I don't blame you. But at least have the guts to be straight about it. You don't want to marry me? Don't. You don't want to have my children? Don't. But at least be straight about it.'

'If you want to have scenes, if you want to play the big movie director, go marry an actress. Go find somebody who enjoys this kind of thing. I can't seem to find any fun in it any more.'

'So you think I'm after your money.'

'I think you're after me *and* my money. Or at least me and *some* money. Certainly not just me.'

'I don't want a cent of your fucking money.'

'Then shut the hell up about it.'

'Fucking money, I said.'

'You're so old-fashioned. Underneath it all, you're so stinkingly old-fashioned.'

'You and Tom York, the glamorous young flyer. I always had the idea you were a couple of kids together. Tom York was pushing forty when you were going with him. You were seventeen and he was forty. And loaded. You made him sound like someone who took over the run through the Andes from Saint-Exupéry. He owned an airline, Nancy Jane. Just a little one, I grant you, but an airline is still an airline.'

'I loved him,' Nancy said. 'Just like I loved you.'

'Ah.'

'Yes.'

'What do I do to get the tense changed? Take out my cheque book? Promise you something?'

'And you wanted to marry me. You actually asked me to marry you.'

'Nice correction. Nothing like accuracy.'

'I find you sickening. Sickening!'

'To think I wanted you.'

'Well now you've got a movie instead. I hope you'll be very happy together. Oh come on—come on—I'm not a fool—'

'Do you seriously — ?'

'Don't I just! Don't I just!'

'Are you going to say *everything* twice? Be careful, it starts off as an affectation and it ends up an affliction up an affliction. What did you do — send the boy round to collect our things from the Gavin Residence? I don't suppose you risked stubbing your toe going there yourself. After all, what do decent manners — ?'

'My God, who's Emily Post suddenly? Have you heard your language in front of the Princess and people?'

'My darling, the Princess is only one more lonely hooker among many.'

'No,' Nancy said, 'no, no, no.'

'Cut it there,' Daniel said, 'cut it there. I'm sorry. I'm sorry.'

'Don't you dare apologize to me,' she said. 'Don't you —'

'Dare apologize to me,' Daniel said. 'Don't worry, I'm beginning to get the rhythm of this thing. I really think you're a terrific woman. I don't care if Tom York was a hundred and forty. What in shit has it got to do with me anyway? You're wrong about the money.'

'Oh no I'm not. You're hurting me. Please stop it.'

'You're beautiful,' he said, 'you're beautiful. Jesus, you've got me doing it now. Just what was *your* motive? Amid all this money-mindedness, all this sinister Levantine greed? Don't tell me it's because you like cock.'

'You're a failure, Daniel. I thought you were a success, but you're a failure.'

'I'm going to be hypnotized in a minute. Careful I don't fall asleep before you drive the last nail in. Did I ever claim to be a success? You should try going to bed with Billy Stern. He's a success, but you wouldn't get much joy out of him. Is that what you wanted, a success?'

'I thought you were dedicated and serious. I don't think you're either thing any more. I thought I could learn something from you. I thought all kinds of things. Things I won't humiliate myself by telling you.'

'You wanted to be the artist's wife and go down to the corner for a pint of sour milk and yesterday's loaf, am I supposed to believe that?'

'You're a failure because you have no heart. You're on nobody's side, not even your own.'

'No heart.'

'No.'

'Because I can't sympathize with some phoney Princess with as much right to be called her Highness as I have to be hailed King of the Jews. Less. Suddenly it's World Refugee Week for a woman who can charter the Q.E.II to come and get her if she wants to. What's the latest idea? Are we still going to smuggle her through customs like she was some Pekingese that might have to go into quarantine? Helping the rich and the famous is whorehouse stuff. It has about as much to do with heart as Heart of Midlothian. A Scottish football club. I was a bit stuck. No heart, that's rich coming from you. You notice nothing. Nothing. You're like those Victorians who used to gather round the railings when some Royal parasite had the sniffles and never noticed the bodies lying in the street.'

'Are you enjoying this?'

'Yes.'

'Because I'm not. I happen —'

'I'm enjoying it because for once I've seen you actually alive. For once this whole relationship has come to life. You know, there are certain kinds of machine, when they go wrong, the dynamo, instead of generating power elsewhere, generates it in itself, the whole thing gets hotter and hotter and finally it blows up. I always think that must be the only moment when it feels the whole goddam thing is worthwhile. You know what Picasso called modern art? A Sum of Destructions. Well —'

'And I'm supposed to have your child?'

'Hullo, it's me,' Larry Pleasure said. 'I hope it's not a bad moment, only I just got the news on 1500 metres from A.F.N. Heraklion. They had an earthquake in Central Turkey just after noon today. First reports say over two thousand dead. When nature turns nasty, it really turns nasty.'

391

'That moody bastard Poseidon again,' Daniel said.

Nancy said: 'Poseidon's not the only one.'

'Has he been beating you again?'

'Hasn't he just?' She put her arm through Daniel's. 'It's all your fault too, Larry.'

'Mine? How mine?'

'For telling him about Tom York.'

'Jesus, that's ancient history.'

'Nothing's too ancient for Daniel to be interested in, is it, sweetness? He goes back centuries.'

'Larry, I want to show you something, while you're here.'

'Gladly. Nancy J., you know I wouldn't —'

'You talk too much, Larry Pleasure, you always did.'

'You're right. Well, well, well.'

'It's interesting, isn't it? But what do you think? Is it a fake?'

'I don't think so. Do you think it's a fake, Nancy J.?'

'It looks very primitive. Daniel! You never told me —'

'I was saving it,' Daniel said. 'I think it probably isn't right, but I thought it was worth a gamble.'

'I don't see why it shouldn't be right,' Larry said. 'Where did you get it? Tselementes?'

'There aren't many secrets round here, are there?'

'He's a good man. It ought to be right. He has good contacts. I had a couple of Bœotian figurines from him and their provenance was as right as right could be. It's nice. You want I should buy you out?'

'After I've sweated blood deciding?'

'I'll give you whatever you paid for it. Cash.'

'Hell, I didn't buy it to sell it again. Certainly not for what I paid for it.'

'It's certainly unusual. What did you pay for it?'

'A hundred pounds,' Daniel said.

'Pity it doesn't have the feet. I'll give you double.'

'You'll give me confidence, you mean. Very nice of you. Of course, if it had the feet —'

'It could still be worth five hundred pounds in the open market. So maybe you fell on your feet, even if it doesn't have any!'

'It'll look much better when it's mounted,' Nancy said. 'Things always do.'

'It's nice. Nice form. Maybe you got yourself a bargain. Who knows?'

The landing-craft hit the beach at about half past ten the next morning. Daniel and Nancy and Astrid and Eleni and Tita were sunning themselves in Larry's private cove when the *Prometheus* approached from Agoria, hesitated and then headed for the beach beside Paniotis' *taverna*. She came in quite slowly, with no one visible except a bald man in a turtle-necked sweater in the bridge-house.

Daniel said: 'My God, they're here!'

The women lifted their heads. 'Who are?'

'The marines. The rescue force.' Astrid was lying next to him in Nancy's black swimsuit. 'We need Larry's glasses.'

'I don't need glasses to know I'm not going in that,' Astrid said. 'They promised me a proper boat.'

Daniel ran into the sea. Nancy stood up, in her turquoise, but sat down when the other women failed to follow. The landing-craft grated on the pebbles, several yards from the shore. Paniotis and Vassili were watching from the terrace of the *taverna*. Davina Long looked up from her new notebook.

Two men in goggles and flippers joined the other man on the bridge. They leaned over the stern of the craft, then sat on the edge of the deck and finally dropped into the water. They swam round and then waddled up the beach to where Daniel had already arrived. As they reached him, they lifted their goggles and winced at the sun.

'Oh my God,' Daniel said. 'I don't believe it, I don't believe it.'

'Daniel, thank God,' Jack Darwin said. 'We hoped you were still here. You got our message?'

'Message? What message? What the hell is this? I *still* don't believe it.'

'The landing gate's gone and jammed,' Paul Mallory said. 'We're in a bit of a fix.'

'What the hell have you got in that thing?'

'Is there a blacksmith or someone in the vicinity? We need someone with mechanical knowledge.'

'But Jack, surely, with your knowledge of modern weaponry—'

'We sent you a telegram.'

'This is the unlikeliest event since the Second Coming. What've you got in that thing, two dozen picked desperadoes armed with jammed gatlings and blunt bayonets dreaming that Greece might yet be free? It's a superb gesture, Jack, it's really superb. Now, of course, I understand what Gil was talking about. He asked had I seen you.'

'We've got Meredith Lamb suffering from gastritis,' Jack Darwin said. 'We've got Francesca Lamb suffering from Meredith, we've got Stuart Melrose, Conservative Member of Parliament for north-east Essex, we've got Victor Rich—'

'An amphibious chat show,' Daniel said. 'I can't stand it. Let's go and have a drink—'

'We've got Gay and Basil Brain, suffering from the green sickness both, and we've got as our doughty helmsman and *chef d'orchestre* the famous London-based American publisher, darling of the Trade Press and champion of lost causes, Norbert Ash.'

'My Christ,' Daniel said. 'Full house aces. Beats full house queens, which is what we've got here. What about your wives?'

'We also have our wives.'

'Janey?'

'And Margaret,' Paul said.

'And all you did was send a telegram. You should've sent an angel. What the hell're you all doing?'

'We also have a clapped-out Volkswagen bus and a crew of three of the sourest Greeks since the retreat from Smyrna.'

'A happy ship,' Daniel said. 'I can tell.'

'I should never have set foot in Greece,' Paul said. 'I knew it was immoral.'

394

'Where are you going? What're you doing?'

'It's all Norbert Ash's idea. Epidauros, Mycenae, Thera, Constantinople and Persepolis.'

'What's wrong with the Thracian Chalcidice?'

'We damned nearly went down with all hands the night before last. I don't know whether you had a storm. We damned nearly sank. I'm not joking. That thing's like going to sea on a canteen tray, I'm telling you.'

'Well at least you're not enjoying yourself, Paul, that ought to make you happy. What do you want to drink?'

'Coffee for me,' Paul said. 'And how are the fleshpots?'

'Fleshy,' Daniel said. 'We've had our ups and downs.'

'Mostly ups if I know you.'

'*Kalimera, Vassili, pos ishte? Kala?*'

'*Kala, kala. I phili sas ine etho? Pirate to tilegraphima sas?*'

'*Ti tilegraphima?*'

'Oh Christ,' Paul said, 'these ex-Classics and their damned Greek. We've had Basil Brain teaching us the rules of transposition ever since we left Piraeus.'

'You'd better get yourselves fit,' Daniel said, 'because the big game's tomorrow. Piers Cobbett's here and we've got the blood match tomorrow against the locals. They massacred the tourists twelve-one last week and tomorrow is Eagle Tag.'

'I've not got my boots,' Paul said.

'Play with your tongue as usual,' Daniel said.

'Oh Christ,' Paul said, 'not already, not already. Where's your woman?'

'On the beach. We're staying with –' Daniel indicated the white towers of Larry's house at the top of the cape.

'Ah the simple life, eh, Daniel? Bloody sybarite. You spoke to Gil then. The script needs work.'

'What I hear I like.'

'What you hear he likes.'

'Toosh,' Daniel said.

Paul said: 'We'd better go and find this blacksmith. They're like chained animals in there.'

'But it seems to be a goer, which is the thing. Obviously the first thing is for me to see a script. I hope you've brought one?'

'All's to talk about,' Jack Darwin said. 'I haven't had the last payment yet.'

'*To tilegraphima.*'

'Ah,' Daniel said. 'A little late, but *efcharisto poli.*' He tore open the telegram. 'Aha, here's a nice surprise, Norbert Ash, Jack Darwin and a few friends are arriving for lunch on the 25th. The 25th? Good heavens, that's today—'

'Oh shut up. I knew he'd never get it,' Paul said. 'We should never have sent it.'

'I hope you're not expecting us to feed you. How many are you?'

'We carry grub. We've got the hairiest cook since Escoffier. He even manages to get his pubic hair into a boiled egg, it's fantastic. We're thirteen.'

'Of course. Himself and the twelve disciples.'

'It's all very well for you,' Paul said. 'But some of us never get the chance to go everywhere with all expenses paid and first-class travel thrown in.'

'Norbert's rates were competitive, were they?'

'Hey there—' Norbert was hailing them from the bridge.

'I wish he wouldn't use that bloody thing. I'm going to throw it into the Hellespont if I get the chance.'

'DANIEL, HOW ARE YOU? ANY JOY?'

'He thinks he's in the remake of *In Which We Serve.*'

'You haven't seen his cap,' Paul said. 'He's got a cap with an anchor on it. He bought it in the Piraeus.'

'I said ANY JOY?'

'He thinks it's nautical. It's actually what the kids wear to go to school.'

'WE NEED A MECHANIC URGENTLY.'

'What's he charging you for this excursion?'

'Don't be so damned insinuating, Daniel,' Paul said, 'all the time. It was a perfectly decent invitation.'

396

'What's he taking you for?'

'Three quid a day per person basic. Travel included. It's not unreasonable. These things cost a packet.'

'Look, we'd better drink up and find this mate of yours.'

'Mate? I don't have any mate. I don't even know if I can find anyone. Oh God, not another phone call?'

Dmitri was standing at the top of the steps, the reins of the little grey donkey in his hand. '*Ti kanome?*'

'*Chriazometha ena michaniko.*'

'I feel an absolute fool,' Paul said. 'I feel completely out of place.'

'What the hell are you doing with a Conservative M.P.?'

'He's a good bloke,' Jack Darwin said. 'Stuart. He was at Virginia's that night. He's the only one who keeps us going.'

'He's a fellow Scot,' Paul said. 'From Aberdeen.'

'Ah well, you and he must have the same sense of humour.'

'What's that supposed to mean? Daniel, exactly what are you insinuating now?'

'WHAT JOY THERE?'

'*Pame,*' Dmitri said.

'*Ela, grigora, Dmitri.*' Daniel gave Dmitri a couple of hundred drachmae. 'If there's anyone to get, Dmitri'll get him, I'll bet I don't get my money back for this. Norbert'll remember he lent it to me at Cambridge.'

'Oh Christ,' Paul said, 'I wish you'd stop this. It's indecently obsessive, this hostility of yours.'

'Nice to see you, Paul, me old son,' Daniel said. 'Cheer up, you may yet be able to strike a blow for the good. I have a little plan in which you and your doughty Argonauts may live to play a vital part.'

'I'm not playing soccer unless I get some decent shoes,' Paul said. 'That's flat.'

'I'm going to go back and start stripping down the gate mechanism,' Jack Darwin said. 'Any idea how long he's likely to be, your chap?'

'Piers Cobbett's here, is he? What's he doing?'

'Enjoying the view and a diet of Coco,' Daniel said.

'Cocoa? In this climate? What are you talking about? He's a Fascist of course, Piers, isn't he?'

'Is he really? A Fascist?'

'He's certainly an out and out élitist. He broke some student's arm, you know, when they had all that trouble. He broke a bloke's arm.'

'But wasn't that — ?'

'They came and tried to break into his rooms and he broke this chap's arm.'

'They'd already burned down Barclay's Bank, hadn't they?'

'It takes a bit of effort to break a man's arm.'

'Presumably they were going to burn his rooms, were they?'

'Daniel, if I said they were black, you'd say they were white. Why not let's leave it there?'

'How would you feel about smuggling a political prisoner out in that contraption of yours?'

Paul Mallory said: 'A political prisoner of what complexion?'

'Well he won't be a Fascist, will he? Not from these NATO-loving shores. A bloke called Akrotiri. Used to be a centrist deputy. They've got him in exile here on Iskios.'

'I'm game,' Paul Mallory said. 'Or is this another of your ill-conceived jokes?'

'Oh, come on. Have you not heard of him? Used to be London correspondent of *To Vrathi*. When are you people leaving?'

'That depends on Norbert and this mechanic fellow. We can't possibly sail until the hydraulics are right and anyway everyone wants a breather. Probably not until tomorrow sometime.'

'After the game.'

'I've got no shoes, man.'

'He can be ready any time. Can you sail at night in that thing? And would there be room?'

'Is he not guarded? Of course we can. We have. It was purgatory, but we did it. They were designed to take a Churchill tank, you know, and sixty men besides. It's been completely refitted though. There's tons of room. It's quite comfortable inside.'

398

'Look, I don't want to buy it, I just want to get this bloke away. His wife's in London, he's a bit desperate.'

'You'd better talk to Norbert. The *Prometheus* has got to go back to Piraeus eventually. If it gets out what we've done, there's likely to be some questions asked. Is it always as hot as this? I never realized you got such heat.'

'This,' Daniel said, 'is the cool. Of course you'd feel it less if you took off your hair shirt. Has Victor got Victoria with him?'

'She's got her patients to think about,' Paul said. 'She couldn't get away. She has her responsibilities.'

'He's happy then.'

'That's a bit of a shit's remark, Daniel, even for you. I'm very much an admirer of Victoria's. She's a woman of character.'

'That may be, but is Victor?'

'You're wrong about so many things,' Paul said, 'you truly are, Daniel. It's this obsessive hostility of yours. It's not healthy. It's also intellectually suspect, which is worse.'

'They all have to come up here,' Larry Pleasure said. 'We have plenty to eat.'

'I've already told Paniotis to give us a big table at the *taverna*. Norbert sent a signal they're out of nosh and would I fix something.'

'Stuart Melrose is actually Lord Melrose,' Nancy said, 'he's the son of an earl.'

'He'll eventually come into most of the counties you've never heard of and one or two you have.'

'Astrid, you should come down,' Nancy said.

'I don't think I will, really,' Astrid said.

'Astrid's very low today,' Nancy said. 'She's beginning to realize how much she's lost.'

'Poor Astrid,' Daniel said. 'Why not come and see how the other half loafs? It might cheer you up; it might even cheer them up.'

'We still haven't heard a word from Athens.'

'It's Sunday, I can't even send a wire,' Tita Ralli said. 'I'm going to try calling Stavro again at lunch time. I'm sure he'll be able to do something.'

'Or someone,' Daniel said. 'So are you coming down or not?'

'Astrid doesn't want to,' Nancy said, 'You can see.'

'Perhaps she'd like to meet a deputation later,' Daniel said.

'He's very naughty, your friend,' Tita said.

'Only I promised I'd go back down. Come on, Astrid, it can't be worse than the commissariat at Culver City.'

'Don't press her, Daniel, she doesn't want to. I think I'll let you go. I don't mind staying one bit.'

'Stuart Melrose will be desolated. Think of all those acres, wilting.'

'I'm not impressed by acres, Daniel.'

'Tonight, Astrid, we live,' Daniel said. 'No excuses. You be ready.'

Paniotis had laid two long tables under the blue sailcloth. The mechanic was working on the landing gate. Shortly before noon, there was a noise of *Prometheus* unchained and the gate fell with a fat splash into the shallows. Norbert Ash, in his sailor's cap, led the expedition ashore, saluting a number of Greeks and tourists who stood ankle deep in the water. 'Ike!' Daniel said. 'You finally made it.'

'That mechanic of yours is using some kind of a sledgehammer in there. I hope he knows what he's doing. I hope you haven't let loose some kind of a maniac, because that's what he looks like to me.'

'Daniel, my dear old son, where's the boozer?'

'Meredith, how are you?'

'Straight ahead? I shall feel better when I've sunk a noggin. Christ, I wish someone would turn the lights down.'

'Is that where we're supposed to be eating?' Francesca said. 'Because Meredith's had the most dreadful stomach. I hope they'll do him something simple. He really needs something like sea bass done in milk, something like that.'

'Why don't you ask them?' Daniel said. 'I'm just the booking clerk. Why the hell didn't you tell us you were planning this?'

400

'Oh listen,' Norbert Ash said, 'this was kind of scratched together at the last minute. I had a whole raft of American publishers were supposed to do this trip with me and Babette and then at the last minute they cried off and I was left with an empty boat—'

'They *all* cried off?'

'They had invited me and then suddenly their tax advisers got jumpy and they said would I take over the booking. They were going to have to pay whether the boat was used or not. So naturally—'

'So are you paying for it now or what?'

'I shall make a fair contribution. Catering's a problem, but I think we should break even. Paul's told me about this prisoner they have here you want us to heist.'

'If you're heading for Turkey, it's a cinch,' Daniel said. 'If you sail tomorrow evening, no one's going to know anything until Tuesday morning. We can put George to bed with a bad headache, fix a dummy in the bed, and come the *matino* you're out of Greek waters.'

'That side of it doesn't worry me.'

'That's because it's my side,' Daniel said, 'no doubt.'

'Daniel, is this a good man we're rescuing?'

'The best,' Daniel said.

'I'm serious. Remember we have a Member of Parliament on board.'

'And Victor. Don't forget to count Victor among the famous. He never does. Why a Conservative, were all the presentable Socialists booked to go to Bulgaria already?'

'Stuart is writing a book for us on Liberty And The Individual.'

'I get you. You don't want to get him messed up at the critical moment in liberating any undesirable individuals. Sharp thinking, Norbert.'

'Daniel, I'm willing to help you, but—'

'Help *me*? Get fucked, Norbert, will you? I don't need your help. George Akrotiri needs *our* help.'

'I'm simply weighing the pros and cons. I'm allowed to do that. Get off my back, Daniel, will you?'

'You don't even have to know who he is. A hitch-hiker.'

'Try telling that to a military court with three goons sitting up there.'

'I was talking', Victor Rich said, 'to someone in Mycenae about the possibility of shooting a version of the whole of the *Oresteia* in English with a mixture of Greek and English actors. He seemed to think think it was a very exciting idea. No one's ever thought of it before. One's faced with the moral issue of whether we should shoot in Greece at all, but against that there's a world-wide market and, of course, we can use frozen money and a local unit. Later on, of course, once we're safely out of the country, we could get Theodorakis to do the music. I shall have to talk to my legal people. In principle, though, what do you feel about it?'

'Sounds very cultural,' Basil Brain said.

'Daniel Meyer, what are you doing here?'

'Gay Brain, what are *you* doing here? I thought this was forbidden land.'

'It is,' Gay said. 'I'm not here to enjoy myself.'

'They haven't got any white fish at all,' Francesca said.

'I promised I'd do a report for Mercy International. I didn't go down to Mycenae. Basil stayed with me and I had a thorough go at the Min of the Int. Without much success. Tight as —'

'Don't complete that simile,' Daniel said. 'I'm waiting to see who's going to pay for lunch. Has Norbert told you I want to spring George Akrotiri?'

'Is George here? Baz, George Ak.'s here.'

'I'm hoping he's going to be a shipmate of yours. Norbert's weighing the pros and cons.'

'Oh my dear, damn Norbert.'

'Another friend of yours is here too,' Daniel said, 'Piers Cobbett.'

'Oh, he's rather bright,' Basil Brain said. 'He once made some comments on a paper I wrote. Quite perceptive. Of course he was wrong in his principal contention, but his errors weren't without interest. What's the *retsina* like here?'

'Just the thing if you've painted your throat recently. Guaranteed

402

to remove all traces. You'll be playing with him in the back four tomorrow afternoon.'

'Football? In this? I shall watch from under my punkah. You must be mad.'

'It cools off about five, that's when we kick off. The locals need taking down a peg or two.'

'I haven't got any shoes.'

'Adidas have hit the island,' Daniel said. 'We'll get you fixed up. Failing that, we'll have you fitted with a pair of spare tyres. No arguments: you play, come what may. Anyway, Gay, you're in favour, are you? All it really means is heading for Turkish waters as fast as your unlikely vessel will carry you.'

'Meanwhile what will you do?'

'I shall stay behind, Sir Percy Blakeney to the last, and play the noble innocent.'

'Are you sure that's still within your powers? And what about Lady Blakeney? Or is your beautiful lady friend no longer with you?'

'Of course she's with me. She's just not to be lured from the heights for the likes of Norbert Ash. Actually we already had a lunch fixed when the invasion fleet showed up. It's true, why are you looking like that?'

'Sounds like trouble to me, Master Daniel,' Gay Brain said.

'It isn't trouble at all, it's Royalty. You know what Americans are like at the hint of the purple. Imagine if Sartre and the Beaver asked you elsewhere, would you be having lunch with us?'

'Don't get violent with me, Daniel. I know your reputation for intimidating ladies.'

'My dear, the last man to try and intimidate you is still recovering from his injuries. If you can call it recovering. New balls take a bit of growing. As a matter of fact, I'm relying on you as an ally. I can just see Norbert Ash chickening out, unless we're really decisive. And in fact one's asking nothing. Surely Playfair, Marks can't do a lot of business with the renascent Hellas?'

'Meredith's the problem,' Gay Brain said. 'He's become such a parody of himself. When we were on Syra and the restaurant charged us by mistake for something we hadn't had, Meredith threatened them with the British Consul if you please. And of course he will insist on speaking ancient Greek to them and then accusing them of being degenerate when they don't understand. The restaurant man nearly divided him in two with a meat cleaver. Meredith then managed to persuade himself that one of the dishes had poisoned him. He's eaten nothing but eggs ever since.'

'Funny, his poison usually comes out of a bottle. Gay, tell me, is Babette not with Norbert, and if not why not?'

'She's got her feet up in London, she nearly miscarried and the doctor said she had to rest.'

'Is she pregnant?' Daniel said. 'I didn't know she was old enough.'

'That's naughty. Babette's a nice little thing.'

'Yes, and I suppose as his first wife was twice as old as he was, it's only fitting his second one should come straight from the makers. On the principle, I suppose, that if you buy the vintage young enough it can mature in your own cellars at a fraction of the cost.'

'Daniel, if I were a dispassionate observer I'd say that you'd had a souring experience. What can it be when you're so happy?'

'I hate people who don't practise what they preach,' Daniel said. 'Especially when their sermons always get published in the Sundays.'

'Where *is* Norbert?' Gay said.

'He's in the kitchen,' Meredith Lamb said, 'sniffing.'

'Our problem, in terms of the cultural market, is how we can ever match a series like "Civilization". That's partly why I accepted this invitation.'

'I'll tell you what, Victor, why not do a series on Barbarism? You could get some tame academic to haul us through history — give him a little money and lots of close-ups — and he can tell us all about the shitty goings-on *in saecula saeculorum* shot in the authentic battlegrounds, execution sheds and producer's offices. You could include the beastly artefacts, the hideous buildings, the dishonest speeches, the false prospectuses of the human race from the tablets

404

of the law right through to the latest election manifesto. Civilization, after all, is for the few, but barbarism's universal.'

'The thing about you, Daniel, is that everything you say sounds like an accusation. How's *The Elephant Man* proceeding, by the way?'

'The spaghetti looks like the best bet,' Norbert Ash said. 'And salad and meatballs.'

'I'm not eating meatballs,' Meredith said.

'I've ordered you an omelette,' Francesca said.

'Don't let them put any pepper in it,' Meredith said. 'It makes me fart.'

'*The Elephant Man* is in good shape; they hadn't quite finished when I left but it should be showable by the time you get back.'

'We want to make a big thing of it in the autumn schedule,' Victor Rich said. 'We want to give it a top slot.'

'So I should bloody well hope. I think it's turned out rather well, to tell you the truth.'

'Bold, uncompromising and calculated to please everybody,' Francesca said.

'Woof, the goalkeeper never saw it,' Daniel said. 'Only you might have waited for the whistle. I was hoping you and I were going to let bygones be bygones, Francesca.'

'Chips?' Paniotis said.

'No chips,' Meredith said. 'Chips! Pardon. No thank you.'

'He belches whether he has them or not,' Gay Brain said. 'And then he criticizes the manners of the young!'

'There's no need for you to take offence in that case, Gay, surely?'

'He's a parody of himself,' Gay Brain said. 'Didn't I tell you?'

'Seriously,' Daniel said. 'Because if you've come all the way to Iskios in order to continue a silly quarrel—'

'I don't honestly know why we have come,' Francesca said. 'Didn't something break down? I've been sitting in what is laughingly called the saloon trying to read Proust—'

'Gallic windbag,' Meredith Lamb said. 'I am the ghost of Marcel Proust/Never laid but often goosed. God, is this an omelette? It looks more like a collapsed enuretic's hot-water bottle.'

'I thought it was time I read him in French. It does make one realize just how bad Scott Moncrieff really was.'

'That alone must make it worth doing,' Daniel said. 'The fact is, I need your help.'

'Oh my dear Daniel, it sounds as if I'm going to enjoy this. Why?'

'Not in your usual capacity as an abortionist,' Daniel said. 'Oh God, come on, if you're allowed to, surely I am. Francesca, this is serious. It's about a political prisoner. I know you and Meredith aren't exactly revolutionaries these days, but this is a bloke who's done absolutely nothing—'

'Sounds just the type to risk one's neck for,' Francesca said.

'Please. He's simply the victim of a fatuous, vindictive régime that surely no one with an ounce of wit can support.'

'No one more quickly reveals all symptoms of galloping fat-headedness than those who regard travel as an opportunity to put the world to rights. Travel is for laughing at foreigners, sampling their booze and consuming their goodies. Anything else is pure fantasy. Pardon. This omelette's been seasoned with Eno's.'

'Why couldn't we have had what those people are having?' Gay Brain said. 'It looks delicious.'

'What other people are having always looks delicious,' Daniel said.

'Which reminds me,' Meredith Lamb said. 'How's that American bint of yours?'

'Delicious,' Daniel said. 'Look, Meredith, Francesca, in spite of everything, you know, whatever political differences we may have, it really is vital you help get this character out. Or at least that you don't try to prevent it. Because what's at stake here isn't really politics at all. The guy's got his wife and children in London and he wants to get to them. The government's stuck him here for no good reason whatever and he wants to get away. Simple as that.'

'Oh why can't you be honest about it? You want us to be part of a lefties' snatch squad. As soon as you get this nondescript, innocuous nonentity, as you so flatteringly describe him, back to London, you'll all be posing for photographs and claiming to have recovered Lenin from the Peter and Paul prison. Don't skulk, Meyer, don't skulk, man. Personally I shall have nothing to do with it. I like the wine, I like the sun, I even quite like the sense of security that comes from living within the confines of a nice, repressive society. It quite revives the appetites.'

'And yours, I have no doubt, take some reviving,' Daniel said.

'That note of asperity, old son, is not seductive and it's not persuasive.'

'If you won't help, at least will you not hinder?'

'I agreed to this trip knowing the company I had to expect. God knows, it's required all one's noted powers of self-discipline to honour the agreement. I'm not going to pay for the privilege of turning my holiday into a pale remake of *Exodus* or whatever that film was called. Personally I make it a principle—'

'Meredith, we all know you're not really the disagreeable old fart you pretend to be. You're really rather an agreeable old fart. Now surely you can't be serious—'

'Heaven knows, there's never been any evidence of it,' Gay Brain said.

'Gay, don't, please. Are you really going to leave a man in exile, possibly indefinitely, because of some *principle*—?'

'Ah, it's the mention of principles that upsets you. That's very common with lefties, I find. If you're a bully or a coward, they have all the sympathy in the world, but show them a principle and they accuse you of being as big a blackguard as ever broke a picket line. Have you canvassed Stuart Melrose yet?'

'He's up the other end,' Daniel said. 'And much as I respect the convention that even a foreigner with a degree in English will never be able to understand a word of our conversation, I don't think it's wise actually to shout about this.'

'Oh come on,' Meredith Lamb said, 'let's open our lungs.'

'Make a change from his flies,' Gay Brain said.

'Do you know Meredith still has his trousers made with buttons?' Janey Darwin said. 'Isn't he a sweet old-fashioned thing?'

'Hullo, Janey, what long ears you've got! How are you?'

'I thought you'd never ask,' Janey said. 'I'm lovely.'

'Lord Melrose—'

'So help me, Meredith, I'll thump you if you do. Right in the nose.'

'Oh don't,' Francesca said. 'It's so puerile, these affectations of virility. I do get tired of them.'

'We need guidance on a question of policy, old son.'

'Then don't ask me,' Stuart Melrose said. 'My doctor's ordered me to give them up during the summer recess. I've got to get my weight down somehow.'

'Sensible fellow,' Daniel said.

'Land Stuart in some sort of political hooha and you'll sell him right down the river. I call it unmannerly.'

'If it's far enough down it'll be just convenient for Westminster, won't it?'

'Unworthy,' Francesca said. 'And also unfunny.'

'Look,' Daniel said, 'if you're really serious about not wanting to get Akrotiri out, why don't you peel off and make your own way home?'

'If you're paying,' Meredith Lamb said, 'I might take you up on that. Only it'll cost you a bob or two. I'm damned if I'm contributing.'

'All right,' Daniel said, 'I bloody will. If you'll go tonight, there is a boat.'

'I don't believe you want to rescue anyone,' Meredith said. 'I think this is pure and simply a plot to get rid of us. I take it this offer is for air travel? I'm not going home by chara.'

'Go home any way you please,' Daniel said.

'Is this offer available to all dissentients?' Basil Brain said.

'It's not an offer,' Daniel said. 'It's Meredith's blackmail. Which on this occasion I'm willing to pay, because it'll make clear to everyone just what kind of a greedy prig he really is.'

'A remark, my dear old son, which the smile does nothing to soften and which I shall not lightly forgive.'

'A remark which the fuddy-duddy tone and the ludicrous clichés equally do nothing—'

408

'What is all the drama about?' Janey Darwin said.

'Nothing that can be packaged in five hundred saucy words and slipped into our Sunday marmalade, Janey, so it's not worth your while to have it explained to you.'

'Except for the sunshine,' Gay Brain said, 'we might as well be in Camden.'

'Except for the additional fact that there actually is a man who needs our help. Of course it's a lot more difficult actually to do something concrete than it is to condemn genocide, capitalism, Comecon, the Pentagon, greed, sloth, accidie and the twelve-mile fishing limit.'

'Daniel,' Francesca said. 'It's hot enough already without having any extra hot air being blown at us.'

'What would you have done if we'd never showed up, old son? That's what puzzles me.'

'He would have found someone else to drag backwards through his thorny conscience,' Francesca said. 'The thing about really good people is that they never reproach others for not being good. That's the particular vice of the morally shifty.'

'Thus speaks the Sister Teresa of the overweight. What would I have done if you hadn't shown up? Rejoiced.'

'And on whom would you have loaded your rather stale burden of guilt?'

'I'd have been scanning the skyline,' Daniel said. 'I might even have taken up the oars myself. I may still have to.'

'What shall we do about the bill, Daniel?' Norbert Ash said.

'You could pay it,' Daniel said. 'Or is that too radical a suggestion? In view of the fact that you chose the cheapest dish, I had hopes we were all going to be your guests.'

'That's a little unnecessary, isn't it?'

'Daniel, how would it be if we all clubbed together to send *you* back to England on the boat tonight?'

'Where'd you get that "all" shit? As Neville Chamberlain said, "I have my friends".'

'And your enemies,' Francesca said, 'and your enemies.'

'Probably the best would be if we divided the whole thing by fourteen.'

'A generous solution and like old Sapt,' Daniel said.

'Old Sapt, did you say, my old son?'

'Sapt, yes; it's a quotation.'

'Of course it's a quotation. And from *The Prisoner of Zenda*, no less. Wait a minute, I'm wrong—'

'You are indeed.'

'Because it's from *Rupert of Hentzau*, in many ways a more spunky production and with a lot less of the kiss-my-fanny about it.'

'It was going to be my first film. At the age of fifteen. The school authorities forbade me to go ahead in case the swords got in people's eyes.'

'One of the best Victorian novels. Sensible style, good plot, heart in the right place.'

'I absolutely agree. Chivalry before advantage, others before self, the chase before the quarry.'

'I couldn't have put it better myself.'

'Granted soon as asked.'

'Look here,' Meredith Lamb said, 'this snatch of yours. It'll take a bit of planning, won't it? A bit of ingenious plotting?'

'Dummies in the bed, well-met by moonlight, secret call signs, the lot, Meredith, the lot!'

'Not forgetting British sang-froid.'

'The whole repertoire.'

'It also means that we can miss out the next stop and get home, with any luck, before my ulcer actually perforates. In a word, forward! Forward, my old son. But not too fast. Not too fast now.'

'It works out at thirty-one drachmae each near enough. Thirty-one and four sevenths actually. That's with wine.'

'I didn't have wine,' Paul said. 'I never do at lunch.'

Francesca said: 'Is there a field somewhere where I can have a piss?'

'There is a loo,' Daniel said, 'or do you only function out of doors?'

'I prefer to piss in the open when I'm abroad because, generally, it's so much more hygienic than the usual black hole.'

'Francesca likes to see what she's doing,' Meredith said.

'Go up the path, if you really mean that, and into the big meadow behind the other *taverna*. It's usually full of cows so I don't suppose you'll be noticed.'

'Daniel, just remember: we haven't signed anything yet.'

'Our word is our bond, isn't it, Meredith?'

'In default of anything better, I suppose it'll have to be,' Meredith said. 'Ideally I'd sooner have cash.'

'It's so nice to get away from them for a bit,' Janey said. 'It's all right having dinner with them in London, but two weeks in a closed boat's another thing entirely.'

'It should give you a whole raft of articles though. Raft, get it?'

'If I'd got it, I'd take it,' Janey said. 'I'd be paddling for dear life.'

'I warned you,' Jack said.

'Do you think that makes it any more bearable? Jack's so phlegmatic. You don't seem to be in the least put out. We haven't even had any real sex since Athens. You can hear every sound and the bunks are so narrow every time you open a leg you're in somebody else's cabin. Norbert keeps telling us it's the cheapest possible way of seeing the Aegean. Seeing it! If you turn round too fast, you're in it. I haven't been in such a confined space since I was last in the airing cupboard. One thing I do expect on a holiday and that's my fair share of greens. At the rate we've been going I shall have scurvy long before we get back to our own bed.'

'All Janey's lamentations, joined end to end —'

'Will make the book of pieces which Norbert is publishing for Xmas after nextMas,' Jack said. 'Nothing is wholly lost.'

'I won't have you ganging up on me,' Janey said. 'It brings out the Women's Libber in me. I shall do something dramatic.'

411

'Go on, throw your bra at me,' Daniel said. 'You know we love you really.'

'I know you do, Daniel, but I don't know about Jack so much—'

'It's this thing about greens, is it? That's made you suspicious? Or has he been wearing your underwear again?'

'I knew we should have shut the cabin door. Seriously, you haven't got a bedworthy bed we could borrow, have you? If we're not sailing till tomorrow, we surely don't have to go back on board the *Bounty* tonight, do we?'

'Thought,' Jack Darwin said.

'Jack, I want you to have a good sniff round this place—'

'Are you sure it's all right us barging in?'

'God yes, Larry dotes on celebrities. And Nancy's dying to see Janey. We were talking about you only the other day in some connection.'

'That's the way she likes to be talked about,' Jack said. 'Why, what goes on?'

'That's what I can't figure out. I'm pretty sure he's in the costume sculpture business. He's got a whole warehouse full of marbles. He says he imports them from Asia Minor, but of course that's because if he's passing them off as genuine he couldn't explain how he got them out of Greece without a permit if they were Greek. They look pretty good to the untutored eye, but if they were the real thing they'd be one of the most fantastic collections— do you know how much a good Hellenistic figure costs in London today?'

'About eight thou, could be more.'

'In which case he's got upwards of a hundred and fifty thousand quids' worth in that building up there alone.'

'Of course it's not the kind of thing you can pop in your handbag.'

'Oh he's got some of that too. Including a Cycladic flute player he says is worth thirty-five thousand bucks. See what a trained eye makes of it, because something's going on.'

'What you fail to understand, Daniel, is that when I write a book I decide on the solution before I plant the clues. You're the sort who goes up to A Well-Known TV Detective and asks him to solve your Aunty Flo's murder.'

'Not likely,' Daniel said, 'when I knocked the old bitch off myself.'

'I must say, Daniel, I've never known you so full of quips. You must be happy.'

'I always said all he needed was the right woman.'

'The right woman, and a kiss from Gil Timmis,' Jack Darwin said.

'He's an old shrewdy Jack, isn't he? So he'd better shut up, hadn't he?'

'Yes, sir, Mr Director. Christ, it's hot. This hill's properly shagged me out.'

'Good training for tomorrow. Don't worry, there's rum and coke at the top. I've never heard Gil so high on a script.'

'We aim to please,' Jack Darwin said. 'You don't mind taking food and drink off this bloke then, even if you do suspect he's a Capo Mafioso?'

'His real name being Lorenzo Piacere? I doubt it. Anyway, he'd be suspicious if I didn't accept his vittles. Actually all I fear he is, is a supplier of bold false marbles to poofy interior decorators who promise their blue-rinsed clients that they've acquired a masterpiece.'

'Hum,' Jack Darwin said, 'we should be able to do better than that.'

'Well here we are, straighten your ties, practise your curtsies, we're on.'

'Welcome, welcome, but where are the others?' Nancy said.

'Just the kind of welcome you hope for at the top of Everest, isn't it? Aren't we enough for you?'

'She really is here then,' Janey said. 'We suspected he'd done away with you and was laughing and joking even as your body was making *fondue* for the sharks.'

'Laughing and joking were you?' Nancy said.

'Through my tears,' Daniel said. 'The rest of them have gone

up to the village, or are threatening to. You were much missed.
I had to hold Meredith Lamb back from scaling the heights and
dragging you down to his level, but it was such a long climb —'

'Oh Danny, stop it, you're like a cold, you run on so. I thought
you and Meredith had made it up.'

'If we did no one would believe it. No, you're right. Anyway,
did you eat and was it all right?'

'Something rather nice has happened actually. Mustapha
showed up.'

'Mustapha.'

'The little puppy. Astrid calls him Mustapha. Daniel rescued a
little puppy from a man who was trying to drown it.'

'Oh how horrible!'

'I thought it was horrible too, but she would have me do it.'

'They're so beastly to animals, aren't they? They had some
baby goats at Piraeus all tied up, I was almost sick.'

'Daniel's told you who we've got staying, I suppose.'

'He's been hinting rather heavily. I suppose it's the Snowdons.'

'Princess Astrid. They've gone to rest, but they'll be out
later.'

'Oh fancy! Why is she referred to as "they"? Is that some
unfamiliar aspect of oriental protocol?'

'There are three of her,' Daniel said.

'Now don't start. Just because Jack and Janey have arrived and
you've got an audience.'

'Start! He's been lashing out the acid like —'

'A Jew with no arms, isn't that the fashionable frankness?'

'That's not what I was going to say. That would mean you
weren't, and you were. And don't bother accusing me of anti-
semitism. Save that for the genuine culprits.'

'What, and risk getting thumped? If you're talking about lunch,
I was only trying to amuse the company.'

'I don't always find compound fractures that amusing.'

'You're no fun any more,' Daniel said. 'I thought you might
like to haul Janey up to see Zeno and Constantine maybe, when it
cools off.'

'It's rather a way,' Nancy said. 'And they may not be there. It is Sunday. Anyway, let's go and sit in the cool for a bit.'

'Talking of a bit,' Daniel said, 'these two haven't been able to have it away properly since they left Piraeus and they're rather keen to join forces as soon as possible. In other words, they want the use of a double bed for the night. You can wait till tonight, I take it?'

'If pushed,' Janey said.

'Oh you poor things,' Nancy said. 'I don't know whether —'

'Couldn't they have a mattress and the squash court, if all else fails? Better than two feet of bunk and Norbert Ash with his ear pressed to the wall on the other side.'

'I'll ask Larry later, if you like.'

'Ask him now, if you like,' Larry said. 'He's right here. How do you do? Larry Pleasure.'

'Jack and Janey Darwin.'

'You couldn't be more welcome. What can I do for you?'

'They're suffering from the green sickness,' Daniel said.

'I don't think we're being very polite to Mr Pleasure,' Janey said. 'Arriving here and — the truth is, Jack and I are hoping to spend the night ashore and we wanted to find a room.'

'Oh well I'm sure we'll be able to fix you up with something. There's always my cottage on the beach.'

'Sounds terrific,' Janey said, 'but we don't want to put you to any trouble. Truly, I have a thing about intruding on people. I hate it when they descend on me and — shut up, Daniel, because I'm serious — I hate to descend on them.'

'That only leaves the lateral approach really, doesn't it?'

Jack said: 'Daniel tells me you have a fantastic art collection here.'

'Are you an expert then, like Daniel?'

'Shit, I'm no expert,' Daniel said.

'I'm no expert at all, but I'd very much like to see the stuff, if it's not a bore to you.'

'Bore? Shall we go now? Mrs Darwin, would you care to come with us?'

415

'Oh Janey and I are going to sit in the cool,' Nancy said. 'Janey, I've got so much I want to talk to you about.'

'Don't worry about me,' Daniel said, 'I'll see myself over the cliff.'

'Don't be so sorry for yourself, Daniel. If you need them you've always got lots of friends who'd be very happy to help push.'

'I believe you.'

'And he does,' Nancy said. 'He really and truly does. Darling, you are silly. You really are silly.'

'Are you here looking for plots, Mr Darwin?' Larry said, as he led Jack away towards the steps going up to the art gallery.

'Because if you are,' Daniel said, 'he can sell you one right on the beach. Listen, I think I'll go over and see if Gavin's at home. I'd like to say goodbye if he is. He'll also be amused to know that I finally bought that damned figure.'

The two women walked on, their figures overlapping as they passed under the archway on to the long terrace. Daniel said: 'You fool, you bloody fool.' He might have been waiting for the chance to be alone with someone he detested. 'Why do you do it? Why?'

He crossed a pebble-dashed courtyard and went down the steps he had first taken with Larry Pleasure. He did not enter the cool corridor. He walked round the rough, hot path. The rock had been coarsely excavated. There were no green flower-beds. All the windows of the house were shuttered and covered with gauze against insects. He lingered, without stopping, at each aperture. What could he hear which could appease his hunger for some clinching evidence? He could imagine for himself more than any chance instance might confirm. The only thing he could not provide for himself was an image of happiness.

Cerberus was breathing smoke. Daniel coughed as he came up the raucous slope, living with cicadas, and past the white dog. The smoke came up from Gavin's place. The fire was on the terrace by the tile table. The fuel was a heap of papers and photographs. There was no one about.

Daniel recognized the pictures he had edited on the floor of Gavin's sitting-room. Gavin had splashed *petrellio* on the centre of the rubbish. A charred cavity had burned quickly down, but the edge of the pile had not caught. Daniel was able to shuffle several almost untouched prints away from the smouldering embers. None of the polaroids of Greece were in the heap, unless they had all been in the middle and had already been consumed. They must have been taken by Bob, Gavin's lover, during their first tour together. All the rest had been sacrificed. Daniel's first feeling was of shock, even anger. He liked to think that he had created something poignant and mysterious, ambiguous and haunting, but when he sorted out what he had salvaged and tried to reconstruct his assembly, the sequence lacked depth or reverberation. The glazed faces stared stiffly. The haunting woman in the garden was an overweight and toothy Gioconda, La Tedesca was no muscular mistress but a horsey blonde with a small face. On El Caballero alone was Daniel now able to put a new construction. Even though he was prepared to believe that Gavin had not realized it at the time, this dark man, with his energetic slimness, was the true subject of the writer's interest. Daniel could now interpret the sequence of the break-up of the ship on the shore more poetically. It symbolized Gavin's own destruction, the destruction of the traveller who had been known to journey round the world in pursuit of a woman he thought he loved, and the break-up of his capacity to conceal his true nature. It would be nice to think that, at the time Gavin was taking it, he had no conscious idea of its symbolic reading. Why were such things moving only when the subject was unaware of their significance?

Daniel stood with the photographs in his hand. For a moment he could believe that he had saved something from the treasure he had travelled to find. When he put them on the tiled table, the wind spilled them. He picked them up and tried the door of the sitting-room. It was locked. He rattled the handle (as if there was someone inside with whom he had had a quarrel) and then he put his shoulder to it. He held the handle and pulled himself hard against the green door. The frame split and he fell into the room.

417

There was no one inside. The furniture, the pictures, the orange carpet, the cabinet, the shuttered windows, everything was as before. Only the little bronzes had gone. He could see Gavin, like a man going through his trouser pockets for the small change he never bothered to take in the days when he was rich, scooping the bronzes into his rucksack; they might fetch a few drachs in the Plaka. Daniel looked round the room with hostility. Did he want to take something or to destroy something? He unhooked a lamp from the wall and took it out to the charred circle by the tiled table. He emptied the reservoir of *petrellio* carefully over the photographs he had salvaged and set fire to them with a match from the box of Argentinian *cerillas* he had found on the ashtray beneath the lamp. He turned the prints like toast, until they had all been burned. At the last second he snatched out the one of El Caballero standing by the *baby-foot* table with Rosa and the beach boys. He waved it like a note rescued from a flood. By the time he reached the village, it was dry.

He walked past the Post Office and the football pitch and sat on the wall overlooking the harbour. Children were playing in the new playground. He winced at the sound of weighted chain rubbing metal.

Daniel said: '*Yasas, Kirie Akrotiri.*'

'*Oh kalimera. Ti kanome?*'

'*Kala, kala.* Can you be ready by tomorrow evening?'

'Ready?'

'To leave. I've fixed for you to go on a boat some friends of mine have brought in to Kalamaki. They sail tomorrow night. There are about a dozen of them. There'll be no problem getting you aboard.'

'You act quickly.'

'I don't have too long. We go back to England ourselves next week.'

'Tomorrow night? Very well.'

'You sound doubtful,' Daniel said. 'If you don't—'

'I said I would play poker,' Akrotiri said.

'Oh well.' Daniel said, 'we all have to make sacrifices!'

418

'Of course.'

'That wouldn't be with Piers Cobbett and that school, would it?'

'You know Piers?'

'*Pos then ton gnorizo*? I know him. I think it might be a good idea if you arranged to have everyone go on thinking you were going to play. The game lasts pretty late, doesn't it?'

'Quite late.'

'All the better. No one's going to be surprised if you don't wake up till late on Tuesday morning. By which time you ought to be in Turkish waters.'

'Saved by the Turks,' Akrotiri said. 'That will be a novel experience.'

'A lot of my friends are turning out in the football game tomorrow, so you'll be able to see who they are. They're mostly London intellectuals, a pretty bright bunch actually, including Professor Brain and Dr Victor Rich, who's the head of one of our commercial TV companies, but actually more of an intellectual than you generally find in those surroundings. I think you know Basil. I can promise you you won't have have a dull trip.'

'No women?'

'Oh some of them have got wives with them. Gay's along. Gay Brain, who's actually a bit of a double agent because she's been compiling a report on the treatment of political prisoners for Mercy. You might be able to mark her card once you're on your way. Quite a bright collection.'

'I know her of course,' George Akrotiri said.

'Oh yes, she —'

'I met her in London and also in Toronto, Canada. I like her very much.'

'She's got guts, Gay. She obviously feels she looks her best in a flak jacket. I like her. So anyway, that's all I can do for you.'

'I'm impressed,' George Akrotiri said. 'And grateful, of course.'

'Can you be down at Robert Gavin's house at nine-thirty tomorrow night? He's gone and he won't be back. The place is deserted. I think it's the best rendezvous near Kalamaki. From there we can easily get to the *Prometheus* without passing too close to any curious eyes. I don't know what you think about diguise. It did occur to me that we could dress you as a woman, but I don't know if it's worth it. How closely is anyone likely to be watching you?'

'At that hour, not very closely. If I wear a skirt I shall only trip – and make myself even more conspicuous.'

'Oh well, lots of women wear trousers these days.'

'In that case, I shall wear trousers and those who like to see me as a woman are welcome to do so.'

'I quite agree. The fewer arrangements we make the less there is to go wrong.'

'The benefits of freedom,' Akrotiri said.

'I'll drink to that,' Daniel said. 'Can I leave it to you to cope with things like a dummy in the bed, if it's necessary? Is there anything you want me to get hold of for you?'

'No, thank you, I shall manage very well.'

'Good. Well, there we are. Good luck.'

'*Efcharisto poli*. I look forward to the football.'

'We're going to take the locals to pieces,' Daniel said.

'*Tha thoome*,' Akrotiri said. 'We shall see.'

'I promise you,' Daniel said.

'I never go to nightclubs,' Larry Pleasure said. 'Not any more. I'm going to have a quiet evening at home. I wish you all the fun in the world. I have some reading to catch up with.'

Nancy said: 'I feel badly, leaving you.'

'Don't feel badly, Nancy J. – just come back! I think it's wonderful you've persuaded her to go out. I really do. You enjoy yourselves and tell me all about it in the morning.'

Only Paul and Margaret Mallory, of those from the *Prometheus*, failed to go with the others to the Poseidon. The party straggled up the long path to the village in groups of three and four. Daniel sought out the Darwins. Nancy looked round and waved to him, but she was with Astrid and Tita and Eleni. He turned his back and waited for Jack and Janey.

'I hear he's fixed you up in the cottage.'

'He was very sweet,' Janey said. 'He really was. And it's so beautiful down there.'

'Feeling better then, are you? You'll be able to do one of your idyll pieces.'

'Idyll widyll,' Janey said. 'Yes, I bloody well will. Why have you got such a thing against happiness, Daniel?'

'Oh don't,' Daniel said. 'I quite agree. It's a terrific cottage. You ought to buy it.'

'It's such a hell of a way from London.'

'Yes, and that's not the only thing in its favour. Tell me though, what did you make of Larry? You know why he won't come to nightclubs, don't you?'

'He was shot in the parking lot of a club just off the strip.'

'You got him talking.'

'Like the tourists get Niagara falling. I don't think he has much trouble turning on.'

'So what's his story, his real story, do you think?'

'You mean what have I made up about him?'

'Listen, *something's* going on in that place of his. Have you met Buck Lehman yet? The muscle man?'

'I've only had a glimpse,' Jack Darwin said. 'He seemed a sort of familiar type.'

'And the little blonde who works on her stomach in the pool? Where does she fit in?'

'Oh she's the C.I.A. man,' Janey said. 'I read my Insight.'

'And the sculpture?'

'Pretty good stuff,' Jack Darwin said. 'I thought. Some of the things he says were salvaged from underwater wrecks were fantastic—all that incrustation. You know, I don't think he'd ever get away with selling fakes to blue-rinsed ladies. Those much abused females have a way of checking and double-checking. Their hair isn't the only thing they have done regularly. Are we nearly there?'

'If you listen carefully, you can hear where we're going.'

'Swinging Iskios,' Janey said. 'Jack, I'm not staying late.'

'We've got a game tomorrow,' Daniel said. 'No one's staying late. And Janey, reasonable demands only tonight, please.'

'He's a fucking fanatic,' Jack said, 'under all that jokey exterior, an absolute raving fanatic.'

'Raving paranoiac. Do you think Larry's going bust? Do you get that impression at all? Because we overheard a strange conversation—'

'When people are going bust, if they're operators like Pleasure, they usually tell you how much money they've got. I think he's more likely to be someone who's actually got plenty, but can't help putting himself in danger by trying to get even more. Is that possible?'

Nancy said: 'Darling, come on, come and arrange where everyone's going to sit. Astrid wants Lord Melrose to come and sit with her. Do you know, it's the first time she's been in a public place since—since it happened. And then I thought you and me and Tita, because Astrid wants someone she knows.'

'Doesn't she know you by now?'

'And Daniel, no remarks, please, darling, tonight.'

Meredith Lamb said: 'I'm not eating anything. I had a boiled egg before we came. Bring on the wine and the dancing girls and that'll do me very well.'

Daniel said: 'You're going to eat, aren't you, Astrid, until things warm up? They're said to be very proud of their *souvlakia*. I trust not on the grounds of their antiquity.'

'What's this,' Piers Cobbett said, 'a training session?'

'That's it,' Daniel said. 'Wine and dance till midnight and then a hundred press-ups by the light of the moon. Look, this is Piers Cobbett. Princess Astrid, Princess Nancy, Princess Tita—'

'Daniel, I particularly—'

Astrid said: 'You can't put a lid on Daniel. I don't mind.'

'And the genuine English Lord Melrose.'

'Hullo Stuart,' Piers Cobbett said.

'Oh Christ, of course, you're both East Anglians.'

'Except when there are any genuine East Anglians present,' Stuart Melrose said.

'Come on, Astrid,' Daniel said. 'I'll wheel you round the floor.'

'I'll never forgive him if he upsets her,' Nancy said.

'Is Coco looking after you? I'll skin him if he doesn't.' Piers clapped his hands and one of the pretty girls jumped round and shouted 'O.K.' above the sound of the amplifiers. 'What do you need? Generous helpings of everything, I presume?'

'Who's financing this exactly?' Norbert Ash said. 'Daniel?'

'I'm not touching anything solid,' Meredith Lamb said.

Daniel said: 'Had you met Larry before?'

'In California, once or twice. He tells me. I'm afraid I had forgotten him. He's very nice, very hospitable.'

'Are you aiming to stay then?'

'Oh no, not at all.'

'How about salvaging your stuff?'

'Oh it's beyond salvage, you know. Most of it was burned, a lot was lost.'

'Overboard, you mean?'

'In the confusion, things were thrown overboard, yes. A lot of my jewellery.'

'But you were insured? I say you were insured?'

'Yes, of course. I hope so.'

'So do I. What about that suitcase, that was found, wasn't it? The one with your stuff in it?'

'With my stuff in it? That was mostly Tita and Eleni's stuff. My cabin was burned out. And then water got in when the fireboat arrived. I think they must have washed a lot of things overboard. It was impossible to check until morning and by then of course –'

'Of course,' Daniel said. 'I may be wrong, but I have a feeling you're not sorry to have been sort of – what? – burned out, like a nest of queen bees. Smoked out; no one could call you burned out.'

'You think?'

'You're a beautiful girl. You're a loss to the world when you're out of commission.'

423

'Thank you.'

'You ought to come to London, you really should. It's a terrific city.'

'Nancy has asked me.'

'That's all damned nonsense, that incognito stuff. First off, my dear, no one gives a shit who you are anyway. London isn't like that any more. Come and be whatever you want to be. If you want to play at secrets, fine, but don't think it's going to do anything for you. Stay at Claridge's for Christ's sake, you've got the cash. If you want to do something secretly, do it publicly; it's so much more fun.'

'You have a wonderful woman in Nancy,' Astrid said.

'You're right,' Daniel said. 'What're you doing, warning me off?'

'Warning you off what?' Astrid said.

'You've got a point there,' Daniel said.

Nancy said: 'Well, how was it?'

'Quite warm once you're in, wasn't it?'

'The music's very loud,' Astrid said. 'But nice.'

'Mantovani in one of his least known moods.'

Stuart Melrose said: 'Mrs Lane?'

'Oh my goodness, Nancy please, Lord Melrose. I don't even know *myself* as Mrs Lane any more.'

'The only people who call me Lord Melrose are people hinting it was time I was kicked upstairs.'

'What will you do when the Earl dies?' Nancy said.

'It's really too early to say,' Stuart Melrose said. 'My old man's still pretty hale. He began his career of paternity quite young. I shan't have to worry for a week or two. I love the Commons, I should hate to give it up, but one never knows. There are other hazards apart from mortality. There could be a swing to the left or one might have a spat with someone. Do you like to hold hands or do you favour just standing and twitching at each other? And then, of course, there's always the bank, someone has to look after that.'

'You must know Charles,' Nancy said. 'My ex.'

424

Piers Cobbett said: 'I have a great belief in the merits of bribery myself.'

Gay Brain said: 'Do you really, bribery?'

'You seem to think that the great British travellers were highly regarded for their aristocratic virtues. In fact, people kowtowed to them because they were willing to hand out the bunce to anyone who pandered to their vices. Even Byron, his very Lordship, whose name every hotel no less than every crusade is willing to take in vain, was listened to in the councils of Greece only because he was the tap through which the funds passed. Lord *Robinet*. If you want to change things, *enrichissez-vous*, and then offer a large denominational bill with every moral nostrum. You'll find the gospel eagerly welcomed. Otherwise, a bloody foreigner you'll remain. And quite right too.'

'The American government itself is largely responsible for the present state of affairs in this country,' Gay said.

'Ah poo,' Piers Cobbett said. 'Are they so? According to what twitch from what divining rod?'

'The scale of aid, in money and equipment –'

'That's far from establishing that the Americans are responsible. If I give you a cushion am I responsible for your sitting down?'

'You encourage me. The history of the C.I.A. –'

'Has yet to be intelligently analysed –'

'If I'm merely interrupting a monologue, pray let me know. The history of the C.I.A. suggests that where leftish governments fall, People in Government, as they are politely known, are seldom far behind.'

'Oh dear,' Nancy said, 'they're talking politics.'

'And what do you do for sex?' Daniel said. 'You're not bereaved, after all, are you?'

'I am not that concerned with sex,' Eleni said.

'You don't expect the court to believe that, do you? I think you're quite interested.'

'I am interested in life, yes, in love too perhaps, but in sex alone, not too much.'

425

'You can't look like you do and not be interested in sex. I'm sorry. You're hiding something.'

'All interesting people are,' Eleni said. 'Aren't they?'

'There seem to be a lot of secrets about, I must say. Do you like this kind of dancing?'

'Not especially.'

'Ballet dancers are always supposed to hate ordinary dancing. Is that true?'

'I'm afraid so, yes.'

'In that case, why don't we — ? We seem to have chosen the one place on the island which is phoney and obvious in which to spend the evening.'

'I thought it was your suggestion.'

'I imagined it was what people wanted. The story of my life. How did the fire start on the *Leto*? What was your first knowledge of it?'

'Oh my dear, we have all that coming from the Insurance, I have no doubt. Do I have to answer now? It was an accident in the kitchen, I think. The first I knew of it, I was standing completely nak'd under the shower — what is funny, please?'

'You're the first person I ever heard who pronounced it like that. As if it rhymed with ached. Nak'd, that's beautiful. That's lovely.'

'How should it be pronounced then, please?'

'I have no intention of telling you. I'm going to kiss you instead.'

'Oh?'

'Did you think I wouldn't? Nak'd! Every time you say nak'd, I intend to kiss you.'

'Are those the only terms?'

'Not if you say not.'

'You are very young really, aren't you?'

'You're very old really, aren't you? Don't say really to me and I won't say really to you. What about Astrid, is she genuinely still in mourning? Or is she just in shock? I'm not making a judgment.'

'I don't discuss her, I'm sorry. We never discuss things, even when we are alone.'

'You and Tita or you and Astrid and Tita or what?'

'At all,' Eleni said. 'Look, a donkey is watching us.'

'Say nak'd again,' Daniel said. 'So you just play canasta and do your noses, do you? And order meals and sail from place to place.'

'Of course,' Eleni said. 'What are you trying to get out of me, and why?'

'My darling, I'm not, I'm just fascinated by you. You're the most attractive woman on the island. And I think you know it.'

'Your fiancée is very beautiful. And very charming. I think you're very disloyal.'

'And you're delighted. No, I think you're absolutely right. She's both, beautiful and charming, all the time. All the time. But she never says nak'd. She never is nak'd either.'

'I like her. I would hate to hurt her.'

'You're a nice woman. Or a clever one. Or, of course, and without contradiction, both.'

'We should go back.'

'No, come on, let's walk. Everyone's very happy, you only have to listen. Let's go up to the windmills. Astrid tells me she lost a lot of her stuff in the fire.'

'Oh I'm bored with the fire.'

'We left you nak'd in the shower—'

'Please, what is wrong with nak'd—how should it be?'

'You're beautiful,' Daniel said. 'I love you.'

Eleni laughed in the darkness, but not loudly, and her hand touched Daniel's elbow and she leaned her cheek against his chest.

'Come on, let's go inside. The door's open.'

'Daniel, what are you trying to do?'

'You know damned well and don't pretend you don't.'

'I never pretend anything. No, Daniel, it's not nice on the floor. I don't like the floor. Please, you don't have to. If you want to make love, why don't you come to my room later, when we get back? I'm too old for floors.'

427

'You're not too old for anything. I love your eyes and I love your mouth. No, I love you. I think you're terrific, I really do. You don't expect a thing from anybody. I think you're fabulous. One of the Gods in disguise, aren't you? Which one?'

'Zeus,' Eleni said. 'So be careful, I'll make you pregnant!'

'You make me laugh, which is even better. It's a long time since I laughed with a woman. You have absolutely marvellous eyes. What the hell are you doing in a ship with black sails?'

'We haven't had time to change them,' Eleni said. 'You're playing with me, Daniel, for some reason. I like you, but I don't trust you.'

'You couldn't have said anything I preferred to hear. Actually, it's not true. I'm playing with you for no reason at all. I love you. I love you at this moment quite fantastically, but I quite agree with you, it doesn't mean anything. On the other hand, doesn't that prove it's the real thing? Besides, feel.'

'You are like a Greek tonight, Daniel.'

'Which is another way of saying that I'm not one. Wittgenstein. Oh listen, I'm like everything, I just don't happen to be anything. How the hell am I going to find you? Will you leave a silken thread on the terrace so I can wend my way through the labyrinth?'

'If you want to come, I'm sure you'll find a way.'

'The invitation stands then, does it? Do you think I shan't take you up? I promise you I will.'

'We shall see,' Eleni said.

'Of course, you could always come to us,' Daniel said. 'I'm sure Nancy'd be glad to see you.'

'That's not nice,' Eleni said.

'Childish, O.K. But true, I'll bet. You know what, we should have done it here, on the floor. It would have been much more to the point. You didn't want to, though, did you?'

'Oh my dear boy!'

'Shit,' Daniel said, 'I shall be forty soon. Forty. *Forty*!'

'It's not so bad,' Eleni said.

'You're not forty, are you?'

'Of course.'

'Then you're right, it can't be so bad. Are you really?'

'Daniel, I think we go back now. Nancy is going to—'

'Are you really that concerned about Nancy? It's too Christian of you. *Ellenitha Christiani!* Or is there someone else who's going to be looking round for you? Are you married, Eleni?'

'Yes, of course. I'm thinking only of the party. They will wonder where we are.'

'You and Tita, both married and both shacked up with Astrid on that yacht for all these months. What's the attraction? Are you lovers, you three? Tell me, go on. I'd give anything to know.'

'Certainly not.'

'Certainly you're not lovers or certainly you're not going to tell me?'

'Of course,' Eleni said.

'It was all a bit of a fizzle,' Daniel said, 'really, wasn't it?'

'I enjoyed it,' Nancy said.

'Then why did you leave?'

'Because I'd had enough.'

'I thought it was a fizzle. A bloody expensive fizzle too, I need hardly tell you. That bloody wog added in the date three times. And got it wrong. You came back with Astrid, did you, because by the time I'd finished getting some air, you'd already buzzed?'

'We felt we'd had enough,' Nancy said. 'You weren't around, so—'

'Well, we've got a big day tomorrow, just as well, I suppose. You know I've fixed for George Akrotiri to leave with the *Prometheus* tomorrow night, after the match.'

'I should think the whole world knows,' Nancy said.

'You disapprove.'

'I think it's ridiculous.'

'Well, I think that's ridiculous.'

'Do you really want to get yourself arrested that much?'

'The whole world doesn't know and no one's going to be

arrested. I shan't have had anything to do with it. Nobody knows about it except—'

'Piers Cobbett knows, because he told me.'

'Well, Piers isn't going to tell anybody.'

'Isn't going to tell anybody? Oh Daniel, I'm really not going to argue with you about it.'

'Anyway I thought I told you.'

'I'm the last person you tell anything to.'

'Probably because you're the last person who wants to hear. Anyway, tell me, how's your romance going?'

'Romance?'

'With Astrid. Did you carry her home safely on her velvet cushion?'

'You upset her very much tonight.'

'Balls.'

'Walking out like that.'

'Crap, she was busy comparing blood samples with the Lord Melrose. He's a quart of lukewarm piss, isn't he? Or were you too busy kissing Madam's feet to notice?'

'What are you trying to do, Daniel? Ever since these people arrived, you've behaved absolutely—I don't know what to say—like a madman, absolutely irrationally.'

'You found me rational before then, did you, doctor? I don't know. I suppose—'

'Well, come on, don't suddenly go reticent on me. You haven't exactly been crippled with self-restraint up until this point.'

'I didn't even expect to find you here. And I want you like hell,' Daniel said. 'The combination—'

' 's a bit embarrassing. I'll *bet*.'

'So there you are. Now you know. Get your knife out and cut along the dotty line. What do you want me to say?'

'You never wanted to love me,' Nancy said. 'And you never did love me.'

'Probably not. You, of course, had nothing but the purest of motives.'

'I was in love with you. I sort of still am.'

430

'Don't pull the hook out cleanly. Leave it loosely in the gills. You never know when you may want to reel me in again. Look, don't bother. I concede your whole case. I'm not reliable, my motives are sordid and muddy; I can't see them clearly myself but the smell is certainly suggestive. Granted, granted. You know what they do or rather what they did on that bleeding yacht all day? They didn't play the Dead March in *Saul* or invent new positions for triple cunnilingus, they played canasta. How's that for kicks?'

'I don't want to hear about it and I don't think you know and I don't see what it has to do with anything.'

'I'll tell you. I'll interpret the subtleties for you. It has to do with the fact that I wanted nothing complicated, nothing sophisticated, nothing beyond the bounds of the ordinary. *Pas du tout.* I wanted to marry you and have a family with you and be a normal person and lead what is laughingly called a normal life. I thought all your crap was something that would wash off. I didn't reckon with it lasting the whole drink through.'

'Now I'll tell you something. Now I'll tell you something.'

'That's two things you've got to tell me already. So start. Start.'

'You couldn't be normal if you tried. That's not what I was going to say. Do you know what happens if we get married?'

'You lose your money, you lose your house, you cease to be the independent Mrs Lane we all know and admire and whose pants are the focus of a hungry world. Right?'

'You don't think it matters how you talk, do you? You think you can talk as dirty as you like. You think everybody else is just a target, just a —'

'Keep going, the tears will come, Nancy J., they'll come if you try long enough and we've got all night.'

'Oh no we damned well haven't.'

'Listen, if you want to cut it here, let's cut it here. Nothing more need ever be said. *Finito. Comme tu veux.* Alternatively, you were about to tell me what happens if we get married.'

'Oh skip it.'

'I'm sorry, did I take your speech? Did I say your lines? Were you really going to tell me about how Charlie would cut you off without a credit card once you got hitched again? Do you think I would've given a fuck?'

'No.'

'O.K., fine. Well then.'

'You'd like nothing better than to see me deprived of every-thing — you'd love me to be defenceless — powerless —'

'Nak'd,' Daniel said.

'What?'

'Skip it. Maybe. Maybe that would be the best thing that ever happened to you —'

'The best thing that ever happened to you, you sonofabitch, you mean — because don't you ever pretend to me for one second that you give a good goshdarn for me.'

'A good goshdarn,' Daniel said. 'Fancy meeting an old friend like that at a time like this.'

'I'm stronger than you think, Daniel, a lot stronger.'

'Good, great. Keep swinging.'

'I thought you were strong, but you're not. You're just cruel, and that's a whole different thing. You keep telling me that you wanted to believe my character was as beautiful as you said I was. I don't believe you believed that at all.'

'Then I shan't be disappointed, sweetie, shall I?'

'You couldn't bear it if I turned out to be this beautiful, legendary creature. You want me to be a bitch and by Christ I can be one.'

'By Christ you can. Why else are we auditioning?'

'I don't want to have your dirty kid,' Nancy said.

'That's good,' Daniel said. 'That's a real harpoon in the lower abdomen. I give you that one.'

'I don't want to be your dirty little proving ground.'

'That only scores an outer, but keep shooting. I just may give you a black eye, but keep shooting.'

'I've said it,' Nancy said. 'I've said it and I've had it.'

'What happens now? A fiery chariot and straight up to heaven?'

'You're actually hurt, aren't you?'

'Yes, isn't that the idea?'

432

'You've said a thousand things. You've done everything you could think of to hurt me and now you're hurt, you want me to say it's all all right. I'm damned if I will.'

'I don't want you to say anything,' Daniel said.

'Liar. You damned well do. You think underneath everything's all right. Well it damned well isn't. Don't smile at me. Don't smile, because I'm not going to smile back.'

'Not even if I put money on the table, Nancy Jane? Don't you have to do what the gentleman wants if he puts his money on the table?'

'You're sick, Daniel Meyer, you're sick and you're disgusting.'

'That is the usual form the speech takes.'

'All your idealism, all your fine sentiments—'

'So much tinsel, you're absolutely right. It takes a pair of blue eyes like yours to see through a scheming shit like me.'

'Damned right. No one's ever worthy of your respect. No one. No one. So live by yourself. Be by yourself. The only person who deserves your company is you and I hope you like it.'

'You ought to be put on patrol in the eastern Mediterranean,' Daniel said. 'The Russians would never pass the Dardanelles again.'

'How does a man's mind work who can say that kind of thing to someone he said he loved? If you'd only shut up for two minutes and think about yourself—you don't deserve to have people talk to you.'

'I'm a big shit,' Daniel said.

'Carried,' Nancy said. 'By a big majority.'

'*Nem con.* What's Piers going to do then? Tip off the authorities?'

'I don't know what Piers is going to do.'

'You ought to marry him,' Daniel said. 'You could collect swastikas. What are you going to do? If you don't want to talk, don't talk. Only if this thing does get out, I shall know who's really been talking. Piers may be a silly Tory romantic whoring after the grand manner, but he's swallowed too much of the old school crap actually to sneak on a chum to the pollis. That leaves you, honey. And if there's any trouble, I should remind you that I was on the *Leto* the night of the fire and what I say to the insurance assessors might prove a lot more embarrassing for your beloved than you don't think, as the French say. Are you really kinky enough to fancy seeing me in gaol? I only ask out of interest.'

'I don't fancy seeing you anywhere,' Nancy said.

'Shall we fuck to that?' Daniel said. 'Do you know where they've hidden the stuff by any chance? Because I'm damned sure something's going on we wot not of. But what? Oh look —'

'Oh no you don't,' Nancy said. 'Oh no you don't.'

'Oh yes I do,' he said.

'You wouldn't have me be anything that I am,' she said, 'would you?'

'Right.'

'If I was the beautiful creature you pretended —'

'I'd run.'

'*You* hit *me*, you bastard.'

'Now the other side,' he said. 'What's wrong with the other side?'

'You'd like to kill me. That's what you've wanted to do from the moment we met.'

'It's dramatic and it's true,' Daniel said. 'But it won't happen.'

'You hadn't got the guts.'

'More a question of time than guts, and we didn't really have the right music either.'

'So you thought you'd marry me instead.'

'Check.'

'You really believe still somewhere, don't you — ?'

'Over the rainbow,' Daniel said.

'Is there anything you're hiding, Daniel, any more? Any deep secret in that inner sanctum you keep hinting at?'

'Is there anyone left in the cave? I don't know. You see, who was it said that in the end everything is true of everybody?'

'I don't know,' Nancy said, 'but I know it isn't true.'

'I'll smile if I want to,' Daniel said. 'Sometimes I recognize the girl I came here with. I rather liked her.'

'Only while you were waiting for the battle to begin.'

'Wars always begin politely with flowers and walks in the sun,

434

don't they? With people behaving *better*, more gently, than they did when they were supposed to be at peace. It's funny.'

'What happened when you went up to the village, when was it, was it yesterday? When you had that call.'

'Nothing. I had that call. I don't think it changed anything.'

'You didn't meet somebody you haven't told me about?'

'Is there an unknown character skulking in the undergrowth? No, there isn't. Nothing changed. Except you didn't want to come to South America. That happened. Look, I'm not blaming you. I know that's not really it. But what is?'

'If you did go over and find Hitler on that island, wherever he's supposed to be, do you know what you'd really do? You'd spend hours trying to get him to admit that he thinks you're a great character. You wouldn't be happy until he told you he was sorry for what he'd done and that he found you a person of such irresistible magnetism that he'd've behaved completely differently if he'd met you sooner.'

'Is that supposed to be wounding? It's probably true. I always said you were clever. You said knowledgeable; I said clever. Promise. You, of course, would merely marry him and help nurse his Eurodollars.'

'You're like the little boy who thinks everyone is going to die except him.'

'I'm like the little boy who thinks no one's going to die except him. Look, Nancy, if we both try and sleep in this bed, we'll neither of us get any sleep tonight and there's not much point in that, so—'

'I shall sleep,' Nancy said, 'when I want to. What makes you so gall*ant* suddenly? I don't even hate you. You won't disturb me.'

'I don't hate you either. That's something else you've deprived me of.'

'As well as?'

'I always thought I was pretty good with women.'

'You are.'

'You don't fool me. It's very nice of you, truly, but you don't. Even on the bathroom floor, it wasn't the real thing.'

'No, it was me,' Nancy said. 'That's what upsets you. To discover there's really somebody else there. I don't think it reflects on you in the least. I don't think it's necessarily anything to do with you. It wasn't *me* who wasn't satisfied. It was you who wasn't satisfied with me.'

'You fascinate me, you know, still. Oh yes. You haven't lost anything. I'd still like to see a film of you from—from the beginning. You deserve the big treatment, sets, clothes, all the old production values. When you're isolated from all of that it's as if some cheapskate's cut you out of your frame. You need a public life, Nancy J.'

'And you, I'll tell you what you are, first, last and always. You're a film director and that's all you'll ever be.'

'I can't believe it, Nancy. It's on my lips and I can't believe it, but I know it's true. You wouldn't still marry me, would you?'

The two helicopters appeared over Kalamaki soon after eleven o'clock the next morning. Most of the party from the *Prometheus* were on the beach near the *taverna* when the Princess, Tita, Eleni, Nancy, Stuart Melrose, Larry Pleasure and Stelio Varis, carrying the luggage, including one of Nancy's white cases specially packed for Astrid, straggled down from Larry's house and across the sand. Daniel carried one of the Tunisian birdcages, empty. Astrid had admired it and Larry insisted on giving it to her as a going away present. The Princess carried Mustapha, the little puppy, clasped in her bosom. Daniel walked behind the others, toting the cage on one finger as if it were the clinching evidence of human absurdity.

'Why does she need two helicopters?' Janey said.

'You know it's vulgar to order one of anything,' Daniel said. 'How was the cottage?'

'Lovely really, except that we had company. A bat. Flew round and round.'

'One doesn't seem to be able to teach them to fly any other way.'

'Jack finally hooked it for six through the open window with the broom.'

436

'It's not every night you win the Ashes. Otherwise O.K.?'

'Absolutely super.'

'How was the captain and the crew?'

'O.K.,' Norbert said. 'Meredith's a bit rough this morning. That omelette didn't agree with him at lunchtime. What do you think we ought to give this chap of yours when he's finished on the gate mechanism?'

'What he asks, Norbert. That's your little bag. I'm not carrying it for you. I've got my hands full with this little number.'

'What happened to the bird?' Janey said. 'Excuse me, but I must try and brown as much of my bum as I can.'

'It flew,' Daniel said.

'Do you think a hundred drachs would be about right?'

'Choose something that divides by thirteen, I should, Norbert. It saves time later. Incidentally you owe me two hundred drachs as it is.'

'You never paid me for the copy I sent you of Meredith's last novel.'

The helicopters clattered overhead. The first pilot veered off and finally came down, on the slant until the last bump, on the leathery grass behind the cottage where Jack and Janey Darwin had spent the night.

Astrid said: 'You know I really don't want to go.'

'What?'

'I really don't want to go.'

'Why does she go if she doesn't want to?' Daniel said.

'Why does anyone?' Eleni said.

When the first helicopter had settled, they saw that there were two men in it. One of them, in a grey suit, with a black briefcase, disembarked and walked away from the party on the ground, shouldering through the empty landscape. His pointed black shoes were as polished as if he were going to a dance.

'Amazing how quickly people who've lost everything manage to have more luggage than they know what to do with,' Daniel said.

'That chopper's a Douglas Wasp as supplied to NATO and other friendly powers,' Jack Darwin said. 'And I think that's a

437

second-hand Boeing Skychair which they tried on the commercial route to the islands last summer. Funny, I'd've thought either would have been ample on its own.'

'Pity we can't pop George Ak. on board one of them,' Daniel said. 'Save a lot of trouble.'

'Yes, I'm sorry to hear your plan means Thera's out.'

'Ask Norbert for a reduction,' Daniel said, 'but actually the sooner you're back in London the better. *Dog Eat Dog*, remember?'

The rotors continued to twitch as the women approached the larger of the helicopters, wincing at the dust. Astrid held down the crown of a plum-coloured felt hat Nancy had brought with her. Tita and Eleni wore silk scarves. All three faces were compressed against the draught; the three women tottered like old ladies as they reached for the hand the pilot extended from the cockpit.

'No one's going in the other one at all,' Daniel said. 'I wonder what it's come for. You don't think Larry's in the drug business, do you?'

'It's an obvious possibility,' Jack said. 'All this traffic with Asia Minor's a bit suggestive. Rather disappointingly banal if true, but then truth sometimes is, isn't it?'

'Hence the systematic sense of let down in the last reel. You're right.'

The women settled in the helicopter. There was so little to do that everyone seemed embarrassed. The blades creamed the air. The dry grass bent and spread. Nancy waved. Janey squeezed her face into an expression of quizzical, but distant, goodwill. Daniel saluted. Jack Darwin was trying to spot whether the chopper was a Mark III or a Mark IV, when it rose, tail-heavy, drifted out over the beach and away. Nancy was stroking Mustapha's head. At the last moment, the Princess must have handed the puppy to her. Perhaps the pilot had forbidden it. Larry took Nancy's arm and they ambled across the field to the beach.

'Kick-off five o'clock,' Daniel said, 'so we'd better be ready to go up at a quarter past four. We don't want to waste our sweetness on the desert sands. I trust you're coming to cheer on the hosts of Albion, Janey?'

438

'If I must,' Janey said. 'My cheering days are largely past. I'll try and manage the odd wistful whoop.'

'I wonder when this chap's coming back for his chopper,' Jack said. 'If he doesn't hurry, he's going to have baked pilot for lunch.'

The pilot of the second helicopter was sitting in the cockpit, his helmet still on, with the sun beating through the perspex. He gave no friendly sign when Jack approached and began to inspect the machine.

'Does Jack know how to work those things?' Daniel said.

'Not the latest ones,' Janey said. 'Jack's thinking of taking Larry Pleasure or whatever his name is up, you know. On the cottage.'

'Is he really?'

'It's so pretty. I'd love it. Jack's got this extra-territorial company set up, which means he doesn't have to pay the property dollar. Makes foreign property rather attractive.'

'Particularly when it's quite attractive already.'

'Well, of course, we wouldn't buy anything—the company wouldn't buy anything—which we wouldn't want to buy anyway. But a place like this, especially when there isn't a landing craft in the way, I can't think of anything dishier, can you? And of course Jack can work where he likes.'

'Except for the next six months. What about you, Janey, or will this be where Janey Darwin comes when "Janey Darwin is on holiday but hopes to resume her articles shortly"?'

'Daniel, I love you ... '

'But?'

'That's it,' Janey said. 'But.'

'Oh Janey, I wish I had you.'

'Daniel, do lay off.'

'I'm not making a pass. Jack, tell your wife I'm not making a pass at her. I'm really so glad to see you both. You're a damned lucky man. I wish I was married.'

'It's an easy club to join,' Jack said. 'It's resigning that's so difficult. They need the subs. I thought it was all fixed between you and Mrs Lane. Have you got problems?'

'No, not problems. The blues. That's all. It's all this damned

439

fine weather. Those other sods are going to turn out, aren't they? Paul and Basil. Where is Basil? And Victor?'

'Basil and Gay went up to the village first thing.'

'Probably to buy shoes. And Victor R.?'

'Victor was last seen threatening to make a pilgrimage to the tomb of Homer.'

'In the hope that the great man had left a message for him, no doubt, designating him *Il Miglior Fabbro*. I'm surprised Norbert didn't go in case there was a lost manuscript lying around, which he could publish as a social service. Foreword by Basil B.'

'Daniel, you know what you need? Some new friends.'

'Or else his friends need a new Daniel,' Jack Darwin said.

'Oh I know what I need,' Daniel said. 'I need to create a masterpiece.'

'Or alternatively to be crucified dead and buried and ascend on the third day and sit on the right hand of God.'

'No,' Daniel said, 'I don't really want to be a critic.'

'He needs a wife,' Janey said. 'It's sad.'

'He'll marry that American woman, you'll see. This is all the bachelor's dying twitch. She's perfect for him.'

Daniel was drinking *ouzo* on the terrace of the *taverna* with Paul and Margaret Mallory when Basil and Gay Brain came down the hill from the village. Norbert Ash, in mask and goggles, was patrolling the bay with his spear gun. 'Hoping to catch one of the Princess's diamonds,' Daniel said. He had forgotten how attractive Margaret Mallory was. She was the sort of woman whom he always remembered as plain and whose pretty good humour seemed, in consequence, rather embarrassing, as if she were conscious of how systematically he belittled her in her absence.

'Here he is,' Gay Brain said. 'The very man. I presume you've heard the news?'

'Meaning you know damned well I haven't, Gay. What news?'

'About George Ak.?'

'If he's suddenly discovered he's got a prior engagement—'

'The amnesty?' Gay Brain said.

'The amnesty.'

'There's been an amnesty. I heard a whisper when I was in Athens, but I thought it might have been one more of those. Anyway, apparently it's true. A Police Major's just arrived to whisk four of them back to Athens. George and another journalist and two old officers.'

'Shut up, Paul,' Daniel said. 'Why do you have to choose this occasion to laugh for the first time in your life? Well, I'll be a sonofabitch.'

'Hardly a novel resolution,' Gay said. 'I'm sorry if you're displeased.'

'George isn't going with them actually,' Basil said. 'If that makes you feel any better. He's stopping behind to play in this match this afternoon and then he's catching the steamer. You know he once had a trial with Panathenaikos? He's turning out for the village.'

'If he scores the winner, I shall strangle him,' Daniel said. 'Well, there we are, aren't we? What a—what a performance! You say you knew this might happen, Gay?'

'Not specifically George. I was told in the Ministry that things were now so well under control, the state of the country was so good that they would soon be able to release most of their critics.'

'Imagine,' Daniel said, 'a country where one can lock up one's critics! Well, there we are then. You can put Thera back on your itinerary.'

'I'm sorry if I've brought bad news,' Gay said.

'I feel a bit of an ass,' Daniel said. 'O.K., O.K. Not a new feeling, I know.'

'No one said a word,' Paul said. 'He's so prickly. You do yourself no service, Daniel, you know.'

'Did you manage to find any shoes, Basil?'

'Piers Cobbett very kindly kitted me out. But I trust this really is just a sort of amiable canter, because I have no intention of doing sliding tackles on solid granite or whatever the local stone is. That pitch looks like concrete.'

'Cultured defence, Basil, that's all we ever ask of you. You provide the culture and we'll do the rest. Paul's going to pop in the winner, aren't you, Paul? Meredith's not turning out, is he?'

'Meredith? He's going to be watching from a bath-chair. He's afraid his ulcer may have perforated.'

'Perhaps he ought to take George's place in the helicopter.'

'I should think he'd like nothing better. Imagine what Turkish cooking's going to do to his small intestine.'

'Turkish cooking's what Greek cooking is really about, isn't that the story, Basil? How long had George known about this, because – ?'

'He had word this morning. You know what these régimes are like; executions and liberations are both sprung on people like birthday treats. It is, in fact, one of the junta's birthday. I forget which.'

'Adolf somebody?'

'The news came this morning, just before the helicopter.'

'Just as well I suppose, in some ways. Probably the whole thing would have misfired anyway and you'd all have been forced to scuttle yourselves in Montevideo Harbour. Ah my *Exeter* and my *Ajax* long ago!'

'He was very nice about you,' Gay said.

'Never mentioned you at all,' Basil said.

'Did you know – thanks – did you know – ? Shit. I have got egg on my face, you must admit.'

'Don't ever wipe it off,' Gay said. 'It suits you.'

'I was going to say, did you know that in the *campo* not too far from B.A. there's a whole township where they speak nothing but German, composed of sailors from the *Graf Spee*? Grid plan streets, the complete Teutonic township.'

'Complete with desecrated synagogue, no doubt,' Paul Mallory said.

'A witty thought,' Daniel said.

'Oh Daniel, for Christ's sake,' Paul said. 'No one's allowed to be funny except you. You act like a spoiled child.'

Gay Brain said: 'Well, he did have a big production all set to roll, didn't you, Danny?'

'They have rather gone and pulled the plugs on me, but then, I suppose, that's show business.'

Basil Brain said: 'I hardly think it signifies the end of worthy causes. There are still several millions starving on the sub-continent and one or two régimes in remote parts of the world, of course, to which rescue operations might be mounted. I'm sure Daniel's missionary zeal can find another outlet.'

'Piss off,' Daniel said, 'Basil, will you, quietly?'

'I'm not going in goal,' Daniel said.

'I don't mind going in goal, if you need someone in goal,' one of the Americans said.

'They've got a bloody strong side,' Piers said. 'Have you ever played in goal?'

'I've never played anywhere,' the American said. 'But I've played American football and I've played basketball. I can catch.'

'There's no sense playing him anywhere *else*, for Christ's sake,' Paul said. 'So he may as well go goal.'

'They're waiting,' Victor Rich said.

'Let them fucking wait.'

The locals had George Akrotiri, who had smiled but not spoken to Daniel, at centre-forward and the Egyptian officer on the wing. Stelio Varis was left-back. The rest of the side was composed of young Greeks sporting Adidas equipment, gold necklets and close-cropped, springy black hair from which the ball, during practice, leaped as if from a trampoline.

'The bloody goalkeeper looks shit hot,' Paul said.

'If he hangs from the crossbar during idle periods,' Daniel said, 'we'll have him medically examined. Dr Rich, you're our resident zoological expert. Is he or is he not a chimpanzee?'

'O.K., so it's Piers, Basil, Danny and me in the back four, right?' Jack Darwin said. 'Paul and Victor the twin strikers. With you — what's your name again?'

'Werner,' the young German said.

'Werner and um —'

'David.' The second American was wearing combat boots, jeans and a T-shirt. He was clean-shaven and his hair had been shaved to the skull. He had sergeant's stripes on his hip pocket.

'David in support.'

'What do I do?' Norbert Ash said.

'Everything else,' Daniel said.

'Are we ready?' The referee was a Swede who operated youth tours to a camp near the harbour. The eleventh member of the tourists' side was a second German, very thin, in black shoes and white socks. He chewed his fingers and waited by the touchline as if he were not sure whether he was playing or not.

The first goal was scored before any of the tourists had touched the ball. Several of them had their backs to the play. The goalkeeper had no need to throw the ball out. It ricocheted from the wall behind him with such force that it was back at the centre circle before there was time for an inquest. Paul refused to kick off. He claimed that the whistle had not yet gone for the beginning of the game and that the goal should be disallowed. The crowd, which was unnervingly numerous, began to shout. Daniel could see Dmitri, sidesaddle on the grey donkey, rolling a cigarette and tittering.

'Come on,' Jack Darwin said.

'I'm not kicking off,' Paul said. 'I'll not play with cheats. I never heard the whistle. It never went. If it's nil-nil, I don't mind kicking off.'

'They're a shower,' Daniel said. 'It was a fluke. So give them a goal start, what the hell?'

Jack Darwin ran up and kicked the ball to Victor Rich. 'Come on, let's get started.'

Paul said: 'You start letting them get away with it and you know what'll happen. It'll be a bloody shambles. We'll need the U.N. to separate the combatants. I've seen it all before.'

The ball bounced and flew from the hard ground at startling angles. The Greeks, of course, were at home in the conditions and controlled the ball with much greater skill, but the back four settled down and fought back with clumsy tenacity. Jack Darwin, accustomed to being the general, had suggested territorial marking, to avoid exhaustion, but the need to crowd the Greeks forced the tourists to change tactics. Man-to-man marking lessened the Greeks'

444

agility and neutralized their ball control. Daniel took it on himself to cope with George Akrotiri. If it was true that he had had a trial with Panathenaikos, he showed few signs of it early on. Daniel was easily able to work the ball past him a couple of times. The first time, Paul called for the ball, Daniel gave it, and Paul was promptly topped and tailed by the tall Greek centre-half. 'You see?' Paul said. 'You see? They're a bunch of bloody cloggers.' He took a long time to get up. The second time, Paul called again, but this time Daniel curved the ball to the pale German standing awkwardly by the touchline. The German stumbled forward and started jogging towards goal. Paul ran up to relieve him of the responsibility, whereupon the German dummied him as if he were one of the opposition, beat the lamp-post of a Greek centre-half, beat the full-back and smashed the ball into the goalkeeper's stomach. Paul disapproved from the floor. 'They never understand team work.'

'Rather useful for a spectator,' Jack Darwin said, 'that bloke.'

'Come on, England,' Janey was shouting from beneath the cypresses, behind the tourists' goal.

'England, she says. We shall lose our best player.'

'I'm not leaving,' Basil said.

'Collect that bloody ball,' Jack Darwin said, 'or you might as well.'

Basil strolled to take control of a high bouncing clearance, missed it and Daniel and Jack Darwin were two against four. A second later the goalkeeper was one against three and a second after that the ball hit the back wall with the finality of a firing squad. 'Sorry, gang.'

'Two-nothing,' Daniel said.

'Not the goalie's fault,' Jack said.

'I know,' Daniel said. 'Bugger him.'

The goalkeeper made a fantastic grabbing save a moment later when the third goal looked certain and went galloping off, apparently with the idea of touching down. 'America their America,' Daniel said, as he counted his testicles in the wall before the lamp-post took the resulting free-kick. The ball struck Werner on the chest and bounced to the centre circle where Paul Mallory was lamenting the aesthetics of the defence to Victor Rich. Stelio Varis charged Victor, who dodged so quickly that the ball skidded unavoidably into Paul's path. Paul, seeing no obstacle between himself and the goal, waited for support, found none, and stabbed the ball under the goalkeeper. 'For Christ's sake,' he said as the team galloped up to congratulate him. 'Where was everybody?'

'Now,' Daniel said. He saw Dmitri, as amused as if the tourists had given a further proof of the absurdity of the non-Hellenic world, and clapped his hands. 'Let's have another.'

It came from George Akrotiri, whose archaic smile was almost as irksome to Daniel as Dmitri's derision. That he had done nothing all afternoon made it even worse. Daniel had relaxed his close marking when Akrotiri trapped a loose ball, beat Basil Brain into a lattice-work of confusion, and lobbed it accurately over the goal-keeper's head.

'Sorry, gang.'

It was still three-one at half time.

'Sorry, gang.'

'No, you're doing very well,' Jack Darwin said. 'Victor, I think you ought to go out on the wing, it'll give you a bit more room, and um I think you should move into the centre a bit with Paul.'

'Wolf,' Werner said.

'Wolf. O.K. And I think I'll try and play a bit more midfield, and you, um —'

'David.'

'Right, help at the back a bit. O.K.?'

'I know that man,' Daniel said. 'The hairless one, but I can't bloody place him.'

'Come on, Victor,' Jack Darwin said. 'Let's see you go.'

'I've got a blister,' Victor Rich said. 'It's these shoes.'

'Pretend the cameras are here,' Jack Darwin said. 'And limp like a man.'

'The secretary-general is all ready to set the second half in motion,' Daniel said. 'If you can call it motion.'

Basil Brain said: 'Someone should have thought of lemons.'

The Greeks resumed with two corners, one headed away by

446

Daniel, the other caught by the goalkeeper who booted it so strongly that the Greek keeper was deceived and only just managed to touch it over the bar. Daniel came up for the corner, headed it down to the frail German and that was three-two.

'He's quite useful, that little kraut,' Jack Darwin said.

'I completely deceived the keeper,' Paul said. 'I did a dummy run, not that anyone noticed. You've got no appreciation. There can be no Art without accurate criticism. That's why we're trailing.'

George Akrotiri took the ball from the kick-off, ambled past Jack Darwin as if he had been cemented into the ground, left Piers hobbling and hit the post with a shot the goalkeeper was still waiting for. He stood with one foot on the rebound as Daniel raced in to tackle. Akrotiri, a smile always on his lips, half turned and caught Daniel in the solar plexus with his elbow. 'Oh, it's going to be like that, is it?' Daniel gritted his teeth and rocked from foot to foot in front of the centre-forward. Akrotiri drove the ball between his legs and bang against the back wall.

'Sorry, gang.'

'We need a keeper,' Daniel said. 'Anyone.'

'You know the people,' Piers said. 'Choose.'

'Try the big kraut,' Jack Darwin said.

'It's O.K., we can still do it. Feed the little bloke and keep it tight at the back.'

The little German cushioned a high ball on the chest, jostled past the lamp-post and hit a shot from twenty yards that bounced in front of the keeper and skidded into Victor Rich, whose hip supplied the clinching touch. 'Four-three,' Jack Darwin said. 'And all to play for.'

'Iskios, Iskios, Iskios.' The crowd began to chant.

The tourists pressed hard. The little German hit the post, Paul Mallory hit the goalkeeper, Jack Darwin headed against the post and Basil Brain ducked under a cross which a less subtle player might have headed home. The clever footwork of the Greeks yielded to petulance and then to recriminations. 'Never travel on a foreign ship,' Jack Darwin said, 'when the bottom begins to fall out.'

Paul Mallory said: 'Daniel, for Christ's sake, part with it occasionally.'

'If you came back and linked up a bit, there'd be someone to part with it to, you big fairy. Accurate criticism!'

Wolf was exercising the Greeks with a series of dribbles. Once he passed to Paul, unmarked on the penalty spot, and was told that he should have shot; the next time, he shot and was told he should have passed. Daniel pursued Akrotiri with flattering diligence. Every now and again, when there was a lull, he tried to smile or make some mild conversation, but the Greek nodded and looked away, always with the same teasing expression on his precise lips. The ball came out to Jack Darwin, ten yards from goal. He hit it so hard that it sailed over the bar and went bouncing down the steps towards the harbour.

Daniel said: 'You've played this game before.'

George Akrotiri shrugged and looked down. 'A long time ago.'

'Congratulations on the news. The amnesty.'

'This, of course, means that there is no need—'

'No. Probably just as well. Does that mean you still—?'

'I wanted to ask you about that. I hear you are leaving Iskios too. Perhaps we could travel to Athens together. I was offered a place on the helicopter, but I refused. My wife—'

'If you still want me to do something, of course I will.'

'Now, of course, it will be much easier. To repay you.'

'Oh, that. That doesn't matter.'

The ball reached Akrotiri as Daniel finished his sentence. Before Daniel realized that the game had re-started, George had laid it off to the Egyptian, who danced down the touchline, leaving Piers in the arms of two large female spectators, and crossed a curling ball. George bent under it and headed up and over the goalkeeper and below the bar.

'Sorry, gang.'

'Just when we were getting on top.'

'I think I should go. I have things I should do,' the keeper said.

'Daniel, go in goal for us.'

'He always holds out the shitty end,' Daniel said. 'Look—'

448

'I really do have to go.'

'Time for his fix,' Daniel said. 'O.K., one goal and then I'm coming out. I didn't even see the ball was back on the field.'

'How much longer?' Basil Brain said. 'Because I shall shortly be in liquid form.'

'Twenty minutes,' Jack Darwin said. 'Ample time.'

'I haven't kept goal since we lost seven-two at Caterham that time Carlo went to Chippenham by mistake and we didn't have a keeper.'

'You're doing a grand job,' Jack Darwin said. 'Seriously.'

Daniel saved a stinger from the Egyptian and all but bumped the ball in his face as he followed up. Daniel's accuracy of kick and throw increased the effectiveness of the forwards. Paul and Werner combined well down the left and Wolf relieved Victor Rich of the need to continue his imitation of a man with courageous cramp. Wolf and Werner engaged in a clever one-two which ended with Werner side-footing the tourists' fourth. Paul Mallory ran to the centre with the modesty of a master. George Akrotiri headed into Daniel's arms and then tried a bicycle kick to a pass from the Egyptian. He missed and landed hard on the ground. 'Take him off,' Daniel said.

Jack Darwin took the ball up, was tripped, took the free-kick, was tripped again, took another free-kick, was charged in the area and put the ball on the spot before the referee blew the whistle: free-kick to the Greeks. The kick hit Victor Rich, cannoned off Paul, and reached Wolf, who made to kick once, made to kick twice and rolled the ball into the empty quarter of the net. 'Five-all,' Daniel said.

'I really have to go,' David said.

'Not now you can't,' Daniel said. 'Jesus Christ, I know who you are. You shaved it all off.'

'By the year two thousand five hundred no one will have body hair,' David said. 'It's actually unvirile.'

'Keep hacking,' Daniel said. 'You're doing a great job. Highly virile. How's Muriel?'

'Who told you about Muriel?'

'I once heard you talking about her,' Daniel said. 'Action stations!'

Jack Darwin scored the sixth. Paul, who had touched the ball at some early stage of its devious progress into the goal, shook hands with Jack like a man who has fulfilled his side of an arduous contract.

'Now,' Piers said. 'Keep a tidy ship and the prize is ours. Six-five.'

George Akrotiri began to go back and fetch the ball more vigorously. First Basil and then David and then Piers chased his ghost around the field. Daniel saved on his knees at the foot of a post and touched a strong shot over the bar. Akrotiri smiled at his boots. The Egyptian took the corner and the lamp-post headed it to where Jack Darwin was guarding the line. He headed it to Werner, who sent a long ball to Wolf, whom only Victor Rich's assistance prevented from scoring.

'One more,' Daniel said, 'and we can all go home with the cup.'

'How much longer, ref?' Paul said.

'Four minutes by my watch.'

The Greeks now tripped Victor Rich in the penalty area. 'An act of conspicuous sportsmanship,' Jack Darwin said, 'though what he was doing there at the time, God only knows.'

'Looking for talent,' Daniel said.

The Greeks refused to give the ball up for the kick.

'Tell them Victor'll take it if they'll let us have it.'

Paul took the kick and sliced it wide. 'The bloody keeper came right off his line,' he said. 'Did you see that?' The Greeks seemed as furious as if he had scored. Akrotiri came through again and this time neither Piers's charge nor Daniel's cry of 'Hoof' as he came out could stop a Greek goal. 'Sorry, gang,' Daniel said. 'Six each. Piss.'

'One more, one more,' Jack Darwin said.

'Jack's somewhat partisan, don't you find?' Basil Brain said.

'Look, I'm coming out,' Daniel said, 'someone else's turn to be the finger in the dyke.'

'You can't, Danny. Not now. Seriously, you're doing a great job.'

Wolf hit the bar. Werner headed the rebound into the cypresses. The Greeks raced into the attack. The Egyptian cut in and slid the ball to the back of the box, with the defence all doing the splits.

George Akrotiri picked his spot and fired. Daniel saw the ball crossing him to the left and swooped confidently, so confidently that for a moment he took his eye off it, looking for an unmarked man to receive the clearance. He got to the ball all right, but with a downward, stabbing motion. In a split second of painless agony he heard his little finger crack and as Jack called out, 'Great save now quickly,' he fell to the ground huddled round his broken hand. Akrotiri gathered the loose ball and tapped it into the open goal. 'Fucking cunt,' Daniel said.

'Sorry, gang,' said the Egyptian officer.

'Shit,' Jack Darwin said. 'After all that.'

'Look, I've done my hand,' Daniel said. 'Rather badly.'

'Let's have a look,' Jack Darwin said. 'See the damage.'

'For fuck's sake.' Daniel twisted himself away from their rough attention. George Akrotiri was smiling among the Greeks. Daniel hobbled away from the goal towards the Post Office where the doctor's surgery was. The building was shut.

'Let's at least have a look.'

'The little finger's practically off,' Daniel said. 'Satisfied? I don't mind Victor —'

Victor Rich said: 'I'm not really a medical man, you know. It's not strictly my field at all. Oh yes, quite a nasty split. You'll have to get some help. Keep the hand up and against the body. Don't try to do anything, whatever you do.'

'I'm trying not to pass out,' Daniel said. 'Look, could someone go and find the bloody doctor. *O yatros, chriazome to yatro oso pio grigora borite.*' He stood huddled on the touchline. The hand hurt. Iskios was never so remote.

Paul said: 'Is that time or what's happening?'

'Shall we play on?'

'We've got five minutes,' Piers Cobbett said. 'Let's not give in before we have to. I'll take over if the goalie can't go on.'

'Go on!' Daniel said. 'Get fucked.'

George Akrotiri said: 'I am so sorry. Is it bad?'

'Bad? Shit.'

Daniel showed his broken hand. The game was going on.

'Danny, what're you going to do?'

'Nice people, I must say,' Daniel said. 'I don't know, find the doctor.'

'You'd better come and sit down and we'll get someone to go and get him,' Margaret Mallory said. 'How can they go on playing?'

'They'd go on playing if I was dead,' Daniel said.

The doctor was a small, dapper man with a plastic Gladstone bag and two-tone shoes. Dmitri Bracheotis brought him on the donkey.

Daniel said: 'Margaret, you are nice.'

'Of course I think you're all completely mad.'

'That's what makes you so nice.'

'Daniel, what's happened? What's happened? Oh my God!'

'It's only broken, it's not actually detached.'

'I was up by the windmills and I saw someone was hurt and of course it had to be you. How did it happen?'

'A cannonball took off his legs so he laid down his arms,' Daniel said. 'Only in the reverse order.'

'Come with me, please,' the doctor said.

The final whistle blew. The tourists had not succeeded in equalizing. A cheer went up from the spectators. 'Bastards,' Daniel said. He read more sadistic curiosity than sympathy on the faces which surrounded him as the spectators moved away from the pitch. 'Look, Victor, I wish you'd come and keep an eye on what our friend's doing.'

'Make sure he gives you a tetanus shot, that's all I can advise.'

'Tetanus?' Daniel said.

The doctor agreed. He unlocked the door of the cold building and signalled Daniel inside.

'You wouldn't come with, I suppose?'

'If you've got a proper doctor in charge, there's nothing I can do.'

'You could hold my hand,' Daniel said. 'The other one, I mean. What do you think he'll actually do? What do you think he *should* do?'

'Set it,' Victor Rich said. 'He must.'

'How did it *happen*?' Nancy said. 'I was up by the windmills.'

452

'The ball hit it, rather forcefully,' Daniel said. 'In here?'

He lay down on the doctor's slab and watched suspiciously as the man arranged a series of boxes and instruments.

'Is it very painful?'

'Yes,' Daniel said. 'Only when I laugh, of course. It's when he starts treating it that worries me. Look, Margaret, there's no need to hang around.'

'I don't mind staying.'

'You're very sweet. What a bugger. God, I wish one of those sodding helicopters was still here. Oh for Neasden General Hospital!'

The doctor said: 'Now, let's see.'

Daniel said: 'This is no place for a Yiddisher boy. If you can give me something to kill the pain, do it. Now.'

'Pardon me?'

'Anaesthetic? *Anesthitiko?*'

The doctor nodded but took the broken hand with a vigour which suggested, to Daniel's anxiety, that he wanted to congratulate rather than treat him.

Nancy said: 'Daniel, I'll be back in a minute.'

Daniel said: 'Listen, I'll be perfectly all right.'

'Sorry this had to happen,' Jack Darwin said, from the doorway.

'Come in,' Daniel said. 'What was the final story?'

'They managed to keep us out,' Jack said. 'But it was a damned close run thing. They just had the edge. Christ, that looks nasty. That looks horrible. What's he going to do?'

'Break it off,' Daniel said. 'And chuck it in the waste basket. I hope that needle's clean. It's tragic to be wounded, but it's farcical to die of the treatment.'

'Tetanus,' the doctor said, squinting at the hypodermic.

'Isn't that stuff supposed to be kept in the fridge?'

'The Greeks invented medicine,' Jack Darwin said.

'I know, but it's supposed to have moved on a bit since then, isn't it? I hope he's been reading *Time* magazine in the meanwhile. Aren't unsterilized needles as bad as rusty wounds?'

'Tetanus,' the doctor said, still squinting

453

'Christ, is he buying or selling? This is definitely not the kind of language game I like to play.'

'Daniel, he speaks English. I'm sure he's very competent.'

'He doesn't speak Cambridge English, Mag,' Daniel said. 'You are a nice girl. I've always loved you. You're a nice patient, sympathetic girl.'

'Daniel, one thing at a time.'

'You're the sort of girl I really like to have when I've got a broken finger.'

'I wondered why it had taken you so long.'

'That's not fair. Oh Christ, here we go. I've always ogled you when I could. Well, tara, if I don't see you all again. Tell them it's been wonderful.'

'Now we take a look at the damage.'

'Look, but don't touch unless you have to,' Daniel said. 'Is everyone as big a coward as I am?'

'I think you're being very brave,' Margaret said.

'I'll drink to that,' Daniel said. 'That hurts rather. A touch of British understatement. Mustn't demean ourselves in front of the natives. Oh fuckaduck. Couldn't we shut that door? The sight of impassive black-robed figures has unfortunate symbolic connotations. Cacoyannis, go away.'

'I will give you something for the pain and then we must set the finger.'

'A nice sense of priorities,' Daniel said. 'Straight old-fashioned story-telling.'

'You are funny, Daniel. Will you go on trying to be funny on your death-bed, do you think?'

'That's a booking I'd sooner not discuss,' Daniel said. 'I don't like to think further ahead than next year on the pier at Yarmouth. At least, with any luck, Jack won't shove me in goal again in a hurry.'

'I wasn't in a hurry this time,' Jack Darwin said. 'Only you would insist.'

'Get stuffed. Is it bleeding?' Daniel said. 'I feel as if it is.'

'The skin is broken,' Jack Darwin said. 'It's rather nasty.'

454

'I haven't looked yet,' Daniel said. 'I'm experiencing the whole thing non-visually. My hand seems roughly the same size as the rest of my body put together. If it is put together.'

'Are you a violinist?' the doctor said.

'My God, my career!'

'Is he a violinist?'

'The man thinks I'm unconscious, but I can hear every word.'

'Or a pianist.'

'*Maestro, addio*,' Daniel said. 'Don't tell me, I'll never play the violin again. My God, imagine if I had been.'

'Please?'

'No, I am not a violinist, a surgeon or a tictac man. My little finger, much as I love it, is not essential to my work.'

'If he is a violinist, he must go to Athens at once.'

'I'm a film director. I need nothing but my eyes and my mouth. Concentrate on saving those and you can have the rest. Oh, except for — Please, just do it, whatever it is.'

A cross-eyed Greek in a white shirt and black trousers came into the surgery, followed by Dmitri. He opened a cabinet and brought out a tray of hypodermics.

'A fine time to start selling antiques,' Daniel said. 'When's he going to give me this bloody anaesthetic?'

'First I give you some morphine,' the doctor said.

'Fine,' Daniel said. '*Avanti*. I always have a shot about this time of day.'

Nancy said: 'You'll never guess who's outside. Mustapha. Aren't animals fascinating? He knows you saved his life.'

'Bless his tiny canine heart,' Daniel said.

'I'm worried about him actually, Daniel. I wanted to talk to you about it, because what's going to happen to him when we go? We shall have to get someone to look after him. I was talking to that peasant you gave the aspirin to —'

'The one who was going to drown him, you mean? Were you really? In what language exactly?'

'He indicated he'd be willing to take him back, Mustapha.'

'Indicated, did he? Under the provisions of the Fugitive Slave

Act, I assume. I presume money came into the indications as well as pity and terror?'

'Obviously we'd have to give him something. But we can't keep Mustapha, can we? We have to do something.'

'We could always have him slipped ashore from a motor cruiser on the beach off Deal. Or alternatively perhaps Astrid would like to smuggle him in for us when she comes incognito. Ow. Listen, do what you like.'

'He said he'd look after him, this peasant. He seemed very fond of him.'

'Then I'm sure everything will be fine,' Daniel said. 'My Christ, what's he planning to inject me with? Byron's bayonet from the Wars of the Liberation? Five minutes from full time. Talk about luck.'

'Soon it will work,' the doctor said.

'God, it's crowded in here,' Daniel said. 'Am I in your way? You'd think bloody Akrotiri might have come up, if only to have a quiet giggle. When are you people leaving?'

'We'll see you all right first,' Jack Darwin said. 'We can always stay till tomorrow.'

'You'd better check with Norbert. After all, it'll mean paying another night's harbour dues. And that's pricey, even divided by fourteen or whatever you are.'

'He's such a bitch, even under sedation.'

'Morphine inhibits the cerebral cortex,' Daniel said. 'Or is cortex an artificial fibre made by I.C.I.? Anyway, it certainly doesn't shut you up.'

'The drug that shuts you up they haven't discovered yet,' Jack Darwin said.

'Are you still here? Where's Janey? Writing a funny piece about me for next week, I'll bet. Big mouth lets one in. Oh shit, I thought this was supposed to make it hurt less. *Ena lepto, sas parakalo.*'

'*Then pirazi,*' the doctor said, '*then pirazi.* Don't worry.'

'How do people endure serious injuries, I wonder? Jack, we must have someone break his finger in our movie. And we'll have great jammy close-ups. All shot with the utmost integrity, of course. No broken fingers for broken fingers' sake. All done to show how much we *hate* broken fingers.'

'The only effective medicine the Greeks ever devised was hemlock,' Meredith Lamb said. 'I certainly wouldn't have the lad take anything else without a proper trial. Where is the poor sod?'

'Oh not him,' Daniel said. 'Please. Tell him I need all the oxygen I can get. He breathes too heavily for a sick room—and too often.'

'Playing games after thirty is sheer rant, so much hot air, and actually trying to stop a ball is purest hyperbole. Pardon. It's still those bloody onions repeating from Athens. Never eat onions south of a line from Cardiff to the Wash. Oh my Christ, look at you. I didn't realize you were actually lying in state.'

'Have a look and then piss off,' Daniel said. 'We've got all the reversed muskets we can use.'

'Francesca insisted I come and pay my respects.'

'Pay them and then go, Meredith, will you, please?'

'We've had our differences in the past, Daniel, but isn't this a time above all for reconciliation? Poised as you are—'

'I've still got one good hand,' Daniel said. 'It'll probably be enough.'

'It may well have to be, old son.'

'Meredith, there really are a lot of people in here.'

The cross-eyed man held a syringe cocked.

'I think now we put you out,' the doctor said.

'I don't mind some of them staying,' Daniel said. 'Nance and Mag and you, Jack.'

'I put you out,' the doctor said, 'and then we operate.'

'This is where I take my leave of you, I get it. Who is this other character? Do you think he's qualified? And for what?'

'They always have an assistant,' Jack Darwin said.

'I thought that was undertakers.'

'Any self-respecting man has an assistant. Relax. We'll make sure he doesn't steal the gold from your teeth.'

'What I can't help wondering,' Daniel said, 'is whether he's qualified—and if so, what as.'

'We shall soon see,' Jack said. 'Some of us.'

'Seek out—less often sought than found ...' Daniel said. 'Good heavens, that's rather nice. A soldier's grave, for thee the best. How does it go on? Goonight, Lou, goonight.'

'Mr Meyer? Mr Meyer? How are you feeling now?'

'Oh hullo. How are you?'

'How are you feeling now?'

'Not too bad. O.K. Oh, that looks better. Not that I saw it before, but I'm sure it does.'

'I am so sorry what happened.'

'Pure accident. I shall be O.K. It's tidy now.'

'I never intended—'

'Look, how could you have? It's not the sort of thing anyone ever could intend. *Is* it? Forget it. When are you off to Athens?'

'Perhaps in a day or two. Mr Meyer—'

'Tell me,' Daniel said.

'I am so sorry when you have only just come round, but there is very little time.'

'I'm sorry,' Daniel said, 'but I'm out of the hundred kilometres walk. Even if it means disappointing the fans.'

'Your friends, are they still going tonight?'

'I don't even know what day it is,' Daniel said. 'They may have gone, for all I know.'

'How do you feel?' The doctor had his head round the door.

'O.K., it looks very neat. Is it all right? What's this you've done? I look like Captain Hook here.'

'Is stainless steel splint. Lighter and better. Very modern from America.'

'Very trendy,' Daniel said. 'But the finger's not straight.'

'Is all right,' the doctor said. 'It's very good. It mend better like that.'

'If you say so,' Daniel said. 'Can I go now?'

'You wait for a while. An hour maybe. Relax. I go now. Your *kiria* is here.'

'Nancy?'

'No, it's me,' Margaret said.

'I come back in an hour,' the doctor said. 'But I have a baby I must deliver. Wait until I come back, please, before you go.'

'If Mag's still here, everyone's still here. Mag, you don't have to stay. I'm O.K. now. You were damned nice, damned nice.'

'I think they are still planning to leave tonight.'

'Look, I'm sorry, um George, but you can't expect me to know, can you? Why, do you want to cadge a lift?'

'Not for myself, no, of course not.'

'Only you've got a mate,' Daniel said. 'Is that it?'

'How goes it, my son?' Jack Darwin said.

'Superman lives. If you can call it living. I'm O.K. How's the outside world?'

'Whirling on.'

'There is another man,' George Akrotiri said. 'Who has not been amnestied.'

'You're really looking for trouble, aren't you? Who's this then?'

'Another political, who was not included. Vassili Ioannides.'

'Why wasn't he included?'

'Who knows? Perhaps malice, perhaps an oversight. Who knows?'

'Well, it's no use talking to me,' Daniel said. 'What can I do? I'm a fucking crock. Jack—'

'Please ...'

'Jack, listen—look, if I don't tell Jack, who can I tell?—George here's got another bloke wants to take up his booking on the *Prometheus*, I don't know what you think.'

'Bit awkward,' Jack Darwin said. 'They've got a piss-up going on. The Greeks all came down to whoop it up. They've got everyone down there.'

'Just as well the Colonels gave the thumbs up for you, George. Jack, are you still planning to sail?'

'I don't know. I suppose so. If there's anyone left sober enough to steer the bloody thing. I daresay we shan't go until morning now.'

Daniel said: 'It doesn't look too promising.'

'This is a dedicated man,' George Akrotiri said. 'A man who will happily hide anywhere he can be hidden.'

Daniel said: 'Honestly, it's not much good talking to me. As you may gather, I'm not the force I was, at least not for the moment. Was Nancy here at all?'

'She was,' Jack said. 'He did quite a nice job on you.'

'I suppose you watched the whole operation.'

'Quite intriguing. Not often you see the methods of Galen in practical use. I don't really think there was that much to it.'

'He is a man who wants to get back into the fight, Mr Meyer.'

'From what you said before, there isn't a fight to get back into. Isn't that what you said? In any case, I don't really know what you expect me to do. If this chap's as determined as you say, I'm sure he doesn't need to rely on a bunch of bloody tourists to get him off the island.'

George Akrotiri said: 'His wife is ill —'

'How come you never mentioned him before? Jack, I don't know what you think.'

'It all sounds a bit last minutish. And we are planning to go to Thera now. Basil knows the chappie who's in charge of the excavations. I wouldn't really want to miss it, if I could help it.'

'God, I wouldn't mind getting in on that myself. If it weren't for this bloody finger.'

'I thought you had to get back —'

'Oh, and that,' Daniel said. 'When do you actually —'

'Of course, Mr Meyer, I am very sorry about your finger.'

'Oh Christ, that's all over and done with now. I just don't think I can act as chief conspirator any more. By all means go and ask Norbert Ash. The bald one, you know. Particularly if your friend's the kind of revolutionary who's willing to share expenses. But don't ask too many people, will you? We still have to get out of the country.'

'Of course. Mr Meyer, there is still one more thing—'

'There usually is,' Daniel said. 'I find.'

'My wife. I would be most grateful if you could still arrange to help her. As I say—'

'I said I would, I will. I don't know how much I can manage, but I'll do what I can. You said five hundred. I'll try and do five hundred. I don't think I can do any more. Unless you need money in Greece, Jack?'

'Not really. Janey and I are thinking of buying one of these cottages of Larry's, but I'd sooner do it through my own channels.'

'Maybe I'll come in with you,' Daniel said. 'I may as well try and save something from the wreck.'

'Why not buy a couple for yourself?' Jack Darwin said. 'Now your ship's come in. Sell one later and live in the other. You'll be quids in.'

George Akrotiri said: 'I hear you bought a Cycladic sculpture.'

'Oh ar,' Daniel said. 'Where'd you get that from?'

'I heard it very confidentially.'

'Well mind you pass it on very confidentially too,' Daniel said. 'Or I shall be in the shit even more than I am already. What else do you hear? Is it a good one? Any word on that?'

'No question,' Akrotiri said. 'Very good.'

'Well, that's something. Look, I'm sorry about your friend, Ioannides, but he has left it a bit late, hasn't he? You'd better let me have your wife's address. And you mentioned something about letters. Do you still want me to take some letters?'

'Now is not necessary, I can manage from Athens very easily.'

'*Opos thelete sis,*' Daniel said.

'Well, *sas efcharisto para poli.* I am so sorry about the hand. Perhaps I see you tomorrow. *Kalinichta.*'

'*Yasoo.*'

Jack Darwin said: 'Sharp little character.'

'I don't trust him,' Daniel said. 'And he should never have been allowed that last goal. Bloody Greeks.'

NOVEMBER

BOOM-TITTY-BOOM. Sun 21 Nov 8.45/Tues 23 Nov 11.15.

Andrew Ford's first film, *Boom-Titty-Boom*, may seem at first viewing no more than another stab at the *cinema-verité* life of a young girl in modern society. There are hints of Godard — in the sequence where the girl, Rachel, is interviewed by a careers consultant and replies, in a dull tone, with answers of so delightful a frankness that the consultant, having made love to her, tells her that she will never find a job until she changes her life-style — and of Ken Loach, particularly when Rachel babysits for a couple who have not been out alone together since their marriage and discovers that doing good also means allowing others to do things ... On closer viewing, however, Andrew Ford shows a remarkable and precocious individuality. The charm of the film comes as much from its refusal to accept that our society can be criticized only by those who can do it neatly (the first half of the film was shot on a shoestring and with often inadequate lighting and sound facilities) as from the candour and charm of Ford's unknown actress heroine, Rachel Davidson, who manages to be at once utterly ordinary and utterly beautiful.

'Yesterday was warm,' Daniel said. 'Today it's cold. It is the year's climacteric. How are you, darling? Sorry I'm late.'

'Well, how's it going then?' Queenie said. 'And what's the continuing story of the lovely Mr Timmis?'

'He seems pretty happy. Camille's film was not all that of a hit at the sneaks, but everyone seems to like her personally. She's coming over next week, they're going to give her a bit of promotion. He's very high on the new script. He's got a few points and so've I, but we're definitely progressing. Jack's really a tremendous craftsman, I must say. So there we are then.'

'So you're happy?'

'Call no man happy, Q, my love. But at least I'm happy about the movie.'

'Buenos Aires here we come! And the money, we've got some lovely money through at last, I hear. They don't hurry themselves any more.'

'And they didn't even then. What're you drinking?'

'I think I'll have a lovely Tio Pepe.'

'Two of those,' Daniel said, 'and the menu when you feel like it. No, I think things are going pretty well really.'

'So when are you off then?'

'Not until after Christmas.'

'After Christmas, what could be nicer? Just when the weather's getting really foul you'll be basking in the sunshine. And start shooting on the first of March, absolutely perfect.'

'God, it's a performance though, a film like this.'

'I do think it's a good script, though, now. I showed it to Mike, after what we said, and I must say I think he'd be mad not to do it. It's really a super part. He's promised to read it over the weekend.'

'I'll bet you he'll say the character's too weak.'

'But I don't think it is. I'm going to have some smoked salmon, I think, and then the *sole Véronique* and that'd be lovely. I think it's just very human. Just the way people behave.'

'That's what actors mean by weak,' Daniel said.

'Green salad, madam?'

'And a green salad.'

'I'll have the *paté Traktir*,' Daniel said, 'and then the *tournedos Boston*. And half a bottle of Perrier and a bottle of the '66 Dom Perignon and that's that taken care of. I like this place, you don't have to sit on strangers' knees. You can, but you don't have to. So what else is new?'

'I had dinner with Billy and some people the night before last.'

'And he sneered at my doing a caper, I suppose?'

'He was rather envious actually. He said all they ask him to do now is—'

'Everything.'

'No, he was saying he'd like to break out and do something more external, so he said. He's a bit off the sensitives, as he calls them.'

'Well, don't tell Gil,' Daniel said. 'Or I shall find myself fifty thousand bucks in and no picture to direct.'

'There isn't the slightest risk,' Queenie said. 'Lovely smokers. Billy's doing a picture in Yugoslavia in April, so there's no risk whatever. I don't think you should worry about Billy.'

'I don't think I should worry about anything, my darling. And once we get started, I shan't. We've had a terrific morning actually, Gil and Jack and I. He's quite bright.'

'He's very bright. And he does get the money, which is the main thing.'

'It's the only thing, frankly. If he didn't, I wouldn't spend ten minutes with the little prick.'

'You're very wicked. And how about the lovely Elephant Man then? Didn't the screening go nicely the other night?'

'Think so? I thought it was O.K. I'm still not that happy with the voice over. I think I shall have to get someone else to do it. I thought Nigel was a bit churchy with it. People seemed to like it. I think it worked.'

'I think it worked a dream. I thought it was lovely. And I'll tell you who else liked it very much and that's Mike. He's always been an admirer of yours, but he really loved it.'

'Victor's supposed to be seeing it next week. They won't give us a definite date until he does. I've asked him three or four times. He's never bloody well here. He's always in Manchester. What on earth does he do in *Manchester*?'

'Perhaps he's got a friend.'

'A friend? Victor? I thought he was the living proof that what the solipsist means is true. He can't actually have discovered that there's someone else in the world apart from himself, can he?'

'That's what I'm told. And then of course they've got this big export thing on. It's not always Manchester. I spoke to his assistant,

465

the beautiful Geraldine, and she adored *The Elephant Man*, so you've got one friend on the dreaded sixth floor.'

'Which is one more than I had before. Is she the lady love? Presumably not. Well, he bloody well ought to like it, it's about all the sort of things he likes—Victoriana, septicaemia, erotica, utopia—Victor's country all right. And pretentious as well. What more can he ask?'

'I didn't think it was at all. Lovely champagne.'

'Oh well, we're not rich all the time. She thought he'd like it, did she?'

'She didn't go that far—'

'Then she didn't go far enough. Are you going to see any of these fillums at the N.F.T. at all? I got the menu this morning.'

'I always mean to go and then somehow I never do.'

'You mustn't get complacent, Q, my love, or that'll make two of us. New clients are there for the picking. Must keep tabs on the up and coming. I know it's too late for personal salvation, but I've decided to make an effort this time to see the Lord's anointed. There's only one way to get good notices these days and that's make films on shoestrings. Nothing touches a critic's heart more than the sight of a shoestring. Their mothers must all have been frightened by *The Gold Rush*. You remember, Chaplin eating his shoestrings like spaghetti? Never mind, darling, you make lovely deals and your flattery always sounds sincere.'

'I don't know whether you're still interested in Greece. I had a manuscript in today from Adam Playfair with a note on it that you might be interested in making it.'

'No one is more interested in making it than I am. What exactly?'

'It's a novel. By a woman called Davina Long.'

'Fuck me,' Daniel said. 'She's a fast worker. She must work every day, the sly bitch. We met her on Iskios. Nancy and I. What's it like?'

'It only came in today. Whatever happened to that book you were interested in by that man?'

'He never wrote it. Robert Gavin. He was too high on this black boy he'd picked up. He's a late convert to the joys of poofdom.

Davina Long, though, what do you know? Get one of your girls to do a synopsis of it. I'd love to know what it's all about, apart from anything else. Is it set in Greece?'

'Set in your lovely Greek island paradise.'

'Only it wouldn't be a bad idea to get something moving for after *The Big One*. It's a much better title, don't you agree? *The Big One*? Rather than *Dog Eat Dog*. Must be better.'

'Much better. Much.'

'Nice and modest,' Daniel said. 'Like you, darling. I was going to say like me, but we mustn't stretch credulity.'

'We must not,' Queenie said.

'Meaning what exactly? Listen, seriously, don't you think really one should go and see some of these Festival films? We might even find someone who could play Pilar — the native girl. And after all, the Chancellor pays.'

'The lovely Chancellor pays, do you see?' Queenie said. 'And what could be nicer than that?'

'Any calls?'

'Torrents,' Wendy said. 'As usual. Shall I begin?'

'Begin, begin. Overwhelm me.'

'Well, Gil called to say that Camille gets in on Monday. Mr Lucas called to say that the interview won't be in this week or next, but it'll almost certainly be in the one after. Because of the Film Festival.'

'He still hasn't shown me what he's going to say, which was the point. Keep after the sod, will you, Wendy, nicely?'

'I will. Queenie's office phoned about your meeting with David and Peter. Ditto about Janet and Michael D. Oh yes, then there was someone called Brian Griffiths from Essex University who says could you come and talk to them Friday night? That's the, um, twelfth.'

'Friday night? Bloody short notice.'

'Billy Stern was going, but he's had to go to America, this character said.'

'Damn all that honesty,' Daniel said. 'Why do they have to tell us things like that. What the hell's he gone to America for, I wonder? Well, fuck that. Hang on; Friday. Have I got anything next Friday?'

'You're lunching, but that's all. And you've got your hair man at three.'

'Essex, that's Colchester, isn't it? I can still do it easily. I've got some friends up that way, that's the thing. What did you tell him? Is he going to call back?'

'I said we'd phone him by tonight if there was any chance.'

'Do you think I should?'

'Do you want to?'

'I don't know what I want. I was hoping you'd be able to tell me. I don't think I want to go, but then again I think I will. So what do I really want?'

'You want to go,' Wendy said. 'I think.'

'You promised me you were intuitive,' Daniel said. 'When you took the job. So I'll take your word for it. Call him up, but be reluctant. And I don't want to eat with them first. I don't mind being stabbed, but I can't bear being poisoned. I don't really think I do want to go, you know. It's a hell of a long drive.'

'Then shall I tell him no?'

'On the other hand, it'll give me a chance to observe the loathsome young at first hand. Christ, Wendy, what am I saying? I'm not young any more. Well, come on, deny it, deny it, what do I pay you for?'

'You're very young.'

'Don't you call me sixteen, you bitch, just because you're whatever you are. Twenty-five?'

'Six.'

'Twenty-six. Are you happy, Wendy Fairfax?'

'Yes, I'm very happy, thank you, Mr Meyer. And five assorted actors also called. I've got their names. And also Mrs Lane.'

'God, you do put things in a funny order.'

'I put them in the order they happen, that's all.'

'You've got no idea of modern narrative forms, doing a thing like that. Go and see *Muriel* at once. What are you, some kind of old-fashioned realist? It's a film by Alain Resnais. What did Mrs Lane want, did she say?'

'She said could you pick her up at the house tomorrow night by any chance? Because that way you could have a drink before you went to the show.'

'Fine, O.K., I'll call her later myself.'

'She won't be there,' Wendy said. 'That's why she called this morning. She won't be there until tomorrow. She's going out of town.'

'I get it,' Daniel said. 'She won't be there tonight?'

'That's what I gathered. At least not until late.'

'I get it,' Daniel said. 'That's why she called this morning. More?'

'Douggie says you can have a fitting any time after Wednesday for the linen jacket and the lightweight trousers. Oh, and Victor Rich's assistant phoned — Geraldine Golding.'

'Ah, the one who liked *The Elephant Man*.'

'Just to say that he'll be back at the weekend and he's asked to see *The Elephant Man* on Monday morning, and could you have a meeting with him on Monday afternoon at three o'clock? She was rather mysterious, but I gather they may want you to do something else for them. She kept muttering about prestige productions for the new year.'

'That means no money,' Daniel said. 'All they want to do is stockpile some boring footage to impress the I.T.A. with their serious concern for quality television. Their licences come up for renewal in '75, don't they?'

'I don't know.'

'You should know these things, Wendy. You also promised me you took a keen interest in current affairs. Honey, don't worry, I'm sorry, I keep forgetting we haven't known each other long. Anything else?'

'That sounds like something now,' Wendy said.

'I'll take it,' Daniel said. 'Hullo. Virginia! How nice! What can I do for you? How are you? I'm sorry, we're fully cast. You should've let me know sooner you were still acting. I'm fine. I'm terrific. It's all going very well indeed. No reason at all why we shouldn't. How's Adam? Ah. I see. Tomorrow night I can't. What about tonight? No present like the present. Well, come here to the flat. What time? Do you want to eat? Do you want to drink? What do you want to do? Well, I'm available. On a part-time basis. No, I know, I know. Of course I don't; I'm flattered. Easily. Gin, I'll see you here tonight about half past six. I'm not doing anything tonight, am I?'

'Nothing planned,' Wendy said.

'I've got scotch, I've got gin, I've got Campari, I've got vodka. Alternatively I can open a bottle of wine or we can go down the road to the Eight Bells.'

'Oh no, I don't want to do that. If you're really going to open some wine, I wouldn't mind a glass of wine.'

'So how are you really and what's going on?'

'Adam's been having an affair,' Virginia said. 'He went to America in August, you know, the usual annual pilgrimage, and I went down to this cottage we were supposed to be sharing with Dick Lucas and his family—'

'Dick Lucas! We did an interview two weeks ago. All his questions were answers and all my answers were questions. How did that go? With that terrible invisible wife of his.'

'They reneged at the last moment. I had to cope with the whole place myself; squalid beyond belief, no indoor loo, three kids, no running water.'

'Where was this place?'

'In the Camargue. My favourite. It belongs to Wyndham Brain, Basil's brother, but they're never there in August, because he does this summer school in Cuernavaca every year. So that was my holiday, boiled alive and harpooned every night by the biggest mosquitoes outside Sci-Fi. The only compensation, of course, was that at least we were in France. But so far from anywhere I only spoke about two words. *Combien* and *merci*. And while I was down there, with three children—and having to pump every drop of water by hand—while we were down there Adam goes and finds this twenty-four-year-old girl in New York. Not only is she beautiful, he also genuinely believes that she's a genius. What's more, he's probably right.'

'I see. Tell me, what does Wyndham Brain *do*?'

'Wyndham Brain? He's only one of the two or three finest copperplate etchers in the world. The house was filled with his things.'

'What sort of things?'

'Mostly people fucking,' Virginia said. 'He's the shyest, most withdrawn man I've ever met and his place is full of these highly explicit, remarkably beautiful erotic etchings. They really are quite extraordinary because they show absolutely everything there is to show and at the same time they have this fantastic tenderness about them. He's got a whole sequence of nothing but a man's head between a woman's legs and they're among the most memorable and touching things I've ever seen in my life. And his Lesbians are utterly heartbreaking. The longing and the anguish he manages to get into them is quite ravishing.'

'Didn't anyone come down and see you?'

'Someone was going to, but they never did in the end.'

'How very frustrating for you! With all those etchings to inspire you.'

'Jean-Claude and his boy-friend,' Virginia said. 'But in the end they went to Hammamet. Strangely enough I didn't find them erotic at all, in that sense, just terribly poignant, the etchings. Terribly *sunt lacrimae rerum*. Somehow it just showed how far you can go and how ultimately you haven't gone anywhere at all. The strange thing, I find, about the explicit is how sentimental it is. The erotic is man's most pathetic attempt to tunnel his way out of life. It's not in the least aphrodisiac.'

'It sounds quite aphrodisiac to me,' Daniel said.

'It may *sound* it, but that's to do with the speech, not the work itself.'

'How did the children react to them?'

'They hardly noticed. I don't think they even knew what they were.'

'*Tu dis*? And you didn't tell them? Spoilsport! Did you know about Adam while you were actually down there?'

'I always have my suspicions when he goes to New York. New York in August, after all. Why on earth would anyone go if he didn't hope for a bit more than a few awful air-conditioned lunches.'

'And Adam's particular bit turned out to be a genius, did she? Where does her genius lie exactly?'

'She's a film-maker,' Virginia said, 'and a poet.'

'And she's got tits like Israeli melons, fuck *her*, I can imagine. Oh Christ, Gin, you know I'm on your side.'

'You're hardly likely to be on Adam's, are you?'

'Meaning?'

'Nothing. Nothing. I'm sorry. It's not you. Don't think it's you. It's just that I've been holding it in for so long.'

'Poor love, don't worry. Let it out. Flood the place, don't be shy. Poor Gin. Come on, there's something about tears. I always propose to people when they cry.'

'Oh God, Danny. Life's so utterly stinking, and I thought it was going to be so marvellous, that's what hurts so much, when I married Adam.'

'Does he want to leave you? Does this girl want to marry him?'

'Marry him? She'd laugh in your face. She doesn't believe in marriage.'

'Then what's your problem? Apart from pain. He'll come back.'

'He hasn't gone yet,' Virginia said. 'Only she's coming over —'

'Her name isn't — hold it a second — it must be — where's that bloody programme? — Mary-Ellen Schwarz. Suggestive! My Christ, she isn't really black, is she?'

'Of course she's black.'

'God preserve us,' Daniel said, 'everybody's doing it. A black genius of twenty-four, looks like you really have got yourself a problem.'

472

'I've got three children and I'm forty next birthday and I don't know what I'm going to do.'

'It's hard to know where to go for laughs, I can see that. Have some more plonk. I hate calling it plonk. Why do we always use language we despise? Have some more of Dr Barolet's mixture. There. So, correct me if Gipsy Meyer is wrong but my guess is she's coming over next week because her film—here we are—*The Dark Tower*—Jesus Christ, well at least it can't be about Adam's if it's dark—*The Dark Tower*, and I quote, "threatens to be the sensation of the Festival". Threats, always threats. Here we go: "A poetic evocation full of ravishing ambiguity." You didn't write this, did you, Gin, by any chance? "A dope pusher, who turns out to be a saint, Lennox Avenue on the day of Malcolm X's murder, corrupt policemen and virgin hookers, the final disintegration of a Jewish liberal lawyer, imagine how trite these ingredients could be and how distasteful in the hands of anything less than a Mary-Ellen Schwarz! If it is too soon to call her a genius, it is never too early to recognize a truly original, compassionate yet defiantly uncorrupted talent. If the similarities with the story of the Passion are never absent, they are never crudely emphasized. The comparison with Ensor's *Entry Of Christ Into Brussels* may seem too obvious but *The Dark Tower* has the right to be measured against the highest standards. Not to be missed." Well! Cheer up, if that doesn't kill it stone dead, nothing will.'

'Norbert's going to publish a full variorum edition of the script and a detailed diary of the shooting. He agrees she's a genius.'

'Oh. Well, that's it then. I suppose you went and recommended the manuscript.'

'Yes, I did as a matter of fact. Wholeheartedly. I think she *is* a genius.'

'In which case I doubt if she'll stay with Adam for too long.'

'Thanks,' Virginia said.

'One genius at a time, surely. Does she want him to go away with her or what?'

'She believes in freedom. She doesn't believe in making claims on people. She believes in them being free.'

'I thought you believed in the same thing. I thought we all did.'

'I do, but I happen to have three children and I'm going to be forty. What chance have I got of being free?'

'What the hell did you recommend it for? You are a bloody masochist.'

'That may be, but I do happen to have certain standards. It's the only thing I do have. I'd sooner die than spurn something I believe in. It's all I've got to hold on to, a certain moral integrity.'

'You could always kill her. That'd be an ironic blow for freedom. I suppose she'd only go and rise on the third day and sit on the left hand of Norbert Ash. He's sitting on the right one himself, of course, which is why he can never pay you what he owes you. I didn't know he was interested in film books.'

'He's interested in quality, whatever its provenance. There isn't that much of it.'

'Well, what does Adam say he's going to do?'

'He'll do whatever she says,' Virginia said. 'She's beautiful.'

'Well, what would you like me to do?'

'I don't want anybody to do anything. There isn't anything anyone can do. She's right. Women are prisoners. Virgin tarts, I must say I do think it's a dazzlingly brilliant image.'

'Forgive me, but when the brilliance has ceased to dazzle, what is a virgin tart and how, to put it bluntly, does she make a living?'

'She sucks, and she gets buggered,' Virginia said.

'Got it,' Daniel said. 'Silly of me not to realize. Highly literal, highly brilliant and also a stock figure from pornography from the year dot, if not sooner.'

'It's impossible to judge genius without seeing it,' Virginia said. 'The point she's making goes beyond porn. It's transcendental. She's talking about the position of women, their denial of their own true sexuality and their place as commodities and fetishes. One of them loves the pusher and there's a scene where she licks his feet. His feet are dirty, filthy, disgusting, and she licks them clean. It's the most moving thing I've ever seen.'

474

'You've seen it yourself, have you, the movie?'

'I've read a very full account. And there are illustrations.'

'It sounds like all it needs is a homosexual drug addict and it'll get four stars from everyone except the *Morning Star*,' Daniel said. 'In other words, a load of pretentious garbage.'

'She's also written the music and the lyrics,' Virginia said. 'Which are probably only going to make her a fortune and which are truly some of the most original I've ever heard.'

'Fuck her,' Daniel said. 'In spades. She does go it a bit. Rich as well as famous. You seem to have got yourself quite a rival. Gin, do you honestly think Adam's going to give up you and his children for the sake of this chick? So he's very high on her at the moment. But these things happen, for Christ's sake, surely. You haven't been faithful to him for the last fifteen years, have you, non-stop?'

'You don't understand, Daniel. What she's doing—what she's done—she's completely altered his whole—his whole—'

'Not his whole consciousness, not that.'

'But she has. She has. It's not just a question of his having an affair, not even just a question of his being in love with her. Because let's be honest, that doesn't usually mean more than a man's fed up with his present setup or he's so besotted he has to say it's something more than sex to justify it. What Adam loves isn't just her body, it's not even her mind, in the ordinary way, it's her whole idea. What I mean is, even when the thing breaks up or when she finds someone else or whatever happens, I'm never going to get him back. He's never going to accept our sort of life again.'

'Do you really want him that badly, Gin? Forgive me, but—jealousy's a hell of a powerful thing. And when it ceases to operate, or if it hadn't started in the first place—put it this way, did you really miss him that much in the Camargue?'

'Having to pump every single drop of water myself?'

'Apart from his qualities as a draught horse. Haven't you always secretly hankered after freedom?'

'I married him because I loved him. I had his children because

I assumed that we were one flesh. I don't pretend that I ever expected either of us to remain technically faithful right through our lives. That sort of expectation is completely alien to anyone of intelligence, both because it's —'

'Darling, spare me a potted history of Bloomsbury. All this ambition of yours, all this literary high-flying —'

'Don't make it sound cheap and facetious, Daniel. I happen to care passionately about books. I always have.'

'A man is judged by the books he keeps, I know. Oh come on, Gin, you've always fancied a bit on the side.'

'This is more than on the side. I admit I have some sympathy for the French convention —'

'Two up and three to play,' Daniel said.

'I'm perfectly willing to accept that adultery is a part of married life. All right, I've sometimes been tempted myself, I may even have fallen once or twice, but this is something completely different. Adam finds our relationship irrelevant.'

'He doesn't even pay you the compliment of deceiving you, you mean, or pretending that he's so passionately in love that you'll simply have to understand — he's not playing the game. He's not flattering you enough.'

'No, he isn't and if you think I'm being a fool to want him to, you may be right, but I can't help it. I'm too old to change. As far as he's concerned, our relationship is irrelevant, anachronistic, whether it's good or not. Whatever I've thought, I never thought he'd — he'd be, well, converted. That's what she's done to him. It's like a religion. She's gone and converted him. I could even imagine him killing himself.'

'Converted him to what? He won't kill himself. Converted him to what?'

'You see, she goes further than Women's Lib —'

'It was only a matter of time before something did.'

'She just believes in Lib pure and simple and of course she's right. It's mere female chauvinism —'

'Oh lovely, at last.' Daniel said. 'I'm beginning to be converted myself.'

476

'Imagining that it's only women who have to be liberated. The liberation of the oppressors is just as important. You get this in Fanon, it's hinted at in Fanon where he talks about the neuroses of the torturers, with quite bewitching insight and compassion. I think it's one of the most deeply imaginative things in modern polemics. Do you know the passage? Well, Mary-Ellen's point is that men are suffering from just as bad neuroses as a result of their repression of women and they need to be understood and relieved as much as we do. It's an enormous intuitive leap for a girl of twenty-four, you must admit. Adam's talking of giving up the agency and I just can't honestly find any arguments against him. You see, I find I agree with most of his basic contentions. Except I don't know how we're going to go on sending the children to Dartington.'

'That does make it a bit of a bugger, I must say. What's he thinking of doing instead?'

'Nothing, at least for a while. Absolutely nothing. He wants to give everything up and be completely open.'

'A Black Mountain Man. And what about Mary-Ellen, is she going to be open alongside him?'

'It's not funny, Daniel. He's right. She's right. They're right.'

'Leaving very little room, of course, for you and me to be anything but wrong,' Daniel said. 'It can't last, Gin, it just can't. I can assure you that Adam will never be able to do absolutely nothing for more than most of a Monday morning. He comes from the most ambitious and competitive generation of carnivores ever to graduate with first-class honours from the Fens. If you suppose that he'll be able to endure sitting by the roadside watching the rest of the traffic whizz past for more than a few minutes, it's only because you've allowed yourself to be panicked stupid. Adam is not the stuff half-nak'd fakirs are made of.'

'Half what?'

'Naked. I met a woman in the summer who said nak'd for naked. Isn't it lovely? I thought it was lovely. I really fell in love with her because of it.'

'I thought you spent the summer with Nancy Lane.'

'I did, but I met this woman all the same.'

'Talented you. And had an affair with her?'

'Yes, as a matter of fact, but only for fun. Sex, not an affair exactly. She was older than me.'

'Oh well, there you are. You are an incredible man. What about Nancy? The last thing I heard you were going to get married. Is that off?'

'I'm not sure. I still see her. I'm seeing her tomorrow. We don't live together but we still see each other.'

'Sounds like the basis for a perfect relationship. Have you ever lost anyone to an idea, Daniel, to a religion, to a gospel?'

'Virginia, I promise you you and Adam will live to see your grandchildren—together.'

'You don't understand, Daniel. I'm intellectually too proud to want him back, if I'm satisfied—'

'He hasn't gone and you don't want him back and actually I do understand very well. The thing being you can't bear him to go either.'

'What I can't bear is that I've wasted my life.'

'Honey, we've all wasted our lives. That's what lives are for. There's very little else to be done with them. Who's looking after the children?'

'We've got quite a good German girl. They're all right.'

'The basis of modern middle-class life always turns out to be quite a good German girl. *O tempora, O herrenvolk.* Why don't you write a book?'

'I couldn't. Now? When I'm just completely upside down?'

'Poor Virginia. Poor, poor Virginia. You know, I'm sorry to say this, but I still think this is just a case of jealousy *à la mode*. Even possibly *avant la lettre*. Are you sure he's actually even threaded this girl?'

'Positive, but that's not the point. The point is, she's right: we do need a completely new sort of world. A completely new attitude. We do need to stop everything and start again. It's true. And yet all I can think of is, if it goes on, I shall kill myself.'

'Why is it that the first sign of a new morality is always a rash

478

of suicides? Don't answer because I can't follow all the French quotations, but it does seem silly. What ever went wrong with Jean-Claude?'

'Wrong? Nothing.'

'I thought you and he were —'

'He's homosexual,' Virginia said. 'I always knew that.'

'Ah,' Daniel said. '*École Anormale Supérieure*. You could have fooled me all the same.'

'Surely you realized? I knew the moment I saw him. Which doesn't mean that he didn't teach me a great deal. He's got an absolutely first class logical French mind. Ice cold and crystal clear.'

'Sounds as if he ought to be declared *d'interêt public*. Like mineral water.'

'I think there's a lot to be learnt from homosexuals.'

'*A Public Life*'s down the King's Road this week. The unending, unbending story of Billy Stern, moralist. I can hardly wait. It's a curious thing about those despised and rejected of men, they always have to go and turn out to be the head of the corner. Either you're down or you're up. One minute we're pissing on them, the next we're licking their goddam feet among other choice parts. It's a thesis and antithesis world all right.'

'I sometimes think perhaps they're the only people who lead a truly adult life,' Virginia said.

'Oh my Christ, you've been reading *Sight And Sound*. Truly adult balls.'

'Do you know, I honestly thought you'd agree with me?'

'Honey, it's not all true what they say about Dixie.'

'Because there's no false sentiment between them. No regrets. No family ties. No compromises for the sake of the children.'

'They *are* the bloody children. Do you know what Billy Stern used to do in the days I worked with him? Never mind. He used to stand in the window of his house and scream at the neighbours. He used to stand and yell at them over the wall. Like an angry little boy. They hadn't necessarily done anything, he was just so steamed up he didn't care where or how he let it go. Is that being truly adult? Is it fuck! Talk about men having the spittoon idea of women, people like Billy have the spittoon idea of the whole bloody world. Truly adult!'

'To tell you the truth, I always think of you leading a life that's basically no different from theirs. That's not a criticism.'

'It's not a criticism, it's a slander. I'll give you just thirty writs to withdraw it. If you think I imagine all my women with spouts on them, you're a long way from the truth. I like women. I'm a sucker for women. O.K., but I am. If I weren't I'd be a dedicated director like Billy is, instead of a conscience-wracked skidzo. You were talking about Nancy. Well, I'll tell you, the main problem between us, when it comes down to it, is that she doesn't want to have any more children. And I can't see the point in marrying if one doesn't have children.'

'You spit in the hope that sooner or later something'll grow out of it, is that it?'

'I want a life,' Daniel said. 'I need a life. Otherwise it's the classic repertory: *Death In Venice* followed by *Dorian Gray* and a late night showing of *Umberto D*. I want to see something grow. Maybe it's vanity, but it's also genuine. Also I want very much, believe it or not, to find something to be faithful to.'

'Even if it has to be a woman.'

'Christ, you really do sound like a convert. You've got that patient, dedicated gleam in your eye, like the Eddystone Lighthouse on a rough night.'

'I'm not accusing you of anything, Danny, you do realize that? Surely we're past thinking of homosexuality as any sort of stigma?'

'Stigma or no, it's actually true that I've never had a homosexual experience in my life,' Daniel said. 'Probably why I hated my school so much.'

'I'm just trying to see the direction things are going. And I am firmly of the view that we're about to see a growing homosexualization of morals. Unisexual morality if you like. Not that it's going to be much help to me.'

'You know one thing which is uncontestably empirically

verifiable and therefore not prejudice, racial or otherwise? These black girls don't weather all that well. They tend to get a bit flaccid here and there. Flummety, Byron called it, of a particular region.'

'She's got nearly twenty years in hand,' Virginia said. 'And anyway, that's not the real issue. The fact is, we've all accepted a morality of bits and pieces, we never really had the courage to think things through to the point that Mary-Ellen has reached. What she accepts, and what she believes we shall have all of us to accept in the end, is the corollary of the old proposition that we all die alone. We all live alone too. And to be truly adult we have to base our morality on the uncompromising acceptance of that premise. Only when we've faced our utter, logically irreversible loneliness can we even begin to give each other comfort or company.'

'But who, as we used to say in philosophy, isn't perfectly well aware of this already? What're we saying here except the old existential bit about life being contingent? We make pacts and we break them, but that doesn't mean we don't sometimes keep them. We can't be sure that people will always keep their word but a surprising number do.'

'What we've done, all of us, is look at the problem, analyse it correctly and then proceed to live by the old false answers. We haven't honoured our own intellectual perceptions, the essential *trahison des clercs*. At the first whiff of loneliness we all bolted for the sanctuary of a double bed like frightened mice. Except you, Danny, and you seem to be *plus bourgeois que la bourgeoisie* all of a sudden. I suppose it's all this money you're making.'

'Oh my dear, I shall probably be off the picture by the time Mary-Ellen's been discovered.'

'What're these for?'

'That's one of my fever charts. That's the form of the film I'm about to make. *The Big One*. Those are the climaxes and those are the scenes leading up to them. In that way I can examine the balance. These are the characters, when they're in and when they're out. It's rather a complicated plot with a good number of leading players. I have to be sure they're kept in the audience's eye often enough to be remembered.'

'I had no idea it was so formal. It's practically like a set of sociological statistics.'

'This is the bare bones of the plot, with all the clues marked out,' Daniel said. 'That way, if we cut a scene I can tell at a glance what vital information has to be fed in elsewhere. The essence of public fiction being that it must play fair. The beauty of the big movie is that it's never critical. It doesn't have references outside itself. Do I make myself obscure? I'm going down to talk to some undergraduates—sorry, students—next week, so I must work myself into the right pedagogical lather.'

'I should never have had children,' Virginia said. 'We all galloped into families too quickly and too unthinkingly. We were so keen to be responsible. It was all that rather forced maturity worship that came out of Downing. We were in much too great a hurry to be mature. There's time enough to be mature when you can't be anything else.'

'Look, I'm going to have some baked beans and another bottle of wine and some garlic sausage. Do you want some?'

'I should go,' Virginia said. 'What nationality was this woman who said nak'd?'

'Greek. She was going round with Princess Astrid, if you've ever heard of her.'

'And you really slept with her because she said nak'd?'

'It was all rather a joke, but yes, I did. It was very enjoyable.'

'No one's ever slept with me as a joke.'

'It was great. The next day I broke my blasted finger. Who says there isn't a God?'

'I must say Victor made us laugh about that.'

'Oh, it was a riot.'

'Meredith's got a piece in next week, in the colour supp, did you know, about Greece?'

'If he puts in about my finger, I'll sue him.'

'One thing I do respect about Meredith, he does research his stuff. Politically he may be a backwoodsman, but he doesn't

482

talk about anything he hasn't experienced personally. That's the strength of his fiction.'

'And its weakness, of course. Are you feeling better?'

'Daniel, please don't.'

'Oh come on, Gin, I'm fond of you. You know I am. I always have been. I've always liked your mouth. It's sort of hot and airless, like the Paris metro.'

'You're the most external man I've ever known. You think of everything as landscape. You're a traveller, not a resident. I don't remember who first made that distinction between people, but I think it's enormously valid, don't you?'

'And you, my dear Gin, what are you but one of nature's critics — forever marking everyone out of ten? I suppose it's the French thing again, there's something of the Jansenist in you, trying to be satisfied by being a Janeite and never quite succeeding. I'm not attacking you. You ought to be living in the Landes, in a great shuttered *domaine* surrounded by unpruned vines and with some lunatic aunt shut up somewhere in an outhouse. You try valiantly to be a Londoner and a free woman, but your heart's not in it. You need to be plugged into some majestic metaphysic complete with promises of glory and doom.'

'My family were Huguenots,' Virginia said. 'What I like about you, Danny, is you're so full of fantasy. One never comes to the end of you. Or the centre. Like Los Angeles. Is there one?'

'Solutions are always a bore. Questions generally provide the most interesting answers. Perhaps I'm the one who ought to be living in the Landes, but you know, I don't believe I have the passion. You could fill your days with meaningful rage and terrible silence, but I couldn't. I should soon begin to wonder what the hell I was doing wasting my time. Unless, of course, I could find an enemy sufficiently resourceful, but sufficiently witty with it, to provide an eternal balance of forces. Like a wife. Then the game would be to guess who would murder whom, but like Cambridge philosophers, we should have to be careful to exhaust all the other possible moves before coming to the final crunch. I've never found anybody I could play that game with, for real, with that mixture of hatred and admiration I really want.'

'I thought I'd found everything I wanted in Adam, I still think so. He's bright, he's ambitious, he's very sensual—'

'I can imagine that—'

'He was rather repressed when I first met him. I felt I knew more than he did. He wanted me, but he also wanted *it*, terribly. When we were first together, I recognized that. I never imagined it was just me who excited him. That was what excited me, to feel all that desire, all that longing to fuck the whole world, and have him channel it all into me. I know it's supposed to be degrading to be a man's spittoon and all that, and I can see how a narrow person can be disgusted, because it is disgust they're talking about. But I don't agree. I loved all that uncontrollable spurting. I knew it couldn't just be me he felt so—so strongly about, if you like— do you mind me talking like this?—but I didn't mind, you know.'

'It's what such a night as this is made for.'

'I felt the whole power of life in him, the whole force of nature. I honestly think it was just a kind of silly petty egotism which made me—women always do it in the end, when they want to hurt someone—'

'What?'

'Oh, reproach him. I told him, just for revenge, after he'd first been unfaithful to me, that sometimes he disgusted me. You know he had a big affair with Cathie Connolly when she first came to London—'

'When she was playing in *The Fair Colleen* at the Adelphi.'

'She was never an actress. Cathie?'

'Was she ever anything else? I was romancing, Gin, as usual. I didn't know actually, though I realize now, of course. Sorry. Go on.'

'I said I was tired of being used, this was when he'd finally come back to me because, well, because of all sorts of things. I said I hated the way he never considered whether I wanted to fuck or not. Make love I said actually, of course, because that was the way we talked ten years ago—'

'Ten years ago!'

'Didn't you know really? I thought everyone knew. The way you men talk.'

'Married men don't talk to bachelors—isn't that a funny word? —and bachelors don't question married men. It's like Catholics and Protestants. There is a bit of communication between Jews of the two persuasions, but not much. Society is highly secular these days, Gin, you know that. There are only the two main faiths: the married and the unmarried.'

'When I think of when we were happiest together, it was when we could be talking and then stop and fuck and then go on talking again afterwards as if absolutely nothing had happened. The worst thing that happens in marriage, in my experience, is when you start trying to make everything tie in with everything else. I'm not hostile to marriage. I'm glad I married Adam. The mistake I made was trying to improve on the imperfect state of our relationship. In relationships, the imperfections are what make them last. I liked him best when I was the means of his expressing his sex, not just the—the partner in it. Partnership, I mean that's an expression from business, really, isn't it? One goes into partnership with a view to profit. It's not a real form of life at all. I shamed him, I bullied him, secretly hoping perhaps that he'd fight back—that's why you made me think of it, talking of your battle in the farmhouse in the Landes—and all I did was go on trying to wish maturity on to us, sense, responsibility. He believed I was right, he believed I was cleverer than he was and all the time I was longing for him to shut me up. I liked him best when he'd take me whether I wanted it or not, even whether I enjoyed it or not. I sometimes did hate him for it, resent it anyway, but at least I knew I hadn't killed him. Deep in my being, I rejoiced in that at least, that I hadn't killed him, that he was still only showing his force in me when he could have shown it in a thousand women, in a thousand ways. I feel powerless now because not only logically, but in my sense of the world as a whole, in my natural conscience you might say, I believe he's right. It's not a narrow intellectual view. I feel it in my whole being; I'm no good to him any more. Our desire

has to be kindled now as if we were conspirators, deep in the basement of a damp house. We fiddle with the works and eventually
the thing starts to burn and then we huddle round it and take
what warmth we can. Before, he was the man, he just came and
he was hot and that was it. Or I was hot and that excited him, but
not because I wanted him, I'm positive of it, because I wanted *it*.
Because I was alive and he'd rise to me. It's only vanity, our damned
conscious, Cambridge vanity, with all its silly reliance on what's
said, what's reasonable, what's civilized, that's killed us both
and made us fiddle about in the cellar every time we want to
warm ourselves. I killed him, he's right to want out. If I wasn't
forty, I'd want out myself, and if I didn't have children to
see through school. God, I hate them sometimes.'

'No you don't. You're just sticking pins in yourself.'

'I hate them. I've known ever since I first had them that they
were a consolation, not a form of life. That's what women who
are vain about their children are always thinking, secretly. Have
you read Bettelheim's *The Children of the Dream*? You really should.
I always think that those who deride sociology or the possibility
of insight through the collation and observation of fact really
ought to read him. You've heard of him, of course?'

'Of course.'

'Because what he says — you'll make me drunk. I shall fall asleep.
He says that the kibbutz was basically intended to be a form of
life for people who weren't going to have children. The idealization
of the communal nursery and so on only came later, because
children came and were rather an embarrassment. The idea of a
serious life was a life without the tedium of child-rearing. Having
children is a confession, really, that adult life won't do. It's unnatural,
but as soon as we concede this, as soon as women begin to have
separate lives, it's not just that they're being mothers, they're
also being children again, and they're banking something in
the way of affection, even of interest, which they know the men
may not give them in the future. The real trauma from the Oedipus
complex is inflicted on the father. After all, in the story, he was the
one who died first. In life, he doesn't die, of course, he just withers

486

away. He dies for the woman, and the child, impotent and craving, is the one who replaces him. Because the child is gelded, he's eternally dependent, eternally devoted, eternally hooked and eternally unsatisfactory. I *knew*, Daniel, I *knew*, as soon as I began to think of my children and the comfort of my old age, that Adam would go elsewhere. It wasn't a reaction, it was a terrible example of—'

'Your old friend the Cassandra complex. You really should have been part of the spoils of war.'

'Also my tits are too small,' Virginia said. 'I think I thought at least when I was pregnant my tits would be bigger and Adam would at least like that. You know, the women's libbers make a lot of men's conditioned horror at the facts of menstruation, when that's not my experience. In Cambridge, Adam and I used to fuck whether I had the curse or not. You can't expect a man of twenty which, after all, is the period of maximum male potency, you can't expect him to hum to himself for four or five days, he doesn't have the patience. I didn't mind. We used to go straight ahead and God knows I never found he minded. Blood on one's penis seems to be quite a triumphant sign to some men, if I'm any judge—'

'If you're not, I don't know who is.'

'To you! Certainly it never worried Adam. I mean, think how many men like the idea of anal intercourse—'

'Gin, you put things so nicely. You make it sound like Euclid.'

'Well, don't they? And why not? I don't blame them. The Incas, and all the Indian tribes along the Pacific littoral, used to make a practice of anal and oral intercourse, I mean they made a positive art of it, and there's no evidence that they were any more degenerate or corrupt than we are. The Spaniards taught them our morals, didn't they? Have you seen any of the erotic sculpture of the tribes I'm talking about? You should.'

'I must.'

'It's not pornographic, that's the amazing thing. It's very touching and personal—'

'Like Wyndham Brain's etchings.'

'Astonishingly so. It's extremely explicit and quite un--what?--undidactic, unproselytizing. It doesn't advertise, it merely, well, *revels* I think is the best word.'

'In that case, I'm sure it is.'

'The thing about Adam when I first knew him was that the whole body appealed to him.'

'Like a French *charcutier*,' Daniel said. 'There isn't a bit of the animal he can't make delicious.'

'One gave oneself to him with absolute confidence. Of course one's intellect did come into it. One knew that when he'd finished making love one wouldn't find oneself strangled because he'd want to go on talking about Proust or Baudelaire or Eliot's *Quartets*.'

'A short menu but a classy one, *à l'époque*. You think he might have killed you otherwise?'

'No, he wouldn't have been himself and I wouldn't have wanted him, certainly not permanently. One's sense of continuity was an intellectual matter, that's what I'm saying. Sexually, one lived from hand to mouth.'

'To name but a few.'

'And that was the wonderful thing about it. The sense of absolute shamelessness. Absolute shamelessness in lovers is what absolute honesty is in argument. It's a deadly mistake to confuse the two and that's exactly what modern morality is leading us to do—'

'Savage disaster lies ahead.'

'I believe it does, Daniel. Who said that?'

'Lawrence, D. H. Some essay.'

'I believe we were monogamous because we were basically so completely promiscuous.'

'*Spiegatemi, prego.*'

'It didn't actually matter who we had, everyone was only an example of the whole of the rest of humanity. *Multum in parvo.* One accepted the single instance because it was easier than trying to grab the lot, but it wasn't basically any different. Our marriages were monogamous on intellectual, not moral grounds. I believe we were genuinely more interested in minds than bodies. The bodies were there and we loved them, but we could have loved another body if it had been attached to a sufficiently delectable mind. I didn't have Adam in bed with me, I had a man. Adam came later.'

'Like a true gentleman.'

'Not always, not in that sense, far from it. But you know, I even liked that, when he came too soon? One could always wait—'

'The tubes ran more regularly in those days.'

'I never minded, until later. Until I didn't—until I wanted to revenge myself. But what I was going to say was about this menstruation thing, what I found was that Adam wasn't at all worried about blood. Sometimes he bit me to draw blood, very nearly anyway. I used to wear high-necked dresses when I went home for the vacs sometimes because I had such marks on my neck. He loved to bite. He loved to do all sorts of things I won't tell you.'

'All lovers do.'

'Oh Daniel, you're so nice to talk to. You're so wise.'

'Darling, go on believing that.'

'What he really reacted to was when I first started to leak. When I first began to secrete milk. He couldn't bear it when my nightie was wet or when I dripped on his chest, it absolutely disgusted him. And of course it's not difficult to see why. It was the first part of my body that wasn't there for his pleasure. It was the promise that I was getting old.'

'Give me a hundred words or so on that point. I'm not quite there!'

'A woman who starts a baby is starting to get old. It's the next stage after youth. After the maiden, the matron. You get this distinction very clearly drawn in primitive societies. Read Lévi-Strauss. You see, it seems as if the woman is getting what she wants. Most men think this is what they think when their wives start talking about babies, but I don't agree. What men realize, subconsciously—'

'Where else?'

'Is that the woman has lost confidence in her ability to hold him by the power of his desire alone. She wants to take something from him, like men do a lock of hair, or used to, before it's too late. And talking about before it's too late means that it's already late enough.'

'Italian lovers still exchange locks of pubic hair, did you know that?'

'Byron and Teresa Guiccioli. And of course there's an interesting connection here between Byron and men like Christie.'

'Christie.'

'The murderer. *Ten Rillington Place*.'

'One of the most disgusting films ever made.'

'I didn't see it. Christie collected the pubic hair of his victims, didn't he, in tobacco tins?'

'Not to smoke, I trust.'

'And after all, there is a sort of line between Byron, the arch romantic, with all his drinking out of skulls and that kind of fetishistic necrophilia, and Christie who actually snipped mementoes from his dead victims. Also—'

'Oh Virginia, you are sweet.'

'Sweet?'

'Such enthusiasm. You're a force of nature. You have the most virile brain I've ever met. You suffer from acute Priapism of the mind. You only have to meet an idea, however fleetingly, and you immediately have the most enormous erection. It's lovely, I mean it.'

'There is a sort of connection between the Byronic search for ultimate experience and the necrophilia of a man like Christie. Christie is Byron without the genius's talent for metaphor. Christie is the literal-minded dreamer, the petty-bourgeois romantic. He was an auxiliary policeman where Byron was an auxiliary revolutionary. Both had dreams about mastering the world, both were caught between ideas of service and ideas of omnipotence. And Byron—'

'Oh darling, if only I had shorthand.'

'Dressing in shrouds, this isn't a very great exaggeration—'

'I know, I know.'

490

'He was obviously dreading the death he also couldn't help flirting with. His Don Juanism and the homosexuality Wilson Knight talks about are all part of the same pattern, the fear of impotence and the longing for peace. Personally, I have no doubt that he was virtually impotent at the end of the Teresa Guiccioli business, which was why he felt himself to be ready for martyrdom. All his life he'd been waiting for the punishment which his sexual prodigality promised him. The Calvinist background comes in here. There's a strong connection, in my view, between his flirtation with avarice—you remember—and his sense of loss, in the sexual sense. I think he hated women partly because they took the vital fluid from him and he flirted with the idea, for a time, that money could replace it. That was his Agony In The Garden. He managed to push temptation aside and went on to his death. That's part of what Wilson Knight ought to mean by talking of his Christian Virtues. He didn't actually have Christian virtues in that sense. He was a sort of Christ, which is staggeringly different. A Christ who had balls and genitals. You remember what Dumas *fils* said?'

'Not *all* of it,' Daniel said.

'When he said that the thing that enabled Christianity to conquer the world, the thing which gave it its ultimate force, was the fact that Christ was a virgin born of a virgin. Without that, he said, Christianity would never have caught the imagination or held the respect of the world. Of course, he had particular reasons for that view. He was an extraordinary moralist, the younger Dumas, for obvious reasons, illegitimacy, the enormous power of his father—'

'All Jesus's problems!'

'Quite a few of them. But Byron somehow disproves that thesis, because of all the figures of the last five hundred years, Byron has the most powerful hold on our imaginations. In many ways, his myth—the allegory his life embodied—is more credible as a diagram of the human predicament than Jesus ever was. Why did women love him? They talk a lot about his looks, but I think it was precisely his bisexual nature which made him so compelling. What is the favourite male fantasy, do you know?'

'You sound like you do. It makes me nervous. What?'

'No, tell me what you think.'

'To be fucking at one end and winning the Nobel Prize at the other all at the same time.'

'I think it's coming between two Lesbians.'

'I'll buy that. I'd go further though—'

'I intend to. Because there's another fantasy involved. It's this: what he wants is to convert the two Lesbians from attending to each other to attending to him. They must admit the supremacy of the male member, but at the same time—'

'The Nobel Prize?'

'He dreams of being a woman too. He imagines them welcoming him as one of themselves. That's the supreme honour, the supreme satisfaction, the supreme act of possession. Going on from there, of course—'

'Oh no, Gin, haven't you really done enough? What do you want beyond a starred first with oak leaves and your own late-night show?'

'Byron's attraction lay in the feeling which women had, the corresponding fantasy that they could win him over conclusively to heterosexuality. They instinctively guessed, sensed that he was unreliable, ambivalent, not emotionally, but sexually, in his deepest being. That was why he challenged them at the very base of *their* sexual being and excited them also because, at a time when women were just beginning to be interested in themselves as women, just beginning to feel the desire for emancipation, he also promised, threatened, if you like, to make men out of them. Now consider why he married Annabella. Can't you see it? He always referred to her as the Princess of Parallelograms and every-one always assumes that this was a sign of how he despised her, that it was mere ironic depreciation; no one realizes how much more thrilling the truth is. He recognized something in her which was desperately attractive, which blew his mind, as they say nowadays, and he tried to bring it off in the context of what seemed a publicly desirable marriage. He tried to find a peaceful, dependable cover for what would have been the supremely ironic and supremely satisfactory event of his life. The supreme act of duplicity. He recognized in Annabella the masculinity which all her intellectual accomplishments, all her emancipated talents, seemed to him to be announcing from the housetops. *She wanted to be a man.* And he wanted her to be, he wanted to assist her, under the guise of propriety, to achieve the dream they both had. He would be married, and thus safe, but to a man, the perfect secret revenge for a secret revolutionary who was also a snob and a member of the British peerage, and equally she would have what he knew in his brilliant heart that she wanted. Now, by way of confirmation, what happened when they actually did marry? Sexually, he behaved outrageously. He forced himself on her. His assumptions ran so far ahead of the fact that he credited her with the wish to live out the fantasies he so clearly perceived latent within her. He completely underrated the force of the superego because he himself, deprived of a father almost from birth, simply didn't have one. It never occurred to him that, even when licensed by public ceremony, she might flinch from her own real desires. You'll remember that before the actual ceremony took place they had a mock wedding up in Yorkshire and the bride was actually a man, they had a sort of camp rehearsal. I ask you, what could be more utterly suggestive and even revealing? It was practically a proclamation. We are told that Byron was full of doubts, but perhaps fears would be more to the point. He longed for the wedding and feared that Annabella wouldn't come up to his dreams. You see, and this is where this is so relevant to the present, he knew, because he was a genius, that he could never say anything to her about it. He could only act. And she had to respond or fail. There was no possibility of explanation. Either she could do it and would do it, or not.'

'He cast her like an old Hollywood mogul,' Daniel said. 'One look and bang, she was in.'

'Exactly. He wasn't apprehensive of the marriage as a public event, he was so excited by what it ought to be sexually that he was in a blue funk in case it wasn't. And when it wasn't, he was furious. He was furious, I do believe, cheated above all because

493

of Annabella's hypocrisy. He knew her nature, as a poet always knows these things. He knew what she really wanted and he hated her, not because she wouldn't give him what he wanted but because she wouldn't take from him what he knew, *knew* that she really wanted. You may remember that one of the things of which she accused him, the main thing according to some people which justified her leaving him, was buggery. She said that he insisted when she was pregnant, on having anal intercourse.'

'P to Q3,' Daniel said. 'A well-known opening.'

'It was what he knew she was ultimately waiting for. It was his real gift of liberation to her and her damned Christian conscience refused to allow her to enjoy what he knew she wanted. Imagine his frustration! He hated her, but never without a countervailing desire to have her back, because in a way he knew that they were perfectly suited. He was never happy again. The Guiccioli was much too feminine, too conventional in every way, to satisfy him. She drained the last of his virility, precisely because she didn't fit his fantasy and so gave him no true satisfaction. Annabella was the absolutely right choice for a bride. He never, before or after, found anyone who could have played the bisexual game so perfectly. She could have cheated society, just as he did with a lordship in which he never truly believed, they could have camped together forever, with a perfect balance. Lord Randolph forgot Goschen; Byron forgot the superego. Imagine how disgusted he must have been when she wilfully frustrated his greatest intuitive insight. When he went to take her anally he must have thought he was offering her the supreme fulfilment of her life. And for a long time afterwards he still believed she might come back to him. Why? Conventional fidelity to a man one had married? *Au contraire*, convention dictated they stay apart. He still dreamed of releasing her deepest being and she obstinately remained false to it. His life was a vulgar shambles forever afterwards, Venice and that boring Guiccioli and the pretty boys at Missolonghi, with whom, if I'm right, he never had any sexual connection. Annabella was the supreme moment and she failed him. And herself. Imagine.'

494

'It makes you think,' Daniel said. 'On the other hand, of course, he did, so to speak, Mr Chairman, want to have it both ways.'

'They could have, they really could have. God again,' Virginia said.

'You blame her, do you, my boy?' Daniel said.

'You remember what Freud said, about every relationship really being a relationship between four people? Well, the perfect marriage is one where there are four people in the bed at the same time. When one and one makes four. That's what Byron saw was possible between him and Annabella. He never had the chance again. He went back to deception and playacting. He proposed marriage, seriously, only once and that was with Annabella. His instinct told him that she was the only one, out of the hundreds he went to bed with, with whom he could have made a foursome.'

'You ought to go back and do a Ph.D. I've always thought you'd have been much happier if you'd been called Doctor. And it too, of course, has the nice element of being a bisexual term. How many comedies have begun with Doctor X turning out to be a woman.'

'I don't want to be in a comedy,' Virginia said.

'They're not really making much else,' Daniel said. 'Unless you want to be in a caper. And the women never count for much in a caper. Furthermore—'

'My tits are too small,' Virginia said. 'I know.'

'Unless you want to be the dykey one. The only artistic thing about the caper is that it deals with the point one per cent of humanity who actually do things.'

'Well, of course, not everyone would agree with you any more that Art is the apotheosis of the atypical.'

'Surely you're not going to provide advance publicity for the new banality, Gin? Let's at least glory in being anachronisms. You exaggerate the importance of tits.'

'No, I don't.'

'Didn't you know that arses are now the big things?'

'*Plus ça change*,' Virginia said. 'Frankly.'

'Gin, are you going to stop the night?'

'Do you always ask people just like that? I don't remember when anyone ever asked me just like that.'

'I mean it quite literally, that's all. You can if you want to. Only I've got a meeting in the morning and quite honestly I've enjoyed this evening enormously, but I've got to look lively in the morning, otherwise they'll think I'm past it.'

'You mean you've got a spare room?'

'Well, you can sleep on the couch if you want to. Or you can sleep with me. Just as you please.'

'You are sweet. You really are. I think it's the nicest thing anyone's ever suggested. *Ma nuit chez Daniel*. Did you ever see that movie?'

'What's that, the drag version of—'

'No, I meant that. *Chez Maud*. I'd like to sleep with you very much.'

'We can still go on talking that way, can't we? Do you want to have a bath?'

'Yes, thank you. I would. I've never gone on the pill. I'm only telling you in case, you know. I haven't actually got anything with me at all. You can see how innocent I meant this evening to be.'

'Well, that's one interpretation. Anyway, I take the point.'

'What I mean is, I genuinely didn't intend to seduce you or anything. I really wanted to talk to you as a friend.'

'Even though I'm not one.'

'But you are. I've always thought of you as being someone I could talk to.'

'Fifteen years ago I wouldn't have been all that flattered at a remark like that.'

'Unfortunately it isn't fifteen years ago. You're not going to marry her, are you? Nancy.'

'Will there be a battle tomorrow? Will the weather be right? Will the other army be there? I don't know. She doesn't want to have a child,' Daniel said. 'I do, if I'm going to marry someone, I mean.'

'Does the fire work in here?'

'If it's clicked properly. Give it a good tug. It takes a bit of a time to actually glow. You know, I'm sorry, but it's a long time since I've been so happy. I suddenly realize how happy I am. Why is it?'

'Because we're behaving like children. Playing houses and things. You see what I mean though, don't you? If they were bigger, it would be nicer.'

'Have you ever tried any of those things they advertise in women's magazines? Especially in France. They're always promising to give you *les plus beaux seins du monde*. Funny they're masculine in French, but then so's *con* of course, so at least it's a set. Perhaps they understand the ambivalences better than we do. I think you look very nice, you're so slim. There's really very little of you at all. I find it very touching. Why don't you leave him and live on your own and have a few affairs? I'm sure you'd enjoy it, it'd give you enormous self-confidence and probably Adam'd be back to reclaim you with the speed of light. You'd have all your options.'

'When a woman reaches my age, the only lovers she can find are her husband's friends.'

'Well Adam's not short, is he? There's the whole eleven for a start.'

'I also have my children to worry about *and* explain things to.'

'Bloody little Puritans. You know, I have a theory that it's the children who repress their parents and not the other way about. I think children incarnate the natural morality from which we escape when we break away from the home we've forced our parents to build.'

'There's no question about it,' Virginia said. 'It's warming up now.'

'You do puncture one's conceit, Gin, don't you? Shut the door if you're cold, there's no need to feel shy about it.'

'I'm not in the least. It's fine. I shall have to make some excuse tomorrow, won't I, to satisfy Candy?'

'Tell her it snowed.'

'She'll know it didn't. She's a poet when it comes to her own life and a statistical know-all when it comes to the rest of the world. Though actually I think she may be turning into a sculptress. She's really done some rather interesting forms.'

'Perhaps she'll be a three-dimensional poetess. Where's Adam tonight?'

'Oh, he went to Paris. Do you want me to run you one when I've finished?'

'Depends how deep yours is. There's not always that much hot water at this hour. I'll have yours.'

'Oh Daniel, will you really?'

'Only to wash in, I'm not going to drink it.'

'You're deliberately making everything as sexy as you can. I do think you're lovely.'

'On the contrary, I'm being a child of nature and just saying the first thing that comes into my head.'

'As Basil would say—"Is there necessarily a contradiction here?" Tell me, did you have some sort of row with her in Greece, your lady?'

'Who's been telling you what?'

'No one's told me anything you haven't made pretty clear yourself. Do you really want to have children? Are you really being honest with yourself? Or are you just so vain you can't wait to see what they're like, like home movies?'

'Why *home* movies? The so-called genuine article isn't any different. Of course that comes into it. It's a funny thing, when I've thought about going to bed with you, I've always come to the conclusion afterwards that I didn't really want to and now that I don't, well—come on, if you get out, I'll get in. You'd make a nice Lady Caroline, but you're no Annabella. We're allowed to kiss. You look so nice wet. It's irresistible.'

'I love you,' Virginia said. 'Off the record.'

'In general, that is the best place. Now don't worry, I won't forget. I've had a lot of practice and I never forget. I never can.'

'Meaning you once did.'

'We once did everything,' Daniel said. '*Non e vero?* Shall I dry you?'

'Daniel, I never realized how romantic you were!'

'With a towel, Virginia, with a towel. Christ, it's a long time since I laughed from sheer pleasure. It is fun. Childish, maybe, but fun.'

'What else is fun? She's got money, hasn't she?'

'Why don't you want me to marry her? You wouldn't be happy with me yourself, you know.'

'I do. Know. I don't want you not to marry her. I just feel you want to and at the same time don't.'

'That, as Pascal would say, is my precise condition. I don't really know which I want to do. You think it's her money. Well, you could be right. I think it's because I want her to admit she's wrong. And then again, I'm not sure. She thinks I want her money. But until she talked about it, I didn't know she had any. In any case she keeps telling me that if she does marry me she'll lose it.'

'And you believe her, I suppose?'

'I damned well do. She's a terrible snob. The worst. Sucking up to bogus princesses. Really, it was embarrassing.'

'Whereas you fuck up to them, which is a lot nicer.'

'A lot more ambiguous. Jesus Christ Almighty.'

'What? What?'

'Oh it can't be true. It can't be true. It's too much.'

'I know you're going to tell me, so you'd better tell me.'

'The cunning bitch. Oh she's too much. I knew she was.'

'Don't play the husband with me, Danny, or I'll smite you.'

'I told you about this girl who said nak'd, this woman?'

'Well?'

'Do you know, I believe perhaps she performed the ultimate service for her mistress and provided her with a—my God, you know, I think she did? I wondered why she insisted on it being so dark. It didn't seem like her. It bloody wasn't her. No wonder she never said anything. Jesus, I wonder how many of them were in it, because—you will remember that one of the charms of the three musketeers is that really there were four of them. It'd be just my luck to have screwed a princess and not to know I had. Never mind about not knowing the mind of another, it's difficult enough to know the body. The funny thing was, her body felt so light, the feel of the colour of her, I thought it was all wrong. I thought it was guilt, but it wasn't. Well, what do you know, I've fucked a princess and never even knew how lucky I'd got.'

'You say *Nancy's* the snob?' Virginia said. 'Is that really the problem?'

'Alternatively maybe she was only the wife of one of the richest men in Greece. Well, either way it's a plus score, right? I heard what you said, Gin, you're pretty clever even with your clothes off. Go and get into bed. I shouldn't advise you to wear nothing because there can be some quite strong prevailing winds on the gallery. You'll find a football shirt of mine in the second drawer down. It's sort of long and romantic, should do you. I mean, please yourself, it's not temptation I'm avoiding, it's sinusitis. She can't really want to be the person she is, I'm talking about Nancy again now. She can't really be that person as exclusively as she seems to be. Am I a snob? Aren't you? Aren't we all? On the way back from Iskios, this island where we all were, oh of course you've heard, well, on the way back from there we were on the steamer and at Naxos, which is one of the stops along the way, a whole party of Greek Orthodox priests got on. Now as you know, the priests and the Colonels are like that. In fact, they were standing on the dock as we came in and they were talking to—need I say?—a couple of army officers. Anyway, we were sitting in a couple of deck-chairs when they came out looking for somewhere to sit.'

'You didn't give up your seat?'

'I did not. I'd have been delighted to have them stand all the way to Piraeus—and back. They're anti-semitic as well as everything else, you know, this lot. Hullo, O.K.? You found it? Terrific, it suits you. You look like George Best; sorry, Georgina Best, if you prefer it. O.K.?'

'If *you* prefer it,' Virginia said.

'Bitch, anyway, they stood around and after a while they started to sing. They took out their music or whatever it was, these pieces of paper, and they started to sing. Jesus Christ, Gin, it was the most beautiful thing I ever heard in my life. These deep voices, no accompaniment except the motion of the sea, such intensity, such commitment, it's the only word; I never heard anything like it. I wished I was one of them. I really did. I would have given anything to have been able to join in. It was—well, it was everything the inaccessible can ever be. And yet at the end, when they stopped and put away their hymn sheets or whatever and formed up to go ashore, I hated them all over again. I still hated what they accepted and what they assumed in order to have the authority to just sing like that, on a steamer, no music, just the divine right to make that sound and the confidence that it would be respected.'

'You get that in *The Portrait Of A Lady*,' Virginia said. 'Only in that case it's capitalism that makes something beautiful and allows it its full flower, only to have it poisoned because the underlying morality is corrupt and ruinous.'

'And you ladies with your firsts, how about you?'

'We're ruined because we have chests and not tits,' Virginia said. 'And because we're the products of books, not of any social system at all, except perhaps competition and the desire to excel—the sublimation of rugged individualism.'

'The other thing which somehow relates to it is that in my luggage I had this Cycladic figure which I'd bought. Well, it's not the usual Cycladic figure as I'll explain in a moment. I had this goddess, if she was a goddess—'

'Perhaps she was only a princess,' Virginia said.

'O.K., anyway, I had this figure, you know, and although I'd paid for it I sort of felt as if I was stealing it. And as they were singing my conscience began to bite like the fox under the Spartan boy's shirt. Not because I was going to smuggle it out of the country if I could, but because, if you like, I couldn't think of anything better to do with it. It was as if I wanted to steal their song and cash it once I'd got it out. I wouldn't have any real use for it, do you see what I mean? I wanted it like a hunter. I wanted to kill it and take it home for a trophy. Which was what I was doing with this figure I'd bought. Not that it has any use any more except as a sort of hard currency. Are you O.K., have you got enough bed?'

'I'm fine,' Virginia said. 'Have you got the figure here?'

'It was very strange leaving Greece. I was rather nervous. After all, even though it hadn't been necessary in the end, I had actually conspired to spring a political prisoner. On Iskios I felt equal to whatever happened. It was a small situation, only seven police on the island, a conveniently manageable cast. Of course that was an illusion, but it was a pretty one. Athens was something else. That's where the hard men are. That's where the *vasinisis* is carried out.'

'*Vasinisis?*'

'Something you don't know, Gin? Torture.'

'I was never a Classic,' Virginia said.

'I was nervous, but I was also something else. Of course. I think it was mainly because of Nancy. I also hoped, in a funny way, that I *would* be arrested. I hoped I'd be released, but I hoped, at the same time as I feared, that I'd be taken away. I wanted her to be shaken up a bit. I wanted her to see that some things are real, that some things really happen, even to people she—I suppose in a way it was flattery. I imagined her as a goddess to whom it can be demonstrated, brutally, that gods don't exist. We spent one night at the Hilton. I wondered what would happen if there was a bomb. Would they take me in then? Some coincidence after all. We went out to Varibobi in the evening and had dinner at Leonidas. It was an extraordinary, romantic evening. Everything that had happened between us—and let's just say it wasn't all good—on Iskios, all of that seemed to be forgotten. She was beautiful, the smell of the pines was blown in over the terrace, it was too much. I acted as romantically, if one can say that, as I could, as charmingly as I could, as falsely as I could? I don't know. I acted as if I were sorry for being harsh and sarcastic, because I had been, on the island. I acted with regretful courtliness. As if I'd realized, perhaps too late, that she was the love of my life—'

'Bastard.'

'I meant it, Gin. I wasn't acting in that sense. It was as if I knew the thing was finished but was proving, like some gallant but doomed prisoner, that the verdict against me could make no difference to my feelings. I accepted the verdict, but I made her—or tried to make her—carry the responsibility.'

'Which is what I mean by bastard.'

'O.K., but beyond all that, beyond all my docile and patient thoughtfulness, as if I were meeting my wife for the first time after her re-marriage, I was waiting for the two courteous but implacable men in identical suits to come across and ask me to go with them. I was dreaming of the moment when I pressed her shoulder, Trevor Howard in *Brief Encounter*, for one inexpressibly poignant moment and then, like Sir Roger Casement, stepped through the green baize door. And all of that, God help me, I dreamed as a proof to her of her vulgarity and her falseness. No one came, of course. We finished dinner, we walked down into the pinewoods and drew breaths of the prickly air, is that a reasonable phrase?'

'Very evocative. A little flowery perhaps.'

'We walked hand in hand back to the taxi and smiled at each other, leaning well back, still hand in hand, as we drove home to the Hilton. She undressed slowly, beautifully, rustling and crackling like a marvellous gift, moving softly about the room, taking a bath in that way which seemed to announce with each mild watery movement exactly which part of her body she was attending to. She came back into the bedroom in the big white towelling coat they give you in those places and sat on the bed to finish drying. I couldn't make love to her. It wasn't a question of trying and failing. I couldn't go near her. My cock was like Graves's famous tassel. And she couldn't come near me, because the evening had been too romantic for a woman to do the leading. It called for me to be a certain kind of man and I wasn't. I was still waiting for the two men in the identical suits. My whole performance — oh all right. Anyway, the next morning we went to the airport. I was embarrassed at my failure, even though Nancy didn't seem especially put out, no demands, no accusations. Smiles, as a matter of fact. She never notices what she doesn't want to. We went through the gate, past the police and we were just going to buy some pistachios and a souvenir bottle of *retsina* when these men came up and said, "Mr Meyer, come with us, please." I said, "Buy the big bag, shan't be a minute," and off I went. Well, here I am, so it's no good playing it for suspense. As soon as we were through the door into their office, I could only think "How dare they?" I wasn't at the mercy of evil, or face to face with the torturers of Hellas, I just thought what bloody little wogs they were and how dare they. I also thought, "I'm completely innocent. This is a complete frame-up. This is typical. They pick on people for doing absolutely nothing." Which, of course, was true, but wasn't really what I wanted to think about this attempt I'd made to smuggle Akrotiri off the island.'

'Paul told me about that.'

'No action qualifies for his approval. He operates on such a lofty plain, Everest is but his footstool.'

'He was full of admiration.'

'Ah poo,' Daniel said. 'Anyway, they weren't secret policemen at all. They were customs officers and they wanted to go through my bag. Well, I couldn't help thinking how bloody silly because all the luggage was on the plane already. It so happened, however, that I hadn't put the figure into my big suitcase because they can snap, these things, if they're bumped down hard. So of course they found it. Where had I got it? Plaka, I said. How much had I paid? A few pounds. It was a fake, I said. A copy. One of them said he'd give me what I paid for it. No, I wasn't interested. It might be a fake, but I liked it. They looked at it and they looked at me, and you know I began to be absolutely convinced that it was genuine. Up till then I'd had my doubts, because it's a funny, very untypical piece—'

'Can I see it?'

'Siga-siga. All in good time. Now, of course, it was a very pretty situation, because these blokes didn't know if it was right or not. They pretended that they knew, but as these people always are, they were much better judges of men than of objects. They judged it by me. Nice situation. The funny thing being, of course, that I didn't know whether I was actually hiding anything or not. I had no evidence it was a fake and no evidence it wasn't. The only way I could get myself to play the scene right was to concentrate on my contempt for them and for the man who'd sold it to me. I told myself that Robert Gavin, who'd been, I realized, extravagantly helpful in arranging the whole thing, was a party to the swindle, if swindle it was, and that he'd fixed for me to be done in return for a percentage of the take.'

'Robert Gavin,' Virginia said. 'Isn't he dead?'

'Dead?'

'I saw it about a month ago. There was a little piece in *The Times*. And the *Observer* did a bit on him. Just initials, but I think it was probably Norbert.'

'I must have been in California. It must have been while I was over there. Are you sure?'

'*A Greek Light*,' Virginia said. 'And *Rats*. Wasn't that him?'

'How the hell did he die? He wasn't murdered, was he?'

'He died in the Marsden, Brompton Road,' Virginia said. 'Presumably cancer.'

'Poor old sod,' Daniel said. 'I suppose he knew at the time. That was why he was in such a hurry over everything. Poor old sod. Well, that's ruined my story.'

'No. Why? Tell me what happened at least.'

'I must've convinced them, after all I convince a lot of people. When Greek meets Hebe and all that sort of thing. I thought of trying bribery, but that would have been a dead giveaway, because you don't bribe people to let you take out a fake. I just waited for the plane to be called. And acted the impatient, wouldn't-you-just-know-these-Woggy-places-weren't-worth-visiting-Englishman-down-there-on-a-visit and eventually they let me through. The really funny thing was, Nancy was carrying an icon in her bag and they never even thought to look. Which suggests somehow, now I come to think of it, that we probably aren't destined to be a couple after all. Fancy Gavin dead. I wouldn't have been surprised if you'd told me that he'd been found in a ditch somewhere in the Peloponnesus suffering from Agamemnon's complaint. A swift dagger in the bath-house. Poor old bugger. He was –'

'What?'

'I can't remember now. Do you realize it's a quarter to two?'

'Well, at least tell me, was it genuine or wasn't it?'

'Do you know, it may sound unbelievable, but I still haven't found out? I've been so damned busy with this film I haven't had time to go down to the B.M. and put it through the lie-detector. I rather doubt if it is. I have got a genuine one though. You're lying on it at the moment. It's under the bed.'

'Can I see?'

'I only show it to *bona fide* customers,' Daniel said. 'And it's too late now. Goodnight, dear Gin. Goonight Lou, goonight, goonight.'

'Proper kiss,' Virginia said. 'Because you're so lovely.'

'Well, we saw it,' Daniel said. 'We finally saw it. *Dopo tanti mesi.* Well, come on: what did you think?'

'Brilliant. I thought it was brilliant. You didn't?'

'I thought it was brilliantly handled,' Daniel said. 'Even if one did tend to get a little weary of Billy's fingerprints all over the silver.'

'You never like anything, that's your trouble. It only has to be by someone you know and you automatically hate it.'

'Rubbish. I can hate perfect strangers quite easily, if they're talented. I thought we'd eat Chinese in honour of the time we first went to see the movie and didn't. The name of this street also happens to be Horryvood Lo, which seems appropriate.'

'Horryvood what?'

'Hollywood Road,' Daniel said. 'When I first called and asked for directions the man who gave them to me was a Chinaman straight off the boat. No, I did admire it. I thought he caught the whole grotesque atmosphere of the mid-'sixties absolutely magnificently. The Macmillan years. Christ, who'd a thunk we'd actually look back on them as a golden era, interrupted only by a few little local difficulties. Billy's very clever the way he manages to flirt with reality without actually touching it. He manages to procure an orgasm without a suspicion of penetration. No wonder the critics like him. He fetches them off without disturbing their clothing. He turns the whole of the Press Show into a kind of sublime gents' Leicester Square, with Art in the place of a fumble and sucks to the plainclothes men.'

'I'm going to have the duck,' Nancy said.

'Oh listen, let's just have them bring the works, it's so much simpler. I must say I did like the sequence when they went to look for a place to hide away in the country and suddenly the hunt came across the fields and you saw the fox twisting and scampering. I thought that was magnificent, obvious in a way, but *England Their England* all right. Woof. Very good. I also liked the scene where he's apologizing to his wife, after the scandal's broken and it's obvious he's going to have to resign, his career's ruined, and she's smiling. That was beautiful. I wonder how much of it was really Billy.'

'All of it,' Nancy said. 'I particularly asked somebody about it at a party.'

'Ah well, there we are then. Proof positive.'

'Daniel, I thought—'

'Sorry, sorry. What do you mean you particularly asked somebody?'

'Well, I was curious—'

'Curiouser and curiouser,' Daniel said. 'Meaning, you've seen the bloody picture before, haven't you? Tonight wasn't the first time, was it?'

'Did I say it was?'

'You could've fooled me. Who did you see it with?'

'As a matter of fact, Stuart Melrose took me.'

'Well, why the hell did we go? Why didn't you say?'

'I wanted to see it again. Daniel, please don't be childish or I shall go home.'

'And how did he like the portrayal of his party?'

'He agreed with what the man in the film said.'

'A great political party is not destroyed by the folly of one man and a common prostitute.'

'Any more than the medical profession is by one doctor who happens to seduce a patient.'

'The Tory Party as therapeutic force, lovely idea. Was he embarrassed by the film at all?'

'Why should he be?'

'That is exactly my criticism. Billy's films are radical only to those who look for the roots above the surface.'

'I'm sure you're being very perceptive, but I'm not with you.'

'Those who are not with me. This is good, isn't it? I like sea-weed. It's like eating mermaid's hair. Pubic hair, of course. Do mermaids have pubic hair or do they have pubic scales? A subject for research. Three years should be enough. Take a Guggenheim, said the Prince. What Billy should have shown but didn't was the degree to which these naughty private arrangements are not just sexual but social as well. The Tories believe in a two-tier system and they always have. What they do is their business and what everyone else does is also their business. What made them so furious with the whole thing was that it exposed the degree of their contempt for the public morality, in every respect, not just sexual, of which they were supposedly such upright—ha ha—guardians. The case *was* a moral issue for that reason. It wasn't a question of sexual degeneracy, it was a case of privilege. And privilege was so taken for granted that even lying to the House of Commons wasn't all that terrible a thing, as long as one could get away with it, and they have got away with it, for centuries. Their hypocrisy is only one more way of lying to the House. That's the point Billy should have made, instead of which he just went all kinky and peculiar on us. He failed to make a morality and he failed, by the same token, to make anything but a bogus work of art. A pretty picture. No wonder Lord Melrose wasn't upset. He'll end up Sir Billy, you'll see. Artist-fartist.'

'Maybe you'll be able to show him how a real artist does things.'

'Next time. Next time. This time I shall simply show him that technically I limp in his footsteps. Only with any luck I shan't show anyone else.'

'Your old age,' Nancy said, 'is obviously going to be thick with masterpieces.'

'When did you go,' Daniel said, 'with Melrose?'

'When you were in California,' Nancy said. 'Daniel—'

'Nancy?'

'I don't know how you're going to take this, but I have to be honest with you.'

'As people always say when they've been dishonest.'

'I haven't been dishonest. I don't like to be accused either. I'm trying to behave like a sensible adult person.'

'You're going to marry Stuart Melrose.'

'Who told you that?'

'No one. I just made it up. Is it true?'

'He's asked me to marry him.'

'*I* asked you, if I remember rightly. And what did you say?'

'I said—I said yes, Daniel. I said I would.'

'To him, you said this, not to me, right? I thought he was married.'

'They're divorced.'

'*O tempora o mores*,' Daniel said. 'I always thought men like that shot themselves. O.K., so marry him.'

'Daniel, I'm sorry.'

'I suppose it's different with him, is it? Dear Charles is so tickled to think of his children growing up under an earl's aegis that he's going to keep up the payments, is that it? Your cake and eat it?'

'We weren't going to work, Daniel, you know it. You thought I was something I'm just not.'

'I thought you were something and by Christ you just are.'

'It comes to the same thing.'

'How is he in the sack, Nancy Jane? Or doesn't that matter all that much? I mean you've seen 'em come and you've seen 'em go, haven't you? And there's always the princess. My Christ, you'll be a countess, Nancy Jane, you'll actually be a fully-blown, copper-bottomed countess. Wow. I see your point. Who could turn down a thing like that?'

'Stuart wants to stay on in the House of Commons. He may renounce his title when the time comes. He's warned me about that very frankly.'

'And you, like the plucky bride you are, have promised him, just like the loyal Tory wife you mean to be, that you'll stick by him through thick and thin, as long as the thin is thick enough, of course.'

'I hoped we could do this in a civilized way. After all, I'm not the one who had doubts first. That was you. I hope you're not going to pretend to be the injured party. I'm not going to apologize for what I feel about Stuart. He had a conscience about seeing me without you knowing, but —'

'You reassured him. I'll bet. No, it's all right. I'm not going to break down or chew the carpet. I quite agree. We don't have a contract.'

'Directors shouldn't marry. Like bullfighters. It only takes their eyes off the main object.'

'And gets them awarded the horns,' Daniel said. 'In the groin, of course. What's the news of Astrid, is she coming to London or not? Or has she got the chop too?'

'I haven't heard a word.'

'Will you take precedence? I suppose you will. What's the story in fact? Will you be Lady Melrose right away? I suppose you must be.'

'I love Stuart,' Nancy said. 'Don't have any illusions.'

'Illusions? Me?'

'Daniel, I still believe in you just as much as I ever did.'

'My price has not drifted lower, despite vigorous trading. I'm relieved. I can do without the benedictions. I've got a film I'm going to do. I can afford to dispense with the fantasy.'

'I mean it. I sincerely think you're the most talented —'

'Oh come on, Nancy Jane. That's the stuff they used to hand out on Lew whatsit's yacht, isn't it? I wish you'd tell me something a bit more concrete. Leftwich. For instance, about Larry. What's Larry's real story? What's he really up to?'

'I don't know. Your guess is as good as mine.'

'I'll tell you what Jack and I think. Jack Darwin. We were talking about it this morning. We think he's a pusher. Our guess is that he deals in fake sculpture. He specializes in items that are said to have been found under water, encrusted with shellfish and barnacles and Christ knows what not all, and he ships them to the States, quite openly, as top-class *bogue*. What he doesn't declare is that they're hollowed out and full of heroin shipped in by high-speed cruiser from Turkey and points east. Clever?'

'Do you have any evidence?'

510

'That old stuff? Of course not. What we do know is that he has a very expensive operation going on and that he's always being pushed for money. I'll tell you another idea, it's that the little blonde girl—what was her name? Buck Lehman's girl—is actually C.I.A. or F.B.I. and is about to blow the whole ring. Nuala. She's in trouble, however, because blowing Larry means discrediting the Colonels as well and so she's in some danger. The C.I.A., if she's F.B.I., are thinking of shopping her to Larry and his friends to avoid a showdown with the Junta. In which case she may end in the underwater museum being nibbled by the *langosta*. Which will later taste delicious at the Pleasure table.'

'I think you must have the most horrible imaginations.'

'Horrible, we do. Let's face it, though, it fits the facts. It fits a lot of the facts. It did occur to us that they probably have a secret warehouse on Hitler's island, otherwise the Pleasure palace would be too ostentatious for comfort. It's meant to attract attention precisely because it's search-proof, more than search-proof, search-bait. Get it? All they have to do is channel the stuff over to Agoria when the heat's on. It did occur to us they could be in the arms business, but I think the loads would be too weighty. Drugs looks like the answer. It's not too original, but how many ways are there of making big money? Of course Buck Lehman could be the C.I.A. man and you can build a number of double-doubles around that, including the idea that the C.I.A. are financing themselves for a takeover by means of the international drug market. Metaphorically, they are the international drug market already, of course.'

'I don't know why you don't turn it into a movie.'

'That's exactly what we were doing. Of course if we were plotting it right, Gavin would be some kind of go-between who was actually murdered but the British government has been black-mailed into making it look natural. In which case O *Mavros* has to be tied into the plot. Shouldn't be any problem. Probably he was M.I.5.'

'You digest everything, don't you? It's scary. I can see myself being processed into some kind of—I don't know—public property. Or have you done it already?'

'No, I haven't. I thought I was going to have you to myself.'

'I never had any such illusions,' Nancy said. 'Personally.'

'So what had you turned me into?' Daniel said. 'You're still so beautiful, that's what's so funny. You're absolutely unchanged. I haven't touched you at all.'

'You'll be much happier without me.'

'I hope so,' Daniel said. 'Oh Jesus, Nancy. Jesus, Jesus. I almost persuaded myself I didn't care. You're quite right. Let's be honest for once, I've been more than expecting this. Looking forward to it. It had already happened, really, before we even left Iskios. I saw you when you heard who he was, Stuart, and it really happened then. The supreme act of vanity is not doing anything, and that was what I did. I really drove you to it. I'm not just flattering myself. You know sometimes when you're shooting a film, you'll do a scene and you'll say, "Let's have one more rehearsal and then we'll do it for real," and you shoot the rehearsal just to make sure everything's working and afterwards you realize that the rehearsal was for real. Then you ask yourself did you mean it to trick the actors or did the actors trick you? Well, anyway, I'm on the verge of thinking you and I were just a rehearsal, you were just a sort of stand-in and by Christ I think back and I think Jesus that was it. That was the real thing. The genuine article. Was it?'

'It was a romance,' Nancy said. 'That's really what it was.'

'Nancy, Countess Stirling,' Daniel said. '*The Portrait Of A Lady*. You know what I'd do if there were only some good reliable clean whores in London? I'd go and have one, right now, as a digestive — and think of you.'

'Goodbye, Daniel,' Nancy said.

'No lychee?' Daniel said.

They parked the station wagon and walked down through the woods. The trees were tall, darkening against an afternoon sky, as lustreless as pewter. The wind had laid a path of chestnut leaves down to the railway which ran along the estuary. As they came to the crossing, with its Victorian warning, fifty words of pedantic cast-iron, a train whistled and came coasting past, three carriages, neat as a parade of prams. They crossed the rails carefully and went down towards the shore. Bernard and Sylvia wore Wellington boots and their children ran ahead, down among the boles of the trees, proving their independence. They could see the knife-edge of the water, glinting among the trees. Sylvia and Bernard looked at each other and smiled, again, as they turned and walked along the hard roadway above the foreshore. There was a solid bed of flint under the mattress of leaves. Soon they came to a large brick building, upholstered in green moss, the colour of cheap furniture. Another sign, of wood this time, rotten and peeling, announced w.d. property. There were rusty gates to the compound. The brick building which had served as a guardhouse had Crittall's windows, glass smashed, frames rusted. Bernard led the way between the green brick walls and the palisade of barbed wire along the shore. They came to a gap where a path slipped down beside the wire to a wild-fowlers' pontoon. The wind flattened the reeds and rattled their stiff stems. Bernard took Sylvia's hand as she lurched on the slick surface. They went between hummocks of beige grass and puddles of brown water. Soon the grass was behind them. Odd tufts were mashed in among the mud. They crossed a dyke, over an uncertain bridge of corrugated iron, and were on the flats where nothing showed beyond a stippling of old cans and flotsam and the pronged footprints of birds. The estuary spread to the right, like a flat silver dish, beneath a pale orange sun so low and so distant that its reflection barely rusted the lifeless water. Bernard showed the children how to twist the heels of their boots to escape the sticky grip of the mud. A couple of shots sounded from their left and the girl, with a cry, protested. An arrowhead of wild duck crossed, one missing from their symmetry, in energetic, outstretched flight. The family stood for a few minutes, breath marking the emptiness, and inspected again, with a kind of comfortable satisfaction, what they already knew so well.

It was raining hard when Daniel left the Morrises. They asked him to stay another night, but the bad weather was almost an encouragement for him to set out. He put some Albinoni in the slot stereo and drove, in a velvet box of sound, through the wet lanes. The long dual carriageway between Colchester and Chelmsford, with its irregular procession of lights, made him dream of an endless journey and from the dream came the idea, inevitably, of a film of the modern Wandering Jew, with his Lotus Two Plus Two and his credit card and his systematically uncompleted business, driving from country to country along a succession of motorways ever more similar one to another. As Europe became one, so the autoroutes became more homogeneous. One no longer knew which country one was in; nothing but international restaurants, international banks, international companies, everyone within the system eloquent in half a dozen languages, eloquent at least in the essential phrases: how much, how long, how often, how soon. The motorways would be fenced off, like Europe itself, from the outside world of farm vehicles, animals and human habitation. Mesh fences guarded those within from the incursions of those without. A man in difficulties on the other side of the wire would be beyond the help of the travellers. The travellers who broke down were equally beyond the reach of the ordinary people outside. Smooth Europe segregated from rough Europe, the motorized, the businesslike, the efficient would circulate as they wished, provided they stayed within the system, provided their credit and their purposes were acceptable. It was not a wholly frightening thought. Daniel could imagine being that Jew, driven onwards not by greed or fear but by the absolute demands of mobility. Such a man, always courteous within the courtesy of commerce, always on time, always in a hurry but never in a rush, in a world where everything necessary was available on a cost-time basis, what would be his drama? His drama would be that he would have none. The failure of such films was that they wanted always to force the man into a revolt against his conditions. The sentimentality of dissent from comfortable continuity, the need for a climax, was what imported falseness into such imagined worlds. If was as if the Swiss should man the barricades. This wanderer would never dissent. His drama would have no climax. He would simply drive and drive, like the vehicle which encased him, until he or his machine, together or singly, fell apart.

The medical depots (at every major staging point) would repair whatever could be repaired for as long as it was reparable and then, what was there but the junk heap? To junk a man painlessly, courteously, when it was beyond doubt that he could roll no further, what could be less callous, less indifferent or less capricious? The soft machine also had its failures and its final, undramatic quietus. Such a film would run on without specific plot, without a form, it would have incidents but they would occur and perhaps recur like the music on the Albinoni tape. The spectator would notice perhaps, with a kind of satisfaction, that the same sequences were coming round again. The form of the film would be that of the tape recirculating, seamless and endless, until some practical person switched it off. The film, seen in this way, coterminous with the life of the watcher, a positive feature of his life, as the cossetting Albinoni now was of Daniel's, would require no cinema, no presentation, no review. To pass comment on it would be like commenting on a river. Better to watch and watch. Instead of the unhappy ending what better than the happy unending? What a mistake to think that the businessman, with his ceaseless repertoire of duties, duties to the durable, to the uncritical, to the whole created world, wanted to break out into a world of feelings, sentiments or passions! He was perfectly accommodated. He wanted nothing different. He changed to fit what was sufficiently often repeated. The world was a teaching machine. He would learn what was presented to him sufficiently frequently. The single instance, the *hapax legomenon*, would always be like a fart in church, which might amuse or embarrass but could never detain or alter him. He was programmed to ignore what did not recur. A love affair, in such a man's life, was a disturbance; even the most reliable installation might have a short-circuit. Such things were put right as quickly as possible. One could not live forever, or for longer than was avoidable, in such a glare. Daniel watched the film through the movieola of the windscreen. The Albinoni was his soundtrack. Had not someone once said that Britain might be the new Venice? (The Venice of Casanova, not of Dandolo.) The new world, like the transistor, needed only to be printed on the surface: roads, junctions, service areas, telex links, all of them could be incised without penetration, on the spherical drum of earth.

He came off the uninterrupted road and extracted the Albinoni. He had reached the sequence of roundabouts in the Essex suburbs of the city. Orange and yellow lights drooped and splashed in the black road. He slowed, the exhaust whipping fog across his back window. As he touched the brakes at a roundabout, the back of the car nudged sideways, like a threatening full-back, but kept its place. The rain filmed the windscreen. The wipers pushed it away in pliable ridges and it quivered in black beans below the arc of their motion.

The Cortina ahead of him eased to the left and took the round-about without hesitation. The road was wide and seemed empty, but before the Cortina had time to get behind the shelter of the roundabout itself, another car, a Viva, had come from the right and slid, as both drivers braked, into the Cortina, broadside on, like a collision at sea. Daniel drove past and parked under a gigantic advertisement for tyres. The driver of the Cortina was a black man. The Viva had a girl at the wheel.

The black man said: 'It was my fault. I just didn't see her. It was my fault.'

Daniel said: 'Thank God for an honest man.'

'You know, it's a funny thing,' the black man said, 'this is the third firm's car that's had this happen in a single month.'

'Not with you at the wheel every time, I hope.'

'Oh no.'

Daniel said: 'Are you all right?'

'It's not my car,' the girl said. 'I had the right of way.'

'Look, it's all right. He's a nice bloke. He says the same thing. Are you O.K.? Are you hurt?'

'I don't know what he's going to say. I had the right of way. He came right into me.'

The black man's fender was bent against the wheel. He was pulling at it with his hands. Daniel bent down to help. The man's hand overlapped his. When he pulled, Daniel's flesh was squashed against the metal. 'Hold it, I'll get a spanner.'

'The third time in a month. I never saw her, you know. Must have been the colour of the car or something like that, because I never saw her at all until the last moment.'

'She was on the roundabout all right,' Daniel said.

'I know. I know. But I never saw her. I've been working all day, I must have been a bit tired.'

'You'd better pull it well away or you'll find you can't steer.'

'What do we do now? We don't need to call the police, do we?'

'Not if no one's hurt,' Daniel said. 'Just pull over and exchange names and addresses.' The girl was still sitting in the Viva. Daniel said: 'Can you just pull over to the side?' She showed him her blanched face. 'It was a bit of a shock,' Daniel said. 'Shove over and I'll see if I can do it.'

'He'll be wondering what's happened.'

'We'll take care of that in a minute,' Daniel said. 'Miserable night. I was just thinking about accidents myself.'

'He's waiting for the car. My Dad. He's waiting for it.'

'It wasn't your fault. He's a nice bloke, he says himself it wasn't your fault. The worst thing is when you're in the right and the other bloke wants to thump you. At least he's honest. You stay here and I'll get him to come over and—'

Daniel went back to the Cortina. The driver had worked the fender clear. He pulled the car in behind the Lotus and the two of them walked to the Viva.

'All you have to do is exchange names and addresses—'

'What happens then?' the girl said.

'The insurance companies sort it out,' the black man said. 'Here, I'll give you my company's card.'

Daniel said: 'You write your name and address and he'll give you his, that's all you have to do. It doesn't look as if the damage is too severe. I'll give you my name and address and then if you need a witness, you can get in touch.'

'You have a very confident manner,' the black man said. 'You must be in show business.'

'I'm a film director.'

'Very nice.'

A police car slid past them and went on down the yellow road.

'Well, I think I'll go now. I'm sorry about it. The third car in a month. They'll laugh about it when I tell them.'

'You must work for nice people,' Daniel said. 'Now listen, what about you?'

'Goodbye then.'

'Goodbye. Nice bloke. They can be such bastards – other drivers, I mean. The car seems to be O.K.'

'Do you think I'm all right to drive?' the girl said.

'He who asks the question is in the best position to answer it. I take it you're doubtful. How far away do you live?'

'A couple of miles. I was just running my boy friend to the station.'

'I'll write a note to your father, if you like. No, listen, I'll take you home. Is there someone there? I'll take you in my car and then perhaps your dad'll come back and drive the Viva. How would that be?'

'It's not the first time,' the girl said. 'It happened to me before and it wasn't my fault then either.'

He took her arm and they crossed the side road to get to the Lotus. 'There are easier and less expensive ways of picking up strange men,' Daniel said. 'Are you all right?'

'I feel a bit funny, that's all. I don't know what my dad's going to say.'

'I'll explain to him what happened. He'll be all right.'

'Because he's waiting for the car.'

'How old are you?'

'I'm nineteen.'

'You have got a licence, haven't you?'

'Not with me.'

'But you have got one? You'll have to direct me, you know. I don't know where you live even though you do.'

'Sorry, you go on down to the garage at the bottom and then you go left. Oh yes, I've got one. I've passed the test.'

'Listen, don't worry. I'm sure your father'll understand. He'll be relieved you're not hurt. And the car's not bad. It's only a bit crumpled. They're only made of tin, you know. They uncrumple as well as crumple.'

'I know. I was only taking my boy friend to the station. This is it, left here.'

'Stop worrying,' Daniel said. 'You'll feel better when you get home.'

'You are kind,' the girl said.

'Sometimes,' Daniel said.

'Hundreds of people wouldn't have stopped.'

'And thousands would,' Daniel said. 'A pretty girl in distress?'

'Right down here. And then on down to the end.'

'I might just have come from murdering someone for all you know. It's strange, isn't it? And so might you, of course, for that matter.'

'I was taking my boy friend to the station. I know I had the right of way. I'm sorry if I'm taking you out of your way.'

'I don't have anything special to do,' Daniel said.

'You are kind.'

The curtains came apart as the Lotus drove up. The house was semi-detached: concrete path from the yellow gate to the leaded hood over the front door, coloured panels in the hall window, Westminster chimes. Mother, father and elder sister were by the door.

Daniel said: 'Mr Hillier? Good evening. I'm afraid there's been a slight accident. It wasn't your daughter's fault. The car's back at the roundabout. She felt a bit shaken so I think it's better if you drive it home. It's not badly damaged.'

'Oh dear,' the man said, 'not again.'

'If you like, I'll run you straight back. It's no distance.'

'I'll go,' the elder sister said.

'Oh dear, oh dear. That wretched car. I wish we'd never bought it.'

'I think you ought to give her a cup of sweet tea and sit her down, Mrs Hillier,' Daniel said.

'I will, I will. Thank you so much.'

'Thank you. You were ever so kind.'

'Pleasure,' Daniel said.

The elder sister got her coat and went with Daniel.

'You'll have to guide me.'

She sat sideways, legs shining, in the far corner of the car.

'You'll have to guide me, I'm afraid.'

She indicated to go straight.

Daniel said: 'It's my fantasy night. Driving pretty girls all over London.'

She indicated left.

'It wasn't your sister's fault. He was a thoroughly nice bloke, luckily. I hope you'll keep the police out of it. I think he was a bit worried in case they got involved.'

She indicated right and then straight on again.

Daniel said: 'Test the brakes before you speed up. It's not much of a night for tobogganing. Listen, I've given your sister my address, so if you need me, call, O.K.?'

The girl sat forward and buttoned her coat. The Viva was in sight.

'Tell me,' Daniel said, 'what does your father do?'

'He's an undertaker,' the girl said.

'Ah. Oh. Well, here we are then. Go carefully.'

'He was probably disappointed not to get any business out of it,' Victor Rich said. 'Excuse me, I'll just take this and then—yes? I can't for the moment. I'm in a meeting. Will you please?'

'How was Paris?'

'Paris?'

'Oh that was Adam, sorry. How was Manchester?'

'Wet.'

'No thanks, I don't smoke,' Daniel said. 'I'm surprised you do. A rational man like yourself.'

'Ought seldom entails does, I'm afraid, in this world. Yes? Oh look, I'll pop out for a minute and see if I can sort him out. Excuse me, but the board want to know something and apparently—'

'Of course,' Daniel went to the window and looked across

London. The Post Office Tower raised a warning finger. Daniel wandered round the big, empty desk and sat creaking in Victor's black chair and toyed with the stenorette. A phone bleeped. It bleeped again. Daniel detached it from its complicated holder.

'The General would like a word.'

'He shall have it,' Daniel said. 'But Dr Rich isn't here at the moment. Perhaps he's on his way.'

'Please tell him to come down to the Board Room as soon as possible.'

'Of course. Will do.'

When Victor returned, Daniel was reading the 1964 edition of the *Film and Television Yearbook*. He was not included.

'The General would like a word.'

'I've just spoken to him,' Victor said.

'I don't smoke,' Daniel said.

'Sorry. Sorry. Now.'

'You saw *The Elephant Man*,' Daniel said.

'What? Oh yes. Yes, I saw it this morning. Daniel, I must tell you honestly how I feel.'

'That's what we're here for.'

'I'm afraid I didn't like it at all.'

'Ah.'

'I'm very disappointed to have to say so.'

'What particularly didn't you like? I'm still not completely happy about the voice over myself.'

'I thought it was all terribly pat.'

'Pat? You mean it had a shape.'

'I don't mean that. I felt completely and needlessly uninvolved.'

'You mean as producer or as audience?'

'Both. Of course there are some things that're very impressive. I'm not denying that. I'm not saying it's not well-directed.'

'You're just not saying it is. You must admit the bit in the blind asylum, the fantasy sequence —'

'To be frank, I thought it went on a bit.'

'If you shorten it, you might as well cut it altogether. Didn't you really feel the pity of it all at the end? The Elephant Man killed by his aspirations just to go to sleep like everyone else? I weep practically every time I see it.'

'Could we cut the prostitute?'

'Afraid of the I.T.A. or what?'

'I'm not afraid of anyone,' Victor Rich said. 'I just think it's questionable. And unnecessarily explicit in the present climate. I'm not even sure that a Victorian prostitute would actually say those things.'

'It's not what she says. She doesn't say anything except "Good evening" does she? It's what she does. Did you hear her say anything else?'

The phone bleeped. 'I thought she said something about—Yes. Speaking. I see. I see. Can you give me five minutes—'

'Look, I'll come back another time.'

'Of course I know. Forgive me, but why is it my responsibility? Yes, I was there but so was Glyn Williams and Turnbull. No, I'm not saying that. It's still too early. Who said that? I see, I see. No, I'm not denying it. I don't feel any need to deny it. I'm not ashamed of it. I understood the main meeting was next week. No, I shan't. Yes, I do. I mean precisely that. If he doesn't agree, he'll have to resign. It's as simple as that. I think it is. Sorry.'

'I still don't smoke,' Daniel said.

'Damned Controllers. They think—'

Daniel said: 'What shall we do? Shall we go through it together reel by reel? Perhaps that'd be the best thing. I mean one can go on generalizing till Kingdom Come, but it never does much good. Didn't you like the way he did Treves? And Clive, you can't have not liked Clive.'

'I'm not all that happy about the music.'

'I'm not budging on the music,' Daniel said.

'Budgetwise,' Victor Rich said.

'Sullivan's out of copyright,' Daniel said. 'What're you talking about?'

'Don't hector me, Daniel, please. What about the orchestrations?'

'Well, they'll have to be paid for whether we use them or not.'

522

'I never authorized that sort of expenditure.'

'Look, we were just two per cent over budget—'

'Daniel, if I were two per cent over my budget I'd be in hot water.' The phone bleeped again. 'Yes. What? I see. He won't. Do they? Who do? All of them? I see. That accounts, I suppose, for why there was no paper in my private loo this morning. General economies all round. I'm not being facetious. Look, I'll come down—'

Daniel said: 'Look, why don't I go? We can always—'

'It's all right, it's all right. I gather it's still about six minutes over length. I think that's something you ought to be worried about.'

'I am worried about it. But I did mention it to your assistant and she thought it'd be better to let you see it first. Assuming you want to use the damned thing.'

'We've put a lot of money into this,' Victor Rich said. 'Of course we want to use it.'

'She also mentioned something about next year.'

'I think we ought to get this right first. My overall feeling is that it's rather self-indulgent. Too in love with itself. Look, I'm so sorry, I must—' He picked up the phone again. 'I thought this would happen. I'll come down. Can you possibly give me five minutes?'

'Enjoy yourself,' Daniel said.

'Because I would like to sort this out. I'll get them to send in some tea.'

'Smashing. Don't worry about it. I've got a book I'm supposed to read.' Daniel waited till Victor had gone and then went to the telephone. 'Can I have a line?'

'I'm sorry,' the girl said, 'there seems to be something wrong with this line. I'm having trouble getting a connection.'

'See if you can get the Dorchester for me.'

The door of the office opened and a man in a grey work-coat put his head in. 'Not here?'

'No,' Daniel said. 'Sorry.'

'Only—' The man came into the room. 'You don't mind if I—?'

'Help yourself,' Daniel said.

'Wanted elsewhere,' the man said. He unplugged the stenorette from the side table. 'Sorry.'

It grew dark. Daniel opened the door and looked to see whether the tea was ready. The secretary's desk was empty. The hood was over the machine. He picked up one of the telephones. It howled uninterruptedly. He went back into the office and turned on a light. He looked up Billy Stern in the *Film And Television Yearbook*. There was a full *curriculum vitae*.

Victor said: 'Good heavens, still here?'

'I never had leave to dismiss, sir,' Daniel said. 'So of course. Everything all right?'

'You know, I never wanted this job,' Victor Rich said. 'It was forced on me and I took it but I never wanted it. You know what I really want to do and that's pure research. I hate the whole commercial rat-race and I always have. I thought this was going to be a creative job, but it never was and they never meant it to be. This company is run by a collection of faceless men with cash-register hearts and I shan't be sorry to say goodbye. Power's never interested me for its own sake. I thought I could do a good job and I told Dick Lucas in that piece he did about me that I wouldn't stay a moment longer if I thought I wasn't going to be allowed to do it. He cut it out of the interview but it's on on the tape for anyone who doubts my word. To sit in an office like this is far from being my idea of a creative existence. I shall be delighted to go.'

'Victor, forgive me if I'm jumping to conclusions, but you sound like a man who's just resigned on a matter of principle.'

'There are more of them than there are of me unfortunately.'

'Unfortunately there always are,' Daniel said. 'Come on, I'll buy you a drink.'

'No, no,' Victor Rich said. 'I'm still on expenses. Look, I'm sorry about this afternoon, sorry to have been so preoccupied, but I'll tell you exactly what I think about *The Elephant Man*, because I'm very clear in my mind about it.'

'Look,' Daniel said, 'I don't doubt you are, but why don't you forget it? I'll argue the toss with the next cunt who sits in that chair. I can't honestly be bothered to do it with you as well.'

524

'They're talking about an autonomous prestige project, something much more in line with what I really want to do.'

'They always do,' Daniel said.

'Danny, you mustn't think I disapproved of *The Elephant Man*. I was simply trying —'

'Victor, let's be honest, I don't give all that much of a fuck what you thought.'

'Daniel, it is confidential, you do understand that, don't you? What's happened tonight. They're preparing a statement for the media, but meanwhile no one knows, no one at all.'

'I think the maintenance man had a clue,' Daniel said.

'Maintenance man? What are you talking about?'

'Come on,' Daniel said, 'take one more deep draught of the warm and invigorating air of corruption and we'll step out into the night.'

'One thing one can never expect from the Philistines,' Victor said, 'and that's gratitude.'

'Sod 'em,' Daniel said. 'I suppose this means your chat show's up the spout as well.'

'No, as a matter of fact. I think I just about managed to get that through the gate before they slammed it. It meant a fairly radical reshape. Above all, I took the view what was needed was a really strong chairman.'

'Who did you come up with?'

'Dick Lucas.'

'Dick Lucas. The living proof that it's still possible to start at the bottom in this country and lick your way up. He should be just what's wanted. Why aren't you doing it yourself? The chairing, I mean.'

'I'm going to go back to research. I've been wanting to for some time now. I'm not really a man who craves the limelight.'

'Of course not,' Daniel said. 'All the same, knowing your luck, you'll probably come up with a cure for cancer within the next ten days to a fortnight. We shall see you Sir Victor yet. And so goodnight.'

*

LIKE STARS ON THE SEA by Davina Long. Report by P.M.D. Alicia Lasalle is a brilliant and beautiful young fabrics designer of twenty-four, making an independent living for herself in London. At a party given by the mysterious millionaire connoisseur Leo Toscani in his Mayfair penthouse, she sees but does not actually talk to the handsome, dark, magnetic-looking Simon Flint, who is one of the most talked-about men in the world of High Finance. Simon, though only in his early thirties, is one of Leo Toscani's greatest rivals and is already the head of a powerful consortium of companies. Alicia is repelled by his egotism and his vanity and leaves the party with Peter Carrington, a young artist, one of whose pictures hangs in the Toscani drawing-room. She and Peter Carrington see more of each other and she feels that she is falling in love with him. Finally, after a trip to the country where both of them do sketches of the same scene, they make love. A few days later, Alicia is telephoned by a young woman who says that she is Peter Carrington's wife. Peter has never spoken of his wife and Alicia is appalled at the anguish in the other woman's voice. Peter begs her to stay with him and says that his wife is not the innocent she seems. But when Simon Flint telephones and asks her to join a party on his yacht for a cruise through the Aegean, she accepts, telling Peter that it is better if they don't see each other for a while. She is shattered by Peter's anger and her own disillusionment. She has given up someone she loves for someone she still finds repulsive, but fascinating. The cruise on the luxurious *Leander* is everything that she has ever dreamed. (Alicia comes from a humble home and has supported herself and her invalid mother since she left Art School.) The clothes which Alicia has designed for herself are a sensational success. The other women, most of whom are older and more sophisticated than she, are impressed by her modesty and her beauty. Simon Flint shows little interest in her, preferring the charms of Mrs Geraldine Davies, a ravishing but diamond-hard divorcée. It is only when they reach the mysterious island of Melissa, with its black beaches and strange, earthquake-ravaged landscape, that Simon Flint finds time to talk to her. She has been offended by his lack of interest, but now the force of his personality almost overwhelms her. He dances with her at a *taverna* and later, on a moonlight walk, he tells her how much he loves the simplicity of the island and the mystic emanations that come from all its centuries of history. She shares his feelings and they imagine an escape from the yacht and a journey to the secret heart of the island, where an age-old city is in the process of being excavated. In the end, however, they return to the yacht. Mrs Davies, apparently out of friendly concern, warns Alicia, when they are alone, that Simon Flint is a seducer of the worst kind, that he is already having affairs with two of the women on board and that he has made a bet with one of the other men that he can seduce her before they reach Constantinople. Alicia is so disgusted by Mrs Davies' revelations that, although she says she does not believe them, she leaves the yacht and hides until the *Leander* has sailed, leaving a bitter note for Simon. While walking along the same path where she and Simon walked in the moonlight she meets a Greek sculptor, Vassili Petrides, who befriends her and shows her the work he has made out of the roasted stones from the volcanic eruptions. The beautiful things he has made out of what has been through the fire inspires her and she stays with him, on a brother-sister basis, and works in stone. He offers to make love to her, but honours her reluctance. They swim naked together and live happily for several weeks. Then Alicia realizes that she must go back to London where her partner Molly Urquart expects her. Vassili accompanies her to Athens. She kisses him goodbye and thanks him for restoring her faith in human beings. In London again, she is so lonely that she accepts an invitation from Peter Carrington to go out with him. His wife, he tells her, has been unfaithful to him with a Hungarian opera critic, one of the most wicked men in London, and he begs her to resume their relationship. Furthermore, he tells her that Leo Toscani has opened a gallery for his work and that he has a big show coming up. Will she help him with the arrangement of the paintings? Success is just around the corner. One day Molly tells her that a man phoned, but wouldn't give his name. It is Simon, who calls again. At the sound of his deep brown voice, her heart turns over. He says, mysteriously, that he cannot see her but that he wanted to speak to her. He asks to be allowed to call her each day. The tone of his voice touches and frightens her. She gives her permission. Peter Carrington meanwhile continues to press himself on her and asks her to marry him when his divorce comes through. She is charmed and attracted by him, but something prevents her from giving a final decision. Simon Flint phones her every day. At first he says that he understands why she doesn't want to see him, but finally she says that she is willing for them to meet and then he reveals the truth. Has she not heard what happened in the summer, after she left the cruise? She explains that she was on the island and heard no news of any kind. What did happen? He tells her that he found out what Mrs Davies had said to her and that he and his mistress, for it was true they had been sleeping together, at Geraldine's insistence, had a terrible row. The night it happened, there was a fire on board the *Leander* and the yacht was gutted. Luckily no one was killed, but Mrs Davies had locked herself in her cabin, with the intention, she said, of dying in the flames and only resolute action had saved her. It is only when she questions him further that she discovers that Simon himself was badly burned in the fire. His injuries, of course, are the result of saving Mrs Davies. He now admits that he has not asked to see Alicia because of his scars, but she insists that she cares only about his real self and not just his looks. (In an earlier episode, she has called at his city office, hoping to catch a glimpse of him, but has been told that 'Mr Flint is not seeing anyone.') 'Please let us see each other,' she says. To which Simon replies, 'Dear Alicia, please come and see me, but I fear I shall never see you.' He is in danger of losing his sight. When Peter and she next meet, Peter is so eager to tell her of the expensive commission he has just won in Texas, that she has to wait until he has finished before she can tell him that she has decided not to marry him. He turns very ugly and says that she has fallen for that crippled Shylock Simon Flint and that she doesn't mind kissing scars as long as their owner has a million pounds. She runs out of the restaurant. Simon is alone in his Barbican penthouse when she goes to see him. His head is still in bandages. He explains how he has had most of his furniture and valuables removed. He lives as simply as possible and thus, in spite of his blindness, he can manage without help. She is deeply moved, but honesty forces her to tell him what Peter Carrington has said about him. He then reveals that Carrington has been blackmailing Leo Toscani because he has provided the old man with young girls (and boys) and that is why he has had the gallery opened for him. Leo thinks nothing of Peter's paintings which are cheap and flashy. As for his own money, his accident has made him realize not that money is not worth having, but that it is worth having only for what it can do. He is creating a vast fund for helping handicapped children and old people. He believes, he tells her, that it is possible to do good in this world and that he wants to do it, while living as simply as possible himself. She tells him that she always knew that she loved him, but that fear and shyness had kept her back. He says that he noticed her the moment she came into Toscani's penthouse and that his only consolation for his blindness is that he will always see her as he saw her then. They fall into each other's arms. Simon says that he is not going to replace the *Leander*, but that he is going to buy a small boat which can be handled without a crew. Of course much depends on the outcome of the grafts being done on his eyes. At first there is a setback, but Alicia promises she will always be with him. He cries, without tears, for the first time since he was a little boy. Eventually a brilliant surgeon succeeds where others have failed and the young couple go on their honeymoon in Simon's new boat, *Eros*. They call on Vassili in Melissa and he gives them, as a wedding gift, one of his sculptures made of roasted rock. They sail away together in the *Eros*, handling the boat themselves, but not before they have bought a tiny peasant's cottage so that they can return each year to Melissa and walk in the moonlight and eat olives and drink wine with Vassili.

'Well, congratulations,' Daniel said.
   'Oh hullo.'
   'May I introduce – this is Queenie Lloyd. Andy Ford.'
   'Hullo.'

'Or should I say Andrew Ford these days? I must say, you've done a tremendous amount to it.'

'It's still not right, really.'

'She was marvellous,' Queenie said, 'the girl.'

'Queenie's with Four Star World International Associates. That's the lot, isn't it, Queenie?'

'That's the lot, until the next amalgamation. I thought the locations were so marvellously well chosen.'

'We shot where we could,' Andy said.

'The new material's really very impressive,' Daniel said. 'Is she here by the way? I haven't seen her.'

'No, she's not,' Andy said. 'She didn't want to.'

'And she thinks she's going to be an actress? Tut tut.'

'She doesn't,' Andy said.

'She looked stunning in *Madame* this week, did you see, Danny? Wearing those hand-printed fabrics? Stunning.'

'Is she in London?' Daniel said.

'Yeah, she is,' Andy said.

'Because I'd like to get in touch with her. She doesn't have an agent, does she?'

'Not that I know of,' Andy said.

'I hear the picture's going to the Academy.'

'Yeah, well, upstairs, you know, in the lumber room sort of thing.'

'Have you got her number? Is she on the phone?'

'Yeah, I could give it to you.'

'If you could, perhaps you would.'

'Andrew, there's a man here from *Cahiers*.'

'They want your views on the early Vincente Minelli, mind how you go. It could be make or break. If you could just let me have the number. And listen, congratulations again. Don't let them rush you into the next thing, if you don't mind a bit of advice. Take a deep breath, because it may be the last chance you get. And if there's anything I can do for you, just give me a call. I don't suppose —'

'I might do that actually.'

'And thanks for the number, because I'd like to congratulate her. She really is a funny girl, not coming. I can't think of another woman in a thousand who wouldn't have been here.'

'Maybe she's being clever,' Queenie said. 'Or is that uncharitable?'

'It just could be both, of course. What did you actually think of it? I saw a lot of it, oh, months ago. I thought it was awful.'

'Had some interesting things,' Queenie said. 'And she looked wonderful.'

'Nice body,' Daniel said. 'And eyes. The eyes, she has the eyes, as my old friend Peppino used to say. I rather thought this Mary-Ellen Schwarz lady might be here. You know, The Dark Tower lady. She sounds rather sensational.'

'I hear it's absolutely diabolical,' Queenie said.

'I was hoping you'd say that,' Daniel said, 'but I'd still like to see her. She's supposed to be having it off with a chum of mine. Well, Adam. You know Adam. That's what I'm told. Well, there we are. Young Mister Ford is the toast of London's poofdom it seems; his career looks to be very well launched. Shall we go and eat? Humble pie, of course. Honestly, though, Queenie my love, generosity to one side and youthful endeavour duly saluted, it really was amateur night, wasn't it?'

'It was a nice little film, Daniel. I enjoyed it.'

'You're just a pushover for any pretty young thing with roses between her cheeks,' Daniel said. '*Pame.*'

They ate at the Ponte Vecchio.

'Do you think she'd do for Pilar?'

'She might. She might indeed. I did have someone—'

'Well, why don't you have her?' Daniel said. 'She doesn't seem to have an agent. I think I'll call her up. I did meet her, you know, in April. That's how I came to see the first cut of chummy's movie. She could be right.'

'She could.'

'I'll see if I can get hold of her. So are you going to come out to B.A. and see me, come the spring?'

'I thought you'd never ask,' Queenie said.

'I wish you would. I shall be the loneliest man on earth.'

'I doubt that,' Queenie said.

'I bloody will. I'm shaking in my *bottes*. It's going to be fucking good though. Listen, I read the Davina Long thing you sent me. I must say it sounds marvellous. By Iris Murdoch out of *Woman's Own* with a faint touch of diabolism behind the ears. Jane Arless to the life. It just could be something rather marvellous, if one could keep a straight face for ten weeks. Have you read it yet, the actual book?'

'I haven't, you see,' Queenie said.

'This girl might even do the part. Rachel Davidson. If she works as Pilar.'

'She might indeed. I must read it.'

'Dear Queenie, you are indulgent. I do appreciate it. Are you happy in your work?'

'Yes I am, you see, that's the whole thing. Aren't you?'

'When I'm working, yes. When I've actually got things going, I think it's the most exciting feeling in the world. That's why you ought to come out to B.A. With any luck I shall be—'

'On the top of your form.'

'*Faute de mieux*,' Daniel said. 'Oh I've no illusions. It's going to be tough sledding. Read this thing, this novel, because I have a sort of strange feeling there might be something in it. Not just as an exercise. It has a kind of macabre credibility.'

'I shall put it at the top of the pile by my bedside,' Queenie said.

'I've never seen your bedside,' Daniel said.

'I make it a rule,' Queenie said.

'I'm sure you're wise,' Daniel said. 'I regret it, of course, but I'm sure you are.'

'I'm very wise,' Queenie said.

He took Queenie to her door and then went to Claridge's. Camille had checked in, but she was not in her room. He left a message (he had already sent flowers) and went to the late movie at the Cinecenta. He left after four reels and drove home to Chelsea and worked on the script of *The Big One*. Reading it for the thousandth time with fresh eyes, he found himself marking weaknesses as briskly as a tailor with a chalk. It seemed as though he knew exactly what the final shape should be. He made coffee and worked on, husking the true grain of the story from its effortful excrescences. It was, as Robert Gavin had said, like doing Latin verses: the assembly of an almost impersonal mental machine. The scansion of the whole piece, its internal cohesion, the variety needed to check mere repetition, all the spontaneous wit which only hard work could provide came easily to him. How important, during the steady hours, *The Big One* was!

'Yes?'

'Daniel?'

'Yes?'

'It's me. Virginia.'

'Yes. Oh Virginia, hullo.'

'Are you busy?'

'I'm asleep,' Daniel said. 'I'll call you back.'

'It's eleven fifteen.'

'I worked all night. What's wrong?'

'Nothing.'

'I'll call you back.'

'It's only can you come to dinner next week.'

'Next week. Why not? What day? What day is it now?'

'Danny. I'm so sorry. Wednesday. I mean dinner Wednesday.'

'I'll call you back. What's up? Where? I mean the dinner. Your place?'

'Yes, of course. The house. As usual. Eight fifteen.'

'Should be O.K. I'll – Yes – unless I can't. I'll call you back.'

'Eight fifteen at the house. Bring someone if you want to. In fact please.'

'Eight fifteen. I'll call you back.'

'Sorry if I woke you. I couldn't know, could I?'

'None of us can,' Daniel said.

'I want to see you.'

'What for?'

'Because I do. I saw the movie the other night. God, last night.'

'You saw it months ago.'

'Some of it. I don't mean I want to see you because of the movie, I mean I saw the movie and I realized I wanted to see you. Congratulations all the same, by the way, but that's not the reason.'

'What is then?'

'I want to see you because I want to see you.'

'All right.'

'Thanks.'

'What's Andy told you exactly?'

'Exactly nothing. Your number. Now what about the address?'

It was in Notting Hill Gate. Daniel went up uncarpeted steps beside a shoe shop. Rachel opened the door.

'Now I understand,' Daniel said.

'It's not a secret,' Rachel said.

'How many months?'

'Seven. That's why I'm being careful.'

'Rachel, Rachel, Rachel,' Daniel said. 'Is it mine?'

'I should think so, wouldn't you?'

'My God. My God. And you never said a word.'

'What word would you have liked me to say?'

'May I kiss you?'

'Yes, of course.'

'I'd forgotten how pretty you were. Do you hate me or something?'

'No. Of course I don't. Not in the least. Why should I?'

'Presumably you wanted it.'

'Of course.'

'This place seems terribly damp.'

'I'll light the fire.'

'Are you all right? Is *it* all right? Have you been going to the right places, doctors and clinics and things?'

'Everything's fine. It's leaping about.'

She was wearing a kaftan with a big Mexican cardigan over the top. He put his head against her womb and his arms round her waist. She let him listen.

'Can I see?' Daniel said. 'It. You.'

She lifted the kaftan up to her breasts. She was wearing long yellow woollen socks, but nothing else underneath. He put his lips there. His tears glistened on her belly. 'Still women's libbing I see,' he said.

'Well,' she said.

'Your own woman, your own baby.'

'Oh, right,' she said.

'Weren't you ever going to tell me, not ever?'

'I hadn't decided,' she said. 'I don't make decisions like that.'

'Marry me, Rachel, please. Please marry me,' he said. 'Don't say anything, don't mock, don't act, don't do anything clever or wise or right or liberated. Just say yes. Please. I swear I'll love you to the best of my ability. I'll do anything you like. I'll stop directing films. I'll break my contracts, I'll never look at another woman as long as I live. I swear I'll be faithful to you. Marry me. I can be what you want. I can. I love you. Don't laugh, don't doubt, just believe. Please.'

'I can't,' she said.

'Oh Rachel, my darling, please don't. Please realize that all this business about female emancipation, female liberation, it's all a kind of imperialism, a kind of threat. You won't be giving yourself to me. You don't have to take my name. You don't have to be faithful to me if you don't want to be. I don't want to hold you to anything, I just want to hold you. Marry me.'

'I can't. Even if I wanted to, I can't.'

'Let me love you and let me love my child. I do and I can. All the rest is just—barnacles, muck, it can all be scraped off just like that.'

'I'm married already,' Rachel said.

'When? Why? Who to?'

'To Andy,' Rachel said. 'This is our pad.'

'Well he ought to be damned well ashamed of himself, keeping a pregnant woman in a place like this when he could be making quite enough to give you somewhere decent to live.'

535

'I'm happy here,' Rachel said.

'Happy? Look at that. Look at that. Green.'

'The doctor says I'm fine,' Rachel said.

'I don't believe you. I don't believe you've married him at all.'

'Yes, I have,' Rachel said. 'July eighteenth at Hendon. You can check.'

'Do you love him?'

She shrugged.

'Does he know who—'

'Do you think I'd marry him without telling him?'

'Why? Why?'

'He needs me,' Rachel said. 'He was unhappy.'

'I'm unhappy. I need you. Why *marry* him?'

'It was what he needed. It was after he'd shown the film. People started telling him how good it was. He got terribly depressed. He was almost suicidal. He needed something to rely on.'

'Rachel, I don't want to hurt Andy. I don't bear him any ill will. I wish him all the luck in the world, but you're carrying my child and I want it. I want you. I have a right—don't shake your head, please don't shake your head. I do. I'm the father. I thought you didn't believe in marriage.'

'I believe in people. He wanted it. It gave him the feeling he needed. He's very weak. Very exposed.'

'Rachel, if I treated you badly—'

'You didn't. Please don't, Daniel. I only used something I wanted from you. You have a nice body. I admired you. I wanted a child.'

'That's why you went with me in the first place. Deliberately—'

'I fancied you, I liked you, I was attracted by you. I only used a spoonful of what you were happy to get rid of into me.'

'I want a child. I've just split with a woman who wouldn't have my child.'

'Ah I see.'

'You damned well don't. It's not like that. I've thought about you again and again these last months. I nearly came to find you in Israel. Then last night something snapped. I knew I wanted you. It's not the baby. It's you.'

536

'I'm sorry,' Rachel said.

'Jesus Christ, Rachel. It's life or death. Yes, it is. Yes, it *is*. You're not seriously going to tell me that you expect me to accept this?'

'No, I don't expect you to at all.'

'O.K. then.'

'But you'll just have to.'

'You don't want the child to have a father.'

'It's got a father,' Rachel said. 'And I'm very pleased.'

'When it's born. Oh for God's sake, you know what I mean.'

'It'll have Andy,' Rachel said. 'And me. That's enough.'

'You intend to spend the rest of your life with this man, do you?'

'Not necessarily.'

'Rachel, I know how you feel about life, about men, about convention—and I agree with you, but don't forget that in the last analysis we're on our own. We're lonely animals on our own and in the end no one's going to help us except ourselves. We're not going to live anyone's life except our own. Brothers and sisters we may be, but when someone wants to spend his life with you, you can't just shrug it away.'

'Is that what you think I'm doing?'

'That's what you *are* doing. Come with me. Now. Please. I've got some money—'

'Do you think that matters all that much?'

'There are things a child needs,' Daniel said. 'I'm not saying I want to buy you. I want to give you things. I want to give him things.'

'Him or her.'

'My child,' Daniel said, 'my child.'

'Do you think I don't know that?'

'Rachel, you make me feel absolutely—How can I persuade you?'

'It's not a question of persuasion,' Rachel said. 'I've given my word to Andy.'

'Underneath it all you're as conventional as—as Evelyn Home. Given your word. All right. Then be conventional enough to give your child a father who really is his father.'

'Would you say that to a girl if you'd met her at a party and screwed her afterwards without taking precautions?'

'No. I wouldn't.'

'We never said we were going to have a child. I wanted one. I used—'

'Oh I know what you used for Christ's sake. I want you. I know now that I want you and I love you and I want to make my life with you. I've tried to do without you and I haven't liked it. I want to get married and have a family and a home. I want to.'

'And so I have to fall in. Daniel, it's not worth arguing, because even if I wanted to—'

'Let me talk to Andy.'

'No.'

'Why not? He's grown up, supposedly. He should be able to stand talking to someone without coming to pieces in one's hand.'

'You'll hurt him. You'll overwhelm him. You'll argue him down. He needs me. We're together. I can't leave him, even if I'd like to. It would be worse than not marrying him in the first place.'

'I'm the father.'

'Daniel, don't thunder, please. You're beginning to sound like Zeus.'

'Why in hell didn't you come to Greece with me? We could have been happy. Rachel, I don't know what I'll do—'

'You'll go to South America. I saw it in the paper.'

'I'll resign. No problem getting another director. There're plenty of vultures perched on the accursed roofs like tame villatic fowl. Billy Stern for a start—'

'Do you think I'd live with you when you'd given up a film like that? I do know a bit, you know. You'd never forgive me. It's no use, Daniel. I refuse to be punished. There's really nothing to be done.'

'Punished! I can't stand it. I can't bear it. I can't—'

'Please don't degrade yourself.'

'I'm not acting, blast you.'

'I'm not going to live with you, I can't marry you. I don't feel guilty and I can't change. I am sorry.'

538

'I don't think he's even a man. I don't even think he's a man. *Is* he?'

'I'm not going to discuss Andy.'

'Was the marriage ever consummated? Except by me?'

'I mean it.'

'Am I going to be allowed to see my own child?'

'Of course. As long as you don't upset it.'

'Rachel, let's just—let me—let's pretend we haven't said any of this. Now. I beg you, I beg you—'

'Don't,' she said.

'On proper bended knee. Will you marry me? Will the mother of my child come and make a home with me and damn everybody? Because—'

'I'm sorry, but no, I won't. I won't. I won't, I won't.'

'I don't know what I'm going to do. This is a nightmare. It's a nightmare.'

'I know,' Rachel said, 'and I'm sorry.'

'A nightmare.'

'It wouldn't work. Don't go thinking it would.'

'Of course it would. If I wanted it to. I can make anything work if I want to. Rachel, come and—'

'I think you should go.'

'Why? Are you feeling—?'

'I'm feeling fine. I just think you should. Nothing's going to change my mind. It can't.'

'What if Andy were dead? What if he had really jumped off that damned roof? What if—?'

'Don't make yourself contemptible, Daniel. I never thought of you as contemptible.'

'I'm not going to do anything,' Daniel said. 'Let me put it this way. If you need me, will you call me?'

'Of course I will.'

'Promise. Will you promise?'

'Happily,' Rachel said.

'Can I call you?'

'If I'm here,' she said.

'You know,' he said, 'I was going to offer you a part in my new movie. After seeing you in *Boom-Titty-Boom*. Don't ever let him use a title like that again.'

'That was nice of you,' she said. 'But I wouldn't have taken it. I'm not going to be an actress. Too many heartbreaks.'

'I don't blame you,' Daniel said. 'Anyway, you probably wouldn't have been right.'

'Thank God we've bumped into you,' Daniel said, 'because I'd really love to know what this evening's all about. Have you got any idea? Is it a wake or a celebration?'

'I gather it's reconciliation time,' Francesca said. 'Apparently Virginia's been having a big affair.'

'Virginia has?' Daniel said. 'Who with exactly?'

'Perhaps I'm speaking out of turn,' Francesca said.

'It's the best place, isn't it?'

'Harold Usborne, you know.'

'Harold *Usborne*? I always thought she despised Harold Usborne.'

'She did,' Meredith said. 'But she suddenly discovered—'

'He had a big one, I suppose. I don't believe a word of it. We'd better keep our voices down.'

'He had a first in geology at Manchester. Apparently he's got a brilliant mind. The rest followed naturally.'

'I don't believe it. So what's the situation now?'

'Large cancellations on both sides of the equation, I gather, leaving the status even more quo than before. Do we know each other?'

'Oh I'm so sorry,' Daniel said. 'This is Camille.'

'Nice to meet you both,' Meredith Lamb said. 'You were at that party in April weren't you, Virginia gave?'

'Yes,' Camille said, 'that was when Daniel and I first met.'

'She's very clever that way, isn't she, Virginia?'

The front door opened. They could hear people laughing inside.

Meredith said: 'Lovely pair on her, Daniel, I must say.'

'Everyone at once,' Virginia said. 'How lovely! Only Gay and Baz to come.'

'I heard you were going to marry that American piece,' Meredith said. 'I take it the wedding's been postponed. Someone told me you were going to be married this month.'

'That's right,' Daniel said. 'November the thirty-first.'